THE EISENHOWER CHRONICLES

M. B. ZUCKER

HISTORIUM PRESS

First Edition published by Liopleurodon Publishing LLC
Second Edition published by Historium Press

Images by Shutterstock & Public Domain
Cover designed by White Rabbit Arts

Visit Mr. Zucker's website at
www.michaelbzucker.com

Library of Congress Cataloging-in-Publication Data on file

Hardcover ISBN: 979-8-2180115-8-0
Paperback ISBN: 978-0-5782880-3-1
E-Book ISBN: 978-0-57882880-4-8

Historium Press, a subsidiary of
The Historical Fiction Company, LLC
2022

To Amanda

You are the finest, loveliest, tenderest, and most beautiful person I have
ever known—and even that is an understatement.

—F. Scott Fitzgerald

To Judy,
Michael Zucker

Table of Contents

Foreword by Yanek Mieczkowski
Presidential Historian and Author of
Eisenhower's Sputnik Moment:
The Race for Space and World Prestige

Imagine having a ringside seat to history.

I once interviewed Arthur Larson, a top aide to President Dwight D. Eisenhower, and in recalling the commander-in-chief, Larson contrasted his views with those of historians who wrote decades after the 1950s. Larson said that he enjoyed an advantage because he had a "ringside seat" to events. He observed Eisenhower up close and in person, without a secondary lens or the filter of time.

Michael Zucker gives readers that coveted ringside seat to history. In this masterful work of historical fiction, Zucker beckons readers to journey with the five-star general and two-term president over the course of his history-making career. Readers will be there as Eisenhower consults with military colleagues like General George Marshall and administration luminaries like Secretary of State John Foster Dulles. The Ike in these pages confides in his wife Mamie, paces the floor while making critical decisions, and struggles with emotions—for example, keeping his volcanic temper from blasting, his face turning crimson and a vein throbbing in his forehead.

Zucker understands the magic of historical fiction. He shows deep respect for accuracy, and the major events he describes all happened. Many of Eisenhower's words here are verbatim quotes. At the same time, Zucker gives historical situations just enough latitude to imagine what Eisenhower might have been thinking or saying in unguarded moments.

The result is a tantalizing tale of history that runs with a higher octane narrative than a standard nonfiction work.

The solid historical grounding to this novel is no accident, because Zucker has studied the 34th president for years. While in college, he grew fascinated with Eisenhower, and he recognized—as increasing numbers of historians do now—that in addition to commanding World War II Allied forces to victory in Europe, the general compiled a sterling record during two terms in the White House, presiding over peace and prosperity, exercising sound judgment at many hinge points in history, and avoiding blunders that, in the atomic age, might have endangered every human on earth. After finishing law school, Zucker has devoted himself to full-time writing, pursuing his passion for historical fiction. In this latest work, Zucker's regard for Eisenhower shines through, and one theme that resonates is Eisenhower's sense of duty to the country and the world, which often led him to sacrifice his home life, even his health.

The Eisenhower Chronicles is especially impressive because Zucker sweeps through the scope of Eisenhower's multi-faceted career. He takes readers on a trek that sees Eisenhower making the tough decision to launch the D-Day invasion, jumping into the 1952 presidential race (despite having never held elective office before), eschewing but subtly undermining Red-hunting Senator Joseph McCarthy, avoiding war with China over the islands of Quemoy and Matsu, dispatching federal troops to Little Rock to defend desegregation, and leading America in space exploration after the Soviet Union launched the Sputnik satellite. In Zucker's rendition, Eisenhower wryly remarks about what he was facing: "Crisis after crisis."

That was the nature of Eisenhower's presidency. During the Cold War, as the world lurched from one tense moment to the next, America burgeoned as an economic and military superpower. Yet as its strength blossomed, the country suffered growing pains. Crises erupted, and Eisenhower had to defuse them. He showed himself a skilled crisis manager, deescalating tensions and finding sensible solutions that adhered to what he called the "Middle Way," steeped in the values of small-town, midwestern America, where he was born and raised.

Zucker captures the ideals and principles that animated the general and president. He also provides a lively, engaging way to experience history. His narrative is addictive—readers will find themselves hooked, wondering what crisis Ike will face next, speculating on how he will find a solution to it. The opening lines of this book start a captivating historical voyage that will grab the reader's attention on every page thereafter.

In 2020, the Eisenhower Memorial opened in Washington, D.C., paying homage to Ike's career with a sprawling tapestry that evokes the sands of the D-Day beaches. (Zucker has worked as a volunteer at this site, the capital city's latest attraction.) The Memorial's centerpieces are marble statues of Eisenhower, depicting him as a general and as a president. To visit the Memorial is to understand the impact of Eisenhower; it enshrines him as a larger-than-life figure, carved into a permanent frieze of history. To read *The Eisenhower Chronicles* is to appreciate that Ike was "just folks," as he liked to say, a mortal man who endured the terrors, traumas, and tears that comprise the human experience—and he bravely faced it all.

Introduction

Welcome to *The Eisenhower Chronicles*. Here, you will experience Dwight Eisenhower's life and career as never before. This biographical novel is told through a series of stories that are both designed to stand alone but, together, bring Ike back to life and present his place in history as the most important individual in defending the world from fascism, communism, and nuclear weapons.

First and foremost, my greatest debt is to Amanda Makhoul Zucker, my wife. We met in law school, started dating by the end of our first semester, and she was the first person I told my idea of an Eisenhower-themed story collection to in June 2019. She always encouraged my dream, proofed the volume more than once, and kept me going. Amanda is my best friend and closest companion, and I will always be grateful for having her in my life.

I would also like to thank Michael Sandlin and Dustin Prisley for editing *The Eisenhower Chronicles*, and to White Rabbit Arts for designing the cover.

Thank you to those who offered their encouragement during this project, including my parents, Dr. Alvin Felzenberg, and my fellow volunteers at the Eisenhower Memorial. As I have also said in the "Further Reading" section, I want to thank the historians whose nonfiction works on Ike were indispensable to my research. Foremost among them were Stephen Ambrose, Jean Edward Smith, Michael Korda, Evan Thomas, David Nichols, Yanek Mieczkowski, Kasey Pipes, Irwin Gellman, Jim Newton, and David and Susan Eisenhower, Ike's grandchildren, and those at the Eisenhower Presidential Library who built the wonderful online archive.

Lastly, I'd like to thank you, the readers. I hope you enjoy *The Eisenhower Chronicles*.

PART I

☆☆☆☆☆

THE GENERAL

Ike's Rubicon

Happiness and moral duty are inseparably connected.
—George Washington

NOVEMBER 10, 1938

LIEUTENANT COLONEL DWIGHT Eisenhower's focus was locked on the ball. His left eye shut; his right narrowed, calculating the distance between the ball and the hole. His large hands gripped the club as he pulled back. He swung forward but struck the ball with restraint.

Ike miscalculated. He had not applied enough force, and the ball, after an initial burst, stopped short. His face briefly flashed scarlet red. Swear words were on the tip of his tongue but Ike restrained himself in front of his golf partner, Marion Huff. He was not comfortable swearing in front of women and fought to control his temper before he embarrassed himself.

Marion teased, "Now you're intentionally slowing us down. I think you want Sidney and I to be late." She leaned on her club as the sun warmed her under her light beige outfit.

"Of course not," Ike muttered. He gripped his club even tighter as he walked to the ball and repeated his process. He shut one eye, stuck his rear out, and calculated how much force was necessary to sink the ball. This time it worked. The ball, once struck, followed Ike's command and tumbled into the hole, vanishing from sight.

"Yes!" Ike's attitude changed on a dime. His face brightened with his signature smile. His chest jutted out and arms pumped.

"Golfing brings out a whole other side to you. You're usually a gentleman," Marion complained as Ike retrieved the ball.

17

"I can't help it. Sports seize my attention like little else," Ike said as he corrected his posture, careful of his back. "If only I was as skilled as I am enthusiastic."

"You're plenty skilled. But I really do have to get back. We can't be late for the President." Her hand jerked as she considered patting Ike on the back before remembering how he hated being touched.

Sweat developed on Ike's shaved head. He walked to her left, letting Marion be in the shade to escape the Manila sun. They moved through the town of middle class, *Bahay na bato* stone houses that reflected native, Spanish, and Chinese influences as they made their way toward the modest homes the Filipino government gave them as officers on General MacArthur's staff.

Ike's golfing excitement receded. It had been a difficult year. Troubles filled his mind as he and Marion walked in silence. Mamie, his wife, had struggled with health issues since arriving in the Philippines two years prior, the deadliest of which was a burst blood vessel in her stomach that put her in a short coma. Ike's health was little better. He'd been hospitalized in January with a bowel blockage. The crisis passed before he was due for surgery, but the pain was excruciating. Golfing with Marion helped him recover.

Then there was work. Ike's admiration for MacArthur when he began serving the general in 1929 had deteriorated. Now, his commander's main use was training for dealing with big egos.

Ike was exhausted of MacArthur's frequent rants about his hatred of communism and the Roosevelt administration. The feeling was mutual. Ike proved too opinionated for MacArthur, such as voicing his disagreement with MacArthur's strategy to prepare the Philippines for independence from the US. Ike thought MacArthur put too much emphasis on parades and other public displays of the army they'd built and not enough on training the army. MacArthur did not appreciate this criticism and had removed Ike as his main advisor. He'd been replaced by Major Southerland, who undermined Ike's position within MacArthur's command and was happy to pander to MacArthur's whims.

Worse still was Jimmy Ord's death. Ike had invited Ord to join him in the Philippines; he became Ike's main partner in building the Filipino Army and an important ally against MacArthur. Ike and Ord decided to teach themselves how to fly planes in their spare time. Both proved natural pilots, though Ike's farsightedness made landing a struggle. Ord flew over the mountains near Manila while Ike was in the hospital. He leaned out of the cockpit to drop a message to his friends below and lost control. The crash claimed Ord's life, increasing Ike's isolation.

These disappointments racketed through Ike's skull.

Can feel the mediocrity in my bones. Might be my worst chapter since Icky died. What has it been? Seventeen years? My God. Can barely believe it. A suffocating darkness. Poured myself into work until Mamie left. I'll turn fifty in a couple years and have no major accomplishments to my name. Sure, I served under great men like Conner and Pershing, but I can see the eyes of my future grandkids rolling over in their heads when I tell them those stories. Dedicated my life to the Army and haven't done anything that would make my family proud. And now I'm stuck in the Philippines without many friends or prospects going forward. Aimless drifting. I'll retire a colonel and with nothing to show for it. It's such a shame I could cry.

Sweat built up under Ike's armpits as he and Marion went separate ways and made their pleasant "farewells." Ike continued toward home, which was a short distance away. His thought attack turned to the state of the world.

Europe and the United States were in relative peace when Ike was born in 1890. Europe's last existential war had ended at Waterloo in 1815; America's at Appomattox in 1865. However, Ike's lifetime had seen a series of global crises. The unification of Germany in 1871 destabilized the European balance of power forged from Napoleon's defeat. That balance, which had prevented major wars for a century, deteriorated and finally imploded in 1914, plunging the world into the Great War. Ike graduated from West Point during the war and hoped to make his family proud by fighting the Kaiser's forces. He was devastated when he spent the war stateside training tank units.

Remember the lazy soldier at Camp Meade? Ike thought. *The one who was more interested in writing than being a soldier? What was his name? Damn, what was that name? Scott—something? I wonder what became of him.*

Ike, a fresh Army officer, had missed the biggest war in history, a career disappointment that birthed his paranoia of retiring unaccomplished.

The Great War triggered an even costlier crisis. The Spanish Influenza killed over twenty million people around the world, including at Camp Meade. Ike quarantined sick soldiers and kept Mamie and Icky sheltered. They, and ten thousand men under Ike's command, survived.

The 1920s were a respite from these crises, other than communism rising in Russia. But the 1930s saw the global economy plunge into the Great Depression. Nearly a fourth of Americans were unemployed, though Ike's Army salary spared his family from the suffering many others felt. Franklin Roosevelt, the current President, guided America through most of the crisis. Ike had mixed feelings about FDR. Roosevelt's signature policies, the New Deal, were large-scale spending and financial reforms that kept America politically stable but did not end the Depression. America still had a 19 percent unemployment rate in 1938. Ike feared parts of the New Deal were unconstitutional and could permanently damage America's entrepreneurial system.

Ike's mind returned to reality as his hand stung on the sunbaked doorknob of his family's Manila residence. He wiped sweat from his forehead with his sleeve; he was eager to shower and change out of his drenched clothes before dinner. Ike felt muggy as he stepped into the front room.

"Such a monstrosity!" Mamie wailed.

I might be sweaty, but I don't smell that bad! She better not be upset by my golfing with Marion. As if she didn't go dancing in Washington before coming to Manila. Maybe it's her health. Or maybe she's concerned about my stupid back again?

"That such things could even happen in the twentieth century!" Mamie shouted from another room.

Ike's eyebrow arched. John entered the room looking distressed, his knuckles white from clutching a newspaper.

"Why's your mom upset?" Ike asked.

John was startled; his lips quivering.

"Haven't you heard the news?"

"What news? What's happening in the world? Something out of Washington?"

"No," John sighed as he handed his father a copy of *The London Times.* "Read this."

Ike's eyes locked onto the opening line:

"No foreign propagandist bent upon blackening Germany before the world could outdo the tale of burnings and beatings, of blackguardly assaults on defenseless and innocent people, which disgraced that country yesterday."

Ike consumed the paper faster than his brain could process it. A Polish Jew had killed the German ambassador in Paris in retaliation for

Germany's anti-Semitic policies. The German government unleashed revenge across the country. Thousands of Jewish synagogues and shops were destroyed in Germany, Austria, and eastern Czechoslovakia, which Germany had recently annexed.

Ike's face turned red. His eyebrows rose, his forehead pinched. A large vein bulged along his temple.

I have Jewish friends in Manila! Some of them came here after fleeing Germany! Ike's thoughts screamed. *I've been so busy trying to build a damn army for the Filipinos! Never paid attention to the rise of these European dictators! That's going to change.*

He looked at a picture of Adolf Hitler, Germany's dictator for five years, printed in the *Times*. A flash of rage boiled in his arms.

Ike knew the basics about Hitler. He was a veteran of the Great War and was wounded by Allied mustard gas shortly before the armistice. He became a far-right demagogue who Germany turned to in desperation after its defeat in the war, subsequent hyperinflation, and the Depression. He transformed Germany into a totalitarian state. Ike suspected the remaining pieces. Hitler's goal was to lead the Aryan race to global dominance. Other races would either be enslaved or exterminated. Hitler foresaw this campaign culminating in an eventual showdown with the United States for world domination.

Ike slammed the newspaper on a nearby table. He fought to moderate his temper so he could think logically. He was furious at Germany, but, for the first time in a long time, he felt something other than disappointment about his own life.

☆☆☆☆☆

A WEEK LATER, Ike and Mamie attended a dinner for American military officers and Filipino government officials. Major Southerland was the host. Neither President Quezon nor General MacArthur were present. Ike poked his squid dish with a spoon, devising a plan of attack on how to eat it. Ike eyed Lieutenant Huff and Marion to see how they approached the task.

Mr. Palma, a Filipino official and former educator, broke Ike's concentration.

"Tell me, Colonel Eisenhower, how goes your work in training the Army?" Palma spoke with a slight accent. He'd been close to the Eisenhowers since they arrived in Manila.

Ike chose to blame his government, determined not to offend the Filipinos who were present, though he felt their countrymen promised everything but delivered nothing.

"The administration won't send us the adequate weapons we need since Roosevelt is appeasing the pacifist lobby." He raised food to his mouth and threw in, "Hopefully that will change soon."

Palma's dark eyebrow raised.

"Why would you want that? Isn't it better for peace?"

Ike felt a twinge of awkwardness. He generally avoided talking politics with anyone he wasn't close to. Ike eyed Major Sutherland, Captain Davis, Lieutenant Colonel Parker, and the Huffs. They gave blank stares. Ike turned to Mamie, who knew of Ike's hesitancy, but gave a slight nod, encouraging him to fire his loaded cannon.

"The United States needs to get ready to fight Hitler."

A shockwave triggered through the group; an awkward silence set in. Ike clenched his spoon; this was why he avoided talking politics. He waited for a response as sweat emerged on his temples for the first time since the cool winter air swept into Manila a few days ago.

The woman to Palma's right, a Filipina of Spanish descent, broke the silence.

"Why wouldn't you like Hitler? He's supporting Franco against the communists and atheists in Spain."

Several Filipinos nodded in agreement.

"What about the Jews?" Ike shot back, digging in his feet. "What about what happened a week ago?"

"Why do you care about them?" Parker asked with a chuckle. "They caused the Depression."

"That's disgusting!" Ike snapped. He turned to Mamie, who he knew agreed with him. She stayed out of the argument. Ike turned to the Huffs. They, too, were silent. Ike returned to Parker.

"Why would you hate a man because of his birth?"

Davis spoke before Parker could respond.

"We need Hitler as a bulwark against communism. Stalin's the real enemy of Western Civilization. Hitler counters the threat from the Kremlin."

Ike violently shook his head.

"Hitler is at least as bad. And he wants to rule the world from pole to pole." Laughter broke out from several Filipinos and military officers.

Ike's eyes bulged against their mockery. "He's already annexed Austria and the Sudetenland. Why would he stop unless he's opposed?"

Sutherland replied, "Those are all in the east. Last time I checked, America, Britain, and France were in the west. So Hitler's not a threat to us. If we're smart, we'll root for him to keep going east until he's in Moscow."

"That's crazy as hell!" Ike exclaimed. "We need to start arming ourselves to oppose Germany!"

"You're an alarmist and a warmonger," Parker responded. "Which is a lot from someone who didn't even fight in the war."

Ike slammed his spoon on the table.

"I wanted to fight!"

"But you didn't!" Parker shouted.

"I still know what it cost!" Ike yelled. "I toured the French battlefields with Pershing ten years ago. I saw the mass graves of thousands of French soldiers. I saw bones sticking out of the ground. I saw the ruins of Verdun and other shattered cities." His hand turned into a fist. "But Hitler and the Nazis are one of the few things in this world worse than war."

Ike saw the look of disagreement on virtually every face in the room. These were his friends. Sutherland quietly said, "You're willing to sacrifice American boys to help the Jews."

Ike's face flashed bright red as his emotions escaped his grip.

"That's racialism! There's nothing wrong with not wanting to see people get hurt because of bigotry! But this is bigger than that! I'm willing to fight Hitler because he's a *global* threat!" Sutherland did not respond. Ike continued, "If you question my morals then maybe we're not friends. I'm not even sure you're fit to be an officer in this army!"

Sutherland's arms shifted into an aggressive posture. Ike leaned forward, calculating how to jump over the table. Mamie turned to Lieutenant Huff, desperate to stop a physical fight from breaking out.

Palma's words cut the tension.

"Maybe you should go."

Ike unclenched his fist.

"Maybe I should," Ike muttered. "Come on, Mamie, let's leave."

Mamie had already grabbed her coat.

☆☆☆☆☆

SEPTEMBER 3, 1939

THE FOLLOWING MONTHS deepened Ike's depression. The argument at Major Sutherland's home, and subsequent arguments about Hitler, isolated Ike from his peers. He'd lost nearly all his friends since November. His bitterness was validated by recent events. Hitler had formed a nonaggression pact with Stalin in August and invaded Poland. It was clear that Hitler had no intention of slowing down and was bent on dominating the world.

"The PM is speaking!" John exclaimed as he turned on the radio to the BBC.

Neville Chamberlain's voice emerged from the radio after a few moments of static. "This morning the British ambassador in Berlin handed the German government a final note stating that, unless we heard from them by 11 o'clock that they were prepared at once to withdraw their troops from Poland, a state of war would exist between us. I have to tell you now that no such undertaking has been received, and that consequently this country is at war with Germany."

The Eisenhowers were grim as they heard a second world war begin in Europe. They feared it would be far worse than the last. Silently, Ike walked to his room and grabbed his diary. He vomited his surging hatred of the German dictator onto the page.

> Hitler is a power-drunk egocentric. His personal magnetism had converted large populations in Germany to his insane schemes and to blindly accept his leadership. Unless he is successful in overpowering the whole world by brute force the final result will be that Germany will have to be dismembered and destroyed.

Ike lowered his pen. He had gone to West Point in 1911 for a free education and dedicated his life to the Army as a result. He had missed the Great War and spent twenty years being mentored by Pershing and his inner circle. Fighting Hitler would be the culmination of his military career.

He continued writing:

> Hitler's record with the Jews, his rape of Austria, of the Czechs, the Slovaks and now the Poles is

as black as that of any barbarian of the Dark
Ages.

Ike closed his diary.

*I was ten years old when my brothers went trick-or-treating.
Desperately wanted to go but my parents denied me the opportunity. I
punched our tree until my hands bled. My father lashed me with his belt
for my outburst. Ran to my room and cried for hours. My darling mother
came to me when I finally calmed down and spoke about my temper. I'll
never forget what she said. "He that conquereth his own soul is greater
than he who taketh the city." That was the most important conversation of
my life. Forged my whole worldview. Humans are selfish creatures. It is
our original sin. Each of us has a duty to overcome that selfishness and
work toward the greater good, for the betterment of humanity and world
peace.*

He heard the BBC continue discussing Britain's declaration of war
from the other room. Ike clenched his teeth when he heard Hitler's name.

*That demagogic monster wants to rule the world and everyone in it. I
cannot think of anyone who has more greatly betrayed humanity's duty to
overcome selfishness. He is an absolute narcissist who has plunged the
world into war. He is nothing but a butcher; no different than Attila the
Hun or Genghis Khan!*

*The Founding Fathers, Washington and the others, were the wisest
group of statesmen that ever lived. Being an American citizen is one of the
world's great prizes. But America has never been in such danger. I know
my countrymen want to stay out of this war, but I'm certain that Hitler
plans to do to us what he has done to Austria, Czechoslovakia, and
Poland.*

Ike reached a life-changing decision. His mother endowed him with a
sense of duty nearly forty years earlier. He now knew that it was his duty
to fight Hitler. He was certain America would be at war within a year, even
if his country didn't know it. He had to do whatever he could to help.

Ike returned to his family in the main room.

"Can you turn that thing off?"

John nodded as he shut the radio.

Ike looked Mamie in the eye.

"It's my destiny to fight him. I have to play my part in this war, no
matter how small." Mamie knew what Ike meant. "We have to return to
the United States."

☆☆☆☆☆

DECEMBER 12, 1939

IKE STOOD ON the pier, monitoring the ship set to return to the US. Mamie and John had recently boarded, and Ike watched the last of his family's cargo get carried aboard. President Quezon had offered Ike a blank check to stay in Manila. Ike liked Quezon; he was a good partner in bridge and fishing. But no amount of money was going to change Ike's mind. Quezon settled for a dinner party to see the Eisenhowers off. He gave Ike the Philippine Distinguished Service Star, which Mamie pinned onto his white dress uniform. Quezon told Mamie she had helped her husband earn that metal.

Ike then received a more interesting assignment offer. A group of benefactors offered him $60,000 a year to resign from the Army and find locations across Asia for Jews fleeing the Nazis to find refuge. He had become known as a fierce critic of Hitler and a friend of Manila's Jews. Ike was tempted; the assignment would allow him to help a lot of vulnerable people while earning a higher salary. Again, though, Ike said his duty was to the Army. He had to do whatever he could to fight Hitler.

"I still think you're making the mistake of your life by returning to the States. You can do a lot more good here than over there as a mere lieutenant colonel."

Ike turned to see General MacArthur standing behind him, his arms folded behind his back.

"I'm aware of your opinion, sir." Ike was glad that Mamie had already boarded the ship; she hated MacArthur for how he treated Ike.

"You're the best clerk I've ever had," MacArthur said as he put his hand on Ike's shoulder. "But the British Navy and French Army will beat the Germans before we're pulled in."

"I disagree, sir," Ike said. He paused. "It was my duty to request a return home."

MacArthur cracked a small smile.

Ike boarded the ship shortly thereafter. The Philippine Army band played on the shore. Two Filipino planes followed the ship as it surged away from the coast. Mamie turned to Ike as they stood on the port bow.

"This could be a big turning point for us. I feel as though our lives are about to change."

Ike nodded. His duty led him home.

A Plan to Save Civilization

I have a feeling that he was a far more complicated man than he seemed to be—a man who shaped events with such subtlety that he left others thinking that they were the architects of those events. And he was satisfied to leave it that way.
—Don Whitehead, on Dwight Eisenhower

DECEMBER 7, 1941

Knock-knock.

BRIGADIER General Dwight Eisenhower shifted in his bed, his right leg kicking slightly. He rolled onto his right side, his exhausted mind clinging to sleep. He dreamt of Christmas vacation. He and Mamie were to see John, who was attending West Point, as Ike had thirty years prior. He felt the warmth of his family, one of the few joys in his own personal world, as fires raged across the outside world. Ike's unconscious mind clung to his family and did not want to return to the dreary, miserable realm of the awake.

Knock-knock.

Ike's eyes opened. He could no longer ignore the noise. He groaned as he rubbed his throbbing eyes and sat up in bed.

That nap didn't last long. Thought I said not to wake me up. Got so sleepy at lunch. Why can't I be left in peace?

He crawled out of bed, wearing an undershirt and casual pants. He opened the door to see Mamie holding the phone.

"What is it, dear?" he asked. "I really needed that nap and asked not to be woken up."

"You need to hear this," Mamie said as she handed him the phone.

"This is General Eisenhower."

"Ike? This is Tex."

"What's happening? Am I needed back at the office?"

"Ike, the Japanese have attacked us at Pearl Harbor."

"They hit us in Hawaii?" Ike asked. *I thought the situation with Japan had stabilized. They must have been lulling us into complacency.*

"In Honolulu, yes. How soon can you get back down here?"

"I'll head over as soon as I'm dressed." *Mamie and I were in Honolulu not long ago. Can't believe the Japanese managed to hit it.*

"See you then." Colonel Tex Lee hung up.

Ike hesitated. *Have to ignore that urge to make vegetable soup. Not sure why bad news makes me want to run for the kitchen.*

"I'm sorry, honey, but I have to go," Ike said as he returned to his room to change into his uniform. *I've been advocating for our entering the war since before Germany invaded Poland. It's our duty, but I didn't think it would happen like this. But there's one thing I know: this is a war for national survival.*

☆☆☆☆☆

DECEMBER 12, 1941

ARMY CHIEF OF Staff George Catlett Marshall impatiently waited for Colonel Smith to arrive. In the days since its attack on Pearl Harbor, Japan was conquering an empire across the Pacific islands and territories that were controlled by the United States, United Kingdom, and the Netherlands. Most importantly, Japan besieged General MacArthur's forces in the Philippines. Marshall desperately needed an expert on the Philippines to advise him on how to defend the islands, an American colony. Smith was to bring a list of ten qualified candidates for the role.

Marshall had attended the Virginia Military Institute after his older brother warned their parents that Marshall would embarrass the family if allowed to go. He quickly emerged as one of the Army's most competent and professional officers. Marshall joined General Pershing's headquarters in the Great War after challenging Pershing's leadership. He became the architect of the Argonne offensive that ended the war and served as Pershing's protégé in the interwar years. He rang the bells of warning as the clouds of war gathered in Europe and Germany prepared to attack its neighbors. A criticism of President Roosevelt, like his criticism of Pershing twenty years prior, led to a promotion, this time, to Army Chief of Staff. He now resided in the Army's headquarters in Foggy Bottom, where they would remain while the Pentagon's construction continued.

Washington had been in a whirlwind since Pearl Harbor, shocked by Japan's actions, appalled by the carnage. Marshall had thought Pearl Harbor was the one spot in the Pacific that Japan was unlikely to attack, though he had alerted its commanders to the possibility. He warned President Roosevelt not to place an oil embargo on Japan because Japan would be emboldened to target the Dutch East Indies' oil supply as an alternative source and attack America and Britain in the process. Roosevelt met with Marshall the evening of the attack and instructed him to mobilize the military and arrange protection for the Japanese embassy and consulates.

President Roosevelt spoke to Congress the following day: his "Day of Infamy" Speech rallied the country to war. Three days after that, Adolf Hitler declared war on America. Hitler blamed the Second World War on Roosevelt and his Jewish masters and claimed the war between America and Germany would "determine the fate of the world for the next ten centuries to come." America was at war with two totalitarian empires that sought to carve up the world between them.

Smith entered Marshall's office without knocking.

"Is that the list?" Marshall asked, impatient.

"Yes, sir," Smith replied, handing him the small sheet of paper.

The list said "Dwight Eisenhower" ten times.

"Is this supposed to be funny?" Marshall asked, his professionalism leaving no room for humor.

"No, sir," Smith replied. "He's the obvious man for the job. He was in the Philippines for five years."

Marshall nodded as he contemplated Smith's suggestion. He had only met Ike once, when they were together in France serving under General Pershing in the late 1920s. They had disagreed on the format for Pershing's memoir, but Marshall walked away from their brief meeting respecting Ike's judgment. Ike's name entered Marshall's little black book of competent officers.

Additionally, Ike recently attracted attention for his performance in the Louisiana Army Maneuvers, a war game Marshall orchestrated in order to see which officers performed well. Ike drafted the strategy for, and was a commander of, one of the two armies that "fought" for control of the Mississippi River. Ike even captured General George Patton's army, though Patton subsequently escaped. Ike, Patton, Omar Bradley, Mark Clark, and others each earned recognition for their performance in the Maneuvers.

"What else do you know about Eisenhower?" Marshall asked.

"He's known as the best staff officer in the Army," Smith replied. "And he's been the Army's biggest advocate for entering the European war since September 1939."

"Interesting," Marshall replied. "Where is he stationed?"

"Fort Sam Houston."

"Call him. Tell him to come here."

☆☆☆☆☆

IN THE FIVE days after Pearl Harbor, it seemed like Third Army headquarters was on fire. Ike and his colleagues dispatched units to the West Coast in case of a Japanese invasion. Citizens called about imagined Japanese warplanes almost hourly, leading to perpetual investigations of potential threats. The Third Army transferred antiaircraft guns and antisabotage measures upon request. It also surveyed the southern border to make sure spies did not penetrate the US.

Ike was simultaneously excited and exhausted. He engaged in all of these activities and more, though his focus kept returning to his dream from the previous night. It had really felt like he was leading American forces against the Germans.

Ike was too busy thinking to hear the ringing of the phone that connected his office to DC.

Hitler is the biggest threat this country has ever faced. George III, Lee, and the Kaiser all pale in comparison. Maybe that explains my dreams. I want to lead troops against his forces over there so I don't have to do it over here. Can you even imagine the look on my future grandson's face as he's sitting on my lap while I tell him stories of how I led troops against the Nazis? It'll be like what I must have looked like to the Civil War veterans in Kansas growing up.

"Ike, can you get that?"

"Sorry, General," Ike replied, embarrassed. He picked up the phone. "Yes?"

"Ike, is that you?"

Bedell Smith? Ike wondered. *What does he want?*

"Yes?"

"The Chief says for you to hop on a plane and get down here right away. Tell your boss that formal orders will come through later."

Ike said he understood and hung up. His heart sank.

They can't do this to me. I spent the entire Great War stateside. I can't spend another world war behind a desk. And what am I going to tell George? He was so excited to have me as his chief of staff. Ike and Patton, together again...

He began dialing his home phone number.

All I want out of life is to make my family proud. The one thing. Not fame, not wealth. I just want—

"Hello?" Mamie answered.

"Hi, dear," Ike greeted. "It looks like I'm headed to Washington. I'm coming home now. Can you pack me a suitcase before I get there?"

"Of course, dear. Just one?"

"I think so. I'm pretty sure Marshall just wants to discuss the defense of the Philippines with me. I'm hoping I'll be back soon."

"Ok. Does this mean I'll be going to West Point to see John on my own over Christmas?"

"I'm afraid so. I hate to do that to you. But remember my wedding proposal: my duty to the country always comes first. That's especially true now."

"I know, Ike. I'll get your suitcase ready. See you soon. I love you."

"I love you too." They hung up. He stood motionless. *My duty always has to come first. Even when every fiber of my being is fighting it.*

☆☆☆☆☆

DECEMBER 14, 1941

IKE WAS EXHAUSTED when he reached Marshall's office. Mamie waved him goodbye as his plane took off, but bad weather forced the plane to land in Dallas. He instead took a train to Washington, riding on many of the same railroad tracks he rode from Abilene, Kansas, to West Point in 1911. Milton, his brother, and Helen, Milton's wife, greeted him at Union Station in DC. He stayed at their home in Falls Church.

"Morning, General," Ike said as he approached Marshall's desk. *This building smells like panicked sweat.*

"Morning, Eisenhower. Take a seat." Ike sat down on the opposite side of the desk from the chief of staff. Marshall began a twenty-minute presentation on the situation in the Pacific. It was grim. "Japan is attacking in every direction. The Philippines, Singapore, the Dutch East Indies, and beyond. Almost everyone I talk to, even people in the administration, are afraid Japan might invade Hawaii or the West Coast. Hawaii's defenses are exceptionally weak at the present time as a result of the Pearl Harbor attack, and Admiral King and I have opted to give Hawaii first priority in terms of reinforcements." He was referring to Navy Chief of Staff Ernest King.

"King has told me that the Navy will not be prepared to participate in major operations for the next few months. The Navy's carriers were not in Pearl Harbor when the attack happened, so they are unharmed and operational. However, all of the Navy's supporting vessels were destroyed. King has insisted the carriers only be used for reconnaissance, unless an emergency demands their attention. King has not given me a date for when he expects the Navy to engage in major operations. This is all while our forces across the Pacific, and most notably MacArthur in the Philippines, are desperately asking for any help we can give them. What should be our line of action?"

Ike was taken aback by the request. He froze for a couple of seconds.

Have to keep my poker face.

"Give me a few hours," Ike requested.

"Alright," Marshall agreed. "You're dismissed."

☆☆☆☆☆

IKE RETURNED AT dusk to his seat on the opposite side of Marshall's desk from the Chief, this time holding notes on yellow tissue paper titled "Steps to be Taken." Ike scanned his notes. *Hope I did this right.* His mind flashed to Fox Conner's mentorship in the early twenties. It was the turning point of his career and made him a competent officer. *Conner told me that Marshall's a genius. And from what I remember Conner made it sound like Marshall likes things short and to the point. No extra rhetoric or glitter.*

Marshall waited impatiently for Ike to begin, his hands clasping with interlocking fingers.

"Well? What do you have for me?"

Ike swallowed.

"I'm afraid I don't see much hope to save the Philippines. We had thirty thousand American soldiers stationed there before the Japanese invasion began. We also had thirty-five B17 bombers and 220 fighter planes. We don't currently know how much of these forces are still active. What we do know is that they can't hold out indefinitely without reinforcements. No amount of heroic resistance by Americans and Filipinos will delay the inevitable.

"Unfortunately, I don't think it is militarily possible or pragmatic to send them the reinforcements they need. We may be able to send some supplies via submarine, but the Japanese have total naval superiority surrounding the Philippines, so such an operation would be risky in the extreme, and we don't have any naval vessels to spare. However, even if we could send some supplies or reinforcements, Japanese naval superiority means that the garrison will be unable to hold out if the enemy commits major forces to their reduction.

"Nevertheless, General, we must do everything for them that is humanly possible. The people of China, of the Philippines, of the Dutch East Indies will be watching us. They may excuse failure but they won't excuse abandonment. Their trust and friendship are important to us.

"Our base must be Australia, and we must start at once to expand it and to secure our communications to it. In this last we dare not fail. We must take great risks and spend any amount of money required. This, then, is my key recommendation to you, General. I believe we must keep our sea lanes open to Australia, which will be our critical base of operations, but also to Hawaii, Fiji, New Zealand, and other Pacific islands. We should also deny Japan control of the Netherlands East Indies if at all possible. The Japanese military, like all modern militaries, runs on oil, and we would be wise to deny the large oil reserves of the Netherlands East Indies to the Japanese.

"To carry out these recommendations, I believe we should not waste our forces in locations where they are not vitally needed. We are currently stretched too thin to do that. That means we should ignore the cries from West Coast politicians who ask for units to defend against an invasion. And we should consider what forces we send to the Philippines and similar situations, since anything short of an armada would likely be laid to waste."

Ike completed his presentation. Marshall continued sizing him up, noting how Ike reacted under the Chief of Staff's judgmental gaze, wondering if the Kansan would squirm.

"I agree with you. Do what you can to save them."

Ike resisted heaving a sigh of relief.

The old man was testing me. He knew what to do all along. Wanted to see if I had the ice in my veins to recognize that we can't save the Philippines, including my friends who are still there. I guess I passed the test.

"I'm appointing you to be head of the Far East section of the War Plans Division," Marshall declared.

"Yes, sir." *Damn it. I guess I'm not returning to command troops after all. I better not be stuck behind a desk for this war.*

"Eisenhower, the department is filled with able men who analyze their problems well but feel compelled always to bring them to me for a final solution. I must have assistants who will solve their own problems and tell me later what they have done," Marshall explained.

"I understand, sir."

☆☆☆☆☆

JANUARY 16, 1942

BRITISH PRIME MINISTER Winston Churchill invited himself to the White House in late December. Most of his top military advisors joined him. American and British leaders deemed their four-week summit the Arcadia Conference, where they organized the top military officials of both countries into the Combined Chiefs of Staff. They also determined that Germany, and not Japan, was the most dangerous Axis country and had to be defeated first, although the US Navy did not agree. Ike spent the conference sitting behind Marshall and witnessing the leaders debate global military strategy.

Marshall and Ike reviewed their notes from the conference, which ended two days prior. Ike was swallowed by work. An aid was luckily able to get Christmas presents for Milton and Helen's kids in his name. It was the least he could do for them for hosting him for so long. Ike wondered how Milton was doing in the War Relocation Authority. His thoughts were interrupted as Marshall explained how the British got the Americans to tentatively agree to Operation Gymnast, an invasion of North Africa.

"Part of what troubles me about this line of thinking," Marshall explained, "is that the British are opposed to my proposal for a unified theater commander. We've successfully divided this war into theaters around the globe. The Pacific will be our responsibility. The Middle and Far East belong to the British. The European Theater will be a combined responsibility, since no one can defeat Hitler alone."

"Right."

"That's why it makes sense for each theater to have an individual, *single* commander," Marshall continued. "The command-by-committee idea the British want will cost us the war. It's far too inefficient. A single commander would erase the fault lines of a coalition."

"It's like a football team," Ike suggested. "Teamwork is the key."

"Can I get a more professional explanation, Eisenhower?"

"Of course, General. Fox Conner once told me that in the future world war he predicted in 1922 that 'Systems of single command will have to be worked out. We must not accept the 'coordination' concept under which Foch was compelled to work in the Great War. We must insist on individual and single responsibility—leaders will have to learn how to overcome nationalist considerations in the conduct of campaigns.'"

Ike had thought of Conner's words for years; he could quote them verbatim.

"That's exactly right," Marshall agreed. "I want you to write a memo giving our argument for a unified commander for our government and for the British."

"Yes, sir."

"The next issue I want to go over is mobilizing the country for the war effort. I don't believe this country has ever been more united in our history than since we entered this war."

"I suspect Pearl Harbor is to blame. If Japan had attacked Singapore or the Philippines it wouldn't have had this effect. But the attack on Pearl Harbor was so unexpected and devastating."

"I agree. Now, President Roosevelt has arranged for the construction of 60,000 planes, 45,000 tanks, 20,000 antiaircraft guns, and six million tons of merchant shipping for 1942. I think he's leaving out the artillery, anti-tank guns, and the machine guns that we'll need. But I can work that out with him."

"It's amazing how we've gone from almost complete military weakness a few months ago to one of astounding strength."

"Well, we're not strong enough yet. I tried to push the President and Congress to build up the military ever since I took this job. The same day Germany invaded Poland. They didn't listen, or at least not much. But hopefully we'll be on the right track at the end of this year. By the way, Eisenhower, I couldn't help but happen to notice that the Plan for Industrial Mobilization was your handiwork. It's just the blueprint we need for mobilizing the population and the economy for a major war. It even covers price and trade controls, raw materials, special agencies that need to be created, transportation. The works."

Ike smiled.

"President Hoover told General MacArthur to write up a contingency plan for mobilization when he was Chief of Staff. He passed it off to me."

"It's very well done."

"Thank you, sir," Ike replied, flattered. "I've long thought that the key to future wars was large-scale motorization and mechanization. Mobilize industry and all that."

"Yes, well, it's clear why your reputation precedes you as a master of logistics."

That's what kept me stateside in the last war. It better not keep me here again for this one, Ike thought.

Marshall shifted tone.

"Eisenhower, I have another issue to discuss with you. Staff officers received the bulk of the promotions in the last war. This time around, I intend field commanders to get most of the promotions."

Ike tried not to show any emotion. His breathing slowed.

Marshall continued. "Take your case. I know you were recommended by one general for division command and by another for corps command. That's all very well. I'm glad they have that opinion of you, but you are going to stay right here and fill your position, and that's that!"

Ike could no longer control his instincts.

Of all the goddamn things to tell me! That's the absolute last thing I wanted to hear! Ike's face turned red. His forehead pinched.

"General, I'm interested in what you have to say, but I want you to know that I don't give a damn about your promotion plans as far as I am concerned. I came into this office and from the field, and I am trying to do my duty. If that locks me to a desk for the rest of the war, so be it!"

Ike got up and marched to the door. *I can't be around him any more right now. Been seeing him almost hourly for weeks! And to treat me that way! He's got a lot of ner—*. Ike paused by the time he reached the door. He calmed down, his body temperature cooling. *He's testing me again, isn't he?*

Ike turned back, smiling. He noted a tiny smile emerge in the corner of Marshall's mouth. It was a cruel ploy to test Ike's temperament.

Ike returned to his desk in the Far East section of the War Plans Division.

That was embarrassing. Anger cannot win. It cannot even think clearly. For many years, I have made it a religion not to indulge myself, but today I failed. I must remember my mother's words: "He that conquereth his own soul is greater than he who taketh the city." My temper is my oldest and greatest enemy. I will fail to oppose Hitler without first defeating it.

Ike put paper into his typewriter and started the memo Marshall had requested on a unified theater commander. He addressed the concerns over national sovereignty that led to the British rejecting Marshall's initial proposal. Ike wrote his memo as an order to an unnamed general.

He instructed the fictional commander that his objectives in the Southwestern Pacific Theater were to first prevent additional Japanese advances, second to secure the sea lanes to Australia, the Philippines, the Netherlands East Indies, and Singapore, and finally to repel the Japanese forces.

Ike restricted the unified commander from interfering with subordinates communicating with their own governments and from restructuring the units from other countries.

When the document was approved and sent, it persuaded both the American and British governments on adopting the unified commander concept.

☆☆☆☆☆

FEBRUARY 2, 1942

IKE WAS ABSORBED in writing another memo when General Gee Gerow, head of the War Plans Division, and General Mark Clark came through a tall, heavy, oak door to Ike's large wooden desk in the division's office in Foggy Bottom. The wall behind Ike's desk sported a huge map that situated the Western Hemisphere as the center of the world.

"One second," Ike muttered as he finished a sentence. He looked up at Gerow and pushed himself back in his chair. "Yes, sir?"

"What are you working on, Eisenhower?"

"The old man has me talking about the vital steps that the United Nations needs to take to win the war."

"Which are?" Gerow asked.

"I'm saying that we need to guarantee that Britain and Russia stay in the war and that we deny the Axis control of the Middle East."

"Go on."

"Well, we need the Brits if we're to ever access the European Theater geographically," Ike began, unsure why Gerow was challenging him so much. "Russia is still pinning down the bulk of the German Army, so that's critical. If they fall, Germany will begin their next phase of expansion and we'll need to start learning German. So it's better to keep the Wehrmacht tied up in Russia. And the Middle East is full of oil that Hitler will use for his war machine, so we have to deny that to him."

Gerow nodded.

"Sounds like you've got it worked out. I hope it's received better than the last one."

"What was wrong with my last memo?"

Gerow handed the memo to Ike. It was marred by a large "Rejected" in President Roosevelt's handwriting.

"I guess the President doesn't want to bomb Germany from air bases in Siberia," Gerow explained.

"Why not?" Ike asked, scanning the memo, frustrated.

"It relies too much on Stalin."

"Are we allies or not?" Ike asked.

Gerow shrugged.

"That's what the President decided. I also wanted to inform you that the boats you requested to be sent to China have been rerouted to Ireland."

Ike's hands fell to his lap, crumpling the old memo. *You're full of good news!*

Collecting himself, Ike asked, "Why would we do that?"

"Europe's been prioritized over the Pacific. You know that."

"That doesn't even make sense, but that aside—"

"Why doesn't that make sense?"

"Gee, you and I both know that military doctrine says you defeat the weaker enemy first. And in this case that's Japan."

"But Roosevelt and Churchill want to keep the Allies united, and that can only happen by targeting Germany first."

"Ignoring military doctrine is going to come back to bite us," Ike replied. "But that issue aside, we're going to regret not helping China more. Especially when there's rumors going around that Chiang Kai-shek might throw in the towel."

"You think China's that important?"

"Of course it is. They're pinning down over a million Japanese troops."

"Japan's still conquering the Pacific without them."

"Yes, but if Japan had more forces available, they could invade Siberia and attack Stalin from the East. Russia has no hope of surviving a two-front assault. That entire hemisphere would collapse."

Gerow nodded as his head bobbed to and fro.

"Fair point."

Ike tossed the old, crumpled memo in a drawer, thinking he could derive some of its details for a future proposal. He coughed. *Don't know why I feel so lousy. I hope it's the flu and not the shingles coming back.*

"I've got one other piece of news for you," Gerow said.

"What is it?"

"I've been assigned to Fort Meade."

Seriously? Gee gets to go work with troops and I'm still stuck behind this desk?

"Congratulations on your parole," Ike replied.

"Thanks. General Marshall is putting you in charge of the War Plans Division now that I'm leaving."

Oh, God. I have to run the whole division now? Tempers are short. There are lots of amateur strategists on the job—and prima donnas everywhere. I'd give anything to be back in the field.

"Don't look so glum, Ike. This is a promotion."

"I know, but I'd rather be with the troops, that's all."

"Don't we all?" Gerow asked. "Maybe don't write so clearly if you don't want to be stuck in Washington. Anyway, you'll do a great job, I'm sure."

"Thanks."

"At the very least it can't be any worse than me. I got Pearl Harbor on the book, lost the Philippine islands, Singapore, Sumatra, and all the Netherlands East Indies north of the border. Let's see what you can do."

Ike smiled.

"Thanks, Gee."

"I'll let you get to it," Gee said as he and Clark left.

Ike sunk back in his chair again. He looked at the gray walls around him and fought the urge to shake his arms in frustration. *I don't want to be here! My parents told me "Opportunity is all about you. Reach out and take it." But this is the opposite! I'm wasting my potential in an office! My grandchildren are going to ask me how I served my Army and country in the war for civilization and I'm going to say, "I wrote a lot of helpful memos!" How pathetic.*

Duty. I have to remember duty. This isn't about me. It's about my duty to the country. It's not the situation that counts; it's about performing my duty in that situation. I must remember that. Maybe then I'll stop rejecting my environment so much and accept that I'm spending the war in Washington.

☆☆☆☆☆

FEBRUARY 6, 1942
SERGEANT MICKEY MCKEOUGH fought to restrain his nerves as he reported to the War Plans Division. He had served with Ike in the interwar years. They had gotten along well. But this was a big assignment, one that could make or break McKeough's career. This followed McKeough's failure to escort Mamie Eisenhower from San Antonio to West Point to see John before McKeough arrived in Washington. Mamie got first class train tickets while McKeough was in coach. How was he supposed to know the trains would separate in Chicago? McKeough spent the next twenty hours terrified of being court-martialed for losing a general's wife. Luckily, he found her in New York, and she was now safely in West Point doting over John.

McKeough saw Ike enter division headquarters.

"Have to be professional," McKeough muttered to himself. He stood at attention and saluted Ike. "Sir! Reporting for duty!"

Ike held out his hand for a handshake instead of returning the salute.

"Hello, Mickey, sure am glad to see you again," Ike said with a smile.

McKeough relaxed and lowered his guard, shaking Ike's hand. It was the same old Ike he'd always known.

"I'm glad to have you on our team," Ike continued, "though I understand you lost my wife on the way here."

"Well… sir…" McKeough stuttered.

"Relax, I'm teasing you," Ike said. "Mamie may have been raised like a southern belle but she's pretty scrappy. She flourished when I was stationed in Panama and the Philippines. Though she certainly preferred Paris."

"But that was before—"

Ike nodded.

"Right. Before 1940."

They walked deeper into the office. Mark Clark approached them.

"Have you heard the news about MacArthur?"

"I heard Roosevelt ordered him to abandon our troops in the Philippines and head to Australia," Ike replied. "But that was a couple days ago."

"Well get this," Clark said with a smile. "Now he's getting the Medal of Honor."

Ike's eyes widened.

"The Medal of Honor? For what? Being unprepared and losing the Philippines?"

"Roosevelt thinks it will help morale."

"Uh!" Ike exclaimed, shaking his head. "Politicians. The President should be making these decisions based on military logic, not public opinion."

Clark shrugged. Ike thought, *Only MacArthur could lose 30,000 troops and an entire country and get the Medal of Honor. He's as big a baby as ever. I can't believe I was stuck under his thumb for a decade. Marshall is so much better. I wouldn't trade Marshall for fifty MacArthurs. Wait. Did I just think that? What would I ever do with fifty MacArthurs?*

☆☆☆☆☆

FEBRUARY 16, 1942

IKE CONCENTRATED ON a logic tree of wartime priorities he was drawing for the Combined Chiefs while hunched over his office desk. *The fall of Britain, or Russia, or India will give the Axis a greater industrial output than the Allies. That can't be allowed to happen. Our industrial power is the key to victory.*

He glanced at a map that hung on the wall. Ike envisioned recent events in his head, picturing the ultimate nightmare if fortune did not reverse and the Axis maintained its momentum.

The Axis currently controls about one-third of the Earth's surface. Nazi U-boats dominate the Atlantic. We're losing dozens and dozens of ships per month. Hundreds of thousands of tons of material. Even our sea lanes to South America are at risk of being cut off. But the situation in the Eastern Hemisphere is infinitely worse. The Nazis are poised to overrun the Soviets in the Caucasus Mountains and Rommel's pushing back the Brits in Egypt. Those two German thrusts can link up in the Middle East and quickly overrun that region. U-boats could then cross the Red Sea and enter the Indian Ocean. The Japanese, meanwhile, are overrunning the Dutch East Indies and could push through Burma and into India. The

Nazis and Japanese could then link up near the Himalaya Mountains. And that would be it. The joining of the Axis armies would mark the entire Hemisphere's fall to totalitarianism. Russia and China will be defeated and forced to surrender. Churchill will probably get thrown out of office with a No Confidence vote and Britain will make a deal with Hitler to avoid total destruction. Before too long the Axis will turn its attention to our Hemisphere. And America, with all its might, won't be able to resist the combined strength of the entire rest of the world, no matter what Lincoln said. Americans will lose their freedoms. Freedom of speech. Right to a fair trial. Everything. We'll all be Hitler's slaves. The whole world.

That's why I don't get what's wrong with this country. Why wasn't it ready? My countrymen aren't stupid. They must have seen what was at stake when Hitler took one country after another. And how could the Navy be caught with its pants down at Pearl Harbor? Because of that Japan has conquered half of the Pacific. How are so many people messing up this badly with this much at stake? What is wrong with people? And the Navy is still messing up. And MacArthur. And...

I need to calm down. We have a lot of smart people here. They're getting a lot of the big decisions right. Like choosing to prioritize Germany over Japan. Roosevelt, Churchill, and the Combined Chiefs were right about that. I was wrong to question them. Yes, military doctrine says to target the weaker enemy first. But in this situation, that's Germany. The Germans have more of their firepower pinned down fighting the British and the Soviets than the Japanese do in the Pacific. And besides, defeating Japan would do nothing to help Stalin. Our top priority needs to be to keep Russia in the war. Especially when there are rumors that Stalin has been asking Hitler for peace terms. If only there was some way to relieve pressure on the Russians.

Ike looked at the map. The Allies needed to slow the Axis advance. But more importantly, they needed to destroy the German Army. The German Army was Hitler's center of gravity. Destroying it would force Germany's surrender. That was the only way to win the war. But how would the Allies do that? Germany ruled the continent. The Allies had no way to even reach the German Army and fight it in a capacity large enough to destroy it.

The British are fighting Rommel in Egypt, but the Afrika Korps is a fraction of the entire German Army. The Soviets are fighting a huge portion of it, but they lack our industrial power and are taking excessive casualties. We need somewhere we can engage the bulk of the German Army and defeat it. I feel like that keeps leading me back to...

Ike turned to General Clark, one of his oldest friends in the Army.

"Can I talk to you?" Ike asked.

"Of course," Clark replied. "What is it?"

"I think I know how we're going to win the war in Europe."

Clark froze. He turned away from his own desk to listen to Ike. A two-star general knew how to beat Hitler?

"Let's hear it," Clark said.

Ike hesitated.

"I think we need to cross the English Channel and invade the coast of France." He had goosebumps saying it out loud for the first time.

Clark's eyebrows furrowed.

"Are you serious?"

"Yes."

"Ike, there hasn't been a successful cross-channel attack since William the Conqueror won the Battle of Hastings in 1066. And there's *never*, in the history of warfare, been a successful attack *from* England and *into* France. What you're talking about is without any precedence in military history. And against the toughest enemy imaginable."

"Hear me out, Mark. When I served in Panama under Conner, he made me study the Civil War in extreme detail. Every general, every strategy. What worked and what didn't. And you know what I learned? That Ulysses Grant was the best general we ever produced. He defeated Lee and saved the Union."

"Which he did through brute force. Grant was a butcher."

"No, he wasn't. His casualties were lower than Lee's. Grant did it by systematically destroying Lee's Army. Not by taking Richmond, the Confederate capital. Not with some special maneuver like outflanking the Confederates. He did it through attrition. He targeted Lee's Army, like Clausewitz wrote about in *On War*, and he destroyed it. That forced Lee's surrender at Appomattox. There's no special button we can press to defeat the Third Reich. I want us to do to Hitler what Grant did to Lee."

"And we'd have to invade France to do that?"

"It's the only land area large enough to engage the German Army on a large scale and defeat it decisively."

"North Africa's obviously not large enough. And there's not enough of the German Army there to fight. What about the Russian front? We could put forces there and help Stalin defeat the German Army there."

"Our lines of approach would be too long."

"We could go through Murmansk from the north or from the Persian Gulf via the Cape of Good Hope from the south. We're already sending the Russians war material that way."

"I don't think we could send millions of soldiers as well. Besides, I don't see Roosevelt and Marshall wanting to rely on Stalin that much. I see them agreeing to a cross-channel attack before they'd ever make that deal with Stalin."

"What about going through Norway?"

"It's not large enough for the type of ground campaign we'd need to defeat the German Army."

"Portugal? Spain? We wouldn't have to go through the Atlantic Wall."

"Maybe. But France is closer to Germany, so it would be closer to the heart of Hitler's empire and engage the German Army faster. Plus, it wouldn't pull Franco into the war."

Clark nodded, persuaded.

"What timeline are you thinking?"

"If Roosevelt, Churchill, and the Combined Chiefs get on board with this now, we can invade France by early next year. The Brits would have to take the lead, since we'd still be building up our military."

"Did you think of this just now?"

"I actually thought of it last September. But the more I think about grand strategy, the more I'm convinced that that's the only way to beat Hitler."

It's strange. I've spent every day thinking about Hitler since November 1938. How he's putting his own selfish interests over his duty to humanity, the threat he poses, how to stop him, how to defeat him. But he's never heard of me. Doesn't know I exist. Life is odd.

☆☆☆☆☆

FEBRUARY 20, 1942

"OUR SHIPS ARE doing no good at the bottom of the Atlantic," Admiral King declared. Marshall had arranged a meeting of the top American officers from all the branches in a Foggy Bottom conference room. Ike sat in the back of the room with the other lower-ranked officers. "We should stop sending convoys to Britain and instead reorient them to the West Coast, which is at risk from Japanese invasion. Let the British and the

Russians deal with Hitler. We should focus on Japan. Get revenge for Pearl Harbor."

Ike rolled his eyes. *The best thing someone could do for this war effort is to shoot King. He's the antithesis of cooperation. He's a deliberately rude person, which means he's a mental bully. Especially to his juniors.*

"Do you have something to add, Eisenhower?" Marshall asked. The Chief had noticed Ike's eye roll.

That's embarrassing. Need to control my instincts better.

"No, sir."

"It seems like you do."

"General Marshall, I'm outranked by everyone in this room."

"Eisenhower, if you have an idea that can help win this war, it is your duty to tell us. I'm ordering you to speak."

"In that case, General," Ike began, "I think we should maintain the Europe-first policy and transform southern England into an enormous armed encampment. Then we'd cross the channel and invade France. This would allow us to push the German Army back across Western Europe and destroy it. We've all read Clausewitz. The German Army is Hitler's center of gravity. If we destroyed it, we'd force Germany's surrender."

The room was silent. No one had expected a proposal that radical, especially from a two-star general. When did the smiling, easy to talk to Ike get so bold?

"Wouldn't a frontal assault against the Atlantic Wall be suicide?" Marshall asked.

"On the contrary, sir, I think not attempting this operation would guarantee Hitler's victory and the end to our way of life."

"But what forces would we need to conduct this operation?"

"We would need massive air power to overwhelm the Luftwaffe. Then we'd cross the channel with two to three million men."

"Those forces don't even exist."

"I think those forces could exist by the start of next year, General."

Marshall studied Ike's face, sizing him up. His protégé had thought this through.

"Eisenhower, the other chiefs and I have been discussing this sort of idea for some time. Some of them still need convincing. So will the President. Write a memo where you explain and flesh out this idea. Have it to me by tomorrow morning."

"Yes, sir."

☆☆☆☆☆

MARCH 10, 1942

IKE LEANED BACK from his typewriter to scrunch his fingers. *Why are they so cramped? Maybe because I've been here for eighteen hours a day, every day, since December 14. Maybe that's why.*

He looked at the message he was writing for President Roosevelt to send to Chiang Kai-shek, the Nationalist Chinese leader. The President expected the letter the following day. *Have to keep working. Otherwise I'm going to miss dinner again. Missed it every night this week. It's nice of Milton and Helen to stay up with me and chat for a bit when I get home most nights. And thank God Mamie's with me now. It's nice that she's taken on the role of making me breakfast in the morning. I miss being in charge of the kitchen.*

Ring!

Ike grabbed the phone on his desk.

"This is the War Plans Division. General Eisenhower speaking."

"Ike, it's Mamie."

"Mamie! I was just thinking about you. How are you, dear?"

"Ike, I have terrible news."

"What is it?" *Is something wrong with John?*

"Your dad's passed away."

Ike paused. *I knew he was sick, but...*

"Ike, are you there? Did you hear me?"

"I heard you. Thanks for telling me."

"Are we going to the funeral?"

"Mamie, I'm needed here. I have to do my duty. I can't go to Abilene. Not even for this."

"Ok, Ike. I understand. Is there anything I can do for you or should I let you be?"

"I need some time to think and reflect."

"Ok, Ike. I love you."

"I love you, too. See you tonight." They hung up.

Ike spent the next half hour reflecting on his father, who was stoic, humorless, and quick to take offense. Little affection passed between him and his sons. Ike's brother, Arthur, had said that their father was absent even when he was home. But Ike loved his father. His father and the Eisenhower boys had read scripture every morning. Ike got his first work experience in the creamery his dad worked for. Once he was finished reflecting, Ike wrote himself a note:

> I have felt terribly. I should like so much to be with my mother these few days. But we're at war! And war is not soft—it has no time to indulge even the deepest and most sacred emotions. I loved my Dad. I think my Mother the finest person I've ever known. She has been the inspiration for Dad's life and a true helpmate in every sense of the word. I am quitting work now—7:30 p.m. I haven't the heart to go on tonight.

Ike wrote a diary entry a couple days later:

> My father was buried today. I've shut off all business and visitors for thirty minutes—to have that much time, by myself, to think of him, he had a full life. He left six boys and, most fortunately for myself, Mother survives him. He was not quite 79 years old, but for the past year he had been extremely old physically. Hardened arteries, kidney trouble, etc. He was a just man; well liked, well educated, a thinker. He was undemonstrative, quiet, modest, and of exemplary habits—he never used alcohol or tobacco.
>
> His finest monument is his reputation in Abilene, Kansas. His word has been his bond and accepted as such; his sterling honesty, his insistence upon the immediate payment of all debts, his pride and independence earned for him the reputation that has profited all of us boys. Because of it, all central Kansas helped me to secure an appointment to West Point in 1911. I am proud he was my father! My only regret is that it was always so difficult to let him know the great depth of my affection for him. David J. Eisenhower 1863-1942.

Ike put down his pen. *My father lived a humble life. But he raised six successful sons. I hope he was proud of that. I wish I had done something in the Army that could have made him proud. Or anyone in my family proud.*

☆☆☆☆☆

APRIL 18, 1942

THE WAR PLANS Division was riveted by the news that Lieutenant Colonel James Doolittle led a bombing run on Tokyo, capital of the Japanese Empire. The attack was mostly symbolic, but it was the first major American operation of the war and boosted Allied morale. However, this victory did not relieve the division from work.

Ike's lunch, a hot dog, sat on his desk while he worked the day away. His morning had been tied up with his recent Australian woes. The Allies feared Japan might invade the distant continent, so Ike told the Australian government he intended to send them a division of African American soldiers. The Australian ambassador replied that his country would prefer white soldiers. Determined that African American soldiers get experience and advancement, Ike informed the ambassador that the African American division was the only unit he was willing or able to send. He received a flood of cables begging for the division.

Ike tracked its journey. The transport ship took off from the East Coast of the United States and narrowly dodged an Italian ship near Brazil. It then made its way through submarine-infested waters as it circled the southern tip of South America.

Sergeant McKeough approached Ike's desk.

"What is it, sergeant?"

"The Chief's returning your memo, sir."

Ike glanced at it. It lacked red marks. Ike's grin stretched from ear to ear.

"I never thought I'd see the day. I got one back with no errors! This is worth more than the Medal of Honor!"

"He also asked for you to go to his office."

"A pat on the back? From him?" McKeough shrugged. Ike entered Marshall's office. "You wanted to see me, sir?"

"Yes, Eisenhower, come in here," Marshall said. "Your stream of memos about the cross-channel attack was extremely well written. No muddled language. You're clearly very passionate about this subject."

"Thank you, General."

"You've convinced me of the wisdom of your plan. Our other top officers are convinced, too. President Roosevelt even signed off on its premise."

Ike smiled, though he stopped it from being too large. *I can't believe the entire military leadership is embracing my idea like this. Can you imagine if it actually happens? I suppose that's something I could tell my grandkids about!*

"Anyway," Marshall continued, "I want to send someone to London to meet with the British chiefs and make sure they're on board with this plan. If they are, we can try to prepare for early 1943, as you suggested. Who would you recommend I send?"

"Major General Joseph McNarney and General Mark Clark would be good fits, I believe."

Marshall held back a smile.

"The position's yours, Eisenhower."

What? I'm going to London? Ike thought, surprised.

"Are you sure, General?"

"Yes," Marshall said. "It's your plan. You should sell it. You also have a good diplomatic touch that I think will go over well with the Brits. Who would you like to bring?"

"Who are my choices?"

"Any officer in this army."

"Can I choose General Clark?"

"Of course."

☆☆☆☆☆

MAY 25, 1942

"I GOT GENERAL Hap Arnold. He's a three star," Margaret said as she finished putting on her uniform for the British Mechanized Transport Corps. "Who did you get?"

"Some two star with a German name that I can barely pronounce," Kay Summersby replied. "Can't believe I got out of bed at 5:00 a.m. for a two star."

"Oh, poor Kay," Margaret replied. The other drivers giggled.

"The German named one?" Nancy asked. "I heard a rumor that he might be Marshall's pick to lead the American forces here."

"Is that supposed to impress me?" Kay asked, frustrated and warm from the lack of air circulation.

Kay inhaled her ration of tea and toast.

"Americans," she muttered. "Flaunting their money. And wankers like Lindbergh trying to keep America out of the war while Hitler enslaves our continent." She bit her toast. "I suppose they did give me my fiancé, though."

"Captain Arnold *is* nice to look at," Margaret replied, getting more laughs.

Kay drove her car to the American embassy at 20 Grosvenor Square. She came from a wealthy family but had volunteered to drive ambulances in London's East End during the Blitz to rescue the dead and dying. She now had the less exciting duty of chauffeuring American officers.

She left her car and entered the embassy for a sandwich. Two American officers waited beside her olive Packard upon her return. One was tall, the other stockier and clearly impatient. Kay was mortified and briskly saluted.

"Are one of you General Eisenhower?"

"I am," the shorter man said. Kay quickly opened the door for the Americans.

"Where to?" she asked.

"We'd like to go to Claridge's, please," Ike replied.

"Oh, really?" Kay asked. "That's only two blocks from here. It would be faster to walk."

"We've opted to drive," Ike replied. "See the city a bit."

"Very well," Kay said. She began driving.

Ike and Clark saw that most of the city was in ruins. Dust hung in the air. They had heard that clothing was rationed. Brits were given four inches of hot water to bathe nightly. They had a few ounces of meat per week. Fresh fruit was considered a luxury. Only doctors and farmers were allowed to drive their private cars.

Ike glumly looked at his clasped hands in his lap. *I wouldn't have driven this short a distance if I knew the conditions here. We can't be seen wasting fuel.*

"I understand why we're here to save Britain," Clark said, looking out the window.

Ike's nostrils flared.

"We should develop a pamphlet for American soldiers coming over here to explain how to get along with the Brits," he said.

☆☆☆☆☆

MAY 27, 1942

"THE AMERICANS OVERESTIMATE the amount of soldiers and war material that they can get across the Atlantic by next year," Lieutenant General Bernard Law Montgomery lectured. "Our cousins must be patient, and follow the directions from our much more experienced British General Staff. That is the only way we will ever achieve an eventual victory."

This tone isn't helping our coalition, Ike thought. He and Clark were among the guests who watched Montgomery's field exercise in Kent and were now watching Montgomery lecture about the exercise. *That gray field coat makes him look even smaller than he actually is.*

Montgomery had distinguished service in the Great War, having survived a sniper round through the lung at Ypres and having fought at Passchendaele. He also helped the British Expeditionary Force escape Dunkirk in 1940.

"The Americans would be wise to join the British in our successful resistance to German and Italian action in North Africa," Montgomery said. "America's military has produced an impressive record of victories in its one hundred and fifty years of existence, but the British Army and Royal Navy were winning wars when—"

Montgomery paused. Ike did not pay attention; he was on the second puff of a cigarette. Montgomery looked at his audience.

"Who's smoking?"

"I am," Ike replied, not thinking anything of it.

"Stop it. I don't permit smoking in my office," Montgomery declared. "I ask you to extinguish it immediately."

Ike's tongue rolled over his upper-right molars. *I've never met a less gracious host.*

"Is that an unreasonable request?" Montgomery asked.

"No," Ike replied as he dropped his freshly lit cigarette to the ground and extinguished it under his boot. "Of course not."

"You might also remove that silver string from your shoulder," Montgomery suggested. "We wouldn't want to appear unprofessional, now would we?"

Ike took a deep breath as he removed the string.

"That son of a bitch!" Ike exploded when he left the session. Kay cringed upon looking at him. His charming smile had been replaced by a fiery red and veins protruding from his forehead like strands.

☆☆☆☆☆

MAY 30, 1942

"HOW'D YOUR MEETING go with," Clark paused, turning to Ike as Kay drove them through the cluttered and damaged London roads. "What was his name again?"

"Vice-Admiral Mountbatten," Ike replied. "It went really well. He put on a demonstration of a practice amphibious landing."

"That's probably useful. We haven't done a landing like that since 1898."

"It was. It's clear that the initial waves of troops must be specially trained in amphibious procedures and cover a front large enough to keep the enemy from immediately focusing his defenses."

"What about the weather?"

"That's a key factor. Bad weather could break an operation."

"Admiral Mountbatten is quite well regarded in my country," Kay said.

"I can see why," Ike replied. "He was vigorous, intelligent, courageous. I could see him leading the invasion of Europe next year."

"That's excellent to hear," Kay responded. "It would be wonderful to have him or one of our other top commanders lead the attack to reverse Dunkirk."

"Well, he certainly seems like a man committed to doing his duty."

"You're quite fond of that word, General Eisenhower."

"Call me 'Ike.' What word?"

"Duty."

"Oh, yes! I think the measure of a man, or a woman, is their willingness to put their selfish interests aside and do their duty for others. For instance—and I hope you don't mind me commenting on your domestic affairs—but it seemed that your King Edward VIII distinctly rejected his duty in favor of his own desires."

"Most of us have harsher things to say about him than that," Kay replied.

"I could say the same about General Chaney and the other American officers in our headquarters here. They're keeping bankers' hours and are wearing civilian clothing! What we need over here is a real commander."

"Maybe you're that commander?"

Ike blushed. He looked out the window and sighed. *I miss Mamie. I know it's only been a few days, but I hate being apart from her. Why do I get the feeling that this war is going to keep us separated? Comes with an Army life, I guess. Duty. I have to remember 'duty.'*

"Here we are!" Kay exclaimed.

Ike and Clark exited the car. Their destination was a sprawling Victorian mansion with golden carvings decorating its walls. Ike looked at the building with wide eyes. Kay giggled, admiring the Midwesterner's curiosity.

Ike and Clark entered the building. Ike's stomach rolled. *No need to be nervous; I've seen the PM a couple of times in Washington already, though this is the first time I'm speaking with him personally.*

"My dear Ike!" Churchill boomed. The Prime Minister was shorter and plumper than Ike but shared his spherical facial features and near-baldness that would lead to supporters saying the two men looked like babies. The military chiefs followed Churchill down stairs.

"Thank you for having us, Mr. Prime Minister," Ike said.

"Oh, but of course!" Churchill replied, his cheeks flush with excitement. "I'm honored to meet the man handpicked by the great General Marshall!" Churchill reached the ground floor. He and Ike shook hands. Churchill escorted him to his war room.

Ike couldn't help but smile. He served in Fort San Houston less than six months ago. Now he met the greatest leader of the age. He saw Churchill as a prophet and a statesman rolled into one, a visionary who foresaw the threat Hitler posed to Europe and then stood up to the monster in 1940.

"I know we come from two different backgrounds, my dear Ike, with me a descendant of Marlborough, and you from Kansas, but we're both military men at heart," Churchill said.

"Agreed," Ike replied. "Shall we take our seats?"

"I prefer to stand. I really am glad you're here, Ike. And I slept the sleep of the saved and thankful the night I heard that Japan had attacked Hawaii. I thought of what our Foreign Secretary, Edward Grey, said over thirty years ago. He said that America was like a giant boiler. 'Once the fire is lighted under it, there is no limit to the power it can generate.'"

Was that a compliment? He was happy when my country was attacked?

"Now, Ike, I understand that your US Army Air Forces intend to conduct daytime bombing campaigns over Europe," Churchill said.

"That's correct."

"I would advise your country learn from the experience of our Royal Air Force. Daylight raids may seem more accurate in targeting, but really they are a waste of resources."

"With all due respect, Mr. Prime Minister, I agree with the view expressed by General Spaatz and the Army Air Forces. Our B17 bombers are called 'Flying Fortresses' for a reason. Each one carries ten .50-caliber machine guns for defense. Flying in close formations will give them a terrific amount of firepower."

"Don't underestimate the Luftwaffe, no matter how much of an ogre Goering may seem! Your air forces lack long-range fighter escorts. Your 'Fortresses' will suffer terrible losses."

"The P-39s and P-40s can escort them about four hundred miles."

"Good luck hitting anything substantial within just four hundred miles," said Alan Brooke, Chief of the Imperial General Staff. His tired eyes and thin mustache were his defining physical features.

"It's longer than your Spitfire planes go."

"Which is why we've committed the Royal Air Force to nighttime raids!" Churchill exclaimed.

"General Marshall and our other chiefs strongly support the daylight raid, even if it is of greater risk. I don't foresee you changing our minds on this point. The real purpose of my being here is that General Marshall wants to confirm that you're committed to the cross-channel attack in early 1943."

Churchill turned to his chiefs and smiled. He turned back to Ike.

"I urge caution, my dear Ike. An attack like that so early is simply impossible."

Will he not cooperate on anything?

"Why wouldn't we be ready, Prime Minister? Your forces will take the lead—"

"British forces are stretched around the world, Ike. We have an entire empire to defend. We lost substantial forces when Singapore fell in February. Tobruk's fall also means the entire Middle East is at risk to Rommel's Afrika Korps. Our focus should be there. We don't have the means to take the lead in an operation as audacious as a cross-channel attack."

"But that means that we'd have to do it!" Ike exclaimed. "And we won't have the manpower by that point! It would delay the invasion to the summer."

"Or until 1944," Churchill suggested.

"Why don't we delay it indefinitely?" Ike asked sarcastically.

"Sounds good to me."

Ike's face turned red.

"What would you rather we do?"

"I suggest we focus on destroying Rommel's forces in North Africa. And then perhaps Norway."

"That won't move a single German division or plane away from the Russian Front! And you've promised to help Stalin! We have to invade France!"

"Any attack between Norway and the Brest Peninsula would end in slaughter. A North African landing near Morocco and Tunisia would allow us to strike Rommel from both sides."

"What makes you think the Vichy French would even cooperate with the British if they land in Morocco after you destroyed their fleet in 1940?"

"They'll be less resistant if we appoint an American commander. They don't hate you. Just us."

"But—"

"I am not prepared to repeat the Gallipoli disaster on the coast of France, Ike!" Churchill exclaimed, referring to his amphibious operation in 1915 that failed to knock the Ottoman Empire out of the Great War. He had been the plan's architect and the Royal Navy's scapegoat when it failed, nearly ending his career. "America may have young boys to spare, but your proposal would have us fight to the very last Englishman! I won't have it! No more Sommes! No more Passchendaeles!"

"Then how would you propose we destroy the German Army?"

"That's not necessary."

"Prime Minister, that's how you *win* a war! You attack the enemy's center of gravity!"

"Only if you're unimaginative, such as your General Grant in your Civil War!"

"Grant was—"

"The generals honored in military history devised a special maneuver to win, a clever trick! They didn't use brute force! Think of Napoleon at Austerlitz."

"Then how would you force Germany's surrender?"

"We can undermine Hitler's empire by attacking its soft points, such as the Mediterranean or the Balkans. That will trigger his overthrow. Then we'll put him on a prison island like we did with Napoleon. That will allow us to restore the conquered countries of Europe."

"Prime Minister, it's very naïve to think that attacking Southern Europe will trigger Hitler's overthrow."

"It might if we let the other Nazis stay in power, assuming they're no longer a threat. A good counterweight to Stalin."

"What! That's no way to discuss an ally!"

"Oh, Ike, now who's naïve?"

"You want to turn Germany into a counterweight against Russia? Is this the sort of old-fashioned European diplomacy that leads to one war after another?"

"How else would you deny Stalin mastery of Europe once Germany's defeated? Britain will be too exhausted to save the continent. And America has been isolationist dating back to your President Washington."

"What to do about Stalin after the war is for you and President Roosevelt to decide. I'm an Army officer. My task is to force Germany's surrender. And I am telling you, the only way to do that is through invading France!"

Churchill paused, satisfied with his verbal jousting.

"What time do you wake up in the morning, Ike?"

"No later than six. Why?"

"There's your problem! You should never leave bed before noon."

"You sound like my wife. At least that was her sleep schedule before the war."

"She would agree with me that your plan is folly."

"Prime Minister, you're going to have to be more flexible than this if our nations are going to cooperate."

"But Ike, why shouldn't the colonies like following the direction of their mother country?"

☆☆☆☆☆

JUNE 20, 1942

"IN CONCLUSION, MR. President, we believe that crossing the English Channel in late 1942 or early 1943 is not only plausible, but necessary, to winning the war," Marshall explained. "It will allow our forces to defeat the German Army in Western Europe and for a speedy thrust into the heart of Germany."

Admiral King and the other Joint Chiefs flanked Marshall. Ike's memos on the cross-channel attack lay in front of them. The memos had convinced King and other American military leaders of the wisdom of invading Europe.

President Roosevelt waited patiently during the Joint Chiefs' presentation. He was the fifth cousin of Theodore Roosevelt and the Assistant Secretary of the Navy to Woodrow Wilson. He had been struck down by polio and had rebuilt himself, reemerging on the national scene as President to stabilize America's political and economic systems during the Great Depression. He was now leading America's effort to save a world enveloped in darkness. The presentation now finished, he turned to each of his chiefs, looking each one in the eye before settling his glare on Marshall.

"Are you out of your goddamn minds?!" he shouted.

"Mr. President!" Marshall began.

"I'm speaking!" Roosevelt asserted. "An invasion of France would be the greatest undertaking in military history! We are *nowhere* near ready for that. We will need at least another year to build up our armaments and to train our troops. You're talking about a head-on assault against Fortress Europe by our inexperienced men and against the greatest army on Earth!"

"Mr. President, I thought you favored a cross-channel attack."

"Maybe eventually! Certainly not in six to eight months' time! *This* is the idea you're proposing to me? Do you realize that the high casualties of a failed invasion of Europe would jeopardize the Europe First policy? The American people would demand we turn our attention to the Pacific."

"Mr. President, we may as well abandon Europe First and go defeat Japan if we don't pursue the cross-channel attack," Marshall replied.

"That's a little like taking up your dishes and going away. The defeat of Japan does not defeat Germany. On the other hand, the defeat of Germany means the defeat of Japan, probably without firing a shot or losing a life."

"But—"

"Are you all secretly Republicans?" Roosevelt asked, "because a failed invasion of France would deliver both chambers of Congress to the former Party of Lincoln by next November. There's no way I'm authorizing this idea."

"Yes, Mr. President," Marshall accepted as he exchanged a look of disappointment with King.

☆☆☆☆☆

JULY 22, 1942

THE NEXT MONTH flew by. Marshall appointed Ike as the American commander in Europe. Ike returned to London to establish US headquarters. He was disappointed that Roosevelt vetoed his idea for invading France in early 1943. News then emerged that Stalin was considering a separate peace deal with Hitler as German forces pushed through southern Russia toward the Caucasus oil fields. Seizing those oil fields would deny them to the Red Army, forcing Russia's collapse. It would also allow Hitler to wage war on America and Britain. The outcome of the war was at stake.

Ike wrote a new memo after returning to Washington, this time arguing for an invasion of France that was designed to fail but that would draw forty German divisions away from the Russian front. Ike explained that there was a one-in-five chance that the invasion force would survive on the beaches of France for more than a couple of months but that it was necessary to keep Russia in the war. Roosevelt grasped Ike's logic and approved of the idea. Churchill and Alan Brooke raced across the Atlantic to stop it.

Roosevelt, Marshall, King, Churchill, and Brooke sat around a conference table in the White House's Cabinet Room. Woodrow Wilson's image hung over the fireplace.

"I admire how your Navy thrashed the Japanese at Midway a few weeks ago," Churchill said to King, "but I'll never agree to this Sledgehammer idea." He was referring to the sacrificial invasion of France.

"Keeping Russia in the war must be our highest priority," Marshall rebutted. "Your proposed Operation Torch, the invasion of North Africa, does nothing to achieve that objective."

Roosevelt listened to the debate, his head turning back and forth as points were made.

"I mean no insult to Joe Stalin, but our biggest priority must be stopping Rommel from becoming a second Alexander the Great by conquering the Mideast!" Churchill exclaimed.

"You just want the Middle East to preserve your colonial empire and route to India," Marshall said.

Churchill appeared like a child caught with his hand in the cookie jar.

"It's not *my* fault that the right strategic decision lines up with our interests."

"As long as I'm Chief of Staff American soldiers will never die for European empire!" Marshall exclaimed.

"And I won't allow you yank cowboys to lead our British soldiers to slaughter on the beaches of France!" Churchill shouted back. A pencil snapped between Marshall's fingers.

Roosevelt knew he needed to intervene to de-escalate the tension between his ally and subordinate.

"Winston," Roosevelt began, "I am determined that American soldiers be on the ground fighting the Germans by the end of this year. It will get the public behind the Europe First policy. Will Torch accomplish that?"

"Absolutely. It's the only operation that's conceivable this year," Churchill nodded.

"How about before the midterms on November 3?" Roosevelt asked.

Churchill smiled. "I'm sure we can give the Democrats the extra boost if we agree to Torch now."

"Then that's what we'll do," Roosevelt replied.

Marshall and King felt the weight of defeat. King crumpled in his seat. Churchill looked at Marshall with a sarcastic smile that read 'I win.' Marshall turned to Roosevelt.

"Mr. President, I don't know if we should be making military decisions for political reasons. The leader of a democracy does not need to keep the people entertained in war time."

"That's not what this is. Maintaining public support for Europe First *is* a strategic decision."

"And Mr. President, you realize that committing to Torch guarantees that we won't be able to cross the channel until the summer of 1943 at the earliest?"

"I know, General Marshall," Roosevelt replied. He knew better than to call him 'George.' "I want your support for this decision, gentlemen."

"You have it, of course, Mr. President," Marshall replied.

"We'll need to pick someone to lead this operation," Roosevelt said, shifting topics. "Shall we take care of that decision now?"

"We ought to pick an American," Churchill diplomatically suggested, offering an olive branch after winning the previous argument. "The Vichy French will react poorly to a British commander. They hate us."

"Eisenhower is the only Army man that the Navy will accept," King said.

Marshall nodded.

"Eisenhower lacks combat experience, but he's the best man for the job."

"Isn't he a staff officer?" Brooke asked.

"Eisenhower's not really a staff officer in the accepted sense of the word," Marshall began, "but rather my subordinate commander who is responsible for operations of Army forces on a global scale."

Brooke nodded, accepting Marshall's recommendation.

Roosevelt shifted subjects again.

"We'll have to break the news to Stalin. He won't be happy about Torch, even if it is the right decision."

"I can do it," Churchill said. "I'm heading to Moscow next anyway. And there's nothing I love more than disappointing a Bolshevik."

"Oh, Winston," Roosevelt said, like a parent simultaneously amused and disappointed with his child's behavior, "it is essential for us to bear in mind our ally's personality and the difficult and dangerous situation he confronts. I think we should attempt to put ourselves in his place, for no one whose country has been invaded can be expected to approach the war from a global viewpoint."

"I'm just having fun," Churchill playfully replied with his arm resting on the table.

☆☆☆☆☆

JULY 26, 1942

"WELL, EISENHOWER, I have good news and bad news," Marshall said. The chief of staff and his protégé spoke from across a coffee table in the lobby of a Foggy Bottom hotel. A bartender in a three-piece suit loudly took a socialite's order, blending with the room's muzak to break Ike's chain of thought.

"What's the bad news?" Ike asked, accustomed to fixing the world's problems since Pearl Harbor.

Marshall was stoic in the face of Ike's cynical response.

"The President has sided with Churchill on Torch. We're hoping to do the landing by early November."

Ike's eyes widened.

"You can't be serious!" he exclaimed. He stood up in agitation, his arms tense and shaking. *Other people may have supported the cross-channel attack. Marshall. Montgomery. Mountbatten. But I would swear on my father's grave that no one supported it as much as me. This was* my *idea that's been rejected. All of that work. And I thought I was finally making my family proud. I'm so stupid for being an optimist sometimes.*

Ike turned back to face Marshall.

"This is the blackest day in history. It's going to cost us the war."

"You genuinely believe that?" Marshall asked.

"Of course!" Ike roared, not caring if he was unprofessional. "North Africa is a sideshow! It does nothing to attack Germany's center of gravity. It's a waste of time. More than that, it's a desperate, passive move. This is the modern equivalent of when Napoleon returned from Elba and then was whooped at Waterloo."

"The President disagrees."

"I mean no disrespect, General, and I hope this stays between us, but he may be the *last* President we ever have because of this. This operation does nothing to help the Russians, who may collapse before the year is over. Then Hitler will be unstoppable. This could be the end of civilization as we know it."

"The other news I brought was supposed to be good news. But it might not be if you feel this strongly about Torch."

"What is it?" Ike asked. *What could possibly be good news after that?*

"You've been appointed to lead Torch," Marshall said with a slight smile.

Ike took a step back, struggling to breathe.

"Are you okay? You're being very dramatic."

"I'm leading an operation?" Ike asked.

"That's right."

"And it's the exact opposite of my own strategic vision?"

"Apparently."

Ike shook his head in disbelief.

"You seem a little pale in the face, Eisenhower. Are you sure you're alright?"

Ike nodded. He turned to Marshall. His brain was already working through multiple issues.

"I only have weeks to prepare."

"I know, Eisenhower."

"I would like Bedell Smith as my chief of staff."

"Done."

"Will invading northwest Africa lead to Franco entering the war?"

"It's possible. We'll have to anticipate that."

"The supply lines across the Atlantic will be extremely hard to maintain. Especially with U-boats still hunting around."

"That's true."

"A beachhead in North Africa might be impossible to establish."

Marshall watched with interest as Ike transformed from opposing Torch to figuring out how to make it work. His duty would be his guide.

☆☆☆☆☆

Dusk set over Washington. President Roosevelt peered out the Oval Office window. He watched as the Jefferson Memorial slipped into the darkness of night. The memorial was originally planned for Theodore Roosevelt, FDR's cousin, but FDR had it switched to his biggest hero.

Daisy Suckley, Roosevelt's cousin and confidant, entered the Oval Office. She approached the President.

"Your guests are arriving. It's time to come to the East Wing and start mixing margaritas," Suckley said. Roosevelt did not respond. "Is something wrong?"

Roosevelt remained silent for several more moments.

"Life. Liberty. The Pursuit of Happiness. We lose this war and those principles are gone forever." He turned to his cousin. "This war is about the survival of democracy. My military chiefs are right. An invasion of Western Europe will prove necessary to defeat Germany. It will be the centerpiece of Allied strategy. Churchill is wrong to think it can be won in the Mediterranean. But the United States is not ready yet. It will take at least a year, maybe two, before we are."

Suckley said nothing and continued listening to the President.

"A new world will emerge from this war. An end to European colonialism. An end to international aggression. At the heart of that world will be the United Nations. That great organization will succeed where Wilson's League failed. It's not just going to end wars, it's going to prevent the outbreak of new wars. That's what we're fighting for. And we're going to have to invade Europe to do it."

Choosing a Supreme Commander

It is difficult to deal separately with the "General" and the "President,"
regarding each without relation to the impact of the one image on the
other. But it could be argued that "the General" is the greatest figure in
American and world history.
—*The Washington Post,* Eisenhower's obituary

NOVEMBER 17, 1943

I'VE THOUGHT IT my destiny to save Britain from destruction since I
was sixteen, while you claim to be motivated by your duty as a
soldier. Nevertheless, I thought it was masterfully conducted. Truly
one of the great campaigns of this war. And you, my dear Ike, were its
Wellington. And not just Wellington in one of his standard campaigns,
such as in India or in the Iberian Peninsula. Oh, no! You were Wellington
at Waterloo! Future historians shall write that the landing in Salerno was
won in the wheat fields of Abilene. I am quite sure of that."

"That's very kind of you, Prime Minister. I'm afraid I don't share quite
so rosy an evaluation of the present campaign."

"Oh rubbish, Ike. I am a descendent of Marlborough and a historian of
our two great nations. I know when an engagement will be seared into the
memory of generations. This was one. It shall stand alongside Blenheim!
Alongside Gettysburg!"

"I think your own favoritism toward an attack through the
Mediterranean, the 'Soft Underbelly,' as you sold it to the President, might
be distorting your judgment."

"His Majesty would not have personally designed a medal for General Alexander and yourself if he did not share in my judgment. Are you suggesting an 'aw shucks' fellow from Kansas knows better than the sovereign of the greatest empire since Augustus and Trajan?"

"If you're going to use that tone with me, Prime Minister, I might be forced to remind you that my forefathers separated from that sovereign's forefathers for a reason."

"Ha! I do suppose you won that round, my dear Ike. Now you must win some more rounds against that awful Kesselring!"

"That's my intention," General Eisenhower replied as he lit a cigarette, his third since the conversation began. "General Marshall takes a polar opposite view of the Salerno campaign, however."

"All the more reason to stand my ground," Churchill replied as he puffed his fat cigar. He was a man of the nineteenth century who had stepped in to save the twentieth.

"He thought we advanced too slowly and gave Kesselring too much time to fortify his defenses." Ike exhaled smoke through his nostrils. "I personally fall in between you and the old man."

"Careful, Ike. General Marshall is six years my junior!"

"And yet he's ten years older in spirit," Ike said with a slight smile. "I think he's been overly critical of how AFHQ handled the Salerno campaign." Ike was referring to the Allied Force Headquarters, which was Ike's headquarters in the North African and Mediterranean theaters. "I don't see how any individual could have devoted more thought and energy to speeding up operations or to attacking boldly and with risk as I did. And, no offense to your generals, but Wayne could only land in Salerno after Monty landed in Calabria."

Ike was referring to American General Mark Clark and British General Bernard Montgomery.

Maybe I'm uncomfortable because Marshall's never criticized me this heavily before. Strange, because I made far bigger missteps in North Africa than I have in Italy.

"Oh, please!" Churchill chuckled as a fly zoomed by his sweaty scalp. "Monty's a bigger pain than Mussolini. He's indomitable in retreat, invincible in advance; insufferable in victory."

Ike laughed. "I couldn't have said it better myself."

"Can I see the medal again?"

Ike handed Churchill the medal that King George VI had specifically designed for Ike and British General Alexander, his deputy. The medal bore an "I" and an "8," signifying that Ike and Alexander were the only generals in history to command the British First and Eighth armies. A small smile emerged on the left side of Ike's lips as he looked at his award.

Never much cared about being rich, but I do admire certain items of high quality.

Churchill had asked Ike to meet in Malta to discuss the state of the Italian campaign so Churchill could have the most updated picture of the war before President Franklin Roosevelt arrived within days. The two titans of Western democracy were then to meet their communist counterpart, the Soviet leader Joseph Stalin, for the first meeting of the Big Three.

"Truly marvelous," Churchill muttered as he returned Ike's medal and took another puff of his cigar. His face flashed a shade of red as he fought back the need to cough. "Damn infection of the *throat*."

Ike nodded. "Mine's been bothering me for a week or so."

"My doctor says it's a respiratory infection and that I am to 'stop smoking.'" Churchill used air quotes, mocking his doctor. "What rubbish. Do doctors nowadays not know that smoking is the key to health? That and drinking and foregoing exercise."

Ike laughed.

"Is that so?" He leaned back in his chair. "And here I've always thought playing sports was good for me."

"Are my Adonisian good looks not all the convincing you need, Ike?"

Ike laughed again.

"I seem to remember putting on weight after my knee injury ended my football ambitions."

"Correlation is not causation!"

Both men suffering from respiratory infections returned their cigar and cigarette to their lips. Churchill's smile faded.

"I again ask you to consider the wisdom of attacking Hitler's peripheries, such as Italy and the Balkans," Churchill said. Ike shook his head. "You've made such strategic gains against that bad man in the past year!"

"Our efforts have been strategically useless. We've only hit non vital areas of the Reich and eliminated bits and pieces of the Wehrmacht, not the German center of gravity."

"'Useless!' What about the fall of Mussolini! What about the German withdrawal from Kursk!"

"Mussolini's ouster led to Kesselring's takeover of Italy. That's worse, if anything. And I'd think Stalin would credit Zhukov for the German withdrawal from Kursk."

"Oh, please! That Bolshevik will only credit himself." Ike laughed, a puff of smoke bursting from his nostrils. "I suppose you still favor Overlord?"

"I do," Ike said diplomatically. "I believe to my core that it's the only way to destroy the German Army, Hitler's center of gravity. And that's the only way to rid the world of that beast."

"My concern is that the Channel tides will run red with the blood of American and British youths, the beaches choked with their bodies."

"With all due respect, Prime Minister, the greater risk is not delivering a crippling blow to the German Army and doing it quickly. While the Allies have gained the initiative through victories like Stalingrad, Guadalcanal, and Tunisia, they've come at great cost. And no one's lost as much as the Russians. The Soviet Union had about twice the population of Germany and Austria combined when the war started. But if we're to believe the estimates of our two governments, and not merely what Stalin tells us, they're still losing soldiers at well over twice the rate of what they're inflicting on the Germans. If we don't land in France next year, the Red Army might simply be bled to death. And then there will be no way to dislodge Hitler from Europe."

"That's purely conjecture," Churchill responded, his jaw tight. "What's not is the generation of British and French boys who were extinguished in the last war at places like the Somme and Verdun. I am determined to stop a repeat of that monstrosity."

"I still believe Grant's victory over Lee in 1865 shows the necessity of destroying the enemy army in modern warfare. And frankly, Prime Minister, you promised our President your support for Overlord at Quebec."

"I did then," Churchill conceded. "But it's far too risky to engage the German Army directly, and so I've changed my mind. I'm a politician. What do you expect?"

Roosevelt, Churchill, and the Combined Chiefs of Staff committed to launching Overlord in May 1944 in Quebec. They also, on Ike's recommendation, authorized the formation of eleven French divisions armed with American weapons. Ike wanted to use this to invade southern France shortly after Overlord.

"You'll be happy to know that I agree with Monty on the need to delay the landing in southern France. We don't have enough landing craft to land in both regions of France simultaneously."

"Perhaps a landing in the Balkans would be wiser than one in southern France. We could prevent the region from falling under the Soviet sphere of influence."

"Stalin's our *ally*, Prime Minister. And I want three army groups on the Western Front. We need overwhelming force to beat the Germans into submission. No repeats of Salerno."

"I'll convince you yet!"

"If you say so, Prime Minister," Ike replied with a Midwestern smile.

"Regardless," Churchill continued, puffing on his cigar, "the command of Overlord isn't formally fixed. I wish it would go to Brooke." He referred to the Chief of the Imperial Staff. "So would he. But we agreed at Quebec that it would go to an American, as your country is putting in the bulk of the soldiers and weapons. That means the decision is up to President Roosevelt, who is much more *casual* about appointing officials to high positions than I ever would have imagined. But I hope he takes the time to make the best possible choice, in this circumstance. The only way that Hitler can still win the war, in my view, is if the Americans and British choose the wrong person as Supreme Commander. History tells us that most coalitions fall apart. Even Napoleon isn't as impressive once realizing his opponents were always coalitions. He could therefore divide his enemies. We British will be glad to accept either you or Marshall."

I didn't realize there was a question that the position was Marshall's, Ike thought. *God, I want to command Overlord! I was its leading advocate. I sold it to Chiefs. It wouldn't be happening if not for me. And I've shown I can command a coalition amphibious landing in North Africa, Sicily, and Italy. Can't let my personal desires overwhelm my duty. Marshall is the greatest American of my lifetime. Probably the greatest since Abraham Lincoln. I have to step aside gracefully and let the greater man get the command and the glory.*

"General Marshall is the greatest soldier in the world today. His superiors used to say that they wished to serve under *him*," Ike said politely. "The command will certainly go to him."

"If that proves to be the case, then General Alexander will be placed in charge of the Italian Front. That way a Brit will run one campaign if an American directs the war in France. It's only fair."

"What does that mean for me?"

"I suppose President Roosevelt will bring you back to Washington to replace Marshall as Army Chief of Staff."

"I would much rather serve as an army group commander under Marshall than to return to Washington and deal with politicians who ignore logic."

Churchill chuckled. "I'm sure you would. And I'll miss working with you. But it is up to Roosevelt."

"Will your generals serve under one of their colleagues? It might be easier for them to continue serving under an American."

"They will if I tell them to. Nice try, though."

"It doesn't have to be me. Bedell Smith could take the role."

"Smith doesn't want the command. He wishes to remain your chief of staff. Unless you think he would serve under Alexander."

"No. Unless he serves as my replacement in this theater, I would have no interest in his leaving me. I'll only yield to the President on that point."

"The lamb flashes his fangs I see."

"Perhaps General Marshall can serve as a global field commander for all American forces in Europe and the Pacific. He could then have deputy commanders lead specific operations."

"That's substantively no different than our current model."

"True. If Marshall is placed in command of Overlord, I have strong opinions on who should be his subordinates."

"I would expect nothing less from you."

"Tedder should be his chief air advisor. He's an expert on air-ground coordination. If anything, Tedder should be his deputy."

"I would expect one of our own as his deputy. Tedder's a fine choice."

"Marshall has told me his plan would be to hit the beach with inexperienced forces and use veterans from the Mediterranean to drive toward Germany. If he adheres to that design then a conservative general like Bradley should command the landing while Patton directs the thrust across Europe. Patton's strength is he thinks only in terms of attack as long as there's a single battalion that can advance. He'd be a poor pick to lead an army group, but I'd recommend him as an army commander under a man who is sound and solid. That man would have to have sense enough to use Patton's good qualities without being blinded by love of showmanship."

"A man like yourself, General?"

"You know I can't promote myself like that, Prime Minister."

"You wouldn't be 'Ike' if you did. I assume you wouldn't want General Clark in Overlord."

"Certainly not. Wayne's far too cautious. As he showed in Salerno."

"Agreed," Churchill replied.

God, I want the command so badly! Ike thought. *I've learned so much in the past year. I have to restrain my feelings. What did Epictetus say? 'Men are disturbed not by things, but by the principles and notions which they form concerning things.' My placement in this war doesn't inherently mean anything. It's how I react to it that matters. The power of my happiness rests in my own thoughts. I must remember that. That's the key to doing my duty.*

☆☆☆☆☆

NOVEMBER 18, 1943

DARLING GIRL,

SOME days have passed since I last wrote. I've been away—and while gone had two days in bed with a heavy cold. You know what I am once I really get a heavy cold. Tomorrow I must start on another journey, and this time by car. How I hate it! It's a journey I could make in an hour by air—I'll take seven by auto, over slippery roads.

I hear the same things about procuring things in Italy that you do! But possibly it's difficult for you to understand that I cannot get time to go browsing around shops like a lot of others can. I have not been in a shop but once (when I sent you the scarf from England) since leaving home. I have to ask someone to get me things. I've sent a frantic request to find me something for your Christmas—but what luck I'll have is something else again. When 'agents' go shopping they think first of themselves. I do hope that the socks I sent you are of good quality.

Your Lover,

Ike

Ike sighed, leaning back in his chair in his Algiers headquarters office. He glanced out the window, where he could see the gentle Mediterranean waves strike Aleppo pine trees and the rocky coast line.

Writing Mamie lets me think on paper, though my hands are better with a pickaxe than a pen. Wish I didn't have to censor myself so much, but I don't trust the censor on my staff. Her anniversary was four days ago.

Ike used the term "anniversary" instead of "birthday" since he said individuals were only born once.

I hate that I've missed it for a second year in a row. God, I miss her! One reason war is so tragic is that it disrupts the nicest relationships mankind can develop. I'm going to run back to Mamie the day Berlin falls. I wish we could run away somewhere where we'd never be found. Barely get any privacy anymore. Maybe if I end up being responsible for losing the war, then people will ignore me! Of course in that case, Hitler would hang me.

It's crazy to think that we met twenty-eight years ago. Stationed at Fort Sam Houston. She said she liked my ruggedness, and I liked that she was saucy about the face. Paid for our dates with my poker winnings. Hit it off with her family. All girls, while mine is all boys. Proposed on Valentine's Day. We've had our ups and downs. The biggest down was certainly Icky's death. Died in my arms. We almost didn't survive that one. I suppose one of the biggest ups, besides Johnny's birth, was my serving under Pershing in Paris in the late twenties. That was quite a trip. We drove around Europe. Really learned the French countryside. Never learned a lick of the French language though. Don't know why I'm so miserable at foreign languages.

Some crazy stuff happened that trip. Saved a Frenchman from drowning in the Seine. Wonder if he's still alive. He better prefer de Gaulle and the Resistance to Petain and Vichy. Then there was our drive through the Alps. What a crazy experience that was! I was driving. Bill—what was his last name?—was my front seat passenger, while Mamie and Helen were in the back seat. My God, did those ladies complain! Saying that they won't be able to eat for a week and claiming they were doomed to have nightmares as Bill and I did our damndest to navigate us through those perilous mountains! To be fair, though, letting Bill take the wheel was a mistake. He tried to pass a bus and our baggage rack became entangled with the bus' wheel. We almost went over the side of the mountain! Had to lean out and beat the baggage rack away from the bus while Mamie was ready to leap out of the moving car! Then we all had to climb to the Grimsel Pass! The ladies' sarcastic jabs subsided, since they ran out of breath, but their silence was almost worse! Bill and I were proud of ourselves. Got us through rough terrain and saw some beautiful sights. But as soon as we were through the ladies started yelping for lunch! That was our clue that they were fine and were complaining for the sake of it!

What a time. Our family was so close then. Now we're spread out around the world. I'm in Algiers, Mamie's in Washington, and Johnny's at West Point. My duty to America and my love of Mamie are the only things that keep me going. I always dreamed of command in the field, but I never figured I'd miss Mamie this much or be separated this long. My heart aches. I hope we have adventures together like that again. We even got to see Ferdinand Foch's funeral. He was a legend back then. The Supreme Commander during the Great War. I suppose whoever commands Overlord will be his successor. That's crazy as hell. I'm in the running to become Foch's successor. Oh, who am I kidding? No, I'm not. There's no way Roosevelt doesn't give it to Marshall. Ugh! I want it so badly! It was virtually my idea! Oh, stop that, Ike! You're not supposed to think that way! Duty, Ike. Duty.

Tap-tap

Ike turned to see Telek, his black Scottish terrier, tapping his paw against the door. Ike's grin stretched from ear to ear. He petted Telek's head.

"Good, boy," Ike muttered. "I could just break all your ribs with a big hug. Never thought I'd be so jealous of a dog. Not a care in the world. Really shows that we suffer more in our imagination than in reality. We're in the same spot, but one of us is happy and the other's miserable. I suppose I don't get to complain, though. No one does, unless they're in a foxhole in Italy. Those boys are as young as Johnny."

Oh, Johnny. I miss him too. Another great companion this war has stripped away from me for the time being. I don't get why he doesn't write to me more. Sometimes I worry a bit about the possibility that he's a bit spoiled. Things have been easy for him. He may dislike writing a letter, but he should do that much in appreciation! After all, suppose he'd have had to start at thirteen or fourteen getting up at 4 or 5 in the morning working through a hot summer day until 9 at night. Day after day. Or doing his winter work with cold, chapped hands and not even gloves. Maybe he'd think writing a letter wasn't so terribly difficult! I don't know why I'm so grouchy. Lonely I guess. I just want him to develop a grounded, healthy outlook, with a keen sense of his obligations, and enjoying his fun more because he has met those obligations. I wonder how he's doing on demerits at West Point. Or if his tennis game's improved.

Ike rose to his feet and picked up his letter to Mamie. He exited his office, one of over four thousand in AFHQ. Ike was never left wanting; all his needs were addressed several times over. This was because every position required an American and British official, so the staff was double what was necessary. He lived in a seven-bedroom villa near Carthage, the ancient city that had fascinated Ike since childhood. Two members of his staff, Captain Summersby and Captain Harry Butcher, Ike's naval aide, were waiting by his door.

Ike handed Butch the letter.

"Can you mail this to Mamie as soon as possible?" Ike asked.

"Of course, sir," Butch replied.

"Thank you," Ike responded. He turned to Kay, who held a riding helmet. "Is that for me?"

"It's far too small for you, Ike," Kay said, her British accent containing a sing-songy reflection. Her dark curls hung under her ears. "This is mine. Must I do everything for you?"

"Is mine by the stable?"

"That's where you left it."

Ike and Kay proceeded to the stable. Horseback riding with Kay had become a daily activity since Marshall ordered him to relax and get more exercise.

"What's wrong, Ike?"

"How do you know something's wrong?"

"You're an open book."

"What genre?"

"*Ike.*"

"I'm sorry, Kay. I just miss Mamie—"

Kay's face dropped before she overrode her instinct and pushed her emotions aside.

She must be missing her fiancé, Colonel Arnold. A casualty of Tunisia. She's Irish and tragic, Ike thought.

"I'm also frustrated about the situation in Salerno."

"The stalemate?"

A vein bulged above his temple.

"We *thought* Mussolini's fall would mean Italy was lightly defended. We *thought* that Kesselring had withdrawn his forces to the Arno River, north of Rome. So we opted not to use overwhelming force. God, I made Ulysses Grant roll over in his grave. We divided our forces to cover more ground. Wayne landed sixty thousand troops at Salerno. We didn't even use a naval bombardment, so Kesselring's forces were intact. Kesselring nearly drove Wayne's Fifth Army back into the sea. What a *catastrophe* that would have been. Roosevelt, Churchill, and Marshall would have been in a race to see who could fire me first. And then there's the thousands of GIs who would have been massacred. Wayne tried to evacuate. I moved *Heaven* and *Earth* to prevent a defeat. Ordered a fleet of B17 bombers and Admiral Cunningham's armada to bombard Kesselring. We flattened him. Overwhelming firepower saved the day. The Fifth Army took five thousand casualties to Kesselring's thirty-five hundred. Realized Wayne's an overly-cautious field commander. Patton would have been a better pick, but he and Brad were already in London preparing for Overlord."

"So do you think it was your responsibility?"

"I *obviously* have to take responsibility for it, since I was the commander. But honestly, I think that some of my subordinates made their own mistakes. I've already ranted about Wayne. Monty landed in Calabria, south of Salerno, and was way too slow in his advance. Then there's Ridgeway and Taylor, who refused to drop paratroopers on Rome. They didn't think the Italians would help us against the Germans when push came to shove. The cowards."

Oof. I shouldn't use insults. At least against my subordinates. They may make mistakes, but at least they're on the right side of this war. They're not like Rommel, Kesselring, or Mussolini. Those three are nothing but stooges for the ultimate villain. Hitler.

"I didn't realize you were *this* critical of yourself."

"I try to evaluate my record objectively. Learn from mistakes. And I *do* think I've learned from the mistakes I've made in the past year. If I'm put in command of Overlord, I'll be ready for *anything*."

"But you think it will go to Marshall?"

Ike was silent. An awkward tension hung over him. They reached the stable. Ike's helmet was right where Kay said it was. They put on their gear. Ike's shoulders, which had been stuck and jutted upward, relaxed as he saw the trail that he and Kay were to ride.

Feel so much better, having vented. Thank God for Kay. I'd go crazy if I had no one to confide in. The other members of my staff, Bedell, Butch,

*and Tex are all great. But Kay gives me the female presence I'm missing
since Mamie's across the ocean.*

Kay smiled at Ike after she climbed aboard her stallion. Ike felt a
punch in the chest. Then he remembered his other duty.

Ike mounted his horse and they began their ride.

☆☆☆☆☆

NOVEMBER 19, 1943

THE *USS IOWA* docked in the French naval base at Mers el-Kebir, six miles
west of Oran. The forty-five thousand ton behemoth wielded dozens of
cannons designed to fire sixteen-inch shells; it was the most powerful
vessel on this side of the Western Hemisphere. Ike was at the front of the
greeting party. Just to his rear and slightly to his right was Admiral
Cunningham. In the rear were Elliott and Franklin Roosevelt, Jr. A light
fishy smell filled Ike's nostrils; a taste of what he may have experienced if
he'd gone to Annapolis, his original choice for a military education.

The arriving party disembarked. President Roosevelt was at the front
of this group. He looked fit and cheerful, excited for his meeting with
Winston Churchill and Joseph Stalin, the latter of whom he was meeting
for the first time. Spectacles lay over his eyes, and a brown fedora sat atop
his dark gray hair. His wheelchair was pushed by an aide. Following the
President was Harry Hopkins, Roosevelt's closest advisor and a man for
whom Ike had great respect. Behind Hopkins were the Joint Chiefs,
including General Marshall, Ike's mentor. In the rear were additional
White House and military aides.

Ike technically met Roosevelt a couple times before, but this was the
first time since Torch and Ike's rise to global fame. Ike didn't adore his
Commander-in-Chief. Roosevelt wasn't his favorite President by any
means. He was no Washington or Lincoln. Ike had mixed feelings about
the New Deal but thought Roosevelt was succeeding as a war leader
despite believing that Roosevelt's order to invade North Africa and the
Mediterranean was a mistake.

"Nice to see you, General Eisenhower!" Roosevelt boomed as the two
parties met.

"It's an honor to see you, too, Mr. President." They shook hands. The
two parties made their way inland to the cars waiting for them. Ike walked
next to Roosevelt as his aide wheeled the President along.

"My plan is to stay in Tunis for the night," Roosevelt explained. "We'll go to Cairo in the morning."

"A night flight, Sunday night, would be better," Ike suggested.

"A night flight?" Roosevelt replied, pleased Ike felt free to give him advice. "Why?"

"Daylight flights are a big risk," Ike answered. "We don't want to have to run fighter escort all the way to Cairo. It would be asking for trouble."

"Okay, Ike. You're the boss. But I get something in return."

"What's that, sir?"

"If you're going to make me stay over at Carthage all Sunday, you've got to take me on a personally conducted tour of the battlefields—ancient and modern."

"That's a bargain, sir."

I've worked with prima donnas like Patton, Montgomery, and de Gaulle over the past year. Making Roosevelt the center of attention will be easy.

☆☆☆☆☆

THE PRESIDENT AND the general arrived at AFHQ. Many of Ike's aides crowded around to see Roosevelt. He'd been President for most of their lives, in some cases. Roosevelt's nose thrusted upward, his grin exuding confidence. Ike stood a few feet behind the President like a beaming father bringing a surprise home to his kids. Roosevelt desired female company after a few minutes of socializing with the crowd of young men. He glanced toward Ike, spotting the general with his peripheral vision.

"Where is Miss Summersby?"

Ike's eyebrows rose in surprise. He turned to Butch.

"Find Kay, please." He turned back to Roosevelt. "She'll be here momentarily, Mr. President."

Roosevelt smiled. Summersby and Butch arrived within minutes.

"Mr. President," Ike began, getting Roosevelt's attention, "this is Captain Summersby, the British girl you asked about."

Roosevelt leaned back in his wheelchair, nose jutting out, his head tilted slightly.

"I've heard quite a bit about you," Roosevelt began. "Why didn't you drive me from the plane? I'd been looking forward to it."

"Mr. President, the Secret Service wouldn't let me drive," Kay replied with an upward inflection.

"Would you like to drive me from now on?"

"It would be a privilege, sir."

"Very well," Roosevelt declared. "You shall drive me then. I'm going on an inspection trip soon."

Roosevelt had dinner with Ike's staff that night. Kay sat next to the President. Roosevelt, the biggest gossip monger to ever sit in the Oval Office, eyed Kay and Ike, monitoring their subtle, friendly interactions. The closeness between them confirmed the rumors he'd read about.

At least something nice came out of this war, Roosevelt thought.

☆☆☆☆☆

"EVERY GROUND COMMANDER seeks the battle of annihilation," Ike explained from the back seat of the car. "So far as conditions permit, he tries to duplicate in modern war the classic example of Cannae."

Kay was driving the vehicle. Roosevelt was her front seat passenger. Ike and Franklin Roosevelt, Jr. were in the back seats.

"Fascinating," Roosevelt replied in response to Ike's history lesson. "Where did you learn all of this, Ike? West Point? Leavenworth?"

"My mom's history books," Ike replied with a chuckle. Roosevelt grinned. "She hid them because I preferred reading to chores."

"But I assume you found the key?"

"Of course!"

"Good man! Innovative! Isn't that what Napoleon said he liked in a general?"

"That was luck, sir."

"What was? Finding the key?"

"No. What Napoleon liked in his generals."

"Aw!" Roosevelt exclaimed, pleased that Ike had passed his test. "You seem to have that as well."

"Thank you, sir."

Roosevelt nodded "you're welcome."

"Did you only read the classics as a child?" the President asked.

"That and the Revolution."

"Naturally. Who was your favorite Founder?"

"Washington."

"Oh, Ike! That's the wrong answer!"

"What would you say is the right answer?"

"Jefferson, naturally."

"We'll have to agree to disagree, Mr. President."

"If you insist, Ike. I suppose this is something I can't make an order."

Telek leapt from Ike's lap and over the chair in front of him, landing on Roosevelt. A smile dominated Roosevelt's face. Kay chuckled at the President's reaction.

"What's his name?" Roosevelt asked.

"Telek," Ike replied.

"Telek? Interesting. Is he American or British?"

"He's British. But he has an American wife."

Roosevelt threw his head back in laughter. His howling contained an aristocratic tone.

"I guess I think as much of him, Mr. President," Ike explained, "as you do of Fala." He was referring to Roosevelt's dog. Roosevelt nodded as he petted Telek's head. He peered out the window as the car drove in silence for several minutes. Finally, the President pointed to something outside.

"There! It's an eucalyptus grove!" The tall trees towered in the distance. Roosevelt turned to Kay. "That's an awfully nice place. Could you pull up there, child, for our little picnic?"

Kay nodded and turned the car toward the trees. The convoy stopped upon arrival. GIs helped situate Roosevelt onto a blanket. Kay reached for the picnic basket.

"No, let me do it," Ike said softly. "I'm very good at passing sandwiches around."

Ike handed Roosevelt a chicken sandwich.

"Thank you, Ike. I love picnics. I go on them regularly with my cousin, Daisy." The old flirt looked up at Kay, who was still standing. "Won't you come here, child, and have lunch with a dull old man?"

Kay did as he requested.

"May I ask, Mr. President, why do you refer to me as 'child?' I'm thirty-four years old."

Roosevelt smiled as he swallowed before speaking. He looked at Kay as if he was her father.

"You are a woman, and therefore, 'child.'"

☆☆☆☆☆

KAY DROVE ROOSEVELT and Ike to the airport that evening. Roosevelt turned to Ike before exiting the vehicle.

"I know what Harry Butcher is to you, but I may have to take him away. Elmer Davis is leaving his position as head of the Office of War Information, and Davis recommended Butcher as his successor. What would you say if I drafted Butch to take over his job?"

Ike frowned.

"Well, Mr. President, I won't pretend it wouldn't be tough. But if you need him, if you give the word, the answer is, 'sure, go ahead.'"

Roosevelt smiled. Ike had given a perfect answer. Roosevelt continued.

"Ike, you and I know who was Chief of Staff during the last years of the Civil War but practically no one else knows, although the names of the field generals—Grant, of course, and Lee, and Jackson, Sherman, Sheridan and others—every schoolboy knows them. I hate to think that fifty years from now practically nobody will know who George Marshall was. That is one of the reasons why I want George to have the Big Command. He is entitled to establish his place in history as a great general."

Ike's frown deepened.

That's it then. The decision's made. It's Marshall. I'll probably be sent back to Washington as Chief of Staff. God, find me a casket now! No, Ike, come on. Control your urges. Duty. Must remember duty.

Roosevelt studied every muscular twitch of Ike's reaction.

He's clearly disappointed, and his face telegraphs his emotions more than anyone I've ever met, Roosevelt thought. *He passed every test I gave him in the past two days. Maybe he's up to the task of Overlord. Maybe.*

☆☆☆☆☆

NOVEMBER 24, 1943

"*HOW DARE YOU!*" Churchill roared. "I am the King's First Minister!"

"That's irrelevant as far as strategy is concerned!" Marshall shouted back. "The Supreme Commander must have command over Allied forces in Europe, the Mediterranean, and the Middle East."

"*Never!*" Churchill barked. "No American will ever have that much power over separate British operations!"

Roosevelt and the other Combined Chiefs' eyes shifted back and forth as the British Prime Minister and American Army Chief of Staff argued, sweat building up on their pale faces.

"You're trying to delay the cross-channel attack! *Again!*" Marshall declared.

"Because a cross-channel attack would be suicide!"

"So, you admit it!"

"Yes, I admit it! I don't want thousands of British and American youths slaughtered on French battlefields for a second generation in a row!"

"It's the only way to win the war!"

"Says the country that had to be dragged into the war kicking and screaming!"

Brooke, who was sitting beside Churchill, was stunned. *Was the Prime Minister trying to wreck the relationship with the Americans that he himself had built?*

"What would you rather we do?" Marshall demanded. "Another useless operation in the Mediterranean?"

"Yes! We must continue to put pressure on the Mediterranean! It's the weak point of the Axis!"

"Okay, then where? Where should we strike next? Since this Italian campaign worked out so well!"

"Rhodes."

"What?"

"Rhodes. It's in the Eastern Mediterranean."

"I *know* where Rhodes is! What would be gained by attacking it?"

"It would draw Turkey into the war on our side!" Churchill grabbed his lapels; his spit curls hanged. "His Majesty's government can't continue to sit idly by. Muskets must flame!"

"God forbid if I should try to dictate!" Marshall shouted. "But not one American is going to die on that goddamned beach!"

The meeting was stunned. Churchill shifted back in his chair, acknowledging Marshall's victory.

Roosevelt eyed both of them, horrified by what he had witnessed.

☆☆☆☆☆

"I THINK WINSTON is beginning not to like George Marshall very much."

Roosevelt lay on his bed; his son, Elliot, had helped his transition from his wheelchair.

"Well," Elliot began, "I wouldn't envy anybody the job of standing up to the PM."

"I'll tell you one man who deserves a medal for being able to get along with Winston. And that's Ike Eisenhower."

"Are you considering him for the Command?"

"After today, absolutely. George and Winston would daily be at each other's throats. Teamwork can't thrive under such conditions."

"But doesn't Eisenhower lack combat experience?"

"Oh, Elliot, please. That might be how professional military men size one another up, but it's irrelevant for conducting a campaign. There's no correlation between commanding an infantry regiment and planning an amphibious landing."

Elliot nodded and put his finger up to his lip.

"Are you serious about giving Eisenhower a medal?"

"Sure I am. But he won't take one. He's not like MacArthur, who accepted a Medal of Honor for *losing* the Philippines. Ike believes medals are only for valor and that he hasn't done anything valorous."

"Perhaps."

"What do you mean?"

"I received a letter from Bedell Smith, Ike's chief of staff. He said Ike would really like to have the Legion of Merit. Anyone in the Army can earn it, and Ike's never gotten one."

"Hm. Could we keep it a secret?"

"I don't see why not."

Roosevelt smiled.

"Good. Send a message to Smith. Have him draw up a citation. North African campaign, Sicilian campaign. If he can get a medal here in time, I'll pin it on Ike myself, before we leave for Tehran."

Elliot nodded and began writing the letter. Roosevelt leaned backward, his body aching.

On the one hand, Marshall's been my right hand since Hitler, that psychopath, invaded Poland. He's directed the military buildup that transformed America from a third-rate power into the greatest war machine in history. He deserves to be the Grant or Pershing of this war. But Pershing himself sent me a letter saying that I shouldn't alter a command structure that's working. Only Marshall can convince Congress to cooperate with my wartime agenda. Ike has no experience in that regard, but he has led three amphibious landings. What better experience could one have for Overlord? Plus he can work with the British, including Winston. The Supreme Commander will need that. Ike's a superhuman diplomat as well as an excellent strategist. He's certainly the best politician among the generals. He can even work with de Gaulle. Whereas Marshall would never be able to work with a prima donna like Montgomery. Not in a million years. He would tell Montgomery "where he could go" after two days.

"Do you think Eisenhower will go into politics after the war?" Elliot asked.

"It's possible."

"What if he's a Republican?"

Roosevelt chuckled and shook his head.

"His politics don't concern me. Any man that smart must be a Democrat."

☆☆☆☆☆

NOVEMBER 26, 1943

THE COMBINED CHIEFS ordered Ike to go to the American embassy in Cairo where he was to deliver a presentation about the state of the Italian Front. Roosevelt requested that Ike visit his cabin beforehand.

Seeing the President over the weekend had lifted Ike's spirits, but the war still ate at him. Marshall hosted a dinner of turkey and cranberries in November and Ike hadn't realized it was Thanksgiving until someone said so. Marshall subsequently ordered Ike to take a short vacation from the war. Ike planned to take his staff to the pyramids. Then Jerusalem. Kay wanted to see the Garden of Gethsemane.

I wonder if the Chiefs will ask about Yugoslavia. I should recommend we give aid to Tito, even though he's a communist. He's at least fighting the Axis. Mihailovic's forces are useless.

Ike arrived at Roosevelt's cabin. A Secret Service guard opened the door.

Roosevelt sat alone in the room. He held a Legion of Merit in his hands, which rested on his lap. The medal contained thirteen white stars arranged within a blue circle. That, in turn, was surrounded by a decoration of overlapping white, gold, and green. The medal was connected to a red ribbon.

Ike's eyes widened as he saw the medal. He froze. Roosevelt smiled. Ike gestured to himself. Roosevelt nodded.

"You deserve this, and so much more, Ike," Roosevelt declared.

Ike beamed at the medal as tears emerged in his eyes.

"It is the happiest moment of my life, sir. I appreciate this decoration more than any other you could have given me."

☆☆☆☆☆

NOVEMBER 28, 1943

THE BIG THREE—Roosevelt, Churchill, and Stalin—sat around a large, circular conference table that did not designate anyone as the head of the table. Soviet secret police stood by every doorway, guarding the room. They met in the Soviet embassy in Tehran. In 1941, Churchill and Stalin had covertly removed Iranian leader Reza Shah Pahlavi, who favored the Axis, and installed his son, Mohommad Reza Pahlavi, who preferred the Allies.

"I am under the impression that I am the youngest of the three of us," Roosevelt declared, his hands clasped and resting on the table. "Therefore, I would like to welcome my elders to this historic meeting."

Behind Roosevelt sat Hopkins and Averall Harriman, the American ambassador to the Soviet Union.

"We must recognize that we hold the future of mankind in our hands," Churchill stated. Foreign Secretary Anthony Eden, military assistant Lord Ismay, and translator Major Arthur Birse, sat behind the Prime Minister.

"History has given us a great opportunity," announced Joseph Stalin. "Now let's get down to business."

Stalin had with him Foreign Minister Vyacheslav Molotov and translator Kliment Voroshilov. The Soviet dictator was a short, stocky man, with a yellow skin tone, bumps on his nose, and a thick mustache covering his upper lip. He looked nothing like the heroic figure displayed in Soviet propaganda.

The Big Three quickly brought up their mutual enemy.

"Hitler is mentally unbalanced," Roosevelt insisted. "He simply took power during the Depression and led Germany astray."

Stalin shook his head.

"Hitler is a very able man," Stalin said through his translator. "He is not basically intelligent. He lacks culture and has a primitive approach to political problems. But only a very able man could accomplish what Hitler had done in solidifying the German people, whatever we thought of his methods."

"Then that is why this must be the last time Germany attempts to conquer Europe," Roosevelt replied, trying to remain in agreement with

Stalin. "How do we make sure that Germany does not recover and start another war, as it did after the last war?"

"Was that not the purpose of your demanding their 'unconditional surrender?'" Stalin asked. "To eliminate another 'stab in the back' theory?"

"That's correct."

"It is clear that Germany must be dismembered," Stalin asserted. "The Germans are a talented people and could easily revive within fifteen to twenty years. Disarmament is insufficient. Furniture and watch factories could make airplanes and shell fuses. We must dismember them as Richelieu had done three hundred years ago."

Stalin was referring to Cardinal Richilieu, a seventeenth-century French statesman who made it France's goal to keep the German states divided. This goal was maintained until Bismarck unified the states under Prussian leadership in 1871.

"My strategy would be to see Prussia, the evil core of German militarism, separated from the rest of Germany," Churchill suggested.

"I think we should go further than that," Roosevelt said. "We can break Germany into five parts and place Hamburg and the Ruhr under international control."

"I prefer the President's plan to the Prime Minister's," Stalin announced.

Churchill's face flashed red.

"If Germany is to be dismembered," Stalin continued, "it would really be dismembered."

"Germany had been less dangerous to civilization when divided into one-hundred and seven provinces," Roosevelt suggested, implying a return to Richilieu.

Churchill's shoulders raised in frustration.

"I would have hoped for larger units."

Destroying German power eliminated it as a counterweight to Russian dominance of Central Europe. It was obvious why Stalin wanted this. But why would Roosevelt? Or could he simply not see that that was Stalin's aim?

"There are other ways of undermining future German aggression," Stalin suggested. "We should execute fifty thousand German officers to stop them from starting another war."

Churchill's jaw dropped, but Roosevelt threw back his head in laughter.

"Surely forty-nine thousand would be plenty," Roosevelt insisted.

Churchill leapt to his feet, his hands slamming on the table. He glared at Stalin.

"I *will not stand* for soldiers being murdered for serving their country!" the Prime Minister shouted. "Nazi war criminals must be *tried* according to the Moscow Declaration!"

"Which you wrote," Stalin countered.

Roosevelt turned to Churchill before he could respond.

"Oh, Winston," the President said, as if to a child, "Uncle Joe is merely joking. He'd never do such a thing."

Stalin smiled at Churchill.

"*Yes*, Prime Minister. It was *merely* a joke."

Churchill's face turned red again. Eden leaned toward him and whispered in his ear.

"Stalin has the President in his pocket." Churchill nodded.

The previous day, Roosevelt had accepted Stalin's invitation to stay in the Soviet embassy while in Tehran after Stalin told him of a Nazi attempt to kill the Big Three. The British were stunned that Roosevelt fell for an obvious lie and allowed himself to stay in a room bugged by the Soviets. But Roosevelt knew it was bugged and wanted to demonstrate goodwill to Stalin.

Roosevelt monitored the other two leaders. *Stalin's a slippery creature. He allied with Hitler in 1939, but I'm sure he was just being pragmatic. I can win him over. I need him to fight Japan and to cooperate in building a new world after the war. Winston wants to return to a world of European empires. But that's over. Woodrow Wilson's vision of national sovereignty and global cooperation must become a reality. The Soviet Union is a progressive regime; it's just further to the left than the New Deal. But Stalin sees the world the way I do and will work with me if I give him what he wants. The British Empire is different and a bigger problem than the Soviets. It has no place in the world we're going to build.*

"Can we now discuss Poland?" Churchill asked.

"What about it?" Stalin replied.

"Britain went to war in Poland's defense in 1939. It's important that it's restored when this war is over." Stalin appeared uneasy. "That being said, I don't particularly care where it's restored." The Prime Minister pulled out three matchsticks from his pocket. "This one is the Soviet Union, this one's Poland, and this one's Germany." He shifted the Soviet and Polish ones closer to the German stick. "We can move them east to west like soldiers at drill executing two steps left, close."

"You're suggesting moving Poland westward?" Stalin asked. "That the Soviet Union would acquire Polish territory and Poland would be compensated for this by taking land from Germany?"

"Exactly."

"How far?"

"What would you like?"

"My preference would be to move Poland's eastern border with the Soviet Union to the line drawn by Lord Curzan in 1920. We could then place the German-Polish border at the Oder and Neisse rivers."

"Interesting," Churchill replied. "So, move it about two hundred miles?"

"Yes."

"That would give Poland access to German industry and detach Prussia. That could work."

"Yes. It would involve relocating Polish and German populations in the region," Stalin replied, now agreeing to put Prussia into Poland.

"I agree. And if I give you this, you'll agree to restore Poland's sovereignty?"

"Yes."

"Gentlemen, if you don't mind," Roosevelt interrupted. "I like this idea, but could it wait until after the 1944 presidential election? There are six to seven million Americans of Polish extraction in the United States and as a practical man I do not wish to lose their vote. I isolated many Italian Americans when I condemned Mussolini in 1940 and I don't want to antagonize the Poles as well."

"I won't complicate it for you," Stalin promised. "I'll wait until after the election. After the war, even."

"Thank you."

"What are your thoughts on the Baltic States?" Stalin asked Roosevelt, referring to three countries that he had conquered in 1939.

"I assume you're interested in their joining the Soviet Union?"

Stalin nodded.

"I could see allowing a referendum in those countries to determine if the people wish to join," Roosevelt suggested.

"I was thinking the same," Stalin replied. "But it must be according to the Soviet constitution. No international inspectors."

"International inspectors are a must!" Churchill declared.

"No, no. That's not necessary," Roosevelt said, paternalistically rebuffing Churchill again. "We trust Uncle Joe, surely."

Churchill folded his arms in frustration. Wasn't Roosevelt the one concerned about self-determination? How was Churchill supposed to stand up to the Soviet tyrant if Roosevelt, leader of the most powerful country on Earth, was playing the role of Neville Chamberlain?

Stalin turned to Roosevelt.

"The Soviet Union will join the war against Japan once Germany is defeated." He knew exactly what the American President wanted to hear. Roosevelt sighed in relief. But Stalin then moved on to the one thing *he* wanted most. "Russia is waging the war against Germany on its own so far."

"That's not fair!" Churchill spat back. "The Western Allies drew Nazi forces away from Kursk when we invaded Sicily!"

Stalin snorted.

"T-34 tanks repelled the Hitlerites from Kursk. The West had nothing to do with it."

"The United Kingdom fought the Nazis for a year alone. Where was the Soviet Union during that period?" Churchill asked, referring to the Nazi-Soviet Pact.

"The Soviets have been fighting the Hitlerites for *two years* alone!" Stalin held up his index and middle fingers so they looked like Churchill's V sign. "And the West isn't helping. We lose before lunch what your countries have lost since the war began."

"The United States goes out of its way to utilize air and naval power," Roosevelt explained. "That helps keep our casualties low."

"So does not fighting the Hitlerites directly," Stalin barked back. "And if we are here to discuss military matters, Russia is only interested in Overlord."

Churchill shook his head.

"We still have alternatives to Overlord, such as Italy, Turkey, and Rhodes." Stalin was unconvinced. "We don't have enough landing craft to invade France."

"We are all agreed that Overlord is the domineering operation," Roosevelt declared, siding with Stalin. "Any operation that might delay Overlord cannot be considered by us. We're looking to launch by May of next year."

"I don't care if the operation occurs on May 1, May 5, or May 20. But a definite date is important." Stalin paused. "Who will command Overlord?"

Roosevelt froze. He was not prepared for such a direct question.

That old Bolshevik is trying to force me to give him a name, but I can't tell him because I haven't made up my mind.

"The matter has not yet been decided," Roosevelt suggested softly.

Stalin dismissively waved his hand.

"Then nothing will come of these operations," Stalin asserted. "The Soviet Union has learned that military decisions cannot be made by committee. One man must be responsible and one man must make the decisions. The Soviet Union will take no part in choosing a Supreme Commander, but merely would like to know who this officer would be and would like to know as soon as possible."

"The decision will be made within a fortnight," Churchill insisted.

"I concur."

Stalin nodded, appreciating his counterparts' candor.

"Should we consider any other operation to launch against Germany next year?" Roosevelt asked. "We can land in southern France *before* Overlord. That could draw some German forces away from the northern beaches. We might even be able to land at the northern tip of the Adriatic to flank the Alps and take Vienna."

"Would this take forces away from Overlord?" Stalin asked.

"No," Roosevelt answered. "We would use soldiers already engaged in Italy.

"We should not detract from the Italian campaign!" Churchill insisted.

Stalin ignored him, keeping his attention on Roosevelt.

"Any of these operations are fine, but they are only to distract Germany from the dual offenses next spring. The Soviet Union remains committed to launching an offensive against the German Army Group Center in Belarus around the time of Overlord."

"Then we shall crush the Nazis between us!" Roosevelt declared. "Just as Ike and Monty did in North Africa!" He decided to address the topic that interested *him* most. "I want to introduce to you my idea for a new mechanism for keeping the peace after the war. To make certain that nothing like this war will ever happen again."

"Continue."

"The new world shall be built around a global organization that allows the family of nations to communicate and settle their problems before resorting to force."

"How is that any different from Wilson's League of Nations?" Stalin asked, referring to the organization established after World War I that failed to prevent World War II.

"This new organization would give greater strength to the major powers. The World Policemen—America, Britain, Russia, and China—will have special privileges that will reflect their role in keeping the world in one piece after the Axis Powers are history."

"The world powers must be able to veto measures that go against their interest."

"We can arrange that."

"The Soviet Union will consider joining if such a veto is established."

"We shouldn't leave France out of the list of World Policemen," Churchill added.

"France collapsed in six weeks in 1940," Stalin countered. "They are no longer a world power."

"France has a glorious history. 1940 was but a setback."

"You just want another European empire to have a veto."

"Perhaps we should give these secondary issues to our chiefs of staff?" Churchill suggested.

"Why?" Stalin asked. "Are we not their commanders, instead of the other way around?"

"I believe we have touched on enough issues," Roosevelt declared, exhausted from the arguing. "We should adjourn for now."

☆☆☆☆☆

DECEMBER 5, 1943

ROOSEVELT SAT BEHIND his cabin desk, which was cluttered with papers that he kept there to always appear busy. Just behind him and to the left sat a large globe, given to him by General Marshall, that the President used to track troop movements. It would return with him to Washington. He was about to make his most important decision of the war.

"General Marshall is here to see you, Mr. President."

"Send him in," Roosevelt replied. *I was hoping to have lunch before having to do this*, Roosevelt thought. *I wish Hopkins could have gotten a straight answer out of him.*

General Marshall entered Roosevelt's cabin. He wore four stars on his shoulders. He carried his cap, his hands clasped behind him.

"How do you do, George?" the President asked.

"It's 'General Marshall,' Mr. President."

"I know, General."

Roosevelt looked Marshall in the eye.

"General, do you remember why I chose you as Army Chief of Staff?"

"I believe it followed my disagreeing with your idea that the Navy should be built up at the expense of the other branches."

"That's right. None of the other top Army generals dared disagree with me. But not you. You spoke truth to power. And that bothered me, to tell you the truth. At least initially. But Hopkins convinced me that was the quality I should want in an advisor. Do you remember what you said when I offered you the position?"

"I believe it was that I would tell you what I believe. Even if you didn't like to hear it."

"That's right. Same principle. And you've always offered me the best advice of any of my military advisors."

"Thank you, Mr. President."

"So now I ask for your personal preference. Would you like to command Overlord?"

Marshall didn't blink.

"You should pick whoever you believe is best."

Roosevelt sighed.

"I want to know if you would like the command, General."

"The President should pick whoever he thinks is best for the country."

"Then it will be Eisenhower," Roosevelt declared. Marshall still withheld his reaction. "I don't think I could sleep at night with you out of the country."

I'm sure the British will have a collective sigh of relief once this is announced, Roosevelt thought. *Just one more thing to do.*

"Can you send a telegram to Premier Stalin announcing the immediate appointment of Eisenhower to Overlord?"

"Yes, Mr. President."

☆☆☆☆☆

"You look like you're ready to burst!"

"I'm sure I am, Kay," Ike replied. "The words keep ringing in my ear."

Ike had returned from escorting President Roosevelt to the *Iowa*. Roosevelt turned to Ike before he departed and said, "Well, Ike, you'd better start packing. You are going to command Overlord."

It was a punch in the chest. *What? Is he serious? I got it? Really!*

Ike was lost for words, finally saying, "Mr. President, I realize that such an appointment involved difficult concerns. I hope you will not be disappointed."

Ike swelled up with happiness and, upon his delivery of the news, the AFHQ staff kicked off a celebration in the Algiers headquarters. Gone was the lingering sadness of Ike returning to Washington. Here was the excitement of a brand-new adventure.

"London, baby!" a colonel shouted. The applause for Ike lasted nearly three minutes.

Kay watched Ike's smile; it was the largest she had ever seen.

Ike's mind started to think as his staff initiated an impromptu party.

I have to wind up my affairs in AFHQ before I fly to London. Need to pick my new deputies. Smith will be my chief of staff. Bradley should run the American Army Group. Maybe Alexander can lead the British one. I should get Tedder as my chief airman, if possible, and have Spaatz run American air forces operating out of Britain.

"This is for you, sir," Tex Lee said as he handed Ike a pair of messages. They were from Marshall.

The first was Roosevelt's message to Stalin informing him of Ike's appointment. Above that Marshall had written: "Dear Eisenhower. I thought you might like to have this as a memento."

Oh my God! What a man! Ike thought. *He deserved the command more than me.*

Ike looked at the second message. It read, "You will be under terrific strain from now on. I am interested that you are fully prepared to bear the strain and I am not interested in the usual rejoinder that you can take it. Now come on home and see your wife and trust someone else for twenty minutes in England."

Ike reread three words a few times. *'See your wife!' Oh, thank the Lord! I can see Mamie! Maybe I can visit John, too, at West Point. And my mother. What a day! I get to see my wife again!*

"How does it feel?" Kay asked. "'Supreme Commander?'"

"Oh, God, Kay. That's too much for a Kansas farm boy. It sounds like 'Sultan.'"

"Better get used to it. That's what people will call you now."

"I know," Ike replied, admiring his emotional rock. "We have to build a strong coalition. It's the only way Overlord will succeed. There shall never be praise or blame for the British as British or the Americans as Americans. We are all in this together as Allies. We will fight it soldier to soldier. Men will be praised or blamed for what they do, not for their nationality."

Kay smiled as her boss was absorbed into his new, ultimate role. Ike looked out the window as the sun set over Algiers.

I spent the interwar years terrified that my family would never be proud of me because I was kept in the US instead of being allowed to fight the Kaiser. Now I'm leading the central operation against a far worse German tyrant. My staff is celebrating now, but the weight of the situation will soon hit them like a ton of bricks. This is the biggest battle of all time. Civilization's survival rests on our shoulders. On mine. I had wrestled with doing my duty in the face of not getting the command or being able to see Mamie. Both of those desires have been satisfied. My duty means something far larger. Larger than I ever could have dreamed.

A Soldier's Meditation

Keep yourself simple, good, pure, serious, and unassuming; the friend of
justice and goodness; kindly, affectionate, and resolute
in your devotion to duty.
—Marcus Aurelius

WHAT KIND OF a man writes a letter to himself?

I keep a diary, but this is different. My stress level has been through the roof lately and I want to think on paper to put events into perspective. 1958 was the worst year of my life. It was consumed by crises. I had to deploy marines into Lebanon to prevent a civil war in that country. At the same time Chiang Kai-shek, ruler of Formosa, tried to provoke a major war between America and Red China. Triggered a goddamned nuclear crisis over Quemoy and Matsu, a pair of tiny islands. Again. Had to reach out to Mao through Poland to restore calm. Third, the Democrats manufactured a scandal that forced Sherman Adams, my chief of staff, to resign, tainting my administration and hurting our ability to function. Those radical spenders used the fake scandal to increase their control over Congress in the midterms. Just pound, pound, pound.

The miserable year ended with the worst news of all. Khrushchev gave us an ultimatum to either surrender West Berlin to the Warsaw Pact or he'd let communist East Germany take it. This is the biggest crisis since Suez. Khrushchev's emboldened after Suez and Sputnik; he thinks he can do whatever he wants and get away with it. Hell, I'd as soon turn West Berlin into a neutral city if it didn't look like appeasement.

Macmillan called me, frantic. Said eight nuclear bombs was all it would take to destroy Britain. Asked if he had enough time to evacuate the British people to Canada and Australia. I see why he's scared. But we must be strong. Can't back down in the face of a tyrant's threats. Tried to tell him that.

The boys who've been advising me, Dulles, Nixon, the chiefs, and everyone else, told me to put more troops in West Berlin in case the Reds invade. That's crazy as hell. Any forces we put there would be squashed by a Soviet invasion. We'd be sending those men to their death. That's something I never want to do again. I've had enough of war. So I withdrew troops instead. Got criticized for that. They said it was appeasement. I'm sure Khrushchev felt differently! I sent a clear signal that we weren't even going to try to defend the city through conventional forces. If he made a move we were going to respond with nuclear retaliation. I bet that made him shake in his kirza boots!

It's interesting that my advisors have been getting less and less comfortable with Massive Retaliation lately. They're starting to say that it's irresponsible to risk a mushroom cloud over Chicago to defend Paris and Bonn. They're even questioning that Harvard man's proposal for using limited nuclear strikes (if there is such a thing) to combat communist offensives as opposed to my Massive Retaliation policy. Maybe rules are starting to codify that will treat the nuclear bomb as more than just another weapon. Nothing would make me happier. It will be a turning point in world history.

That good news isn't helping me calm down. I even threw my golf club at Dr. Snyder the other day. Nearly broke the poor man's leg! Maybe I'm a more emotional creature than I tell myself. Or maybe even I get nervous when my decisions will shape the world's survival or its end. This isn't the first time. There have been more nuclear crises since I took office than I care to count. And there was the war before that, of course. That was probably even worse. That wasn't the hypothetical of millions of deaths. That was ordering millions of young boys to kill and die in battle. All because an even worse tyrant also had dreams of global domination and sought to smash the world into submission.

That's what this letter's about. That war. Specifically, the big crisis of that war. The most stressful day, or pair of days, in my entire life. D-Day. Operation Overlord. The defining moment of my life and career. I've written about it in *Crusade*, but I want to write a personal account just to put this Berlin crisis into perspective. No one's eyes are supposed to see this but mine. I have to remember to crumple it up and throw it out as soon as I'm done. I must be as honest with myself as possible and write a full recounting of the day, as best as I can remember it from fifteen years ago.

The SHAEF (Supreme Headquarters of Allied Expeditionary Force) planners and I were at Admiral Ramsay's Portsmouth Headquarters at 0400 on June 5, 1944. We could hear the forty-mile-per hour-wind blowing from inside the compound. Rain pelted the ceiling and windows. The invasion was originally planned for May 1, but I delayed it until early June so we could have adequate landing craft. On June 3 I rejected launching the invasion on June 5, because Group Captain Stagg, SHAEF's chief meteorologist, had described the menacing weather we could expect in the English Channel for that day. Air support and naval gunfire would have been useless. Our armada was already at sea, but I ordered it to stand down.

The current meeting was our last chance to launch an invasion on June 6. Delaying again would mean our next chance would be June 19 because the Channel weather that summer was the worst of the century. The weather was a bigger enemy during Overlord than Hitler.

My heart sank as Stagg entered the room. Was he going to give me the same bad news that he had six hours before and four hours before that? Instead, he had a smile across his face as he began the most important weather report of all time.

"I think we have a gleam of hope for you, sir," Stagg said in his Scottish accent. "The mass of weather coming in from the Atlantic is moving faster than we anticipated. We predict there will be fair conditions beginning late on June 5 and lasting until the next morning, June 6. But the weather will close in again on the evening of the sixth."

A break in the storm? Was it possible? Was this the almighty endorsing our cause?

"How long will the storm last?" I asked, my right arm leaning on the conference table. "This is life or death for a quarter of a million kids."

"I can't say at this time," Stagg replied. "But there should be a window of about twenty-four hours with tolerable conditions."

Should. The fate of civilization rested on the word 'should.' I would be mortified if other eyes read this, but I sometimes wonder if more weight was ever placed on a single man, a single decision, in all of human history, as was placed on me in that meeting. Failing to launch the operation would complicate our advancement across Europe before the winter set in, as well as demoralize our troops and anger the Soviets. But launching it under bad weather could mean our troops and landing craft would end up at the bottom of the Channel and doom the invasion.

"Do the Germans know about the break?" I asked.

"No, sir," Stagg answered. "We have weather stations west of the British Isles. They do not. They probably think there's no chance of an attack in the next days."

My eyes narrowed as I considered the possibility that we knew of a break in the weather and the Germans did not. We could take them by surprise. I decided to poll my advisors. I turned to Bradley, who was leading the American forces on two of the invasion beaches.

"What do you think, Brad?"

His soft eyes looked at me through his glasses. His jaw was visibly clenched.

"It's too questionable. I would probably say 'no.'"

Admiral Ramsey chimed in next.

"Whatever you decide," he said to me, "the signal must be flashed to the fleet within half an hour if the invasion is a go."

More pressure! Ramsey turned to Stagg.

"What's the wind velocity over the Channel?"

"It should be stable during the window."

"Remember, Ike," Air Chief Marshal Leigh-Mallory said to me, "bad cloud cover will cause the paratroopers to be dropped over too large a region in Normandy. That will divide their strength. The Germans will annihilate them. The beach landing will die without the paratroopers blocking German reinforcements. We could lose half a million men and our one shot to win the war."

That was comforting to think about! Tedder, my deputy and Marshal of the RAF, spoke next. He had a pipe between his teeth.

"Additionally, we won't be able to use our heavy or medium bombers."

"We can use a large force of fighter-bombers instead," I suggested. Tedder looked to Stagg.

"What will the weather be on D-Day in the Channel and over the French coast?"

"To answer that question would make me a guesser and not a meteorologist."

I turned to Bedell Smith, my chief of staff.

"What do you think, Bedell?"

"It's a helluva gamble, but it's the best possible gamble."

I turned to General Montgomery, my co-architect of Overlord and the commander of all ground forces during the invasion. I asked for his opinion.

"If I were you, I would say 'go!'" He paused. "Luckily for me, I'm not you."

I sighed.

"The question is how long can you hang this operation on the end of a limb and just let it hang there?" I asked.

Waiting on the other side of the Channel was German Field Marshal Erwin Rommel, protégé to General Heinz Guderian, the architect of the Blitzkrieg that conquered Europe. He was waiting to kill my men. Then again, I was trying to kill his. But my men were fighting to defend systems of self-government, not for the whims of a tyrant. Rommel beat my men at Kasserine Pass in February 1943. I was determined that he would not do that again on the coast of France. He and I were lifelong soldiers, but our similarities ended there. It's not just that I spent my career as a staff officer while he'd been a line officer. He was impatient, a loner, and a so-called solitary genius who scorned his Italian allies, while I'm known as a team player and an optimist.

Our intelligence reports told us that Hitler considered our forces, three million strong in southern England, a greater threat than the Soviet Union. Maybe that's why the bulk of his advanced units were in Western Europe, as well as his rockets, heavy tanks, planes, and submarines. Then there was the Atlantic Wall, a colossal series of fortifications that stretched from the Arctic to the Spanish border. The Soviets may have fought the bulk of the German Army, but we faced most of the Germans' industrial output and advanced units. I dreaded sending young boys who should have been playing baseball and dancing with girls to fight this enemy, but Hitler had made all of Europe his slaves. We had to free them, or else he would have made the rest of us his slaves before too long. And he was tightening his grip on Europe in 1944. I feared the Soviet army would be bled to death on the Eastern Front. He was digging out resistance forces like rats. Train shipments to his camps in the east were increasing every day. It felt like the whole world was on fire, and I was tasked with putting it out.

Delaying until June 19 would have likely thrown away any hint of secrecy. A German spy would have figured out that Normandy was the target site by then. Or the Germans would have spotted our buildup in southern England and fired their rockets at it. And that was assuming that the weather would have even allowed for a June 19 landing, which it turns out it would not! So it would have been delayed into July!

We sat in silence for five minutes as I wrestled with these ideas and more. What if Stagg was wrong and the weather doomed our men to dying in capsized landing craft? What if our paratroopers were blown all over the countryside and were massacred? Would we lose the war? It was a real possibility. Hitler could regain the initiative. Allied unity and determination might collapse. But what if the break in the weather was real, and this was our one chance to secure a foothold in Western Europe? I could barely breathe as the outcome of the war rested on my judgment, and mine alone.

The calculation was simple in the end. Delaying the invasion made it doomed for failure, and the Nazis would rule Europe forever. Launching the invasion at least gave it a chance of success. My knuckles were white as I reached the decision, feeling both somber and content.

"Ok, we'll go."

The SHAEF planners absorbed the words for a moment. Some felt dread, the others excitement. Monty, naturally, was the first to speak.

"Well done, Ike!" he exclaimed.

All of my subordinates stood up and left the room. Each had a role to play that day. I was left alone. Events had passed from my control. The largest and most complex operation in military history was now underway. There was no turning back. I thought of Lincoln's Second Inaugural Address. He said of the Union and Confederacy:

"Both read the same Bible and pray to the same God, and each invokes His aid against the other. It may seem strange that any men should dare to ask a just God's assistance in wringing their bread from the sweat of other men's faces, but let us judge not, that we be not judged. The prayers of both could not be answered. That of neither has been answered fully. The Almighty has His own purposes."

Lincoln was right. God can't be for and against the same thing. We were about to learn which side of the war He was on.

☆☆☆☆☆

OUR LANDINGS IN the Cherbourg-Havre area have failed to gain a satisfactory foothold and I have withdrawn the troops. My decision to attack at this time and place was based upon the best information available. The troops, the

air and the Navy did all that bravery and devotion to duty
could do. If any blame or fault attaches to the attempt it is
mine alone.

I reviewed this note twice more before putting it in my pocket, having
dated it July 5. I suppose my mind was elsewhere. It was the note that I
prayed I wouldn't have to give to the press, though I wrote such notes
before every operation.

I put away my pen and turned to Bedell, who sat with me in the back
seat as Kay Summersby drove us to see the 101st Airborne Division near
Newbury, Wiltshire, twenty-five miles south of Oxford. Leigh-Mallory
estimated that they would suffer a 70 percent casualty rate. I had to see
them—look them in the eye—before they were deployed.

My hands clasped in my lap as I wrestled with anxiety. My brain
slushed around beyond my control. I fought to think about something
more positive—before Bedell and Kay noticed my growing distress—a
commander's worries should be reserved for his pillow! I tried thinking
about a letter I received from a woman back in the States. She objected to
my calling the recent weather "damnable" in an interview. She said since
God sent it I shouldn't curse it. Gave me a chuckle at the time. Lost its
potency. Aw well.

Bedell glanced at me, my efforts in vain.

"How do you think today and tomorrow will be remembered by
posterity?" he asked. I didn't respond. I was just trying to get through the
day. The history books were precisely what I *didn't* want to think about at
that moment. "I think it will be remembered as the beginning of a new
age. The day civilization triumphed over barbarism."

I nodded ever so slightly to acknowledge Bedell's efforts to cheer me
up. He tried again.

"I'll never forget how you stood up to Churchill and Bomber
Command over the dispute of whether to bomb French infrastructure or
German oil reserves. I'm certain we'll be proven right that targeting
railway lines and bridges across northern France will undermine German
logistics and benefit the invasion. We only won that argument because you
threatened to resign. I was never prouder of you."

I smiled.

"This invasion is the greatest challenge our military's ever faced," I
muttered. "A head on assault against Fortress Europe. We overcome that,

and we face the fiercest army in history. We cannot afford an indecisive blow."

"I know, Ike. That's what I'm saying."

"We shouldn't complain about Bomber Command. They're not as bad as de Gaulle. He still thinks Overlord's a bad plan and refuses to deliver the speech SHAEF wrote for him to give to the French people. He's the only one the French Resistance will listen to, and we need them to help our paratroopers. The problem is he knows it. Thinks he's Joan of Arc. I suppose now I know why they burned her at the stake."

Kay chuckled awkwardly from the front seat. I took out a cigarette, and then put it away. I smoked three packs a day during the war. It was my only bad habit.

Silence set in as we continued on our way. My mind raced over the details of recent weeks. Convincing the Big Shots to increase the landing from three divisions to five and add the jumpers. Patton stepping in controversy with his claim that America and Britain will rule the world after the war—excluding the Russians. His punishment was that he was now running a fake army to convince Hitler that the real target was the Pas de Calais, instead of Normandy. Fox Conner, my mentor—the man who rebuilt my life after Icky's death—he was still alive in 1944. What did he think of Overlord? He taught me everything I knew about my profession. Everything I used to plan that invasion. He even predicted that the war would happen two decades prior. Predicted that Marshall and I would be at the forefront. Was he proud to see his vision—

Seventy percent. That number roared back into my consciousness. It had been a week since Leigh-Mallory gave me that number and it still shook me. That number seemed high, based on our paratrooper operations in Sicily and Italy. But he was the expert. I had to trust him on the numbers, at least to a point. He wanted to cancel the paratrooper drop the night before the invasion. But we needed that drop to allow VII Corps to move inland from Utah Beach and seize the port of Cherbourg. Because without Cherbourg the whole operation acquired a degree of risk, even foolhardiness that presaged a gigantic failure, possibly Allied defeat in Europe. I rejected his advice. Told him to put his view in writing so he could protect himself in case I was wrong. The responsibility was mine. For everything that went wrong. That was my duty that day. Every needless death caused by poor planning was my fault. He was the expert, and I had disagreed. If his predictions proved accurate, then I would carry to my grave the unbearable burden of a conscience justly accusing me of the stupid, blind sacrifice of thousands of the flower of our youth. Committing to the paratrooper drop was the hardest decision of my life until launching the invasion.

I remained quiet as we saw the jumpers' gliders in the distance. We'd arrived at Newbury. My stomach rolled into knots as the car slowed. I'd read a poll of American forces in Britain a few weeks before about what's the one thing they would ask me if they could. The most common response was when they'd be able to go home. I would have asked General Marshall the same thing if I could. I was sure the jumpers would be annoyed to see me, since they probably blamed me for their present circumstances. I got out of the car and saw the 101st Airborne gathered together, getting ready for their operation. They didn't notice me yet. Seventy percent. Of twenty-nine thousand. My God. That's the number I expected would never see their loved ones again. What kind of a butcher was I?

I clasped my hands behind my back and walked toward the jumpers, saying nothing to Kay or Bedell. As I approached the warriors I noticed that many of them had painted their faces black. That served two purposes. It helped to camouflage them at night when they would meet the enemy and helped them feel brave. Some jumpers on the outer rim of the group glanced at me, then looked again to confirm the sight. They stood at attention.

"Hey, it's Ike!" one shouted.

"Look, the Supreme Commander's here to see us off!"

"Holy cow, Ike's here!"

Soon dozens, if not hundreds, of jumpers excitedly ran toward me, encircling me in a large group. I've never seen so many excited faces. I can't think of a more humbling experience. These men were the real heroes. They were about to risk their lives to defeat a racist monster. Yet they were excited to see *me*, who couldn't compare to their bravery and duty.

"At ease! Come on!" I exclaimed. "Gather around!" I glanced at the crowd, looking as many jumpers in the eye as I could. "Smoke if you got 'em, jumpers!"

They laughed; many pulled out cigarettes and lighters. I decided it was finally time for me to enjoy one too. I pulled out my cigarette, only to realize I'd left my lighter in the car!

"Anyone got a light?" I asked. They laughed again.

"Here ya go, Ike!" one exclaimed with a thick southern accent. He lit my cigarette and I thanked him.

"You men ready to get the ball through their endzone?" I asked. That lit up their faces. They loved that their general spoke the way they did.

"You ever play ball, Ike?" one asked.

"I did at West Point!" I answered.

"You any good?"

"I nearly tackled Jim Thorpe!"

That led to some "ohs!" from the group.

"Nearly?" another jumper asked.

"Yup," I replied to some laughs.

"Your team win?"

"Not exactly." More laughs. I turned to the jumper closer to me.

"Where you from, Corporal?"

"Brooklyn."

"Brooklyn, huh? You a Yankees fan?"

"That's right!"

Dozens of jumpers groaned. I joined them. I asked a few others. A handful of states were mentioned. New Jersey. Arizona. California. Ohio. Virginia. I wanted to find one from Kansas, preferably Abilene. That would have been a hoot!

"Anyone from Kansas?" I asked after I gave up on trying to be lucky. No one responded beyond a few shaking their heads 'no.'

"That's a shame," I said. "I'm going to need a job after we've hit Berlin!"

Some jumpers cheered.

"Don't worry, General," one said. "You can work at my ranch in Dallas!"

I smiled and nodded, pretending to consider the option. He continued.

"If I'm not there after the war you can ask my Pa. He'll give you a job."

I frowned. That burst the comradery, if for a moment. The reminder of coming death. For them and not for me. I toured several other groups of jumpers over the next hour or so before they took off. No other war in history so definitely lined up the forces of arbitrary oppression and dictatorship on the one hand against those of human rights and individual liberty. And they were the best of our side. They were plunging into the most vicious warfare imaginable, not only for America and Europe, but so the whole world could live in freedom and peace. They had no options of retreat. They had to succeed or die. I felt like a father to those young men when I was among them. But what kind of father sends his boys to kill and die? And they had real fathers waiting at home, anxious that their sons would return in one piece. And I took them away. No, I didn't. Hitler did, by trying to rule the world. How can one man be so selfish? He was the ultimate example of narcissism. And those jumpers were the ultimate example of duty. I couldn't be prouder of them.

"How about you?" I asked another jumper.

"What about me, General?"

"Where are you from?"

"Michigan."

"Michigan," I repeated. "How's the fishing up there?"

"It's great, sir."

"Michigan's a beautiful state. I've been fishing up there several times."

I made a demonstration of my preferred fly fishing technique. That led to a brief discussion on the topic. I became solemn again.

"Are you scared?" I asked the Michigander.

"No, sir!" he declared.

"Well, I am. Many of you boys ain't coming back."

"We're well briefed, sir. We're ready."

I smiled.

"We're going to achieve full victory and nothing less. I can't stress enough upon you all the historic magnitude of this undertaking. Your service will save the world."

That led to more nodding—more determination of spirit!

My eyes filled as the last planes flew beyond my ability to see them a short time later. I wiped the tears with my sleeve and slowly made my way to the car.

"Well, it's on," I said to Kay. She said nothing. "It's very hard to look a man in the eye when you fear you are sending him to his death."

I sat in the car.

"I hope to God I know what I'm doing."

☆☆☆☆☆

KAY AND I sat in my trailer that night outside of Portsmouth. I held a western in my hands, trying to pass the time until I received an update on the jumpers. I wasn't actually reading though; my eyes stared at the same paragraph for longer than I could count. My mind was elsewhere.

"How do you read that rubbish?" Kay asked. I ignored her. My mind wasn't with her words, either. She stood up and slowly made her way behind me. She touched my neck, which was taut as a drum. She tried to massage it, but my knots were gordian. Nothing was getting through. She gave up after a few minutes, complaining that her hands hurt. Oh, Kay. I could have spent that night chatting with Churchill or de Gaulle. But I chose to wait with Kay, my closest companion of the war. I'd have lost my mind if not for her.

Anxiety ate at my bones and a terrible pain throbbed in the back of my head. I looked to Kay with bloodshot eyes and asked for a cigarette. Maybe it would clear my head. Kay handed me my pack, but my body was vibrating, and a couple fell out and onto the floor. I picked one up, against all odds, and grabbed my lighter. I must have spent two minutes trying to light it before giving up. I lived ten years a week during that war, but never more than that night.

"I hope de Gaulle did his duty," I managed to say. "He better have sent a message to the French Resistance to cooperate with the jumpers. I'll have gambled my career for nothing by defying Roosevelt and telling him he can liberate Paris if he doesn't do it. That's a terrible thing to say. Mustn't think of myself right now."

Kay watched me silently, not sure if I was speaking to myself or to her.

"God, I hope Stagg was right about the weather! The goddamn weather! The fate of the world rests on the same factor as deciding if it's a good day to play golf or go to the ballgame. I can't imagine what it will be like if those boys have to land during a storm. They'll all die in the Channel. They'll all die because of me."

"No, Ike—"

"Even if they do hit the beach they'll have to overcome the German defenses. And what if it's more than machine guns? What if it's something we can't imagine? General Groves sent a scientist over here a few weeks ago who said the Germans might use some sort of radioactive fallout against our forces. I don't even know what that means exactly, but there'd be no way to protect them from that if it happens. Why hasn't Mallory given me an update on the 101st? There must be a report on early casualties by now. Why is he leaving me to soak in anxiety?"

My eyes shifted to my hands, which sat on my lap—still vibrating.

"We'll have a million soldiers on the continent within weeks, assuming tonight and tomorrow go well. That's too much for Monty to lead on his own. Bradley should have equal authority. I'll need to step in for overall command. Monty won't like that. It's necessary, though."

Kay continued watching me monologue.

"I wish this war could end without having to send our youths into harm's way. A man must develop a veneer of callousness that lets him consider such things dispassionately, but he can never recognize the fact that back home the news brings anguish and suffering to families all over the country. War demands real toughness of fiber. It's not only the soldiers that must endure but also those in the homes that must sacrifice their best. But it's so damn hard. What if something I hadn't thought about happens and men *die*? I feel like my mind should be able to process more than it does. Something's holding me back. And I hate that. A mental block. Maybe if Washington were here. Or Lincoln. Or Grant—"

"They wouldn't have done any better," Kay reassured.

"My son, Johnny, graduates from West Point tomorrow. What if his father destroying the world overshadows him?"

"You didn't *start* World War II, Ike. You're trying to end it."

I nodded.

"Tomorrow we get revenge for the Blitz," Kay said. "All those bodies I pulled out of the wreckage. You're getting revenge for us."

"This isn't about revenge, Kay."

"What's it about then?"

"Justice and peace."

She looked at me with sadness in her eyes. I didn't know what was going on in her head. Never do with women. I suppose she was also feeling the weight of our potential failure. Or maybe she was prematurely mourning the end of our friendship if we did win the war, which is what eventually happened. We shook hands when the time came, and that was it.

My emotions overwhelmed me again, for the hundredth time that day. What if the invasion failed? So much death. So many young men lost in their prime. *My fault*. It would all be *my fault*. And what would happen to the war? Roosevelt would lose the election in the fall. No question there. America would throw in the towel in Europe and turn to Japan. Get revenge for Pearl Harbor. Churchill would be thrown out on a No Confidence vote. Then Hitler would make a peace deal with Stalin and divide Europe between them. They'd probably go to war again within a decade, but either way, tyranny would rule Europe forever. It was wrong to think of myself that day, but I couldn't help but know that history would condemn me forever as the epitome of failure. The man who threw away humanity's last chance to defend itself from the ultimate villain. A man who wanted the Aryan race to dominate the world for a thousand years. All others would be enslaved or destroyed. That would happen because *I* failed.

Kay relieved me of this self-inflicted suffering. She turned on the radio before leaving my trailer to find her own bed.

"This is the BBC!" the radio announced. "Our Berlin Division says Allied paratroopers have landed in France. We now take you back to London!"

I rested my arms on a desk, trying to slow down their vibrations. I was losing that fight.

A French woman said a few words over the radio. Then de Gaulle's voice appeared. I never expected it to sound like angels coming through the clouds, but there it was. The English translation ordered the French Resistance to cooperate with the Allies. A smile burst on my face. I raised the radio's volume and consumed his beautiful words. My arms stopped vibrating.

Lives were saved!

☆☆☆☆☆

THE MORNING WAS sunny, thank God. Stagg was right.

I lay in bed, smoking a cigarette and reading a western. I had nothing to do all day except to listen for updates about the landing. Fifty-nine convoys were stretched along one hundred miles of English coastline. I had written a letter that was sent to each of the soldiers, sailors, and airmen, wishing them luck and telling them to do their duty. I was happy with the short note, but I heard later the men considered it too impersonal. Oh well.

Seven thousand ships crossed the English Channel in the largest armada in the history of warfare. Ten thousand planes dominated the skies over Normandy. One-hundred and sixty thousand soldiers landed on the five beaches.

Brrring! Brrring!

I picked up the phone. Admiral Ramsey called to say that everything was going according to plan. Four beaches had fallen easily. We had only lost two destroyers to mines when the armada crossed the channel. That was much lower than SHAEF expected.

God, what a day!

I decided to pay Monty a visit. I left my trailer and saw some GIs passing by.

"Good morning! *Good morning!*" I sang in a cheer. I saw another soldier reading the morning edition of the Portsmouth paper. I asked to see it. The main story was about Allied forces capturing Rome, Mussolini's old capital, instead of the Normandy landing.

Oh well.

Montgomery was happy and smiling when I saw him. He was wearing a gray sweater, if memory serves me. He said he wanted to cross the Channel to be with his men and did not have much time to talk to me. He was intent on establishing a headquarters in Normandy on D-Day. I asked if he wanted to speak to the world press representatives. He did, naturally. I told Butch, my aide, to arrange the press conference.

I visited Bradley next, around 1330. He had a bandage over his nose and glared at me when I entered his headquarters.

"We're busy here, Ike."

"I know, Brad. I was just hoping to get some updates."

"Can it wait?"

"Why do you look so out of it?" I asked. "Everything's going as planned. The airborne target sites have been secured, although some jumpers are still scattered across the Normandy countryside. I haven't heard anything about casualties yet, but it sounds like it's less than seventy percent. The Navy's swept the channel of mines, and—"

"Ike, I am asking you to go!"

My face flashed red. Why was he acting this way?

"What's happening, Brad? What should I know that you're not telling me?"

"One of the beaches has gone to hell!" he shouted. Some of his subordinates turned to stare at him. They were not used to the GI's General losing his cool. Neither was I. He rushed me into a small office so we could speak privately.

"What do you mean?" I asked. "Which beach?"

"Omaha. Everything that could have gone wrong *has* gone wrong."

"How wrong?"

"I think we're going to lose the beach."

"*What!*" I shouted. "We can't lose *any* beaches. We need all five for the invasion to work."

"I know!"

"And we especially can't lose Omaha. It's the link between Utah and the Anglo-Canadian ones! Without it Rommel will keep our forces separated and the Americans will be slaughtered before we can take Cherbourg!"

"I *know*, Ike! That's why I'm panicking! We're only holding a hundred yards of the beach."

"Did any amphibious tanks make it ashore?"

"Five, from what I can tell."

"*Five?* We sent thirty-two to Omaha!"

"I know! The others all sank!"

"What the hell happened? Why is Omaha such a disaster?"

"A whole bunch of things! It was a perfect shitshow storm!"

"Care to list some?"

"The seas were choppy," Brad began. "I put the men in the landing craft twelve miles out."

"Brad, it's supposed to be seven!"

"I thought twelve put them out of range of the German artillery!"

"Their artillery was supposed to be destroyed by a naval and aerial bombardment!"

"Yeah, well, Rommel built their bunkers below cliffs and it was cloudy, and we couldn't hit them. I called off the bombardment after forty minutes."

"It's supposed to be four hours!"

"There was no point in that!"

"So, you sent them in landing craft for twelve miles, against intact German artillery, and in choppy seas? How much did you feed them this morning?"

"A lot."

"Oh, my God! The landing craft must have been full of vomit!"

"I know!" Brad shouted. He wiped sweat from his forehead. "I don't know what you want me to say. We had no choice but to take the beach. It was necessary for the invasion to succeed. But the sea was choppy and the German positions couldn't be hit by bombardment. So, I decided to take the German units with head-on assaults on their strong points."

"*What!*" I shouted. "That's insane! Did you learn nothing from Sicily or Salerno?"

"I asked General Marshall for his advice, and that's what he told me to do."

"General Marshall hasn't led an operation since 1918! He's using a foolish theory and this isn't a textbook."

"I don't know what you want from me!" Brad snapped. "My post has been in crisis for hours, and you're here, and you're judging me and my decisions after the fact. It's not fair!"

"What the *hell*," I said, exacerbated. I folded my arms, then unfolded them. He was right. I was criticizing him in hindsight. That wasn't helpful. Now we had to find a way out of this nightmare. "What's our next step?"

"I want to evacuate Omaha."

"Out of the question."

"We *have* to."

"No, retreat is impossible. And losing Omaha will leave Utah isolated from the other beaches. Then Rommel will divide the Americans from our allies and conquer us both."

"Ike, a German offensive will push our men into the *sea.* They'll *all* die."

"I *forbid* a retreat." He looked at me in exacerbation, unsure why I was putting my foot down. "I'm serious. We're not losing Omaha."

"Well then what do you propose?" he asked. "I've already asked Montgomery if I can evacuate my men on Omaha to Gold Beach and he refused. The bastard."

My eyes narrowed as I put my finger to my chin. There must have been some way to hold the beach. That required delaying a German offensive. How could we do that? We had already destroyed most of the infrastructure in Normandy and northern France in bombing campaigns. Plus, our jumpers were surely disrupting various German operations. But we needed a guarantee.

"I could authorize Leigh-Mallory to bomb the beach again. Try and take out the German positions," I muttered.

"And kill all our men!" Brad explained.

"I'm thinking out loud. We could also threaten a German position. Like how we bombed Berlin back in March to force the Luftwaffe to defend it so we could then destroy the German planes with the Mustangs? We could do something like that."

"What would we threaten that would be prioritized over pushing our forces back into the Channel?"

"Maybe if Monty puts pressure on Caen. From Caen we can take Paris. Rommel won't give that up easily. I'll tell Monty to put any pressure on Caen that he can to distract German reinforcements from Omaha."

"And what should I do?" Brad asked, his face pale and sweaty.

I shrugged. My arms vibrated slightly. I doubt Brad noticed.

"Pray?"

"That's helpful," he muttered.

"I think it's up to the men on Omaha now. Individual sergeants and lieutenants to rise to the occasion."

"To clean up our mess." Brad nodded in agreement.

I left his headquarters shortly thereafter. I kept imagining the surf at Omaha red with the blood of American soldiers. I couldn't get it out of my mind. I was sick in my concern for those young people. They were in a hell I couldn't imagine. I chose that beach. I selected Brad and Gerow, his subordinate. I failed them, and with them, the invasion.

☆☆☆☆☆

THE FIRST DROPS of rain pelted the windows at Ramsay's fleet headquarters. I put out a cigarette. My body was otherwise still. Exhaustion had replaced anxiety in my bones. Ramsay, Tedder, and Leigh-Mallory sat with me around Ramsay's conference table.

"We achieved complete tactical surprise," Tedder read from a report. "The next ninety-six hours will be crucial. V Corps is still ten miles from Gold Beach. Seven from Utah. We'll have to link those forces in the next days to form an unbreakable and united front."

"How much of Omaha do we hold now?" I asked.

"Only a sliver. But at least we secured it. General Theodore Roosevelt, Jr., landed on the beach in a landing craft when he saw the crisis. He led Rangers and the First Infantry Division over the cliffs and broke through."

All four of us let out a sigh of relief. Heroism of individual soldiers whose names will surely be lost to history saved the day.

"How many did we lose there?" I asked.

"A thousand dead," Tedder answered.

I shook my head. A thousand American young men who will never grow old. A thousand grieving families who lost their loved ones.

"What were our total casualties for the day?"

"Ten thousand. According to our estimates. Lower than we expected."

"A lot of good that does for those among the dead and maimed."

"It's war, Ike. We didn't start this."

I nodded, though I wasn't sure that made me feel any better. I hate war. But I did, and still do, hate the Nazis even more. I've mentioned Lincoln's

Second Inaugural in this letter. His most famous line is "With malice toward none, with charity for all." It's amazing he could say such things at the end of the Civil War, that he could have such compassion, even for the Confederates. I don't know if I could say the same thing about Hitler and the Nazis. I'd like to think that I tried not to hate them. But I can't help it. Turning the other cheek just wasn't possible for what they did to our youths and to the world. Maybe a better man could feel differently.

Leigh-Mallory signaled my attention.

"As long as we're discussing casualties," he began, "It's hard to admit when one is wrong, but I am proud to do that now. You made the right decision regarding the drop. I am sorry for having contributed to your worries."

I nodded, accepting his apologies. The paratroopers had a 20 percent casualty rate. That was so much better than 70 percent. Again, though, that still is thousands of mothers and girlfriends who will never see their loved ones return.

"It really was a masterwork of logistics," Ramsay said, leaning back in his chair. "A miracle it succeeded."

"Of course Overlord did not fail," I countered. "How could it? With so many fine young men and women from all corners of the Earth determined to do their best to free a world gone half mad."

"Amen," Leigh-Mallory replied.

"Can we turn back to Omaha again?" I asked. My subordinates nodded. "The Germans had the chance to throw our forces back into the sea. But they didn't." I paused. "Was it because of Monty threatening Caen?"

Tedder shook his head.

"There weren't any German reinforcements to launch the counterattack."

"How were there no reinforcements? Did the jumpers do that good of a job disrupting them? Or did we just bomb the local infrastructure so much it was unusable?"

"Those were factors. But so was the fact that the Germans were genuinely unprepared. They didn't see the break in the weather and thought the invasion was impossible. Their U-boats were not conducting any patrols."

"But there must have been alerts about the jumpers and beach landing."

"Our intelligence," Ramsay began, "suggests that Rommel was out of town celebrating his wife's birthday. Lulled into complacency by the weather."

"The weather's becoming my best friend!" I exclaimed. "What about Hitler though?"

"We think he slept until midday. His aides were too scared to wake him. When he did wake, and they told him the news, he refused to believe this was the real invasion."

"He was that fooled by Patton's fake army?"

Ramsay smiled and nodded.

"This was the most successful deception since the Trojan Horse. Hitler thought this was a diversion and the real attack was still targeting the Pas de Calais. In Hitler's defense, though, he unleashed his Panzers toward Normandy in the afternoon. But they won't reach the beaches until tomorrow. I guess he finally realized we played him for a fool."

"Never say 'in his defense' and 'Hitler' in the same sentence again, Admiral," I ordered.

"Yes, sir," Ramsay replied.

"Did you hear the news from General Marshall today?" Leigh-Mallory asked me.

I shook my head.

"Apparently his wife picked up the phone and called him in from the garden. He listened to it for about five seconds, said 'thank you,' and then returned to his garden. His wife asked what that was about. He said that we've landed in Normandy. She asked frantically if he should do something. And he said, and I quote, 'from this distance don't you think that's Eisenhower's problem?'"

We all laughed. I shook my head, still exhausted.

"That sounds like the old man."

I yawned.

"I want to go to bed soon. I know it's early, but this has been the longest day of my life. I want to cross the channel to visit the beaches in the morning. See them myself."

"Do you think the war is over? Now that the beachhead's secure?" Tedder asked.

I shook my head.

"What did Churchill say after Monty beat Rommel in Egypt? That it was the end of the beginning? Well, today was the beginning of the end."

That elicited smiles. We were just getting started. The Western Front, the decisive front of World War II, in my view, had begun. It was a religious crusade against the forces of darkness. The Supreme Overlord saw us through D-Day and would see us through to victory in Europe eleven months later.

I feel a lot better now, having reviewed the most stressful day of my life. This situation over Berlin will resolve itself peacefully. Those boys in the Kremlin don't want to die. They're just making noise. Unlike Hitler, who set the world on fire. If I could face Hitler and Rommel, Khrushchev shouldn't scare me.

Hitler and Khrushchev. The two biggest foes I've ever faced. Each sought world mastery, each driven by a blend of narcissism and an insane ideology that led them to think they could tear down this civilization that was painfully built over thousands of years and build utopia in its place. No matter the millions who died in the process. And standing in their way were the soldiers, sailors, and airmen of the Allied nations, jointly motivated by their duty. Duty. The most beautiful word I've ever heard. No man can always be right. So the struggle is to do one's best, to keep the brain and conscience clear; never to be swayed by unworthy motives or inconsequential reasons, but to strive to unearth the basic factors involved and then do one's duty.

This letter must be burned if it is ever found. I would be more embarrassed than I can imagine if it was ever read by another soul. How can I complain about the stresses of the day? I didn't confront death in the form of a German machine gun. I was selfish for thinking about how success or failure would affect my place in history. Men that day lost any history they would ever have. How can I write a letter about the anxieties of the day when men who killed and risked death in battle did not? They are greater men than I. That is not to say that veterans who did write their memoirs are lesser men. But how can I, who did not face a shot fired in anger that day, claim any worthiness to write of the anxieties of the day?

I can't.

I ran for President to make sure that nothing like that day or that war ever happens again and no future generations have to endure what those men did. I think and hope and pray that humanity will learn more than we had learned up to that time. But those people gave us a chance. They bought time for us so we can do better. Every time I think about those beaches or that day, fifteen years ago now, I think that we must find a way to gain an eternal peace for this world.

The Tragedy of
Leroy Henry

Soldiers were fighting the world's worst racist, Adolf Hitler, in the world's
most segregated army. The irony did not go unnoticed.
—Stephen Ambrose

JUNE 16, 1944

I BELIEVED IN America.

Don't know why. My people came to the "New World" in chains. My own granddaddy was a slave. And he wasn't freed willingly. Only done through force. I can't believe I ever thought America was a good place to live as a black man. That I'd have freedom and apple pie. It's a sham.

I was drafted to serve my country. It was attacked, it needed help, and I was drafted. Didn't love that I was uprooted and taken halfway around the world. Didn't mind it too much though. It was an adventure. I'd live the rest of my life knowing I'd served my country and fought the monster that the press told us about. It was something I'd be proud of for years. But now I don't got years.

I'd made some friends in the Army. Learned some skills. Been with a pretty girl. Least that's what I thought. Still can't believe…

They dragged me to this country. We was gonna "save" it from conquest. This country. Which itself conquered most of the world. Let that sink in, Leroy. And that I was dragged here to save it, and now they're gonna take my life.

113

Henry's arms wrapped around his legs in a fetal position. He breathed slowly, calmly. He sat on a small bed, barely above the ground, on a thin mattress. The springs poked his sides every night. That denied him sleep at first, but he got used to it. The walls around him were made of gray stone with a hint of blue. It may have been pretty in a different context. Here it only reinforced the suffocation. In the corner sat a small toilet. He didn't even have books to pass the time. Henry was only semiliterate, anyway, but at least having *a* book would have been a nice gesture.

The Brits are supposedly different, in a good way. They lack America's race issue. Strange, since they brought my ancestors to America in the first place. But they do seem different. Thousands signed petitions on my behalf. That's nice. They get it. Then again, a Brit is why I'm here in the first place, so they still got some making up to do.

These countries are the good guys. America and Britain. Jim Crow and a huge empire are the good guys. You believe that? What does that tell you about the Germans?

Not sure why I've been talking to myself so much lately. Maybe working through my thinking makes it all hurt less. That once I understand what I'm feeling the feeling goes away. Or maybe it distracts me from the inevitable.

I admired Ike so much. He was gonna save the world from darkness. Still is, probably. Like how Honest Abe freed my granddaddy. And he was supposed to save me. But he's either too busy or he doesn't care. How could I have been stupid enough to put my faith in a white man born in the 1800s? I expected him to care about a black boy? Talk about naïve.

Tears emerged in Henry's eyes as his frustration mounted. He squeezed himself tighter.

My daddy told me that real men don't cry. I tried to live up to that. Can't help myself anymore. It's all too much. I'm sorry, Pa.

Wanted to serve my country. Then I'd marry a nice black girl. Have a couple of kids. Live an honest life. Go to Heaven.

I'm trying to maintain my faith, but goddamn it! I just want to get my way! For once. Reality must conform. Just once. This cell is suffocating. Can't breathe. I didn't ask the world for much. But this time it needs to conform to what I want. Just this once. Can you do that for me, Jesus? Just this once. I know I disappointed you. But you're supposed to be merciful. That's what I was taught.

One mistake. All this because of one mistake. All this weight. Suffocating. And this was ONLY a mistake. Not the crime they accused me of. Convicted me for. Killing me for.

I'm so scared. I want Pa to save me. Want Ma to comfort me. I'm so alone. I hate being alone. Especially now.

I always tried to act tough. Especially with my buddies. Leroy wasn't scared of nothing. But it's easy to act tough when things are easy. It all goes out the window once pressure's applied.

☆☆☆☆☆

MAY 5, 1944

PRIVATE LEROY HENRY smiled, his head on the pillow, his thumbs twiddling. Never had barracks been so relaxing. Training was done for the day. He could rest, his mind at peace, his breathing calm. The only obstacle to his tranquility was his plans for the evening. But that was cause for excitement, not distress.

"What are we doing tonight?" Private Washington asked. "We got some time off. Let's enjoy it."

"Do we gots to do something?" Private Davis replied.

"This'll be one of our last free nights before the invasion. We should take advantage of it."

"Ok," Davis said as he sat up, his legs dangling over his bunk. "How about a movie? I heard the Army is putting on *The Big Bonanza*. Should be good."

"I could do that," Washington responded.

"And there's a dance at Avenue Hall this evening. We could go to the movie and then the dance. Bound to be some colored WACs to have fun with."

WACs were the Women's Army Corps, the female branch of the Army.

"Sounds great. And you didn't want to do anything. I see what game you're playing. How about you, Leroy? You interested?"

Henry, in the bunk above Washington, pulled himself out of his semicatatonic state.

"You guys go on without me."

"Come on, Leroy!" Washington exclaimed. "Don't do this!"

"You tired?" Davis asked.

"Nah," Henry replied. "I got other plans for tonight."

Washington and Davis were quiet for a moment. Then Washington started laughing.

"Alright, I know what you're doing. You're seeing that prozzer again."

"Maybe," Leroy said with a smile.

"You're not serious," Davis said.

"Come on, man. Let Leroy have some fun. You mad because she's thirty-three?"

"No, you dope. She's white. Leroy's asking for trouble."

"Don't be such a slow poke," Henry said, turning to face Davis.

"Yeah, don't be a slow poke," Washington agreed.

"I'm being realistic. The white soldiers don't like it when we have fun with white British girls. They don't get why the Brits don't share their ugliness."

"They're not that bad," Henry replied.

"Not if you know your place," Davis said.

"No, I'm serious," Henry insisted, sitting up. "I was a truck driver in Missouri. Now they trained us as Army technicians."

"They won't even let us fight."

"I'm not saying everything's equal, but I like being in Quartermaster Gas Supply Company." Henry chuckled. "That's a mouthful. But we gonna be doing important work after the invasion. We're gonna bring fuel to the Army units so they can fight the Germans."

"I know, but that's still support work. That's all they think we're good for."

"You're being too hard on them. We're doing something important here. America's come a long way since our granddaddy's dads' time."

"Not as far as it needs to go."

"I'm not denying it doesn't have its problems, but Hitler's not gonna solve them."

"Didn't say he would."

"And Ike's leading the invasion. He's a good man."

"He's just another old white man."

"I admire him."

"Me too," Washington agreed.

"You can have your own opinion," Davis said. "I just think y'all aren't appreciating that a segregated army is going to fight the world's worst racist."

"I ain't denying that," Henry replied.

"What time's the movie?" Washington asked.

"We should get going soon if we want good seats," Davis said.

"You guys get going. I have an appointment to keep."

"Be careful, Leroy. I care about you."

"Yeah, yeah."

☆☆☆☆☆

HENRY MADE HIS way from Somerset to Combe Down, which was southwest of London on a ridge above Beth. Combe Down contained Bath stone villas from the eighteenth and nineteenth centuries. The village's defining feature was its mines, which supplied the materials that built Buckingham Palace, among other buildings. Its geography was scarred by the Blitz.

Henry arrived at a modest stone house tucked into an English garden. Within an hour they were lying in bed together. He smiled as she covered her torso with the blanket.

"You're so cute."

"Bug off," Julia Spencer replied in her West Country British accent. Her blonde hair hung over her shoulders.

"No, I mean it."

"This isn't about that."

"I know," Henry said, disappointed. He rubbed his nose with his index finger. Julia's eyebrow rose.

"Lovely."

"Sorry. I find I act on habits without thinkin'. Then I make mistakes when I'm not lookin'."

"It just wasn't attractive is all. Not a big deal. We already did it."

"That was it for tonight?"

"We'll see. As long as my husband stays downstairs."

"Good," Henry said with a smile. He took Julia's hand in his and kissed her knuckles. "Can we start over?"

"With what?"

"Our conversation. I don't know if I'll see you again after tonight. The invasion is coming soon."

"Thank God."

"You don't want me around?"

"No, I'm saying the war will be over soon and this accursed rationing will end. I can live like a human again."

"You want to pick the next topic?" Henry asked, trying to stay positive.

"Sure," Julia said. She took out a cigarette that Henry had given her last time but put it back.

"I would love to be in America. You can be anything you want there. Pluck money off the streets. I know it's probably different for a Negro."

Henry shrugged. "I don't really want that much in life. So, I can't complain. Might be different if I were more ambitious."

"Is what you want what we just did?"

Henry laughed. "Pretty much." He kissed her knuckle again. "What would you wanna be in America?"

"Maybe an actress. I've always loved the idea of being on stage. Don't know if I'm any good. Never tried anything. Or I could be a teacher."

"You couldn't be a teacher here?"

"I guess I can, but it seems like you Americans don't struggle as much. What's the saying? 'Americans are overpaid, over-sexed, and over-here.'"

"'And you Brits are 'under-paid, under-sexed, and under-Eisenhower,'" Henry said with a smile.

"Pff." Julia rolled her eyes. "He seems like a nice man, but I'm not sure he has anything between his ears. How the British Empire is following orders from a Kansas bumpkin I'll never know."

"I like him. You want to go again?"

"I've changed my mind. I'm too tired."

"Come on!" Henry begged. "This is comin' out of my paycheck. I could have gone to the dance at the Avenue Hall, but I chose to come here."

"The Avenue Hall?"

"Yeah."

"I was there one night during the Blitz."

"Really?"

"Oh, yes. We heard the air-raid sirens and left the dance hall to get to my cousin's home. We hid in her basement during the first raid."

"Could you hear the bombing?"

"Of course! The first raid lasted for two hours. I was simultaneously praying that our cousin's house be spared and that, if we were hit, that death come quickly."

"I've thought similarly once I'm in France. Either make it through without a harm or make it fast."

"I'm telling my story. Stop interrupting."

"Sorry."

"It's okay. That night was the first time I've seen a Luftwaffe plane up close. It was gray with black markings. I'd seen the fires and broken bodies of other raids, but I'd never seen a plane before. One of theirs, that is. We made our way home after that. I think we helped our local dentist before we reached home, though. His children were trapped under a collapsed building. Anyway, our home had no gas or water after that. The electricity wasn't affected, I don't think."

"Was that before or after you met Mr. Spencer?"

"Before. That was 1940. I met him in '42."

"Wow," Henry muttered. "You sure you don't want to go again?"

"Yeah. But we should talk payment.

"I have the pound." Henry turned to his wallet.

"It's two this time."

"What? Why?"

"I'm raising my price. I need two pounds to get the things I need."

"That's not fair!"

"Neither is rationing!" Julia shouted. "Now pay up!"

"I only have one pound!"

"Listen here," Julia asserted as she pointed her index finger at Henry. "You're going to pay me the two pounds, or I'm telling the US Army you raped me."

"That's not funny!"

"I'm not joking. It's one or the other. Now pay up!"

"I don't have two pounds!" Henry pleaded. "I'm happy to pay you the one."

"John!" Julia screamed, getting her husband's attention.

Henry leaped out of bed.

"Are you crazy?" he shouted.

"John! This colored boy raped me! I need your help! He has a knife!"

Henry froze as Julia crawled out of bed and lunged for the door, unsure if he should try to stop her.

"John!" Julia screamed again. "He raped me! Help!"

"You crazy bitch!" Henry shouted as he sprinted to the window. His strength came to him as he pulled the window open. He looked below. He was on the second story. *I could break my—*.

"What Negro's here?" John asked as he arrived in the room.

Henry leapt without thinking. He somersaulted, per his training.

Thud!

Henry was dizzy. The world spun around him. *Have to rest.*

"Don't you move, you black bastard!" John shouted from the second floor of the house. He started climbing down the stairs.

Got to get out of here. Henry summoned his strength once again. He pushed himself to his feet. His run started slowly but picked up speed. *Nothing seems broken.*

Henry ran a couple blocks. Then he collapsed on a bench and passed out.

☆☆☆☆☆

MAY 30, 1944

I DON'T UNDERSTAND why my memory keeps replaying what happened, and yet most of it remains a blur. I guess that happens when I get stressed. Everything becomes a blur. Probably not a good trait for a soldier. Not that that matters anymore.

Let's see. British police woke me on that bench in Combe Down after a couple hours. They told me I was under arrest for raping Julia, which was nonsense. Then they realized I was a GI and handed me over to the US Army, who put me here.

Henry was in his cell in Shepton Mallet, a British civilian prison that was loaned to the US Army during the war.

"Private Henry?" the lawyer had asked.

"That's me."

"I'm Major Drew. I'll be representing your defense."

"I didn't know there were any Negro JAGs." Henry stood as they shook hands. Drew laughed.

"There aren't many of us. But you're in good hands."

"At least *you're* confident."

"One of us needs to be. Do you want to tell me what happened?"

"You gonna tell anyone else?"

"Whatever you say is protected by attorney-client privilege."

"What does that mean?"

"It means that whatever we discuss can't be requested by the prosecution in discovery. That doesn't mean they can't get the information through other means, but that these conversations are protected."

"Sounds good," Henry said. He hesitated. Drew waited. "I didn't rape that woman."

Drew kept a poker face.

"Now, I did sleep with her. Paid her, too. Thought I was having some fun before the invasion. I didn't know this would happen."

"Soliciting prostitution is still a crime," Drew replied. He was surprised how quickly Henry disclosed this fact. He must have been desperate for help.

"I know, but it isn't rape! You can see the difference between those, right?"

"Of course. But you admitting that you hired a prostitute in court will still lead to charges."

"I understand! But there's no way it's as serious as rape!"

Drew nodded.

"The victim, Mrs. Spencer, is claiming that you broke into her home and raped her at knifepoint. You're saying there's no validity to that?"

"Not even a little!" Henry shouted.

"You might want to lower your voice."

"I'm being serious!"

"I understand that, but we don't want anyone overhearing us."

"Ok. Sorry."

"That's okay. But what's your version?"

"The *truth* is that this was my third time seeing her, but this time she wanted two pounds, where normally she just wanted one. I didn't have two, and she ran to her husband claiming I'd raped her."

"Do you have any witnesses who can attest to that?"

"No. Other than my buddies who knew I was seeing a British whore."

"What race are your buddies?"

"They're Negros. Like us."

"That doesn't help us then," Drew replied as he pushed his glasses up the bridge of his nose.

"Why is it the Army who's charging me? The 'victim's' a Brit."

"Parliament passed the Visiting Forces Act, which lets the US Army handle its own criminal cases unless the Army waives that right and hands it over to the British legal system. The Army chose not to waive that right in this case."

"What's the worst-case scenario?" Henry asked.

"Of what?"

"Of getting convicted. How long could I be in the stockade for?"

Drew hesitated.

"Rape is punishable by death under Article 92 of the current US Army Articles of War."

Henry's face sunk. It took a few seconds for the word to sink in. *Death?* He looked Drew in the eye.

"You knew that law's name off the top of your head?"

"I looked it up when I was assigned to your case."

"What are my chances?"

"An American Negro accused of rape versus a British prostitute? I'd like to say this could go either way. I'd like to, at least."

☆☆☆☆☆

NEXT WAS JULIA'S testimony. Talk about popping my bubble.

"He appeared in our home. He was lost, asked for directions to Bristol, I think."

"Were you alone?" Captain Cullison, the white prosecutor, asked.

"No, my husband was with me at that point."

"Okay, so the defendant asked you for directions. What happened then?"

"I offered to go with him so I could direct him on how to get to Bristol."

"You went with him?"

"Yes."

"All the way to Bristol?"

"No, just a block down. So I could give him directions."

"Did your husband mind your doing this?"

"No. He was fine with it."

"What happened next?"

"We had walked about a block when he pulled out a knife and forced me over a wall. Then he raped me."

"Were you afraid for your life?"

"Yes."

"How did you get home?"

"My husband came out and found me. He was worried after I'd been gone for so long."

Henry glared at Julia during her testimony. How could she not care about his desperation after what she'd been through during the Blitz? He kept trying to stop glaring at her. It didn't look good to the panel, who were seven white officers and one black captain. But it happened instinctually unless Henry caught himself. Then his mind would move on and he would glare at her again.

Drew opted not to cross examine Julia, attempting to impeach her testimony instead. He had Henry, Washington, and Davis testify in support of his effort by admitting to a preexisting transactional sexual relationship between Henry and Julia. Cullison had Julia's husband testify in response. Drew made a desperate last roll of the dice with a hearsay objection, but the panel preempted Drew's effort by accepting Julia and her husband's testimonies as fact. The presiding colonel overruled Drew's subsequent objection and instructed the parties to make closing statements.

Cullison's closing statement was the worst. Like living in one of those horror stories my pa told me. Being told you're one way, with fancy words, even though you know you're not. But what was it worth if I knew something but everyone else disagreed? Made me feel like my opinion didn't matter—even if I was the subject.

"Your Honor, rape is a crime under Section 148(b) of the Manual for Courts-Marshal. The defendant's actions clearly fall under Section 148(b). That section defines rape as 'the unlawful carnal knowledge of a woman by force and without her consent.' That gives us two elements to be met— carnal knowledge and lack of consent. There is no dispute of fact as to whether carnal knowledge occurred. The defendant has admitted such and a medical exam of the victim confirms it. The point of contention is the lack of consent. The panel accepted the victim and her husband's testimony that the defendant put a knife to the victim's throat, forced her over a wall so they would have greater privacy, and coerced her into having sex with him at the threat of stabbing. This clearly fulfills this element.

"Additionally, Your Honor, Section 148(b) does not state a specific mental state. However, the defendant's actions clearly satisfy Knowledge, if not the higher mental state of Purpose."

☆☆☆☆☆

Drew's waste of breath—whoops—I mean closing argument, was less impressive, to put it mildly.

"Your Honor, the defense argues that the panel acted inappropriately in making its findings of fact in this case. The defense contends that the victim *was* a part-time prostitute who offered sexual favors in exchange for money and that she began this conduct as a result of wartime rationing.

"As the prosecution stated, medical examinations of the victim demonstrated that the victim engaged in sexual activity, but he left out that this activity did not occur forcefully. If this does not prove that the victim's testimony was not credible, as this court has held, it does nonetheless suggest that the defendant's innocence must be assumed until greater evidence proves he is guilty under Section 148(b) of the Manual.

"Testimony by the defendant's friends, such as Privates Washington and Davis, demonstrated that the defendant and the victim knew each other before the night of the supposed encounter. This contradicts the victim's testimony.

"The defense also contends that the defendant did not meet Knowledge or any other mental state, as the event did not occur as the victim claims.

"This war is about preserving our rights as American and British citizens from foreign tyranny. One of those rights, particularly in America, is 'innocent until proven guilty.' The prosecution has not given enough evidence to prove beyond a reasonable doubt that the defendant committed the crime of which he is accused. Ruling in favor of the defendant, in favor of justice, will show the world why we're fighting."

☆☆☆☆☆

THE PANEL FOUND Henry guilty.

He lost his breath when he heard the judgment and sank back in his chair. *This isn't happening. How can they not see she's full of it? And one of the officers on the panel was a Negro! How could he...*

The colonel presiding over the tribunal asked the panel to give its sentence. The spokesman said:

"Article 92 of the US Army Articles of War of June 4, 1920 reads, 'Any person subject to military law who commits murder or rape shall suffer death or imprisonment for life, as a court-martial may direct; but no person shall be tried by court-martial for murder or rape committed within the geographical limits of the States of the Union and of Columbia in time of peace.' The exception clearly doesn't apply in this case since it's wartime and this trial is not in the United States. Consequently, we sentence the defendant to death by hanging."

Colors around Henry blurred as his head dropped. He did not hear Drew say, "I'm sorry." He only heard a buzzing sound. The rest of the world did not matter. Tears did not rise in his tear ducts. He couldn't think. Finally, vomit surged into his throat. Henry instinctually forced his body under control, refusing to retch in the courtroom.

He started shaking. Drew tried grabbing his arm. Henry pushed him away.

What is this? What kind of system is this? I didn't do it! I honestly— ah! Suffocating. What kind of country sentences an innocent man to death? Where's the justice here? Where's the hope?

☆☆☆☆☆

JUNE 3, 1944

I WONDER IF the Lord is mad at me for sleeping with a prostitute. Maybe that's what happened. I sinned and now I'm being punished. That's the only way that this is justice.

Henry was sitting in his "Condemned Cell" in Shepton Mallet. He would be hanged in a week. *I wonder if I'll live to see the invasion. Goddamn. Not only was I going to witness history, but I was going to be part of it. And now—*

An African American man in a three-piece black suit who had a mustache and glasses arrived at Henry's cell. The guard let him in. Henry eyed the man with suspicion. His ability to trust died in his trial and conviction. The man placed his briefcase on the bed and looked at Henry like a concerned father.

"Private Henry?" Henry nodded. "My name is James Miller. How are you holding up?" Henry didn't move. "I'm with the NAACP. Have you heard of us?" Henry shook his head. "It stands for 'National Association for the Advancement of Colored People.'" Henry's stare remained blank. "I'm a lawyer. I help Negroes whose only real crime is the color of their skin. I'm a colleague of Thurgood Marshall. Have you heard of him?" Henry shook his head. "That's okay. You will one day."

"I don't got many days left."

"You do if I have anything to say about it."

"What do you mean? I had my trial. I lost."

Miller smiled. "I am not licensed to practice in Britain. But I talked with Major Drew, your lawyer. We've appealed your case."

"What does that mean?" Henry asked desperately.

Miller chuckled. "Normally, a case is appealed to a higher court in the jurisdiction. But we appealed your case to General Eisenhower. Your execution has been frozen in the meantime."

Henry stopped himself from jumping off the bed.

"Ike?" he exclaimed. Miller nodded with a smile. "Ike can control my case?"

"The NAACP determined that, as commander, Eisenhower has authority over the military justice cases in this theater of operations. It's a way to guarantee that his conduct of the war isn't undermined by the military justice system."

"Will he save me?"

"There's cause for hope."

"That's not a 'yes.'"

"I can't guarantee you anything, Leroy. But the British people have rallied to your cause."

"A British couple is why I'm here."

"You can't blame the actions of one or two individuals on an entire group, Leroy. That's the mentality that led to your case of injustice."

"Fair enough. What actions have the British taken? Major Drew told me I'm not in their legal system, so what can they do?"

"They're putting public pressure on General Eisenhower to revoke your sentence."

"How?"

"A local baker named Jack Allen started a petition on your behalf that's gotten thirty-three thousand signatures. Thirty-three thousand people who you've never met who don't want you hanged just for being a Negro."

"Anything else?"

"Have you heard of Cecil King?"

Henry shook his head.

"He's a columnist for the *Daily Mirror*, which is the largest newspaper in the world. Their circulation is over five million. He wrote a column this morning that said that you've received a harsher punishment than a white soldier would have received."

"Is Ike going to read that?"

"Maybe."

"Are you serious? He's 'bout to lead the biggest operation of the war. He aint reading British newspapermen or caring about a Negro convicted of rape."

"I need you to be more optimistic and hopeful. We've got a shot here. We've appealed to the man whose job it is to destroy the world's biggest racist."

"Excuse me if I don't feel hopeful right now. My entire life's been ripped apart, and in a week I'm going to hang for a crime I didn't commit. I'm actually pretty *not* hopeful right now." Tears welled up in Henry's eyes. "I'm scared, Mr. Miller. I upset Jesus, and He—"

"Hey, hey! You did not upset our Lord, my boy. He forgives you. You have to believe that."

"How!" Henry shouted, tears now streaming down his face. "How would I believe that?"

"He loves you, Leroy. He's going to get you out of this."

Henry shook his head. "No. I'm from an evil country. I thought it was good, but I was wrong, I—" Henry was too choked up to speak.

Miller sat on the bed next to Henry. He had seen this mindset a thousand times before.

"I understand how you feel, Leroy. You feel powerless. You feel like the whole system's rigged against you. And guess what? It is. You live under Jim Crow. The British have an empire across the world, and even they don't understand it! But that doesn't matter. I need you to stop wallowing in self-pity. You're a soldier. A fighter! You're a part of the great Arsenal of Democracy."

Henry shook his head, lacking control of his emotions.

"You need to have faith in Christ, Leroy. He'll make sure Eisenhower does the right thing. Eisenhower's the hope of Europe. You need to have hope in him, too."

Henry shook his head again as he finally breathed normally. "Don't —" He paused.

"What was that?" Miller asked softly.

Henry looked Miller in the eye. "Don't give me hope."

☆☆☆☆☆

JUNE 19, 1944

GENERAL DWIGHT EISENHOWER, the Supreme Commander of the Allied Expeditionary Force, marched through his headquarters at 20 Grosvenor Square. General Walter "Bedell" Smith, his chief of staff, and Colonel Tex Lee, his aide de camp, trailed him. Ike lit a cigarette as he entered his office. Lee closed the doors behind him.

"What's the situation on the front?" Ike asked Smith. The Normandy invasion occurred two weeks prior, on June 6. Hitler had refused to allow the German forces to retreat, causing a stalemate of attrition.

"Continual Allied attacks are confronting fierce German resistance," Smith began. He carried a report of the day's relevant news in a folder. "Montgomery's Twenty-First Army Group is still stuck at Caen—"

"He was supposed to capture Caen on D-Day!" Ike asserted.

"I know, Ike. On the bright side, the air campaign is restricting fuel to the Germans by crippling their infrastructure."

"Any conclusions from Bradley or Montgomery on the hedgerows?"

"No. Other than they're making the advance difficult."

"I already knew that." *We spent too long worrying about taking the beaches. Didn't put enough time planning on how to advance inland.* "The Ninth Infantry Division cut the Cotentin Peninsula yesterday. Any news from that part of the front?"

"Bradley estimates that 40,000 Germans are defending Cherbourg, which is still thirteen miles away from the Twelfth Army Group."

"How far away are they from St Lo?"

"About five miles."

"We can try to break the German line there."

"Perhaps."

"Don't give me 'perhaps,' Bedell! Thousands of men are dying! How are our supply lines?"

"We've landed 218,000 tons of supplies on the continent since D-Day."

"That's thirty percent *less* than planned."

"I know."

"Are the men getting their rations?"

"There's been difficulties. But French peasants are selling them eggs from their farms."

"Any other news?"

"A German V1 bomb killed one-hundred and twenty-one people at the Guards Chapel of Wellington Barracks yesterday."

Ike frowned. *We've got to take out these V weapons. I had to go into an air-raid shelter nineteen times yesterday morning.*

"What about weather?"

"The Weather Division predicts the oceans will remain calm."

"Thank God." *Especially after the storm at the beginning of the month nearly wrecked the invasion.*

"I agree. They say a cold front is descending from Iceland and the Mediterranean's restless—"

"Those don't sound calm."

"They say they won't matter."

"Let's hope they're right. It's only the fate of Europe that's at stake. And thousands of our men."

"That's everything I have to report."

Ike turned to Lee. "How about you, Tex?"

"I have two things, General. A SHAEF study found that the average Londoner could expect to be within a half mile of a V1 detonation once a month."

"All the more reason we have to reach the Pas-de-Calais and knock out that launch system," Ike replied.

"Yes, sir. The other article I have deals with an appeal we received a couple weeks ago."

"An appeal from who?"

"A Negro soldier was convicted of raping a British woman and is sentenced to hang."

"Was the soldier one of ours?"

"Yes."

"How does this fall under my authority?"

"You're the senior officer of this theater."

"Do we really have time to discuss this?" Smith asked. "We're talking about the life of one man while the entire Western world is at stake."

"We have time," Ike replied. "The front is a stalemate. Montgomery's running the ground war so far. Tedder and Leigh-Mallory are managing the air campaign. And Ramsey is directing the sea fighting. So we have a few minutes. Maybe we can do some good."

Lee continued. "The British public is rallying to the Negro's defense."

"That's irrelevant," Smith interjected. "Public opinion doesn't affect the outcome of trials."

"Why are the Brits supporting him?" Ike asked.

"They lack our racial consciousness. Except for the ones in cities and the wealthy."

"Has SHAEF's Law Division reviewed this yet?"

"Yes. They think there's a lack of evidence for the conviction."

"Is that the case file?"

"Yes," Lee replied. He handed the NAACP folder to Ike.

"It's inappropriate for you to interfere with the judicial process, Ike," Smith asserted.

"Color me intrigued," Ike replied. "Can you gentlemen give me an hour to read this file?"

Smith and Lee agreed.

☆☆☆☆☆

A PILE OF cigarettes sat on an ashtray on Ike's desk. He paused from reading as his ears rang once again. He closed his eyes and exhaled until the pain ceased. *This damn war's eating my body. My ears, my back. I can barely walk some days.*

An hour had passed since Ike began reading. Smith and Lee entered the office. The folder sat open on Ike's blue desk.

"You boys were keeping time, weren't you?" Ike asked.

"What do you think of the case?" Lee asked.

"I'm not a lawyer," Ike began, "but this seems like pretty thin evidence for sending a man to his death."

"We can't risk undermining our institutions," Smith said. "People will question them. Faith in institutions matters."

"I know, Bedell," Ike replied. "And you know I'm fine with the death penalty. But I don't think it serves our institutions to allow a man to die for a crime he didn't commit." He turned to Lee. "Can you get Summersby and Moaney?"

"Yes, sir," Lee replied as he left the office.

Ike lit a cigarette.

"Ike, I really think you're stepping out of bounds if you revoke the conviction. The JAGs did their job."

"That's what I'm wrestling with, Bedell," Ike said as he blew a puff. "But we also can't deny that there's been tension between our white soldiers and Negro soldiers since our buildup in Britain started two years ago. Our white soldiers don't understand why British girls are going out with the Negroes. Maybe I should have kept my press ban on these types of stories in this theater."

"We thought that would look bad in a war to save democracy."

"So does letting an innocent man hang. Stopping that sort of thing from happening is why we're fighting this war."

"You don't actually know he's innocent."

"That evidence is pretty thin. It seems more likely that there was anger that they had interracial sex and they were taking it out on him. Now, I think miscegenation is inappropriate, but you don't kill a man for it."

Lee, Kay Summersby, and Sergeant John Moaney arrived in the office.

"Has Tex filled you in on the situation?" Ike asked.

Kay and Moaney nodded.

"This case comes down to his word against hers. I'm not sure that's enough evidence to hang a man."

"Ike, you're not saying you think she's making it up?" Kay asked.

Ike shrugged. "Very little of either of their claims are provable."

"A woman doesn't make up something like this. You'd be letting a rapist go free."

"Or letting an innocent man die," Ike replied. "I'm not saying this is easy."

"Why would she lie?"

"The file says he wouldn't pay her. Maybe this was revenge."

"Oh, please! Don't be a chauvinist!"

"That's not fair, Kay. I'm operating on remarkably little evidence on either side. Neither have witnesses."

"What about the victim's husband?" Lee asked.

"I don't know his deal," Ike said, "but the file says the defendant admits to sleeping with the victim. I remember the anxiety of when I was stationed in the Philippines and Mamie remained in Washington for a year. And we have a good marriage. Then there's the rumors about you and me, Kay, and what that's putting Mamie through. I know what jealousy can do. He too might want revenge on this Negro boy."

"So, his testimony doesn't matter?" Smith asked.

"It might be biased," Ike replied.

"He was under oath!"

"So was the defendant!"

"It's so typical that a *man* wouldn't believe the woman," Kay muttered. "I've never heard of a woman *lying* about something like this."

Ike turned to Moaney, his African American aide.

"John, does this happen to Negroes back home?"

Moaney stood stoic. He looked Ike in the eye.

"More than ya' would want to know, Gennul."

Ike nodded. He'd suspected as much. *I remember seeing the paratroopers a couple of weeks ago. The ones who landed in Normandy.*

Twenty percent became casualties. Leigh-Mallory thought it would be seventy percent. And I met them. Shook their hands. Learned their stories. It's very hard to look a man in the eye when you think you're sending him to his death.

"This war's causing enough corpses," Ike said as he turned to Lee. "Write this down." Lee took out a paper and pen. "The defendant's conviction and sentence are hereby revoked because of a lack of evidence. He is to return to his duty."

"Yes, sir," Lee replied as he wrote down Ike's order.

Ike turned to Smith. "Let's get back to the war. Put me in touch with Bradley's HQ. We need to discuss the thrust to St Lo."

☆☆☆☆☆

"Has he heard?" Miller asked.

"What do you think?" the warden replied.

Henry was in a fetal position, sitting on his bed in the "Condemned Cell."

A guard unlocked the cell door. Miller entered, a smile slicing across his face like a crescent moon. Henry, lost in thought, did not notice Miller.

I need to accept that reality doesn't care what I want. It's indifferent. I could ask for one thing and make peace with a hundred, and it won't be enough. The world takes and it takes. I shouldn't expect anything. Not even justice. And the injustice isn't from a random person. It's from soc—

"Leroy?" Miller asked, peering down at him.

Henry looked up, his eyes bloodshot. "What are you smiling about?"

"I have good news for you."

Good news? I haven't had good news in over a month.

"General Eisenhower revoked your conviction."

Henry didn't move. He stared at Miller. "Can you repeat that?"

"Happy to. Eisenhower revoked your conviction."

"What does that mean?"

"It means he threw out your case. Lack of evidence."

"So I'm gonna live?"

Miller nodded. "To a ripe old age, God willing."

Henry's eyes filled with tears. He broke out into laughter, unable to control himself. "I'm gonna live!" he shouted.

"Congratulations, Leroy!" Miller said. "You've also been ordered back to duty with the Gas Supply Company. So you need to pack up.

You're going to France." Henry nodded. "Are you okay with serving your country, after all it put you through?" Henry nodded again. "Really? I'm not sure I'd be so forgiving."

Henry looked up, tears in his eyes. "I don't forgive it. This has changed my opinion of America for the worse. Its flaws are deeper than I knew."

"Then what am I missing?"

"That Ike's a good man. And that someone like him can be in a position of power means that America can change. That separates it from the Germans. That's worth fighting for. That gives me hope."

The Soldier versus The Tyrant

Calamity acted on Eisenhower like a restorative and brought out all the greatness in his character.
—Alan Brooke

FIELD MARSHAL WALTHER Model looked up from the maps that were laid out across the table. With a monocle covering his right eye, he watched the other generals study the plan that was meant to save the Third Reich from the fate it deserved.

Standing with perfect posture, Model said, "This is by far the boldest plan that the Fuhrer has ever devised. I am not confident in its ability to achieve the objective." He was one of the most revered German generals of the war for his mastery of both offensive and defensive tactics. He did his best work as a "Mr. Fix It" on the Eastern Front and was fanatically loyal to his Fuhrer, but he knew that leading this offensive would be his greatest challenge.

Marshal Keitel, standing across the table from Model, shook his head. "I agree that the Fuhrer is making a gamble that cannot succeed."

Model watched Keitel closely. He knew that Keitel was pessimistic and considered surrendering himself to the Allies.

"How dare you!" barked Reichsmarschall Hermann Goering. Once the second most powerful man in the Reich, Goering lost most of his influence after the Luftwaffe was nearly annihilated by the Allies. "*Operation Watch on the Rhine* will save the Fatherland from its enemies!"

"The Russian Army is only three hundred miles from Berlin!" Keitel shouted. "We should be putting all of our reserves on the Eastern Front to try to hold the Bolsheviks back for as long as possible!" Keitel turned to General Jodl and sought validation. "What do you think?"

Jodl wiped sweat off his bald head.

"Honestly, I don't see what we have to lose," he said. "If *Operation Watch on the Rhine* succeeds, Germany will be saved from destruction. And if it fails, we will lose the war four months sooner than expected."

Keitel bit his lip, fighting off the words he wanted to say. They all missed the great German victories from 1940 and 1941. Even a year earlier, the Nazis had controlled all of the land from the Atlantic Ocean to the gates of Moscow. Now, France, Holland, and Belgium had been liberated. The Soviets had captured Warsaw and were closing in on the German border. German cities were bombed every day and the Allies dominated European skies.

"The Fuhrer is coming!" a guard outside the chamber shouted. Two black-clad SS guards opened the doorway before the generals had time to react. All of the generals stood at attention as the Nazi dictator, Adolf Hitler, entered the room.

The generals held up their right arms in their Nazi salute and shouted, "Seig Heil!" Hitler briefly raised his right arm as he made his way to the head of the table. Hitler was in poor physical shape. Taking his cap off his head, he failed to control the shaking of his right arm after a ten-year struggle with Parkinson's. His infamous rectangular mustache had grayed. His eyes, known for their hypnotic stare, had lost their blue shine and were now swollen and red.

Hitler's eyesight was poor due to a battle wound that he had suffered during the Great War; his hearing was damaged after an assassin placed a bomb under his desk in July 1944. Hitler had exacted revenge for the assassination plotters by having dozens of officers shot by firing squad and hundreds more hung with piano wire.

Hitler said nothing for several minutes as he looked over the maps. He had been planning *Operation Watch on the Rhine* for several months. He knew the Allies would soon invade Germany from all sides. His armies had suffered their highest casualties of the war following the Allied invasion of Normandy. But like an aggressive, cornered animal, he decided to lash out one last time.

"Gentlemen, we have been given an exceptionally lucky opportunity. As our forces retreated across Western Europe, the Americans and British pursued us and foolishly stretched their supply lines. And, like the barbarians they are, they continue to fight at the Siegfried Line. Similarly, Soviet Marshal Zhukov has also stretched his supply lines. As our enemies recover from their idiocy, we have gathered everything that remains of the German War Machine for a massive offensive!"

Hitler grabbed a long pointer and gestured to a map of Belgium on the table and discussed the plan.

"We now have over three-hundred thousand men and nearly three thousand vehicles in the Eiffel. In four days, they will attack through the thinly held Ardennes Forest. We will fight our way through the American armies and cross the Meuse River." Hitler gestured to a river that flowed through the northern part of the forest. "We will then make another push, continuing northward until we capture the port of Antwerp."

Once that happened, the Nazis would surround Bernard Montgomery's Twenty-First Army Group, which was made up of thousands of British and Canadian troops.

"With the Americans crushed and the British surrounded, we will have crippled the enemy's advance. We will then turn our attention to stopping the communist hordes in the east."

Hitler hoped that Stalin, his former ally, would make peace with Germany after being abandoned by the West. The Red Army had suffered a six-to-one casualty exchange in Hitler's favor and Hitler believed he could fight the Soviets to a stalemate.

"We must show the Americans what terrible casualties we can still inflict. I don't care if all of Belgium is destroyed in this battle," Hitler concluded.

"My Fuhrer, I believe that we shouldn't attempt to capture an objective as audacious as Antwerp. I have a plan that may be more realistic," Field Marshal Model said.

The Fuhrer slowly turned his head. Hitler greatly respected Model, though he usually resented generals challenging his decisions.

"What do you propose?"

Model pointed to the Ardennes Forest.

"We should still launch one attack from the Ardennes, and another from Aachen. In a great pincer movement, we would smash all American forces in the region, but stay to the east of the Meuse River. The pincer would form a large barrier that the Allies could not penetrate, and hold them away from the Fatherland. This operation would cause less stress on our supply lines."

"There is a fatal flaw in your plan," Hitler said, with distaste. "With all of our men forming a barrier in the West, we would be completely exposed to the Bolshevik offensive." He used his pointer to highlight Poland and said, "Nothing would stand between the enemy and Berlin."

"My Fuhrer, barely anything stands between the Soviets and Berlin now! I do not understand why we are not trying to push back the Marxists!" Keitel shouted.

Hitler snapped.

"You fool, that would only cause history to repeat itself! In 1917, Germany and Austria defeated Russia, but we were still subdued by the devils in the West and forced to sign the accursed Treaty of Versailles!"

Nobody said anything for a few minutes. Silence filled the room as the generals submitted to their master. A sinister smile slid across Hitler's face. He believed the Ardennes offensive would complete his obsession of dividing the American and British armies. *Operation Watch on the Rhine* would be a masterstroke and would reverse the tide of the war as if by magic.

Keitel broke the stillness.

"If only Roosevelt was not such a fool. We could have been allies against the Marxists."

"I will never be allied with the Americans! Not after what they did to me in the trenches!" Hitler snapped, referring to being injured in an Allied mustard gas attack in 1918 that temporarily took his vision. He took a deep breath to regain control of his temper and turned to Model. "Field Marshal, you have my full approval for the paratrooper operation. If we can drop a thousand paratroopers behind Monschau, then we can block American reinforcements from reaching the Ardennes until it's too late."

"Yes, my Fuhrer." Model nodded obediently.

Hitler's hand trembled. Frustrated, he put his arm behind his back to hide his physical weakness. He continued after a few moments.

"Also, I would like an update on the preparations of Skorzeny's operation."

Model cleared his throat.

"Skorzeny feels that, while his men are ready and that they have ample amounts of enemy uniforms, he does not possess enough disguised vehicles."

"Tell him he must make do with what he has," Hitler muttered, still trying to regain control of his arm. He recalled meeting the man the Allies called "the most dangerous man in Europe" in East Prussia on October 22.

Hitler had explained his plan for the Ardennes offensive and that he wanted Skorzeny to "command a group of American and British troops and get them across the Meuse and seize one of the bridges. Not, my dear Skorzeny, real Americans or British. I want you to create special units wearing American and British uniforms. They will travel in captured Allied vehicles. Think of the confusion you could cause!"

Skorzeny was captivated by his Fuhrer's scheme. Hitler then explained that he wanted a small unit of these disguised agents to make their way to Paris and kill General Eisenhower and his staff. "That would be the last nail in the coffin for the western enemy. Between dividing the Americans from the British and gutting that race traitor, that entire unnatural coalition will implode. We will restore our grip on the continent. It is strange. Eisenhower is a mindless, military bureaucrat who has not once thought for himself as he serves his Jewish masters in their mission to destroy his own homeland, but he has somehow managed to bind the dying British Empire and its former colony in a coalition. I am convinced that no one else could do this. So killing the traitor must be our highest priority."

Hitler's arm finally stopped shaking. Placing both hands on the table, he leaned forward, appearing wolf-like and ready to pounce. The Nazi warlord eyed each of his commanders, one by one.

"This battle will determine whether we live or die. All resistance must be crushed in a wave of terror."

☆☆☆☆☆

DECEMBER 15, 1944

GENERAL DWIGHT EISENHOWER celebrated with his staff. He'd been promoted to a five-star general after President Roosevelt submitted the request to Congress earlier that day. He lit a cigarette and turned to gaze at Paris. He marveled at this beauty of the Western world as the sun shone over the Eiffel Tower. Having recently returned from a meeting in London with Churchill, Ike decided to leave his headquarters in Versailles to visit the French capital, which he had liberated in August.

He turned his attention back to his staff, grabbing the bottle of wine and pouring another glass for Kay Summersby. She took a sip.

"Thank you, Ike, and again, congratulations."

Sergeant McKeogh, sitting beside Kay, lit a cigarette and smiled. McKeogh had even more reasons to celebrate than Ike. He was getting married tomorrow to a sergeant in the Women's Army Corps, also on Ike's staff. Ike was a doting father to the young couple. He had arranged for the wedding to occur in the Chapel of Louis XIV in Versailles and planned to give them a $100 war bond as a gift.

Ike took a puff of his cigarette as his anxiety caught up with him.

We've lost track of the Sixth Panzer Army. Allied intelligence insists the enemy lacks the logistical support to launch a counter offensive—that Overlord and Bagration left the Wehrmacht a shadow of what it was. They should know by now how dangerous underestimating Hitler can be. There's no way he gives in without putting up one more fight. The obvious target is Antwerp, since its capture would deny us our key port for supplies and reinforcements. The larger question is when such an offense would occur. The weather team says Europe is about to endure its worst blizzard in decades. Hitler will probably have to wait until spring or else—

"General Bradley has arrived to congratulate you, sir," an aide interrupted Ike's thoughts.

Ike nodded.

"Very well. Send him in."

The aide saluted before turning to leave.

Of course it's Brad who's here. My vital subordinate in this war. I suppose it makes sense. George's telegram offered congratulations but said he wants to focus on the Third Army's upcoming offensive toward the Saar. Monty, meanwhile, won't show his face because of Market Garden. Still hasn't gotten him to shut his mouth about his narrow thrust proposal. Doubt anything could change that mind.

General Bradley walked past a bust Goering had placed of himself in the building in 1940 that Ike had turned to the wall. Bradley saluted Ike, who returned the salute and then held out his hand.

"Congratulations on your fifth star, Ike," Bradley said.

"Thank you, but do you remember the last time I was promoted?" Ike asked.

Bradley nodded.

"Of *course* I do. Rommel attacked us at Kasserine Pass almost immediately. But Ike, the Germans no longer possess enough strength to launch a counterattack. I wouldn't be surprised if they used all of their resources to stop the Russians." Ike made no response, taking another puff of his cigarette. "Have you told Mamie the news?"

"Not yet."

Bradley chuckled.

"I still can't believe it. You went from a lieutenant colonel to a five-star general in three years."

"Is that all it's been? I feel like I'm a thousand years old."

Bradley chuckled again. His smile dissolved as he handed Ike a form he had held under his arm.

"An updated casualty report from the fall."

Ike took the form and scanned it.

"Two thousand losses per division per month," he muttered. "Two thousand three hundred for the Germans. Isn't that higher than the Eastern Front?"

"It's over twice as high for the Germans," Bradley replied. "It's also higher than comparable units on any front of the Great War."

Ike felt sick as he thought about the carnage since Normandy.

These numbers can never be statistics. Each one is a human being with a grieving family back home. Letters from families worried about their boys had reflected many of these casualties. Ike had answered each of those letters. *I can think of no more effective means of developing an undying hatred of those responsible for aggressive war than to assume the obligation of expressing sympathy to families bereaved by it.*

The casualty report fueled Ike's hatred of Hitler and his warped Darwinian worldview that races must expand or be consumed by other races, a diametric opposite of Ike's views on duty.

"The outcome of this war has to be worth it, Brad."

"How do we do that?"

"By securing a lasting peace."

☆☆☆☆☆

THREE HUNDRED THOUSAND German soldiers waited in the Eiffel. Each had socks over their boots and blackened faces for stealth. With them were over two thousand tanks and other vehicles. Much of the infantry carried newly invented assault rifles, far more accurate than any other gun on the battlefield.

None of the German soldiers understood why they were in the Eiffel until an order arrived from Field Marshal Model: they were to attack through the Ardennes Forest at dawn. Many of the soldiers cheered. They felt unbearable hatred for the Americans and this was a chance to get revenge upon the nation they despised most.

"Men, this is our chance to 'thank' the Americans for their destruction of our cities and the murder of millions of our people. We will chase the yanks not only from the Fatherland, but off the continent of Europe forever!" one officer shouted.

A short distance away, troops of Skorzeny's special unit, Panzer Brigade 150, were launching their own operation. Each man was disguised in an American uniform. Most were meant to cause confusion behind Allied lines and capture a bridge on the Meuse River. Gefreiter Wilhelm Schmidt's unit had a more ominous objective.

"Gather around," Schmidt ordered his unit of twenty disguised assassins. "Our objective is to kill that race traitor, General Eisenhower, and his staff. We're going to his headquarters and will end his campaign to exterminate us and replace Germany with a Jewish empire. Does everyone remember their training for this operation?"

"Those of you who don't know any English should say 'sorry' if an American tries to talk to you," instructed Oberfähnrich Günther Billing. "You can also open your trousers and run to a bush. Pretend you're having a diarrhea attack. The yanks won't come near you!"

"That's right," Schmidt added. "Now let's do a brief review of the American way to salute, shoot, and smoke. Because don't forget, the privileged yanks still have cigarettes. Theirs weren't all destroyed by B-17s."

The unit finished its review after a few minutes.

"Let's go kill that traitor," Pernass said as the unit entered the Ardennes. "Eis-en-how-er. Such a German name for such an evil man."

The Ardennes Offensive, Germany's great counterattack, began as hundreds of thousands of soldiers entered the forest. A nearly unstoppable force was unleashed as liberal democracy collided with totalitarianism like rarely ever seen before or since. The fate of Western Europe, perhaps even the world, hung in the balance of this ultimate showdown.

☆☆☆☆☆

DECEMBER 16, 1944
IKE SAT IN his office as he studied the map. The enemy was attacking across an eighty-five-mile front in the Ardennes. The Waffen SS spearheaded the attack; Ike knew this offensive was going to be Hitler's greatest attempt to turn the tide of the war. Involved in the offensive were the Fifth and Sixth Panzer armies, as well as the Seventh Army.

Ike's desk was organized in a neat, spartan manner. A black phone sat in the corner. An ashtray was suspiciously empty; Ike's habit was to throw his ashes into the carpet. Two pictures, one of Mamie, one of President Roosevelt, smiled at him.

General Bradley entered the room and saluted Ike. Ike did not bother to return the salute.

"I'm not convinced this isn't a spoil attack. The Germans want to throw us off guard," Bradley said as he walked to a chair next to Ike's. Ike shook his head. "Well, maybe it's a diversion. Maybe the real attack is coming elsewhere."

"No, this is it. Hitler's put everything he has left into this offensive. I knew he was going to try this, I just didn't think it would be so soon!" He slammed his fist onto his desk. "I should have known he'd attack during a blizzard so we couldn't utilize our air power."

"What should we do?" Bradley asked.

The lessons Ike learned from Conner returned to him. Clausewitz. Grant. Center of gravity. The German Army had been hiding behind the Siegfried Line all fall, and now the brainless Hitler was giving it to Ike on a platter.

"Any reinforcements that we send into the Ardennes will immediately be destroyed. We need to pull back our forces for a counterattack." Ike pointed to the map. "We need to let Hitler stretch his supply lines to the breaking point. But not too far!" He turned to his friend. "We can't retreat past the Meuse River. Also, since the attack is directed toward the north, we have to remain on the defensive in that area."

"What about the south?" Bradley asked.

"That's where we take the offensive. Our forces are like crocodile jaws. The northern forces are our top jaw and the southern ones are the bottom jaw that will swing shut. We'll have Patton take the Third Army northward."

"He'll resist canceling his Saar offensive."

"I don't see an alternative. The Third Army is the best weapon we have to strike the German attack." Ike paused. "Eventually we'll have to bring down the other flank."

"But my headquarters are in Luxembourg. Who would you put in command of my troops north of the offensive?" Bradley asked.

"What about Montgomery?"

Bradley shook his head.

"No, Ike, you *can't* do that to me! You cannot put my Army under the command of that British narcissist!"

"If putting Monty in charge of the American armies helps limit our losses, then you better believe I'll do it!"

Bradley turned away from Ike.

Ike looked at the map. He asked, "Has the 101st Airborne recovered from Market Garden?"

Bradley nodded.

"Yeah. I think they have."

Ike did not speak for several minutes. He stared at a small town in the Ardennes. It had many roads traveling through it. The Germans would be greatly slowed down if the Americans could hold it.

"We have to move the 101st to Bastogne."

Bradley turned back to Ike.

"Okay, but the fog is bad. They'll have to drive there."

Ike nodded.

"Whatever it takes." He lit a cigarette. "This battle is going to make Kasserine Pass look like a skirmish."

☆☆☆☆☆

DECEMBER 17, 1944

"DID YOU HEAR what happened at Malmedy this morning?" Pernass asked Fritz Christ.

"That the Waffen SS killed eighty-five yank POWs?" Christ replied.

"Exactly. A couple machine guns in the back of their trucks and they, you know, mowed them down," Pernass said, raising his arms as if manning a gun. "That's what they deserve for coming to Europe."

The jeep's tires skid on the ice. Pernass shifted leftward, smashing into Christ, who grabbed the bullet-riddled side of the jeep to avoid being flung out of the vehicle.

"Watch it!" Christ exclaimed. "Is Kay Summersby driving this thing?"

"Drop dead!" Billing ordered, briefly taking his eyes off the road to look at his backseat passengers. "You should still be thankful I got us away from the Luftwaffe. Still can't believe we were strafed by our own air force."

"They think we're Americans," Schmidt replied from the passenger seat. "Who can blame them? At least that means Skorzeny disguised us well."

"Yeah, well, he didn't exactly give us enough fuel to get to Eisenhower's headquarters," Billing said. "Permission to stop at that yank fuel depot?"

He pointed to a large American outpost that had a large tarp covering several barrels of gasoline on its left flank.

"Granted," Schmidt replied. "The rest of our unit will follow. They may as well get fuel from the yanks, too."

Christ felt his stomach clench as the jeep slowed down, skidding along on the ice farther than Billing intended. The four other jeeps, with four assassins in each, followed Billing's lead. No one arrived. The assassins sat in silence.

"The yanks have terrible manners. What do we have to do to get any service?" Billing asked.

"Honk your horn. We need their attention," Schmidt barked. Billing did so.

An American lieutenant and sergeant emerged from the outpost. The lieutenant eyed his guests suspiciously. Why were they driving four men to a jeep? Two per jeep was the standard practice in the US Army.

"Greetings!" Schmidt exclaimed in English.

"How can we help you boys?" the lieutenant asked.

"Do you mind telling me where we are now?" Schmidt asked.

"The Aywaille outpost."

"Aywaille, that's right," Schmidt muttered. The lieutenant narrowed his eyes. Schmidt turned to Billing. "Ask him what he came for."

"Do you have any petrol to spare?" Billing asked in English.

The Americans exchanged a glance.

"What did you call it?"

"Petrol?" Billing asked.

"You mean *gas*?"

"*Gas*!" Billing exclaimed, raising his hands into the air to seem pleased. "Please excuse me, sir. I was born at Harvard with their fancy words."

The lieutenant turned to the sergeant.

"Go get I Company and come back here."

The sergeant returned to the outpost.

"Is there a problem?" Schmidt asked.

The lieutenant ignored him and turned to Christ.

"What's your name, son?"

"Lieutenant Charles Smith," Christ responded rapidly.

"Where you from?"

"Detroit."

"What state is that in?"

Christ's eyes widened. Why were there so many states?

"Minnesota?" Christ asked.

"You grew up in Detroit and think it's in Minnesota?"

"He meant Michigan," Schmidt interjected, giving a brief glare at Christ. "You know, the poor American school system and all that. It only started to receive federal direction under the New Deal."

"Uh huh." The lieutenant heard the footsteps of over a hundred soldiers from I Company walk up behind him. "Tell me," the lieutenant began, looking Schmidt in the eye, "what's the password?"

"Excuse me?" Schmidt asked, leaning forward slightly.

"Every unit in the Army knows the password. It lets us know you're not krauts in disguise."

Schmidt's eyes widened. He didn't think the Americans were capable of coming up with something like a password.

"Rita Hayworth?" Schmidt asked while trying to appear confident.

"That's wrong," the lieutenant replied. "Do you at least know who won the World Series?"

"The Yankees of course! Go New York!"

"That's also wrong." The lieutenant turned to his subordinates. "Arrest these men."

"What!" Schmidt shouted. "You can't do that!" Schmidt and the other assassins in his car reached for their weapons. They paused when dozens of American guns rose at them. Schmidt raised his hands over his head.

All twenty assassins were lined up as prisoners within minutes. Schmidt stood at the front of the group, his head hanging in shame. They were captured after a day. What kind of assassins were they?

"You do know that dressing in enemy uniforms to commit sabotage is a capital offense under the Geneva Convention?" the lieutenant asked.

Schmidt's eyes narrowed.

"Yes."

"And you think switching road signs and the like is worth that?"

"We weren't committing sabotage like that."

"What was your objective then?"

Schmidt bit his tongue and turned his hands into fists in frustration.

"I can't say."

"Just tell me. You're already captured. It doesn't matter now."

Schmidt's eyes shut. He wasn't supposed to, but the words felt so good in his mouth, playing to his darkest emotions.

"We were going to kill that *monster*, Eisenhower."

"What!" the lieutenant screamed. He turned to his subordinates. "Call SHAEF! We've got to warn them! The krauts are trying to kill Ike!"

☆☆☆☆☆

IKE'S EARS RANG, as happened several times since D-Day. He didn't hear the dozens of military police (MP) marching down the hall until they burst through the door into his office.

"The hell is this?" Ike roared. He saw Walter "Bedell" Smith, his chief of staff, among the MPs. "Bedell, did you authorize this?"

"I did, Ike."

"Why?"

"The Germans are trying to kill you. A group of assassins disguised as Americans were intercepted near Aywaille not long ago." Smith pushed his glasses up the bridge of his nose. His eyes darted at every corner of the room. Smith was even tempered. Always angry.

"I don't believe for a second that the Germans are trying to kill me," Ike replied.

"We have complete and positive proof. A hundred MPs have been assigned to guard you and escort you around. Sorry, Ike, but you're under lockdown."

"This is crazy as hell," Ike muttered. "Do we know where these assassins came from?"

"They're from Skorzeny's unit."

"Does that mean Hitler's involved?"

"It was probably his idea."

Ike folded his arms and leaned back in his chair. His forehead pinched. He knew this meant he wouldn't be able to visit the front.

"I'll accept these guards if it makes the War Department feel better. I still can't believe Hitler's trying to kill me." He paused. "This better be over by Christmas. I don't want to spend my holiday under lockdown or make these men work."

"No promises," Smith replied. He pulled out a cigarette. "You should know, Ike, that a double of you is being sent to walk around this area. It'll throw off the Germans."

"What!" Ike barked. "That's immoral! Another man shouldn't die because of me!"

"Marshall said that keeping you alive is too important for the war effort. He's willing to risk it."

"I don't approve," Ike said.

"You don't have to," Smith replied. "The old man outranks you."

☆☆☆☆☆

A BLACK CAR waving a Union Jack raced toward the US checkpoint. Field Marshal Montgomery jotted some notes as his car slowed. An American private approached the car.

"Proof of ID?"

"ID!" Montgomery exclaimed. He leaned forward in his seat, his beret atop his perfectly combed hair. "Do you not recognize me, young man?"

"You're Monty. Or at least you look like him."

"What the devil does that mean?"

"Skorzeny's spies have infiltrated Allied lines. A group of assassins tried to kill Ike. And another checkpoint intercepted someone who was dressed like you."

"I'm flattered," Montgomery replied. "But there is only one Field Marshal Bernard Law Montgomery, First Viscount Montgomery of Alamein. And he is me." Montgomery stared into the private's eyes. "I order you to let my car through."

"Not yet, sir," the private said, turning his eyes from Montgomery's gaze. "I need to check with my superiors. I'm sure we can straighten this out."

"I'm not putting up with this nonsense!" Montgomery roared. "Driver, keep going!" The driver hesitated for a moment, but accelerated the car through the checkpoint. "That takes care of that. Silly yanks. Don't they know they need me at the front to raise their morale since Ike is under house protection?"

Bang! Bang! Bang!

The car came to a screeching halt.

"Are they mad?" Montgomery screamed. He glanced out the window to confirm that the Americans had shot out his wheels. "How dare they!"

The private returned to the window.

"You do not ignore a checkpoint, sir!"

"Young man, I will have you court martialed for this!" Monty spat.

"We can put him in that barn until we're certain he is who he says he is," a corporal said.

"You'll do nothing of the sort!" Montgomery snorted.

"Sorry, sir, but we're not taking any chances right now," the corporal replied.

"How dare you not recognize me!" Montgomery shouted. "I'm the one winning the war for your generals!"

Montgomery spent the next several hours in the barn against his will. He was only released when a British captain managed to confirm that he actually was the hero of El Alamein. Montgomery was furious at the Americans for detaining him. When Ike heard the news, he said this was the best thing for which Skorzeny had ever been responsible.

☆☆☆☆☆

DECEMBER 19, 1944

VERDUN WAS KNOWN for the terrible battle that had engulfed the city during World War I. Hundreds of thousands of French and German soldiers tore each other to shreds for almost a year. Three decades later, several Allied generals met at Verdun to discuss their strategy for winning another terrible battle, against another generation of Germans.

Ike stood at the head of a long conference table. Beside him was Air Chief Marshal Tedder, as well as Generals Bradley, Devers, and Patton. At the other side of the table sat several British and French officers.

Ike began the meeting.

"The present situation should be regarded as one of opportunity and not of disaster. There will only be cheerful faces at this conference table."

They all look calm—but concerned. Probably doesn't help that I have 100 MPs stationed around the perimeter.

Patton quipped, "Hell, let's have the guts to let the sons of bitches go all the way to Paris. Then we'll really cut 'em off and chew 'em up!"

George Patton wore his oversized helmet and had pistols in his belt. He'd earned a reputation as the most aggressive and unpredictable American general. He turned the Germans' Blitzkrieg back on them, attacking so quickly and incessantly that they did not have time to fortify their positions. This meant Patton had among the lowest proportion of casualties of any general on the Western Front.

Ike and Patton originally met in 1919. They tested innovative tank tactics together, believing tanks could become more than mere infantry support. Their superiors reprimanded them, but their ideas were successfully implemented in World War II. It was through Patton that Ike met Fox Conner, the mentor who molded Ike into the officer he was now.

Ike ignored the laughter Patton received.

"The Germans are concentrating their attack in the north, toward Antwerp. We must remain on the defensive in that area to slow them down. The 101st made it to Bastogne, the Ardennes' transportation center. Hitler won't risk destroying it in combat, so we can expect the Germans to surround the town. The German offensive will be crippled if we can hold Bastogne and control the supply line. Those jumpers will need relief and need it soon. George, how soon do you think you can disengage the Third Army from combat, turn it northward, and attack the Bulge?"

"I can attack with three divisions within two days," Patton responded.

Feet shuffled. Tedder and Bradley stared at Patton in disbelief. Ike heard a British officer say, "These Americans know nothing of warfare."

Ike ignored him.

"George, don't joke with me. A move like that would be impossible."

A sarcastic, almost sinister smile slipped across Patton's face.

"I'm not kidding. My Army is ready. I can get one core going in forty-eight hours, and I have more coming right behind it."

"How?"

"You're not as clever as you think, Ike. I gave the order before coming here."

Ike smiled.

"Keep moving northward after you reach Bastogne. I'll try to help you in any way possible."

"Please, once my Fourth Armored Division enters the battle, the Germans won't know what hit them."

Ike frowned but turned back to his other generals.

"Hopefully the blizzard will be gone within a few days. Then we can attack from the air."

The meeting was over shortly thereafter. Ike briefly relaxed before his next conference—he had to call Montgomery.

☆☆☆☆☆

DECEMBER 20, 1944

MONTGOMERY WAS STILL peeved about being detained by the Americans. Even worse, Churchill had refused his demand to be put in charge of all

Allied soldiers in the Ardennes, despite Monty explaining how he was the only one who could stop Hitler's offensive and prevent the collapse of Western Europe.

He paced around his office, waiting for a phone call from Ike. It finally arrived.

"Hello?"

"Monty, I need your help. You're the best man on the northern part of the Bulge. Since Bradley's headquarters are in Luxembourg, I want you to take command of all American forces in that region. I need you to launch a counterattack within a short time."

Montgomery smiled.

"I can't quite hear you properly," he claimed. "I shall take command straight away!"

The British general then hung up on his superior. Ike, agitated, hung up his own phone.

This was the high point of his role as a coalition general. Putting Montgomery in charge of American forces proved he was an Allied commander, not merely an American one.

He rubbed his eyes.

I hope he has enough tact not to make a big show out of leading our men.

When Montgomery arrived at the first meeting with his temporary American officers, his car was waving the largest Union Flag his subordinates could find.

☆☆☆☆☆

DECEMBER 21, 1944

HITLER STUDIED AN updated map of the Ardennes battleground in the Eagle's Nest. His offensive pushed the American armies back for miles. Hitler had received word via telegram, which now rested beside the map, that the Americans had withdrawn from Saint Vith. This allowed the Germans to strengthen their advance in the northern part of the forest. He was disappointed, however, that the Allied occupation of Bastogne slowed the Germans' center.

When Hitler planned the Ardennes offensive, he thought it would take Ike three days to make a strong counter. It had now been five days and he had not yet had occasion to move the American tokens.

"The mongrels are incapable of organizing the simplest maneuvers."

Ike's armies were in disarray and the Germans were advancing rapidly through the Ardennes. He hoped they would soon cross the Meuse River and then fight their way to Antwerp. Ultimate victory over Ike was within his grasp.

☆☆☆☆☆

My darling:

This is the year's shortest day— how I pray that it may, by some miracle, mark the beginning of improving weather!

From your papers you'll know that we are extremely busy—in fact that's an understatement. There are so many things about this war that can't be told now—possibly never—but they should make an interesting talk between you and me when we're sitting in the sun, taking our elegant ease in our reclining days. But you'll probably be sick of hearing war—so maybe we'll just sit and fish or listen to the radio, or go visit John! With four grandchildren, I hope!

I've been advanced in rank, with the title of "General of the Army." Haven't received the regulations concerning insignia, etc. Five stars will be awkward unless I can get someone to embroider them on jackets.

Not long ago I had to come through Paris, and the driver happened to bring me past Pont Mirabeau. I saw our old apartment house, from the bridge. It is a bit dingy looking; otherwise unchanged. The river was overflowing its banks.

Well Sweet, I do hope you and John have a nice Christmas. For me there will be none—but that's part of this dirty business. But next year we'll be together if God is good to us.

Loads of love,
Ike

Ike sighed as he placed his pen down and folded the letter. His hand was cramped from holding the pen, a frequent occurrence for the past months. He looked at the photo of Mamie on his desk.

Must hold back the blue devils. But it's becoming harder and harder.

☆☆☆☆☆

DECEMBER 22, 1944

THE PARATROOPERS WAITED patiently in Bastogne. This was their third day of being cut off from American forces. German loudspeakers repeatedly taunted, "Hey, Americans, do you want to die for Christmas?" That morning, the Germans had demanded that the 101st Airborne surrender or the Nazis would destroy the entire town.

The paratroopers gathered around to hear General McAuliffe's response to the ultimatum. They stood in a crowded circle. An officer finally emerged from a tent. "The response is simple: Nuts!"

The paratroopers erupted into laughter.

One soldier, confused, turned to another. "'Nuts?' What does that mean?"

"It means, 'go to hell.'" He looked at the trees that blocked the Americans' vision. "They have us surrounded. The poor bastards."

☆☆☆☆☆

DECEMBER 23, 1944

SMITH WALKED INTO Ike's office to see Ike praying by his desk, on his knees, eyes closed, head down. Smith stood as silently as possible, his hands behind his back. Smith could not look away from Ike's hands, which were grasping each other in front of him. His knuckles were white from intensity.

Ike opened his eyes after a few moments.

"Hi, Bedell."

"Hello, Ike." Ike grabbed a crutch and put it under his shoulder. Smith grabbed Ike's other arm, helping to raise the Supreme Commander to his feet.

"Thanks," Ike said, making his way to a cot in the corner.

"You're welcome," Smith replied. It was a familiar sight. There were times in the past months Ike couldn't walk or sit up. He was in constant pain. He occasionally used crutches, as now, to maneuver when in private.

"I take it the air offensives have begun?" Ike asked, letting his weight drop on the cot. The blizzard passed that morning.

"They have. But that's not why I'm here."

"You want to discuss Private Slovik?"

"If you don't mind."

"Of course." Ike fumbled for a cigarette. "Do you think I should accept his plea or authorize the execution?"

"You would be the first person to authorize the execution of a soldier since President Lincoln."

"At least I'll be in good company," Ike replied, now fumbling for his lighter.

"This is serious, Ike!"

"I know. But so is desertion. There are over eight hundred thousand GIs fighting in the Ardennes. I bet all of them would desert if they could. No one wants to kill and die, especially in this weather. But it must be done to end the war. And Slovik deserting his comrades in their darkest hour couldn't be more offensive to me."

"It's offensive to me, too! But there are enough corpses. Can't we spare this man? Throw him in the stockade?"

"It's not fair to the men who *are* doing their duty. Slovik was offered a chance to return to the front and drop his charges *three* times."

Smith sighed, turning his gaze in another direction.

Ike closed his eyes and took the first puff of his cigarette. The generals were silent for a moment.

"We need to discuss the fact that Marshall hasn't sent enough reserves. Reserves we need for the Ardennes."

"He's doing the best he can," Smith replied.

"It's not enough. But I think I've figured out a solution."

"What's that?"

Ike took another puff.

"I'm going to order General Lee to start deploying colored troops into combat."

Smith was stunned.

"The Negroes are only for supporting roles! You can't send them into combat!"

"I feel that in the existing circumstances I cannot deny the Negro volunteers a chance to serve in battle. We both know they've been requesting the chance to serve their country."

"That's irrelevant!" Smith declared. "It's illegal! It goes against Marshall's policies!" Smith's hand moved through the air like a knife, with all his fingers extended, to make his point.

"This is an emergency. The most important thing is defeating the German counteroffensive."

"You're exploiting this emergency to promote your own views. This is social engineering. The press will kill us."

"Careful, Bedell, I'm your boss. You can't talk to me like that," Ike smiled.

"All I'm saying is that I worked with Marshall and the War Department's policies don't create an exception for emergencies on this issue."

"I'll worry about General Marshall," Ike replied. "Besides, the units will re-segregate once the German offensive is beaten."

Smith calmed down and looked at the floor.

"This is the first time since George Washington we'll have integrated Army units," he muttered. "Do you think it will lead to an integrated military?"

"Maybe someday," Ike mumbled. *That's still good company.*

☆☆☆☆☆

DECEMBER 24, 1944

THE BATTLE OF the Bulge entered its second week. The head of the German offensive, made up of Panther and Tiger tanks, was less than ten miles from the Meuse River. The Nazis penetrated over fifty miles into the Allied lines. Tens of thousands of people had already died in the fighting.

The massive tank force at the front of the offensive had crushed everything in its way for the past week. The single vehicle leading the advance through the Ardennes, a huge Tiger, rumbled to a halt. The group of tanks following it also stopped. They needed to refuel. A report came in after several hours of waiting: no gasoline would be able to reach them.

Ike's plan had worked. The Nazis had stretched their supply lines. Combined with the great American aerial attacks of the past two days, the German tanks had run out of gas. The Battle of the Bulge reached a turning point, but it was far from over. Thousands were dying every day in the Ardennes. The battlefield would be littered with American and German dead as the combat intensified.

☆☆☆☆☆

IN THE EAGLE'S Nest, Field Marshal Walter Model was informed that the German offensive had lost its momentum. He knew the battle was lost. He planned to inform the Fuhrer and request a retreat at the first opportunity, which came immediately. Hitler entered the room, using a cane as he made his way to a chair.

Hitler put on his glasses and looked at an updated map of the battle.

"Good, by tomorrow we shall have crossed the Meuse. Then we will continue our advance to Antwerp."

Model watched his Fuhrer carefully. "My Fuhrer, I have bad news." Hitler continued looking at the map. "Due to American aerial attacks against our supply lines, we are unable to refuel our tanks at the front of the offensive." Hitler was impassive. "I am requesting permission to withdraw."

Hitler took off his glasses, his hand shaking. After a few moments of silence, he shouted, "You want to retreat? We've pushed the enemy back eighty kilometers and you want to *retreat*?"

Model took a step back as Hitler rose from his chair.

"My Fuhrer, we cannot continue our advance. The Americans will soon counterattack. We should pull back our armies to avoid further losses."

"How dare you suggest such treason?" Rounding the table, Hitler waved his hand in the air and shouted, "If enemy planes are the problem, then we will find a way to retake the sky! But how are we unable to defeat the American hordes?

"It's simple; my generals are incapable of the most basic tasks! They have always been the greatest obstacle on my way to victory! Goering was unable to crush the Royal Air Force. Paulus did not guard his flanks and was captured at Stalingrad. Von Manstein idiotically fell into Zhukov's trap at Kursk. And Rommel was not able to defend Normandy when he possessed an army of *two million men*!"

The Nazi dictator beat his own chest.

"I *crushed* France and forced Britain from the continent in six weeks. I nearly obliterated the Red Army in four months. I was able to hold the Americans in their own hemisphere for nearly a year, and would have continued to do so if it weren't for Admiral Donitz! I have been betrayed and let down by my generals time and again, and they wonder why I don't trust them!"

Hitler slammed his fist onto the table.

"Now, our offensive toward Antwerp is not even going to reach the Meuse River!" He gritted his teeth. He looked up at Model apologetically after a few minutes. He said in a much quieter voice, "If we lose the battle, we lose the war." He looked down and mumbled, "I will not let Germany be destroyed. I will not…"

☆☆☆☆☆

DECEMBER 28, 1944

IKE WAS ON a train headed toward Hasselt, near Montgomery's headquarters. He left his hundred guards behind.

I already lost my Christmas because of all the security. Makes me not care about getting killed anymore. God, that smell. Rotting flesh from across the Ardennes. Horrid.

Ike reached into his pocket and placed seven coins between his fingertips. He rubbed the coins together. A little girl sent him the coins after he became famous in November 1942.

My godmother. My pen pal. I miss her, too. Maybe after this campaign I can write to her again.

Thrilled to hear that Patton reached Bastogne. Relieved the 101st. Doesn't quite make up for the loss of the Leopoldville *though. Five hundred—drowned—because of a U-boat in the Channel. I needed those men in the Ardennes. Oh, God, Ike, don't think like that. Mustn't let this war take my humanity. Not more than it already has.*

Monty secured the northern flank of the Bulge, but he's procrastinating on launching our counterattack. It's been three days. Need an answer from him.

The train stopped. The doors opened, and Field Marshal Montgomery boarded the vehicle. He wore his tank beret.

"Nice to see you, Ike!" Montgomery said cheerily.

"You too, Monty," Ike answered. Both men took their seats. "I want to know how your preparations for the northern offensive are coming."

Montgomery hesitated.

"Fine, I suppose. There is much to be done."

Have to be direct with him. Otherwise he'll drag this out.

"Monty, why haven't you launched the attack yet? Our counterattack was supposed to have begun days ago."

"My intelligence," Montgomery began, "believes the Germans are going to bring more men into the Ardennes and could launch another thrust northwards. If I were to start my own offensive, the number of casualties could be appalling."

Ike sighed. *There's over half a million German soldiers in the Ardennes Forest. He can't seriously think the Germans will attempt another thrust?*

"What if your intelligence is wrong? How long would it take you to start your attack?"

Montgomery paused.

"I plan to begin my attack in six days, on January third. Is that alright?"

Ike sighed again. *More delays. More death.*

"Fine."

Montgomery smiled.

"As long as you're here, I would like to ask you again about my plan to invade Germany once this battle is over." He continued before Ike could respond. "I would act as overall ground commander, and I would direct a British-led thrust through the north to attack the Ruhr. Patton would act as my support, and we would capture Berlin before the Russians."

"That's not the strategy I want to follow." *He's relentless.* "More importantly, it's not the strategy President Roosevelt wants to follow. The American people are unhappy to have a foreign general commanding their soldiers in that way. We're lucky there hasn't been a bigger fuss about what's happening now."

"But Ike, Napoleon's victory at Austerlitz isn't legendary because he destroyed the Russians and Austrians through attrition. It's legendary because he only deployed a minor force and coaxed the enemy into thinking he was weak before striking their flank with his main force!"

"I know what Napoleon did at Austerlitz. I taught it at Leavenworth. But it isn't 1805 anymore. We're in the twentieth century. You can't defeat an enemy by bypassing their Army and taking their capital. That's what McClellan, Hooker, and so many other Union generals got wrong. Grant figured out that in modern, industrial warfare, you have to destroy the enemy's center of gravity, usually their Army. That's what we're doing by pushing the Germans back across a broad front. It may not be creative, but it'll destroy their Army and guarantee an end to the war."

"Maybe. It also stretched our forces so thin across the front that we didn't have any reserves to counter the German offensive. Besides air power, that is, which was grounded for days because of the blizzard. Not to mention that we took such high casualties from your war of attrition that our divisions have been under strength since September."

"Something like the Ardennes Offensive striking the flank of your narrow thrust would have been a catastrophe!" Ike growled. "We'd be lucky to meet the Red Army at the Rhine, let alone Berlin."

Montgomery, frustrated, said, "I will launch my attack on the third. Then we will crush the Nazis and erase any sign of their offensive."

He stood up and left, planning to renew arguments for his plan the next day. Ike lit another cigarette as the train started to take him back to his own headquarters.

☆☆☆☆☆

JANUARY 3, 1945

HAVE TO KEEP my arms steady. Exciting day, but I'm spilling brandy everywhere. Winston won't be pleased.

The Allied counterattack was imminent. Churchill waddled into Ike's guarded bunker to celebrate. The Prime Minister smoked his cigar as the Supreme Commander lit a cigarette. They clinked glasses.

They conversed until General Charles de Gaulle, the towering French hero with the thin face, drooping nose, and skinny mustache barged into the room.

"What do you mean you're moving the defense of Strasbourg?"

Oh, God. Never a moment of peace.

"I believe the American soldiers protecting that city would be more helpful if they were deployed to the Ardennes. We need as much help as possible in the battle."

De Gaulle slammed his hands onto Ike's desk.

"Strasbourg is one of the most honored cities in French history. It will be recaptured if you move its defenses. That would humiliate the French people!"

Insides feel like an inferno. Hope my face isn't red as a beat.

"If Strasbourg were to fall again, we would liberate it as soon as the fighting in the Ardennes ended."

"It has been a symbol to France ever since Bismarck captured it in 1870. It would cause a political crisis if it falls again." De Gaulle straightened his posture. "I will not let that happen. I will order the entire Free French Army to protect Strasbourg if I have to."

Ike locked eyes with de Gaulle.

"If the French Army disobeys my orders, I will sever all of its ammunition and food supplies." He immediately regretted making that threat. De Gaulle spent the next three hours lecturing Ike and Churchill about the full history of Strasbourg and its importance to France.

Ike and Churchill drank several bottles of wine, brandy, and vodka as they were forced to listen. Ike looked at Churchill, whose expression begged *make him stop!*

Ike finally looked up at de Gaulle and asked, "If I promise not to move the defense of Strasbourg, will you let the Prime Minister and I return to our meeting?"

"Of course," de Gaulle smiled.

Churchill chuckled after the Frenchman left.

"I think you've done the wise and proper thing." The Prime Minister blinked several times, intoxicated and hoping he chose the correct words.

Ike shook his head and lit a cigarette.

"A political crisis could hurt my lines of—" He couldn't think of the word. Ike rubbed his eyes and gave up. Churchill knew what he meant.

You know who I should think about more? Hannibal. Loved him when I was a kid. He led a coalition. Just like me. Wonder if his colleagues were as annoying as mine.

Montgomery launched his attack from the north shortly thereafter. The Anglo-American force smashed the Germans and started fighting its way southward. Bradley and Patton were still advancing from the other direction.

Ike's counterattack had begun.

☆☆☆☆☆

HITLER WAS FURIOUS when he heard about the Allied counterattack. He studied a map of the Ardennes and could not find a way to stop the enemy offensive. It was only a matter of time before the Nazis lost the battle. Hitler tried to control his arm. Everything was failing. Worst of all, the assassins assigned to kill General Eisenhower, the man he hated most in the world, had been intercepted. Germany's last chance of winning the war was vanishing.

The Nazi warlord took off his glasses and turned to Bormann, his secretary. Hitler's voice was weak.

"Our submarines dominated the Atlantic. We had the Caucasus oil fields in sight." He turned back to the map. "Where did it all go wrong? My dream of a thousand-year Reich! Revenge for the Treaty of Versailles! A world freed from the Jews!" He calmed down. "What happened?"

Bormann finally looked up from his work.

"My Fuhrer, you failed in your mission the day you declared war on America."

Hitler remained seated and did not reply. He pondered the idea for a few minutes. He slowly spoke.

"The mission of the National Socialist movement…" His voice rose several octaves. "…was to stand up to the United States!"

He leapt from his chair.

"Only the German people are capable of stopping the Americans and their Jewish masters from dominating the Earth! We are the only ones who can save European civilization from obliteration at the hands of American conquerors!"

Hitler wandered around the room.

"It was American Jewry who started the Second World War! They used their economic puppet strings to turn all the powers against each other, weakening one another, so they could swoop in and enslave them all!

"A great German nation already existed in the heart of Europe by the time Columbus discovered America. Von Steuben is the only reason the Americans are even independent. Then the mongrels freed their slaves. The biggest mistake they ever made. Now they've started a world war. America belongs on the ash heap of history."

☆☆☆☆☆

JANUARY 8, 1945

"WHY CAN'T I see the letter?" Ike asked. General Guingand stood silently, holding the letter in his right hand. "I order you to give me the letter."

Guingand bit his tongue and he raised the letter so Ike could take it.

"Remember, Ike, I warned him not to write or send this."

Ike quickly scanned it. His face turned red. His forehead pinched, and a large vein became visible along his temple.

"What the *hell is this*?" Ike shouted at Guingand. "Monty has to confirm our last conversation in writing because I 'have a habit of changing my mind following previous conversations?' That's an attack on my integrity! You can question a man's logic but not his integrity!"

"I know, I tried to warn him—"

"And I didn't agree to his becoming the overall ground commander after the Bulge! That's an outright lie! I explicitly said the opposite! In fact, General Marshall wrote me on this very topic a couple days ago and ordered that 'under no circumstances make any concessions of any kind whatsoever.'"

Ike, whose diplomatic skills made the Anglo-American coalition possible, was at his breaking point.

"I'm sure if you wrote him and said—"

"This is insufferable. I've been putting up with that son of a bitch since June 1942 and I'm done with it!" Ike moved to his desk and grabbed a pen. "I'm going to tell the Combined Chiefs that they have to choose. It's him or me! And I can tell you right now that they're going to pick me, because I'm the Supreme Commander. They're going to replace that psychopath with General Alexander. That's who I've wanted from the beginning!"

Guingand left Ike's headquarters as quickly as possible and returned to Montgomery. Montgomery looked at his chief of staff with curiosity.

"Why are you so sweaty?"

"I warned you, sir," Guingand said as he approached Montgomery. "I warned your letter would cause a crisis, and it's really going to hit the fan now."

"What are you talking about?"

"Ike's furious. You misquoted him and questioned his morality. You need to eat the humble pie and apologize."

"I'll do nothing of the sort. My letter was entirely truthful and reasonable. It's illogical that it would upset him."

"Just this once, Monty, you have to see things from his point of view."

"Don't be so dramatic. This will all blow over."

"It won't, sir. General Eisenhower said he's going to write the Charlie Charlies!" Guingand said, referring to the Combined Chiefs. "He's going to give them an ultimatum to choose between the two of you. You're not going to win that fight."

"Who could they possibly pick to replace me?"

"He thinks they'll choose General Alexander."

Montgomery froze.

"Alexander? They can't do that to me! Get me a pen and paper. I have to write Ike!"

Montgomery's new letter asked Ike to rip up the previous letter. He signed it as, "Your loyal subordinate, Monty."

☆☆☆☆☆

JANUARY 15, 1945

A BLACK MERCEDES-BENZ 770 descended from the Eagle's Nest, slowly making its way down the road that descended to the train tracks below.

Adolf Hitler brooded in the shadowed back seat. The Nazi dictator had his field-green wool cap with a brown leather visor on his lap. Bormann sat beside him. Neither man spoke during the car ride. Hitler struggled to control the tremors in his arm.

Hitler turned his head to look out the window, waiting for his personal train to arrive. He was going to return to Berlin now that he had lost the Battle of the Bulge. Bormann eyed his Fuhrer. Hitler analyzed everything that was happening.

Montgomery and Patton had convened on Houffalize, pushing the Germans back to their original line. *Watch on the Rhine* was a disaster. The Luftwaffe no longer existed. Over a hundred thousand German soldiers had been lost. Thousands of tanks were destroyed, the last glimmer of hope extinguished, the last exit route cut. Nothing could save Germany now.

Hitler heard a plane flying in the distance. He knew it was the enemy's. It was a reminder of his defeat. He felt frustration overtaking him and drew a deep breath.

"We possessed the most advanced technology in the world! Weapons that Eisenhower and his mongrels could not even imagine!"

He turned to Bormann.

"But it is not the pilots' fault! It is Goering's, and his foolish leadership!" He gritted his teeth. "And Model, he is as incapable as the others! My generals are the scum of the German people!" He slammed his fist into his leg. "That's the thanks I get for decorating them! I have been betrayed and thwarted by the military since the beginning! National Socialism will no longer exist! Western imperialism and Bolshevism will rule the world."

Hitler turned to look back out the window. He was in a similar position to the Kaiser's over two decades ago. He was not going to make the same mistake.

"We will not capitulate—no, never! We may be destroyed, but if we are, we shall drag a world with us—a world in flames."

If the German race had lost the struggle for existence, it should be destroyed. Hitler was determined to squeeze every last drop of blood from the enemy and his own people. There would be no negotiations, no repeat of the Versailles Treaty. Since Germany had failed to conquer its enemies, the only alternative was annihilation.

Hitler's thoughts returned to reality as the train finally approached. He waited for it to stop and exited the car. He held his hat in his hand and placed his weight on his cane. Bormann waited by his side. The train door opened, and the Nazis climbed aboard. The train resumed its journey to the Reich's capital.

The German Army, weak from its defeat in the Battle of the Bulge, was unable to defend the nation as the enemy invaded. This pushed Hitler deeper into the depths of insanity. On April 30, 1945, the same day that the Soviets captured the Reichstag, Hitler entered a small room with his recent bride, Eva Braun. His last known words were, "Tomorrow, millions of people will curse me, but fate has taken its course." Hitler then swallowed a cyanide capsule, brought his Walther pistol to his temple, and pulled the trigger, finally bringing an end to his tyranny.

☆☆☆☆☆

IKE COUGHED AND looked up from the map. His eyes closed from the pain —too weak to control his breathing. The Battle of the Bulge was a decisive Allied victory, but it took its toll like no other period of the war. He rested his forearm on his desk as his back and knee throbbed. He was powerless to stop his physician's words about surgery—which Ike was desperate to avoid—from playing in his ears.

He wiped tears from his eyes as he studied the map. A series of blue arrows represented his offensives. All three army groups were in Germany, systematically destroying what was left of the Wehrmacht. Modelled on Hannibal's victory at Cannae, Montgomery and Bradley would soon encircle the Ruhr valley, Germany's industrial heartland. There, Model would commit suicide to avoid surrender.

Ike's subordinates would then race to the Rhine and enter the heart of Germany. The things he would see there confirmed the worst fears he felt after learning of Kristallnacht years before.

He presided over Germany's surrender on May 7, ending the war in Europe and dissolving the Nazi regime. Ike's SHAEF staff tried to put together a dramatic message to announce the war's end. Ike rejected their proposals. Like Grant's message to Lincoln at Appomattox, Ike's telegram to Marshall was brief: "The mission of this Allied force was fulfilled at 0241 local time, May 7, 1945."

Marshall's response was the most meaningful praise of Ike's career:

> You have completed your mission with the greatest victory in the history of warfare. You have commanded with outstanding success the most powerful military force that has ever been assembled. You have made history, great history for the good of mankind and you have stood for all we hope for and admire in an officer in the United States Army.

Ike had fulfilled his duty in the face of the ultimate threat. He could return to Mamie and retire to enjoy his golden years, knowing that Allied victory set the foundation for a post-war peace.

He hoped.

PART II

☆☆☆☆☆

THE PRESIDENT

The Office Once Held by Washington: Part I

The middle of the road is all of the usable surface.
The extremes, right and left, are in the gutters.
—Dwight Eisenhower

NOVEMBER 5, 1951

IT'S OBVIOUS TO anyone who doesn't have a silver spoon in their mouth or an Ivy League diploma on their wall that Taft is a more honorable man than Dewey," President Truman explained, "but we have a responsibility to keep the isolationists out of the White House. They'll destroy everything we've built, including NATO."

Truman sat behind the Oval Office desk that once belonged to Theodore Roosevelt. The other Roosevelt, Franklin, peered into the distance in a photograph hanging from the wall off Truman's right flank. Round, full-framed glasses shielded the President's eyes. "The Buck Stops Here" read a sign on Truman's desk. General Eisenhower, the Supreme Commander of NATO, sat on the other side of the desk, wearing a light gray Army uniform.

"I agree," Ike replied. "We can't let them take us back to '41. You'd think we'd have learned the lessons of Pearl Harbor."

"You're the best man to make sure that doesn't happen," Truman said, maintaining constant eye contact. "You could have this office by acclamation if you say the word."

Ike chuckled, glancing at his hands clasped in his lap. His cheeks flushed.

"You've been in the sun too long."

"That's bullshit, Ike, and you know it," Truman insisted. "No other Democrat can stop Taft. I'll have to run for a third term if you don't run next year."

Would stop Taft or help him? Ike thought. *Truman's approval rating is just over 20 percent. His mishandling of Korea created a bloody stalemate that's keeping millions of our boys away from their families, including my son. I'm unsure he's any better than Taft.*

I can't believe people are talking about me becoming President. Me! In the office once held by Washington, maybe the greatest man who ever lived.

Ike had hoped to retire after the war and become a college university president, like Robert E. Lee after Appomattox. But Columbia underwhelmed him. Ike was out-of-step with the East Coast Ivy League faculty. They focused him on fundraising instead of educating students to be good citizens. That's why he jumped on the chance to organize the US, Canada, and Europe into the North Atlantic Treaty Organization.

"Don't you want history to remember you as a President?" Truman asked. He twiddled his thumbs, playing to Ike's ego.

"I'm sorry, Mr. President, but I think I pretty well hit my peak in history when I accepted the German surrender."

"Ok, Ike, here's the deal," Truman began, shifting in his seat and parting and re-parting his hair. "You'll recall that I offered you the presidency the first time we met, dodging shell-craters on the Autobahn. I even said I'd become your Vice President. I offered it again in '47 when my numbers were in the tank. You turned me down, claiming it was unacceptable for a soldier to seek office. But I'm asking you a third time. Will you run? We have to have a Democrat who will continue the policies that Roosevelt and I started and you're the man who can do it."

Ike's eyes darted about. Right, left, right diagonal. His teeth lightly bit the tip of his tongue. *How do I say this without upsetting him?*

"I'm sorry, Mr. President, but you can't join a political party just to run for office."

"What do you mean?" Truman asked, his eyebrows arched. "Are you not a Democrat?"

"What reason do you have to think I have ever been a Democrat? You know I have been a Republican all my life and that my family have always been Republicans."

"The Republicans opposed our entry into World War II," Truman pointed out, frustration in his voice. "I seem to remember you feeling otherwise."

"I agree with a lot of the foreign policy that you and Roosevelt have done. The opposition to Nazi Germany and the Soviet Union, the support for the United Nations and NATO."

"Sounds like a Democrat to me."

"But I think the Democrats are too liberal on economic issues."

"You favor Wall Street fat cats to working Americans?"

"I don't think it needs to be one or the other."

Truman scoffed. Ike clenched his fist. It had been a long day. Lucius Clay, an old Army friend and war colleague, tried to talk Ike into running as a Republican a few hours before.

"Besides," Ike continued, trying to pacify the President, "America needs a change of party in the White House. The Democrats have been in power for twenty years. We're on track to becoming a one-party state."

"What's wrong with that, as long as it's the Democrats?" Truman joked. "You're comfortable belonging to the same party as Joe McCarthy?"

"And Abraham Lincoln."

"Lincoln and Teddy Roosevelt would be Democrats by now."

"I disagree."

Truman turned away from Ike. He put his finger to his lips, contemplating. This election was a referendum on his presidency and the most popular man in the country was ready to join the other side. The President looked back up at the general.

"My own position is in the balance. If I do what I want to do, I'll go back to Missouri and *maybe* run for the Senate. If you decide to finish the European job, and I don't know who else can, I must keep the isolationists out of the White House. I hope you'll let me know what you intend to do. It will be between us and no one else."

Ike smiled.

☆☆☆☆☆

I'LL GIVE THIS statement to the press if he agrees to support NATO, Ike thought as he sat in the Pentagon's cafeteria. Ike felt the folded paper in his pocket; it read, "Having been called back to military duty, I want to announce that my name may not be used by anyone as candidate for President—and if they do I will repudiate such effort."

"I hope I'm not late, General!" Senator Taft exclaimed as he held out his hand. Taft wore a three-piece suit, tight around the gut, and glasses that rivaled Truman's.

Ike stood to shake Taft's hand. "Not at all!"

"When do you return to Europe?" Taft asked.

"Tomorrow."

"I'm honored you took the time out of your brief visit to the States to meet with me."

"The pleasure's all mine. I'm always happy to meet the son of a former President."

Their conversation quickly turned to the issues of the day.

"I know the liberal elites in New York and Washington scoff at me," Taft said, "but Americans must learn to eat less. It will bring down food prices and inflation."

Ike nodded. *It's weird that I'm agreeing one hundred percent with an archfoe of Roosevelt, Truman, and Marshall.*

"What do you think of the war in Korea?" Taft asked, peering from behind his glasses. "Or the 'police action,' as the man in the White House calls it."

"I supported our initial involvement," Ike replied, his forearms resting on the table.

"So did I."

"North Korea's invasion of South Korea was part of communism's worldwide aggression. Failing to take a firm stance would have resulted in a dozen Koreas. Stalin would have expanded relentlessly, like Hitler after the Munich Agreement."

"Allowing the Reds to take South Korea was unacceptable, but I don't love how Munich has become an excuse for our present offensives around the world. And Truman should've been impeached for usurping Congress' war powers."

"I assume you think Truman shouldn't have let MacArthur go north of the Thirty-Eighth Parallel?" Taft nodded. "I agree. We'd completed what the Security Council authorized once South Korea was liberated." *Maybe I really don't have to run for President. He seems like he's got a good head on his shoulders.*

"And now thousands of Americans are dying for his mistake. Your son is in Korea, right?" Taft asked.

"That's right. He's in the Fifteenth Infantry."

"You must be worried about him."

"Every day."

My heart aches just thinking about it. Icky, my first son, died of scarlet fever when he was three years old. John's a father now. But he wanted to prove himself by serving his country. Oh boy, can I relate to that. I spent the interwar years determined to make my family proud and I thought serving in combat was the only way. But I couldn't stand to lose him. It would kill me. I barely survived losing Icky. I can't lose John too. He probably thinks I'm heartless for telling him he has to fight to the death or commit suicide instead of being captured. But that's what Stalin's son did in World War II and I can't let Stalin use my boy against me or the Free World. But by God, I haven't been so desperate about anything since I waited for news on June 6, 1944.

"You must dislike Truman more than I do," Taft inquired, his chin swaying from side to side ever so slightly.

"He's my Commander-in-Chief."

Taft chuckled. "Mum's the word. But he deserved impeachment for firing MacArthur." He was referring to when President Truman fired General MacArthur, the original commander of UN forces in Korea, for publicly disagreeing with Truman's decision not to fight Red China with nuclear weapons after that country entered the Korean conflict.

"There we disagree," Ike replied.

"Why?"

"MacArthur was challenging civilian control of the military. That principal goes back to George Washington."

"He was a hero. Who was Harry Truman to fire someone like that? He's a haberdasher from Missouri."

"Not everyone is the son of a Medal of Honor winner or a President," Ike declared, defending his humble Kansan roots. He blanched. "I hope that wasn't out of line."

"No big deal," Taft replied.

"Can I ask you a question?"

"Of course. That's why we're here."

"Is it true you opposed the war with Nazi Germany?" Taft nodded. "Even after Hitler declared war on us?"

"Japan attacked us. We had to fight them. But Hitler was Europe's problem. We could have become a fortress in this Hemisphere and let him have that one."

"You don't think he wanted to conquer us next?"

"No, I think he only wanted to destroy communism."

"But what about the Jews and other minorities he was slaughtering?"

"I don't think American boys should be dying for charity. We would always be at war somewhere in the world."

"And you think Fortress America could withstand Hitler?"

"Just as much as I think it can withstand Stalin. That's why I want to see us pull out of NATO. No offense. We'll become the Gibraltar of freedom."

"In the nineteenth century Gibraltar was a great stronghold, but today it is one of the weakest military spots in the world. It could be reduced to nothing by a few modern guns posted in the hills and concentrating their fire on it." *I should know! It was my HQ during the North Africa invasion!*

"We don't need the world."

"But what about the free nations banding together for mutual defense against tyranny?"

"That's rhetoric to get us involved where we don't belong. Helps the weapon manufacturers get government contracts."

"I entirely disagree with that assessment."

"I know." He chose to twist the knife in further, muttering, "I don't know if I shall vote for four divisions or six divisions or two divisions for NATO."

Ike grit his teeth. NATO had lacked military forces, headquarters, or a command structure when Ike and Mamie arrived in Europe in February. He'd built it into an alliance that bound the West together and deterred Stalin's aggression. Taft would throw it away.

"NATO's bad for weapon manufacturers, if anything."

"How's that?"

"It keeps the peace. It stabilizes Europe."

Taft laughed tactlessly.

"Stabilizing Europe! What are you, Augustus?"

"No," Ike replied, his eyebrows pinched. "Europe will eventually have to be defended by the Europeans. We can't be a modern Rome guarding the far frontiers of empire with our legions."

"That's what Democrats like Truman want. Police the world."

"And I disagree with them. But we *should* defend countries from communism who are willing to defend themselves. That's different from an anti-communist crusade. Measures like the Marshall Plan—"

"The Marshall Plan was a global giveaway. Much too large!" Taft snapped, accidentally spraying spit onto the table.

"It was an investment in peace."

"*Baloney.* It's going to get Europeans addicted to our aid." Taft crossed his arms. "Truman's National Security Council doesn't know any more about foreign policy than I do. Bradley said we needed $13.5 billion in the military in 1950. Now he says $50 billion isn't enough." He was referring to Omar Bradley, Chairman of the Joint Chiefs and Ike's most important subordinate in World War II.

"That's because of Korea."

"Then why do we have an army in Germany?"

"Why are you willing to let the Soviets undo the results of World War II? We fought hard to free Europe."

"Because the policies of the past twenty years betray our history. The New Deal. Running the world. All of it. I'm going to spend my presidency dismantling Roosevelt's legacy. And I'm going to enjoy every minute of it."

"I doubt that platform could win. The Democrats are unpopular, but the only people who would support what you're talking about are those who want to retreat from the world because of Korea."

Taft scoffed again. Did this old soldier think he knew politics better than the son of a former President?

"Are you even a Republican?" Taft asked.

Ike smiled. "While growing up in Abilene, the locals referred to Democrats the way they would the town drunks."

Taft cackled. A new line to poke fun at the other side. He always said, 'the point of the opposition is to oppose.'

"That's good. But what's your history with our party?"

"Well, I'm not known as 'Mr. Republican,' like you, but I did march in a pro-McKinley rally when I was six."

"Do you consider yourself a conservative?"

"I don't like rigid labels like 'liberal' or 'conservative.' I try to examine each issue individually. The pundits will hang labels as they may."

"But how would you describe your political philosophy, if you needed to?"

"I've used the term 'Middle Way.'"

Taft shook his head. "A moderate. Like that wimp, Tom Dewey."

He's really a piece of work! Have to stay diplomatic. He isn't worse than Montgomery was during the war.

"I determined my support for the Middle Way while at Columbia," Ike said.

"It's spineless fence sitting."

"It's endorsed by the Almighty!"

"What does that mean?"

"The standard statistical distribution curve of issues like humans' height or weight has the bulk of cases fall near the center."

"That endorses *political* moderation?"

"It shows that the right answer usually avoids the extremes."

"I don't think that's relevant. Moderation has been the death knell of this party. Saying 'me too!' every time Roosevelt opened his mouth is why Willkie and Dewey kept losing."

"Moderation takes decent ideas on the left and right and finds a middle ground that captures the strengths while minimizing the weaknesses of each side. An easy example is taxes. Too high, and they stifle growth. Too low, and the government can't pay for things society deems necessary."

"What have you thought of Truman?" Taft pushed.

"What have we been talking about since you sat down?"

"You're the hero of our time!" Taft flattered. "I'm interested in your thoughts."

Ike hesitated. *Need to criticize Truman or else he'll use it against me.*

"Poor Harry Truman!" Ike exclaimed for effect. "He's a fine man who, in the middle of a stormy lake, knows nothing about swimming."

Taft nodded, suspecting Ike's appeasement.

Ike had to be careful; Taft would use whatever he said against him in a primary, regardless of the content. He was honest about Truman, though. Ike agreed with the Marshall Plan and NATO but thought it a mistake to drop the atomic bomb since he believed Japan would have surrendered anyway. Then there was Korea and Iran, which was going communist and about to let Stalin control the Persian Gulf. Worst of all was Truman's authorization of NSC 68, which predicted the Soviets would hit the US with nuclear bombs within a few years and led to a restoration of permanent wartime defense spending to continue the fight. This caused a surge of inflation and treated nuclear war as inevitable. Truman's Cold War strategy was on the brink of collapse. Forfeit or nuclear war were the only outcomes.

All these issues stemmed from the fact that Truman was no match for Stalin. Ike liked the Soviet leader during the war but he'd become as dangerous as Hitler ever was. Nazism had little appeal outside of Germany while communism appealed to the impoverished around the world. Stalin had spies everywhere; he'd even penetrated the Manhattan Project.

It wasn't supposed to be like this. The victory over Germany was supposed to lead to global peace and cooperation. The Allied coalition was meant to continue into peacetime. Instead, tension between America and Russia had escalated more and more since before the ink on Germany's surrender was dry. The world hurtled toward World War III. Four more years of the Democrats would lead to more wars like Korea and America bankrupting itself on defense spending. Not that Taft and his isolationist Republicans were any better. They'd withdraw America from the world. The Soviets would conquer Europe and Asia. That, too, would start the Third World War.

How was it that either option would lead to a global cataclysm far deadlier than Hitler?

"You mentioned Washington earlier," Taft said. Ike nodded. "You know he would be on my side."

"About what?" Ike asked.

"Washington was an isolationist. He warned us about 'entangling alliances.'"

"Jefferson coined that term."

Taft shrugged and Ike frowned. Ike tore up his written statement after the meeting ended. He couldn't give it to the press. His stomach knotted in anxiety as he and Mamie returned to Europe.

☆☆☆☆☆

FEEL DISGUSTING. So sweaty. Bet I could see my chest hair through my Ike Jacket right now. Because of how soaked I am. Don't look at it. Why am I wearing my full uniform and jacket in this heat? Where am I?

Ike's gaze rose from the ground to the grassy fields. White oak and magnolia towered over him, though their shade did not diminish the heat or humidity. Gardens stretched in every direction. A large estate loomed in the distance, a great wooden mansion at its center. Its roof was bright red, and its walls were white wood. A circular dirt path sat in front of the building surrounding a large patch of trimmed grass. Single-story wings flanked the mansion on each side.

Why does that building look so familiar? Shouldn't trespass. But I'll pass out if I don't get a drink of water.

Ike stumbled toward the mansion, every step a struggle. No sooner did Ike begin his quest than a man on horseback intercepted him. He wore a corn yellow worn-out vest and a black tricorn hat that shaded his shoulders. Sweat shone on his forehead. His black horse *neighed* as he came to a stop. Ike looked up at him.

What the hell is he wearing? Either he's out of fashion, even for a farmer, or I'm so old I missed the new look.

"What's your name?" the man on horseback asked, his knuckles white from gripping the reins.

Ike felt an unconscious jolt; he'd been famous for a decade. This was a nice change of pace.

"I'm General Eisenhower."

"A general?" the man asked. "Did you fight in the war?"

"Yes, sir," Ike replied politely.

"Where?"

"I commanded the European Theater."

"Europe? You mean you were with Dr. Franklin?"

What?

"That's a strange uniform for a general," the man said.

"You don't like my jacket?" Ike asked as he glanced at it briefly. "I know it's a sweaty mess, but I designed it myself." He looked the man in the eye as his horse trotted to his right. "You haven't given me your name yet."

"Joseph Cash," the man said, still suspicious. "I assume you're here for a visit."

"Sure," Ike muttered quietly. "Where am I exactly?"

Cash's eyebrow rose.

"You're on the most famous estate in the country. Maybe the world."

"That's not helping."

"Mount Vernon."

Mount Vernon? How the hell... alright. I guess that explains why he's dressed like he's from another century. Must be a tour guide or something.

"Can I get a glass of water before my tour?"

Cash ignored him.

"I don't think he's very busy right now. Not sure he's had many visitors today. You can probably see him if you want."

"Who are we talking about?"

"General Washington."

"Come again?"

"George Washington. The general and President. You're not from around here, are you?"

Washington? The George Washington? Can't believe it! My God! Oh my God! Stomach's doing a somersault! How in the hell... I don't know. But this fellow is right in front of me and saying I'm about to meet George Washington, who I've idolized since I could read. I wonder if I can confirm the cherry tree story.

Ike looked up at Cash.

"I would be honored to see him."

Cash escorted Ike toward the mansion. "The general enjoys socializing with visitors. Though he's busier now that President Adams has appointed him Commander-in-Chief due to the crisis with France."

The Quasi-War of 1798, if my history serves me.

"He pretends to ignore the attacks from the Jeffersonian press but it eats at him."

How could anyone criticize George Washington? He's the ultimate hero! Always admired his stamina and patience in adversity. His indomitable courage, daring, and capacity for self-sacrifice. Talk about doing your duty. He personifies 'duty.' The beauty of his character. Always inspired me. His Farewell Address, his counsels to the rebellious Army officers at Newburgh, exemplified the human qualities that I adore and strive to emulate.

I don't know how I can meet him. I've met the biggest figures of my time. Roosevelt. Churchill. De Gaulle. But George Washington is in his own category. He's the turning point in the world's history of democracy. The Roman Republic became a dictatorship of Julius Caesar. England's attempt at a republic became a dictatorship of Oliver Cromwell. The French Revolution fell into anarchy and became a dictatorship of Napoleon. All of the failed attempts in Latin America that either fell into chaos or became tyrannical. But ours didn't. It wasn't perfect, but it created a stable republic. And the reason why is that it was led by the greatest leader of all time.

Ike noticed slaves in the fields.

I can barely stand this weather. Can't imagine what they're going through. We really are a fallen race.

Cash noticed that Ike was staring at the slaves.

"We have about three hundred at the plantation. One hundred work across the five farms. We've been growing primarily wheat for years now.

Except the accursed Hessian flies, those dreaded pests, are terrorizing our crops."

Ike did not reply. He simply stared.

"Look alive, Ice-en-hower. You're about to meet him."

Ike smiled from ear to ear. His spirit rebounded as he saw the huge figure lazily seated on the mansion's front porch. *I've dreamed of this day since I stole my mom's key and read the history books she hid from me so I'd do my chores.*

George Washington had deep creases under his eyes, his hair gray. He wore a puffy white shirt and rested in his chair, watching the landscape.

"This is General Ice-en-hower," Cash explained. "He's here to meet you."

Ike tried to contain his excitement.

"Care to join me?" Washington asked as he gestured to the chair next to him.

Ike nodded as he leapt up the stairs. Washington bowed his head.

"A pleasure."

"The pleasure's all mine, sir. Honestly."

Cash smiled. "I'll leave you two alone." He turned his horse about.

Ike sat down, resting under the shade. Washington studied him, raising his strong jaw, sizing Ike up, tapping his fake molars together. Ike tried not to shiver in anticipation. Washington was used to such reactions.

"What was your name again, son?"

"Dwight Eisenhower," Ike responded. *He knows my name!*

"Is that German?"

Ike nodded.

"When did your family arrive in the country? Or the colonies?"

"1741. They settled in Pennsylvania."

"Oh really?" A hint of a smile emerged on Washington's lips. "Did they serve in the Revolution?"

"I hate to disappoint you, Mr. President, but they were Mennonite pacifists."

Washington nodded. He wasn't surprised. Less than half of the population supported the war.

"That's an interesting outfit you're wearing."

"I'm sorry it's so sweaty and gross. It's not usually like this. I try to keep it reasonably clean."

"It's an Army uniform, I suspect. But not from here. Its materials look…" Washington's inflection fell. "Are you from the future?"

"How did you know?"

"Your clothes! The most gifted seamstress, even Martha, couldn't produce stitching like that."

Ike glanced at his jacket. "I can't complain."

"What year are you from?"

"1952."

"Fascinating."

How did he accept that so easily? What the hell is going on?

"A lot must have happened in the past hundred and fifty-four years."

Ike nodded. *He must be as fascinated with my being from the future as I am in meeting my hero. Must have a million questions. He'll probably ask what day he's going to die. What was it? Think it was December 1799.*

"What is the state of dentures in your time?" Washington asked, massaging his jaw while Ike was engrossed in his own thoughts.

Ike was caught off guard.

"Uh," Ike muttered, pausing for time. "I don't have a lot of personal experience, but I think they've improved a lot. They're no longer made of wood."

"Mine are Hippopotamus tusk, actually, the horrible things. Do you know from what material they're made in your time?"

"Some sort of plastic, I'm sure."

"I've not heard of this."

Oh, true! He doesn't know what plastic is. How do I describe it? Ike asked himself. "Plastic is a new type of material. Everything is made of it from my time."

"Do you have any on you?"

Ike felt his pockets. He pulled out his wallet.

"I might have some plastic cards in here."

Washington played with Ike's wallet for a moment and returned it to him. A serious expression conquered his face.

"How does the country remember me?" he asked with anxiety in his voice.

Ike smiled. "We worship you."

Washington relaxed. He tried to smile, though his dentures made it difficult.

"Really?" he asked, seeking affirmation.

Ike nodded.

"You're the father of our country. Every schoolboy and schoolgirl knows you. You're our biggest hero, along with another President named

Abraham Lincoln. You're on the one-dollar bill."

Washington was content. He'd spent his life obsessed with his reputation and this man from the future told him it was secure. He looked at Ike.

"Do the people of your time think I'm stupid compared to the other leaders of this age? Such as Jefferson and Franklin?"

He's awfully insecure. Always thought Washington was a titan of confidence. Also thought he was guarded with his feelings. Must be making an exception since I'm from the future and he wants to know his place in history.

"No one in my time thinks you're stupid, Mr. President."

"What about my record as a general?"

Ike shrugged. "I mean, we don't think you were a military genius like Alexander or Caesar, but that's not what—"

"They were given professional armies!" Washington exclaimed. "I built the Continental Army from scratch!"

I never knew he was this sensitive. Makes me feel less insecure about my temper and moodiness.

"I take it the country still stands." Ike nodded. "What's the standard of living like in your time?"

"The average American citizen lives better than a king in your time."

Washington nodded. "The national prosperity was my first and only concern as President. I worked on infrastructure, the fiscal system, and Western expansion for our booming population. It appears that effort succeeded."

"You wouldn't believe the technology we have in 1952. Many citizens can cool their homes or wash their clothes at their convenience with machines that run on electricity."

"Fascinating."

"And communication has increased, too. We've invented flying machines that can carry people across oceans to visit other continents. And we have devices where someone can talk to another person even if they are on the other side of the world. The world has shrunk from your time."

"I assume the world doesn't run on steam anymore."

"No. Industrialization has advanced. Coal was the dominant source of power in the last century. In my time everything runs on oil."

"Then that would be a good investment. What role does religion play in public life?"

"It's declined during my lifetime."

"That's worrying. Faith is key to a nation's character, and a nation's character is key to its success."

"I find that much of that deals with controlling the degree to which one desires things for their own selfish interest. Having preferences is fine but wanting things at the expense of your duty toward others is destructive. I've long seen you as the quintessential model of duty."

"You flatter me. What is the state of the government?"

"The Constitution of 1787 still exists and is in force."

"Really? Still?"

"Yes. Although one of our political parties bends its interpretations of it to increase government powers to a level not even Alexander Hamilton could have dreamed."

"The structure of society must be very different in your time. The government must be trying to adapt. That's why the Constitution has a mechanism for amendments. But I do not conceive that my generation is any more inspired—or have more wisdom—or possess more virtue than those who come after us. You mentioned Hamilton. What happens to his fiscal systems, such as the national bank?"

"It launches us into industrialization, although it ends in the 1830s."

"What comes of our economy?"

"It shifts from agriculture to industry, especially in the north. People move to cities. A new central bank called the Federal Reserve is established in 1913."

"How does it work?"

"It regulates the banks and sets interest rates. I can do my best to explain it in more detail, but I'm a soldier, not an economist."

"We must be aware of our own limitations. Who wins the next presidential election?"

"That's in 1800?"

"Yes."

"Thomas Jefferson."

Washington's face turned a shade paler. "That French partisan! And the republic survives?"

"More than that. He doubles the country in size."

"Really?" Washington asked.

"Oh, yes. He buys all of the land from the Mississippi River to the Rocky Mountains from France."

"Good for him. The west is the key to our future. I explored the frontier as a young man, and I've always recognized the potential for new towns and cities. The vast lands. The rich soils. The rivers. We will outpace the growth of Europe."

"That's exactly what happens," Ike said, validating Washington's life mission.

"What happens to the situation in France?"

"You're familiar with Napoleon Bonaparte?" Washington nodded. "He seizes power and wages wars across Europe."

"I did not see how France could go from monarchy to republic so quickly. From one extreme to the other. It makes sense someone like that would take power to restore stability. How does history view him?"

"The consensus is that he revolutionizes warfare but lacks your strength of character. His defeat leads to a century of relative peace in Europe."

"What about our country? Please tell me it remains at peace."

"I'm sorry, Mr. President, but it wages several wars between your time and mine. James Madison becomes President after Jefferson. He gets us into another war with Britain that ends the peace and prosperity secured by your Jay Treaty." Ike referred to the treaty that Washington's administration negotiated that kept America out of war with Britain.

"The fool," Washington muttered. "He's a brilliant thinker but a mediocrity at world affairs."

"We then get into a war with the Spanish colony to our south. We conquer much of its territory."

"What?" Washington demanded. "Our nation is to act with character and justice! To seize land from another country..." he muttered as he shook his head.

"That in turn leads to the crisis of the 1850s, since North and South argued over whether the new states carved from that conquered territory should allow slavery to be legal."

Washington froze and then looked Ike in the eye. "Did you just say that slavery is still legal in the 1850s?"

"Yes."

Washington looked as though his loved one died in front of him. He shivered with disgust. He did not speak for several moments.

"I failed," he muttered with a shortness of breath. "Slavery was to disintegrate in the next few years. It must destroy the republic if it lasts that long."

"It almost does."

"Almost?"

"America has a civil war in the 1860s. It's the defining event of the nineteenth century."

"A civil war? So, my worst fear comes to pass. My countrymen ignore my warning of sectionalism." A few minutes ago, Ike was the man who had validated Washington's hope of westward expansion and prosperity. Now he validated his fear of civil war.

"The South secedes from the Union to protect slavery. The North and South go to war. The North wins. It preserves the Union and ends slavery, under the leadership of President Abraham Lincoln."

"Lincoln," Washington said the name quietly. "You mentioned him earlier. Who is he?"

"Lincoln is our other biggest hero. He grew up with nothing and rose to the presidency. He led us through the Civil War. He is the Savior of the Union and the Great Emancipator."

"He sounds like a great man. I do not have children of my own, but what side do my stepfamily's descendants take in the war?"

Ike paused.

"Do you remember Henry Lee?"

"Of course. He was a subordinate of mine during the Revolution."

"His son marries your wife's great granddaughter, if memory serves me."

Washington grimaced, highlighting the creases under his eyes. He was not sure how he felt about his family marrying into the Lee family.

"President Lincoln asks Lee's son to lead the Northern armies in the war."

"So, my in-law saves the Union?" Washington asked.

"No, I'm sorry to say. He decides to lead the South's armies instead."

Washington turned paler than he did when he learned of the Civil War.

"You're telling me that the man who marries into my family fights to destroy the Union I helped build?"

"Yes," Ike muttered. "In his defense, secession was a controversial issue at the time that lacked a clear answer."

Ike hoped this nuance would appease Washington. It did not. Washington's face turned red.

"How *dare* you defend an act like that? He's as bad as Benedict Arnold! The man you've described failed in his duty. Nothing is more shameful."

Duty. My hero just used my favorite word. Duty.

"He felt his responsibility was to Virginia, not the Union."

"Damned nonsense!" Washington boomed. He pointed at Ike. "You will not defend him in my presence. I regret knowing that he is a future family member of mine."

"You'll be happy to know he loses the war."

Washington paused. "How?"

"The North deploys overwhelming force to destroy Lee's Army."

"So, he did not learn my lessons of war either?"

"What do you mean?"

"I outlasted the British by preserving the Continental Army. It sounds like the South fails to preserve their Army and therefore fails to outlast the North."

"That's correct."

"The fools."

"In my time what you're describing is called 'center of gravity.' A faction at war must destroy the enemy's center of gravity. Like what the British failed to do to you and what the North succeeded in doing to the South."

"Fascinating," Washington replied.

"It's based on the writings of a Prussian general from the 1800s."

"You said slavery doesn't survive the war?"

"Correct. Lincoln adds an amendment to the Constitution that abolishes it forever. He's murdered shortly thereafter."

"A pity. What is the state of the Negro in your time?"

"They're still treated as second-class citizens."

"Even in 1952?"

"I'm afraid so."

"An even greater pity. Since the Revolution I've believed that this can become a biracial society, unlike Jefferson, who hopes to send the slaves elsewhere. The Negros will be our equals once they are educated. I hope to free my own slaves before I die, but Virginia makes it difficult. I want to create a fund that will educate the young ones while providing care for the elderly."

Ike smiled. *Now that's the George Washington that I know.*

"You spoke of our westward expansion. What happens to the Indians?"

"They suffer greatly as the white man displaces them."

Washington looked sullen. "A stain on our nation's character. I had so hoped they would be spared by our expansion and integrated into our society." He glanced at the sky as the sun hung overhead. "What happens after the Civil War?"

"Women and non-landowners got the vote by the early twentieth century. And America grows into an industrial giant." Washington smiled again. "The policies of you and Hamilton, as well as Lincoln, lead to our growth into a major world power by the turn of the twentieth century. I was born in this period. There are some issues as wealth becomes concentrated in the hands of a few."

"So, Mr. Adams' predictions about a new aristocracy of wealth are correct."

"Yes. The early twentieth century is also when the European peace ends."

"How?"

"The European nations wage a terrible war against each other. An entire generation is killed. America is pulled in at the end."

"So, my warning about getting involved in European affairs is also ignored?"

"They were closely followed for a century. But it became difficult to remain neutral as we became a world power. We were able to project our power abroad and try to defend human freedom."

"I suppose my warnings were primarily meant to guide the country until it had completed its westward expansion and grown into a great power. What happened after the war?"

"The President at the time, a man named Wilson, tried to build a global organization where countries would peacefully resolve their differences instead of settling them on the battlefield."

"That sounds like it defies human nature. Nations, like the people who form them, are fundamentally self-interested. Did this scheme succeed?"

"It did not, primarily because the Senate refused to let America join the organization. They thought it betrayed your principles."

Washington frowned. On the one hand, he was honored that the country still cared about him and his ideas. On the other hand, he did not want to be blamed for the missteps of future generations.

"Continue," Washington asked, gently.

"The 1920s boomed but the 1930s saw a terrible economic crash. It spread around the world. The result was that very militant governments took over several powerful countries."

"What do you mean, 'militant governments'?"

"Monarchy is no longer the dominant force in the world in my time. Now there are competing systems of government. On one side was 'fascism,' which glorified the nation, the all-powerful leader, and conquest. On the other side was 'communism,' which sought to create a worker's utopia through violent and expansionist means. Both are hostile to each other and to America's republic."

"Utopian dreams can only become nightmares. I've seen it so many times since our prudent revolution. France, Poland, and St. Domingue all imploded."

Ike nodded.

"The fascist countries plunged the world into another war."

Washington shook his head, aghast at all the terrible news from the future.

"I see that global trade did not banish war from the Earth as I hoped."

"It did not, although there is still hope in my time that trade will raise living standards around the world and preserve stability."

"Tell me about this next war."

"It was the most terrible war ever fought. Tens of millions died. Most of this was because of Germany, which slaughtered millions of civilians."

"A shame. The home of von Steuben, my friend. Though my experience with the Hessians leaves me with little surprise they would succumb to an evil government. What role does America play in this war?"

"It tries to stay out at first but eventually plays a leading role in defeating Germany and its allies."

Washington smiled, though he wrestled with his feelings of isolationism that evolved over his career with the radically different circumstances of the future. He glanced at Ike's uniform, which was covered in dried sweat. Ike had said he was born around the turn of the century and came from 1952. He said that the war occurred after the economic crisis of the 1930s. The dots connected in Washington's mind.

"What role did you play in the war, Eisenhower?"

Ike bit his tongue. *How do I explain that? Is it bad character to talk about myself?*

"If it's all the same to you—"

"You are ordered to speak," Washington declared to the subordinate officer.

Ike took a deep breath. *I hope he doesn't think me of poor character.*

"I played a leading role in America's war effort. I directed the campaign against Germany and led American and British armies across Western Europe. I accepted Germany's surrender at the end of the war."

Washington tried to smile again.

"Do you feel you did your duty?"

Ike's eyes watered. "I'm sure I didn't do it as well as you would have, sir, but I did the best I could." He turned away from Washington, fighting back the tears. *I can't cry in front of him. Even though no one's opinion matters more to me.*

"We've only spoken briefly, but I suspect you performed your duty with distinction."

A tear ran down Ike's cheek. "I'm sorry, sir," he muttered as he wiped it with his finger.

"Quite all right," Washington replied. "You said the Germans surrendered. What happened next?"

Ike regained his composure. "Europe and Asia were destroyed in the war. America, in the past few years, has grown into the most powerful country on Earth. Maybe the most powerful of all time."

Washington was pleased once more. "My efforts were to transform America into a powerful and prosperous republic. One of the great nations on Earth. What you describe transcends my imagination."

"We even have an explosive capable of destroying an entire city."

"That's terrifying."

"I don't mean to glorify it. I'm just explaining how powerful America is in my time."

"But the country remains a republic despite its power?"

"Yes, though there is concern about whether it can maintain a large-scale military and remain a republic for long. Some, myself included, fear it will devolve into a garrison state."

"Like most issues, it seems the answer would lie in balancing the various goals. Of having a large military and projecting power in the world without degrading the republic. An informed citizenry is the key."

"I agree."

"And America is entirely unrivaled in your time?"

"We do have one rival. Russia rules ten nations in Eastern Europe."

"Russia? Do the Tsars still rule?"

"Worse. He's more tyrannical. A communist, an ideology I mentioned earlier. Britain and Western Europe now rely on us for defense. America leads the free world."

"What do you mean, 'free world?'"

"There are more countries living under systems of self-government than ever before in history. And America is their leader. But we have tense relations with Russia that have been escalating since the Second World War ended. We now risk a Third World War. America is currently fighting one of Russia's junior allies in Asia. I, and many people, fear a war involving those 'city-destroying' explosives I mentioned earlier."

Washington shook his head again. "You've told me a terrible tale. I am glad I don't live in your century. Your time's leadership has taken on the role of running the world. It risks bankrupting the republic."

"The world has shrunk since your time. The wars against Germany showed what happens when America renounces all foreign entanglements."

"So, you would have America wage wars against all potential threats around the world? Sounds more like Caesar than Publius."

"We can't allow countries like Russia to attack other countries unchecked. They'll come for us eventually. Free countries have a duty to cooperate to contain Russia and the world as a whole has a duty to cooperate toward peace."

"You sound like I did when I said the various states had a duty to resist Britain together and cooperate to build a republic. Cooperation among the states was the key to the Revolution. The notion of global cooperation is foreign to me, though."

"I think that's because of our two different times. Modern Presidents have broken from your approach to foreign policy. They have sought to transform America into the world's leader and are willing to deploy force around the world to enforce America's vision."

"Sounds like we've become the British."

"Again, the conflicts with Germany and Russia—"

"But you've gone from one extreme to the other! Like France did with its revolution!"

Ike froze. *Extreme? Why does that seem so familiar? I usually hate extremes. Is he suggesting applying the Middle Way to foreign policy? Like playing a role in the world while maintaining his avoidance of unnecessary wars? That would maximize world peace. It would let us check dictators' aggression through global cooperation and fight only when we must. I feel like I know this, so why—*

Ike noticed a small smile emerge in the corner of Washington's mouth. He had led Ike to the proper conclusion. The proper approach to America's role in the world. Truman's overreaching was not the answer. But neither was Taft's isolationism.

This is crazy as hell. We have almost identical views of foreign policy. I had never seen my worldview merely as an update of Washington's Farewell Address, but he's shown me how to bridge the gap between his views and the modern world. My world.

"How are you going to implement this policy?"

"What do you mean?"

"You know what the answer is for your time. Now what will you do?"

"Some people who admired my role in the war want me to run for President. But I don't want to and think it would be inapp—"

"'Want?' What kind of a word is that? What about 'duty?'"

"I was taught in the Army to never get involved in politics."

"Your community has taken up a cause. It is your duty to put yourself and everything you have and are at that cause's disposal."

"But—"

"You've described your world on the brink of destruction from those terrible weapons. You have a duty to save it."

"But the Army—"

"*I* was in the Army. *I* was a general, like you. And *I* became President."

"You're different."

"I'm a citizen. Not a god."

Ike sighed, unsure what to do. "Can I promise to consider it?"

Washington nodded. Both men slumped back in their chairs, letting the sunlight shine on their faces. They sat in silence for several moments. Ike tried to clear his mind and not think about his problems so he could relish his hero's presence.

"We can now enjoy the rest of our day together," Washington suggested, breaking the silence. "I hope you'll stay and have dinner with Martha and myself. We'd be most honored by your presence."

"It would be an honor."

"We can share a bottle of Madeira. Then I can show you the key from the Bastille that Lafayette sent. An artist by the name of Jonathan Trumbull has sent me beautiful paintings of the War of Independence. We can look at them together and discuss the war. Soldier to soldier."

"Sounds like something I've always dreamed of."

"Tell me about yourself. Are you married?"

"Yes. Almost forty years."

"Good man. Where did you grow—"

☆☆☆☆☆

THUD!

IKE WAS disoriented as his eyes sprung open. His soldier's instincts activated as he looked up for action. His hands became fists. His tired eyes peered through the darkness.

Something woke me! But what?

He noticed Mamie's head laying on his chest.

"Mamie!" he exclaimed.

Mamie groaned. "What?" she softly muttered, too tired to process what her husband was doing.

"I was about to have dinner with George and Martha Washington! And you rolled into me and woke me up!"

Mamie's half-open eyes glared at Ike for a moment, unsure what he was talking about. She looked like she was seeing an alien.

"I'm going back to bed," she announced as she rolled away.

☆☆☆☆☆

FEBRUARY 16, 1952

"WELCOME TO OUR humble abode!" Mamie exclaimed as she greeted Jacqueline Cochran, the night's guest. Mamie was pleased to show off her newly curled bangs, which would soon become her signature look.

"Delighted!" Jackie exclaimed as she shook Mamie's hand. Jackie's short blonde hair was set off by her pleated black dress with a matching belt. A blue bag hung around her arm. She was a famous aviator who created the Women's Flying Training Detachment. Her husband was Floyd Odlum, a financier. She turned to greet Ike, who stood a few feet behind Mamie. His hands were clasped behind his back, a smile dominating his face.

Ike and Mamie were staying in Rocquencourt, a French village. Ike had 250 subordinates as the Supreme Commander of NATO. Bernard Montgomery was his deputy commander. They worked without friction, unlike their collaboration during the war. Ike and Mamie mostly socialized with other American officers and their wives. They rarely visited Paris, spending most of their time in Rocquencourt.

Mamie directed the trio away from her bodyguard, Monsieur Meechem, an Irish police officer who had been assigned to the Central Intelligence Division of the US Army. She glanced at Meechem as he stood in the corner of the room with his hands in his pocket. She regained her focus as her husband bored Jackie.

"Our garden did really well last season! Our corn did better than any other vegetable we planted!"

"I was hoping to talk about your *other* exciting news."

"What's that?" Ike asked.

"Ike!" Mamie exclaimed. She turned to Jackie. "Our family has been blessed with Susan's birth on New Year's Eve."

"Oh, right!" Ike exclaimed. "We can't wait to meet our granddaughter the next time we go to the States."

"How soon would you like that to be?" Jackie asked. "You know there's—"

"*Please* don't ask me about the presidency. I'm sorry I interrupted you, but we've been getting two hundred letters a day, mostly about that topic."

"Your country needs you, General."

"Both parties have been trying to get me to run since '43. My answer is still 'no.'"

"But you don't need to worry about *both* parties anymore," Jackie insisted, swallowing. "Last month, Senator Lodge announced that you're a Republican and you affirmed his statement."

"I know," Ike said. "But that doesn't mean I want to be a Republican *President*."

Jackie reached into her bag. "I think this will change your mind."

Ike's forehead scrunched. "What is it?" She pulled out a film canister. "Is it a movie night?"

"Floyd made this for you. It's an event we put on."

"What sort of event?"

"Will you just watch it?"

Ike agreed, and the trio watched a rally in Madison Square Garden with thousands of people cheering in the stands. There were hundreds of signs and banners that read, "I like Ike!" or "We like Ike!"

An entire rally dedicated to him. Ike was transfixed. So was Mamie. Firefighters and police officers tried to contain the overwhelming crowd.

I didn't realize I was a symbol of hope for thousands. I knew the political parties wanted me to run because they wanted to win. But this really is a movement. I've long thought that the office should seek the man. Like it did for Washington. That seems to be happening. Maybe I do have to run.

Tears emerged in Ike's eyes. Dozens of powerful men wanted the presidency, but these thousands wanted Ike. Jackie could read his mind.

"There were twenty-five thousand people there." She could see he couldn't take his eyes off the screen. "Tom Dewey put this on." Jackie had been afraid the rally would be too hokey, too much of a stunt. Her fears were misplaced.

Celebrities like Humphrey Bogart, Lauren Bacall, and Clark Gable spoke to the crowd. The film finally ended. The trio sat in silence. Ike couldn't have thought of a stronger sign of his duty. George Washington was right. His subconscious had sent him a message, but he had tried to dismiss it as a dream. Ike was ready to listen.

Jackie turned to him.

"I'm as sure as I am sitting here and looking at you that Taft will get the nomination if you don't declare yourself."

Ike said nothing, his jaw clenched, his eyes staring at the screen. He finally turned to an aide.

"Tell General Clay to come over for a talk. And tell Bill Robinson that I am going to run."

Jackie smiled as he said the words. She was there for the decision, the biggest he'd made since D-Day.

"I'll have to go to King George VI's funeral in London before I can return to the US," Ike explained as his aide poured them wine. Jackie lifted her glass.

"To the President!" she toasted.

Ike burst into tears. No one had called him that before.

"I wish my mother was here to see this day."

The Office Once Held by Washington: Part II

Any man who wants to be President is either an egomaniac or crazy.
—Dwight Eisenhower

MARCH 15, 1952

I HOPE I'M not late," Sherman Adams said as he entered the house. Adams wore a bowtie around his long neck. His snow-white hair was cut short.

"Not at all, Governor," Herbert Brownell, a lawyer, said from the couch. "We're just starting."

Ike was meeting several top Republican leaders in the New York home of Thomas Dewey, the Republican presidential candidate in 1944 and 1948. Along with Sherman, Brownell, and Dewey, Ike was joined by Henry Cabot Lodge and Lucius Clay, whom he had met in the English countryside after Ike decided to run for President. This group of politicians formed the leadership of the Republican Eastern Establishment, the moderate wing of the Republican Party. They had been trying to recruit Ike for months and were at their wit's end when he finally agreed.

"What were we discussing?" Adams asked as he took his seat.

"We decided that Mr. Lodge should be the frontman for the Eisenhower-for-President committee," Dewey explained. "He supported Senator Vandenburg for the Republican nomination in '48, so he's the least associated with me. The Taft forces hate me and we need someone who wasn't for me last time."

Ike glanced at Lodge and Dewey. Dewey had publicly endorsed Ike for President on *Meet the Press* in 1950, increasing the pressure for Ike to run. Lodge had put Ike's name on the New Hampshire primary ballot without Ike's permission. Ike won the primary, increasing his stature as a potential candidate.

"Minnesota has already pledged for Harold Stassen and California has pledged for Earl Warren. We're in trouble no matter which way I do the math. It might be too late to stop Taft," explained Clay, who had an emaciated-looking face and thinning hair. No one had put more pressure on Ike to run. Clay was an old Army friend who helped administer the American zone in Germany after World War II. He was also the architect of the Berlin Airlift after Stalin blockaded that city in 1948.

"How many delegates do we need to win?" Brownell asked.

"Six hundred and four," Dewey answered his former campaign chairman. Dewey was only five-foot-eight but had believed becoming President was his destiny. It was written in the stars in 1948, but Truman's surprise upset stole it from him. He was determined to prevent Taft, his nemesis, from getting the Republican nomination and to put Ike, who saw the world the way he did, in the Oval Office. "We have to prevent Taft from getting that number. Then it will come down to a fight at the convention."

Ike studied Dewey. *He's as cold as a February iceberg. Alice Roosevelt Longworth was right about him. He does look like the little man on the wedding cake. But he's spoken to me several times about halting the Democrats' drive toward socialism. I'm not sure I'll be able to win the presidency without him.*

"Do we know who the Democrats will nominate?" Clay asked.

"Let's worry about our party's nomination for now," Dewey said.

"We need to be aggressive," Brownell suggested. "Our passiveness last time is why we lost. Truman was calling you a Nazi," Brownell said, turning to Dewey, "and you never responded. You looked weak."

"I agree. We have to respond to Taft's charges. And quickly."

"What sort of charges?" Ike asked, engrossed in the political discussion, a fish out of water.

"His team is saying that you deliberately let the Soviets take Berlin first," Adams answered.

Ike's face flashed red. *Is Montgomery giving Taft his talking points?*

"Would Senator Taft like to pick the hundred thousand mothers who would have sacrificed their sons for Berlin?"

"You can't let personal attacks rattle you as President," Lodge suggested. Ike nodded and calmed down.

"Don't worry, General," Dewey advised. "You're a popular war hero with a winning smile. There's nothing Americans like more."

☆☆☆☆☆

JUNE 4, 1952

"LADIES AND GENTLEMEN!" Ike exclaimed. "We are today experiencing some Kansas showers." The crowd chuckled. "But I can assure you we are not experiencing half as much water today as there was in the English Channel eight years ago today." His reference to D-Day received polite applause. "Moreover, we here in Kansas can use this rain here today. It's okay by me!" The crowd remained silent.

Ike wiped the splatters of raindrops from his gray zyl glasses as he tried to maintain his speech's pace. The energy had dramatically dropped since he first arrived at his campaign announcement in Abilene. He had been greeted by multiple "heys!" and "yahoos!" He stood in a small stadium that was less than half filled.

"With my brothers, I am indebted to you because there is a building in this town that's a memorial to our parents and their family. It is dedicated to all of the servicemen of World War II. Greater than any statue of bronze or stone is the purpose that monument will serve: the advancement of the responsibility and the privileges of American citizenship. Its sponsors seek to inflame within our generation the spirit of the Founding Fathers. They seek to lead a crusade for the mass comprehension of what America is all about.

"The real fire within the builders of America was faith. Faith in the provident God that prodded and guided them. Faith in themselves as the children of God, endowed with purposes beyond the mere struggle for survival. Faith in their country and its divined principle that proclaimed man's right to freedom and justice. Rights from His divine origin."

Ike's generic platitudes underwhelmed the crowd. He lost his place more than once in the prepared text. He struggled to finish.

"Forty-odd years ago, I left Abilene. Since then, I have seen demonstrated in our own land and in far corners of the Earth, on battlefields and around council tables, in schoolhouse and factory and farming communities, the indomitable spirit of Americans. From this rostrum, looking back at the American record through these years, I gain

personal inspiration and renewed devotion to America. There is nothing
who can frighten or defeat a people who in one man's lifetime have
accomplished so much."

The crowd lightly applauded.

"Ladies and gentlemen, I believe we can have peace with honor,
reasonable security with national sovereignty. I believe in the future of the
United States of America!"

The crowd cheered louder with "yays!" and "woos!"

Ike took a deep breath. *Thank God that's over. I was afraid I was
going to hate running for President. Now I'm sure I am.*

Dewey and Brownell were pale a few feet away.

"That was appalling," Dewey muttered, rain dripping down his
mustache. "Taft is going to crush us."

"I don't know," Brownell said slightly higher than a whisper. His eyes
narrowed.

"Are you kidding?" Dewey asked. "Did we watch the same speech?"

"Yes, but he was stumbling because he was reading from a speech. He
kept getting lost. He looked constrained."

"So, he'll be better if he talks off the cuff?"

"Probably."

"Then never give him a speech again."

☆☆☆☆☆

JULY 11, 1952

"WHAT DID I eat," Ike wailed. He laid on his bed in the Blackstone Hotel in
Chicago, clutching his stomach.

"You've eaten nothing but trash on the campaign trail," Milton, Ike's
younger brother, argued.

"Go peddle your papers," Ike muttered. Mamie laid next to Ike, ill and
barely conscious.

Knock knock.

"Can you get that?" Ike asked.

"I'm on it," Milton sighed. He opened the door. Dewey and Clay
entered the room.

"Any updates from the convention?" Ike asked.

Dewey chuckled. "Just got screamed at by a bunch of Taft forces."

"What do you mean 'screamed at'?" Milton asked.

"Exactly what he said!" Clay exclaimed. "They were collectively shouting at him. Like a hundred angry guys and gals. All at once."

"Why?"

"Why?" Clay laughed. "Don't you know anything about the Republican Party? Taft hates Dewey and Dewey hates Taft. They were put on this Earth to torture each other. Taft's forces were shouting that Dewey cost the party the '44 and '48 elections. And he sat there and took it like a champ. It was beautiful."

"I will admit it was one of my better performances."

"I'll root for anything that makes Taft red in the face," Ike muttered.

Taft and his proxies had attacked Ike for months. They claimed he was Jewish, which he did not mind, and an anti-Semite, which he did mind. They claimed he was a communist for befriending Soviet General Zhukov after World War II. They attacked his character by claiming he had an affair with Kay Summersby, his driver and friend from the war. Worse still, they claimed Mamie was an alcoholic since she sometimes became dizzy from an inner-ear disorder. In summation, Taft's forces saw Ike as a pawn of an un-American Paris-London-New York axis.

"You don't mean that," Milton prodded.

"Yes, I do."

"No, you don't. You don't hold animosity toward anyone."

Ike scoffed. "Politics is a lousy business. Where's MacArthur?" He was referring to the general from the Pacific Theater of World War II and the Korean War who was a right-wing firebrand. Ike served under MacArthur through the 1930s, but they'd subsequently grown apart.

"I believe he left after his keynote speech flopped," Dewey suggested. "Maybe he won't be Taft's VP pick after all."

"He won't be happy unless he's President himself. Or dictator," Ike said, losing strength. He let his head rest on the pillow behind him, sweat dripping off his bald scalp.

The phone rang with startling intensity that caused Milton to jolt in his seat.

Dewey grabbed the phone. "Hello?" He turned to Ike with a grin. "Brownell says you need to write your acceptance speech!"

Milton and Clay applauded the news.

"I don't want to!" Ike cried.

"Do you want to be President?" Dewey asked, his head tilting to the side as if disappointed by a child.

"I'd prefer it if my guts calm down. I won't be able to concentrate."

Dewey put the phone to his mouth again.

"He says he's too sick to write the speech. Okay. I understand." He turned to Milton. "Turn on the television."

Milton did as he was told. The convention floor came on the black-and-white screen. The delegates were voting for the first ballot.

"Taft will get close but not enough," Dewey muttered, still loosely holding the phone.

"Just watch!" Brownell audibly shouted so everyone could hear him.

Ike won 895 votes, far more than the 604 he needed to win. Taft only won 280.

Milton and Dewey were stunned. Dewey put the phone to his ear.

"What did you do? I pulled in most of the New York delegation, but how did you put us over the top by this much?"

"You have no idea what it's been like down here. Our Fair Play idea really worked," Brownell said. He was referring to Brownell and Lodge's plan to accuse the Taft campaign of "shenanigans" and claim that the Georgia and Louisiana delegations were biased. Taft said this was unfair, but the Convention supported the Fair Play Amendment, removing many of Taft's delegates.

"That doesn't explain how we won by such a large margin," Dewey said.

"We got down to Wisconsin on the roll call and we were still not over the top and we had thrown in all our reserve strength. Then Minnesota flipped and everything was fine. Getting the California delegation on our side didn't hurt either," Brownell said slyly.

"California!" Dewey exclaimed, jumping. The television had been turned on after California's votes were counted. "How'd you get California to switch from Warren?"

"Senator Nixon's an Eisenhower supporter. He's an internationalist and thinks the general is the best man to take back the White House. He convinced the California delegation to switch."

"You're a genius," Dewey congratulated.

The television showed the delegate count on the screen. Political commentators discussed the Fair Play Amendment and how Ike won on the first ballot. Ike lifted his head from the pillow to look at the television, leaving a sweat stain behind. He was the calmest man in the room.

"That was an awfully close call, wasn't it?"

☆☆☆☆☆

"WHERE ARE YOU going?" Clay shouted from the Blackstone Hotel's entrance. Ike, the presumptive Republican nominee, ran across the street, his gray fedora awkwardly tilted to the right.

The crowd around the hotel bursted with applause as their hero ran by. A group of die-hard supporters carrying signs that read "Hitch-Ikers" waved their signs with enthusiasm.

"Where am I going?" Ike shouted back. "I'm going across the street to say hello to Mr. Taft. I just called him and asked if I could come over." Clay and Brownell took off after their candidate, trying to keep up with the sixty-one-year-old who had been bitterly sick moments ago.

I won this contest against Taft but that doesn't mean I should rub it in his face. I need him and his supporters on my team if I'm going to win in November. It's like Germany in the war. I defeated them and then brought West Germany on the side of liberal democracy.

Ike neared the Hilton that based Taft's headquarters. Teary-eyed Taft supporters glared at Ike with confusion as he ran by. Ike took the elevator up to the ninth floor and knocked on Taft's door. His former rival emerged within moments, pale and distressed from defeat.

Ike was also agitated. *It took ten minutes to cross the street!*

They spoke for a few minutes and then went out to see the press.

"I want to congratulate General Eisenhower," Taft said courteously. "I shall do everything possible in the campaign to secure his election and to help his administration." Ike's light gray suit was distinct from Taft's black one and Ike's downcast demeanor surprisingly contrasted with Taft's upbeat energy.

☆☆☆☆☆

IKE HAD DINNER with Brownell and Clay that night to celebrate their victory. They quickly discussed Ike's first decision as a presidential candidate.

"Have you put any thought into who you want as a running mate?" Brownell asked as he raised food to his mouth.

Ike's brow furrowed.

"I thought that was up to the convention. I didn't realize that was for me to decide."

Brownell and Clay exchanged a look, exacerbated once more by their political novice of a candidate. Brownell turned back to Ike.

"Yes, sir, General, that is true insofar as balloting is concerned. But I am sure that the delegates will look to you exclusively for guidance."

Ike smiled, happy he could choose his own protégé.

"If you give us your choice," Brownell continued, "I will convey it to the other leaders of the party. We'll see to it that the selection is done smoothly at the convention." He gestured to himself and Clay.

I suppose I have been kicking around a few ideas in the back of my mind on who should be my John Adams, my Hannibal Hamlin. He began listing off names on his fingers.

"My first pick would be Charles Wilson, the president of General Electric. Seems like a bright guy. Next would be C. R. Smith, the president of American Airlines. They both seem like they have good executive ability. They'll need that if something were to happen to me or if they seek to succeed me."

Businessmen are so much more respectable than politicians.

Brownell and Clay exchanged another glance.

"General, these are all fine men," Brownell began gently, placing down his fork, "and I am sure they would make excellent Vice Presidents, but we really need a name that will be recognizable to the average delegate on the floor. Someone they can relate to."

Ike nodded, following along.

"In view of your age, we will want a young man. Preferably someone from the West Coast. Someone with political experience who can balance the ticket. General Clay, Governor Dewey, and I have discussed this. Unless you object, we recommend Senator Richard Nixon from California."

Ike nodded some more.

"Nixon," he said the name softly. "He's the congressman who managed the Hiss Case, correct?"

"That's correct," Brownell affirmed.

"I was really impressed with his handling of that issue. He dug up a Soviet spy who worked in the State Department and who was an aide to Roosevelt at Yalta. I could certainly see him becoming my Vice President."

"Awesome!" Brownell exclaimed, leaning back in his chair, relaxed. Clay leaned forward to push the point further.

"Republicans see you as an ally of the Eastern Establishment. Nixon's young, moderately conservative, and a Californian."

"Sounds wonderful," Ike said. "Clear his name with the party leaders. We can invite him over and tell him, if you'd like."

Clay breathed a sigh of relief. Nixon would not be surprised by this decision. Lodge, a Senator from Massachusetts, had approached Nixon on the Senate floor and offered him a deal: the Vice Presidency in exchange for the California delegation. Ike's team would have burned a bridge if the candidate rejected him as a running mate.

☆☆☆☆☆

DEWEY AND NIXON joined Ike, Brownell, and Clay.

"It would be an honor to be your Vice President, General," Nixon said. Nixon's suit, gray, was a shade lighter than Ike's sport's jacket. Nixon's tie had cartoon lightbulbs running down its front.

"We should celebrate with a nightcap!" Dewey exclaimed. The former New York governor prepared the drinks. He turned to Nixon. "Make me a promise. Don't get fat, don't lose your zeal, and you can be President one day."

Nixon smiled at the thought. He could leave his mark on history, like his heroes, Disraeli, the Roosevelts, Wilson, Churchill, and de Gaulle.

Ike felt a lump of sadness in his throat during the celebration.

I'll be officially nominated tomorrow. That means I'm going to resign from the Army. It's been forty-one years. From such an honorable profession to such a dirty one.

☆☆☆☆☆

JULY 12, 1952

PICTURES OF ABRAHAM Lincoln hung around the arena as Ike and Mamie stood center stage. Nixon and his wife, Pat, stood right behind him. The crowd boomed, "We like Ike! We like Ike!"

Ike beamed at the crowd, his smile stretching from ear to ear. He raised his hands and gave two "V for Victory" gestures, his raised arms forming a third V. It was based on the V symbol Winston Churchill used in World War II.

Ike looked slick in his black suit. Mamie held a bouquet and had a white cap and strings of pearls. She wore a belted, button-down pleated shirtdress. Nixon wore a gray khaki suit with a polka-dot tie. Pat wore a white patterned dress with a black collar and black belt, and her white beret was similar to Mamie's cap.

Ike began his acceptance speech once the furor died down.

"Mr. Chairman. My fellow Republicans.

"May I first thank you on behalf of Mrs. Eisenhower and myself for the warmth of your welcome. For us both this is our first entry into a political convention, and it is a heartwarming one. Thank you very much.

"Ladies and Gentlemen, you have summoned me on behalf of millions of your fellow Americans to lead a great crusade—for Freedom in America and Freedom in the world. I know something of the solemn responsibility of leading a crusade. I have led one. I take up this task, therefore, in a spirit of deep obligation. Mindful of its burdens and of its decisive importance. I accept your summons. I will lead *this* crusade."

The crowd applauded what would become a central theme of Ike's campaign. His campaign for the presidency was a crusade for peace in the world and moderation at home.

"Our aims—the aims of this Republican crusade—are clear: to sweep from office an administration which has fastened on every one of us the wastefulness, the arrogance and corruption in high places, the heavy burdens and anxieties which are the bitter fruit of a party too long in power.

"We are now at a moment in history when, under God, this nation of ours has become the mightiest temporal power and the mightiest spiritual force on earth. The destiny of mankind—the making of a world that will be fit for our children to live in—hangs in the balance on what we say and what we accomplish in these months ahead.

"We must use our power wisely for the good of all our people. If we do this, we will open a road into the future on which today's Americans, young and old, and the generations that come after them, can go forward —go forward to a life in which there will be far greater abundance of material, cultural, and spiritual rewards than our forefathers or we ever dreamed of.

"Ladies and gentlemen, my dear friends that have heaped upon me such honors, it is more than a nomination I accept today. It is a dedication —a dedication to the shining promise of tomorrow. As together we face that tomorrow, I beseech the prayers of all our people and the blessing and guidance of Almighty God."

The crowd cheered as Ike concluded. His eye was set on the highest office in the land, the office once held by Washington. He did not want that office just to hold power. He had one aim—to make sure that nothing like World War II could ever happen again. His son was still fighting in Korea. The world looked like it was hurtling toward global destruction in a nuclear inferno. Ike was the only one who could build lasting peace.

Nixon grabbed Ike's arm, lifting both of their arms over their heads. The crowd went wild. Nixon pointed at Ike, highlighting the Republican candidate for President.

☆☆☆☆☆

AUGUST 16, 1952

"I DON'T SEE the point of getting me on the campaign trail before Labor Day," Ike argued. "I suspect I have the energy for eight or nine good weeks of campaigning. We should save that for the end. I don't want to burn out and look like an old man near election day."

"But General," Clay began, "holding off until September will lead to accusations that you *are* too old to be President. And you *will* be the oldest President ever elected, breaking William Henry Harrison's record. And we all know what happened to him."

Clay referred to the ninth President, who died after a month in office due to catching pneumonia from not wearing his coat during his inaugural address, which occurred in a blizzard.

"I think campaigning around the country for eight or nine weeks with long hours every day and without breaks will show that I'm fit for my age," Ike stated, his arms crossed.

Ike and his team were staying in a cabin owned by Ike's friend, Aksel Nielson, in Fraser, Colorado.

I'm loving this elevation. 8700 feet. This looks like a good team. Dewey. Brownell. Adams. Clay. Lodge. I suppose they're my subordinates for this rodeo. Kind of like Bedell Smith and Tex Lee were my key subordinates at SHAEF during the war. Think I'll conduct this operation the way I did Overlord. Hold the reins for overall strategy but let these boys deal with the details. This campaign has to go all-out if we're going to end twenty years of Democratic control of the White House. And we have to to end the Korean conflict and prevent World War III.

"I heard Stevenson's acceptance speech on the radio," Ike said, switching topics. "He sounded pretty good. How hard do we think it will be to beat him?"

The Democratic convention was held in the same arena in Chicago as the Republican convention had been two weeks earlier. They nominated Adlai Stevenson, the popular governor of Illinois, based on Truman's endorsement. Stevenson portrayed the Republicans as the party of Herbert Hoover and the Great Depression. Though he claimed to be FDR's heir, Stevenson's centrist politics were closer to Ike's.

Adams scoffed, his weight resting on the circular wooden table sitting between the team.

"Don't worry, Stevenson's too accomplished an orator. He will be easy to beat."

That sounds awfully cocky, Ike thought. *Overconfidence cost Dewey the '48 election. We can't make that mistake again.*

"We could exploit the fact that Stevenson is divorced and single, while the General is happily married," Brownell suggested. "That will certainly increase our appeal to women voters."

"Because if he couldn't make one woman happy, how could he make all of them happy?" Lodge asked.

"That, and it makes him less relatable and approachable. It also opens the door to rumors we could spread about his sexual orientation."

"What do you mean?" Dewey asked.

"You know," Brownell suggested. "We could imply he's a queer."

"Not on my watch!" Ike declared, his face giving a scarlet hew. "I'll have nothing to do with a campaign that attacks an opponent on those grounds. Personal issues like that are no one's business."

The room was awkwardly silent, unsure what to make of the candidate's outburst. Was he going to be like this the entire time?

Adams broke the silence.

"We should discuss some of the lighter issues of the campaign. Have we settled on 'I Like Ike' as the slogan?"

"It's simple enough," Dewey replied. The group nodded.

"Our polling suggests the voters trust Ike to be an adult and keep them safe. They also think he'll fulfill his promise of ending the Korean War. They care less about his opinions on various issues. That's why I think it makes sense to emphasize people's innate trust in him," Adams explained.

Everyone nodded, though Ike frowned. *Why don't they care about my views? I want to break this country from the road to socialism that Roosevelt put us on and set it on the path of moderation and balanced budgets. How can I do that if the people don't care what my views are? I bet they'll care if they see my policies working.*

"I'll instruct the manufacturer to mass produce 'I Like Ike' buttons and pins," Adams said, looking at his notes on a legal pad. "They'll also make accessories for our female supporters."

"Like what?" Clay asked.

"Earrings, dresses, and sunglasses with 'Ike' written on them. Stuff like that," Adams answered.

"Would a woman be interested in something like that?" Mamie asked, having just sat down and unsure how she felt about other women wearing her husband's name.

"I've already been getting hundreds of requests for that sort of paraphernalia," Adams replied. "It'll be a good way of locking down the women's vote."

Mamie remained unconvinced. Adams turned back to Ike.

"I also think we should move ahead with the three Cs as your campaign message."

"What were they again?" Ike asked.

"Communism, Corruption, Korea."

"Doesn't Korea start with a K?"

"I don't think the average voter knows that. Three Cs sounds better than two Cs and a K."

"I'm not sure we should be treating the American people like they're stupid," Ike replied.

"I thought you were doing three Ps, not three Cs," Mamie said to Ike.

"What are the three Ps?" Adams asked, getting frustrated and giving Lodge a glance that sought validation.

"I thought my husband was running on Peace, Prosperity, and Progress," Mamie answered.

"What difference does that make?" Adams asked.

"It's more positive," Mamie replied. "It shows we're trying to move the country in a positive direction instead of just being negative toward the Democrats."

The men looked at each other. That was a good point. Ike smiled.

Why do I get the feeling that Mamie is a better campaigner than all of us men?

"I still think 1K 2C highlights Ike's strength at national security and his promise to clean up Washington. I'll keep that in my notes for now," Adams said, annoyed that the candidate's wife was besting a governor and campaign chairman. "Let's move on to living arrangements on the campaign."

Ike sighed, fighting to control his frustration. *This part of work is so boring. It's almost a deterrent to starting new jobs.*

"We'll mostly be staying in hotels every time the train enters a new city. I'll stay in the room next to the general. Mamie can stay in a room further down the hall," Adams explained. "That will give me access to the candidate at my convenience."

"Not if I have anything to say about it!" Mamie snapped. "I'll be staying in Ike's room. I want to be able to pat his bald head whenever I want to!"

Adams glared at Ike as if to plead, 'why is your wife so demanding?' Ike smiled back; he enjoyed seeing Mamie torture these conceited politicians.

Adams turned to the group.

"I suppose I can alter the arrangements."

Mamie smiled.

Lodge watched the interactions between Adams and Mamie with a mixture of sadness and relief. He was glad he didn't have to deal with Mamie's demands but sad that he had to hand over the position of campaign chairman to Adams. Lodge was too busy defending his Senate seat from Democratic congressman John Kennedy.

"Speaking of altering the arrangements," Lodge began, "I'm confident that I can have Massachusetts locked up by November. How do we feel about Pennsylvania?"

"It may be close there," Dewey said.

"Could we add a campaign stop?" Lodge asked.

"I would love to make an appearance in Philadelphia," Ike said with a smile. "The city of the Declaration and Constitution."

"I can draw up a plan for adding Philadelphia to the campaign in September or so," Adams offered, trying to get back in Ike's good graces. "It shouldn't be more than thirty-five pages."

Ike's eyes widened in surprise. He laughed.

"Politics is a funny thing. Thirty-five pages to get me into Philadelphia. The invasion of Normandy was on five pages." Adams shrugged. "When am I going to the South? I bet they have great food there."

The politicians looked at each other in surprise. Brownell, who had a light touch with the political novice, broke the news.

"General, the South has been solidly Democratic since the Civil War. Republicans never campaign there. It's a waste of time and resources. We'll be more competitive elsewhere."

Ike looked like a stubborn child. He rumpled his eyebrows.

"What do you mean I'm not going to the South? I'm running for President of all the country, aren't I? I'll tell you, gentlemen, I'm going to go into the South right after Labor Day."

Adams threw his legal pad on the table.

"This changes everything! I have to make a whole new schedule!" He left the table to start making phone calls. "So many arrangements!"

The other politicians turned back to Ike.

"This will have to change your message in the Southern states," Brownell said. "Like the Negro question, for instance. How vocal do you want to be in supporting racial integration during the campaign?"

"Wouldn't it be more strategic to not put that issue center stage and focus on it once we're in the White House?" Ike asked. "It's so divisive, where attacking the Truman administration's corruption isn't."

"I agree," Brownell said. "I still like the ideas we've talked about where we can desegregate the District of Columbia and appoint pro-integration judges as a way to advance that issue in a quiet way that won't draw too much attention." Ike nodded. "What about the Texas tidelands issue?"

Brownell referred to a controversy between Texas and the federal government over which had authority over tidelands located in Texas.

"The treaty gives them to Texas, right?" Ike asked, his left arm now casually laying over the side of the chair. "I feel that settles the issue."

"That will upset voters in the northeast."

"I'm compelled to remark that I believe what I believe and won't tailor my opinions and convictions to the one single measure of net vote appeal," Ike replied. Mamie smiled.

"If you say so," Brownell said.

"What about religion?" Dewey asked. "That's particularly important in the South." The governor had risen to his feet and now paced around the room. "What's your denomination?"

"I don't have one," Ike answered nonchalantly.

"That's a problem," Dewey replied, his hands behind his back.

"I try to be a nonconformist. Like my brothers. We've always been that way."

"That won't help if you're trying to win southern votes." Dewey turned to Mamie. "What about you? What's your denomination?"

"Presbyterian."

Dewey turned back to Ike.

"How would you feel about becoming a Presbyterian?"

"That seems like an awfully big commitment to win a political campaign."

"It would be easier to say you're a Presbyterian than to say you're a Christian that doesn't belong to a denomination," Clay argued.

"I think I'd rather maintain my independence."

Adams returned to the room, looking confused.

"I started making the calls to alter the schedule when I saw some nuns outside. I think they want to see the candidate."

Ike smiled. *Talk about religion!*

"We don't have time for that," Dewey said.

"Oh, please!" Ike exclaimed as he stood up. "When I consider the dedication of those people, the least I can do is pay my respects." He exited the cabin to meet his supporters, his famous 'Ike grin' charming all.

☆☆☆☆☆

SEPTEMBER 15, 1952

"THIS IS WHAT your dollar was worth twenty years ago!" Ike exclaimed from the back of *Look Ahead, Neighbor*, his personal campaign train. Several microphones reached just below his mouth so the large crowd could hear him. He lifted a four-foot block of wood over his head to represent a dollar in 1932. He then placed the wood down and grabbed a small saw.

The crowd cheered. The saw was one of their favorite campaign stunts. Ike sawed the wood in half. Or roughly in half. He lifted the new two-foot piece of wood over his head.

"This is what twenty years of Democratic rule has done to your dollar!" he shouted. "The Democrats don't appreciate what deficits do to inflation and *your* savings!"

The crowd cheered again.

"A new administration that balances the budget and reduces our debt will restore your purchasing power!"

The crowd cheered once more. It was time for Ike to play his last, strongest card. He placed the wood down.

"Now do you want to see my Mamie?"

The crowd boomed with approval. Signs went up saying, "I Like Ike but I LOVE Mamie!" Mamie walked onto the platform from within the train and waived. The crowd cheered for her far louder than they had for Ike and his wood gimmick.

Ike beamed with satisfaction and approval as his wife received adoration.

Look how she waives at them. Still saucy about the face. She's a better campaigner than I am. That's because she sounds more like a woman with common sense than an average politician's wife. She's helpful in identifying when my speeches are in character, even though she's more conservative than me. She's so good with our fans, even writing seventy-five letters a day in response to the flood of mail we get.

☆☆☆☆☆

SEPTEMBER 18, 1952

LOOK AHEAD, NEIGHBOR hurtled noisily down the tracks to Kansas City.

Ba-dump, Ba-dump, Ba-dump.

Harry Truman must be the most partisan President since James Polk, Ike thought as he read a campaign document. President Truman had invited Stevenson to the White House. There, the Democratic candidate received a briefing from Chairman of the Joint Chiefs Omar Bradley and CIA Director Walter "Bedell" Smith on the state of the world. Ike had not received a similar invitation.

He sees the world in black and white. When he thought I was a Democrat he was ready to give me the presidency. But now that he knows I'm a Republican he's declared war. He's campaigned more than Stevenson so far.

Ike put the campaign document aside and grabbed his notes for the speech he planned to give on honesty in government. *I wonder if I should discuss patronage. Such a wicked word. I could mention that Milton won't be given a position in my administration even though he's more than qualified. But patronage cannot be allowed in an honest government.*

Adams came over with his aide, Robert Cutler, and with Jim Hagerty, who ran the campaign's media relations.

"We have a problem," Adams said, a panicked look on his face.

"What is it?" Ike asked. *I've barely done anything today. What could be so bad?*

Hagerty handed Ike a telegram.

"Peter Edison of the *Washington Post* has reported that Senator Nixon has a slush fund made up of campaign donations that he uses for personal purposes," Adams explained.

Oh my God, Ike thought. *Cleaning up corruption is a key plank of my campaign, and that fool goes and does this?*

"How much are we talking about?" Ike asked.

"The *Post* says $18,000."

"Do we know where he got it from?"

"A handful of California millionaires. For some speeches and letters he's signed. Stuff like that."

Ike frowned and leaned back in his seat.

Dick's been a problem since this campaign started. I tried to teach him trout fishing when we were in Colorado in August, but he couldn't do an outdoor activity to save his life. On the other hand, he's been a good lightning rod on the trail. I've been doing my best to keep above partisanship and Dick has done a good job in keeping the pressure on Stevenson and Truman. But that also means that he's been on the receiving end of most of their attacks. They've been getting nasty, especially Truman.

"Is it all in the fund or has he received any of it personally?"

"The story says it's all in the fund."

"That's good, at least. What should we do about this?" Ike asked.

"Normally," Hagerty began, speaking for the first time, "we wouldn't comment on a *Post* story. But Senator Nixon was asked about the issue at a campaign stop in Marysville, California. He appears to have felt differently."

"What did he say?" Ike asked in anticipation.

"He said the story was a communist conspiracy against him."

Ike threw his head backward, his eyes wide. He was dumbfounded.

"This is bound to get the story a lot of attention," Hagerty continued.

I might have to get him off the ticket. I do my best to be a man of character. It's not always easy. I have a temper and humans are fundamentally self-interested. But I try my best. Dick having a slush fund as my running mate undermines that. On the other hand, he's been popular with the Republican base. They might turn on me if I fire him. That could kill my chances in November. Maybe I need to get him to resign out of honor?

"Telegraph this to Dick," Ike ordered Hagerty. Hagerty put pen to paper to take notes. "'I suggest immediate publication by you of all documentary evidence, including amounts received in full, all payments from it, and the exact nature of the speeches, letters, addresses and documents for which expenses were met out of fund. The fact that you never received a cent in cash is of the utmost importance and should be made clear in the evidence given the public.

"Our train schedules today seemingly prevent a telephone conversation, but you know I am ready to consult with you on the matter whenever it is physically possible."

Hagerty nodded as Ike finished. The candidate turned back to Adams.

"If Nixon has to resign, we can't possibly win this election," Ike said. "Let's make our mistakes slowly."

"If we did have to replace him, do you have any ideas on who you'd want?"

"Should probably stick with a Californian. What about Earl Warren?"

"He should work. Popular with liberals and moderates."

"But we're trying to maintain support from our right flank. Bill Knowland might be better since he's a Taft supporter from California. We should get this Nixon business approved by Senator Douglas on the Ethics Committee, as well. He's a Democrat. That will give it more credibility."

Ike's advisors walked away. He put his finger to his lips.

This could get as bad as the Patton-slapping incident in '43. I want all the information available on this before I make a decision. And this will be my *decision.*

☆☆☆☆☆

"I AM DISTURBED by this news of so-called 'slush funds!'" Ike declared at a campaign stop in Kansas City from the back of *Look Ahead, Neighbor.* "Senator Nixon is the type of young leader this country needs! But he must prove himself!"

The crowd applauded in agreement.

"Anyone associated with our crusade to restore honest government to Washington must be of the highest character! Of what avail is it for us to carry on this crusade against the business of what has been going on in Washington if we ourselves aren't as clean as a hound's tooth?"

☆☆☆☆☆

SEPTEMBER 21, 1952

IKE PACED BACK and forth on *Look Ahead, Neighbor*. Nixon never resigned and critics were questioning Ike's character for not removing him from the ticket. The Democrats were on the attack, although Stevenson was oddly quiet. Adams called Senator Knowland, who was inbound from his Hawaii vacation to potentially replace Nixon. The Republican National Committee arranged for Nixon to have airtime on the major channels. Dewey instructed Nixon that he was to use the airtime to resign from the ticket. Nixon refused, saying he needed to hear the instructions from Ike himself.

He's undermining my crusade. I ran for President to build a lasting peace in the world and I'm going to be denied that because of some senator from California who isn't even forty. The ethics report isn't in yet. These are difficult days.

Ike stopped pacing when Hagerty came into the room.

"We have him on the phone."

Ike nodded and followed Hagerty. He took the black phone and its cord in his hand.

"Hello, Dick," Ike said. "You've been taking a lot of heat the last couple of days." There was a pause.

"Yeah, it's been pretty rough," Nixon replied.

"I haven't made a decision." Ike tried easing Nixon's anxiety by telling him what he was thinking but Nixon remained silent. *I sent millions into harm's way. Why is deciding about one man's career so hard?*

Nixon refused to speak. Declaring his innocence would not win Ike's empathy. And he wasn't about to offer his resignation. Ike would have to be the butcher if he wanted him gone.

"I don't want to be in the position of condemning an innocent man," Ike continued, finally breaking the awkward silence. "I think you ought to go on nationwide television and tell them everything there is to tell, everything you can remember since the day you entered public life. Tell them about any money you have ever received."

That was easy for Ike to say but hard for Nixon to do. Ike was asking him to throw away any privacy that he and Pat enjoyed.

"Will you endorse me if I do that?" Nixon asked, desperate for approval.

Ike hesitated and sighed in frustration.

"This is an awfully hard thing for me to decide," the man who launched Operation Overlord explained. "You are the one who has to decide what to do. After all, if the impression got around that you got off the ticket because I forced you off, it is going to be very bad. On the other hand, if I issue a statement now backing you up, in effect people will accuse me of condoning wrongdoing."

"General," Nixon began, "do you think after the television program an announcement could be made one way or the other?" He was desperate for the uncertainty to end and resented Ike perpetuating it.

"We will have to wait three or four days after the television show to see what the effect of the program is."

Three or four days! That was too far for Nixon. How much did Ike expect of him? How much was he willing to endure to be *Vice* President? How could Ike expect him to humiliate himself in front of the world and not then say enough is enough?

"General, the great trouble here is the indecision. There comes a time in politics when you have to shit or get off the pot."

Ike's eyebrows furrowed. *What did he say to me? No one's talked to me that way in years. Not Montgomery. Not even Patton.*

They hung up shortly thereafter. Their problem was not yet resolved, though Nixon had survived his phone call with Ike. But his greater test was still to come.

☆☆☆☆☆

SEPTEMBER 23, 1952

IKE, MAMIE, MILTON, and Ike's team arrived at the Cleveland Public Auditorium to watch Nixon's speech on television. It was to be broadcasted at 9:30 PM ET, after the Milton Berle show. Ike sat between Mamie and Bill Robinson, an executive for the *New York Herald Tribune* and one of Ike's closer friends. Ike held a legal pad in his left hand and a pen in his right. They were in the auditorium's manager's office.

A lot had happened in the past few days. The ethics report was released and cleared Nixon of any wrongdoing, though most Americans were still suspicious of his actions. A report then revealed that Stevenson possessed a fund of $69,000, far larger than Nixon's.

Dick put me through hell with this scandal. I know he's also struggling, but my character's been challenged because of his stupid mistakes. I hope Dewey made clear that he needs to resign during his speech when they spoke a couple hours ago.

Nixon's speech finally started. The image was in black and white, and Nixon's gray suit blended him into the gray background.

Hope he learns from that mistake, Ike thought.

Nixon began.

"My Fellow Americans,

"I come before you tonight as a candidate for the vice-presidency and as a man whose honesty and integrity has been questioned.

"Now, the usual political thing to do when charges are made against you is to either ignore them or to deny them without giving details. I believe we have had enough of that in the United States, particularly with the present administration in Washington D.C.

"I have a theory, too, that the best and only answer to a smear or an honest misunderstanding of the facts is to tell the truth. And that is why I am here tonight. I want to tell you my side of the case.

"I am sure that you have read the charges, and you have heard it, that I, Senator Nixon, took $18,000 from a group of my supporters.

"Now, was that wrong? And let me say that it was wrong. I am saying it, incidentally, that it was wrong, just not illegal, because it isn't a question of whether it was legal or illegal, that isn't enough. The question is, was it morally wrong? I say that it was morally wrong if any of that $18,000 went to Senator Nixon, for my personal use. I say that it was morally wrong if it was secretly given and secretly handled.

"And I say that it was morally wrong if any of the contributors got special favors for the contributions that they made.

"And to answer those questions let me say this—not a cent of the $18,000 or any other money of that type ever went to me for my personal use. Every penny of it was used to pay for political expenses that I did not think should be charged to the taxpayers of the United States.

"One other thing I probably should tell you, because if I don't, they will probably be saying this about me, too. We did get something, a gift, after the election.

"A man down in Texas heard Pat on the radio mention the fact that our two youngsters would like to have a dog, and believe it or not, the day before we left on this campaign trip we got a message from Union Station in Baltimore, saying they had a package for us. We went down to get it. You know what it was?

"It was a little cocker spaniel dog, in a crate that he had sent all the way from Texas, black and white, spotted, and our little girl Tricia, the six-year-old, named it Checkers.

"And you know, the kids, like all kids, loved the dog, and I just want to say this, right now, that regardless of what they say about it, we are going to keep it."

Mamie teared up as Nixon discussed Checkers. Ike, who was growing more and more frustrated that Nixon disobeyed his orders, fought to not roll his eyes at his wife's response.

"I think you will agree with me—because, folks, remember, a man that's to be President of the United States, a man that is to be Vice President of the United States, must have the confidence of all the people. And that's why I'm doing what I'm doing. And that is why I suggest that Mr. Stevenson and Mr. Sparkman, if they are under attack, that should be what they are doing."

Ike's face flashed red. *Goddamn it! He didn't name me, but he's thrown me under the bus too! The public will demand my personal finances. That will include any proceeds I earned from* Crusade in Europe. *I paid capital gains taxes on that book, not income taxes. That was IRS policy. That saved me a fortune, but the press will attack me for it anyway. Why the hell did he have to go and say that?*

Ike slammed his pen on his legal pad in frustration. He returned to listening to his running mate's speech.

"I think my country is in danger. And I think the only man that can save America at this time is the man that's running for President, on my ticket, Dwight Eisenhower.

"You say, why do I think it is in danger? And I say look at the record. Seven years of the Truman-Acheson administration, and what's happened? Six hundred million people lost to Communists.

"And a war in Korea in which we have lost 117,000 American casualties, and I say that those in the State Department that made the mistakes which caused that war and which resulted in those losses should be kicked out of the State Department just as fast as we can get them out of there.

"And let me say that I know Mr. Stevenson won't do that because he defends the Truman policy, and I know that Dwight Eisenhower will do that, and he will give America the leadership that it needs."

Nixon's speech ended a few minutes later. Mamie was on her third tissue as she kept wiping away tears. Ike turned to Arthur Summerfield, the chairman of the Republican National Committee.

"Well, Arthur, you certainly got your $75,000 worth."

He did it. He beat me. I thought I was smarter than all the politicians after I beat Taft. But that junior senator made it so I couldn't fire him even if I wanted to. And now I have to disclose my own finances. He's smart. But now I'm not sure if I can trust him going forward. What is it the Democrats call him? Tricky Dick? That fits more than I realized.

Milton turned to his brother.

"You know you'll have to cooperate when it comes time to disclose your finances, right?"

It was one thing to think on his own what he must do. It was another to hear someone else say it. Ike's face turned red.

"I'll not do that! Not ever!" he screamed. He stomped around the room. *The press will never let me hear the end of it if they see what I paid in taxes on* Crusade.

☆☆☆☆☆

"WE WANT NIXON! We want Nixon!" the Cleveland crowd chanted as Ike came on stage. He had planned to speak on inflation, but there was only one topic anyone wanted to hear about.

"I have seen many brave men in tough situations," Ike began once the crowd stopped chanting, "but I have never seen anyone come through in better fashion than Senator Nixon did tonight."

The crowd cheered for their hero. They loved his speech and his honesty, especially about his daughters' new puppy.

"I am not intending to duck any responsibility that falls upon me as the standard bearer of the Republican Party. The final decision is mine, and I have not yet made up my mind. It is obvious that I have to have something more than a single presentation, necessarily limited to thirty minutes."

Ike was reminding the crowd who was in command. But they were demoralized to hear that their new favorite politician was still at risk of losing his position. Ike renewed their spirits by reading the telegram he had sent to Nixon, praising his speech, and proposing they both fly to Wheeling, Virginia, to meet the following night.

The old general gave his subordinate a direct order for the whole country to see.

☆☆☆☆☆

IKE STOOD ON the tarmac as Nixon's plane landed. A crowd of supporters waited behind him. They clamored with approval as Nixon and Pat slowly made their way down the steps of the airplane. The couple was exhausted from the experience, humiliated that their privacy was annihilated and angry at Ike for putting them through it. Pat glared at Ike as he took Nixon in his embrace.

"General," Nixon said in confusion, "you didn't need to come to the airport."

Ike smiled. His opinion of Nixon shifted overnight. *He may be making me disclose my finances, but he also went through hell, which shows what men are really made of. And Dick passed with flying colors.*

"Why not?" Ike asked with a huge grin. "You're my boy!"

The underdog had won the fight; his popularity greater than ever. But Ike asserted who was in charge.

☆☆☆☆☆

OCTOBER 3, 1952

BA-DUMP, BA-DUMP, BA-DUMP.

Look Ahead, Neighbor raced toward Milwaukee, Wisconsin, where Ike was to give a campaign speech while sharing the stage with the state's Republican leaders. He smiled as he reviewed his notes, enjoying his sense of calm after the previous crisis-filled weeks.

We can finally get back to the issues now that Dick's fund scandal is behind us. This campaign is important. Can't get bogged down in such nonsense. I have to keep my eye on the ball, on the ultimate goal. A lasting peace. Nothing like the world wars can ever happen again and my administration must diffuse East-West tension to make World War III impossible. Then the world, and particularly the United States, can reduce defense spending. It's disgusting how much this Cold War with Stalin is costing us. Once we reduce that expenditure we can pay off the national debt that's been building since the Great Depression. The debt threatens our economy and the value of our money and savings. It's irresponsible to pass it down to future generations and my administration will set in motion its elimination. World peace. Disarmament. A national surplus. That's why I'm running for President. That's why I have to win.

Wisconsin Governor Walter Kohler approached Ike's sitting area. He had thin hair and a large nose and wore a gray pinstripe suit with a diagonal stripe tie.

"Can I join you?" Kohler asked.

"Of course," Ike replied. Kohler sat down.

"It's an honor to campaign with you, General."

"The honor's all mine."

"Do you mind if I look at the speech you're going to deliver later? I'd like to know what to expect. This is a normal procedure in political campaigns."

"I understand. This might be my first election, but I've been on the campaign trail for weeks now. Every Governor I've done an event with has wanted to clear my speeches in advance."

"Thank you for your understanding."

Ike handed his speech over to Kohler. Kohler glanced it over, nodding along as he read. He paused, then reread the same paragraph. Then he read it a third time. He finally looked up at Ike.

"Can I ask you about this particular section?"

"Which one?"

"This one here." Kohler pointed his pen at the page so Ike could see.

The paragraph read, "There have been charges of disloyalty against General George Marshall. I know him, as a man and a soldier, to be dedicated with singular selflessness and the profoundest patriotism to the service of America."

Ike smiled. "That's my favorite part of the speech. What's wrong with it?"

"It's obvious what you're doing, General. You can't say that. Especially in Wisconsin."

"Why not?" Ike asked glibly.

"You know why. *He's* sharing the stage with us at the event later today."

"Joe's not even mentioned."

"The reference is clear. You're defending Marshall in McCarthy's backyard. While he's on stage with you."

Ike's jaw shut tightly. *Of course that's what I'm doing. Because how dare anyone say such a thing about General Marshall? He is a perfect example of patriotism and loyal service to the United States.*

"McCarthy deserves it. He said General Marshall was in bed with Stalin and part of the largest conspiracy in history."

"You can disagree with him all you want. That's not my business. But you *can't* say this in a speech *in* Wisconsin. It will divide the local Republican Party. We'll lose the state. We already lost it in '48 and this will make us lose it again. Hell, *I'll* probably lose reelection if you say this."

It took long enough for him to name his actual concern. It was bad enough I had to sit in the same room as McCarthy in that hotel last night as my team and Kohler's went over the plan for today. Had to restrain myself to not gut him for what he said about my mentor.

"I don't owe McCarthy a damn thing," Ike declared. "He supported Taft in the primary. And he's hurting me with Democrats who might support me otherwise. Eleanor Roosevelt said she'd never support me just for joining the same party as McCarthy."

"I don't care what that old woman says. Her husband's administration was an insult to American values and the Constitution."

"You can believe what you want," Ike retorted, throwing the Governor's words back at him, "but I *will* defend General Marshall today. He's the greatest American of my lifetime."

Kohler sighed. He turned and shouted, "Adams!" There was a pause. "Adams!"

A staffer approached Kohler.

"Do you need anything, Governor?"

"Can you find Governor Adams?"

The staffer left. Adams arrived within minutes.

"What's the problem?" Adams asked.

"Have you read the General's speech for today?"

"Not this one, no."

Kohler handed him the speech. Adams scanned it and paused, as Kohler had done. He looked at Ike.

"You can't say this about Marshall."

Damn politicians always stick together.

"This is important to me, Sherman."

"Do you know what this will look like if you insult McCarthy while he's on stage with you?"

"The man's a curse, both domestically and in the world."

"I don't like him any more than you do. But we shouldn't throw away Wisconsin just to feel good about ourselves."

"If anything, McCarthy is *helping* the communist cause because the Soviets are using him in their propaganda."

"I'm not arguing with you."

"Well, wait," Kohler jumped in. "Communist infiltration of the federal government *is* a problem."

"Oh, I agree," Ike said as Adams nodded. "But he's approaching it the wrong way. Terrorizing people in hearings and such. It's un-American. And it's clear he cares more about the publicity than actually solving the problem."

"But that doesn't change the fact that we'll lose the state if you say this today," Adams asserted as he shook the speech in his hands.

Ike paused. *Adams is smart. I trust him. But this seems unethical. Throwing away the chance to defend a hero like Marshall and repudiate a villain like McCarthy. Then again, losing Wisconsin hurts my chances to win the presidency. And all those goals I was thinking about earlier. Peace. Disarmament. Debt reduction. They'd all be lost. I think General Marshall would understand.*

"You *really* think the paragraph should be removed?" Ike asked, his face and neck turning purple from frustration.

"Yes," Adams answered.

"Well, drop it."

Kohler took a sigh of relief, slumping back in his seat.

"I handled the subject pretty thoroughly in Denver," Ike said, justifying himself. "There's no reason to repeat it tonight."

☆☆☆☆☆

"COMMUNISM HAS INSINUATED itself into our schools, our public forums, some of our news channels, some of our labor unions, and, most terrifyingly, into our government itself."

Ike lacked his famous smile during the campaign event and the energy of his convictions during his speech. The Wisconsin crowd was visibly underwhelmed as they watched the candidate with blank faces. Mamie, Adams, Kohler, McCarthy, and others standing behind Ike on stage tried to make eye contact with one another, without it being obvious, to get affirmation that he was doing as poorly as it looked.

"It has infected virtually every department, every agency, every bureau, every section of our government. The loss of China and the surrender of whole nations in Eastern Europe was due to the Reds in Washington."

Every word was a strain. Mamie shook her head, distraught that her husband was proclaiming things he didn't believe. McCarthy's face wore a smug grin; his party's presidential candidate was making a speech he could have given on the Senate floor.

"Their penetration of the government meant—in its most ugly triumph —treason itself. Freedom must defend itself with courage, with care, with force and with fairness. I call for respect for the integrity of fellow citizens who enjoy the right to disagree."

Even this line, which was a veiled criticism of McCarthy, was delivered as a prisoner reading their captive's notes.

"The right to question a man's judgment carries with it no automatic right to question his honor."

The crowd lightly applauded. This was one of the most mediocre campaign speeches they had ever seen.

Ike was on autopilot as the speech ended and he exited the stage. He paused as several other officials and campaign leaders crowded near the stage's exit, all desperate to get off. Someone tugged on Ike's arm. His body shifted in the tug's direction, though his eyes were slow to follow. His stomach rolled as he realized McCarthy was gripping his arm with his left hand and extending his right.

You're kidding me. He wants to shake my hand?

Ike noticed that hundreds of people in the crowd were still watching the stage.

Oh, no. I can't let them see—

He glanced at McCarthy, whose lips formed a sinister grin.

This son of a bitch! He knows what he's doing. I either have to shake his hand, and therefore endorse him, or risk upsetting the crowd. God damn it!

Ike slowly, reluctantly, raised his arm. McCarthy clasped Ike's hand and vigorously shook it. The crowd applauded. That caught Mamie's and Adams' attention. Their mouths dropped at what they saw.

Ike pulled back as soon as he thought the crowd was satisfied. He raced off the stage, his face bright red.

Ugh! I don't remember the last time my skin crawled this much! Why do I feel like I shook hands with Hitler?

☆☆☆☆☆

"Although he clearly lacked enthusiasm about campaigning with McCarthy, General Eisenhower did bow to the Wisconsin Senator's urging and eliminated from his Milwaukee speech tonight a defense of his old friend and chief, General of the Army George C. Marshall," wrote William Lawrence of the *New York Times.*

Ike seethed as he read the newspaper aboard *Look Ahead, Neighbor.* He was humiliated. Jim Hagerty, who handled the campaign's media relations, had distributed the Milwaukee speech to the press *before* the defense of Marshall was removed. Reporters noted its absence from the event. The Democrats pounced, once again. They attacked Ike's character. No one hit harder than President Truman.

"I had never thought the man who is now the Republican candidate could stoop so low," the *Times* quoted Truman as saying. "A man who betrays his friends in such a fashion is not to be trusted with the great office of President of the United States."

Why did I make the stupid decision of running for President? Ike asked himself. *I'm unworthy of the office of Washington and Lincoln.*

"This is not the only shameful act that the Republican nominee has taken as of late," Truman's words continued. "He also refuses to reject the endorsement of Republican Senator Pat McCarran. McCarran, as everyone knows, defends the racist immigration laws established by Republican Presidents Harding and Coolidge. Those laws benefit immigrants from Western Europe at the expense of Eastern and Southern Europeans, Jews, and people from Asia. McCarran and other Republicans defend these laws because they believe Western Europeans are the master race, just as Hitler and the Nazis did. I suppose Eisenhower, who General Marshall put in charge of liberating Europe during the war, agrees with them."

How low can you get? Ike thought. *Implying that I'm a Nazi! This is worse than when he claims I'm a Wall Street stooge. He's probably mad that I declined coming to the White House for a foreign policy briefing, as Stevenson had done. Had to reject his peace offer because I have to keep Taft and his supporters on my team if I want any hope of winning this election.*

He continued reading.

"General Eisenhower notified Senator McCarthy of his intent to defend Marshall during their meeting the night before the Milwaukee speech. McCarthy told Eisenhower that he had no particular objection to General Eisenhower's saying anything he wished to say, but he believed a defense of General Marshall could be made better before another audience."

That's not true! Damn McCarthy! He fed the press this lie. I know he did. I'm not going to forget this. Not any of it! Not the handshake, not the lie, not making me look like a jerk. He's made an enemy, a big one!

I'm going to have to make this up to General Marshall. Be extra sweet to him if I do become President, which looks doubtful now. He's the most sensible man I've ever known. I'm sure we can bridge this misunderstanding. I just can't believe I did this. It might be the worst mistake I have ever made. Not something stupid from when I was a teenager or a fresh Army officer. But now, when I'm a sixty-one-year-old man. And Marshall's done so much for me. He convinced President Roosevelt of my idea for a cross-channel attack in World War II. He advanced me through the ranks and gave me a big role in that war. Those were better times, for me, anyway.

This is the worst moment since I declared my candidacy. Between this and Dick's scandal, we're really off track. And my character, my sense of duty to those close to me, has been dragged through the mud because of these episodes. I'm sure I'm no longer seen as the honorable war hero in the public's eyes.

We might lose. Four more years of Democratic rule will lead to national bankruptcy and World War III. I can't allow that to happen. I have to do something to regain our momentum. Something big to remind the people why they drafted me to run for President.

I know exactly which issue to use.

☆☆☆☆☆

OCTOBER 24, 1952

THE MASONIC TEMPLE in Detroit, Michigan, contained sixteen floors and was 210 feet tall. A freemason himself, George Washington's tools were brought in to help construct the huge building in the early 1920s.

Ike stood on the stage of one of the Temple's three theaters. Thousands of supporters and dozens of journalists eagerly waited for him to begin. Ike had slipped in the polls following the McCarthy incident, but his campaign stabilized his decline via round-the-clock television ads. Stevenson, meanwhile, had thought using television to help his campaign demeaned the presidency.

Ike smiled as he saw several children carrying "I Like Ike" balloons. Children were among his campaign's biggest supporters and volunteers.

Young people give me hope for the future. It fills my old heart with joy to see them engaged with the political process. Although they might like that I look a bit like they did a few years ago, Ike thought.

The crowd settled down. Ike began the most important speech of his campaign.

"In this anxious autumn for America, one fact looms above all others in our people's mind. One tragedy challenges all men dedicated to the work of peace. One word shouts denial to those who foolishly pretend that ours is not a nation at war.

"This fact, this tragedy, this word is: Korea.

"A small country, Korea has been, for more than two years, the battleground for the costliest foreign war our nation has fought, excepting the two world wars. It has been the burial ground for twenty-thousand dead Americans. It has been another historic field of honor for the valor and skill and tenacity of American soldiers.

"We are not mute prisoners of history. That is a doctrine for totalitarians, it is no creed for free men.

"There is a Korean war—and we are fighting it—for the simplest of reasons: Because free leadership failed to check and to turn back communist ambition before it savagely attacked us. The Korean War—more perhaps than any other war in history—simply and swiftly followed the collapse of our political defenses. There is no other reason than this: We failed to read and to outwit the totalitarian mind.

"I know something of this totalitarian mind. Through the years of World War II, I carried a heavy burden of decision in the free world's crusade against the tyranny then threatening us all. Month after month, year after year, I had to search out and to weigh the strengths and weaknesses of an enemy driven by the lust to rule the great globe itself.

"World War II should have taught us all one lesson. The lesson is this: To vacillate, to hesitate—to appease even by merely betraying unsteady purpose—is to feed a dictator's appetite for conquest and to invite war itself.

"That lesson, which should have firmly guided every great decision of our leadership through these later years, was ignored in the development of the Administration's policies for Asia since the end of World War II. Because it was ignored, the record of these policies is a record of appalling failure.

"The first task of a new administration will be to review and re-examine every course of action open to us with one goal in view: To bring the Korean War to an early and honorable end. This is my pledge to the American people.

"For this task a wholly new administration is necessary. The reason for this is simple. The old administration cannot be expected to repair what it failed to prevent.

"Where will a new administration begin?

"It will begin with its President taking a simple, firm resolution. The resolution will be: To forego the diversions of politics and to concentrate on the job of ending the Korean War—until that job is honorably done.

"That job requires a personal trip to Korea.

"I shall make that trip. Only in that way could I learn how best to serve the American people in the cause of peace.

"*I shall go to Korea.*

"That is my second pledge to the American people."

The crowd exploded with joyous applause at that pledge. Ike let the approval soak in. He needed it, after the tough, previous month.

The Truman administration denounced Ike's speech. Several officials, including Omar Bradley, Chairman of the Joint Chiefs, said Ike should tell them his plan to end the war so they could implement it and save lives. The truth was that Ike did not have a plan. Not yet. But Ike's speech was the last nail in the coffin of Stevenson's campaign.

The hero of World War II, the conqueror of Hitler, had promised to bring the boys home from Korea. One of those boys was Ike's son.

☆☆☆☆☆

NOVEMBER 4, 1952

KNOCK KNOCK.

"COME in!" Ike ordered, ever the old general.

Brownell entered the room. Ike spent election night at Columbia University's President's House at 60 Morningside Drive in New York City.

"How's your head doing?" Brownell asked.

"Better," Ike replied, briefly touching the bandage that covered the back of his head with his large fingers. "It isn't throbbing anymore."

Ike had spent the previous night filming a live television spot with Mamie and the Nixons. They discussed the campaign and what they sought to accomplish in the White House. The special also had several clips of voters explaining why they were voting for Ike. Answers ranged from his pledge to end the Korean War to his commitment to reducing inflation. The event ended with a cake carrying seven candles—Ike's lucky number.

The television studio asked Ike to take a photograph under a large clock once the special ended. They said it would signal Election Day. Ike agreed, although he said the idea was corny. The clock came loose and landed on Ike's head. He said he hoped that wasn't a bad omen for the election.

It wasn't.

"Did you hear Stevenson's concession speech?" Brownell asked.

Ike grunted. "I have no interest in listening to that monkey."

"He quoted Abraham Lincoln."

"How?" Ike asked, jealous of one of his heroes.

"He reminded his supporters of the little boy who had stubbed his toe in the dark. He was too old to cry but hurt too much to laugh."

Ike snorted. *My respect for Stevenson has dissolved during this campaign.*

Brownell noted a painting in the corner of the room. It was still drying.

"Did you just do that today?"

"Yes," Ike replied. "I still don't have the hint of talent, but it lets me be alone for hours and interferes not at all with what I call my 'contemplative powers.'"

Brownell nodded.

"How many states did we end up carrying?" Ike asked.

"Thirty-nine of forty-eight. With fifty-five percent of the popular vote. A landslide."

"Which ones did we lose?"

"They were all in the Deep South. None of them have ever voted Republican. Though you did win Tennessee, Virginia, Florida, and Texas. Probably because you campaigned in the South, even though we all told you not to. This might be a turning point for the party's competitiveness in that region."

Ike smiled.

"You should come downstairs, Mr. President-elect," Brownell suggested, the first to use that salutary term for Ike. "Your supporters want to celebrate with you."

"I'll come down in a minute," Ike instructed. "I want to reflect a little."

Brownell nodded. He headed toward the door.

"Herbert," Ike began, interrupting him.

"Yes, sir?" Brownell asked, pausing.

"I want to have a chief of staff in the White House."

"Like in the Army?"

"Yes. It will make the command structure more familiar to me."

"That makes sense. I'm sure it can be arranged."

"I want you as my chief of staff."

Brownell smiled.

"That's an honor, sir, truly. But my principal interest in life is to be a lawyer. I want to continue in the law."

Ike put his finger up to his mouth.

"You want to be a lawyer?"

"Yes."

"How about attorney general?"

Brownell's jaw dropped. He took a step back, unprepared for such an offer. He rubbed the back of his head as he searched for words.

"I," he began, filling an awkward moment. "I'll need to talk to my wife. Check my finances. Make sure we can last four years with me in government service."

Ike nodded approvingly.

"Sounds good. Let me know when you're ready. I'll be downstairs in a minute."

Brownell nodded as he left, greeting the Secret Service agents who now guarded the door.

Ike rose to his feet and paced around the room.

I'm surprised my old joints didn't creak as I got up. It's been quite a journey since I left Abilene. I grew up in near poverty. Now I've won the office once held by Washington. Something like that could only happen in America.

This was the easy part. Now I have to be President of the United States. Stand up to Stalin. End the Korean War. Avoid World War III. Secure a lasting peace for all mankind.

My dream where I met George Washington happened almost a year ago. But I still remember what we discussed. America in the modern age must lead the world. But it also must avoid unnecessary wars. That's what I'll have to do as President. It won't be easy. Communism has never been more aggressive. And our own government is looking for a fight. It will take everything I have to keep the peace.

World War II was the culmination of my military career. I wanted to retire after the German surrender. Get fat and brown under the sun with

Mamie. But the nuclear bomb poses an existential threat to humanity. I never wanted to be President. But Washington was right. It was my duty.

Better Scared than Dead

The 1950s were boringly peaceful only because Eisenhower made them so. His ability to save the world from nuclear Armageddon entirely depended on his ability to convince America's enemies—and his own followers—that he was willing to use nuclear weapons. This was a bluff of epic proportions.
—Evan Thomas

SEPTEMBER 17, 1953

PRESIDENT EISENHOWER'S JUBILANT attitude faded as the meeting droned onward. He put the finishing touches on his doodle of Defense Secretary Wilson. Ike tuned out what Treasury Secretary Humphrey was saying and instinctively reflected on the great achievement of his young presidency—the Korean armistice. Ending the Korean War was the centerpiece of Ike's 1952 presidential campaign. He fulfilled the promise by sending Secretary of State Dulles to India and giving Prime Minister Nehru a message to pass along to Red Chinese leaders Mao Tse Tung and Chou Enlai. The message implied that the United States could no longer accept casualties along a static front and would use nuclear weapons to break the stalemate in Korea if the Red Chinese did not renew armistice talks. The threat worked and an armistice was finalized in July. The troops, including Ike's son John, came home. The armistice was a step toward world peace, Ike's ultimate goal.

Unfortunately, the National Security Council was discussing a small recession that developed from the armistice. Veterans were looking for work and weapon manufacturers had to lay off employees now that the war was over.

"Congress is set to vote on a $7 billion tax cut for the middle class. That's in addition to extending unemployment benefits for four million eligible workers. These bills undermine the administration's stated goal of balancing the budget and will upset parts of the party's Old Guard," Secretary Humphrey reported as light reflected off his bald scalp.

Ike instinctively grabbed at the air to raise his adrenaline. He stopped once he saw what he was doing and sought to be professional.

"I know, George, but this deficit spending is only temporary. Or at least that's what Arthur assures me," Ike said, referring to economic advisor Arthur Burns.

"We can afford this limited deficit spending now that inflation's dropping," offered Vice President Nixon, the youngest man in the room. "But we'll have to renew our efforts to balance the budget when we submit next year's budget proposal or risk losing the midterms."

"You know my rule about using policy for political purposes, Dick," Ike shot back. "That type of talk has no place in a responsible administration."

Nixon leaned back in his chair.

Ike looked at the clock. It sat on a mantle below a painting of George Washington.

This meeting feels particularly long.

Part of the reason Ike's NSC meetings were so long was the regimented, systematic approach to policy analysis and discussion that Ike brought from the military into his administration.

"What else is on our agenda? Today's schedule could kill a horse and my putting green misses me."

"We should at least mention the latest update from Iran," replied CIA Director Allen Dulles, jumping in before his brother, the Secretary of State, could get a word in.

"Please proceed, Allen."

Allen glanced at his notes.

"Prime Minister Mossadegh suspended his parliament and is ruling the country through emergency powers. Aid shipments from the Soviet Union have also begun entering the country. We have contacts with MI6 and the Shah but we're still working on a plan to counteract Mossadegh's moves."

Ike lightly closed his teeth over the tip of his tongue as he considered the problem. He knew much of his administration wanted to follow

Churchill and MI6's lead in taking covert action against Mossadegh.

Winston's still mad that Mossadegh nationalized Britain's oil supply. That's no reason to take action against a country. Hell, that's Victorian. But Mossadegh is playing footsie with Moscow and Iran falling to communism could lead to the region falling. The Middle East has 60 percent of the world's oil so that means a vital interest for the West is at stake. Still, intervening in a country violates my belief in the equality of nations. On the other hand, covert action is far less costly than a Korea-type of war, which may prove necessary if Iran really does fall under the Soviet orbit.

Ike altered his grip on his pen and shifted in his seat.

"How do the Iranian clerics feel about this?"

"They hate Mossadegh and think his Tudeh Party are a bunch of atheist communists," Allen replied.

"Do they favor the Shah?" Ike asked.

"Probably."

"Confirm that and get back to me. Keep me updated on this subject. We can't let Moscow take the Persian Gulf. We'd lose the whole region and that's not happening on my watch," Ike said defiantly. "Do you have anything, Foster?"

"On this topic?" Secretary of State Dulles asked, determined, as always, to have Ike's approval.

"On any topic," Ike replied.

"Your trip to Spain is in its final preparations," Dulles said.

Wilson shifted in his chair away from Dulles and toward Admiral Radford, escaping the Secretary of State's infamous bad breath. Dulles ignored the insult.

"My team is also finalizing the remarks you'll make when meeting Franco."

Ike took his glasses from his face and fiddled with them, showing his restlessness once more. He did not like the idea of making nice with Franco, who favored Hitler and Mussolini during World War II. Ike lost several nights of sleep in 1942 worrying Franco would join the Axis in response to Ike's invasion of North Africa. That didn't happen but Ike did not like the notion of shaking hands with Hitler's pal. Nonetheless, Spain had been diplomatically isolated since the war and was no friend of communism. A rapprochement with Spain was the pragmatic choice, even if it made Ike's skin crawl.

"Sounds appropriate, Foster. Anything else?"

"Have you read the briefing on the Soviet H-bomb?"

"Of course," Ike replied. "Though I noticed the Policy Planning Board didn't reach a consensus."

"We're working on it, Mr. President," said Robert Cutler, the assistant to the president for national security affairs and the administrator of the National Security Council. "The team's been working overtime on this one."

Ike gripped the temple of his glasses between his fingers and spun it in three-quarter circles. The Soviets testing their first hydrogen bomb was a major step for the Soviet nuclear program. The US had tested its hydrogen bomb in December 1952, between Ike's election and inauguration. He decided to keep the weapon classified. But the Soviet bomb increased the probability of a strike on the US mainland.

"We shouldn't let this spook us into reversing the demobilization of Truman's military buildup," Humphrey said. "NSC 68 will bankrupt the country if we let it."

"It ought to spook us!" Dulles exclaimed. "Paul Nitze may be a Democrat and a Truman guy, but the Reds getting the H-bomb confirms his theory that '54 will be the Year of Maximum Danger and that the Soviets will launch a nuclear first strike on our cities."

"We shouldn't use that term, 'Year of Maximum Danger,'" Ike replied. "We need to think of the Cold War as a long-term problem, not something that'll be solved in a year. And George is right. NSC 68 is way too expensive. It's not sustainable for the long-term. We need a strategy that will be. Otherwise, we'll forfeit the Cold War."

"With all due respect, Mr. President," Dulles began as he pushed his glasses up the bridge of his nose and leaned forward in his chair. "The Cold War is far more dangerous than it was in the last administration and continues to get more dangerous. The policy inherited from Truman is collapsing and the Soviet government has been paralyzed since Stalin died in March. I think that's why they ignored your Chance for Peace speech." He was referring to a speech Ike gave in April that called for an end to the Cold War and global disarmament. He had opened his hand to the Soviets and was rebuffed. "Even worse, Mao's no longer tied down on the Korean Peninsula and is on the move across Asia. He's eyeing Formosa and is backing the Reds fighting the French in Indochina. The Russians getting the H-bomb is the cherry on top. It's as powerful as thirty Hiroshima bombs and they're going to hit us with it next year."

Ike weighed whether or not to start doodling a coffee mug.

Foster's right. The communists are more aggressive than ever and give no sign of slowing down. But these boys, as bright as they are, act like they're looking for a fight with the Soviets and Red Chinese. That's to say nothing of the boys at the Pentagon, the Republican Old Guard, Truman's old nest of trigger-happy wonks, and every other commentator and academic who doesn't get why I don't drop an atom bomb on the Kremlin. A dangerous overcorrection of the pre-Pearl Harbor isolationism that vexed Roosevelt years ago. Mankind has the power to destroy the world for the first time in history. Yet everyone in this room seems to think these atomic weapons are a tool of first resort that can be used without consequences. That dropping them on a Soviet ally won't be reciprocated. Or that it won't make the use of these weapons acceptable or routine in international relations. Men are stupid.

☆☆☆☆☆

THE RINGING PHONE interrupted Ike's reading. He did not mind putting down his memo about the fighting that broke out around West Berlin as NATO units resisted the Soviet Army.

"This is the President speaking."

"Mr. President, it's happening! We're under attack!" Admiral Radford's voice screamed through the phone.

Ike leapt to his feet. "What do you mean?"

"Just what I said!" Radford shouted. "The conventional fighting around Berlin has escalated! I thought it would stay contained but I was wrong! The Reds are hitting us first! Can I retaliate?"

"Of course!" Ike shouted. "Hit them with everything we have! And send more troops to West Germany! We threw away our whole system to have this Garrison State! It's time to use it!"

Ike slammed down the phone. He frantically turned and looked outside the Oval Office to see David and Susan, two of his grandchildren, playing in the grass. Ike's stomach somersaulted.

"Sherman!" he screamed. "Sherman, goddamn it, get in here!"

Chief of Staff Sherman Adams flew past Ann Whitman and poked his head in the Oval Office.

"Yes, Mr. President?"

"Get my grandkids inside!" Ike shouted. "The Russians are attacking!"

Adams turned and ran as fast as he could. He wasn't fast enough. A light flashed in the sky. The last thing Ike remembered was the Washington Monument being vaporized. He regained consciousness hours later to find nothing but ash where America's capital city had been.

"David?" Ike shouted as he crawled his way through the ash. "David? Mamie? Did anyone make it?"

Ike saw movement under a charred piece of wood. He ran over on his hands and knees, ignoring his burns, and lifted it so Ann Whitman, his personal secretary, could crawl out.

"Ann! Ann, I'm so sorry! Are you okay?" Ike asked as he knelt next to her.

He was stunned when he saw that half of her face had been burned off. She looked up at him with her remaining eye.

"Mr. President?"

"I'm here, Ann!" Ike exclaimed as his knees sank into the ashes. Even the worms in the ground were destroyed in the attack. "How can I help?"

"Mr. President," Ann said softly through coughs. "We trusted you to keep us safe. *I* trusted you. You said you wanted peace. How could you let this happen?"

Ike cried but drops of blood were all that fell onto Ann's forehead. Ike felt a crushing weight of failure and defeat as he shifted his weight onto his rear and looked at the smoke that filled the sky. He didn't know how many Americans were dead but the Armageddon he had sought to prevent had come to pass. He wanted to find Mamie, but his energy drained from his body as he struggled to breathe. He changed his mind and decided to shoot himself. There was nothing left to keep him going. He'd failed his duty and wanted his suffering to end. As soon as that thought of death crossed his mind, the world around Ike dissolved and he was released from his nightmare.

☆☆☆☆☆

SWEAT RUSHED DOWN Ike's forehead as his body contracted. His elbows hit his knees and his arms shook. His face felt cold until his breathing slowed to a normal pace. Ike sat up in bed and reached for a cigarette on his nightstand. But Ike had quit smoking five years ago.

Ike ordered himself to gain control of his emotions and restore his calm. He wrapped his arms around his knees to feel warm. *That wasn't real. Only a dream.*

"Ike, are you okay?" Mamie asked, awakened by her husband's scare. She put her hand on his bald head. "You're covered in sweat. Should we call Dr. Snyder?"

Ike shook his head. "That isn't necessary. I'm sorry I woke you."

"It's okay, Ike. But I want to help."

"Just hold me?" Ike asked.

"Of course," Mamie replied. She shifted her hips and wrapped her arms around him.

Ike's breathing stabilized and he rested his cheek on her forehead. He tried to calm down but could not take his mind off his nightmare.

That's the stakes. That's what I have to avoid. Another war means human extinction. I know that dream came from the discussion on the hydrogen bomb. I have to find a way to prevent that catastrophe. The whole world depends on it.

☆☆☆☆☆

SEPTEMBER 24, 1953

"GENTLEMEN, THE PRESIDENT!" Cutler's Boston Brahmin accent cut through the air. The entire National Security Council stood as Ike entered the Cabinet Room.

"Be seated," Ike muttered curtly. His advisors sat down and noticed Ike's brown plaid suit. That suit was a terrifying sight in the Eisenhower White House. It was the President's signal that he was angry and not to be trifled with. Ike sat at the head of the table.

"I want to start with what we discussed in last week's meeting. The issue of the Soviet H-bomb and the likelihood that they'll hit us with it in the near future."

"I fully believe this prediction will come to pass. It's why we need to roll back communism. Or contain it at the very least," Nixon interjected, determined to assert himself as a competent foreign policy thinker among the older, more experienced statesmen.

"It's too expensive, Mr. Vice President," Humphrey replied. "The Treasury Department's analysis shows that NSC 68 will lead to a debt crisis by the decade's end. We've avoided one already only because we ended the war in Korea and Truman's wage and price controls."

"Can we review what NSC 68 entails?" Ike asked. "We should be on the same page with what we're dealing with here." He turned to Cutler. "Robert, do you mind?"

"Of course, Mr. President," Cutler replied as he glanced at his notes. "NSC 68 marked the final culmination of the Truman administration's Cold War strategy. The document was written by Paul Nitze in 1950 and predicted that the Soviets would launch a nuclear strike on the US homeland in 1954 and that the US needed huge conventional forces to carry on the fight against communism after the Soviet strike. President Truman implemented the document after North Korea invaded South Korea in 1950, legitimizing Nitze's predictions of a global communist conspiracy for world domination. This authorization quadrupled military spending to around sixty billion dollars by 1953. That dwarfs the annual level of defense spending during World War II."

"And it will *bankrupt* the country if we maintain that level of spending for much longer," Humphrey stated, slowly emphasizing each word and moving his thumb and index finger together as one unit. "We need to change the way we think about this situation. Opposing communism abroad and our finances at home are part of the same challenge. We need to think of the national debt as a greater threat to national security than the Soviet Union."

"That's absurd," Admiral Radford replied. Radford was the architect of the US Navy's aviation program during World War II and had recently succeeded Omar Bradley as Chairman of the Joint Chiefs of Staff. "The Reds are a bigger threat to the Free World than the Axis ever was. They threaten our security more than Robert E. Lee did 90 years ago. No amount of spending is too much in crushing them and their mission of world-wide tyranny."

"I agree with George," Ike responded. "We can't afford to bankrupt ourselves in search of security. We'll lose our freedoms and everything we're trying to defend from the communists if we do."

"I respectfully disagree, Mr. President," Radford replied.

Ike frowned as he leaned forward in his chair. Most of the government thought the Soviets intended to launch a nuclear strike on the US within a year. Ike was skeptical of that prediction but knew they had to oppose communism. At the same time, he knew everyone but Secretary Humphrey and himself was prepared to spend as much as possible on the military for the duration of the Cold War. Ike believed that threatened America's democratic way of life. But his nightmare from a few days ago had led him to think of another option for this situation. He decided to play the devil's advocate to provoke a debate on his radical idea.

"I want us to consider the following thought experiment: Would it be morally wrong *not* to attack the Soviets before they have the capacity to hit the US? It looks to me as though the hour of decision is at hand, and that we presently have to face the question of whether we would throw everything at once against the enemy. The question can no longer be ignored. It's our duty to answer it. Otherwise, we risk the likelihood of a giant nuclear Pearl Harbor."

A grim silence sucked the life from the room. The prospect was horrifying. No one knew how to approach this hypothetical.

Dulles broke the silence. "To clarify, Mr. President, you're talking about a preventive strike intended to destroy the entirety of the Soviet Union?"

"That's correct, Foster. It's the only way to guarantee that we're neither hit ourselves nor that we're forced to bankrupt ourselves."

"Wouldn't we also have to destroy the rest of the Iron Curtain? And Red China?" Allen Dulles asked, twirling an unlit pipe between his fingers under the conference table.

"We could consider that," Ike replied. The men were tense for several long moments.

This time Radford broke the silence.

"This idea is logical. Communism must be opposed but the President and treasury secretary believe containment is too expensive. It is inevitable that the Soviets will hit us within a year or two if we don't act preventively. They have a nuclear arsenal but lack the capacity to strike our mainland. We should take advantage of this fact before they develop that capacity." The Dulles brothers, Nixon, and Cutler all nodded with Radford's words. Ike folded his arms as the Chairman of the Joint Chiefs continued. "When I led a carrier group in '45, we firebombed Japanese cities where the buildings were made of wood and paper. It caused an inferno, but we were tasked with killing the bastards scientifically. We can now do the same with the Soviets."

Ike's stomach clenched. He wanted to vomit and felt his temples sweat as his insides somersaulted. He did not expect his advisors to consolidate around the idea of destroying Russia so quickly.

If I pull the trigger on this, that's my legacy. Not Overlord, not the lasting peace I wanted to build. But the destruction of over 100 million people. And that's only if we stop at Russia. These monkeys will want to take out the entire Eastern Bloc and China too. It will be far worse than the two World Wars combined. The story of this century will be of two wars that propelled America to world leadership and within ten years of that leadership America committed by far the greatest atrocity in the history of our species. My name will be permanently condemned as a butcher who made Hitler look saintly in comparison.

"You're all on board with this?" Ike growled.

"We have to deal with the world as it is. Not as we would like it to be," Dulles replied.

"This may very well be our best option. We can't let the Soviets win or risk their hitting us on the one hand, but on the other we can't afford to contain them with NSC 68," Nixon said.

What credentials does he even have to give that type of advice? Ike thought, glaring at his Vice President but holding back his criticism.

"Should we notify the NATO allies of our intentions?" Wilson asked.

"It's far too early for that," Ike replied. "This concept is still in its cradle."

"It would be the financially responsible thing to do," Humphrey said, throwing in his two cents.

Ike turned to his treasury secretary, with whom he usually agreed on most issues.

"We're talking about hundreds of millions of lives, George. This is about more than money."

"I don't understand, Mr. President," Humphrey replied as he shifted his posture. "You raised this idea as an alternative to NSC 68. You wanted a way to protect the free world from communism without bankrupting ourselves and sacrificing the Constitution to a Garrison State. Why shouldn't we weigh the financial costs?"

"I want us to keep in mind the Ukrainian villagers that would be incinerated by this idea. There's more at stake than money," Ike responded.

"No one wants to incinerate Ukrainian villagers," Dulles interjected. "But our foremost job is to protect Americans. And the American people face an imminent existential threat that will lose no sleep incinerating *them* at the first opportunity. We have a short window to prevent that, and I think we should take it. It's not our fault that Ukrainian villagers live under an atheistic, demonic ideology that seeks to destroy us."

"But must this be so zero sum?" Ike asked, his temper rising. "Must this be our lives or theirs?"

"President Lincoln, the wisest man to ever hold this office, once said that a house divided against itself could not stand—" Nixon began.

"He didn't say that two houses constructed differently, of different materials, of different appearance could not stand in peace within the same block. So, Lincoln's analogy doesn't apply to us and the communists."

"Mr. President," Wilson began, "You did what was necessary to defend freedom when you invaded Normandy in '44. That was the largest operation in history. Millions were involved. I don't understand the difference between that and this idea."

"That was clearly necessary," Ike replied. "I want to make sure that there are no alternatives before we contemplate something so horrible as this option."

"I don't see what our alternatives are," Humphrey said. "The Reds know they can only truly defeat us by attacking our economy. NSC 68 plays directly into their hands on that point."

"I would add that allowing the Soviets to develop the capacity to hit us with atomic weapons would be incredibly irresponsible," Radford stated. "History will draw comparisons to President Buchanan allowing the South to secede before the Civil War. So, to return to the Vice President's Lincoln analogy, doing the preventive strike that you originally suggested might be the Lincolnian position here."

Ike continued to feel sick as he thought about this conversation.

It's insane that they've all jumped onto this idea so quickly. I'm still not convinced that the Russians plan on hitting us and triggering a nuclear exchange. They fought tooth and nail to defeat Hitler and the boys currently running the Kremlin survived Stalin's terror. They're not suicidal. They're survivors. It doesn't make any sense that they would provoke their own destruction. But that still leaves the problem of NSC 68. George is right that it is way too expensive. It'll bankrupt the country, which must be avoided if democracy is to survive. But that doesn't mean we can simply give up on containment. Moscow would rule the world in no time. The nation of Washington and Lincoln cannot be allowed to fall to the ideology of Marx and Lenin! If only there was another option to allow us to contain communism without breaking the bank on such large-scale forces. It doesn't help that maintaining such a huge military creates the ability, and therefore the pressure, to wage more limited wars like Korea. I have to find a way to keep us out of war without giving up on containment and without bankrupting the country.

Ike flexed his mental muscle to calm his stomach as he leaned forward. "We've beat this subject to death. Let's move on to another. We should make our mistakes slowly and proceed cautiously."

☆☆☆☆☆

IKE RESTED ON a lawn chair in the White House's solarium, a sunny, leafy penthouse on the third floor of the mansion. The sun shone on his face and hands as Ike's eyes were closed. This helped Ike keep his ruddy complexion and made him look less pale on television. The actor Robert Montgomery, his television coach, advised him to do this.

Squawk!

Ike winced as Mamie's canary, which sat in a cage beside Ike, disturbed his peace.

The only thing I hate as much as birds are monkeys. If this creature weren't Mamie's it would make good target practice.

Ike tried to restore his calm as Cutler, Dulles, and Bedell Smith entered the room. Smith had been Ike's chief of staff during World War II, just as Cutler had been George Marshall's. He was now Undersecretary of State and kept an eye on the Dulles brothers on Ike's behalf.

Ike opened his eyes as he heard the footsteps approach.

"Here come the conspirators," he said as he smiled at his trio of advisors.

"We were having dinner at Foster's house last Sunday and discussed the NSC meeting from the previous Friday," Cutler began. "We decided it would make sense to think outside the box on this issue of containment and should start drawing up different options and strategies to replace NSC 68."

Ike leapt to his feet.

"I love that!" he exclaimed. "What would be even better is if we could recruit some bright young fellows to collaborate on these alternative strategies."

"Where do we want to do this?" Smith asked.

"How about in the National War College?" Ike suggested.

"I'm sure they'll make room for us," Cutler replied.

☆☆☆☆☆

THIS IDEA CULMINATED in a presentation to Ike in a projection room in the White House basement a few weeks later. Three teams were tasked with drafting alternative strategies to NSC 68. George Kennan led Team A. He was the country's leading expert on the Soviet Union and had been a key advisor to President Truman; his inclusion in this strategy session showed

Ike was approaching the Cold War in a bipartisan manner. Kennan was the father of containment; his Long Telegram to Truman in 1946 argued that the Soviets sought to dominate Europe and Asia and that, should they be prevented from expanding, would collapse under the weight of their centrally planned economy. This was a wise alternative to World War III.

"In conclusion," Kennan said to Ike, "our team thinks your administration should largely continue the Truman Administration's strategy of containment but not through the massive military spending that NSC 68 requires. Containment should be centered in Europe by strengthening the Atlantic Alliance. We should maximize political solidarity within NATO. We can strengthen our ties with the rest of the noncommunist world by continuing to lower trade barriers. This would improve the economies of the underdeveloped world and make an alliance with the West more attractive than an alliance with Moscow. This vision of multilateralism will reduce containment's costs, which this administration takes into consideration."

Ike nodded and took notes as Kennan finished. He liked Team A's emphasis on Europe and multilateralism. Ike worked with the Europeans to free the continent from Hitler during World War II and saw NATO as the centerpiece of America's global leadership. He also saw multilateralism as vital to world peace.

Vice Admiral Richard Conolly, the leader of Team B, began his presentation.

"Our team agrees with the prior team that the Soviet Union is an existential threat to Western Civilization. We believe that, unlike Nazi Germany and Red China, the Soviets can be negotiated with. That does not mean that we can go easy on them. Our team was particularly bothered at how Secretary of State Acheson had drawn a line across the Far East and said we'll only defend countries on our side of the line. He placed South Korea on the other side of the line, inviting communist aggression toward that country and leading to the Korean War. We have to make clear that communism is not allowed to spread *anywhere* in the world."

Conolly paused to catch his breath.

"The main problem we sought to solve was the cost that NSC 68 imposed on the US. We can't afford such a large-scale military expenditure. It would either cause a debt crisis or force us to wage World War III to prevent a debt crisis. Therefore, our team recommends shifting containment away from conventional weapons that can only wage limited Korea-type of wars. Instead, we believe the administration should invest in a large nuclear deterrent. The threat of a catastrophic nuclear attack will deter any large-scale communist aggression. In addition, we recommend giving authority over the nuclear bombs to field commanders who are facing vis-à-vis the communist forces in Europe and Asia. This could only help to increase the threat of a nuclear response in the face of communist aggression. The only drawback to this brinkmanship approach is it might scare some of our allies, so we might have to pursue it unilaterally."

Ike jotted down notes. The idea of a nuclear deterrent reminded him of the threat he implied to Mao that had ended the Korean War. He also recognized how a large nuclear arsenal would be far cheaper than the huge conventional force that NSC 68 required. However, Ike objected to surrendering his sole **authority** to use nuclear weapons. He also thought a purely unilateral foreign policy was unnecessary and that a nuclear deterrent did not require America losing all its allies.

Air Force Major General James McCormack led Team C and explained the importance of rolling back communism, not merely containing it. Either militarily or covertly, the US should try to detach the Iron Curtain from the Soviets' grip and force a regime change in Red China. Ike was more skeptical of this proposal. Either of those goals would trigger World War III. But rollback could be contemplated in less vital, weak parts of the communist world. Allen Dulles and the CIA were already discussing a covert operation to remove Mossadegh and strengthen the Shah in Iran.

Ike jotted down some final notes as the presentations ended. He wrote next to his doodle of a coffee cup:

GLOBAL DEFENSE OF FREEDOM/
ALMOST A CONTRADICTION IN TERMS
3 PLANS/ BEAUTIFULLY PRESENTED (ALL SEEM TO BELIEVE)/
C CONTAINS B

Ike looked at his notes for a couple more minutes before putting them down and standing up. He walked toward the center of the room.

"I wish the three teams could have developed a single plan," he muttered.

Kennan was stunned at what happened next. Ike spoke for forty-five minutes. He restated what the three teams had presented into his own words and thinking. He blended the three options together into a single strategy.

"Global cooperation and a nuclear deterrent will both be necessary for containing communism. Multilateralism increases our strength, and the nuclear deterrent will allow us to make the price of communist aggression higher than any sane person would consider. It will also allow us to shrink the conventional military and balance the budget, bring down the debt we inherited from Roosevelt and Truman, and secure America's long-term financial stability.

"I agree that the nuclear arsenal should be given to the military. It should be placed within the Air Force. This will increase the communists' likelihood of taking the deterrent seriously. I'm afraid that Team C's ideas on rolling back communism in Eastern Europe and China may be too aggressive but we can certainly use the concept of rollback in less vital places. The nuclear deterrent can check major communist aggression while we covertly roll communism back in secondary areas.

"I am very pleased with your work. You all did an excellent job. We've crafted a strategy that will avoid more wars like Korea and is sustainable for the long-term. Preferably, the Soviets will understand this and agree to nuclear disarmament. But if they don't, we will contain them until they eventually collapse under their own weight. Western Civilization and liberal democracy will outlast that crude autocracy as long as we avoid a large-scale war.

"Robert," Ike said, turning to Cutler, "have the Policy Planning Division write out what I explained into a formal document for the NSC."

Kennan couldn't believe it. He, like many Democrats, had dismissed Ike as a lightweight; he now realized Ike was the smartest person in the room. He wondered if Ike even needed the presentations to devise the strategy. Kennan suspected Ike organized these strategy teams and presentations merely to get his administration on board with the strategy he had already formulated. It worked.

☆☆☆☆☆

DECEMBER 4, 1953

"I HOPE YOU'LL forgive our disagreement earlier with regard to American protection of the Suez Canal," Ike said as he took a seat, wearing his bathrobe.

"What was that?" Churchill asked, also in his robe. "I can't hear you properly."

"Are you sure you don't want your hearing aid, Winston?" Ike asked, straining his voice.

Churchill closed his eyes and shook his head.

"I assure you it's not necessary. That contraption is nothing but a *bloody* nuisance." Churchill saw Ike frowning as his eyes opened. The statesmen were in Ike's cabin in the Mid Ocean Club in Bermuda. "My people say that their beds look like they're from old ships. Reminiscent of Lord Nelson."

"Is that the speech?"

"What?"

"Is that my speech?" Ike asked, louder.

"Yes! Here you are."

Ike took the draft and scanned it to see the extent of Churchill's editing. His administration, after initial hesitancy from Dulles and Wilson, had consolidated around nuclear deterrence. However, before authorizing this shift in strategy that he and Dulles were calling the New Look to differentiate it from Truman's containment, Ike wanted to give the Soviets another chance to end the Cold War. He planned to propose nuclear disarmament and cooperation on peaceful nuclear energy for the world.

"What did you think of it?"

Churchill tried not to look underwhelmed.

"It wasn't bad. I mostly removed some obnoxious lines about what you called the 'colonial model.'"

Ike had his first smile of the conversation.

"It's part of America's philosophy to oppose colonialism." Ike could tell that Churchill didn't hear him. "It will be good for Europe to make peaceful atomic power its main energy source. Not be reliant on Near East oil."

Churchill nodded.

"Would you be offended by a change of topic?"

"Of course not."

"I'd like to ask about Russia. Do you think Stalin's death changes anything?"

"Russia is a woman of the streets," Ike replied. "Whether its dress is new, or just the old one patched, it's the same whore underneath."

"But what will you do if they reject your proposal?"

"Disarmament must remain our ultimate goal, but in the meantime, we must make clear that we're free to use the atomic bomb to defend the free world."

"Can you repeat? I think I misheard you."

"I said we have to make sure they know that we'll use nuclear weapons to defend ourselves and our allies. For example, we'd use atomic strikes if China violates the Korea armistice."

Churchill raised his head and looked Ike in the eye. Was his old war colleague a mere ventriloquist doll for Dulles?

"Are you trying to make the rubble bounce?" Churchill asked. "What you're talking about would be even worse than the war against Herr Hitler."

"It's the only way we can contain communism. The plan my administration inherited from Truman was too expensive."

"Expensive! I'm not sure you appreciate how new and terrible atomic weapons are. England would never survive what you're talking about. We must play nice with the communists. A summit is the best move."

"I know you want to relive World War II, Winston, but we can't let the Reds coax us into complacency. Besides, all weapons become conventional eventually."

Churchill's eyes widened as far as Ike had ever seen them.

"And we'd better *make* an exception!" he stuttered.

Ike studied the panic on his ally's face.

☆☆☆☆☆

DECEMBER 8, 1953

IKE'S STOMACH WAS in such a knot he was ready to vomit. His insides bothered him for days leading up to his speech to the United Nations General Assembly. That is what normally happened before he had to give a major speech or during a stressful event.

He looked out at the delegates of the UN member states from behind his podium, put on his glasses, and took a few deep breaths to calm his nerves. Sweat already built on his temples.

"On July 16, 1945, the United States set off the world's first atomic explosion. Since that date in 1945, the United States of America has conducted forty-two test explosions.

"Should an atomic attack be launched against the United States, our reactions would be swift and resolute. But for me to say that the defense capabilities of the United States are such that they could inflict terrible losses upon an aggressor, for me to say that the retaliation capabilities of the United States are so great that such an aggressor's land would be laid waste, all this, while fact, is not the true expression of the purpose and the hopes of the United States.

"To pause there would be to confirm the hopeless finality of a belief that two atomic colossi are doomed malevolently to eye each other indefinitely across a trembling world. Surely no sane member of the human race could discover victory in such desolation. Could anyone wish his name to be coupled by history with such human degradation and destruction? Occasional pages of history do record the faces of the 'great destroyers,' but the whole book of history reveals mankind's never-ending quest for peace and mankind's God-given capacity to build.

"It is with the book of history, and not with isolated pages, that the United States will ever wish to be identified. My country wants to be constructive, not destructive. It wants agreements, not wars, among nations.

"The United States would seek more than the mere reduction or elimination of atomic materials for military purposes. It is not enough to take this weapon out of the hands of the soldiers. It must be put into the hands of those who will know how to strip its military casing and adapt it to the arts of peace.

"I therefore make the following proposal.

"The governments principally involved, to the extent permitted by elementary prudence, should begin now and continue to make joint contributions from their stockpiles of normal uranium and fissionable materials to an international atomic energy agency. We would expect that such an agency would be set up under the aegis of the United Nations.

"The responsibility of this atomic energy agency would be to devise methods whereby this fissionable material would be allocated to serve the peaceful pursuits of mankind.

"To the making of these fateful decisions, the United States pledges before you, and therefore before the world, its determination to help solve the fearful atomic dilemma—to devote its entire heart and mind to finding the way by which the miraculous inventiveness of man shall not be dedicated to his death but consecrated to his life."

The assembly was silent as Ike spoke. It exploded into applause as he finished. Ike had outlined the vision of a better world, a world he had dreamt of since World War II ended eight years earlier. It was a world where the United States and the Soviet Union would cooperate to guarantee international peace and prosperity. It was a world where the UN would finally replace the hostile alliances and saber rattling that had been the mainstay of diplomacy. It was a world where the UN would control the few nuclear weapons in existence and peaceful nuclear energy would be an option for all nations. World peace and environmental sustainability would be secured for generations.

Even the Soviet delegation cheered. The whole world came together behind Ike's vision of peace in that moment. A tear emerged in his eye.

☆☆☆☆☆

DECEMBER 31, 1953

IKE IGNORED THE drizzling rain as he lined up his club with the ball.

"Have to remember to stick my butt out," he muttered. Ike shut his left eye as he calculated one last time. He swung and missed. "Damnation!"

He was in a foul mood as his first year as President came to a close. The congressional Republicans continued to appease Senator McCarthy, who threatened Ike's domestic agenda and the careers of thousands of civil servants. More importantly, the Soviet Union had rejected his Atoms for Peace proposal that would have brought about global disarmament and clean nuclear energy to help the world. Ike could have retired at the end of his term and not run for reelection had it succeeded. Now, the Cold War would go on. The Soviet Union and its communist allies would continue to try to spread around the world. The United States would have to contain them. The nuclear arms race maintained its grip of fear over humanity.

Not even visiting the National Golf Club in Augusta, Georgia could cheer Ike up. Nor the prospect of playing bridge with his friends or of fishing when the rain stopped. Adding to his woes was that Mamie was under the weather and resting in the Eisenhowers' cabin instead of spending time with Ike.

The administration had recently announced the New Look, given the failure of Atoms for Peace. Dulles gave a speech to the Council on Foreign Relations where he declared the US would inflict Massive Retaliation upon the communist world if it tried to expand its influence. Dulles explained how a nuclear deterrent was cheaper than containment through conventional forces, giving the US "more bang for the buck." Ike had secretly written the most chilling line in the speech: "The basic decision was made to depend primarily upon a great capacity to retaliate, instantly, by means and at places of our choosing."

The speech was designed to make Dulles seem like he enjoyed the capacity to unleash an apocalypse. Ike, meanwhile, sought to look like he was more interested in golf than governing. He wanted the world to think that he did not know what using nuclear weapons would mean and that his warmonger Secretary of State was leading him along. The world knew that Ike was the architect of Adolf Hitler's defeat and so was not afraid of the colossal forces involved in Massive Retaliation.

Ike had to convince the American people and the communists that he was willing to use nuclear weapons while doing everything in his power to prevent their use. His countrymen would be frightened of atomic war; children would spend his presidency hiding under their desks in safety drills in preparation for a Soviet missile attack on their city. But it was better for them to be scared than to be dead.

Critics would say that the New Look, by relying on a nuclear deterrent to contain communism, increased the risk of nuclear war. Ike believed the opposite. He believed that limited wars like Korea were the most likely source of escalation toward nuclear war, especially since most of the world saw atomic weapons as a weapon of first resort that *could* be used to resolve international problems, like how it forced Japan's surrender in World War II. The polls still wanted to drop the bomb on Moscow and Peking. The Pentagon and his advisors clamored to use nuclear weapons whenever the Kremlin or Mao looked at them funny.

Threatening all-out war would preserve the fragile peace. It would take all of Ike's efforts to play the three-dimensional chess game against the communists and his own advisors that was necessary to keep the peace and avoid Armageddon. Massive Retaliation was an enormous gamble that Ike desperately hoped could save humanity from World War III, which he ran for President to prevent. He hoped he could achieve a breakthrough toward nuclear disarmament before leaving office that would make the New Look unnecessary and guide the world toward a just and lasting peace.

The Road to
McCarthywasm

He was a far more complex and devious man than most people realized, and in the best sense of those words. Not shackled to a one-track mind, he always applied two, three or four lines of reasoning to a single problem.
—Richard Nixon, on Dwight Eisenhower

FEBRUARY 18, 1954

BRIGADIER GENERAL RALPH Zwicker sat behind a large black table in the Federal Building in Manhattan. His black officer's uniform was spotless. His hands were clasped, and his hair parted just over his left eye. His files were laid out before him and organized so as to be readily available to him at a moment's notice. The room was dimly lit; a thin layer of dust forced Zwicker to take short breaths so as to not irritate his throat. Zwicker graduated from West Point almost thirty years prior. He performed a reconnaissance mission at Omaha Beach on D-Day a few hours before landing on that beach as part of Operation Overlord as an Army Ground Forces observer and the chief of staff for the Second Infantry Division. He led troops at the Battle of St Lo during the breakout from Normandy, some of the most ferocious fighting in history's biggest war. He received the Silver Star and Bronze Star and then served at NATO headquarters.

Zwicker's eyes followed the dark figure hunched over a table on the other side of the room. The man finally put down his papers, glared at

Zwicker, and restrained his excitement as he made his way toward the general. This was the drug upon which he fed.

"Thank you for joining me this morning, General Zwicker."

"I was instructed to comply with your subcommittee's subpoena, Senator."

"Unlike that coward, Peress, who just pled the Fifth. Are you familiar with the circumstances surrounding Peress' promotion and dismissal from the Army?"

"I was informed of the relevant controversy before coming here today."

"Then you know who promoted Peress?"

Zwicker made no response, his expression stoic. Senator Joe McCarthy, his five o'clock shadow clearly visible to Zwicker now, allowed himself to smile and show his excitement.

"Who promoted Peress, General?"

"I know nothing about that matter. It was a routine matter dictated by statute."

McCarthy winced at Zwicker's splitting of hairs. He leapt forward awkwardly, his ankle still throbbing from a car accident the night before that put his wife in the hospital. His pupils narrowed and fled from the expanding whites of his eyes as he repeated his question, angrier than before.

"*Who* promoted Peress?"

"I don't know," Zwicker answered with no change of reflection in his voice.

"Well then, he must have been promoted by a silent master who decreed special treatment for communists!" McCarthy declared as he turned from Zwicker and threw his arms in the air. "Or how else would you explain how a man, drafted to serve his country while it's fighting Reds in Korea as a *dentist* and who refused to take his loyalty oath when he was a *known* member of the American Labor Party, a communist puppet organization, gets promoted to Major before being *honorably* discharged?"

"That was all according to statute, Senator. It was a routine matter for a soldier who declined to take the loyalty oath."

"Well, you know that somebody has kept this man on, knowing that he was a communist, do you not?" McCarthy spat as he raced back to grab a yellow note pad off his desk.

"I am afraid that would come under the category of the executive order, Mr. Chairman." Zwicker was referring to a 1948 executive order that allowed his superiors to instruct him not to give any names or secure information to a Congressional committee.

"You're hemming and hawing," McCarthy asserted.

"I am not hawing," Zwicker refuted, showing his frustration for the first time. "And I don't like to have anyone impugn my honesty, which you just did."

"Either your honesty or your intelligence," McCarthy shot back. "Who ordered this discharge?"

"The Department of the Army."

"Who in the Department?"

"I can't answer that."

"Do you think, General, that anyone who is responsible for giving an honorable discharge to a man who has been named under oath as a member of the communist conspiracy should himself be removed from the military?"

"He should by all means be kept if he were acting under competent orders to separate that man."

"You have a rather important job," McCarthy flattered insincerely. "I want to know how you feel about getting rid of communists."

"I'm all for it."

"Anyone with the brains of a five-year-old child can understand that question," McCarthy stated, his eyes darting back between his notes and Zwicker, who fought to contain his temper as this former Marines intelligence officer insulted him. McCarthy put his notepad behind his back and strode to Zwicker.

"Do you believe, General, that a man who gives an honorable discharge to a *known* communist should remain in the military? I ask you again."

Zwicker could smell the bourbon on McCarthy's breath.

"I do not think he should be removed from the military."

"Then, General, *you* should be removed from *any* command. Any man who has been given the honor of being promoted to general and who says, 'I will protect another general who protected communists,' is not fit to wear that uniform, General!"

Zwicker's face flashed red, his shoulders dropping under the verbal assault. McCarthy grinned, feeling he had the upper hand.

"I ask again, and I ask *nicely*, why did *you* give an honorable discharge to a man known to be a communist?"

"Because I was ordered to do so."

"In other words, anything that you are ordered to do, you think that is proper?"

"That is correct," Zwicker replied, a growing anger in his tone. "Anything that I am ordered to do by higher authority, I must accept."

"What is your considered opinion of this order forbidding you assist this committee in exposing the communist conspiracy in the Army?"

"Sir, I cannot answer that, because it is signed by the President. The President says don't do it and therefore I don't. I won't answer that because I will not criticize my Commander-in-Chief."

McCarthy's jaw clamped shut in excitement. Those were the exact words he wanted to hear. The President. The Commander-in-Chief. His great enemy. McCarthy took a few small steps away from Zwicker, giving him room to breathe.

"That's why we're in our *twenty-first* year of treason," he muttered. "You will return here on Tuesday morning, at 10:30. And contact the proper authority who can give you permission to tell the committee the truth about the case before you appear Tuesday."

"Sir, that is not my prerogative, either."

"You are ordered to do it!" McCarthy pointed his index finger in Zwicker's face.

"I am sorry, sir, I will not do that."

"Dismissed!" McCarthy declared. He returned to his table. Zwicker's uncooperativeness didn't matter. McCarthy's national approval rating was over 50 percent. That allowed him to announce a major speaking tour across the country that the Republican National Committee agreed to sponsor. The party was within his grip. His power was surging, which he would need as he closed in on his ultimate target: the five-star general in the White House.

☆☆☆☆☆

PRESIDENT EISENHOWER SAT behind his desk, his jaw clenched as he wrote a letter to Edgar. Edgar, who was far more conservative than Ike, had written his little brother a letter that criticized Ike for opposing the Bricker Amendment, a proposed amendment to the Constitution which would revoke the President's ability to negotiate executive agreements with other countries and require treaties to receive enabling legislation from Congress. In short, it would move the President's power to negotiate with other countries to Congress.

"You seem to fear that I am just a poor little soul here who is being confused and misled by a lot of vicious advisers," Ike wrote.

> I am aware that Senator Bricker might marshal some legal support for his arguments, but I do not see why this should impress me. Lawyers have been trained to take either side of any case and make the most intelligent and impassioned defense of their adopted viewpoint. The counterarguments are much stronger in this case. How am I, as the President of the United States, supposed to build alliances with other free countries to oppose the international communism that we all fear if I cannot make agreements with them without asking Congress' permission at every step? I do not think that either you nor Senator Bricker have enough experience in conducting difficult negotiations looking toward necessary and essential executive agreements to have a thoughtful opinion on this issue.

Ike put down his pen, unsatisfied with his letter.

Such a hard time focusing on this, he thought. *My subconscious attention is elsewhere, on all the issues on my plate. Congressional Republicans want a tax cut for wealthier Americans despite the deficit. They claim the tax cut will pay for itself by increasing revenue, but I'm not convinced that it will stimulate businesses enough to justify the cost. They also oppose my proposal for Hawaiian statehood, want to restore the Smoot-Hawley Tariff that exacerbated the Depression, and even proposed an amendment that would end the separation of church and state. It is beyond me why anyone should choose to be a Republican. I thought they would be excited to cooperate with the first Republican President in twenty years, but they seem to have forgotten what cooperating with the President even means.*

Then there's the foreign problems. Communism has taken over Guatemala. The French are refusing to ratify the European Defense

Community and oppose letting the West Germans into NATO. Then there's the Italians and Yugoslavs saber rattling over Trieste. But nothing compares to our problems in Indochina. That region has plagued me for years. The French refused to give me the forces I required when I was at NATO because they were trying to make Indochina their colony again after Japan took it during World War II. Truman poured billions into the French effort. He saw French colonialism as less evil than the communist insurgency who wanted the French gone. I personally think they're both evil. Communism wants to rule the world and must be stopped, but people are allowed to choose their own government and it's unacceptable in today's day and age for Europeans to try to make African and Asian peoples their puppets. It was clear when I was in Panama and the Philippines how much resentment colonialism builds. We're going to push these underdeveloped countries to the communists if we defend colonialism. Even though colonialism produces a higher standard of living for these people than communism ever could.

The French have half a million soldiers in Indochina. They're losing a third of the graduating class of Saint-Cyr every year over there. That's crazy as hell. And now they're putting their forces in a fortress village called Dien Bien Phu so they can fight the communists in a set-piece battle. That's suicide. They'll be surrounded from all sides and won't be able to resupply their forces, even by air.

The French government and my own advisors have started talking to me about intervening to help the French forces. I suppose Indochina is a vital national interest to us. Its fall could condemn millions to communist enslavement and put Thailand at risk, as well as Burma, East Pakistan, and Indonesia. But we must be careful about waging a land war in Asia, as Korea taught us. The French would have to agree to Indochinese independence after the communists' defeat for me to even consider intervening. I would want a coalition of our traditional allies and other countries in the region so it's clear that we are not another white colonial army. But Churchill is already fighting communists in Malaysia and Kenya. He doesn't want another war.

To go unilaterally into Indochina, or other areas of the world which are endangered, amounts to trying to police the world. If we attempted such a course of action, using our armed forces and going into areas whether we were wanted or not, would cause us to lose all our support in the Free World. Army Chief of Staff Ridgeway is warning against an intervention, and I agree with him. Air Force Chief of Staff Twining, on the other hand, is advocating for a tactical nuclear strike against the communist forces. I suspect my other advisors, including Foster Dulles and Bedell Smith, probably agree with him. They're crazy as hell. Using nuclear weapons would open the door for further use of those terrible things, by us and by others, in the future. They forget that the nuclear deterrent is just that—a deterrent! It's not to be used except in the most *catastrophic scenario.*

What would have happened if Senator Taft won the nomination in 1952? He unfortunately died of cancer last year. It was an open secret that he wanted Douglas MacArthur, my old boss and pain in the neck, as his Vice President. That means MacArthur would be President right now and dealing with this crisis. He pushed to use nuclear weapons in Korea. That, plus the pressure from his advisors and the French—come on, Dwight. Don't get into hypotheticals that stack ifs on top of ifs.

Ike had put the earpiece of his glasses into his mouth to suck on without realizing it. He took them out, wiped off his saliva, and placed them on his desk. He then looked at his fingernails without thinking. He had cut them last night with foot long scissors and a letter opener and then covered them with three coats of clear polish so they wouldn't crack.

The Oval Office door opened and four advisors entered the room: Undersecretary of State Bedell Smith, White House Chief of Staff Sherman Adams, Attorney General Herbert Brownell, and UN Ambassador Henry Cabot Lodge. They took their seats without being told.

Smith locked eyes with Ike. His face was long with exhaustion. Smith had been Ike's chief of staff in World War II and was then the first director of the CIA. He now kept an eye on the Dulles brothers at the State Department but was worn out from serving Ike for over a decade and from being labeled a communist by Senator McCarthy even though he was as conservative as you could get.

"Why the long faces?" Ike asked his staff.

"General Zwicker's testimony just ended," Brownell explained. Ike grimaced.

"How did it go?"

"McCarthy said he 'had the brains of a five-year-old' and 'wasn't fit to wear his uniform,'" Adams answered for the group.

A vein bulged in Ike's temple. He gritted his teeth.

That lousy son of a bitch! To talk to a distinguished officer—wait, Dwight, slow down. Don't lose your temper. That doesn't hurt anyone but yourself. You want justice for the Army you served your whole life, but right now, you want emotional stability even more. Can't think straight when you're angry. Ok. I'm calmer now.

"What's wrong with him?" Ike asked. "Doesn't he know that you can't keep communism out of the United States by destroying Americans?"

"The Europeans see him as the American version of fascism," Smith chipped in.

"Not surprising," Brownell replied, "when he called those prosecuting Nazi war criminals 'communist conspirators' and lobbied against the execution of Waffen SS officers who massacred our POWs during the Bulge."

"I'm still mad at myself for failing to defend General Marshall from him. My biggest error in judgment. How does a tail gunner in the Pacific attack the patriotism of the greatest American of our lifetime?" Ike asked rhetorically.

Ike leaned back in his chair.

We've got to do something about this rogue Senator, he thought. *How selfish can he be to attack an administration, of his own party no less, when it's trying to prevent nuclear war and build a lasting peace in the world? I don't even want to be President; I would rather be practicing chip shots on the South Lawn. I have a duty to pour my energy into waging peace and building prosperity for our people, but I have to waste time dealing with this secondary issue because one demagogue wants attention.*

Ike looked at his advisors.

"I was hoping we could ignore him until we'd ended the Cold War. His rise in 1950 happened because China fell to communism and the Soviets got the bomb. But the Soviets rejected our proposal for mutual nuclear disarmament with the Atoms for Peace thing. Therefore, McCarthy's power isn't going away any time soon. Too many people's careers and reputations have been destroyed. The horror. Good, duty-bound Americans who dedicated their lives to national service have lost everything because of his accusations. We can't ignore him anymore. We've got to stop him."

"Ok, but how?" Brownell asked.

"War is all about centers of gravity," Ike explained. "We have to protect our center of gravity while destroying his. Ours is my bipartisan popularity and my credibility as a leader. His is his following. We have to detach it from him."

"The right wing and the Catholics will never abandon him."

"I'm willing to bet that support will fade if they see he's a bully. I'm willing to bet on the goodness of the American people."

"He wants to challenge you for the Republican nomination in '56," Lodge began. "Taft's old guys never forgave you for beating him in '52. Now they're using Joe to try and destroy you."

"This guy McCarthy wants to be President," Ike affirmed. "He's the last guy in the world who'll get there if I have anything to say about it. Can you imagine what a *President* McCarthy would do? The domestic division would be unlike anything we've seen since the Civil War. And his rabid anti-communism, his always acting with his gut rather than his head, could get us into nuclear war. Especially when most of the government seems predisposed to use the bomb anyway. With an extremist at its head…"

Ike's words trailed off. His advisors exchanged a glance, unsure what to make of the President's remark that they and their colleagues were predisposed to use nuclear weapons in response to foreign crises. Lodge was the first to speak.

"The credibility you have as a leader, which you were just referring to, may unravel if he keeps digging into the Army and our administration with claims that they're infested with communists."

Ike's eyebrows pinched.

"We've set up a vigorous mechanism for identifying and removing security risks within the executive branch. Even loyal Americans are being dismissed if they are at risk of blackmail for reasons of instability, alcoholism, homosexuality, or having previously associated with communist front groups."

"I know, Mr. President," Lodge said softly, "and objectively you're correct. But McCarthy doesn't care about objectivity. Only his own power and influence."

"That's why we have to attack his popularity," Ike said, returning to his earlier point. "And I think we can do that by making clear to the American people that he is a bully in the first degree. Americans hate bullies."

"Why not say so in a speech?" Adams asked. "The press has been calling for you to denounce McCarthy since you were inaugurated last year. Why not finally do it in a big speech that will be remembered by history?"

"Because, Sherman, it may be remembered as the point of no return in his rise to power and taking the presidency."

"I don't follow, Mr. President."

"No one cared about McCarthy's initial speech about 205 communists in the State Department until President Truman dared him to prove it. That propelled McCarthy into the headlines. If I denounced him in a speech it isn't clear to me who would win."

"But you're *General Eisenhower!*" Brownell exclaimed. "You can't compare yourself to *Truman!* The people love you!"

"You also won a hundred thousand more votes in Wisconsin in the '52 presidential election than McCarthy did in his senatorial election," Adams pointed out.

"I will not make a mockery of the presidency by getting in the gutter with that skunk!" Ike shot back. "You boys seem to forget that this is an election year and we're only holding the Senate by one vote! Do you want me to split the party wide open?"

"How do you plan to attack him then?" Smith asked.

Ike smiled as he turned to his wartime Chief of Staff.

"Bedell, do you remember Operation Fortitude?"

Smith returned Ike's grin.

"When we gave Patton an inflatable army so the Nazis would think we were targeting the Pas de Calais instead of Normandy?"

"Exactly. I know of two effective ways to attack an enemy. The first is overwhelming force. That's how we liberated Europe from the Germans. I don't think that will work against McCarthy. But the second is to attack an enemy through covert means. Through indirection. Like how we helped the Shia clergy remove that communist Mossadegh from Iran last year."

"What's your proposal?" Smith asked.

"McCarthy is like Napoleon on his wintry march toward Moscow. We let his ambition destroy him."

"I'm still not following," Adams said.

"We let him dig into the Army as much as possible. As *publicly* as possible. That will destroy his credibility and he'll collapse. Can you imagine him attacking the army that destroyed Hitler and Tojo less than ten years ago on live television? No one could survive that. We have to make that happen. He thinks attacking the Army will bring *me* down because I'm a general. But it's going to bring *him* down. Joe's not as invincible as he thinks."

Ike's advisors exchanged another glance, reflecting on their leader's plan.

"It's certainly ruthless," Lodge said. "Will it work?"

Ike shrugged.

"I may be one of seven sons, but I'm not the seventh son of a seventh son. So I'm not a prophet."

"He's hardly Napoleon," Brownell muttered. "Joe never plans a damn thing. He doesn't know one week to the next. Not even one day to the next, or what he's going to be doing. He just hits out in any direction."

"That's why we can encourage him to escalate his attacks on the Army and he'll bite without thinking about it," Ike replied.

"The press will accuse you of cowardice."

"I can take it. Even though ignoring their criticisms proves it's *not* cowardice. To my mind, giving in to the critics smacks more of foolishness than leadership. This is not namby-pamby. It is certainly not Pollyannaish. It is just common sense."

The advisors quieted again, thinking about how they were committing to an unconventional strategy for targeting a political rival. Adams broke the silence this time.

"Two roads diverged in a wood, and I—I took the one less traveled by. And that made all the difference."

☆☆☆☆☆

FEBRUARY 24, 1954

MCCARTHY BIT INTO a fried chicken drumstick, nudging a drop of saliva off the corner of his mouth with his tongue. His eyes were locked on his adversary, Army Secretary Robert Stevens. Stevens had white hair, round tortoiseshell glasses, a gray suit, and a dark blue tie with orange and yellow diagonal stripes. He held his own piece of fried chicken in his now greasy hands.

"Joe, I am going to prevent my officers from going before your committee until you and I have an understanding as to the kind of abuse they are going to get. I won't have a repeat of what you did to General Zwicker."

Stevens had McCarthy knocked on the back of his heels. The American Legion and the Veterans of Foreign Wars both issued public rebukes of McCarthy's treatment of Zwicker. Ike had publicly praised Zwicker and recommended him for a presidential citation. These 'backhanded' responses to McCarthy's actions meant he was vulnerable, and Stevens sought to become the administration's hero by sealing the peace deal.

"Go ahead and try it, Robert!" McCarthy taunted with food in his mouth. "I am going to kick the brains out of anyone who protects communists. If you go ahead with this I guarantee you will live to regret it. I don't give a goddamn whether an officer is a general or what he is, when he comes before us with the ignorant, stupid, insulting aspect of those who appeared, I will guarantee you that the American people will know about it!"

"I've already notified your fellow committee members that General Zwicker will not be appearing on Tuesday."

"I am through with all this covering up of communists!"

Stevens quickly sucked some fried breading off his thumb and then grabbed a napkin to wipe off the excess grease. He was a professional businessman who had been chairman of J.P. Stevens, a large textile manufacturing plant, before Ike asked him to administer the Army. Surely, he could tame this drunken firebreather.

"I admit that the Army mishandled the Peress promotion. We made several mistakes. We'll make reforms to make sure that doesn't happen again. But that doesn't excuse how you treated General Zwicker."

Senator Karl Mundt, McCarthy's friend, intervened before McCarthy could respond.

"What do you propose, Mr. Secretary?"

"That we make a deal."

"What sort of deal?" McCarthy asked, his eyes narrowed.

"That the Senator from Wisconsin agree to act responsibly and respectfully if I allow General Zwicker or any other officers to testify before his committee. I'll instruct Zwicker to give you the name of who promoted Peress if you agree."

Mundt turned to McCarthy, one of his eyebrows raised.

"Does that work for you, Joe?"

"It does. Investigating the Army would be so much easier if I weren't so fond of you, Robert." McCarthy put his finger in his ear without realizing it and scraped out some dead skin.

"Excellent!" Mundt exclaimed. "I'll write it up!" He took a minute to write out some terms. "Point one says that the Army and the committee agree that communists must be rooted out of the armed forces. Point two says that both parties agree that the Secretary of the Army will complete the Peress case and hand over the responsible officer to the committee. Point three just notes that the committee may call on General Zwicker again."

"Those are just concessions on my end," Stevens replied, his words slurred from chicken grease coating his teeth. "What about Joe's agreement to treat the officers better?"

"You have my verbal pledge," McCarthy answered, putting his hand over his heart.

"Can I trust that sort of promise?" Stevens asked.

"Of course!" McCarthy replied.

"That'll work."

"Do you both mind signing? It will strengthen the agreement," Mundt suggested. Both men complied.

"Wonderful!" McCarthy exclaimed. "Just wonderful! You won't regret this."

"I'm sure I won't," Stevens responded. Both men stood and waded toward the door of Mundt's office. Fifty reporters emerged once the door opened. Stevens' eyes widened, a goldfish in a tank of barracudas.

McCarthy handed a reporter the paper agreement. Stevens' jaw dropped in horror, unable to stop him. The reporters glanced at the agreement and then barraged Stevens with questions. He was a deer in headlights, too stunned to respond.

McCarthy turned to a reporter so he was out of Stevens' earshot.

"Stevens couldn't have surrendered more abjectly if he had gotten down on his knees!"

☆☆☆☆☆

FEBRUARY 25, 1954

"WHAT WERE YOU thinking?"

Ike paced back and forth across the Oval Office, his jaw tight. His back was sore; it was more and more these days. Stevens sat near the room's frame, his face red and sweating. His jaw rested on his fists, which vibrated. Brownell, Vice President Nixon, and Press Secretary Hagerty were also milling around the room.

"I wasn't even informed about your meeting yesterday until I read that my administration surrendered to McCarthy in the newspaper!" Ike barked.

"I'm just a dog," Stevens whimpered, desperate to put his head in his hands and disappear from the world. "I'll resign immediately."

"That isn't necessary," Ike snapped.

"I want to."

"Denied. Draft a statement that gives your side of the story. You'll read it from the White House. *I'll* edit it to make sure it's what we need."

Stevens nodded obediently, desperate for his embarrassment to end.

"It was a bear trap," Hagerty offered. "You couldn't have known that would happen." Stevens nodded, the reassurance helping.

Ike's eyes bulged in his skull, telegraphing his displeasure.

Of course he should have known. Letting McCarthy outsmart him like that, Ike thought. "Of all the godd—"

He caught himself, resisting his subconscious urge to swear. He would not do so while in the Oval Office.

"I smell presidential ambitions," Ike said. "Joe keeps calling the Democrats traitors, knowing that will defeat us in the long run because we must have Democrats to win. Consequently, he will go around and pick up the pieces. He's crazy if he believes that."

"It seems like my efforts to keep the peace between the administration and Joe have failed," Nixon offered, stating the obvious. His exposure of Alger Hiss as a communist spy in the State Department had helped give McCarthy's crusade its credibility.

"Mr. President," Hagerty began, "it may be time for you to denounce McCarthy."

Ike glared at his press secretary.

"You're madder than a wet hen."

"Why?"

"Because, Jim, it will divide the party," Brownell explained, now agreeing with Ike's plan.

"I'm sorry, Mr. President," Stevens spoke, "but I don't understand why you don't publicly defend General Zwicker by making a formal speech. That sort of thing."

"No!" Ike shouted. "We stick to the plan! Calling McCarthy out publicly would just increase his stature and force a head-on collision."

"Which you would win."

"We don't *know* that!"

Hagerty studied Ike as he argued with Stevens. Something was afoot. The President was having a much stronger emotional reaction to this situation than he had to other, seemingly greater crises, such as the Korean

War. Hagerty, as press secretary, was up to date on classified material. The disjointed pieces *clicked* in his head. He leapt to his feet, so now he and Ike were the two individuals standing.

"Goddamnit, sit down!" Ike ordered, failing to check his subconscious urges.

Hagerty ignored him, raising a finger instead and moving it to-and-fro.

"I *know* what game you're playing, Mr. President!" Hagerty announced excitedly. "It's not the party! *You're* worried about the Oppenheimer situation becoming public!"

Stevens and Brownell turned white as they expected Ike to rip Hagerty in half. Instead, Ike smiled, finally relaxing, his secret out.

"Very good, Jim. Pretty clever for a man who got his pants stuck in fishing lines."

"With all due respect, Mr. President, that was almost a year ago."

"I'm just teasing you, Jim."

"I'm sorry," Stevens interrupted, "but what's the Oppenheimer situation? I assume we're speaking of J. Robert Oppenheimer, the father of the atomic bomb?"

"Correct," Ike affirmed.

"The President withheld Oppenheimer's top-secret clearance because he tried to delay the construction of the hydrogen bomb," Nixon explained.

"McCarthy will hit us on having had Oppenheimer in the government and will paint all of my scientists as Reds," Ike continued, his voice tired from stressing over this and so many other issues that ate at him while he fought to keep the world at peace. "We need them to keep us ahead of the Soviets technologically. Scientists can have idiosyncrasies, even in politics, but Oppenheimer made it clear he's not on America's team anymore. He had to go off the Atomic Energy Commission. But the fact he was here at all gives McCarthy the chance to inflict a huge scandal on this administration."

Brownell stood up, shaking his head, his hands vibrating. He breathed heavily.

"Oh my God! This is a disaster!" he exclaimed. "We are so screwed! He's going to find this and he's going to kill us with it!"

"Calm *down*, Herbert!" Ike ordered.

"Mr. President, you had a *communist* designing our nuclear weapons. And after the Rosenburg debacle! Do you know what he's going to say about us? About you? Will we even be hirable after this?"

Stevens leaned forward in his chair while Ike was still watching Brownell.

"We have to give Joe *whatever* he wants! *Anything* to end this!"

Ike slowly made his way back to the Oval Office desk.

"What are you so scared of?" Nixon asked. "We *removed* Oppenheimer."

"You think that will stop him?" Stevens demanded to know. "You don't know what this guy is capable of!"

"Our administration is going to implode!" Brownell wailed. "All of our efforts are—"

Bang!

Ike slapped the Oval Office desk. The others turned to him.

"I have had enough," Ike asserted quietly. "I have had enough of you all pussyfooting around and I sure have had enough of McCarthy doing this to us and to everyone else!" The President walked toward the center of the group.

"America operates on the *world* stage now! It's *our* responsibility! We are trying to prevent a *global* Armageddon and I am *not* letting that *creep* get in our way. Now I need you all to *toughen* up. This battle is *not* lost. Not yet. He doesn't know about Oppenheimer. And I want to keep it that way."

"It's just a matter of time before Joe cracks it wide open and everything hits the fan," Hagerty replied. "If this breaks it will be the biggest news we've had yet. Real hot."

"That's why we *can't* hit him directly. He'll use the Oppenheimer case against us. We have to make him think that I'm appeasing him so he doesn't dig too deeply. But I still have to protect the loyal men and women in the executive branch from his reach."

"How do you plan to do that?" Nixon asked.

Ike turned to Brownell, his chief legal advisor.

"I suppose the President can refuse to comply with a congressional subpoena, but when it comes down to people down the line appointed to office, I don't know what the answer is. I would like to have a brief memo on the relevant precedent. Just what I can do in this regard."

Brownell put his finger to his chin as he thought.

"There's no legal precedent for that that *I'm* aware of. But that doesn't necessarily mean it's *illegal*."

Nixon watched the conversation between the President and Attorney General, fascinated.

"If there's nothing stopping me," Ike said with a chipper inflection in his voice, "then I want to prohibit anyone in the Army, or any Army document, from going before McCarthy's subcommittee."

He turned to Stevens.

"Is that understood?"

"Yes, Mr. President."

"Good. I'll save this executive privilege for the entire executive branch for later on. A card up my sleeve. This might convince McCarthy to increase his attacks on my administration. He may even identify the Oppenheimer issue. But doing nothing guarantees that he'll tear through the administration until it's a husk."

☆☆☆☆☆

FEBRUARY 28, 1954

MCCARTHY'S STARE WAS dead as his Old Crow bottle left his lips. He put the bottle on the counter, next to his gun that was always with him as protection against potential threats. He'd been up drinking all night, seething in anger from the news.

"I can't believe that son of a bitch told the entire Army not to talk to me," he said to Roy Cohn, his right-hand man and a twenty-five-year-old lawyer. "Without information from the Army officers or their records all of my efforts will come to a halt."

"It just goes to show that the law is a joke," Cohn muttered. "The establishment would never allow a conservative to get away with this. Who's in power is all that matters."

"Exactly," said McCarthy. He picked up his whisky bottle, pausing before it reached his lips again. He gritted his teeth.

"And that wimp, Stevens, complaining to the Democrats on my subcommittee and getting the *Chicago Tribune* to tell his side of the chicken lunch. It just shows that they're all in on it. The establishment. I mean, even *Nixon's* in on it! Nixon! He should be on *our* side! He's more like us than he is like Ike's Ivy League hacks like Brownell and Adams. But he thinks blowing smoke up Ike's ass will put him in the Oval Office one day."

"We have to hit 'em!" Cohn declared. "The law's irrelevant! We need to hit 'em! Attack!"

McCarthy chuckled.

"Is that the best you got?"

"What?" Cohn asked, defensive.

"Nothing. I think I just expected a bit more from someone who partook in the Rosenberg prosecution at twenty-two. But I guess you haven't been yourself since Schine was drafted."

That name sent a shiver down Cohn's spine.

"I miss him so much," Cohn said as his head dropped.

"Relax, you fairy."

"You shut up!"

"God, Roy, relax. David was a miserable little Jew, anyway. I'm not even sure what the Army wants with him."

Cohn leapt to his feet and stormed toward the door.

"Get back here, you baby," McCarthy ordered. Cohn did as he was told. "We're having a serious conversation here." McCarthy's tongue clicked without his realizing it.

"We have to rid the world of that liberal in disguise, Eisenhower. He's a pawn of the Eastern establishment. He gets cheered on by Henry Luce's magazines and the *New York Herald Tribune.* Then a *real* conservative can be President. We have the Midwest and the Sun Belt on *our* side! The oil billionaires are on *our* side! We can still win this!"

Cohn nodded.

"We have to find a way to circumnavigate Ike's order to the Army," McCarthy said. "Any ideas?"

Cohn put his finger to his chin.

"Well, the law *is* artificial. Nothing more than a social construct. We can tell the Army officers to ignore Ike's order and report directly to you on issues dealing with graft, corruption, communism, and treason."

"Will that work?"

"Why not? The content of the law depends on who's in power. And one day that will be us."

"Do you think your mom will finally love you once you're my Attorney General?"

McCarthy stuck the knife in again.

"Dumb bitch," Cohn muttered, McCarthy pressing his buttons. McCarthy's eyes shifted to-and-fro.

"We're going to vanquish those elitist pricks!"

☆☆☆☆☆

MARCH 9, 1954

IKE'S FACE WAS bright red, his eyes bulging as he fought to control his temper. Hagerty, Stevens, and John Adams—who was an Army JAG, Stevens' counsel, and shared a name with the second and sixth Presidents—sat before him.

"I never thought I would see this," Ike muttered. "Not since the South seceded... This is the most arrogant invitation to subversion and disloyalty that I have ever heard of. I won't stand for it for one minute. He's no different than Hitler."

"That seems a bit extreme," Hagerty suggested softly.

"No, Jim, it isn't!" Ike boomed. "McCarthy is making the exact same plea of loyalty to him that Hitler made to the German people. Both tried to set up personal loyalty within the government while both were using the pretense of fighting communism!"

Ike shifted back in his chair, trying to restrain himself. McCarthy, like Ike's other enemies, including Rommel and Mao, would always be measured against Hitler, his nemesis.

"McCarthy is trying deliberately to subvert the people we have in the Army, people who are sworn to obey the law, the Constitution, and their superior officers. I think this is the most disloyal act we have ever had by anyone in the government of the United States."

Ike leapt to his feet and then sat back down, not sure how to channel his frustration without losing his temper.

"Saying Army officers should ignore my order and come to him directly! The nerve! He's crossed the line. If he isn't stopped our whole system of government, of being a nation of laws and not of men, will be in jeopardy!"

Ike looked Hagerty in the eye.

"If such an invitation is accepted by any Army officer and we find out who that officer is, he will be court martialed on the spot. And fired on the spot if it's a civilian."

He slumped back in his chair again. His belief in duty had been nurtured within his subconscious since he'd sworn loyalty to America and the Army at West Point forty-three years prior. McCarthy's selfishness and pleas for others to ignore their duty ate at Ike in a way he couldn't appreciate on a conscious level.

Ike finally calmed down and allowed his lips to form a subtle smile.

"My whole strategy against McCarthy is predicated on my belief that the American people will reject him once they see what a bully he is. And you know what? Some Americans have already been writing to me to express their disapproval of him."

"That's good," Stevens encouraged softly.

"Yeah, but they keep asking me to fire McCarthy!" Ike exclaimed. "Makes me think the people don't understand how their government works!"

The others laughed. Ike, who had shifted from anger to joy, now became somber.

"The Republican Party is supposed to be the party of Abraham Lincoln and Theodore Roosevelt. We have to free it of its reactionary elements. Isolationism and McCarthyism. The people who still deify Calvin Coolidge and who never forgave me for befriending Marshal Zhukov after the war. We have to unify and moderate the party after Joe's beaten. Then we'll have saved it from his influence."

"Lodge told me today that Senator Barry Goldwater is interested in a summit of party leaders where you and Joe can bury the hatchet."

"We're way past that point, especially with his declaration that the Army should report to him despite my order. We've gotten to the point where one of us has to go down. Him or me. And I'm determined that it won't be me."

"That's what we're here to discuss, Mr. President," Stevens chimed in. "Mr. Adams here has finished his report. I think you'll find it very interesting."

"What report?" Hagerty asked.

"Roy Cohn, McCarthy's counsel, has badgered the Army since November regarding David Schine, who was Cohn's aide before he was drafted into the Army."

"Badgering them how?"

"He's demanded that Schine get special treatment. Weekend passes, an excessive number of phone calls, relief from kitchen duties, and so on. He even threatened to, and I quote, 'wreck the Army,' if we don't comply with his demands."

Hagerty's eyes widened. He turned to Ike to see if Ike shared his excitement about this news. Ike's expression didn't change. Did he already know? Or was he keeping a poker face?

"Cohn has pestered me repeatedly about granting Schine an officer commission, but I told him that Schine isn't qualified," Stevens explained.

"What's so special about Schine?" Hagerty asked.

"Nothing," Adams answered. "His only accomplishment is that he wrote a pamphlet denouncing communism that he put in his dad's hotels. But we think he and Cohn might be a couple of pixies together and that's why every strand of Cohn's thinking comes back to this issue."

Ike exhaled as he rested his arms on the Oval Office desk.

"This is it. They're already attacking the Army. Now we'll hit them with a corruption charge of trying to get special favors for their friend. The committee will have to investigate, possibly with public hearings. That will let the people see McCarthy in action against one of our most respected institutions. Especially if we can get it on television. You think McCarthy's a nasty piece of work when he's on offense? Just wait until we get him on defense. His center of gravity is his base of support. We're going to rip it out from under him. And affirm the decency of the American people in the process."

Hagerty watched in awe as Ike explained his strategy as if he were a mob boss planning to kill a rival.

"How do you plan to leak it?" Ike asked.

"We were thinking of giving it to Democratic Senator Stuart Symington and to the reporter Joe Aslop."

"Ugh," Ike shook his head in disgust. "Aslop is one of the lowest forms of animal life on Earth." Aslop was Ike's worst critic in the press.

"I already have an established relationship with him," Adams explained.

"Whatever's easiest."

☆☆☆☆☆

MARCH 24, 1954

IKE EMERGED FOR his press conference in the Indian Treaty Room, a lavish area filled with rich blue and brown designs from the marble floors to the tall windows, from the intricate balcony railings to the high ceiling. A display with the presidential seal was placed in front of a large rectangular window with a round top. A podium stood before dozens of reporters tightly packed into the room. Ike approached the podium, wearing a light gray suit with a white shirt and a red and blue foulard tie. The reporters noted he wore red, white, and blue.

"Good afternoon, ladies and gentlemen," Ike said. "Before we begin, I want to confer a statement made by Puerto Rican governor Marin. He expressed regret for the tragic attack by Puerto Rican terrorists upon our

Capitol Building at the beginning of this month. He also expressed pleasure that the terrorists were quickly subdued. With that behind us, I'll happily take your questions."

Hundreds of hands raised. Ike pointed to his first choice.

"Robert Spivack, *New York Post*," the reporter introduced himself. "Mr. President, in the State of the Union message, I believe the figure of 2,200 security risks was used, and I wondered if there is any breakdown available now on that since the 1,456 figure?"

Ike frowned; the press had been harping on his statistic for the number of federal employees removed as security risks for nearly two months.

"No detailed report has yet been made to me, and it is perfectly understandable. The Civil Service Commission has a very hard job. There were 2,200 people against whom the government intended to move because they believed them to be security risks, remarks already on their records showing that there was some doubt. Those 2,200 have gone in one form or another."

"Thank you, Mr. President," Spivack replied.

Ike moved on to a reporter on the right side of the room.

"Clark Mollenhoff of the *Des Moines Register*. I would like to ask a couple of questions about the situation with what's called 'McCarthyism.'"

Ike gritted his teeth. *Here it goes. Must be steady. Downplay him. Tell the country he doesn't matter. The press usually deserves respect and stature, but they keep obsessing over McCarthy's cheap sensationalism. They're half the reason he's as powerful as he is. And then they want me to clean up their mess.*

"I never talk personalities," Ike replied. "But go ahead."

"Thank you, sir. My first question regards your decision to have the actress Lucille Ball and her husband Desi Arnaz for dinner at the White House a few days ago. As the Senator from Wisconsin has made apparent, Ball was registered as a communist in 1936—"

"I believe," Ike interrupted, "that Ms. Ball made clear that that occurrence only resulted from her desire to gratify her grandfather. I believe Ms. Ball said exactly that in her Senate testimony."

"Yes, sir," Mollenhoff continued, "but my question is whether the decision for you and your wife to have dinner with Ms. Ball and her husband did not somehow result from a desire to signal to the country your faith in her *not* being a communist after Senator McCarthy's accusations against her."

"Not any more than the fact that her show gets more views than my inauguration did last year!" Ike chuckled.

The reporters laughed.

"May I ask another question?" Mollenhoff asked.

"Please," Ike replied.

"Thank you, Mr. President. I want to get this on the record. Do you believe that Senator McCarthy threatens our system of government?"

"When the notion is stated as baldly as that, then it instantly becomes ridiculous."

Many reporters exchanged a glance with their colleagues. Why did the President never appreciate the threat McCarthy posed to American democracy?

"One more question, Mr. President. Governor Stevenson claimed in a recent speech that the Republican Party is divided against itself and cannot stand because it is half-Eisenhower and half-McCarthy. He's clearly referring to President Lincoln's famous speech. I know that Vice President Nixon gave the administration's formal response to Stevenson, but I was wondering if you would like to say something yourself on the topic."

"At the risk of sounding egotistical, I say 'nonsense.'"

Mollenhoff ceded his place to another reporter.

"Milton Friedman, *Jewish Telegraphic Agency*. I also would like to ask a couple of questions related to Senator McCarthy."

Ike nodded, hiding his frustration.

"As I'm sure you know, Mr. President, it has recently come to light that Senator McCarthy and his legal advisor, Roy Cohn, are accused of pressuring the Army to gain privileges for their friend who is serving in Fort Dix. This is resulting in a forthcoming hearing, which was delayed because of the terrorist attack on the Capitol Building a couple weeks ago. Senator McCarthy accused the Army of blackmailing him so that he will end his investigation into the issue of communists in the Army. The Subcommittee of Investigations, of which Senator McCarthy is a part, has asked him to step down for the duration of the hearings. The Senator, however, insists on maintaining his right to vote as a member of the subcommittee. I would like to hear your response to the Senator's claim that he should remain on the subcommittee during the hearings."

Ike chuckled.

"That was a very long question!"

The reporters laughed. Ike's cheek pinched as he thought of how to word his answer.

"I believe it comes down to this: in America, if a man is a party to a dispute, he does not sit in judgment of his own case. Does that answer your question?"

Friedman nodded.

"Yes, it does. Thank you, Mr. President. I would like to ask you one more, if you don't mind."

"Will this one be shorter at least?"

"Yes, Mr. President," Friedman replied with a laugh. "Senator McCarthy has accused your administration of delaying the construction of the hydrogen bomb for eighteen months. How do you respond to that charge?"

The moment of truth, Ike thought.

"I never heard of any delay on my part. Never heard of it."

"Did you listen to the Senator's speech on the subject?"

Ike smiled.

"I never even knew he made a speech!"

The reporters laughed. Ike became serious.

"I would like to say a few words on this general topic. We know we value the right to worship as we please, to choose our own occupation. We know the value we place on those things. If at times we are torn by doubt by unworthy scenes in our national capital, we know that we are Americans. The heart of America is sound."

Many reporters nodded in agreement.

☆☆☆☆☆

MARCH 28, 1954

"So, MR. WELCH, I hear that you're taking the government's case pro-bono," Ike said with a chipper tone in his voice. He stood in the middle of the Oval Office.

"That is correct, Mr. President," Welch replied. "This is quite a case. And to be perfectly honest, the publicity my firm is going to get if we win is more than worth it."

Joseph Welch was a six-foot-tall trial lawyer from Boston. He had a folksy demeanor and wore a gray, striped three-piece suit with a bow tie that belied his reputation for going for the jugular. Welch turned to a man a generation younger who stood behind him, slightly to the left.

"Mr. President, I would like to introduce you to my aide, Mr. Fischer."

"A pleasure to meet you, young man!" Ike exclaimed as he shook Fischer's hand.

"Mr. Fischer is indispensable to my practice," Welch explained, "but if I am being completely honest with you, we are a bit nervous. See, Mr. Fischer was a part of the National Lawyers Guild at Harvard, which Senator McCarthy has claimed has communist ties. He may use that against us."

Ike folded his arms over his chest.

"If he does, you can claim outrage that he is attacking such a responsible young man. Claim that he's being unfair."

"An interesting idea," Welch muttered as he rubbed his chin.

"If you excuse me, gentlemen," Brownell interrupted, "but I must have a word with the President. I am sure that Secretary Stevens and Ambassador Lodge will be more than happy to converse with you in the meantime."

Brownell took Ike to the side of the Oval Office.

"What is it, Herbert?" Ike asked.

"I just wanted to inform you, Mr. President, that both Senate Majority Leader Knowland and Minority Leader Johnson have agreed to your request to televise the hearings in the name of 'transparency.'"

Ike's face lit up.

"Excellent! The American people will see McCarthy for what he really is. He is now battling corruption charges and is in a full pissing match with the US Army on live television. If that doesn't destroy him, nothing will."

"I agree, Mr. President. But party leaders will want the hearings to end as soon as possible. Otherwise, the Republicans will get hurt in the midterms."

"No!" Ike declared. "The party isn't as important as the country. I want these hearings on the air every day and night until McCarthy is discredited in front of the world!"

"I understand, Mr. President," Brownell agreed, his eyes wincing from the President's ruthlessness. "One other issue is the rumor that McCarthy will subpoena Sherman Adams."

"Why would he do that?"

"Because Adams instructed Stevens and John Adams to write the Schine report."

"I *won't* let that happen. I'll use executive privilege. McCarthy will *not* destroy the separation of powers on my watch. My people and their documents will *not* be subpoenaed."

"Yes, Mr. President," Brownell affirmed before returning to Welch and the others.

Ike remained in place, staring at Welch admiringly. Welch was his Patton in this battle against a new demagogue. The Army was Ike's proxy in his feud against McCarthy. It was time to counterattack.

Only one could emerge the winner.

A Dove
in Hawk's Clothing

I believe that Ike's most singular contribution to our history is his repeated
refusal to resort to nuclear weapons during that period. It was not only
plausible but I think logical to suggest that you use the weapons. Truman,
obviously, had used the bomb twice to end World War II. It was Ike who
again and again overruled the advice of his military and diplomatic
advisors and said "no." And I must say that had he done so and if nuclear
weapons and the use of those weapons had become a routine matter of
military force in the period, we might not be here today.
I think that's his great contribution.
—Jim Newton

SEPTEMBER 3, 1954

PRESIDENT EISENHOWER LEFT his muddy boots by the cottage's front
door, his smile stretching from ear to ear. He was at Byers Peak
Ranch, outside Fraser, Colorado. The log cottage, owned by Ike's
friends Aksel Neilson and Carl Norgren, was small, like the adolescent
aspen stands that surrounded it. Snow had already built on the peaks of the
surrounding mountains.

Ike put away his tackle box and fishing pole and made his way to the
cottage's front room. The cottage had premodern furniture. He sat on a
wooden chair with limited cushioning, a lampstand by his left arm.

*Fly fishing is so much more challenging and rewarding than worm
fishing, he thought. Fishing, like golf and hunting, requires planning and*

plotting. They take you into the fields. They induce you to take, at one time, two or three hours to think about the bird, ball, or wily trout. They make this job so much easier. I don't understand politicians like Dick Nixon or Lyndon Johnson who don't have hobbies to relieve the stress of politics. How are their entire lives devoted to something so repugnant?

"How was fishing?" Mamie shouted from the other room. She had spent the day with her mother and grandchildren.

"Good," Ike replied, shouting back. "I caught a ten-incher. Maybe Delores can prepare it for lunch." He was referring to Delores Maloney, an African American woman who, like her husband, John, had served Ike and Mamie since World War II.

"I think she's already in the kitchen working on something."

"What?" Ike asked, unsure what his wife said from the other room.

"I said she's already making lunch!" Mamie shouted louder.

"Ok," Ike replied.

"Are you in for the rest of today?" Mamie asked, her voice softer again with a falling inflection.

"I was hoping to go golfing before dinner with Ellis and Clifford," Ike answered, referring to two members of his friend group he called "the Gang." The Gang were made up of wealthy businessmen who befriended Ike after the war. Their schedules catered to his and some joined him on his vacation from the White House. "We want to get a few rounds in before the temperature drops below freezing this evening."

A moment passed.

"No problem," Mamie answered. "Just change out of your fishing clothes before you sit down. They stink up the cabin."

Ike frowned. He was already sitting and did not want to move. *Not even the President is safe.* He took off his white cap, which he wore outside to protect his bald scalp from the sun. Sweat had built up on the parts of his scalp pressed against its fabric. He pinched his white shirt, which had a rough, bumpy texture, and brought the cloth to his large nostrils.

Ike's eyes narrowed. *It doesn't smell that bad. I'll change later. Just sat down.*

He picked up *The Narrowing Circle*, a whodunit murder mystery, off the lampstand and leaned back in his chair. *Need to catch up on reading. This year was exhausting. The McCarthy hearings,* Brown v. Board, *the St. Lawrence Seaway, the French defeat in Dien Bien Phu, the fall of communism in Guatemala. I'm even working six days a week on this vacation. Have to relax more.*

Ike read for the next forty minutes. He paused as a female character entered the narrative. He frowned. *I've always preferred men's company. Being one of the guys. Don't know why I get awkward and shy around women. Always been that way. This book's okay. Not the best mystery I've ever read. Hell, even I could probably write better mystery novels than some of what my aides get me. I should tell them to get me a good Western. That's definitely my favorite genre. That and military history. Whodunit mysteries are up there—*

"Mr. President." Colonel Andrew Goodpaster entered the room, interrupting Ike's thoughts. "The Secretary of State is calling." Goodpaster was wounded in Italy during World War II and was now Ike's Staff Secretary, meaning he managed the paperflow and major documents for the President and his senior staff. He had a skinny face and his hair parted just to the left of his head's midpoint.

Ike sighed. *What does Foster want?* He groaned as he willed himself to his feet. He took the phone, attached to a black cord, from Goodpaster.

"Thank you, Andrew."

"Sir," Goodpaster said with a nod as he left the room.

"Hello?" Ike asked after he put the phone to his mouth.

"Mr. President?" Dulles asked.

"That's right, Foster. What's happening?" Ike cut right to the chase. That was fine with Dulles.

"What we've feared would happen has come to pass."

"Regarding Formosa?"

"That's right."

"Which island did they hit?"

"Quemoy."

"I see," Ike replied. Tension between Formosa and Red China had been building. The communists had defeated the Nationalists in 1949, causing the Nationalists to flee to Formosa and create their own government. Both sides vowed to destroy the other's government and unify Formosa with the Chinese mainland. Red China was an ally of the Soviet Union and an implacable enemy of the US. Formosa was anticommunist and a US ally. "I suppose Chiang's promise to liberate China from communism is what provoked this." He was referring to Chiang Kai-shek, the leader of the Chinese Nationalists and Formosa.

"That and our efforts to create SEATO as a Southeast Asian equivalent to NATO," Dulles replied, referring to defensive organizations where nations allied together to resist communism. "Chou En-Lai vowed to 'liberate' Formosa from Chiang a few days ago. We predicted this attack was coming." Chou En-Lai was Red China's Premier and Minister of Foreign Affairs.

"What did they hit Quemoy with?"

"Some artillery rounds."

"Do you think this is preliminary to an invasion?"

"If we don't take action."

Ike smiled. *There's only one man I know who has seen more of the world and talked with more people and knows more than he does—and that's me.* Ike was unique in this high opinion of Dulles. Most people thought he was arrogant, even grotesque. Churchill had summed up his opinion as, "Dull, Duller, Dulles."

"Do we know who gave the order to launch these things?" Ike asked.

"Who do you think?"

Dulles was right. Ike did not actually need to ask that question. The answer was obvious.

Mao. The most dangerous man on Earth since Stalin died. Hell, he might be the most dangerous since Hitler fled to South America. He's the biggest adversary I've faced as President, along with McCarthy. And now he's attacking Formosa. This is going to take us to the brink. Formosa is small and so far the Reds are only bombing a tiny island that sits between the two countries. But Formosa is a staunch ally against communism and it can't be allowed to fall. We gave half of Vietnam to communism at this year's Geneva Accords and Formosa's fall would convince the world that all of Asia is falling. That can't happen. This is a vital interest of the United States. I need to talk to Congress and our allies about the prospect of war. Even nuclear war. The Europeans will think we're insane to wage World War III over some islands, but we have to defend our vital interests from communist aggression, even at the risk of war.

"Should we alert the Joint Chiefs that we'll likely need to deploy the Strategic Air Command?" Dulles asked, referring to the part of the Air Force that controlled America's nuclear arsenal.

"No," Ike replied. "Not yet."

"When can I expect you back in Washington?"

"I'm not going back."

"Sir?"

"We don't want to cause a panic. You come here. Bring the Joint Chiefs."

"Ok. We'll come out as soon as possible."

"Sounds good, Foster. Keep me updated.

"Yes, Mr. President."

"Ok, goodbye."

"Goodbye." They hung up. Staying in Colorado would make the American people think Ike was a detached President, which he intended. It led people to think Ike didn't understand the consequences of using nuclear weapons, giving his nuclear saber rattling more credibility. It also led the people to think Dulles, a staunch Cold Warrior, was in the driver's seat.

This wasn't Ike's first showdown with Mao. That was Korea. President Truman led a UN coalition to save South Korea from the North. Mao intervened to help North Korea. A stalemate emerged and Ike ran for President to end that stalemate. Ike threatened to escalate the war with nuclear weapons if Mao didn't agree to an armistice. That worked, but Mao wasn't tied down on the Korean Peninsula anymore. He was on the move, trying to spread communism across Asia. He was a fanatic and totally devoted to communist revolution and expansion. He fought the Nationalists and the Japanese for over twenty years, pulling off impressive feats like the Long March across China. Mao defeated Chiang and founded the communist government, despite being outnumbered.

I think what makes me the most nervous about him is that he defeated General Marshall.

The war between Mao and Chiang resumed after Japan's defeat in World War II, and Truman sent Marshall to broker a ceasefire. Marshall insisted that Chiang take some communists into his government and Mao used this to undermine the Nationalists' military position.

My God, how the hell am I supposed to defeat Mao if Marshall couldn't? Marshall built our military into a colossus and rebuilt Western Europe after the war. But Mao outsmarted him. What chance do I have?

I can't believe we're looking at the prospect of another world war. War is humanity's greatest evil. I toured the French battlefields of World War I, such as Verdun, when I served under General Pershing. Bones stuck out of the ground. Millions perished. And for what, an assassinated archduke and some convoluted alliances? Then there was World War II. I had to make life and death decisions that affected millions. Sent boys younger than my son to kill and die. In Falaise I could smell the rotting flesh of dead armies. You couldn't step in any direction without stepping on a German corpse. Not that World War II wasn't worth it. Of course it was. I saw the Germans' camps. Millions slaughtered just for existing as religious minorities. The survivors were walking skeletons. I've never seen such a clear picture of man's barbarity and evil. The Nazi regime had to be destroyed for civilization to survive. But the fact that a government could even behave that way shows man's stupidity and selfishness.

It's going to take everything I have to protect Formosa while avoiding World War III. I can already predict what my advisors and the military are going to say based on the advice they gave me during the crises in Korea and Indochina. They'll want to go nuclear. They always do. They think nuclear weapons are the tool of first resort in the face of communist aggression. Anything less is appeasement in their minds. I'll have to trust my own judgment on this. I won't be able to bounce my ideas off anyone or have my decisions validated. I can't even talk to Mamie about this. It's just me. George Washington wasn't this alone. He had Hamilton, Knox, and others. Lincoln had Seward and Grant. Roosevelt had Churchill, Marshall, and myself. Even I had Bedell Smith and Omar Bradley during the war. But this is different. I have no one. Let that loneliness sink in. Have to be wary. My advisors will be as dangerous in this situation as Mao. I'll have to be ready for them if I'm going to deter communism while keeping the peace.

'Lord, make me an agent of thy peace.'

☆☆☆☆☆

SEPTEMBER 12, 1954

"CHIANG KAI-SHEK HAS his Nationalist forces on three islands that sit between Formosa and Red China," explained Admiral Radford, Chairman of the Joint Chiefs. "He has fifteen thousand troops on the Tachens, fifty thousand on Quemoy, and four thousand on Matsu. Quemoy blocks Xiamen, a Chinese port that is less than two miles away. Chiang is using these islands to disrupt Red Chinese shipping. All three of the islands were historically part of China."

"And now the Reds want them back," Dulles said, his chin resting on his fist. "How far is Formosa from Red China?"

"About one hundred and fifty miles," Radford answered. "Formosa is key to our defense strategy in the Pacific." The Joint Chiefs were meeting with President Eisenhower and Secretary Dulles in Ike's office near his cottage in Fraser. The office was neat and well organized.

"Especially since the French defeat at Dien Bien Phu cost us half of Vietnam," Army Chief of Staff Matthew Ridgeway chimed in. "The West can't be seen retreating from Asia for a second time this year." Ridgeway had replaced MacArthur as the UN commander in the Korean War, reversing MacArthur's retreat down the Peninsula following Red China's intervention. The war became a stalemate, but Ridgeway opposed Ike's decision to accept an armistice instead of escalating with nuclear weapons.

"We must be careful of Chiang," Ike said. "He dreams of reconquering the mainland. He wants to draw us into a war with Red China."

"Mr. President, it's wrong to draw a moral equivalency between Chiang and the Red Chinese," Radford replied, his chin jutting out. "Chiang is an ally in containing communism and saving the world from atheist tyranny. Mao's aggression is a continuation of World War II."

"I'm just saying that we should be wary of him. His interests aren't the same as ours," Ike answered. His nostrils flared with annoyance at Radford's challenge.

"We're all united in stopping this horrible business that Mao and Chou are starting," Dulles said, trying to unify the room. Dulles' grandfather and uncle had also served as Secretary of State. Dulles escorted his uncle to the Paris Peace Conference at the end of World War I, where he provided legal advice to President Wilson's delegation. He became an international lawyer and served in the State Department in the interwar years. Dulles had supported American membership in the League of Nations but opposed its involvement in World War II until the Japanese attacked Pearl Harbor. After the war he became the leading foreign policy spokesman for the Republican Party and joined Eleanor Roosevelt as a delegate to the UN where he worked on the UN Declaration of Human Rights. He then negotiated the peace treaty with Japan that restored Japan's independence in 1951. Ike hadn't considered anyone else when choosing a Secretary of State in 1953.

"What do you suggest we do?" Ike asked Radford, on edge in anticipation for the Chiefs' recommendation. *These boys will no doubt push to go nuclear, like they always do.*

Radford leaned forward in his seat.

"We want to put American troops on the three islands. Quemoy, Matsu, and the Tachens. It will beef up Chiang's defenses and give the

Nationalists a morale boost."

"It will also put our boys in the middle of the Chinese Civil War," Ike replied. "It's way too risky."

"We're talking about a limited deployment," Air Force Chief of Staff Nathan Twining answered. "This wouldn't cause much of an escalation. The cost-benefit analysis is in favor of this move."

"I disagree," Ike stated. "War is a mutating monster that can't be predicted. Small wars have a tendency to become big wars."

"We shouldn't be afraid of a big war," Twining replied.

"I agree," Dulles chimed in.

Foster wants to use force. Shocker, Ike thought sarcastically.

"We also think that you should pledge to defend the islands with aerial forces. Including nuclear weapons," Radford said.

There it is, Ike thought.

"Who's 'we?' Do you all agree with this?"

"I don't, Mr. President," Ridgeway said.

"But the rest of you do?" The Joint Chiefs nodded. Ike clamped his molars down tightly in frustration. *Have to disapprove without making them question my gumption.* "I'm distressed that you all lack a basic understanding of the President's constitutional powers. I can't start wars or make promises that could lead to wars whenever I want. The United States has no treaty with Formosa. I would need Congress' approval to make such a promise."

The Joint Chiefs exchanged a confused glance, their eyes scrunched.

"Mr. President," Radford began with hesitation, not wanting to upset the President again, "President Truman entered the Korean War without Congressional approval. He said it was a police action and that he could act without Congress."

"Which I think was a dangerous precedent that can lead to future wars. Truman's action was unconstitutional."

"This is beside the point," General Shepherd said. "We *need* to make promises like this because your administration has dramatically cut defense spending. You've put what little you do give us into the Air Force. We lack the ability to deploy substantial forces anywhere in the world at any time of our choosing, like we did in the prior administration."

"And the prior administration got our country stuck in a three-year stalemate in Korea. I'm trying to avoid such a situation from recurring," Ike answered, making a point of maintaining eye contact.

"Are you suggesting you're intentionally handicapping our ability to fight communism?" Shepherd asked.

Ike half-smiled with the right part of his lips. "I'm just prioritizing debt reduction. It ballooned under Roosevelt and Truman."

Radford sighed.

"We can't get distracted by issues like Congress or the national debt, as important as they may seem. This is *the* showdown with Red China. I can't speak for my colleagues, but I think we should be prepared to drop nuclear bombs on Red Chinese airfields and gun emplacements. That would disable Mao's ability to invade Formosa."

Dulles and the other Joint Chiefs slowly and silently nodded in agreement. Ike eyed each of them. The senior military and diplomatic officials in the strongest country in history were advising him to unleash the most powerful weapons in history against the most populous country in history for bombing a few tiny islands.

How would Adlai Stevenson have resisted this pressure if he won in '52? Ike thought. *I have the stature of the man who led Overlord and accepted Germany's surrender and I'm barely holding firm. I wonder if they would have pushed him into some kind of nuclear war.*

"I know for a fact that the Chinese airfields near Formosa are near population centers," Ike said, his eyebrows pinched. "Our tactical nuclear bombs are the equivalent of fifteen kilotons of TNT. That's not a small bomb. Civilians would be caught in the inferno."

"That's a risk we have to take," Radford replied. "I ordered the Navy to firebomb Japanese cities made of wood and paper in World War II. I don't think this is any different."

"I'm not willing to deploy nuclear weapons or make promises that would tie my hands to their use," Ike responded, making his voice louder than Radford's.

Radford cleared his throat unnecessarily.

"Conventional bombs would not disable the Chinese airbases and gun emplacements for long. A nuclear strike would. Frankly, Mr. President, if the islands fall before America acts your administration would be subject to a 'Pearl Harbor-style' inquiry."

The Joint Chiefs were quiet, confused why the President, a military man most of them had known and worked with for over a decade or more, was opposing them and so unwilling to use military force.

A vein bulged in Ike's temple, feeling betrayed by the Joint Chiefs' predictable and extreme recommendation.

"We're not talking about a brushfire war," Ike began. "We're talking about going to the threshold of World War III. If we attack China, we're not going to impose limits on our military actions, as in Korea. And if we get involved in a general war, the logical enemy is Russia, not China, so we'll have to strike there."

The President's vision sent a shockwave through the chiefs. A war with Russia? The Soviet Union had a nuclear arsenal, which China did not. The President knew that a strike on China would escalate to World War III, so the US may as well start by attacking the Soviets.

The Joint Chiefs started chattering among themselves. Some shifted their thinking after what Ike said. Some did not. The chiefs' division reduced the pressure on Ike, who took a deep breath in relief.

☆☆☆☆☆

NOVEMBER 2, 1954

IKE HAD A highball in his right hand as he slumped into his chair. Vice President Nixon, sitting beside the President, held a glass of red wine. Ike's collar was open. He glanced at Nixon.

"You don't have to wear a suit and tie," Ike suggested. "We're in the East Wing. We're not working."

"I always dress this way, Mr. President. Even at home," Nixon replied.

What a strange man, Ike thought. Ike and Nixon were not used to socializing since Ike treated his subordinates like he was still in the Army and he was their superior commander.

Ike turned back to the news on the television. The midterm election results were incoming, and it was a bad night for the Republicans. The GOP had held a slim majority in both chambers for the first two years of Ike's presidency, but the Democrats were on track to take both houses of Congress.

The Democrats are radical spenders. They're going to fight my efforts to reduce the debt and demand an increase in defense spending. On the other hand, McCarthy and the isolationist Republicans will be less powerful now, Ike thought.

Nixon broke the silence.

"This is my fault."

Ike's eyes were glued to the television. It took him a second to register what the Vice President said.

"No, it isn't, Dick," Ike consoled. "You're a good speaker."

"No, it's my fault. My heart wasn't in this race. Campaigning hasn't been any fun since the fund crisis in '52."

"Don't take this personally."

Nixon's jaws clenched, vibrating his jowls.

"Pat wants me to leave politics. I'm considering it."

"Oh, Dick! Don't do that. You can be President one day. You're not ready yet, but you will be by the time I leave office." Ike had sent Nixon on several foreign trips to get him foreign policy experience. It was part of his efforts to mentor Nixon and make him presidential material.

"You really think so?" Nixon asked.

"Of course," Ike replied. "I'm not going to leave you outside the loop, like Roosevelt did with Truman and the Manhattan Project."

Nixon's cynicism sank deeper.

"That doubt. It's still inside me. It still exists."

Ike sighed. He felt awkward about being Nixon's therapist. *If I have one instinctive passion in my dealings with others, it is the right of every individual to his or her privacy in heart and mind. Humans are more emotional and sentimental beings than they are logical and intellectual. When, therefore, they are shocked or hurt in their deepest selves, others who care about them should, as I see it, stand by but refrain from probing, advising, or even—in a verbal sense—sympathizing.*

Ike glanced at Nixon; his face sank lower and lower as insecurities and thoughts ate at him.

"You know, Dick, setbacks can often be opportunities to prove yourself."

"What would we prove from this experience?"

"That we can work with the other side. That we have the character to get back up after being knocked down."

Nixon snorted at Ike's efforts to cheer him up. Ike ignored it.

"We lost this election because of all the mossbacks in our party. We're supposed to be the party of Abraham Lincoln and Theodore Roosevelt."

Nixon nodded. "There were too many turkeys running on the Republican ticket. Plus, McCarthy imploded in the spring and Robert Taft is no longer here to promote the Old Guard. That's why this happened."

"Exactly."

"It still doesn't change the fact that I've only slept five hours a night for the past five weeks."

"You did your duty, Dick. You couldn't control the outcome."

"I know, but it makes Stevenson's remark about me being 'McCarthyism in a white collar' sting worse. We can't rub our victory in his face."

"That's not what this is about."

"It's part of what it's about," Nixon muttered softly.

"I'm not kidding about the conservative wing of the party being a problem, though," Ike said. "I sometimes wonder whether we should form a third party that subscribes to the Middle Way and avoids the extremes. We could call it the Whigs. Although I have never actually been able to find out what that word meant."

☆☆☆☆☆

DECEMBER 12, 1954

WE ALL NEED to learn more about China to get through this crisis. I just hope this presentation is accurate. The State Department's China division is weak from years of McCarthy claiming it's filled with communist traitors. It's not hiring as much quality or quantity as it should be.

Walter Robertson finished organizing his forms.

"Mr. President, Mr. Vice President, thank you both for having me here. It's an honor to speak to you both."

"The pleasure's all ours," Ike replied with a hint of a smile.

Robertson, a State Department expert on China, had for years been a leading defender of Chiang Kai-shek and was an architect of American recognition of Formosa as the real China. His bulky bronze class ring *clinked* when he let his hand drop to the table. Ike, Nixon, and Dulles sat on the opposite side of a White House table.

"The first thing to know if we are to understand China's perspective," Robertson said, "is that China is a civilization pretending to be a nation state. Think of the entire Western World, including Greece, Rome, Britain and France, us—all those countries and more make up Western Civilization. China is the equivalent of all of those countries combined in terms of its history and culture."

And yet so many of my advisors want to hit them with nuclear weapons. How can they destroy an entire civilization? Ike thought.

"How continuous is their society?" Nixon asked as he adjusted his tie.

"Continuous in what way? Their government?"

"No," Nixon replied. "Their culture. How static has it been over time? At least until Mao seized power?"

"I would say they have remained about the same over the millennia. At least as far back as the record shows. For example, Mr. Vice President, the Chinese alphabet has remained remarkably consistent for thousands of years. Modern Chinese can read Confucius."

"Fascinating," Nixon muttered. Learning about China stimulated his interest, as if they were another species. "What's China's origin story?"

"They don't have one, unlike America's little revolution—"

"Little?" Ike asked.

"I mean they don't have an event comparable to the American Revolution, Mr. President. Though, like the United States, China has a unifying philosophy."

"Communism?" Ike asked.

"Confucianism," Robertson replied. "Confucius' writings were adopted by the Han dynasty as official state philosophy. His writings were the equivalent of the Bible and Constitution combined."

"What did he teach?" Nixon asked.

"Confucius' main goal was social harmony. He preached compassionate rule, the performance of rituals, self-restraint, and learning. He believed in social hierarchy. Confucius cared about the middle path and used only moderate reform when necessary."

Ike unconsciously nodded.

"Why doesn't Red China seem to reflect Confucian philosophy?" Nixon asked.

Robertson instinctually put his hands in his pockets but took them out to appear professional.

"I believe you answered your own question, Mr. Vice President. We're dealing with *Red* China. Mao wants to remake Chinese society, as well as the world order. He wants to destroy Confucianism to make way for communism. Where Confucianism prizes stability, Mao prizes perpetual revolution and upheaval, both domestically and around the world. He thinks stability brings stagnation and hierarchy, which he hates."

My God. Intentionally causing instability. I can't think of anything as opposed to my worldview. What kind of a leader hates stability and likes permanent crisis? How are people supposed to live in chaos? I wish I could get in Mao's head, like I did with Hitler.

"Does Mao have any personal heroes?" Ike asked. "Mine are Washington and Lincoln. Who are Mao's equivalents of them?"

"Qin Shuhuang and Karl Marx," Robertson answered without missing a beat.

"I've heard of Marx. Who was the other name?" Ike asked.

"Qin Shuhuang. He unified China for the first time and ended the Warring States period. He defeated his rivals, burned books, and persecuted Confucians."

"Sounds like a nice guy," Dulles muttered, speaking for the first time.

"Mao wants China to be a blend of Qin Shuhuang and Marx. He sees himself as a philosopher king."

"Like in Plato?" Ike asked.

"That's correct," Robertson replied, surprised that the old soldier knew *The Republic*.

Ike smiled. Fox Conner had him read *The Republic* in Panama.

"Can you go more into Mao's foreign policy views?" Ike asked.

"China has historically seen itself as the center of the universe. This is the core of its identity. It doesn't like our Western notion that it is one state among many. This Sino-centrism is blended with world revolution in Mao's foreign policy thinking."

"How does China take orders from Moscow if it thinks it's the center of the universe?" Nixon asked.

"A lot of China scholars are skeptical that China is as subordinate to Moscow as most American politicians think."

"What does Mao think of us?" Ike asked.

"Of the United States?"

"Yes."

"Mao characterizes his enemies as 'imperialists.' As in colonists, like the old European Empires. He thinks the US is the leader of global imperialism and that we intend to invade China and Asia."

"Nonsense," Nixon muttered.

"If this is an American invasion," Ike began, "why is he attacking Formosa?"

"China's military strategy is different from the West's," Robertson explained. "They focus on victory through psychological advantage. Think of how Mao won over the Chinese peasants as part of his strategy to defeat Chiang in the Civil War. They don't rely on brute force, like we do."

Like how I fought the Nazis by destroying their Army, Ike thought.

"So, Chiang holding these islands is a psychological insult?" Ike asked.

"Correct."

"And so, Mao thinks he's acting defensively, even if we think it's aggression?"

"Yes."

"And Mao's defensive maneuvers are triggering our system of deterrence?"

"Exactly."

"This is ridiculous!" Dulles exclaimed. Ike and Nixon shifted away from Dulles to escape his halitosis. "This is masking the fact that Mao is trying to destroy Chiang. It's no different than Hitler occupying the Rhineland, Mussolini invading Ethiopia, or Japan conquering Manchuria."

"I don't disagree with you," Ike replied. "But we still need to consider Mao's perspective."

"How can we consider his perspective?" Dulles asked with a deep breath, "when he's more dangerous than the Russians and as fanatical as Hitler?"

"How is that?" Robertson asked.

Dulles turned to his subordinate.

"You couldn't negotiate with Hitler. Neville Chamberlain proved that. And you can't negotiate with Mao."

"What would you recommend?" Ike asked. *Let's get his cards on the table.*

"We'll probably have to use nuclear weapons against China this time. There's no other way to save Formosa. And losing Formosa is a key step toward communist victory in Asia."

Foster wants to drop nuclear bombs on China and Mao's the fanatic? I can choke on this much hypocrisy, Ike thought. *I wonder if Mao sees Foster as a partner in some crazy game of combative coexistence.*

"A nuclear strike would slaughter millions and plunge the world into war for the third time this century. We have to look for a less destructive solution before it comes to that. It's our duty as a nation," Ike argued.

"I agree with Secretary Dulles," Nixon chimed in, desperate to seem as thoughtful a foreign policy thinker as Ike and Dulles. "Red China must be stopped before it conquers the world. The bomb ended the Japanese threat, it will end the Chinese one too. We should alert NATO of our intentions."

What is wrong with my advisors? Do they not grasp what they're saying? Am I the last sane man left on Earth? Why do I get no one reasonable to talk to about this situation?

"No, Dick, we can't do that. The best-case scenario is that this will validate the bomb's use going forward. The worst case is an all-out nuclear exchange with the Soviets."

"At the very least," Dulles began as he pushed his glasses back up the bridge of his nose, "we need to establish a naval perimeter around Quemoy and Matsu. That will display strength in the face of Mao's warmongering."

Have to restrain him softly, Ike thought.

"I'll order the Seventh Fleet into position to do some reconnaissance. But I'm going to tell it not to be too aggressive. We can't be the ones who escalate this situation." He turned to Robertson. "I'd like you to go to Formosa to hold Chiang's hand during this crisis. Keep him on a leash so he can't do anything too brash."

"Yes, Mr. President."

Ike rose to his feet. *Have to find a way to save Formosa while keeping the peace. I have to. And I have to do it alone.*

☆☆☆☆☆

JANUARY 20, 1955

THE CRISIS ESCALATED. Chiang and Chou each announced that war between Formosa and Red China was imminent on New Year's Day. Red Chinese forces landed on Ichiang, an island seven miles from the Tachens, on January 18. The communist forces quickly overwhelmed the Nationalist defenders. An attack on the Tachens appeared inevitable. This prompted Ike to invite Congressional leaders from both parties to the White House to discuss the crisis.

"I'm tempted to ask Chiang to abandon the islands while fortifying Formosa," Ike explained after he and the Congressmen exchanged pleasantries.

"You can't do that!" Senator Knowland exclaimed, air whistling through his nostrils. Knowland became leader of the Republicans' conservative wing and the Senate Majority Leader after Robert Taft died in 1953. The midterm elections reduced him to being the Senate's Minority Leader. "Chiang will never abandon the islands! It would destroy the Nationalists' morale!"

"We should be more concerned about this situation escalating out of control than we are about Nationalist morale," Ike countered.

"That's appeasement!" Knowland responded. "Senator McCarthy is already accusing your administration of appeasing Red China. This would only confirm his claims."

McCarthy, Ike thought, frustrated to hear the name of one of his greatest enemies. *If the New Look is appeasement that can only mean that he wants a nuclear war with China. That's what he'd do if he were President. Thank God the Senate censured him in December.*

"Please don't use McCarthy's name in my presence," Speaker of the House Sam Rayburn requested. "Now that he's been censured, I never want to see that right-wing demagogue again."

"Amen to that," agreed Senate Majority Leader Lyndon Johnson.

"He shouldn't be an issue going forward," Vice President Nixon chimed in.

"I suppose the islands will probably survive anything short of a direct invasion," Ike replied, trying to agree with Knowland.

"We can't let this situation get to that point," Knowland countered, his eyes fluttering. "We should launch a preemptive nuclear attack against Red China and the Soviet Union before they can invade Quemoy and Matsu."

Oh my God, Ike thought. *Who actually thinks that Knowland would carry that thesis to its logical conclusion and present that resolution to Congress? I don't believe he would for a second. Knowland's foreign policy is to develop high blood pressure whenever he says 'Red China.' You can even see his cheeks get pink. I'm looking at it right now. What a guy.*

"I will not consider a preemptive war. Not for one second," Ike rebutted, his jaw clamped shut. "America has a duty to be a moral nation and preemptive war is the doctrine of Adolf Hitler." Awkward tension set in.

"We at least need to be ready to launch a nuclear strike on Red China if Mao invades Formosa," Johnson said to break the silence, standing with the other party's leader in the Senate. Johnson was a large Texan whose hair was brushed backward.

This is going around in circles. Wish I could start doodling. Would they really mind? Ike wondered.

"We can consider that option, Lyndon," Ike replied, throwing the new Senate Majority Leader a bone. "If we did that, we would need to stop Chiang from attacking the communists. That would force our hand."

"You want him to stop resisting the Red invasion of Ichiang!" Senate Minority Whip Leverett Saltonstall exclaimed. Saltonstall was a centrist from Ike's wing of the Party.

"I mean that we can't let him attack Red forces in an offensive manner. He obviously should defend the islands if he's determined to hold them," Ike replied. *I hate to say this, but my dealings with Chiang, South Korean leader Syngman Rhee, and other Oriental leaders make me question if Orientals think logically, like we do in the West. They're so willing to wage war against stronger countries, thinking they can draw us into helping them. Then again, I suppose that was Churchill's strategy in 1940.*

"Do you support the statement that we'll strike Mao with nuclear weapons if he invades Formosa?" Johnson asked.

"The hard way is to have the courage to be patient. We must not be too quick to say what we want to do."

"So that's a 'no?'" Johnson asked.

"I didn't say that."

"Then what are you saying, Mr. President?"

Time to make my move, Ike thought. "I want Congress to pass a resolution that gives me full authority to use military force to defend Formosa."

Johnson's eyebrows scrunched. "What sort of resolution?"

"One that would serve as a middle ground between a declaration of war and my acting without any Congressional authorization."

"That isn't necessary," Rayburn replied, peering through his rectangular glasses. "The President has all the powers he needs to deal with this situation. A joint resolution at this particular moment would be unwise because the President would be saying in effect that he did not have the power to act instantly."

"Launching a nuclear strike on China would be an act of war," Ike replied. "The Constitution gives Congress the power to declare war."

"President Truman set a precedent that the President can take military action abroad when he intervened in Korea without consulting Congress," Rayburn said.

"And I believe his action was unconstitutional," Ike rebutted.

"Why do you want to weaken the presidency?" Johnson asked.

"I want to uphold the Constitution," Ike said. "It's our inheritance from the Founding."

"I believe President Eisenhower simply has a more conservative view of executive power than some other Presidents," Nixon interjected, trying to help his boss. "This might be because he himself comes into the office as a general. He feels the desire to share responsibility with Congress more than a civilian President would."

And because I actually care about the Constitution and am trying to restrain some of the excesses Roosevelt established with the New Deal and court packing schemes, Ike restrained himself from adding.

"The President is asking for a predated declaration of war," Rayburn replied, shifting his weight to the left side of his seat.

"It's not a declaration of war," Ike rebutted. "It's an authorization for the use of force."

"What's the difference?"

"I'm trying to avoid a war, so declaring war would be the opposite. But an authorization to use force would give me the Constitutional authority to manage the situation and threaten a nuclear response while still being short of war." *It's insane that they're opposed because they think it's too constraining instead of too broad. What's wrong with Congress? What happened to Henry Clay and Daniel Webster?*

"It isn't necessary," Rayburn declared.

"I agree," Johnson said. Knowland was torn; he had a conservative view of the Constitution but didn't want to constrain the President's ability to use force against communism.

"We can agree to disagree," Ike replied, trying to be diplomatic. "But the resolution would eliminate any doubt about my powers. It would make clear the unified and serious intentions of our government, our Congress, and our people. I believe this would serve to deter continued Chinese aggression by showing Mao that we are locked and loaded if he escalates his attacks."

"That's an interesting thought," Rayburn said. He rubbed his chin. "Would it be just for Formosa or for the islands too?"

"I think it should be contingent upon Chiang evacuating the Tachens. That will de-escalate the situation. The resolution should be ambiguous on Quemoy and Matsu."

"Why?"

"It will keep Mao guessing on what we'll do. It keeps our cards close to the vest."

Rayburn smiled.

"Now that sounds like the man who invaded Normandy."

Ike chuckled and continued, "I do not suggest that the United States enlarge its defensive obligation beyond Formosa, but the danger of armed attack directed against the area compels us to take into account closely related localities which, under current conditions, might determine the failure or success of such an attack."

"Wow," Johnson muttered, still unused to Ike's jargon. "I can ask George to introduce the resolution."

Georgia Senator Walter George, who was on the Foreign Relations Committee, introduced the resolution on Ike's behalf. It passed 83 to 3 in the Senate and 410 to 3 in the House. Opposition came from Democrats who said that the President's executive authority meant that Ike did not need the resolution. But the world, including Mao, now knew that Ike had the authority to take whatever action he wanted.

☆☆☆☆☆

IKE AND MAO'S standoff continued into the spring. Mao continued bombing Formosa and prepared to invade the country. World leaders feared it would escalate into World War III. Ike received a letter from Churchill that criticized Ike for being too aggressive toward China. If Sino-American tensions led to a war between NATO and the Soviet Union an atomic bomb would be dropped on London. Why risk that over some tiny islands? *Sometimes I wish those damned little offshore islands would sink*, Ike thought as he put away Churchill's letter.

The Joint Chiefs did not share Churchill's fear that Ike was being too aggressive. Quite the opposite.

"I'm afraid to say that we disapprove of the Formosa Resolution," Admiral Radford explained. "It is too ambiguous about what actions we would take to defend Formosa."

"That was the point," Ike replied, "to keep Mao guessing."

"Predictability is key to foreign policy," Radford countered, his thumbs twiddling. "Our allies and enemies need to know what we'll do in specific situations."

"I disagree. We don't want to make commitments we can't keep. And our enemies should be on their toes."

"A Chinese invasion of Formosa is imminent. I assume that we'll strike back with nuclear weapons once that happens."

"I would make no such assumption," Ike replied.

"Then how is this any different than Chamberlain at Munich? Are you trading away Formosa for 'peace in our time?'"

Idiot. I'm trying to save Formosa while avoiding war, Ike thought.

"Formosa will not fall on my watch."

"But you're not taking sufficient action to save it!" Radford shouted, exacerbated. How could the President, who was as important as anyone to defeating Hitler, not grasp that this was a binary choice?

"I disagree," Ike replied, his molars pressing together as he sought to keep his cool. "I've recently ordered Admiral Felix Stump of the Pacific Fleet to evacuate Nationalist forces from the Tachens, as well as any civilians who wish to leave."

"That's retreat!"

"No, it's being cautious!" Ike declared. "You may not remember the devastation of the last world war, but I do!" He paused. "I'm going to tell Robertson, a State Department official I sent to Taipei, to tell Chiang not to attack the Chinese mainland without our approval."

"Frankly, Mr. President," Admiral Carney, Chief of Naval Operations, began, "I believe that evacuating the islands will be a more difficult job for the Navy than defending them. It also leaves us unprepared to engage Mao's naval forces once their invasion begins."

"If we can deescalate this situation, we might be able to prevent an invasion," Ike suggested.

Radford and Carney scoffed. Radford said, "Your actions are more likely to help Mao's invasion than prevent it."

Ike's face flushed red. *Our government is pushing for war. Nuclear war. And Mao's not backing down. I'm the only thing that stands in the way of global Armageddon. But everyone is united in their readiness for war—is there a chance that I'm wrong? Get that stupid thought out of your head, Dwight. You've seen war. The piles of corpses. The letters to and from grieving families. Never again. I can't let that happen again. I wanted to be President to avoid war. That's what I have to do. For the sake of millions. Maybe billions. That's what I have to do.*

☆☆☆☆☆

THAT NIGHT, TWO members of The Gang, George Allen and William Robinson, came to the White House to help Ike relax. They rewatched *High Noon*, Ike's favorite film. It was about a sheriff who had to defy public opinion to do what's right.

Ike was now with his friends and Mamie in the East Wing. They played bridge. Allen and Robinson were partners. Only Mamie dared partnering with Ike and his volcanic temper. In bridge, partners compete to form a contract, which specifies how many tricks they need to receive points. Players make calls in a clockwise order, where they can pass, double, redouble, or state a contract that the partnership will adopt. The player with the highest contract wins the contract for their partnership. It requires partners to be able to anticipate one another's actions.

Ike glanced at his cards. *I have a 1 and 4 of Clubs and a 5 of Diamonds. Bill played a 5 of Clubs. George played a 1 of Hearts and a 3 of Clubs. Mamie must have the 2 and 6 of Clubs. If she plays the 6, we'd be 6 beyond 6. That means we'll win.*

Ike took a deep breath. He eyed his wife, whose blue eyes studied her cards. He also peered at her shoulders, which were bare in her outfit. He had to stop himself from staring. *She looks lovely in that outfit. I love when her shoulders are out like this.*

The fireplace crackled. *Love that sound.*

He looked back at Mamie, who still waited to call.

I wonder what she's thinking. She must know that playing a 6 will win this round for us. I guess I shouldn't presume. I can try to read her mind and intentions all day, but that doesn't mean I'll be right. Have to try though. Just like this thing with Mao!

Ike froze. Was that an epiphany?

Wait. That's it. Mao and I are locked in a massive game of bridge. We're each trying to read the other's mind and anticipate the other's moves. We can restore the peace if we play our cards right. This whole time I've thought Mao was my enemy. But he may be my ultimate bridge partner. And the stakes aren't bragging rights. They're humanity's survival.

Mamie's nose wrinkled. *She's so cute.*

He sighed. *Can't be too soft with him. He's still trying to spread communist totalitarianism and destroy liberty. He's threatening a vital American interest. Regardless of what everyone thinks, I have no intention of backing down. Formosa's not falling, not on my watch. But war is only a last resort if a vital interest is threatened and all peaceful alternatives fail. But they haven't all failed. Not yet.*

Bridge is fun, but there's another card game I've played even longer. Poker. Bob Davis taught me poker when I was a boy in Abilene. Poker's all about the bluff. I'm the best poker player I've ever met. Became my main hobby at West Point after I injured my knee and had to quit the football team. Except I had to quit poker, too, because too many people owed me money. But there's something about reading your opponent's mind and bluffing to win.

Nuclear poker. The New Look, with its nuclear deterrence, is essentially nuclear poker. I ended the Korean War by making Mao and Chou think that I would escalate with nuclear weapons. And they folded. We got the armistice and my son came home from the war, along with millions of other sons. But Mao seems determined not to fold this time.

I don't know if I can hold out much longer. It looks like Mao might invade Quemoy and Matsu within days. I don't think I could hold back Congress, the Joint Chiefs, Dulles, Nixon, and everyone else much after that. I can't even imagine how horrifying a nuclear war will be. We'll have to dig for worms in the ashes for food. I don't know why everyone else doesn't get that.

Mao said last week that he's not afraid of a nuclear war. He said that, even if hundreds of millions of his own people, and of other people's, die in the mushroom clouds, that that's okay with him. Because capitalism will be destroyed in the exchange between us and the Russians while communism will claw out of what's left and endure. It's a terrifying thought that he's ready for a nuclear war. But I don't believe him. Not for a second. Mao's a monster, a tyrant, a butcher. But even he is not that heartless and crazy. He's bluffing. And so will I. I need to put the fear of death into him.

Poker and bridge. Bluffing and reading minds to make a deal. I'm going to need all my skills in both of those games to save Formosa while avoiding war. I need to read Mao's mind, like I did with Hitler.

Mamie smiled. She placed a 2 of Clubs on the table. She looked satisfied with her decision.

Ike's jaw dropped. His eyes widened. He looked his wife in the eye.

"Why did you play that card!" he demanded to know.

"Because I felt like it!" she fired back.

Ike slumped back in his chair.

Hopefully reading Mao's mind will go better.

☆☆☆☆☆

MARCH 15, 1955

"WHY DID THE *LA Times* send me to witness this test?" Gene Sherman, a reporter, asked. "I've seen several atomic bomb tests before."

The colonel standing beside him chuckled.

"What's so funny?" Sherman asked.

"This test will be different. The brainiacs call what you're about to see an 'H-bomb,' or a 'hydrogen bomb.'"

"Fancy name," Sherman muttered. "But once you've seen one of these things, you've seen them all. I only got three hours of sleep because of this."

"I'd bet good money that you'll take that back once you see it go off."

"I wouldn't count on it."

One thousand soldiers from Camp Desert Rock and twenty journalists were standing in a trench in the Nevada desert, waiting for the test. Everyone present wore a helmet. The journalists had been invited to the test by the Atomic Energy Commission.

Sherman noticed that the soldiers did not seem anxious. They mostly joked with each other. Sherman wondered how many had seen a hydrogen bomb test before.

"It's time," the colonel said to the soldiers. They started taking the precautions that the Atomic Energy Commission had instructed them to take.

Twenty-five hundred points of TNT were detonated an hour before to test the site's calibrations. Equipment deemed unnecessary was removed thirty minutes after that. Sherman looked up and watched as three B29 Superfortress bombers droned over the target.

"This is H minus five," a loudspeaker explained. "The mushroom cloud will be at an altitude of approximately forty thousand feet eight minutes after the detonation." Sherman felt a knot in his stomach. "You gentlemen are privileged to be closer than any of our troops have ever been—closer than any American troops in history. This is the first time you may get hurt if you don't obey orders. Two miles is mighty close. Gentlemen, this is the greatest show on earth. Relax and enjoy it." The loudspeaker squeaked as it shut off.

The whole group knelt to the bottom of the trench. Sherman's helmet bumped the side of the trench as he lowered himself. Everyone put their head down.

"Five... four," the countdown said, "three... two..." Sherman couldn't shut his eyes to protect them from the flash. "One."

The first thing Sherman noticed was the powdered sand around him turn white. He wasn't sure why he noticed that in the corner of his eye, but he did. Then he saw the brightest flash that he, or anyone in the history of the world, had ever seen. It was the brightest flash to appear on Earth since the asteroid hit the Yucatan Peninsula sixty-five million years ago.

Sherman was unsure he was breathing as he stared at a much larger mushroom cloud than any he had ever seen. It far exceeded what his peripheral vision could take in. Never before had he been in such awe.

The United States government had tested its first hydrogen bomb in December 1952, which was between Ike's election and inauguration. He ordered it to be classified and kept secret from the American people. That had now changed. He had ordered a hydrogen bomb test and told the Atomic Energy Commission to invite reporters to watch. That way all Americans, and the world, would know what was in the US arsenal. Mao would know what he was up against.

☆☆☆☆☆

MARCH 23, 1955
IKE AND PRESS Secretary Jim Hagerty stood behind the door of the State Department Auditorium as reporters swelled the seating area. Ike's stomach did somersaults. He was always nervous before going on television, but this time was especially perilous. The world was on the brink of nuclear war. The hydrogen bomb test increased tensions and fears that were already reaching a breaking point. Dulles contributed to the atmosphere by giving an interview a few days ago where he discussed nuclear war in positive terms. Senator Knowland then declared "no appeasement!" in the halls of Congress. Fear gripped the American people as the prospect of World War III settled in on them.

Ike bit the earpiece of his glasses. Hagerty, with his hair slicked back and with rectangular glasses covering his eyes, looked grim as he told the President more bad news.

"Are you sure this came from Radford?" Ike asked about the Chairman of the Joint Chiefs.

"Yes, Mr. President," Hagerty answered. "He told reporters that there is a 'distinct possibility' that war will break out at any time."

"My God," Ike sighed, his face pale, "this has got to stop. There is always a danger in the Far East, but we are trying to keep the peace. We are not looking for war."

"I know, Mr. President."

Ike kept chewing on his earpiece, his expression hopeless. Then his sunny Eisenhower optimism kicked in and his frown flipped into a grin. He turned to Hagerty.

"I would tell those reporters that you are not normally a betting man, but that if any of them wanted to bet a thousand dollars that we would be in a war within the next month that you would be happy to let them."

Hagerty chuckled.

"If you let me say a hundred, I'll do it."

"That's a deal!"

Ike turned to the door. His anxiety toward being on television returned. It was almost time.

"You know they're going to ask about this situation in Formosa, right?" Hagerty asked. Ike nodded. "Some of the people in the State Department say that the Formosa Strait situation is so delicate that no matter what question you get on it, you shouldn't say anything at all."

A small smile of determination emerged on Ike's lips.

"Don't worry, Jim. If that question comes up, I'll just confuse them."

Hagerty smiled.

"You're on."

Ike entered the State Department Auditorium. He walked toward the podium as cameras flashed and dozens of reporters shuffled in their seats. Camera equipment hummed.

"Morning, gentlemen," Ike said with a smile. Light reflected off of his bald scalp. The conference started. An early question from NBC was why journalists were allowed to witness and report the hydrogen bomb test in Nevada.

"Oh, that sort of thing is too complicated for a dumb bunny like me!" Ike exclaimed. "You'll want to ask Lewis Strauss from the Atomic Energy Commission about that. I'm sure he knows the answer." Strauss did know, since Ike had told him what to tell the press that morning.

A man stood up, holding a pen.

"Charles von Fremd of CBS! Can I ask a question?"

"I couldn't possibly say no to CBS."

Fremd smiled.

"I would like you to comment, if you would, Mr. President, on Secretary Dulles' statement that, in case of war in the Far East, that, and I quote: 'we would probably make use of small tactical atomic weapons.'"

Sweat built on Ike's temples. He had handled the press well since World War II, but this had to be the performance of his life. The fate of the world was at stake.

"Yes, of course they would be used. In any combat where these things can be used on strictly military targets and for strictly military purposes, I see no reason why they shouldn't be used just exactly as you would use a bullet or anything else."

The reporters were breathless. Did the President compare nuclear weapons to bullets? While the world was on the brink of World War III?

I've got to make Mao and the world think I don't know what waging a nuclear war would mean. I've got to. My grandchildren's future, the world they won't be able to grow up in. It's all at stake.

Fremd stuttered before he asked his next question.

"But…" he paused. "Would the United States itself be destroyed in a nuclear war?"

Ike looked impish.

"Nobody in a war or anywhere else ever made a good decision if he was frightened to death. You have to look facts in the face, but you have to have the stamina to do it without just going hysterical."

Several reporters exchanged glances of amazement and shock. What did he say? This was the President? This buffoon defeated Adolf Hitler?

Another reporter stood up.

"Joseph C. Harsch from the *Christian Science Monitor*."

"Morning!" Ike exclaimed.

"Yes, good morning, Mr. President," Harsch quickly said, as confused as anyone in the room. "I would just like to clarify, Mr. President. Would the United States use nuclear weapons to defend Quemoy and Matsu?"

Ike fought to control his nerves.

"I believe the great question about these things comes when you begin to get into those areas where you cannot make sure you are operating merely against military targets."

"Did that even answer the question?" one reporter audibly asked another. What was this? Every reporter in the room remembered, and some witnessed, Franklin Roosevelt address Congress the day after Pearl Harbor. It was a majestic performance. They had thought Harry Truman's conferences and speeches were less dignified, but they were at least intelligible, unlike this amateur golfer in the White House. He commanded the nuclear arsenal?

Harsch was clearly dissatisfied with Ike's answer. He tried again.

"I'm sorry, sir. I am a little stupid about this thing."

"Well, I'm glad you didn't say *I* was!" Ike laughed.

Small nervous chuckles filled the room for a moment. Then grim seriousness. Harsch asked directly, "If we got into an issue with the Chinese, say over Matsu and Quemoy, that we wanted to keep limited, do you conceive of using this specific kind of tactical atomic weapon in that situation or not?" He could not be more precise.

This one must be a masterpiece of gobbledygook, Ike thought.

"Well, Mr. Harsch, I must confess that I cannot answer that question in advance. The only thing I know about war are two things: the most changeable factor in war is human nature in its day-by-day manifestation; but the only unchanging factor in war is human nature.

"And the next thing is that every war is going to astonish you in the way it occurred, and in the way it is carried out.

"So, for that man to predict, particularly if he has the responsibility for making the decision, to predict what he is going to use, how he is going to do it, would I think exhibit his ignorance of war; that is what I believe.

"So, I think you just have to wait, and that is the kind of prayerful decision that may someday face a President. We are trying to establish conditions where he doesn't."

The press was silent; unsure how to decipher that. The world would think that the President of the United States did not grasp how destructive a nuclear war could be. On top of that, this was the general who led the Allies to victory on the Western Front. He wasn't afraid of massive military force. That was a scary combination. But his answer also contained a ray of hope for Americans scared of the crisis. He had said war was unpredictable and that it was up to the President to make the right decision. And deep down, despite his butchery of the English language, they knew he was Ike. He was 'dad.' An adult. They could trust him to keep them safe from communism and nuclear weapons.

The reporters reluctantly accepted that they weren't getting a decent answer out of Ike on this issue. They moved on. Ike returned to Hagerty once the press conference was over. Both men beamed.

"I've never seen anything like that. Well done," Hagerty said, breathless.

Ike smiled, proud of himself.

"I must have given fits to the Russian and Chinese translators trying to explain to their bosses what I just said."

☆☆☆☆☆

APRIL 4, 1955

IKE RELAXED IN satisfaction as he leaned back in his large brown leather chair. His plan had worked. The Chinese government was unsure whether

Ike would use nuclear weapons to defend Formosa. They scaled back their aggression, ending the crisis. The situation stabilized by April; the shooting stopped. Chou En-Lai attended the Bandung Conference of Asian and African leaders in Indonesia. He said at the conference that China sought "friendship" with the American people and would only try to liberate Formosa through "peaceful means."

The last months replayed in Ike's mind again and again. He joyfully laughed.

It worked. My strategy actually worked. I'm so tired from these months of effort, but I don't care. I even have Democrats like Johnson calling for peace after my press conference. I trusted no one's judgment but my own. I had no other choice. The advice I received was unanimous in pushing to use nuclear weapons. And I said "no."

I'm only disappointed that no one, and I mean no one, understands what I did. I'm not getting a pat on the back. There's no victory parades, like I had when I returned in '45. Most Presidents, like Lincoln, are great for inspiring the people, whereas I held the country back from making a horrible mistake. And no one will understand or applaud that. Not that that's what this was all about. It was my duty.

Vice President Nixon entered the Oval Office.

"You wanted to see me, Mr. President?"

"Yes, Dick, I do. Take a seat. I have an idea I want to discuss with you. I thought of it the night we watched the midterms together."

"Oh, God, why'd you remind me of that night?" Nixon asked with a chuckle as he took his seat. "Did you hear that Khrushchev criticized Mao in public? He said Mao should have either taken the islands or not started the crisis."

"I'd have preferred the latter."

"Me too," Nixon replied as he wiped some sweat off his forehead. "What idea did you want to bounce off of me?" He was honored Ike wanted his advice.

"I want to talk about where we go from here with Red China."

"Okay," Nixon replied tentatively.

"Do you think there'll ever be a diplomatic rapprochement between the United States and China?"

"Not in my lifetime," Nixon answered. "Maybe in 2000. Or 3000."

"You're that pessimistic?"

"Of course!" Nixon exclaimed. "Mao's a fanatic. We can't do business with him. We have to contain him and his forces."

"That's what I thought about the Germans. Except instead of containing them we had to conquer them."

"In World War II?"

"And World War I for that matter. But especially the Nazis. I hated them. They wanted to rule the world from pole to pole and slaughter minorities on a mammoth scale."

"Of course, Mr. President. Your heroism in the war brought you to the White House."

"And yet," Ike continued, "Now we're friends with Germany. Or West Germany, at least. Chancellor Adenauer is one of my favorite world leaders to work with."

"That's true," Nixon conceded.

"He's very fond of you. Hopes you succeed me."

"I know."

"So, if we can go from Operation Overlord and the Battle of the Bulge to a state where the German Chancellor is rooting for your election, is it impossible that we'll one day befriend the Chinese?"

"I suppose not."

"Doing that would also divide the Chinese and the Soviets. That would strengthen our position vis-à-vis both of them. They might even compete for our friendship."

"I understand."

"Good," Ike said. "Because treating China, or any country, for that matter, as a permanent enemy of mankind makes a lasting peace impossible. I'm not saying it will happen while I'm President. The Cold War's too intense. Temperatures need to moderate. But maybe it can happen within the ten years or so after I leave office."

"It's an interesting thought," Nixon said, not completely convinced but not wanting to argue with the President.

"I think so, too." Ike leaned back. A rapprochement with China, like so many other issues, was in the future.

Right now, I want to relax. Let the hair down, if I had any. Because I stood up to Mao. And I won. I kept the peace. Again. Without any help. Well, that's not true. There was one being I could turn to during this crisis. Thank you, Supreme Overlord. I couldn't have done this without You. I am an imperfect man, but I am Your instrument.

He makes wars cease to the ends of the earth; He breaks the bow and shatters the spear; He burns the shields with fire.

Ike turned and looked out the Oval Office window.

"It's lovely outside today," he muttered to Nixon. "Must be around sixty degrees. I would love to go out golfing. Or fishing."

The Outbreak of
World War III

The problem is not merely man against man or nation against
nation. It is man against war.
—Dwight Eisenhower

OCTOBER 22, 1956

MONSIEUR LE PREMIER Ministre. You're the guest of honor. You open the discussion." The assembled functionaries and diplomats fell quiet.

David Ben-Gurion studied the smiling face of French Prime Minister Guy Mollet, his eyes behind dark-rimmed glasses, his hair thinning except on the sides, his expression delighted to host his Israeli counterpart. They were seated in an ivy wrapped brick villa owned by the Bonnier de la Chapelles family in Sèvres, out of sight of American or Soviet intelligence.

Ben-Gurion had driven to Sèvres, after landing in France, in an unmarked car. He'd worn a large hat by way of disguise. Mollet, for his part, had gone home for the day and then driven to Sèvres in his personal car to remain undetected. Ben-Gurion placed his index finger to his lips as he pondered his first move of the secret summit. He extended his king's pawn.

"I would like you to explain to me when you in France stopped teaching Latin and went over to French," Ben-Gurion said in a thick Yiddish accent. The Israeli Prime Minister suffered from a receding hairline but more than made up for it with the puffs of snow-white hair that jutted over both ears.

"What is this!" Mollet exclaimed, turning to British Prime Minister Anthony Eden for help. Moshe Dayan, Chief of Staff of the Israeli Defense Forces, shook his head behind Ben-Gurion.

"Or would you rather discuss why France fell in 1940?" Ben-Gurion asked.

"Mon Dieu!" Mollet slurred. "Need I remind you that France has considered Israel an ally in Algeria? That it has sent Israel weapons in violation of the Tripartite Declaration?"

"Perhaps we should dip our toe into our main topic for the evening?" Eden asked, glaring at Ben-Gurion. The British Prime Minister's graying, swept-back hair matched neatly the trim moustache which had adorned his upper lip since his years serving in the First World War. Eden fought at the Third Battle of Ypres and during the Spring Offensive. He subsequently served as Foreign Minister on three separate occasions where he opposed Chamberlain's Munich Agreement, acted as Churchill's protege, and, along with Vyacheslav Molotov, was the only person to dine with Franklin Roosevelt, Winston Churchill, Joseph Stalin, and Adolf Hitler.

"Gladly," Mollet replied with a newfound venom in his voice. "One man unites us."

"Nasser," Eden confirmed.

"Exactly. I know why Anthony and I are here. What of you, Monsieur le Premier Ministre? What has Nasser done to Israel that brings you to us today?"

"He's allowed the fedayeen to attack my country from the Gaza Strip." Ben-Gurion referred to Palestinian guerillas. "The IDF has done its job but tensions have escalated between us and Egypt since last February."

"And that leads you to seek Nasser's destruction?"

"Nasser's Egypt is the most powerful of all the enemies that surround Israel in a web of aggression. Not even the American State Department could defuse the situation."

"Oh, don't get me started on the Americans!" Eden shouted. "Foster Dulles is a fanatic who would gladly sacrifice Europe in his crusade against communism. This mess is his doing!"

"Only because the American President was in the hospital," Mollet said.

"*Please*," Ben-Gurion muttered. "The Dulles brothers were already running American foreign policy."

"Touché." The verbal sparring belied the fact that the three were attended by a gaggle of silent functionaries whose trained response was impassivity.

Nasser seized the Suez Canal in June in response to Dulles ending funding for his Aswan Dam, which in turn was a response to Nasser's recognition of Red China. The Canal was the most important waterway in the world. 100 million tons of material went through it in 1955. It brought oil that Europe relied upon from Saudi Arabia, Iran, Kuwait, and Iraq.

"To conclude this little history lesson," Eden continued, getting the meeting back on track, "there's no way the *Egyptians* can successfully operate the Canal for long."

"This is no different than when Hitler occupied the *Rhineland!*" Mollet exclaimed with a rising inflection in his voice. "Never again!"

"Britain had the largest share of ownership in the Canal since *Disraeli* held my position in '82," Eden said, turning his right hand into a fist. "We can't let Europe become dependent on an Arab dictator for oil."

"What are British reserves for the pound sterling?" Ben-Gurion asked.

Eden hesitated.

"$2 billion."

"That's it? You *are* desperate."

Eden's face flashed red.

"This is a *vital* interest for my country."

"Mine too," Mollet concurred, his nose tilting upward.

"That's all good and well," Ben-Gurion shot back with frustration, "but this is an issue of Israel's *survival*. Nasser managed to buy 200 million dollars of weapons from the Eastern Bloc, ignoring the fate of the Guatemalan communists, and the Americans refused to send us the adequate weapons to defend ourselves. Which is why, Prime Minister Mollet, I truly am grateful that your country looked past the foolish Tripartite Declaration, despite my repartee."

"*Britain* has led Europe many times in the fight for freedom, against despots such as Phillip II, Louis XIV, Napoleon, the Kaiser, and Hitler. I'd like to add Nasser to that list of the vanquished."

"Do you intend to lock him up in Scotland once this is done or put him in Saint Helena?" Ben-Gurion asked. Mollet squinted his eyes at the insult to Napoleon.

"I'd rather he be dead in a ditch," Eden replied with a cheer.

"Who will replace him in Egypt?"

"I don't care."

"What if Egypt falls into anarchy?"

"I don't care. I just want Nasser murdered."

"If that's the case, I recommend we attack Egypt through the Sinai together in a week's time. We can retake the Canal and topple Nasser."

"I don't believe Britain and France should engage Egypt until after your forces reached and secured the Canal."

"Out of the question. I won't let Israel be the aggressor so you can play peacemaker. And I have no interest in seeing Egypt or the Soviet Union do to Tel Aviv what Hitler did to London and Coventry."

"I don't want our collaboration to be too obvious."

"The Soviet reaction to our offensive in Egypt will be negative and likely dangerous. It would be better if you started bombing Egyptian airfields the day after we made our move."

"We can do it within a week. That's the best I'll give you. Our countries can offer an ultimatum ordering both you and Egypt to cease combat in order to protect the Canal. When Nasser refuses, we'll intervene."

"Done."

Dayan smiled; the allied attack on Egypt had been his idea. Plus, he loved witnessing Ben-Gurion's decisiveness. It was the Israeli founder's outstanding character trait. This was his most important decision since agreeing to the UN's 1947 partition plan that divided Israel and Palestine.

British Foreign Secretary Lloyd, an easily missed presence, sat silently behind Eden looking like he'd caught a whiff of something foul. Lloyd, like most of Eden's advisors, believed diplomacy could resolve the issue with Nasser.

"May I ask a question about your operational plan?" Eden asked.

"Of course," Ben-Gurion replied.

"Your invasion of the Sinai—will it amount to a real act of war?"

"What does that matter?"

"If it doesn't then we may not have a credible *casus belli* for military intervention."

"What would resolve that issue?"

"If your government declares war on Egypt."

"That isn't necessary. The armistice from the '48 war was nullified when Nasser let the fedayeen attack us."

"We will not declare!" Dayan shouted. "We will simply strike!"

Ben-Gurion turned to his advisor and raised his index and middle fingers, signaling him to be silent.

"I see," Eden grimaced.

"There are more opportunities here than just destroying Nasser and restoring the Canal," Ben-Gurion said with a smile and with his hands clasped on the table.

"Such as?"

"It has come to my government's attention that oil sits under the ground in the southern and western Sinai. We should tear this peninsula from Egypt. It doesn't truly belong to her. You Brits stole it from the Turks when you thought Egypt was in your pocket."

"What do you propose we do with it?"

"I suggest we lay down a pipeline from the Sinai to Haifa to refine the oil."

"Interesting," Mollet muttered, resting his chin on his fist.

"I'm not sure I want to redraw the map of the Middle East," Eden said softly.

"On the contrary, I think destroying Nasser gives us a fantastic opportunity to reorganize the region along lines that make more sense than what Sykes-Picot gave us."

"Like?"

"Jordan should be partitioned."

"Why?"

"It's not a viable state. Iraq can have the East Bank upon a promise to settle the Palestinian refugees there and making peace with Israel."

"What of the West Bank?"

"It will be attached to Israel as a semi-autonomous area. We could also make Lebanon a homogeneous Christian state by expanding Israel to the Litani River."

"You would absorb that many Muslims?"

"Yes."

"Any other ideas?"

"Of course. Israel will assume responsibility for freedom of navigation in the Straits of Tiran in the Gulf of Aqaba."

Eden chuckled.

"You really are a born land grabber."

"Israel is but a continuation of ancient Judea! Or did you prefer it when we were at the world's mercy?" Ben-Gurion grit his molars as he stared Eden in the eye, daring him to back down. This was an alliance of convenience. Eden had never been friendly to Ben-Gurion's mission, whether by opposing Jewish immigration to Palestine during the

Holocaust or opposing Churchill's ideas to bomb the railroad tracks leading to Auschwitz. "And you're one to talk about land grabbing. Or should we go to India and ask Nehru about Britain's record as—"

"Enough bickering, gentlemen!" Mollet exclaimed.

Ben-Gurion's body stiffened as he lay back in his seat. He turned to Dayan and then back to Eden. Calmer, he resumed pressing his case.

"Under my design, your country would restore its hegemony in Iraq and have a continuous supply of oil from the region. And your country," Ben-Gurion said as he turned to Mollet, "would no longer have to worry about Nasser arming the Algerian rebels. Even America might support us as it would solidify regional stability and prevent Soviet penetration into the Middle East."

"Let's talk more about America," Eden suggested, waving his right hand casually before him. "What do we think will be Washington's reaction after your offensive next week? And of the United Nations for that matter?"

"The UN will be too weak to stop us," Mollet interjected before Ben-Gurion could speak. "We'll veto any measure in the Security Council."

"As for America," Ben-Gurion began, "you'll notice that the operation will begin a week before the presidential election. Eisenhower will be unable to react without risking defeat and losing the Jewish vote."

"Very clever," Eden said, nodding softly.

"We in Israel were disappointed when he won the last election. Truman and the Democrats were supportive of the Zionist project. Eisenhower's a pragmatic military man, not an idealist. Like his mentor, George Marshall, who opposed Truman's recognition of Israeli statehood because he feared it would drive the Arabs into Stalin's arms."

Mollet scoffed.

"In France we call him 'the Liberator,' for what he did in the war. But he's been a miserable ally as President. He let the communists defeat us at Dien Bien Phu."

"An American nuclear strike would have been a *disaster*," Eden rebutted, his arms folded. "But he has warned me multiple times about using force against Nasser. He may feel betrayed and react poorly."

Ben-Gurion dismissively waived his hand.

"Oh, please. He's not going to let himself get voted out of office over Nasser. As far as I'm concerned, Eisenhower's hands are tied."

☆☆☆☆☆

OCTOBER 23, 1956

HENRIKA KATO CHECKED her gray backpack one last time. She'd packed four shirts and two pairs of socks. It was most of what clothing she owned. Her eyes glazed over the pockets as she zipped and unzipped both multiple times, her subconscious paying more attention to her future than to her present. Satisfied that she possessed what she needed, at least until she joined her allies, she erected her posture, her thin black hair resting lightly on her shoulders, her pale face frowning as she saw her husband, Fernao, sadly watching her.

Husband and wife locked eyes in a silent, awkward standoff that refused to break. They studied each other's faces. Fernao had a five o'clock shadow, his bangs dangling over his forehead. He finally broke the silence.

"Were you planning on saying goodbye?"

She gulped her guilt back into her chest.

"Don't make this harder than it already is."

Fernao shrugged.

"You don't have to go."

"It's my duty."

"Your duty's here. With me. With Pacifico."

Henrika glanced at her son's room. The door was closed, but he was surely listening on the other side. She turned back to Fernao.

"Come with me."

"I can't."

"It will be like the old times. Like when we met. During the war. You were so brave."

"Were?"

"My wording stands for itself."

Fernao's jaw clenched.

"I was twenty. You were seventeen. That age has long passed. We're parents now. Our responsibility is different, but it's no less real."

"Hungary needs us! The Nazis are gone, but we're still ruled by foreign tyrants!"

"*Shh!* They could be listening!"

Henrika nodded. Of course she knew not to talk about such things, but there were times her subconscious instinct leapt forward despite her better judgment. She made her way to a record player, her family's one source of entertainment. Louis Armstrong's "What a Wonderful World" played at top volume.

"I have to go," she muttered.

"We're not finished!" Fernao exclaimed in a sort of screaming whisper.

"Yes, we are! I'll not let the damn Soviets make Pacifico an orphan the way the Nazis did to me!"

"And you think protesting will help with that?"

"We have to get *rid* of them! We can barely feed ourselves under communism!"

"I know."

"But you're not doing anything about it!"

Fernao sighed.

"How narcissistic can humans be that the last 200 years have been a string of failed utopias and they think that was just because 'those' people weren't good enough?"

"You mean the Soviet Union?"

"No, I mean *you*. Thinking you can save the world on your own."

Henrika slammed her fist into the wall, causing a dent in the weak material.

"Because I don't want to be Khrushchev's slave? Kiss my ass!"

Fernao's head dropped before her. He put his weight on his back leg.

"You know I would. For you."

Henrika smiled.

"We can leave Pacifico with a neighbor. He's not a baby anymore. Let's relive our youth."

"Those days are gone, my love."

"They don't have to be."

Fernao nodded.

"Why are you content as a *slave*?" Henrika slurred, her hands tightening.

"*You* were happy being a slave to Stalin!"

"I *know*! But it was after the war! We didn't know the things we know now!"

"What? From Khrushchev's speech?"

"Yes!"

They were referring to a secret speech that Khrushchev gave in the Kremlin a few months prior that denounced Stalin's brutality in an attempt to outmaneuver Stalin's conservative allies. The Mossad acquired it and gave it to the CIA, who in turn gave it to the *New York Times*.

Fernao opened his hands before her. She took them, clutching his fingers.

"That speech told me that the Russians are nothing but thugs. We have to free Hungary."

"You're angrier at the Russians than when they raped your sister in '44."

"This is serious. The protest today is going to restore Nagy to power. You remember how great it was when he was in charge? He's going to push out the Soviets, restore our free speech. Things like that."

"And how exactly does he plan to push out the Soviets?"

"You think I'm stupid, don't you?"

"Of course not, but I wonder if you think things through all the time. You always act with your gut."

She squeezed his fingers.

"I'm not going to leave Pacifico without a mother. The Americans will save us when push comes to shove."

"The Americans?"

"Yes. They'll intervene. Like they did in the war. And no average American is President. Eisenhower defeated the Nazis in Western Europe. He'll free Eastern Europe from slavery next. The protest might even be the catalyst."

"You never learn!"

"What?"

"You're doing the same thing again! You worshipped Stalin and thought he would solve all your problems. That bubble burst but you're repeating the process with Eisenhower!"

Henrika threw his hands away. Her eyes bulged in her skull.

"Stop saying I'm stupid!"

"I'm not!"

"You're implying it!"

"You need to realize that no one's coming to save us! We only have each other! And I don't want to *lose* you!"

"Coward! You're a coward!"

"How am I a coward?"

"You're too afraid to fight! You're not the man I married!"

"You don't mean that!" Tears emerged in his eyes again.

"Yes, I do! And you're selfish! You don't care about our son! You're clutching me like I'm your property and you're too much of a coward to come with me!"

Fernao's face turned three different colors before he pointed to the door.

"Go! Show how much you don't care about this family!"

"Baszd meg!" She stomped to the door and opened it. She paused and turned back to face him. "I'm sorry."

His eyes begged her not to go but his voice said nothing. He mustered the words.

"At least say goodbye to Pacifico." He paused. "Just in case."

Henrika's instinct was to snap again; to criticize Fernao for even suggesting that she wasn't coming back. Instead, she caught herself, her mind calmer than before. She hesitated before putting down her backpack and knocking on Pacifico's door. He made no response. She entered anyway.

Pacifico sat in the corner of his room, a gray, flannel shirt draped over his shoulders. Henrika went down on her knees, raising her arms for an embrace. Pacifico watched her, like a wounded zebra eyeing a lioness, but didn't move. Henrika swallowed the saliva in her mouth. Her eyes begged Pacifico to come to her.

"Mommy has to go for a little bit," she said, "but she'll be back. Please give Mommy a kiss."

Pacifico still wouldn't move.

"Please come to me, Pacifico."

He stared at her but did nothing.

"Please."

Pacifico's eyes shifted to Fernao, his father, seeking guidance. Fernao, standing behind Henrika and outside her field of vision, nodded to Pacifico. Finally, the boy slowly rose to his feet and came to Henrika. Tears emerged in Henrika's eyes as she pulled her son to her chest, squeezing his head like a boa constrictor.

"This is the right thing," Henrika whispered to Pacifico. "I know you can't see it now, but you will when you're older. I'll be back soon. And by that time, we'll be *free*."

☆☆☆☆☆

TWO HUNDRED THOUSAND protested in Kossuth Square, near the Danube in Budapest.

The scale and noise reminded Henrika of the war.

A member of Hungary's intelligentsia spoke to the crowd, which was made mostly of workers and peasants. All sectors of Hungarian society marched in solidarity.

"Our complaints are many!" the intellectual shouted. "The Soviet occupation must end!"

The protestors shouted their approval.

"The secret police must end!"

The protestors shouted again. A large force of AVH, Hungary's communist secret police force, stoically watched but did nothing. The intellectual knew how to press the crowd's buttons.

"We must end communism's attacks on the Catholic Church! We must free Cardinal Mindszenty from their prison!"

The crowd's noise increased tenfold.

"Down with Gero! We want Nagy!" Henrika shouted with half the crowd. "Out with the Russians!" shouted the other half.

"And so, with these goals in mind," the intellectual said, once the crowd's noise had lowered again, "we must remove this monument to the *beast* who put us in chains!"

The crowd's attention turned to the statue of Stalin that stood behind the intellectual. A group of protestors tied a pair of ropes around Stalin's neck and pulled.

"Down with Gero! We want Nagy!"

"Out with the Russians!"

"Down with Gero! We want Nagy!"

"Out with the Russians!"

The statue toppled; the crowd became its loudest yet. Henrika felt a surge of adrenaline as she fed off the crowd's energy and saw her *former* hero fall. One must wonder whether she thought a statue of Eisenhower would take its place.

She, and many others, shook their fists in the air at the AVH. She felt like she did during the war against the Nazis, like she was seventeen again, and more importantly, like she was right about the revolution, and that she was smarter than Fernao knew. He would admit he was wrong when Hungary was sovereign once again and Pacifico would grow up in a democracy.

No more poverty. No more AVH. No more hungry nights in Hungary.

No more pain.

Hungary's communist council capitulated by the end of the day. Imre Nagy took power for the first time in over a year. Moscow was blindsided. Nagy called for the protests to end.

They didn't.

☆☆☆☆☆

October 29, 1956

President Eisenhower squirmed in his seat on stage. Mamie sat to his right. To his left was the television moderator and seven women who CBS picked to ask Ike questions for this campaign event. Mamie chuckled as she watched her husband contain his nerves; he remained, as always, more comfortable in men's company.

The moderator introduced the program. Ike then delivered his prepared text.

"Ladies, I am grateful that you should take time to come in today to talk over with me some of the critical questions of the day. There was a time, you know, when they called this a man's world, but at least in the political scene this has long ago ceased to be true. In the last election we found that fifty-two percent of the votes were cast by women, and they instantly demonstrated that far from being confined to managing their homes they were going to have a big voice in managing the government.

"So today, in order to get at some of the things that may be on your minds, I suggest we handle it sort of like a press conference and each of you ask a question in turn. I think it would be best to start on the left and we go in turn right around. If that's all right, we'll start with you."

The first woman began.

"Mr. President, I am Irene Martin from Allen, Maryland, and the mother of twelve children and seventeen grandchildren. I would like to know what is the future for our families in this atomic age. Specifically, I wondered if you could talk about Governor Stevenson's proposal for a ban on nuclear testing."

Ike overcame the urge to roll his eyes.

Stevenson. How did the Democrats nominate him after I defeated him in the last election? Who wanted to see a rematch? He and Kefauver are the weakest ticket the Democrats could have assembled, Ike thought.

"I'm afraid I consider the governor's proposal to be political theater," Ike replied. "The world must find peaceful solutions for the problems that used to be turned over to the arbiter of war. We can never have a hydrogen war, as I see it, and still have a civilization such as we now know. And now, if you don't mind, Mrs. Martin, may I ask *you* a question?"

Mrs. Martin nodded.

"Who do you plan to vote for next month?"

"Why, Governor Stevenson!"

The panel laughed.

"I thought so!" Ike exclaimed. "Now why would that be?"

"I voted for the governor four years ago and everything's been fine!"

The panel laughed louder.

The second woman began.

"Hello, Mr. President. My name is Margarite Laurianti. I'm from Cleveland, Ohio. My question is about whether you think the situation in the Near East will remain stable until after the election."

"The progress made in the settlement of the Suez dispute recently at the United Nations is most gratifying. Egypt, Britain, and France have met, through the Foreign Ministers, and agreed on a set of principles on which to negotiate. I don't mean to say that we are completely out of the woods yet, but I talked to the Secretary of State just before I came over here tonight and I will tell you that in both his heart and mine at least, there is a very great prayer of thanksgiving."

Ike could barely catch his breath before the next question.

"I am Mrs. Helen Dormitzer, from Chicago, Illinois. My question deals with the domestic situation in America today. Specifically with regards to the economy. Governor Stevenson has suggested that, in light of your heart attack last year, you may not be able to complete a second term. Do you believe you could manage the domestic issues that this country faces for another four years?"

Ike and Mamie laughed.

"Well, first, let me just address the question of my health. My doctors have given me a clean bill of health and say that I am in good enough shape for my age to complete a second term and to treat the presidency as a full-time job. And, frankly, I would have run even if they warned me not to!"

The panel laughed. Mamie jokingly shook her head in disapproval and squinted her eyes at Ike. Ike saw his Staff Secretary, Colonel Andrew Goodpaster, signaling him from off the set. Goodpaster fought in the Italian theater of World War II and now managed the paper flow and major documents for the President and his senior staff. Ike turned back to the panel.

"As for the economy, it is clearly in a period of prosperity. For one thing, I signed the Interstate Highway Act, the most important bill of my presidency, this year. This highway system will allow Americans and goods to travel the country like never before. The government is projected to receive in taxes six times what it invested in the project. That will allow us to lower income taxes and pay down our national debt, which in turn increases the spending power of *your* money. On top of that, the bottom twenty percent of income earners have grown more in their proportion of wealth than the top twenty percent have under my administration. That is the only time in American history that that has happened."

☆☆☆☆☆

IKE AND GOODPASTER left the CBS recording building together once the show was over. They made their way toward the *Columbine*, a plane which was to take Ike to his next campaign event. Mamie followed suit. Goodpaster clutched a State Department memorandum in his hand.

"What's wrong, Andrew?" Ike asked. Ike had been achy since his heart attack the previous September and his abdominal surgery in June. He was about to feel worse. Much worse.

"An Israeli force of fifty thousand has entered the Sinai."

Ike's eyebrows scrunched.

"I thought they might attack Jordan."

Goodpaster shook his head.

"No, Mr. President. They're in Egypt. A parachute battalion landed in the Mitla Mountain pass forty miles east of the Suez Canal. A second force is driving through the Sinai to reinforce them. A third is directed toward Ismaila, a fourth is attacking Egyptian bases at Rafy and El Raish."

"Near Gaza," Ike muttered. Goodpaster nodded.

"The fifth and final thrust is moving down the west coast of the Gulf of Aqaba and is targeting the Sharm el Sheikh."

"They'll control the gulf once that happens. How many reserves do they have?"

"Two hundred thousand. Plus some heavy artillery and jet fighters."

"Any bombers?"

"No."

"What do the Egyptians have?"

"Seventy-five thousand troops. Ninety MiGs and fifty twin-engine Ilyushin bombers."

"I see," Ike muttered. He looked away from Goodpaster as he reflected.

This is it. I ran for President in '52 to end the Korean War and prevent World War III. I can feel in my bones that, more than the crises in Indochina or Formosa, that this is going to mark the start of the Third World War. This is 1914, when Franz Ferdinand was killed and Europe's decayed alliance system imploded. It's 1939, when Hitler's aggression lit the world on fire. The United Nations might collapse. It risks the entire Muslim world turning against the West or the Soviets exploiting the situation for their own advantage. Wait a second. A risk? More like a guarantee.

There's no way that Israel's acting alone. Our U2 flights over Israel have shown the French selling them Mystere jets, in violation of the Tripartite Declaration. I expected them to hit Jordan, not Egypt, since Israel's been launching border raids into Jordan as of late. Must have been a diversion. An intelligence failure, like Pearl Harbor and the Ardennes. I have to remain cool, like I did in the Ardennes. Can't let my emotions rule me. That's an important rule for life, but especially now. At least those surprise attacks were from the Axis, an alliance of monstrous regimes who wanted to carve the world between them. This time it's my own allies. A betrayal.

There's no way Eden's not in on this. He hates Nasser and is obsessed with retaking the Canal. I warned him that he needed to exhaust all peaceful options first and only then use force if peace was too great a price. But he's using his emotions, not his logic. How does a man of his stature succumb to that? Emotions are so dangerous.

Ike boarded the *Columbine*, which he directed to return to Washington, DC. His thoughts continued stewing.

Why did I have to have those medical issues? The heart attack and the ileitis attack? Each one put me out of action for weeks. I like Foster Dulles, but I try to keep him on a short leash. And I didn't appreciate the gravity of the decisions he made regarding Egypt during those periods, or even when looking at them afterward. Especially cutting off funds for Nasser's Aswan Dam. So Nasser's trying to compete with the pharaohs' pyramids. So what? Foster hates that Nasser wanted to be neutral in the Cold War. I agree that it's foolish, but if you are waging peace, you can't be too particular about the special attitudes that different countries take. We were a young country once, and our whole policy for the first 150 years was, we were neutral. We constantly asserted we were neutral in the wars of the world. We can't assume neutral countries don't deserve aid.

We're in the atomic age. A Third World War means human extinction. I'd hoped to only be a one-term President. That way I'd retire. Spend time with Mamie and the grandkids. But the damn Soviets rejected Atoms for Peace, which would have brought about nuclear disarmament and made peaceful nuclear energy available for the whole world. The Soviets decided that world domination is more important than their duty to humanity. So the Cold War kept going. Then there was the summit in Geneva in 1955. I proposed Open Skies, which would have let us and the Soviets fly over each other's country and inspect one another's nuclear capabilities. Imagine how much that would have done for trust and peace! The Soviet bosses seemed interested in it, too. All except for one.

Khrushchev.

The real source of power in the Kremlin. He's dangerous. A bully with dreams of world mastery. Who does that sound like? He vetoed Open Skies. So the Cold War kept going.

Then my damn health problems killed any chance of my ending it during a single term. God, I was so depressed when I could barely move after my heart attack! And I was depressed that I was depressed! All men die, but not all men die whining. I met with my family and advisors to discuss whether I should run again. They were unanimously supportive of my doing so, besides Milton. I didn't think another Republican could win. Still don't. And I'm horrified by the rise of Khrushchev in the Kremlin.

Khrushchev's actions are not useful for peace. Khrushchev, however, does not want peace, save for on his own terms and in ways that will aggrandize his own power. He is blinded by his dedication to Marxist theory of world revolution and communist domination. He cares nothing for the future happiness of the peoples of the world—only for their regimented employment to fulfill the communist concept of world destiny. He is not a statesman, but rather a powerful, skillful, ruthless, and highly ambitious politician.

Can you imagine if communism does take over the world? How miserable that world will be? No religion. No freedom. Everyone in crushing poverty. The only thing worse than that is an atomic war. There will be no coming back from that. Probably no life left on Earth.

This is the fight of my life. I just hope I'm up to it.

☆☆☆☆☆

"WHERE'S FOSTER?"

IKE and Goodpaster marched through the White House halls toward the Oval Office. A vein bulged over Ike's right temple. Saliva sat on both corners of his mouth. The Secretary of State appeared as they turned the corner. His thin-rimmed glasses sat halfway down the bridge of his wide nose.

"Foster!" Ike barked. "Send a message to Tel Aviv!"

Dulles nodded, signaling that he was listening.

"Foster, you tell them, Goddamnit, that we're going to apply sanctions, we're going to the United Nations, we're going to do everything that there is so we can stop this thing!"

"Right away, Mr. President."

"Doesn't Ben-Gurion know that we're obligated to defend Egypt? The Tripartite Declaration says we must defend *any* victim of aggression in the Middle East."

"I've already begun an evacuation of all non-essential Americans in Jordan, Syria, Egypt, and Israel."

"Good."

"Our U2 flights detected Israeli mobilization, but we thought they would strike Jordan, not Egypt."

"I made the same mistake. At least I'm in good company."

"The Anglo-Jordanian treaty probably prevented that attack and caused Britain, France, and Israel to agree on an Israeli strike against Egypt."

"You think the Europeans are in on it?"

"Absolutely. The Israeli strike is a pretext for Britain and France to 'protect' the Canal. In all probability, these moves were concerted; the French did the planning, the British acquiesced, and the French, in violation of the 1950 agreement, covertly supplied the Israelis with arms."

"That's my understanding of the situation too."

"The British and French will want our support on this."

"What would they think if we were to go and aid Egypt to fulfill our pledge! Nothing justifies double-crossing us! I don't care whether I'm elected or not! We *must* make good on our word. Otherwise we are a nation without honor."

"They probably consider the Canal to be a vital interest."

"I don't *care*. That doesn't *justify* their intervention. Ben-Gurion's aggressive actions are obviously the result of his belief that we won't act during the election. He's *gravely* mistaken. Winning a domestic election isn't as important as preserving and protecting the *peace*. And in the long-term, Israeli aggression cannot fail to bring catastrophe and such friends as he would have left in the world, no matter how powerful, could not do anything about it."

Ike took a step back as he saw Goodpaster return with a collection of his advisors: Chairman of the Joint Chiefs Admiral Radford, CIA Director Allen Dulles, Treasury Secretary Humphrey, and Defense Secretary Wilson.

Got to calm down, Ike thought. *I'm going to need to control my temper if I'm going to restore the peace.*

Ike turned to his advisors.

"This international aggression is totally unacceptable. Even by an ally."

They nodded. He focused on Radford.

"How many days will it take for Israel to overrun the Sinai?"

"I would guess 'three.' That will be the end of the issue."

"No," Foster Dulles rejected bluntly. "It is far more serious than that. The Canal will be closed in this conflict. Oil exports from the region will end. Then Britain and France will intervene. They appear eager for it and may have even concerted their action with Israel."

"We've picked up a spike in communication between Paris and Tel Aviv in the last week or so," Allen Dulles added.

"The Europeans will want our support," Wilson offered.

"I intend to uphold the Tripartite Declaration," Ike repeated. "It is our only honorable option. We can't be trapped by our traditional alliances. Not this time."

"Won't it hurt our standing in the world if we betray our allies? They won't depend on us going forward."

"We stand for *peace*," Ike declared. "I don't care who caused the aggression or who received it. As long as I'm President, America will stand for *peace*. No matter what. This move was totally unnecessary. I'm going to stop it. Besides, the Soviets might try to defend Nasser to secure a foothold in the region, and I'm not looking to start World War III by election day. Ending the attack on Egypt is essential."

"The European economies haven't recovered from the war with Hitler," Humphrey chimed in. "This Israeli operation risks their oil supply from the Near East. We may need to prop them up so they don't suffer financial crashes."

"I have no trouble seeing them go under," Ike shot back. "Those who began this operation should be left to work out their own problems. To *boil* in their own oil. I have no intention of subsidizing them. At least while this stupid military campaign is ongoing."

"But it will hurt NATO in the long run if—"

"George, you are not going to get a ceasefire by saying 'everyone please stop.' Look for options to put as much financial pressure on all three allied countries as possible. It's our best source of leverage on them."

"I'm confused, Mr. President," Radford said.

"With regard to what?"

"Nasser wants to build an Arab super-state. He intends to conquer the Mideast like he's Alexander the Great or Rommel. We should take this opportunity to break him."

"I don't like Nasser any more than you do. Or any more than Eden, for that matter. He's a demagogue. But he embodies the emotional demands of the region for independence and for 'slapping the white man down.' Supporting this sort of unjustified aggression against him will turn the whole Muslim world against us. From Dakar to the Philippines."

"Wouldn't the Arabs and Muslims realize that the Europeans are responding to a seizure of their property?" Allen Dulles asked.

"I imagine they're playing the smallest violin on Earth for the loss of property by their former colonial rulers. And as I understand it, Nasser had every legal right to nationalize the Canal under eminent domain. The Canal is within Egyptian territory. And he paid the Europeans a just compensation."

"What if we put the Canal under an international consortium?" Foster Dulles asked. Foster was a successful international lawyer before becoming Secretary of State.

"How would we like an international consortium running the Panama Canal?" Ike asked.

"With all due respect, Mr. President, America does not possess the same position in the world order as Egypt."

"That's irrelevant. All nations are created equal. At least with regard to treatment and their rights under international law. No matter how big or small. No matter if they're for us or against us. Besides, America will be much more popular in the Third World if we are on the right side of the colonialism issue. This is a last gasp of European Victorianism. It reads to me like Churchill might be behind it."

"Should we not support Israel as the sole democracy in the region?" Wilson asked.

"I don't think it's fair to hold the Arabs' antidemocratic tradition against them. I served in North Africa during part of World War II. I worked with the Arabs and learned a bit about their culture. They've lived under one form of dictatorship or another for centuries. So our concept of human rights, as interpreted by Locke, is irrelevant to them. What I came to understand is that the Arabic peoples, generally speaking, are an emotional people who are prone to violence and are prejudiced against white people. And I can't say I blame them with how the Europeans abused their region after the Ottoman Empire collapsed."

Ike turned to Foster Dulles.

"What do you think the Saudis will do in this situation?"

"I suspect they'll take Israel's side. The Saudis and the Egyptians hate each other."

"The fact that Nasser's a secular nationalist and the Saudi King is medieval may be part of it," Ike replied. "Keep me updated on any communication from Riyadh. We need to turn our attention to the elephant in the room. The Soviet Union. Our top priority must be to keep the Soviets out of the Middle East without triggering a war."

His advisors nodded.

"Mr. President!"

Ann Whitman, Ike's personal secretary, burst from around the corner in an area adjacent to the Oval Office. Her short, curly blonde hair shook from her exertion.

"What is it, Ann?"

"Mr. Adams is in the Oval Office. He has the British ambassador on the phone for you."

"Oh, thank you!" Ike exclaimed as he made his way to the Oval Office. His advisors trailed him. They had difficulty keeping up, even though he was a sixty-six-year-old man who recently endured multiple surgeries.

White House Chief of Staff Sherman Adams stood near Ike's desk, which had once belonged to Theodore Roosevelt. He held a phone in his hand.

"J.E. Coulson's on the line for you, Mr. President!"

"Thank you, Sherman," Ike replied as he took the phone. "Good evening, Ambassador!"

"Good evening, Mr. President," he said in an aristocratic tone.

"Ambassador, I'm very disturbed about this thing in the Sinai. The prestige of the United States and the British is involved in these developments. I feel it is incumbent upon both of us to redeem our word about supporting any victim of aggression. Last spring, when we declined to give arms to Israel and Egypt, we said our word was enough. In my opinion, the United States and the United Kingdom must stand by what we said. In view of the information regarding the number of messages between Paris and Tel Aviv in the last few days, I can only conclude that I do not understand what the French are doing."

"I do not know about the messages."

"If I have to call Congress in order to redeem our pledge, I will do so. We will stick to our undertaking."

"Would the United States not first go to the Security Council?"

"We plan to go to the United Nations first thing in the morning. When the doors open. Before the USSR gets there."

"I think it is better if we keep this as an internal dispute within NATO than letting the Soviets get involved."

"Of course I agree. But this may spiral out of control. And fast. Communicate that to Eden and Lloyd if you're able."

"I understand, Mr. President."

The call ended soon after. Ike took a moment to pause as he looked out the Oval Office window.

I need a dual strategy. Get the allies out of Egypt and make sure the Soviets don't get involved. I have to play my cards right. No matter how impossible it seems. So many pieces at play. The allies. Moscow. The Arab world. My advisors, who have a track record of advocating for the use of force, even nuclear force. My health. The election. It's overwhelming. Have to remain calm. Or at least as best I can.

Normandy. The Bulge. Korea. McCarthy. Formosa. I've risen to the occasion before. I have to do it again. And this time, more than any time since Normandy, it really counts.

☆☆☆☆☆

OCTOBER 30, 1956

"STATE HASN'T HEARD anything yet from London or Paris," Foster Dulles explained as he rested his right arm on the Oval Office desk, sitting a short distance from Ike. "They're leaving us in the dark."

"What about the ultimatum?" Ike asked.

"The ultimatum is about as crude and brutal as anything I've ever seen."

"Can you explain it to me?"

"What's the point? They're *going* to act on it no matter what."

"I'd like to know anyway."

Dulles sighed.

"Eden and Mollet instructed Ben-Gurion and Nasser to call an immediate ceasefire and to back away from the Canal Zone and allow Britain and France to occupy it. If the belligerents don't agree, the Europeans will take the Canal Zone by force."

"My God," Ike muttered, leaning back in his chair. His large nostrils couldn't help but to pick up the stench of Dulles' breath.

"They also vetoed the resolutions that Ambassador Lodge and the Soviets both issued at the Security Council that condemned Israel's actions."

"Of course. Issue cables to both capitals that advise Eden and Mollet to renounce the ultimatum."

"Yes, Mr. President. I don't have any updates regarding the protests in Hungary at the present time. There are still skirmishes between protesters and the pockets of troops that Moscow left in the country."

"I see."

"It's a shame this Suez business is occurring simultaneously with Hungary. We have the opportunity to push back Soviet colonialism in Eastern Europe and the world is focusing on European colonialism in the Mideast."

Ike shrugged.

"The world doesn't care as much about whites oppressing other whites as it does whites suppressing nonwhites."

"True."

"Any news about Czech opinion on the protests in either Hungary or Poland?"

"We have very little information out of Czechoslovakia. Ambassador Bohlen recently saw Bulganin and Khrushchev together at a reception in Moscow. Khrushchev, he said, had never looked so grim. His days may well be numbered. Possibly it will fall to Zhukov to choose his successor; in fact, Zhukov himself may succeed Khrushchev."

"I doubt Khrushchev is going to fall that easily. He, if anything, is the real brain in the Kremlin these days. Bulganin's merely his pawn. This is a dangerous moment. The communist bosses in Moscow might feel insecure about losing the Eastern Bloc. They lost Yugoslavia under Stalin. Now they might lose Poland and Hungary. They might even start a world war to hold onto them. We have to watch that situation with the utmost care."

"Yes, Mr. President. You might consider going on television to explain each of these situations to the American people."

"I'd rather avoid that. The damn FCC principle. Stevenson would get equal time to respond."

"I understand. Maybe a statement would be useful, then, to notify both the people and the Arab world that we're not part of this conspiracy against Nasser."

Dulles pressed his left rib cage.

"I'll instruct Hagerty to give a message to the press. Are you okay?"

Dulles nodded, though his eyes were shut to mask a growing pain.

"Yes, Mr. President. I'll be okay. Let's continue."

"You don't look good, Foster. Come on. Let's get you looked at."

"That isn't necessary," Dulles replied, the volume in his voice plummeting.

"Yes, it is. Come on. On your feet," the old general ordered. Dulles slowly stood up. Ike guided him toward the Oval Office door. Ike, too, was physically weak from his recent health issues. "We can't let the Soviets take the lead at the UN," Ike muttered. "They would win the confidence of the Third World. Ann! I'm going to need some help here!"

"Yes, Mr. President!" Whitman exclaimed from the other room as she slowly made her way to the Oval Office.

"We also need to release some sort of statement regarding sanctions on Israel if their aggression doesn't halt—"

The weight on Ike's shoulder dramatically increased as Dulles collapsed to the floor. Ike grabbed his advisor and sought to blunt his fall, though the pain in his abdomen surged in the process.

"Ann!" Ike screamed.

Thud!

Whitman sprinted to the President and Secretary of State. She helped Ike to his feet. He was disoriented.

"I'll call the Medical Unit!" Whitman exclaimed.

Dulles was soon on his way to Walter Reed Hospital.

★★★★★

BEN-GURION AGREED TO the European ultimatum a few hours later. Nasser ignored it. British and French air forces initiated attacks on Cairo, Port Said, and Alexandria. They were launched from an allied military buildup near Cyprus, the largest naval concentration in the Eastern Mediterranean since World War II. The British had three aircraft carriers and 45,000 troops. The French had 6,000 troops. Allied bombers attacked airfields, ports, railways, communication centers, and the radio towers of the Voice of the Arabs at the Abu Zabel near Cairo. They only faced disorganized Egyptian antiaircraft fire. Nasser proved more successful in sinking a 320-foot-long freighter loaded with cement into the narrowest part of the Canal, blocking it.

The American Sixth Fleet arrived in the Eastern Mediterranean the following day, as yet unsure of its enemy.

☆☆☆☆☆

NOVEMBER 1, 1956

"Now, AS WE have witnessed in these very weeks momentous events throughout the world, we have applied these principles by which America must ever live—and strive to lead."

Ike was at his final campaign event before the election, speaking to a Republican gathering at Philadelphia's Convention Hall.

"In Eastern Europe, we have seen the spirit of freedom—swift and strong—strike through the darkness. The peoples of Poland and Hungary, brave as ever through all their history, have offered their lives to live in liberty. And as the people have risen, so have new governments—and so has new hope.

"In all of this the true intent of the Soviet Union seems not yet clear. It is timely to ask: How have we practiced our principles at this historic moment? We have welcomed these events seeking for no selfish advantage. We seek from these people neither material gain nor military alliance. We seek simply their freedom—for their sake, and for freedom's sake.

"The United Nations—within forty-eight hours of its being called to consider the matter of Soviet forces in Hungary—was called to judge the use of foreign forces in Egypt. I, as your President, am proud—and I trust that you are proud—that the United States declared itself against the use of force in not one, but both these cases.

"And now, a few words about the principles that we have followed in making particular decisions. First, we cannot and we will not condone armed aggression—no matter who the attacker, and no matter who the victim. We cannot—in the world, any more than in our own nation—subscribe to one law for the weak, another law for the strong; one law for those opposing us, another for those allied with us. There can be only one law—or there will be no peace.

"My fellow citizens, we look beyond these days, and we say: We shall continue to practice the peace that we preach. We believe that humanity must now cease preying upon itself. We believe that the power of modern weapons makes war not only perilous—but preposterous—and the only way to win World War III is to prevent it."

☆☆☆☆☆

BA-DUMP, BA-DUMP, BA-DUMP.

Ike's eyes were half open as US Car No. 1, a train used by all Presidents since Coolidge, made its way to Washington. Goodpaster and Sergeant John Moaney, Ike's African American aide, sat near him in silence on chairs with green and yellow stripes around a shiny brown table. Ike had just finished a late dinner—it was almost midnight—and held his fourth scotch in his right hand. His left hand had sunk into his suit jacket pocket. He felt something touch the tips of his index and middle fingers. Ike's eyes scrunched, unsure of what he put in his pockets. He grabbed the small piece of paper and scanned it with his exhausted, tipsy eyes. He chuckled.

"What is it, sir?" Moaney asked. He had been with Ike since World War II.

Ike took a moment to raise his head and answer.

"It's from my tailor. He spent time in the Nazi camps during the war. Came to America after. I think he appreciates my role in destroying the Hitler regime. I frequently find that he puts little notes in my clothing after cleaning them."

"What sort of notes?" Goodpaster asked.

"Foreign policy advice, mostly."

"Really?"

Ike nodded.

"This one's asking me to stand with Israel and against Egypt."

"Is that appropriate?"

Ike shrugged.

"I don't mind. You know, I don't think I knew any Jews when I was in Abilene. They just—they didn't live there—for whatever reason. I remember, when I was a boy, a friend of mine said to me that there weren't any Jews on Earth. That they were all in Heaven as angels."

Goodpaster and Moaney exchanged a confused glance. Ike chuckled.

"I didn't understand what he meant. Still don't. But I made plenty of Jewish friends between the world wars. Especially when I was stationed in the Philippines in the '30s. Some had families who'd been there a while. Others were refugees from Hitler. That's why I was outraged when he launched an assault on Jews across Germany in November of '38."

"*Mmm*," Goodpaster grunted. "I remember that. Big backlash in the States."

Ike nodded.

"I hadn't paid much attention to the fascists until then. But after that I was obsessed with stopping Hitler and his evil schemes until we accepted Germany's surrender at Rheims in '45. That's around when we saw the full magnitude of what the Nazi government had done. Georgie Patton asked me to see a camp near Gotha. The day Roosevelt died, if memory serves me. It was the most horrible thing I'd ever seen. And I've seen a lot in my life, mind you. Especially in the previous couple of years. But I saw piles of corpses. Living humans who looked like skeletons. Artwork made of human skin. Crematoriums filled with the bones of children. Bradley said my face was stark white. And Patton—old blood and guts? He vomited. I still can't—"

Ike paused as his indigestion seemed to rise into his throat. He coughed and sipped his scotch to get it back down. Goodpaster and Moaney waited. Ike shook his head in disbelief.

"God, Hitler was a monster. The ultimate one. Him and his followers. Murdered a million Jewish babies just for existing. What the Nazis did to the Jews was the biggest atrocity in human history. The *biggest* atrocity. In our own lifetimes. I can't think of a bigger betrayal of man's duty to fellow man. That's why it was so important that we documented what happened there. Marshall let me bring in reporters and Congressmen. The world must never forget."

"What'd the Germans say?" Moaney asked. "The ones who weren't Nazis?"

Ike gave a sarcastic chuckle.

"That's a whole hornet's nest. Most claimed they didn't know. I'm not quite sure how they couldn't have known, but that was what they claimed. And I ordered the locals of the area to help bury the bodies. Gotha's mayor and his wife killed themselves after seeing the camp. I remember being pleased with that at the time. It meant Germany's conscience may have survived Nazism. That it could be redeemed."

"Do you think it can?"

Ike nodded.

"Look at West Germany today. Under Adenauer."

Moaney sighed.

"No country's perfect. But can ya' imagine your country havin' done *that*?"

Ike grimaced.

"I remember one painful experience when I attended a Yom Kippur service in '45 at a Displaced Persons camp near Feldafing. I thought it would be mournful. The war and the German oppression had ended only a few months prior. The Rebbe had other plans."

"What happened?" Goodpaster asked.

"The Rebbe had lost his whole family at Auschwitz. And his sermon claimed that America and Britain shared the German guilt for not bombing the camps or the railroads to the camps. And he pointed to me and stated that I was personally responsible for not having done more to stop what Hitler was doing."

"That's not exactly fair," Goodpaster argued. "The camps were in Eastern Europe and we were based in Britain. And railroads are the hardest target—"

"I know, Andrew," Ike interrupted. "And I lacked full authority over the aerial forces. But—"

Ike dissolved into his seat. He glared at the ceiling as his eyes filled with tears.

"His emotions were real. No matter the rational arguments that could be made—he didn't care. His emotions were *real*. And he blamed me. Despite my best efforts to do my duty. That was one of the most painful moments in my entire life."

"What did ya' do?" Moaney asked.

"I cried," Ike replied, as he wiped away a tear. "What could I have done? His emotions were real." Moaney and Goodpaster nodded. "That's why it's so important to combat racism." Ike glanced at Moaney. "Here and everywhere. That sort of thing can never happen again. Especially while I'm President. It can't happen on my watch."

The three men sat in silence for a few moments before Ike spoke again.

"I became responsible for thousands of displaced Jews who were liberated from the camps when I was governor of the American-occupation zone in Germany. Had to figure out ways to provide shelter and clothing and food. Medical care. Truman and I sent more letters than I can remember back and forth on how best to care for these people who had gone through the worst form of hell that I can imagine. Beyond what I could imagine. We gave them some housing and farms we repossessed from the Germans. Though most of Germany had been flattened in our bombing campaigns.

"It was in that period that I first met Ben-Gurion. He was a leader in the global Jewish community. We got along okay, back then."

"If you don't mind me asking, Mr. President," Goodpaster began, "how did you feel when Ben-Gurion and his followers established Israel after the war?"

"At the time I was critical of the idea. You're probably wondering 'why' after the things I saw after the war."

Goodpaster nodded.

"It wasn't that simple," Ike said. "The UN partition led several Arab states, *led by Egypt*, to try and push the Jews into the sea." He emphasized the words 'led by Egypt' as a reflection of the current crisis. "The Israelis won that war because they were better organized and they managed to defeat the Arab armies, one at a time. They even gained more territory than the UN had given them. That led to even more Arab resentment.

"Now, Israel's founding led to a couple of issues. One was that it hurt the local population: the Palestinians. A lot of them were displaced from their homes during that war. My hope is that a peace agreement can let the refugees reintegrate into Israel. If we can't figure that out, we'll have to find a way to integrate them into other Arab countries.

"More importantly for American foreign policy, Israel's founding created a situation where we could either let the Jews be crushed by their neighbors, which was unacceptable, obviously, or to support Israel and have the Arabs all turn to Moscow for friendship. That would be a disaster, too. The Mideast might be the most important region on Earth, in a strategic sense. We have to keep the Soviets out. But that means we're stuck in a balancing act. Because Israel is now a historical fact and must be protected from harm, as any country should be. Especially since the Jews have been oppressed for over two-thousand years.

"That's the problem with Ben-Gurion, though. He doesn't get that supporting Israel's security is different from condoning Israeli aggression against Egypt. That Albert Einstein-looking midget is an extremist. He cares more about acquiring more land than he does about peace. Israel will never have peace that way."

Moaney glanced at the table, troubled by the situation in the Sinai. Ike finished his glass and eyed the scotch bottle. Goodpaster spoke before Ike could grab it.

"What happens if the sanctions on Israel don't force them back?"

Ike dragged the scotch bottle closer.

"Then the use of military force goes on the table. Congress won't like it, but they're not in session."

"Couldn't that hurt you in the election?"

Ike shrugged.

"I have to restore the peace. No matter the political cost. If I lose reelection, you can be sorry for anyone in the world besides me."

☆☆☆☆☆

November 2, 1956

"*Mmm. What is it?*" Ike asked as he returned to the world of the awake. The President's Bedroom was pitch-black. "Who's there?"

"Colonel Goodpaster."

"What time is it?"

"It's four in the morning. But we've had some updates you need to hear."

Ike nodded as he begrudgingly crawled out of bed.

"Let's take this outside. I don't want to wake Mamie."

Mamie didn't move, deep in REM sleep.

Goodpaster began once they were outside the President's Bedroom.

"First of all, we've heard from Walter Reed. Secretary Dulles has had abdominal surgery and is in a stable condition."

"Thank God."

Goodpaster nodded.

"Our ceasefire resolution at the UN General Assembly passed sixty-four to five."

"Five? Britain, France, Israel. Who else?"

"Australia and New Zealand."

"Interesting."

"The Canadians are sponsoring a resolution that will create an international police force to protect the Canal."

"Good on Louis." Ike was referring to Canadian Prime Minister Louis St. Laurent.

"The small countries are thrilled with you. Standing up for Egypt against our traditional allies. Your standing in the world has never been higher, except maybe for VE Day."

"I'm glad, but that's not the point. And I feel that I'm about to lose my British citizenship."

"A lot of Brits agree with you."

"How so?"

"Eden's resolution for intervening in Egypt only passed 270 to 218 in Parliament. Labour is up in arms."

Ike shook his head.

"I wouldn't dream of taking this country to war on such a vote. It doesn't even make sense. If one has to fight, then that is that. But why get into a fight where you appear a bully to the whole world and in which your own people don't support you?"

"I don't know. I think Eden's obsessed with Egypt, if you ask me. One last piece of news before you can return to bed."

"What is it?"

"The Kremlin released a statement that called for equality between the Soviet Union and the satellite countries. That Soviet troops can only be stationed in other countries with those countries' consent."

Ike squinted.

"I thought you'd be happier," Goodpaster said, his head hurting from exhaustion. "This is the most important statement to come out of Moscow since World War II."

"Maybe," Ike muttered. "If it's true."

Goodpaster shrugged.

"That's all I have for you right now. Sorry I had to wake you."

"You did what you're supposed to. I'll see you in the morning."

"Yes, Mr. President."

"Life gets more dangerous by the minute," Ike declared before Goodpaster left. "I could really use a good bridge game."

☆☆☆☆☆

NOVEMBER 4, 1956

HENRIKA LEANED FORWARD, her elbows resting on a shelf protruding from a wall in what was an indoor market and was now a resistance base. Dusk was setting outside, darkening the base's interior. A small food stockpile sat in the market's back left corner. Multiple shelves had been moved around to form obstacles in case any wall was breached by the enemy. Twenty resistance fighters occupied the facility; almost all were men, leading to a musky stench filling the air from days of exertion with little time to shower. The base was crucial to the rebels; it was their last stronghold in Central Budapest. Its fall would break vital communication lines between other rebel groups, allowing the Soviets to divide and conquer them.

Henrika's mind didn't notice the pressure on her left butt cheek at first; her mind was elsewhere, imagining the excitement of visiting New York City once Hungary was free. Where would she go first? She *had* to see the Statue of Liberty. And Disneyland! Was that in New York? Probably. Were visitors handed money as soon as they arrived? They must be; everyone in America lived a lifestyle more lavish than any Hungarian king. The pressure increased, and even Henrika could feel stubby fingers shifting in every direction. Her throat constricted as she turned and slapped the man's right cheek with her full body weight.

The man took a step back, unprepared for Henrika's rage. He rubbed his cheek for a moment, disoriented.

"How *dare* you touch me? I'm a married woman!" Henrika's eyes bulged as her body felt warmer and warmer.

"So? Marriage is a social construct." The man wore a collared shirt with three of the buttons through their respective holes. A tie sat across the back of his neck, carelessly resting on his shoulders.

"So are language and laws, you idiot! That doesn't mean they don't matter!"

Henrika felt like her core person, her essence as a woman and as a human, had been violated. Her stupid brain wandered around everywhere but in reality, as it always did, and she failed to take the necessary precautions to protect her womanhood from the creeps she'd known all her life. And this man, if you could even call him that, took advantage of her failure. How dare he interject himself into something so special, so personal? Without thinking, Henrika reached for her machine pistol. The man saw what she was doing and turned his right hand into a fist. Good. Henrika was ready for a fight.

"What's happening here?" asked a mustachioed man in a soldier's uniform. A collection of strings hung from his cap from where he tore off a red star.

Henrika could barely think clearly enough to articulate her words.

"This *kurva fia* touched me where he shouldn't have!"

The old soldier turned to the man with the fist.

"That's no way to treat a lady. Now put some room between the two of you. There's not a lot of space in this market, but there's enough for you two to not have to see each other."

"Gladly," Henrika muttered. The old soldier stayed next to Henrika, putting a wall between her and the other man. He inspected his own machine pistol. "What's your name?"

"They call me Attila. You?"

"Henrika."

"A lovely name."

"Were you a soldier?"

"Yes. Most of us defected once the revolution started."

"Good. We'll need all the help we can get against the Reds."

"It's not all communism that's bad!" the other man claimed. "The Soviets just did it wrong. We'll do it the right way once they're gone."

Attila spit on the ground.

"Communism should have never been more than a small food for thought in shaping society. It should never have prevailed."

The other man dismissively waived his hand at Attila.

"And what would you prefer?"

"I want what America has," Henrika interjected.

"America's a sham," the man replied. "Over there the capitalists run everything."

"At least *they* don't have to wait in line for toilet paper!"

"I wouldn't mind the American model. But it would be better to elect kings than Presidents or Prime Ministers. Like Matthias Corvinus."

The other man laughed. Henrika squinted.

"I'm not sure who that is," she admitted softly.

"He was from the Renaissance!" the man laughed. He turned back to the old soldier. "That's why they call you Attila! You want to go back in time."

"I would prefer almost any time in Hungary's past to the present," Attila declared.

"So, you want to go back to the war? When the Nazis ruled everything?"

"The Nazis were a bit overbearing," Attila replied, "but at least they protected us from the communists and Jews."

"You probably supported the White Terror of 1920."

"Supported it? I was part of it. Happily."

"Fascist."

"Communist."

"You act like that's an insult."

"It is to any thinking person."

"You don't know what you're talking about. You're living in the Stone Age."

"You really are an obnoxious shit. Get out of my sight."

"Happily. I shouldn't associate with fascists."

The man left the market that served as a rebel base.

Attila turned back to Henrika.

"Am I correct to assume that you're married?"

"Yes."

"And your husband still lives?"

"Yes."

"Why isn't he here?"

"He's scared. He fears we'll leave our son an orphan if we fight the Soviets."

"And you disagree?"

"Yes. Hungary must be free. And I believe that the Americans will step in if we need them."

"I suspect they will. Eisenhower and Dulles hate the Reds."

"It's a shame what happened to Nagy. Who would have guessed that he was a Soviet puppet?"

"Oh, please. A rock could have seen that one coming. And your husband needn't worry. Stick with me, and I'll get your soft little head back to him in one piece."

"Thank you. I'm sure he'd appreciate that. Unlike that handsy procs."

"You have quite a mouth for a married woman."

Henrika smiled.

The other man leapt back inside the market.

"Back so soon?" Attila asked.

The man's eyes were wide and desperate.

"They're coming! The Soviets! The Soviets are coming!"

"Everyone to your stations!" Attila ordered.

Henrika leapt to a corner of the market, looking through a hole in the wall. She could see a group of Soviet soldiers in the distance, hugging the sides of buildings as they advanced toward the rebel base.

"Don't shoot until you see the whites of their eyes," Attila advised her.

Henrika nodded. A hot pain emerged in her stomach. Soviets? Here? She didn't think Bulganin and Khrushchev had it in them. Was Fernao right? Maybe there was genuine danger in partaking in the revolution. No, that's a terrible thought. She was not going to leave Pacifico without a mother. She had a guardian angel. Not Attila.

Dwight Eisenhower. He would save her. She did not question that truth.

☆☆☆☆☆

"THE STATE DEPARTMENT estimates that over two hundred thousand Soviet troops have crossed the border into Hungary, as have four thousand Soviet tanks," Undersecretary of State Herbert Hoover, Jr. explained to the National Security Council in the Cabinet Room. A painting of George Washington hung on the middle back wall, above the fireplace, which in turn was flanked by busts of Washington and Ben Franklin. Hoover was the son of the former President and was a businessman in the oil industry before agreeing to serve under Foster Dulles, who he now temporarily replaced as Dulles was in Walter Reed.

Overwhelming force, Ike thought. *Bulganin and Khrushchev took a page out of my playbook. Got to find a way to help the rebels, but...*

"I didn't think Bulganin would go this far," William Jackson, National Security Assistant to the President, muttered. He had served as an intelligence officer for George Marshall, Omar Bradley, and George Patton, during World War II. He'd also served as Deputy Director of the CIA under Bedell Smith.

"Do we know where Imre Nagy is as of now?" Defense Secretary Wilson asked.

"We *think* he's fled to the Yugoslav embassy. But we don't know that with certainty," Hoover answered.

The National Security Council was tense, taken aback that another major crisis was thrust upon them, not wanting to stare at Ike but desperate for him to take the lead. He finally spoke.

"We have two options, as I see it. To do nothing means that these brave Hungarian rebels will be massacred. But *to* intervene risks an awesome escalation of tension with Moscow. It will mean intervening *behind* the Iron Curtain."

I knew this Hungarian revolution was too good to be true, he thought. *What the hell is going on in the world? Crisis after crisis. I consider myself a high-energy individual, but I'm not sure how much more of this I can take. I feel so drained. Can barely focus.*

I said to Colonel Goodpaster and Sergeant Moaney not long ago that I would never allow something like the Nazi slaughter of the Jews to occur again. And yet here we are, and I have to choose between preventing a potential massacre and a showdown with Moscow.

How am I supposed to weigh Hungarian lives—rebel and innocent— against my dual strategy on Suez to remove the allies and keep out the Soviets? If I act in Hungary, will that make the Soviets more or less likely to intervene in Suez? Will it even matter at that point? I can't see a scenario where American forces enter Hungary in some capacity and the Soviets don't escalate toward catastrophe.

Then there's the issue of the American boys who will be sent into harm's way. I usually say that only the defense of a vital interest can possibly justify military action. Is this a vital interest? It's probably not a security interest, but it is a moral one. Can a moral vital interest justify sending young boys to their deaths?

"It seems like we really *don't* have an option besides trying to save them," Wilson said as he uncrossed his legs and leaned forward. "Between the humanitarian aspect and the fact that we've staked our credibility on helping to liberate Eastern Europe—and they'll never be a better opportunity than this."

What a disappointment, Ike thought. *I thought having the CEO of General Motors run DoD was a novel idea. But he's really a shallow man and leaves me to do his work for him. I'll probably replace him if I get reelected.*

"Additionally," Hoover began, "the State Department has been encouraging resistance to Moscow since Foster acquired his position. The protests are *our* responsibility."

"Makes sense," Ike replied. "How do you propose we send our forces there?"

Hoover looked at the globe that sat on the side of the room that was easily accessible to the National Security Council. The globe was a little over two feet in diameter and sat on a dark mahogany lobed oblong stand. Clearly, Hungary was landlocked: it had no ports from which to invade by the sea. Additionally, it was surrounded on all sides by Soviet client states. Austria was an exception, but needless to say, Vienna was not going to risk Soviet retaliation by allowing the Americans to use it as a staging ground for their operation.

"I'm not sure," Hoover admitted. "Surely you or Admiral Radford would have a better idea."

Ike turned to Radford to see if he had anything to say. Radford made a fist and put his thumb to his chin as he pondered the options. He cleared his throat.

"We may be able to deploy a small force. Through Yugoslavia perhaps?"

"A small force?" Ike asked, pretending to be startled. "Against a couple hundred thousand Soviet troops?"

"You think that's unwise?"

"Yes. We shouldn't consider intervening unless we can dominate the situation. To do less puts our boys in harm's way without doing everything possible to achieve our objectives and bring them home as quickly as possible. Which would not only be a bad idea but a disgusting one, as far as I'm concerned."

"We risk the slaughter of thousands of Hungarians who are on the *right* side of the issue by sitting on our hands," Wilson argued. "That's also disgusting."

Slaughter, Ike thought. *Seeing flashes in my mind right now. Prisoners so starved they can't even be fed, because their bodies lost the ability to digest food. Human heads shrunken to be paperweights. Train cars filled with the corpses of those left to die.*

"I agree. But let's get creative here. Hungary is as inaccessible as Tibet," Ike shot back. "I'm not even sure it is logistically *possible* to put troops there without attacking the *whole* Eastern Bloc!" Ike breathed heavily, fighting to keep his composure, his chin quivering.

"We could ask the British and French for help," Hoover suggested.

"They would reject that idea even if we *weren't* at odds over this Suez business," Ike replied. "They don't want to risk war with Moscow."

"What about an expedition with the West Germans and the Italians? They fought the Reds only eleven years ago. We could get to Hungary through Czechoslovakia. Liberate Prague in the process."

"Out of the question."

Feeling cold. This is overwhelming. Another foreign crisis. Seriously? On top of Suez, the election, my health, Foster's health? I don't know if I can take this. I mean, really, has any President, ever, faced such a complicated situation with such high stakes? Have to calm down. Steady thinking's the only way to resolve this with the Earth in one piece.

"I don't understand how we can let the Soviets crush a client state and massacre friends of freedom in good conscience," Radford interjected. "The protestors are essentially like our minutemen in 1776 who resisted foreign domination."

It's like they all want to be the most moral person in the room. Consequences and reality be damned.

"I agree with you, Arthur," Ike replied. "But let's be logical. Reducing tensions with Moscow must be a higher priority."

"That's appeasement! What if the Soviets attacked Israel? Would we still say that not upsetting the Kremlin is more important?"

"Israel is *outside* the Soviet sphere of influence. Hungary *isn't*. Thwarting Soviet expansion is different than intervening within the Eastern Bloc itself." Radford looked annoyed. "What do you think is the worst-case scenario of intervention?"

Radford thought for a moment.

"I suppose it would depend on one's thoughts about a nuclear exchange. Or of a general war in Europe. Like a repeat of 1939 to 45."

"Do you really think we would have a nice sweet 'World War II' type of war?" Ike asked. "I suspect we would devastate civilization as we know it."

"The President's right," Jackson said. "The situation with Hungary is tragic, but stability between the superpowers is essential."

"More essential than helping those trapped under the boot of communism?" Wilson asked.

"There may be a third option," CIA director Allen Dulles muttered as he lit a pipe. Ike always referred to Allen as a special kind of genius and sought to forge cooperation between the CIA and State Department by placing a pair of brothers in charge of them.

"Yes?" Radford asked.

"We could airdrop weapons to the rebels without putting our own troops on the ground."

"*Hmm*," Hoover and Wilson grunted simultaneously.

"That's an interesting idea," Radford said. "It would be like Roosevelt's Lend-Lease program during the war. Send arms to an ally so we don't have to get involved ourselves."

The entire National Security Council nodded. Except for Ike.

That would still cross Khrushchev's red line. The situation in Suez is bad enough in risking a world war. I feel like doing almost anything in Hungary is unacceptably dangerous, Ike thought. *Can't let emotions get in the way of logic. No matter how terrible a decision it seems. Remember what mother said to me as a boy. "He that conquereth his own soul is greater than he that taketh the city."*

Ike's stomach felt a chill. He pressed his index and middle fingers into where the surgeons had cut in June.

"We could explore launching such an operation from the Neubiberg airfield in West Germany," Radford suggested, taking the lead. "Or something from Turkey, possibly."

"We can probably count on support from Tito and Mao," Allen Dulles said.

"Really?" Wilson asked. "From Mao?"

"Yes. He and Tito both approved of the Polish protests. He may support the Hungarian ones as well."

"We could exploit this to divide the communist world," Wilson said, fancifully. "Like how the Free World is divided over Suez."

"We're going to save the Hungarians and isolate Moscow all at once!" Hoover exclaimed. "Separate them from China and the satellite countries simultaneously."

Allen Dulles smiled as he puffed on his pipe, his idea taking hold.

"I'm sorry to burst everyone's bubble," Ike interjected, "but I have no intention of approving of such an operation."

How am I going to sleep tonight?

"Mr. President!" Radford shouted before lowering his octave. "We can't waste this opportunity!"

"Dropping weapons into Hungary *still* risks an escalation with Moscow that I'm not willing to accept."

Radford's body locked up in tension. How was the President, a former general no less, obstructing an operation that could turn the tide of the Cold War decisively in America's favor? In Radford's eyes, as in the eyes of most of the Council, Ike was an obstacle.

"Mr. President," Wilson began, "you used to tell me that you supported sending weapons to the satellite states because you didn't want them dependent on Moscow for the rest of their lives."

"I know, Charlie, but this is different. Bulganin and Khrushchev will see this as an act of war. And world tensions are too high right now to risk anything that could go nuclear."

"We shouldn't fear nuclear weapons," Radford shot back.

"That's crazy as hell."

"We can't ignore our *duty*, Mr. President." Ike's face flashed red at the charge. "We come from different branches, but we swore an oath to the country decades ago. And we've upheld that oath. But to give communism a victory is to turn our back on—"

"If there is *one* thing that I will *not* be questioned about, it is my *duty*, Arthur," Ike snapped, at wit's end. His eyes bulged. The other members of the National Security Council turned to Radford to watch a response that did not come. Ike took a moment to push his anger back inside and calm down. "Our only *true* option is to write a letter to Bulganin and demand he withdraw Soviet troops from Hungary. Nothing more."

"He'll still say that we're interfering in Soviet domestic affairs," Hoover replied.

"I know," Ike said. "But America recognizes Hungary as an independent sovereign state. We have never asked for a people to rise up against ruthless military force. We simply insist upon the right of all people to be free to live under governments of their own choosing."

Several members of the Council shook their heads. Ike concluded.

"We'll be ready for refugees once this is over."

The meeting ended shortly thereafter, with most of the National Security Council visibly disappointed in Ike's decision.

☆☆☆☆☆

IKE BREATHED HEAVILY as his large nostrils flared. He knelt by the side of the bed in the President's bedroom, his eyes closed, his head down. His body locked up as competing emotions battled in his psyche. Ike's face flashed red, then pale. His arms couldn't help but vibrate. His mouth opened as if he were about to cry, only to grit his molars in anger. The intensity of his breathing continued to escalate until he finally calmed. It slowed so much it nearly stopped. His body vibrated a few more times until he finally opened his eyes. A tear slid down his cheek that he wiped away with a large index finger. Ike swallowed saliva that had built up in his mouth and let his weight sink backward. His tired blue eyes, with a hint of bloodshot, shifted back and forth a couple of times. He did not feel like getting up yet. He finally realized that Mamie stood on the other side of the room, watching him.

"I didn't want to disturb you while you were praying," she said softly. He nodded a 'thank you' as he pulled himself up enough to sit on the bed. He was still visibly distressed. "Are you nervous about the election?"

Ike shook his head.

"It has nothing to do with that. But you know I try to leave my work at the office. Not bother you with the issues that land on my desk. Whether I'm an Army Major or a President."

"I know, Ike. But you can talk to me if you need to."

Ike shrugged.

"I'm just so tired, dear. So drained. I'm not sure I'm going to last until the election."

"Sure you will."

"How do you know?"

"Because if anyone can do it, it's you."

"This week is particularly brutal. I just had to make a terrible decision, but I had no other options. Like, I try my best to be logical, but it isn't easy when you know people are going to get hurt and hate you for it."

"But this has been your life for so long now. Surely it must get easier."

"It's never easy to make life and death decisions. At least it shouldn't be. I don't know, I wondered sometimes about Roosevelt and Churchill. They seemed to act like characters out of Homer. Throwing lightning bolts as they pleased around the world." He placed his clasped hands in his lap. "I feel like I just sacrificed a *country* to save the *planet*."

Mamie put her hand on Ike's bald scalp.

"My, you are *sweaty*."

"You know, I'm still haunted some nights by what I saw in the German camps. I thought I could stop that from ever happening again. But I feel like I just let it happen. This reminds me of how I felt after Icky died."

Mamie grimaced at the mention of their first son's passing. She wanted to help her husband, her life partner since she was nineteen. And she knew what to do. He just gave it away. If he felt like he did after Icky's passing, she would use the same thing that helped them recover from that ultimate personal crisis.

"Do you remember when I went into labor with John?"

Ike took a moment to respond. He squinted.

"Vaguely. I hate to say it, but my emotions have been all over the place since my heart attack. It seems more distant than it used to."

"Well, let me jog your memory. We were stationed in Panama and my parents had me return to Denver with them. You were visiting when my water broke and you put me in a jeep, along with one of my sisters. You were so excited that you hit the gas and couldn't understand why the car wouldn't move. I had to tell you through my contractions to start the ignition!"

Ike laughed. His body finally shrunk as he relaxed. Mamie wrapped her arms around him, relaxing him more.

"I guess I remember that. Now that you mention it," he said quietly.

"Frankly, you weren't much more useful when our grandkids were born."

"What do you mean!" he exclaimed playfully.

"Oh, please! Like when Barbara Ann was born!"

"What did I do wrong then?"

"You and John were disappointed it was a girl because you two wanted to build a *football* team, of all things. I could have killed you both."

"I think my complaint was warranted!"

She tapped his forehead with her index finger.

"No, no," she muttered. He smiled as he enjoyed her embrace. "Please don't worry too much, Ike. I know the decisions are hard, but I've never met anyone as downright obsessed with doing their duty for the greater good as you. You said so when you proposed to me all those years ago. That's why you left me for three years during the war."

Ike chuckled. Mamie continued.

"You even turned down the chance to make a film about Normandy because of your duty. The money didn't even cross your mind. Do you remember how you explained it to me in a letter?"

"Not really."

"You said 'it's fun to be poor!'"

Ike laughed.

"It is when we do it together." She kissed his forehead. "So tired. Can we pray together?"

"Of course," she answered. They slowly made their way to the side of the bed, where they knelt down.

☆☆☆☆☆

"THEY'VE ALREADY TAKEN the Soroksári road, south of here," Attila explained as Henrika and the man who had touched her butt whose name she had yet to learn knelt on the ground of the market. "If they take this building, they'll control the Vaci road. That means they'll cut Budapest in half. We have to make sure that doesn't happen."

"Agreed," the other man said.

"Then Eisenhower will step in," Henrika said, soot having darkened her pale face, desperate for her words to be true. Attila glanced at her in the darkness of night but said nothing. The market was full of bullet holes from when the rebels repulsed a Soviet thrust a few hours earlier. He expected another attempt to capture the building before fighting stopped for the night. Every rebel in the market was exhausted.

"Take the window," Attila ordered the other man. "You'll be responsible for holding that flank." The man nodded. "By the way, I'm not sure we were properly acquainted when we got off to a bad start earlier. What's your name?"

"Does it matter? We probably won't survive the night."

"I'd like to know."

"Lael."

"An ironic name for an atheist."

"Irony's one of life's beauties. It's my favorite virtue."

"Fair enough. Pleased to meet you, Lael."

"Likewise."

They shook hands. Lael left to man his post with his machine pistol. He waited there with three other rebels. A dozen filled the market. Several designed Molotov cocktails with palinka.

Attila and Henrika waited by the market's other flank. She stayed low on both knees; he sat slightly over her as his right knee knelt into the ground and his arms rested on his left knee, which stood at a ninety-degree angle.

"Tell me more about your family," Attila asked.

"What do you want to know?"

"Does your husband treat you well?"

"Like a queen. I could ask him to cut his hand off for my mild amusement and he'd do it gladly."

"And yet he refused to come."

"Yes. I'm not sure of another time he disobeyed my request."

"Is he truly a man if he is so obedient?"

"He is if it is his wife he is obeying."

"You really believe that?"

"Yes. Are you married?"

"I was."

"What happened to her?"

"Not important. How old is your son?"

"Seven."

"Is he forming his own personality yet?"

"Ha! That rascal was born with one. You never saw a needier baby."

"How do you mean?"

"He had two moods: receiving attention and crying."

"And you gave in?"

"Every time. He had both of us around his finger from the moment I birthed him. His first word was 'more.'"

"My kids wouldn't have gotten away with that. Nothing a few good licks couldn't cure."

"We wouldn't have dared. At least until he becomes a teenager and starts mouthing off."

"Just you wait."

"I'm sure."

"Are your parents alive?"

"No. They died in the war."

"Did the Nazis kill them?"

"Yes."

"Why?"

"My father refused to surrender his horse to them. That horse was the apple of his eye. Even more than me."

"And they killed them for that?"

"They killed people for less than that."

"Hmm."

"Did you support them?"

"I did until they tried to annex us."

"Why?"

"Why did I support them? Because the communists want to destroy our society. Every tradition. Every belief. They want to start us at year zero."

"And you value our traditions?"

"Of course. I love this country. I don't like the modern world. No one has honor any more. No one respects authority. Life moves too fast. Too squishy. I'd take us back to the Renaissance. If not earlier."

"The modern world isn't so bad."

"Easy for you to say. You're a woman."

"So?"

"So, there are those who want to destroy the traditional relations between men and women."

"What's wrong with that?"

"Wouldn't you prefer your husband be the one here and you the one with your son?"

"I suppose so."

"That's what I mean."

"I don't know. Talk to me about it tomorrow. Or whenever I sleep again."

"Why? Do you reinvent yourself every day?"

"It feels like that sometimes."

"I've noticed that about you."

"What do you mean?"

"Your behavior adjusts itself as you take in new information. I'm not even sure you know you're doing it. It's fascinating."

"What does that mean?"

"It means you're guided by your gut and not your brain. You absorb ideas into yourself which affect your emotions and actions. I don't know if it's a woman thing or a *you* thing."

"I'm more than just a woman, you know."

"Oh yeah? What are you then?"

"I'm someone trying to build a better world for my family."

"A noble notion. How do you plan to do it?"

"By killing every communist that I find. Then I'll return to my family and go to Heaven when I die."

"Is that so?"

"That is so. I just wish my husband was here with me. We had so much fun together during the war."

"You found that war fun?"

"More than anything in my life. It forged our love. And this new battle is driving us apart."

"Maybe I'm not the only one who misses the past. Wait a second. I hear something."

Attila looked through the window. He saw motion in the distance as dark blobs hugged the shattered buildings and moved toward the market.

"It's the Soviets," Attila said as he raised his machine pistol until it was under his chin. He peered through the window again. The blobs stopped. Attila's eyes narrowed. "What are they doing?" he whispered. His question was answered as the sound of an enormous engine emerged. "Can't be."

Attila turned to Henrika.

"They have a tank."

"What?"

"Don't say 'what.' You heard me. They're done playing after we fought them off a few hours ago."

Henrika looked through the window to see the advancing T-54. The thirty-six ton monster headed right for the market.

Henrika froze. She swallowed what little saliva was in her mouth.

"Eisenhower's not saving us, is he?"

Attila blinked a couple times, amazed she was asking this question. He shook his head. Tears emerged in her eyes.

"I'm so stupid," she muttered as she shifted her weight to her rear.

"What are you doing?" Attila demanded to know. "Get up!"

Henrika ignored him. She put her face in her hands and bawled.

"I'm going to leave my son an orphan. All because of that *bastard*!"

"We don't have time for this!" Attila shouted. Henrika remained unresponsive. Attila shifted to another location to eye the tank. He then came back and grabbed Henrika's arm, trying to lift her. Either he was too tired or her posture made her too heavy. He struggled to drag her. "Stand! Now!"

The world disappeared for Henrika. One thing occupied her mind. Fernao was right. And she was stupid for putting her faith in Eisenhower. She felt worthless. Worse than worthless, she left her family by pinning her hopes where they didn't belong. Again. She tried to think things through, like Fernao appeared able to do, but somehow she repeated the same mistakes over and over again. The decisions made sense to her, but others could see her folly in advance every time.

Two rebels lit Molotov cocktails and ran past Attila and Henrika. They tried to stay near the sides of buildings as they charged toward the tank. Soviet troops shot at them, delaying their advance. Their cocktails went off before they reached their target.

Attila tripped and fell to his knees, giving up on dragging Henrika. He ran to another spot along the wall to watch the tank. He dropped his machine pistol and left it behind. Attila fell to his knees as he slammed against the wall, a clumsy, panicking mess. He hyperventilated; dust gripped his eyes.

Henrika didn't notice when Lael shouted "Sic semper tyrannis!" as he fired on Soviet troops. His throat was struck by a burst of Soviet machine gun bullets. He bled out, grabbing his throat, his body spasming in a puddle of blood. Nor did she notice when three more rebels threw Molotov cocktails at the tank, only to be repulsed by Soviet troops.

"My son," she cried. Her mind felt like it was on fire. She wrapped her arms around her legs in a fetal position. What was wrong with her? Why couldn't she see things as clearly as Fernao did? Just this once, she wanted to be the one who could say "I told you so." Though she'd give anything to *hear* him say that now.

"I want to see my son again. And Fernao. I'm so sor—"

The tank fired at the market. Henrika didn't notice.

"Look out!" Attila screamed as he leapt back to her aid. The roof collapsed.

Everything went black.

☆☆☆☆☆

November 5, 1956

Secretary Humphrey could see statues of Alexander Hamilton and Albert Galatin from his office in the West Wing of the Treasury Building. Humphrey's bald head had led Ike to tell him they parted their hair the same way upon meeting following Ike's election in 1952. Humphrey remained one of Ike's closest advisors, to the point where Ike said, "When George talks, we all listen." He remained the administration's leading advocate for balanced budgets, tax cuts, and deregulation.

He reviewed a White House memorandum that explained that Israel had completed its conquest of the Sinai and had captured Tiran and Sanifar, two islands in the Gulf of Aqaba that Egypt used to blockade Eilat, an Israeli port. Israel had captured thousands of Egyptian prisoners during the operation, including two Egyptian artillery battalions, despite most of Egypt's weapons coming from the Soviet Union. Egypt's Air Force was destroyed.

Humphrey's secretary notified him that the call he'd expected from British Deputy Prime Minister Rab Butler was now on the line. They exchanged pleasantries and Butler explained Britain's poor financial situation amidst the Suez conflict. He asked if America could give Britain a loan. Ike had anticipated this move and had prepared Humphrey on what to say.

"The United States is willing to offer the United Kingdom 1.5 billion dollars. Interest would be deferred."

"That's wonderful, Mr. Secretary!" Butler exclaimed in his posh accent.

"I'm not done," Humphrey asserted. "There's strings attached."

Butler was silent for a moment.

"What strings?"

"The loan is conditioned on an immediate British withdrawal from Egypt." Butler became silent again. "You and the French have two hundred ships off the Egyptian coast. Paratroopers are already landing in the country. President Eisenhower is willing to grant your country this loan on the condition that you withdraw."

"There's no way I can sell that to the Prime Minister."

"Then I suppose your government will have to do without a loan from us."

"Be reasonable, Mr. Secretary. Nasser is in Russian hands the way Mussolini was in Hitler's. It is in neither of our countries' interests for him to remain in power."

"Perhaps. But the President believes that Western aggression against Nasser will only turn the Third World against us and into the Kremlin's arms. Your country and France look like bullies to the world."

"We don't even have a set exit strategy as of now."

"That isn't the fault of this government."

"Does the President understand what his financial actions are doing to the British economy? We are America's closest ally. We're going to run out of oil if we don't get this loan."

"Then I suggest advising the Prime Minister to withdraw. Exit strategy or not. Or at least halt your offensive. If we could have for the next two or three days a period of relative calm while your troops did nothing but land, we might much more swiftly develop a situation that would be acceptable to both sides and to the world."

"I will discuss this with the Prime Minister. I hope that these disagreements and actions do not permanently strain relations between our two governments."

"As do I."

The conversation ended shortly thereafter. The British government received another headache as the Labour Party organized protests in Trafalgar Square in London against "Eden's War." The protestors called for Eden's resignation.

☆☆☆☆☆

"Ambassador Andropov informs me that the situation in Hungary is now under control and that Soviet vital interests are secure," Nikolai Bulganin, Premier of the Soviet Union, said behind his elongated brown table in his Kremlin office, an office which featured two chandeliers hanging from the ceiling, oak paneling along its rectangular walls, and windows located to the left of the Premier's table. Bulganin himself wielded white hair and goatee; his tie was black with white dots. Two red flags stood behind him.

Two officials sat across the table from Bulganin. The first was Nikita Khrushchev, Secretary of the Communist Party, a stocky, bald man with an impossibly spherical head and porcine features—a noticeable double chin among these. He was the most dangerous opponent America ever faced. The other was Georgy Zhukov, the most revered man in Russian military history, who battled the Nazis at Moscow, Leningrad, Stalingrad, Kursk, and Berlin. Stalin sacked him after Russia's victory and assigned him to the command of the Odessa district in Ukraine. But Stalin's death in 1953 allowed Khrushchev to pluck Zhukov from irrelevance. Together they destroyed Lavrentiy Beria, who Stalin once said was the Soviet Heinrich Himmler, before Beria could seize power for himself. Zhukov was now the Soviet Minister of Defense.

"It was a terrible decision," Zhukov added, "but it was necessary. The fascists in Hungary left us no choice. With that operation complete, we can now turn our attention to saving Nasser in Egypt."

"The Israeli government is criminally and irresponsibly playing with the fate of the world and with the fate of its own people," Bulganin said. "They are sowing hatred that places in question the very existence of Israel as a state. We must, at this moment, take steps to end the war and restrain the aggressors."

"It still amazes me we didn't see this coming," Zhukov muttered with disgust.

Bulganin shrugged.

"The KGB bugged the American embassy, but the Americans weren't involved in the conspiracy. This time."

"The situation in Egypt gets worse and worse by the hour," Khrushchev declared, beating the point to death. "Nasser has asked for our military assistance. How easily could we get our Navy or Air Force to Egypt?" Khrushchev squirmed in his seat, his perennial kidney stones tearing at his sides.

"Are we really going to fire upon British and French units?" Zhukov asked, his eyebrow raised. "That could spin out of control."

"Our relationship with Nasser is the centerpiece of our efforts to expand our influence across the Third World. *We* stand by Egyptian self-determination and against colonialism, while America has tied itself to the European empires. If we let Nasser fall, our credibility will be lost."

What Khrushchev did not say was that his own place within the Kremlin's hierarchy would also be lost. Khrushchev had removed rivals beyond Beria. He'd isolated and removed Vyacheslav Molotov, Stalin's old Foreign Minister and the architect of the Nazi-Soviet Pact who remained incessantly hostile to the West in the early Cold War. Khrushchev also manipulated the removal of Georgy Malenkov and the ascendancy of Bulganin as Premier following Stalin's death.

"I'm not disagreeing with you on that point," Zhukov countered, "but I question whether we even have the means to deploy a force to Egypt. We lack a surface fleet, because, with all due respect, it was *your* idea to invest in submarines."

"Are you suggesting we lack *any* capacity to deploy a force to Egypt?" Bulganin asked.

"Yes," Zhukov answered.

"That is most troubling. Because Nikita's right. The imperialists in London and Paris are grasping for what's left of their power in the Near East. By defending Nasser, we can throw off their yoke and gain a decisive foothold in the region. That would be our greatest victory against imperialism since Hitler's carcass was burned."

"I just don't see how it's logistically possible, or even desirable. We would have to cross the Black Sea and enter the Eastern Mediterranean without a warm water port and without a fleet to carry our men and equipment. Furthermore, I was under the impression, Nikita, that we agreed that man is essentially good at heart and will follow our lead as the world's most progressive state as soon as they throw off their militarist overlords."

Khrushchev ignored Zhukov's challenge. His double chin sat atop his finger as he pondered how to save Nasser. His small eyes squinted as a sinister thought formed in his mind.

"What about the R-5M?"

Zhukov jumped back in his seat. His face scrunched. He looked to Bulganin, who had no expression, and then back to Khrushchev.

"You can't be serious." Khrushchev maintained his poker face. "Tell me you're joking, comrade."

"When have you ever known me to joke?" Khrushchev asked. Air whistled through his nostrils as his body locked up, the weight of his idea setting in.

"You want to launch nuclear missiles at the imperialist forces in Egypt?" Zhukov asked. "Are you trying to save Nasser or turn him to ash?"

"I'm not talking about firing at Cairo."

"Where then?"

"London. Paris. Tel Aviv. The R-5Ms that we have stationed in the satellite states can reach all three cities. We can tell all three governments to withdraw from Egypt or face destruction."

"Is the R-5M even ready?" Bulganin asked.

"It became operational quite recently," Khrushchev answered as he leaned forward, smiling.

"Hmm," Bulganin grunted as he put his two hands together under his white goatee.

"What of—"

"Global tensions are like a wine glass," Khrushchev interrupted Zhukov, feeding on the adrenaline of his idea. "Tensions are rising to the rim of the glass. This forms a meniscus. We just can't let it overflow."

"Overflowing meaning war?" Bulganin asked.

"Yes. But by threatening war we can keep our *enemies* off balance. We can't let our enemies live peacefully. Imagine the influence we'll earn across the Third World if we threaten *nuclear war* to save Nasser!"

"And what happens if Eden and Mollet call our bluff?" Zhukov asked.

"Then we show them we're *not* bluffing."

"That risks national suicide! You think America will stand by any of this?"

"I do. Foster Dulles is in the hospital."

"What about Eisenhower?"

"Eisenhower is a wimp," Khrushchev declared. "At Geneva he showed he was obsessed with peace at *any* price. The brainless soldier doesn't even *think* for himself. Dulles whispered in his ear *more than once* during that summit. What kind of a leader lets himself be seen allowing his advisors to guide him like a puppet?"

"And what if he chooses to stand by America's allies anyway?" Zhukov asked.

"The key," Bulganin interjected before Khrushchev could speak, "would be to drive a wedge between Eisenhower and the Europeans."

"How?"

"We offer to let Eisenhower in on our operation."

"Against the Europeans and Israelis?"

"Precisely. We send our threat to the aggressors and *simultaneously* we offer to cooperate with Eisenhower in forcing them out of Egypt. Eisenhower's hands will be tied. He can't claim to care about *peace* if he rejects cooperation with us while we're trying to save Nasser. We'll be neutralizing Eisenhower as a threat."

"That's brilliant," Khrushchev said, his forearms now resting on Bulganin's desk.

"Is it?" Zhukov asked. "Eisenhower's still mad at us for the operation in Hungary."

Bulganin waved his hand dismissively.

"We're never going to let him take away our buffer zone so the motherland can be invaded again. Not after 1941."

"But what if Eisenhower refuses an alliance? This is opening the door to another world war. One worse than the last one."

Khrushchev laughed.

"*I'm* tougher than Eisenhower. With Dulles gone, he'll *fold* like a house of cards."

☆☆☆☆☆

HAROLD MACMILLAN, CHANCELLOR of the Exchequer, entered Prime Minister Eden's office. Macmillan was a veteran of World War I and, like Eden, a Churchill protégé. He was fastidiously dressed. His receding hairline revealed age spots above his right ear. Bags sat under his eyes; his mustache was grayer by the day. Eden did not look up at first, a slight grin reflecting his contentment.

"You know, Harold, I've convinced myself that historians will write that Nasser's brought this upon himself. I'll be standing up to a thug and will be seen as the opposite of Chamberlain. This whole thing will preserve our nation as a major power in the world. Why do you look so glum? What's that envelope?"

"It's from the Foreign Office."

"What is it?"

"A cable from Bulganin."

"Can I see it?"

Macmillan handed Eden the letter. Eden's face turned white as he read it.

"What does it say?" Macmillan asked.

Eden took several moments to respond. Sweat built up on his mustache. His lips opened and closed several times until he forced himself to say the words.

"He says... He says that the Soviet Union is determined to, and I quote, 'crush the aggressor and reestablish peace in the East by using force.' Then he brags about Soviet rocketry and, I quote again, 'all types of weapons of destruction.'"

Macmillan said nothing. Eden slammed the letter on his desk and seethed.

"This is nuclear *blackmail*!" he shouted. His arms vibrated, unsure if he wanted to stand or not. "He has the blood of how many *thousands* of Hungarians on his hands, and he accuses *me* of aggression? Threatening us with national *destruction*!"

Eden stood up, then shook his head violently, then turned his hands into fists. He shivered uncontrollably.

"How dare he! How *dare* he!"

"Do you think he's serious?"

"What do you mean?"

"I mean if you think he's serious. Hitler threatened our existence, but do you really think Bulganin will begin World War III over Egypt?"

"Do you have any idea how *obsessed* the Russians are with replacing us in the Middle East? Since the Great Game—"

"I don't need a hist—"

"We have to take this threat seriously."

Macmillan sighed. He put his fist under his lip. His head shook slightly to and fro.

"What?" Eden asked.

"What should we do?" Macmillan asked desperately.

"I haven't a clue," Eden muttered as he sank back into his chair and stared at the ceiling. "Pray for a miracle?"

☆☆☆☆☆

"JESUS CHRIST," WERE the first words Colonel Goodpaster heard as he passed Ann Whitman's desk and entered the Oval Office. He left the door open behind him, not thinking about such a menial issue. He found Ike, Allen Dulles, Radford, Humphrey, and Hoover waiting for him. He feared they would be angry waiting for their subordinate, but they had started without him.

"What's happened?" he asked. Ike, his arms folded and his weight against the Oval Office desk, turned to Hoover to explain the situation. Hoover cleared his throat.

"We received a cable from Bulganin. It says that the Soviet Union intends to expel the allies from Egypt. Probably through force."

"Jesus Christ," Goodpaster muttered.

"There's more. He's proposed that the United States join the Soviet Union in the operation."

"Nothing but window dressing," Radford muttered.

"I had hoped," Ike began, "that Bulganin's rise within the Kremlin hierarchy would lead to peace. He's a fellow military man. He knows the cost of war. But he's nothing more than Khrushchev's pawn."

Goodpaster studied Ike's face. He had never seen the President so drained, at least since his heart attack and surgery. Ike's face was paler than usual: he had dark half-circles under his eyes. His mouth hung open, revealing his yellowish teeth. Goodpaster looked to Ike's other advisors. The CIA Director. The Chairman of the Joint Chiefs. The Secretary of the Treasury. The Acting Secretary of State. All were in over their heads.

Ike wandered toward a wooden pelican on the side of the room to think. Goodpaster wondered what transpired in the President's mind. Then he looked back at the blank stares of the President's advisors. Allen Dulles rolled a pipe between his fingertips. Hoover put his hands in his pockets and then pulled them back out. He glared at Allen Dulles.

"This is your fault!"

Allen Dulles looked askance; his head shifted back momentarily. He was in no mood for such an accusation.

"What the *devil* do you mean by that?"

"It's your job to anticipate the actions of other countries. And you screwed up. And now we're looking at a possible Soviet intervention into the Middle East. And possibly against our European allies."

"At least the CIA didn't *create* the conditions for this mess!" Allen Dulles shot back. "Unlike the State Department! Cutting off aid for the Aswan Dam! Not making it *crystal clear* that we would oppose an attack on Nasser!"

"That was your own brother's doing! He can share the blame with you!"

"Don't you dare attack my brother!" Allen Dulles spat, waiving his pipe in Hoover's face. "Not while he's in the hospital! What kind of a man are you?"

"Me? You and your brother, with your damn Manichean worldview, have put all these countries, like Egypt, in a position where they have to choose which side of the Cold War they want to be on. And guess what? That *increases* tensions! First bribing Egypt with aid and then cutting it off for recognizing Red China. Look where it's brought us!"

Allen Dulles looked flustered, unsure how to respond.

"You have a lot of nerve attacking my family after what your *father* did as President!"

"Are you serious!" Hoover roared.

Humphrey's bald head shifted back and forth every time someone spoke. He appeared like a child desperately watching his divorcing parents.

Goodpaster turned to Radford.

"Shouldn't we stop this?"

"Quiet, *Colonel*. Not now."

Ike ignored the argument. His arms were folded as he paced around in circles.

My abdomen is killing me. I can feel my surgery scars bulging. Have barely slept for days. Can't stand up straight anymore. I've been fragile since the surgery, but this week drained me of everything I had left. Could fall over if someone so much as breathed on me.

The Israeli attack on Egypt was the outbreak of a Third World War. That was clear from when I first heard the news in Richmond. Putting that global catastrophe back in the box required a dual strategy. Phase one was to put diplomatic and economic pressure on our traditional allies to withdraw their attack. That has yet to succeed, but likely will. Phase two was to hold back the Soviet Union from taking advantage of the situation. The Soviets were distracted by Hungary for a few days, but their standard opportunism is kicking in. They want a foothold in the Middle East. That's what Russia has always wanted. It would be a devastating defeat in the Cold War if that happened. They would have a chokehold on the world economy. I doubt the Cold War will stay cold in that case. Or else the end of freedom. The Soviets will do almost anything to make that happen. They might even destroy Israel or attack Britain and France, which Bulganin implied in his letter. I still can't believe he wrote that.

I can't defend Western Europe with non-nuclear forces. The Soviet Union has 175 divisions in Eastern Europe. The United States has twenty total, five of which are stationed in Europe under NATO. Overlord would be useless in the atomic age. If I want to stop the Soviet intervention, I only have one choice. The strategy that I've used to keep the peace since September 1953.

Massive Retaliation. The New Look. The idea that I would unleash an all-out nuclear response against the Soviet Union in response to aggression. Truman had designed the containment of communism to depend on maintaining a World War II-sized, 60 billion-dollar plus military that could intervene anywhere in the world in response to aggression, as he did in Korea. That would bankrupt the country and result in a Garrison State. Truman said it was necessary because he accepted that the Soviets would launch a nuclear strike on the US mainland, and we would need the military to carry on the fight. I rejected such fatalism, such inevitable doom. Instead, I built up the nuclear arsenal to act as a deterrent.

The New Look has kept the peace, so far. My threat to use nuclear weapons against Red China ended the Korean War. My advisors unanimously pushed for me to use them when the French were fighting communists in Indochina. I managed to make Mao unsure if I'd go nuclear or not when he was bombing the islands near Formosa. Any intervention to help the Hungarian rebels would have depended on Massive Retaliation.

But this time is different. I'd be making a direct threat to destroy the Soviet Union. This is Massive Retaliation's ultimate test. I've done everything I can to make my threat of nuclear war as legitimate as possible, in order to keep the peace. I've pretended to misunderstand translators when meeting foreign leaders and butchered my words at press conferences in order to appear stupid and so not appreciate what a nuclear war would mean. I even had Foster Dulles whisper some gibberish in my ear when meeting the Soviets at Geneva, because I wanted them to think that I'm being led on a leash by my saber-rattling Secretary of State.

To threaten Massive Retaliation in this situation is taking us right to the brink. If Bulganin and Khrushchev refuse to back down, I'll be pulling the trigger on the apocalypse. Am I seriously willing to wage a nuclear war? Really? I've sent millions to kill and die before, but this is a magnitude I can't even fathom. Can I stomach being responsible for so much suffering? The ultimate suffering to ever be inflicted on this world? Makes me want to vomit just thinking about it. Have to stay strong. Calm.

I hoped I would never have to know. But I may have to find out, and quickly. Such a monstrous thing. The end of all things. Maybe I shouldn't do this. Just let the Soviets win here. Surely, it can't be as bad as World War III. The whole Eastern Hemisphere would fall. The Middle East. Europe, most likely. Mao would run rampant over East Asia. The Western Hemisphere is all we'd have left.

No. I have to try. I owe it to humanity. The chance to live in freedom instead of tyranny. It's my duty. Mamie said she never met anyone as committed to their duty as me. Duty. My duty has been my whole life. I have to do this. I have to! Even if it gambles everything. How does that feel? Putting my finger on the nuclear trigger? Pointing it at Moscow? I'm staring into the abyss this time, praying they blink.

Ike slowly returned to his advisors.

"I wasn't even *at* the CIA at that point!" Allen Dulles screamed, his face red. "You can't hold me responsible for missing North Korea's attack on the South! And again, that was State—"

"You may not have been in charge at the time!" Hoover conceded. "But you share—"

"Gentlemen!" Ike barked. His advisors fell silent. They turned to him, desperate for leadership. They got it. "The Soviets are trying to distract us from Hungary. Those boys in the Kremlin are both furious and scared. Just as with Hitler, that makes for the most dangerous possible state of mind. And we better be damn sure that every intelligence point and every outpost of our armed forces is absolutely right on their toes. If those fellows start something, we may have to hit them—and, if necessary, with *everything* in the bucket."

Ike's advisors stared at him with lifeless eyes. They'd disagreed with many of his decisions in this crisis. Opposing the allies. Not helping the Hungarians. Now he implied he was prepared to pull the trigger on Massive Retaliation? They awaited what he said next.

Weird feeling in the back of my head, Ike thought. *Like I'm in a deja vu or something. Can't put my finger on it. I know! Haven't felt it in years. It's that feeling I had when I launched the Normandy landing.*

Ike turned to Allen Dulles.

"I want continuous U2 flights over Israel and Syria. We have to know if the Soviets have any nuclear bombs in Syria. They might be bluffing. The British and French would have reason to bomb Soviet planes or any other units. But I don't want them to know that we'll invoke Article Five of NATO in their defense, if need be. We'll let the Soviet threat increase their likelihood of withdrawing from Egypt."

Ike turned to Radford next.

"Is the SS-3 operational yet?"

Ike was using NATO's term for the Soviet R5-M missile. Radford turned to Allen Dulles.

"It's unclear from U2 photographs over Russia."

"That's okay," Ike replied. "I don't want any U2s going over the Soviet Union at this time. Tensions are high enough. The SS-3 is the only tool the Kremlin has, as far as I'm concerned. It would be geographically impossible for them to reach the Mideast through non-nuclear means."

"I agree," Radford responded. "They have the aircraft to put troops in the region, but it's more likely they'd use nuclear missiles."

"Put all navy commands on nuclear alert," Ike ordered.

"Yes, sir."

"I'll notify the rest of the Joint Chiefs to do the same for the other branches. Especially the Strategic Air Command. We need to send a clear signal to the Kremlin that we mean business."

"The Sixth Fleet is already in the Eastern Mediterranean," Radford offered. "Task Force 64 has nuclear capabilities."

"Good. Have the Fleet sail near the British and French fleets, so an attack on one will be an attack on all. Does the Fleet have atomic antisubmarine weapons?"

"Yes. Task Force 69 has nuclear depth charges."

"Wonderful. I'll have Hagerty release a White House statement. We need to not threaten Bulganin directly while still making it clear that it's unthinkable for the Americans and Soviets to work together or for either military to enter the region except under a United Nations mandate. If they try, we will oppose any such effort. We have to make it a certainty that they know they'll be committing suicide."

"How long will a nuclear war last?" Goodpaster asked.

"At least a month or two," Hoover responded.

"*What!*" Ike shouted. "That's nuts. In World War II, countries kept fighting even after the point of devastation. Assuming World War III will be over in a month or two is as serious as the idea of a race between Secretary Humphrey and myself to the moon."

Humphrey, having been mentioned, spoke next.

"We should devise a contingency plan for restoring the dollar after the nuclear war."

"Wait a minute, George. If this happens, we're not going to be reconstructing the dollar. We're going to be digging for worms."

That caused Ike's advisors to pause. Hoover broke the silence as he tapped the knuckle of his index finger to his bottom lip.

"What do you expect our casualties to be?"

"The Policy Planning Division of the National Security Council has told me that sixty-five percent of Americans will be dead or wounded. After this war, you might as well go outside and shoot everyone you see and then shoot yourself."

Ann Whitman gasped from outside the Oval Office, eavesdropping through the door that Goodpaster left open. The advisors became quiet again as the magnitude of World War III set in. Ike continued explaining his vision.

"The Army will be in charge of law and order because the federal government will be destroyed. The states will have to rebuild a new form of federal government. The country will literally be in the business of digging ourselves out of the ashes and starting again."

Depression hung over the room. None of the advisors wanted to think about life after the nuclear war. Not that any of them would be alive to see it. They wanted to go home. Hug their wives and children. Whatever parents they had left. Maybe for the last time.

Ike turned to Goodpaster.

"Can you determine something for me?"

"Whatever you want, Mr. President." Goodpaster's voice was weak and tired.

"How many hydrogen bombs can we detonate before we knock the Earth off its axis?"

☆☆☆☆☆

KHRUSHCHEV'S FACE WAS pale as he waddled into Bulganin's Kremlin office. Armpit stains were visible on the Party Secretary's shirt, his black sweater vest was crumpled, his fingers curled like claws. Bulganin did not look in his direction; the Premier lifelessly stared ahead, his sweaty palms placed together at neck-level. Khrushchev slammed his hands on Bulganin's desk, sweat dripping from his face and onto the wood like rain.

"I take it you've read the White House's statement?" Bulganin asked.

"Yes," Khrushchev muttered, out of breath and exhausted from recent events.

"What is your recommended course of action?"

"Is that a serious question?"

"Yes."

"We do nothing."

"Nothing?"

"I'm not even sure I'm *capable* of much else at the moment. My butt is so tense right now I'm surprised I could even run here."

"Lovely. But I'm not ready to give up on the gains in the Near East we'd envisioned earlier."

"What? Eisenhower just threatened nuclear war. We can't cross him if he's serious."

"I thought you said he was a wimp."

"I thought he was!"

"And what do you think now?"

"That he's a moron who can barely complete a sentence and who doesn't appreciate that a nuclear war will kill us *all*!"

"Surely he's not that dumb."

"Have you looked in his eyes? He has nothing between his ears! He gets led along by his militarist masters like a puppy! And don't forget, this is the man who launched Operation Overlord in World War II! He isn't afraid of *others* deaths."

"Coming from the man who found his calling during Stalin's purges."

"I may be ruthless, but I'm not stupid."

"You're asking us to give up our chance to dominate the Eastern Mediterranean! Name one Tsar who wouldn't have dreamed of this opportunity!"

"Nikolai, I'm begging you. We mustn't make a move."

"Won't this destroy our prestige in the region? Backing down like this?"

"We'll still increase our prestige."

"How so?"

"We'll say that our nuclear threat is what got the allies out of Egypt."

"How are you so sure Nasser will survive if we do nothing?"

"Because Eisenhower is going to get the imperialists and Israelis out of Egypt. He's already pressuring them. He's a capitalist pig who is placing the will of American oil companies over his friends."

Bulganin leaned back in his chair, his sweaty back causing a stain.

"*Hmm.*"

"Let's let Eisenhower resolve the situation," Khrushchev implored. "I'll tell *Pravda* to claim the credit for us once it's over."

☆☆☆☆☆

NOVEMBER 6, 1956

EDEN SAT AT the huge table that dominated the Cabinet Room in 10 Downing Street. His ministers watched as he continuously fidgeted, distraught by recent events. He barely had the strength to speak.

"I spoke to Prime Minister Mollet on the phone last night, before retiring for the evening. He's panicked over the Soviet nuclear threat."

"That seems to be receding," Foreign Minister Lloyd suggested.

"Regardless," Eden continued, "Mollet is desperate to hand the Suez conflict over to the Security Council, so long as the Americans, and not the Soviets, sponsor the resolution."

"The Canadians have taken the lead on that issue."

"He also pushed for free elections in Egypt so the allies could negotiate with someone other than Nasser."

"I see virtually no chance of that happening."

"I am simply the messenger," Eden replied faintly. His was the face of the defeated. It was about to get worse as he turned to Macmillan.

"How is the financial situation?"

"We've passed the end of the rope."

"Meaning?"

"I can no longer be responsible for Her Majesty's exchequer unless a ceasefire is ordered immediately."

Eden regained his energy as his face turned red.

"And why would *that* be!"

"Because, Mr. Prime Minister, our country has exhausted its remaining oil reserves."

"I thought we were going to buy oil from Venezuela since imports from the Mideast have ceased and the Americans cut us off."

"We lack the money to buy from Venezuela. It's been spent on the war in Egypt. Under the Bretton Woods System that Keynes designed, we would need to ask the IMF for our deposit back."

"Only if there's a decrease in the global demand for pounds!" Eden spit.

"Which there is now that the American Federal Reserve is selling pounds at a rate far above what's necessary," Macmillan answered professionally.

"Then let's request the withdrawal from the IMF!"

"We did. The Americans vetoed the transfer."

Eden struggled to breathe. He put his face in his palms, fighting back tears in front of his colleagues. Macmillan eyed Butler, his rival, and turned back to Eden, who breathed heavily, his dreams destroyed and his world imploding around him. Macmillan stated his conclusion.

"Eisenhower has been one step ahead of us the entire time. Cutting off oil and loans. Using American dominance of the global financial system to deny us access to the IMF. He's going to let our economy crash unless we withdraw from Egypt immediately."

The words felt like dirt in Macmillan's mouth; he had been Ike's political advisor during the North African campaign in World War II. Eden hyperventilated. His head bobbled as he became dizzy and slouched to the side. He spoke softly and primarily to Macmillan.

"He's ruined me. I'll have to resign. How will history remember me? A miserable failure following giants like Churchill and Attlee. Churchill, who won the war. Attlee, who founded the National Health Service and the welfare state."

"You had a great career in the Foreign Office and in the war," Macmillan consoled. Eden shook his head.

"No one will remember that. They'll only remember my little war in Suez."

☆☆☆☆☆

IKE AND MAMIE exited Marine One, his helicopter as President of the United States, to see Colonel Goodpaster waiting for them on the White

House lawn. It was election day, and they had voted in Gettysburg, Pennsylvania, where they had a home.

Why did I have to rush back to Washington so quickly? Ike wondered. *Have the Soviets made their move? Has World War III finally come? The anxiety since threatening nuclear war has been killing me. Had to call Dr. Snyder last night because my blood pressure was through the roof. Said my heart was skipping beats. I suppose one way or another, my threat will resolve* that *problem.*

Goodpaster joined Ike and Mamie as they walked toward the White House.

"What do you have for me, Colonel?" Ike asked.

"CIA has said that the U2s haven't picked up any Soviet forces moving into Egypt or Syria."

"Really? So, it's over?"

"It appears so."

Ike smiled and looked to the sky. There were clouds, but no mushroom clouds, thank God. Tension strong enough to break a lesser man melted from his body.

"Anything else?" Ike asked.

"There's news from Hungary."

"Yes?"

"The State Department estimates that tens of thousands of Hungarians have been killed since the Soviet invasion. Hundreds of thousands of others have poured into Austria as refugees."

"My God. I'll send Nixon over there as soon as possible. He's tired from campaigning around the country, but he can evaluate the situation and design a program to bring refugees to America. Have we tracked down Nagy yet?"

"Uh, yes, Mr. President. The Soviets got him. They executed him."

"I see," Ike muttered glumly. The trio entered the White House. Ann Whitman caught Ike's attention as he entered the West Wing.

"The British Prime Minister is on the phone for you!"

Ike lit up. *We can finally end this thing. Right now.*

They exchanged pleasantries. Eden cut to the chase and informed Ike that Britain would accept the ceasefire proposal at the General Assembly.

"Anthony," Ike said, ready to burst, "I can't tell you how pleased we are that you found it possible to accept the ceasefire."

"We are going to cease firing tonight," Eden repeated, submissive and defeated.

"Without conditions?"

"We cease firing tonight at midnight unless attacked."

"That's wonderful news, Anthony. How soon will all British forces be withdrawn from the area? I hope it will happen quickly."

"I would hope some forces could remain in the area as part of a peacekeeping force. It would help me save face. Our men could help clear the Canal of the obstructions Nasser put in it."

"No," Ike replied curtly. "I would like to see none of the great nations in it. I am afraid the Red boy is going to demand the lion's share. I would rather make it no troops of the big five." He was referring to the five permanent members of the UN Security Council: America, Britain, France, the Soviet Union, and China, whose seat was held by Formosa. "The Canadians have volunteered a large force for the operation."

"I don't know," Eden muttered.

Time for some tough love! Ike thought.

"Anthony, if you don't get out of Port Said *tomorrow*, I'll cause a run on the pound and drive it down to *zero*."

The line was silent for a few moments. Then Ike heard heavy breathing.

"Ok, Ike. You win."

Ike breathed a sigh of relief. He closed his eyes, grateful that the nightmare was finally ending. His eyes opened as he explained his thinking further.

"Once UN forces are in the region, any act of aggression will be aggression against the entire UN. No one would *dare* such a thing. The sooner you and the allies withdraw, the better able we are to prevent Nasser from delaying the UN's entry."

"Can we move on to another topic?" Eden asked.

"Of course."

"What do you make of this Soviet nuclear threat?"

"I believe the threat has passed."

"You do?"

"Yes, thank God. Their threat is just words now. Of course, if I'm wrong, and Britain *is* attacked, you should know that you and your family are always welcome in the United States. This Suez business was nothing more than a family spat."

"Thank you," Eden replied awkwardly to the warm gesture predicated on his country's destruction.

"You're welcome," Ike replied, not understanding Eden's tone.

"How's Foster doing?"

"He's stable in Walter Reed."

"Splendid. Do you have a sense how the election over there is going to go?"

Ike chuckled.

"Our whole thought has been on Hungary and the Middle East. I don't give a damn how the election goes."

The conversation ended shortly thereafter. Mollet called an hour later for a similar conversation. Ike told Goodpaster that Israel would be more difficult. He was right. Ben-Gurion insisted that Israel hold onto the Sinai for the time being. Ike threatened to increase sanctions on Israel, including the stopping of any Jewish philanthropy. If Ben-Gurion still refused to budge, Ike would have Israel expelled from the UN. He even hinted that the US would not defend Israel from Soviet aggression. With that threat, Ben-Gurion, like everyone else, folded to Ike's will.

☆☆☆☆☆

"STOP POUTING!" MAMIE ordered.

"I'm allowed to pout! I'm the President of the United States!" Ike shot back.

"You can be a real *child* sometimes!"

"What do you want from me? I was looking forward to golfing in Augusta! I'm allowed to be disappointed!"

Mamie laughed as she patted Ike's bald head. She returned to her seat. They were at the Republican headquarters at the Sheraton Park Hotel, along with members of Ike's staff and friends, watching the election results.

I'm so drained of energy I can barely keep my eyes open. I know Mamie's here. And Ann Whitman, which is interesting, because Mamie usually avoids her like the plague. Must be in a particularly good mood. I don't care to bother figuring out who else is here. I could sleep for days. Like during that break I got in March 1945.

Ike regained his focus to look at the television screen. He was on track to win an even bigger landslide than he did in 1952. Ike smiled. The American people were scared by the Suez and Hungary crises, but they had had full faith that Ike knew what he was doing and would pull the world back from the brink. Stevenson's claims that Ike was too old and frail to be President had melted away.

Whatever indifference I had to the outcome of this election I've shed like snake skin. When Admiral Nelson lay dying at Trafalgar, he looked around and asked, 'Are there any of them left?' And when I get in a battle, I just want to win the whole thing. Six or seven states we can't help, but I don't want to lose any more. Don't want any of them left, like Nelson. That's the way I feel.

Ike's friends cheered as state after state entered his column. Ike was at peace as he reflected on the crisis that was now history.

The Democrats—Truman, Stevenson, Eleanor Roosevelt—they criticized me this week for not standing by our allies, especially Israel. What would have happened if they were in power, instead of me? The Soviets would have felt obligated to save Nasser as we supported his destruction. I'm too tired to think of what that could have caused. Instead the world keeps spinning, and our nation is beloved across the Third World. I can't help but wonder how this would have played out if I weren't President. Like if the lightning strike that hit me during World War I had killed me. Careful, Ike. You're entering into morbid and less than humble territory.

Four more years of this prison sentence. It must go to good use to justify delaying the retirement I want so desperately. A world without war. A world where every individual can build the life they want. A world where everyone does their duty for the greater good. This week proved, once more, that international law is the means to that beautiful end, and that all nations must be treated equally. It might even involve a limited surrender of sovereignty of all nations to a sort of joint agency who can justly settle disputes between nations. It would have the power to enforce those decisions. But that's the work of my second term.

Son of Father Abraham

I hope to "stand firm" enough to not go backward, and yet not go forward
fast enough to wreck the country's cause.
—Abraham Lincoln

DECEMBER 31, 1956

PRESIDENT EISENHOWER SHIFTED his weight into the back of his chair
as he scanned the happy faces scattered around the Cabinet Room.
He had won a landslide reelection on November 6 by a margin of
nine million votes. It was the biggest victory since FDR demolished Alf
Landon in 1936. Ike fought to contain his joy and not seem prideful. The
American people validated his administration with a second term. And
why wouldn't they? He gave them an era of peace and prosperity
following twenty years of perpetual crises under Roosevelt and Truman.

Several of Ike's cabinet secretaries surrounded the brown oval table.
Secretary of State John Foster Dulles sat on Ike's right flank, while
Treasury Secretary George Humphrey sat on his left. Vice President Nixon
sat opposite Ike, while Attorney General Herbert Brownell, Defense
Secretary Charles Wilson, and Health, Education, and Welfare Secretary
Oveta Culp Hobby were scattered throughout the room. All were excited
to plan out the beginning of the President's second term. The Republican
Congressional leaders, such as Senate Minority Leader Bill Knowland,
Minority Whip Everett Dirksen, and House Minority Leader Joseph
Martin, looked less thrilled. In a historical aberration, the Republicans lost
seats in both chambers of Congress despite their party nominee's landslide
in the presidential election. The aberration's explanation was an open

secret in Washington; the American people liked Ike, but that devotion did not transfer over to his political party.

"The situations in Suez and Hungary have deescalated, and no longer risk turning the Cold War into World War III," said Chief of Staff Sherman Adams. "This, along with the President's reelection, gives us a lot of political capital to accomplish the administration's objectives at the start of this term." Adams completed his presentation and noticed the bored faces. Adams was not popular in Washington, even among his Republican allies. He had a reputation for bluntness and for keeping visitors away from the President.

"How do we plan to spend this capital?" Knowland asked. He sat beside Nixon, trying to keep his distance from his rival for GOP leadership after Ike retired. "The Democrats control Congress, but I think I could talk Johnson into a tax cut for high income earners. Give the economy a little more juice."

"The President and I don't want to cut taxes again until after the debt is lowered," Humphrey replied.

"Legislation is Congress' prerogative," Knowland said. "Not the executive's. Roosevelt isn't President anymore, and the Constitution will be respected again."

"President Eisenhower's popularity is the only leverage congressional Republicans have in this day and age. You'd be wise to remember that," Nixon said.

"This bickering must stop, gentlemen," Ike declared, intervening before the debate escalated. *Why's Dick picking on Congress? He's the President of the Senate,* Ike thought. "Senator Knowland, I agree with Secretary Humphrey with regard to taxes. I would like our first step in 1957 to focus on foreign policy. Particularly the Middle East."

"What about the Middle East?"

"Britain and France are withdrawing from the region after their Suez adventure. The Middle East is now ripe for Soviet hegemony if we sit on our hands and don't act quickly. I want Congress to pass a resolution giving the President the power to send economic or military aid to any Middle Eastern country resisting communism."

"Military aid? Wouldn't that press against the Constitution's provision that Congress has to declare war?"

Ike sighed. *What's wrong with the Old Guard? I'm trying to bridge the gap between the Founders and the twentieth century, but Knowland still wishes it were 1787.* "The resolution I'm proposing would respect

Congress' duty to declare war without actually doing so and give me the authority I need to stop Bulganin and Khrushchev from extending the Iron Curtain into the Middle East."

"I'm sorry, Mr. President, but I'm not convinced that satisfies what the Constitution requires," Knowland replied. "Blame Madison."

"Can you try to take a less strict interpretation?" Ike asked. "Truman set a precedent that the President could launch a military 'police action' when he intervened in Korea without congressional approval—"

"Which was impeachable," Knowland interrupted.

"I agree that it was outside of Constitutional bounds," Ike replied, rephrasing Knowland's comment. "What I'm proposing would give greater respect to the Constitution while also allowing the President to manage national security on a day-to-day level without seeking Congress' permission every five minutes."

"*I* see," Knowland said, placing emphasis on the word 'I' as he leaned forward, putting his forearms on the table. Adams, strict about improper use of furniture, glared at the Minority Leader. "This is part of your middle way philosophy. You're playing centrism with the Constitution."

A blood vessel in Ike's temple rose to the surface as he fought to control his temper. Luckily, Dirksen intervened, "We'll see what we can do, Mr. President. What other business would you like to discuss?"

Ike regained his composure. "Would you like to tell these gentlemen, Herbert?"

The Attorney General shook his head.

"I think this is better coming from you, Mr. President."

Ike smiled. *Herbert really is one of the finest men in my administration. He has excellent character, even after a lifetime in politics and law. He'll make a good President one day.* Ike turned to face the congressional leaders.

"I want to start my second term with Negro voting rights."

Dirksen ruffled his eyebrows. "Is that really what you want to spend your political capital on, Mr. President?"

"That's exactly what I want to spend it on. The right to vote is fundamental to democracy. It's unacceptable that a segment of our society can't partake in that right because of something foolish like skin color. We're the party of Lincoln. We need to make this right."

"Excuse me, Mr. President," Brownell began, "but are you sure you *only* want to focus on voting rights? Negroes face various other issues in their daily lives, especially in the South. Should we not also address the segregation issue?"

"Herbert, we've talked about this," Ike replied. "The country can only take so much at once. One civil rights issue will be controversial enough. More than that will only increase the opposition to our bill and drive a bigger wedge between Southerners and the rest of the country." He paused, not trying to make Brownell uncomfortable in front of the other officials. "Besides, voting rights will give Negroes the political leverage they need to secure other civil rights."

"I think Negroes like Reverend King might get frustrated if they see we're only tackling one issue at a time," Brownell answered, his bald, egg-shaped head reflecting the lamplight. Brownell met Ike in 1952, when Ike was Supreme Commander of NATO, and helped convince him to run for President. But Brownell was still trying to figure him out. He knew Ike's heart was in the right place on civil rights but occasionally wondered if Ike could lead on the issue.

"Herbert, didn't Aesop teach us that the tortoise beat the hare? Moving too quickly will only make things worse. Societies, especially democracies, only reform and evolve incrementally. It's why Lincoln took four years to end slavery. Besides," Ike chuckled, "Churchill told me that courage was the best virtue, but I always thought it was patience. I was a staff officer for decades before I got anywhere in the Army. And patience with fortitude is how we'll outlast the Soviet Union, not by forcing a premature showdown. Patience allows the right side to win in the long-term. Of course, the exception to this rule is the hot war. In that case, you want to use overwhelming force to defeat the enemy quickly and get your troops out of harms' way."

Ike stopped. He was rambling and shifting to topics he found more interesting.

"I've expressed my view, Mr. President. Do you want me to explain the bill?" Brownell asked. Ike nodded. Brownell turned to the other officials. "The bill is essentially the same one we tried to pass a few months ago, before it got buried in Senate committee hearings under the threats of filibusters." He glanced at Knowland. "The bill contains four parts." He began listing them on his fingers. "It will create a bipartisan civil rights commission, a civil rights division in the Justice Department, give the Attorney General authority to get court orders—"

"Pardon my interruption, Mr. Attorney General, but wouldn't that isolate the old Taft wing?" Knowland asked, referring to the conservative wing of the Republican Party.

"I'm confident you can get your ducks in a row."

"I wouldn't be so sure. You know of my commitment to Negro rights. But a lot of conservatives will be concerned with a bill that gives the federal government this much authority. They don't want to see states' rights constrained."

Honestly, what decade is Knowland living in? Ike thought.

"You don't think the booming economy will help soften resistance? Americans have never had it so good," Brownell said.

"Have you seen the South's response to *Brown*?" Knowland asked. "To say nothing about the fact that Democrats control both chambers. And Southerners are particularly strong in the Senate."

"Johnson wants to run for President in 1960," Nixon interjected. "He won't isolate the other parts of the country by defeating a civil rights bill."

"I also don't think we should let the Democrats' control of Congress deter us," Ike said. "Most of them are good people who see that things need to change for Negroes. And besides, my boxing coach at West Point told me that if I wasn't smiling when he knocked me down, he would walk out of the room."

The other officials did not absorb Ike's attempt at optimism.

"If I could interject," Humphrey began, "The South has a delicate social structure that's taken a long time to recover from the War Between the States. It's not going to appreciate the federal government interfering in its business, especially over the Negro issue. They remember Reconstruction."

"I agree," said Hobby, the only woman in the room.

Southerners, Ike thought.

Brownell answered his colleagues, "There are nine hundred thousand adult Negroes in Mississippi. Seven thousand voted in the election last month. We're the world's leading democracy. This is unacceptable."

"Were those Negroes Republicans or Democrats?" Knowland asked.

"Oh, Bill!" Ike exclaimed. "This isn't about elections."

"Then what's it about?"

"Justice."

"As long as we're talking about social issues, could we also consider the Equal Rights Amendment?" Hobby asked.

"The amendment for female equality?" Nixon replied.

"Yes. It would make women equal in the Constitution."

"Where are women not equal?" Ike asked. Hobby's eyes narrowed, not sure what to say. "Women make up the majority of voters. If anything, they have the majority of the political power in this country."

"Mr. President, I think the issue has less to do with voting rights and instead reflects concerns among some women that their opportunities in the workforce and in education are restricted because of their gender," Hobby replied.

"Oh," Ike said, giving his brain a moment to think. "Of course women should have equal opportunities to pursue their dreams. And equal access to education will allow them to become doctors, lawyers, teachers, and scientists, but most importantly, to become good mothers and voters."

Hobby nodded in agreement.

"Why wouldn't the Fourteenth Amendment already cover women?" Humphrey asked.

"Women weren't meant to be included when it was written in 1868. Even the Radical Republicans weren't ready for that. Nor were the women at the time, for that matter," Hobby answered.

"But it still says 'persons,' does it not?"

"I like the idea of an Equal Rights Amendment," Ike said. "A woman should have every right that a man does. But as I said earlier, I think we should focus on Negro voting rights. One thing at a time."

☆☆☆☆☆

MAY 29, 1957

"BUT ISN'T IT common knowledge that Stonewall Jackson was the best general of the Civil War?" Nixon asked. He went out of his way not to lean on the Oval Office desk since he did not want to provoke Adams' wrath. "The second best general would be Lee. But Jackson used a similar tactic to Patton in World War II, where he was so aggressive that he took apart larger armies piece by piece. That's why I think Jackson's the best general of the war."

Ike shook his head.

"I wouldn't say that, Dick. In fact, I think it's not a very reasoned opinion. You forget that Grant captured three armies intact, moved and coordinated his forces in a way that baffles military logic yet succeeded, and he concluded the war one year after being entrusted with that aim. I'd say that was one hell of a piece of soldiering extending over a period of four years, the same time we were in the last war."

Adams shifted his attention back to Nixon, anticipating the Vice President's rebuttal against the war hero. Nixon was silent.

Ike continued, "Furthermore, Grant had noteworthy common sense and picked good subordinates. That's an aspect of generalship that the public doesn't understand. And Grant picked top-tier subordinates like Meade, Sherman, and Sheridan. And then he wrote the best military memoir in history."

Ike smiled; he enjoyed talking about Grant, his role model for a general.

"If only he had been a more successful President," added Fred Morrow, an African American lawyer who was the first African American to serve on a President's executive staff. "Though I'll give him credit for trying on civil rights."

"The military occupation of the South couldn't go on forever," Adams replied. "And if the Supreme Court hadn't ruled the 1875 Civil Rights Act unconstitutional Grant might have succeeded."

"Then we wouldn't be discussing another voting rights bill right now," Morrow agreed.

"Speaking of which, where'd Herbert run off to?" Ike asked. "He's late." Ike had little patience for tardiness.

Brownell entered the Oval Office, right on cue.

"I'm sorry I'm late, Mr. President."

"Let's get started," Ike growled. Brownell placed a stack of papers on the Oval Office desk. Ike's desk was characteristically organized.

"Here's the final draft for the voting rights bill."

"Can you walk me through it again?"

"Of course, Mr. President." Brownell counted the parts on his fingers. "Part 1 appoints a bipartisan civil rights commission. Part 2 creates a civil rights division in the Justice Department. Part 3 will give the Attorney General authority to, and I quote, 'seek from the civil courts preventive relief in civil rights cases.' End quote. Part 4 will protect voting rights by allowing for federal civil suits. That's the broad picture. I'll spare you the legal details."

Ike nodded.

"And I'll spare you details about the Strategic Air Command!"

Morrow shifted in his seat, uncomfortable by the President's lack of interest in civil rights issues, even if he was pursuing them. It was clear to

Morrow that Ike's brain understood that civil rights needed to happen. Every American deserved equal rights and opportunities. But Morrow wondered if Ike's heart feared the instability of social change. Ike was a conservative, not a revolutionary. Morrow watched as Ike's heart and brain wrestled over how to approach the issue affecting his people.

"I understand foreign policy is your real interest, Mr. President. You were a general after all," Brownell replied, "But I think this bill's cause would be helped if you take a greater interest in it and push it publicly. Like, this desk. It belonged to Theodore Roosevelt. Think of how much he was able to achieve by wielding the Bully Pulpit embodied in this office."

Brownell was referring to TR's idea that the presidency was a powerful office from which to advocate for a cause.

"I'm not convinced that would be the right approach here," Ike responded. "Truman tried that and failed. He made minimal progress on this issue. I've approached it indirectly and I would say we've gotten a lot farther on it. We ended segregation under federal jurisdiction and have made sure every judicial appointee supports civil rights. *Brown* and the other integration cases have gone a long way to bring the protest movement into the American mainstream. And we did that without making the South hostile to us. I know this indirect strategy may not be what wins applause from the 'sophisticated' liberals at the *New York Times* or Harvard, but for practical purposes I think it's been a lot more successful than making a lot of noise on the issue."

"Some of the moves the administration made were more public," Morrow chimed in. "You declared segregation a national security issue, because the Soviets use it in their propaganda."

"I know, Fred, but I fear the President attacking the South head on with this stuff would upset them. I'll lose any image I have as a neutral arbiter who can coax them along."

"What about a meeting with civil rights leaders?" Brownell asked. "You could get their advice and they can endorse the bill. It would calm liberals' fears that it isn't strong enough."

"It would depend on who we're talking about," Ike replied. "If we brought the extremists here, I might have to meet with some Klansmen to still appear neutral."

"Mr. President!" Morrow exclaimed, trying not to lose his temper in the Oval Office. "That's a false equivalency! You can't compare activists fighting injustice to those inflicting it."

"That's not what I'm doing, Fred," Ike replied. "Obviously the activists in the civil rights movement, regardless of how extreme, have their hearts in the right place, while the Klan does not. What I *am* saying is that extreme rhetoric, regardless of where it comes from, does not help this or *any* issue. It hurts discourse and inflames tribalism. The only acceptable outcome of this movement is that we are one cohesive country where every citizen has equal rights and can pursue their dreams, regardless of race. But we won't *be* a cohesive country if extreme rhetoric polarizes different segments of our society. We would have escalating hyper-partisanship and each side seizing power to enforce its will on the other until our whole system deteriorated."

"Let me ask you this, Mr. President," Morrow began, "how would you respond if someone said that World War II or the Cold War was the fault of 'both sides'?"

Ike's eyebrow raised in skepticism.

"Southern whites, for all they need to learn, are not Nazis." His face flashed red.

"That's not the point I was trying to make, Mr. President. Oppression is oppression. One side is right, and the other's wrong."

"All I was saying is that the extreme wing of the civil rights movement isn't pure good, especially in the eyes of public opinion. Martin Luther King and his faction, sure, we'll agree there. But the more extreme side is hurting its own cause."

"They still shouldn't be compared to the Klan." Morrow bit his tongue and stopped himself from saying the comparison was unjust; he did not want to insult the President.

Ike was unsure how to respond.

"I believe I said they're equivalent in terms of public perception and discourse. That's all. Don't forget the Klan called me a traitor to the white race for what I, and this administration, have already done for civil rights."

"That should be a badge of honor, sir."

Ike smiled. Morrow was back in his good graces. He turned to Nixon.

"Obviously we'll have to confront the Southern Democrats over this bill. How do you think the Northern Democrats will react?"

"My sense is that they'll both criticize it as not strong enough but avoid breaking with their Southern brethren. Play both sides of the fence," Nixon answered.

"Can someone explain the Democrats to me?" Ike asked. "One wing wants to socialize the country. The other is the most reactionary group within American politics. It doesn't make any sense."

"The Democrats started as a party based in the South," Adams explained. "Wilson and FDR embraced big government policies, so now there's a delicate balance between the two wings. And that's before mentioning how the New Deal brought Negroes into the party. They're in the same party as those who oppress them."

"That makes even less sense," Ike replied.

"The bigger contradiction is how America was founded on freedom while still having slavery. We never had the chance to be the republic of liberty our Founders envisioned," Nixon said.

"The man who wrote 'all men are created equal' owned slaves himself," Morrow chimed in, highlighting the contradiction Nixon mentioned.

"That's why this bill is so important," Brownell said, bringing the conversation full circle. "We'll help America become the country it was *meant* to be. This will be the first civil rights bill since Reconstruction."

"Not true," Adams said. "Benjamin Harrison proposed a voting rights bill in the early 1890s, I believe. It was defeated in Congress."

Ike raised his eyebrows, learning a new fact.

"Who knew?"

☆☆☆☆☆

SENATE MAJORITY LEADER Lyndon Johnson spoke with Majority Whip Mike Mansfield in his Senate office a few days later. Johnson's large frame hung over his desk as his hands gesticulated.

"I hear what you're saying, Mike. I support rights for the Negroes as much as Dr. King himself!"

"But you said you want to remove Part 3 of the President's voting rights bill! I refuse to believe you can't see the inconsistency!" Mansfield exclaimed, his brown hair resting gently over strands of gray that flanked each side of his head.

"What I'm saying is that it's dangerous to let a Republican President pass a bill that secures Negro voting rights. FDR won the Negro vote fair and square, and now Ike's trying to steal it back. Well, we won't *let* him." Johnson said every word of that sentence slowly.

"Votes aren't stolen or won in that way, like pieces of a board game. That's putting the party over public service."

"Oh hell, Mike, that's *exactly* what the Republicans are going to say. And they're at least full of it, you're just being a dummy!" Johnson said, trying to sound funny rather than insulting. "Ike and the Republicans are playing nothing more than a partisan game to get *votes*. And we're going to play the game too and *stop* them. They don't care about Negroes. They haven't since Hayes withdrew the Army from the South and left them at the South's mercy."

Johnson was referring to the Compromise of 1877, when a stalemate in the Electoral College led to a deal where the Republican Rutherford Hayes got the White House in exchange for the end of Reconstruction.

"How—"

"Frankly, Mike," Johnson interrupted, "the Republicans will probably take a lot of liberal Northern whites with them if we don't stop this thing."

Mansfield's jaw stiffened, frustrated at being interrupted and at his Majority Leader's behavior.

"How do you plan on explaining it to the country though? Eisenhower will appear to be pushing for civil rights, and you're undermining him. They won't believe you when you say it's politics. He's not partisan like the rest of us."

"Goddamn, Mike, don't pretend you're dumber than you actually are!" Johnson exclaimed. "I'll tell the Northern crowds they had to compromise to get any civil rights bill at all, and I'll tell the Southern ones I undermined it as best I could. Simple."

"And you do mean *you'll* do it. For your presidential run in 1960."

"Now you're catching on," Johnson said, pointing at Mansfield with his right index finger and smiling.

"You're not worried about opposing Ike on this? He's a popular war hero."

"Bullshit. FDR won that war from his wheelchair. Ike didn't do shit. And I have the Silver Star from my service in the war. He doesn't. So, who's the *real* war hero here?"

"Now you're having fun."

"Maybe," Johnson said coolly. "But I'm serious when I say I'm not going to let Ike destroy the electoral coalition that Roosevelt built. I'm not sure how that titan built a coalition between Southern whites and blacks within a single party, but it was a stroke of genius that's made our party stronger than ever."

Johnson wanted to become President, like his heroes Abraham Lincoln and Franklin Roosevelt. But he wanted to surpass them, not just follow in their footsteps. And he would do that by ending poverty and legalized racism, which he sought to be his legacy ever since his 1955 heart attack. That meant he needed to keep segregation alive as a political issue. Then he'd destroy it from the Oval Office and put FDR in his shadow.

Footsteps approached Johnson's office, walking past Johnson's secretary.

"Is that Uncle Dick I see?" Johnson asked, leaping to his feet like a schoolboy. Georgia Senator Richard Russell, Johnson's mentor, was dismayed as Johnson's arms grasped his thin frame for a bear hug. "What brings you over here, Uncle Dick?" Mansfield noted that Johnson's Southern accent grew thicker as he spoke to Russell.

"It's that Eisenhower bill for the coloreds! It's unacceptable! What is he thinking, promoting divisions within the South?"

"Don't you worry, Uncle Dick! I've got a plan to take care of it! Don't you worry about those colored boys!"

"Do you have the votes to kill it?"

"Now, Uncle Dick," Johnson said, sounding like a disappointed parent. "I can't kill it outright. How would that look to the Negroes and Northern liberals we need in future elections?"

"Then what's your plan?"

"Gut it!" Johnson exclaimed as he slapped Russell on the back. "You'll see, Uncle Dick. We don't have a thing to worry about from old Ike Eisenhower."

☆☆☆☆☆

SERGEANT JOHN MOANEY, an African American man twenty-four years Ike's junior, held Ike's undershorts open so Ike could step into them. Moaney grabbed a shirt for Ike to wear. Ike's tired eyes watched as Moaney helped him get dressed.

Ike was more than capable of doing this activity himself, but Moaney became his personal valet and servant in World War II and Ike grew accustomed to his assistance in daily life. Dressing Ike was a precise, half-hour ritual. But the public debates about the voting rights bill made Ike uncomfortable.

Why am I the one who's been a general and President and not him? I went to West Point and paid my dues to rise through the Army ranks, but is that all that's happened here? Why I'm in my position and why John's in his? He was a good farmer before being drafted, and he chose to stay with me all these years. But why does this feel different now? Like this was never a fair competition?

Ike pushed his arms through the sleeves as Moaney held them open.

"John," Ike paused.

"Yes, Gennul?"

"How long have we been together?"

"Since August '42."

"Is that right?"

"Yes, sir."

"That's a long time. You know you're the most important person in my life, right John? Besides Mamie, I mean."

"Thank you, Gennul. It's been an honor serving you all these years."

Ike felt tears swell to the surface of his eyes, but he fought to hold them back.

I wish I could ask him his opinion about the bill, but he'll never be objective with me. He loves me too much. He might be the one person I can talk to about these things in total honesty.

"Do you think I've always treated you fairly?"

"Of course, sir."

"No differently than the white staff?"

"Of course not. That's not the kind of man ya' are." Moaney opened pants for Ike to step into.

"I know the Negro community wants me to speak out more. But I feel in my bones that that will inflame Southern whites."

"Ya' do what you think is right, Gennul. I trust you."

"You do?"

"Of course, sir. Ya' defeated Hitler. Ya' can take the South."

"I feel like other Negroes don't share your trust in me."

"They see ya' as an old white man. They don't know you like I do."

Ike again fought the tears.

"I feel like I've fought my whole life to be good and decent to the black man. My parents expected no less. I'm sure I've told you the story of when my high school football team played the team from another school. The other team had a Negro player. I played opposite him when no one else would. I shook his hand before and after the game."

"I know, sir. Ya've told me this story lots of times."

"Did I ever tell you about the Negro soldiers I commanded after graduating West Point?"

Moaney was stumped.

"I don't recall."

"The year was 1916," Ike began. "Poncho Villa was crossing the border and causing trouble, so President Wilson mobilized the Army. General Pershing ended up invading Mexico with 40,000 troops or so. Patton was one of them. But I was in charge of training a Negro unit. It was a miserable experience. They clearly had no idea what they were doing, and I was so disappointed in them."

"What went wrong?"

"That's the issue. At the time I assumed they must not be smart enough. They weren't as smart as the white soldiers I'd worked with at other times." Ike's face turned red, his arms shook, his hands in fists. "Of course that's not what it was! It was wrong for me to think that way! No one had taught them the basics of being a soldier! That's why they didn't know any better." Ike could not hold back the tears any longer. They poured down his cheeks. "Can you ever forgive me?"

Moaney smiled. "Of course, sir. Ya' don't have a bad heart." He finished pushing Ike's belt through his pant loops. "Besides, you're going to make things better."

"What do you mean?"

"With your bill, sir. It's going to do a lot of good for Negroes. Then they'll see in you what I see."

Ike smiled. His head dropped; he tried to stop Moaney from seeing him cry.

"You're better than I deserve, John."

☆☆☆☆☆

"UH. WHAT?" BROWNELL asked, groggily emerging from sleep.

"I hear something," Doris, his wife, replied. "Go look."

"It's the middle of the night."

"Herbert, I'm a minute away from calling the police on whatever's out there. Please go and look."

Brownell's senses returned to him as he fully regained consciousness. He nodded and summoned the will to stand. He grabbed his son's baseball bat and waddled to the front door.

A sharp smell fully woke Brownell. He gripped the bat and pushed his way out the front door. The night was pitch black, but Brownell could clearly identify several hooligans running away, frightened by his presence. He took in the smell one more time and went back inside.

"What is it?" Doris asked. "What's out there?"

Brownell grabbed the phone, his arms shaking from adrenaline and fear for his family.

"They spilled kerosene around our home and ran away. I'm calling Hoover."

☆☆☆☆☆

JUNE 15, 1957

"IS HE ON the line?" Ike asked.

"Yes, Mr. President," Ann Whitman said.

Ike picked up the Oval Office phone. He heard a buzzing sound and then a click.

"Hello?" Ike asked, hoping to hear a voice.

"Hello, Mr. President?" Johnson asked, his Texan accent coming through clearly.

"Lyndon, hi." Ike sighed. "How's the Senate? I haven't spoken to you since the House passed the civil rights bill two weeks ago." *At least Johnson's someone I can do business with.*

"Oh God, Mr. President. Tempers are flaring and they could get worse over here."

"Really? But it passed the House so easily."

"These things always pass the House easily," Johnson explained, as if to a political novice and not the President. "The Senate is where blood gets spilled. I've got Humphrey and his pack of liberals wanting one piece of me and Russell and his segregationists wanting another. Rayburn has no idea how good he has it." He was referring to the Speaker of the House.

"When do you think the Senate will vote on the bill?"

"Well, Mr. President, I've got to tell you, I'm hoping to pass fifteen appropriation bills before we get to your civil rights bill."

"I see."

"Once we're through those appropriation bills, you can let us fight July and August and if necessary, into September."

"I've got to tell you, Lyndon, I'm honestly a little struck back on my heels by how much resistance this bill is facing. It really is the mildest civil rights bill possible," Ike said, trying to make it sound nonthreatening.

Johnson chuckled.

"Welcome to the United States Senate, Mr. President."

☆☆☆☆☆

JUNE 19, 1957

NIXON WAS FRUSTRATED as he sat in his chair as President of the Senate, one of his duties as Vice President. He had spoken with Senator Hubert Humphrey, leader of the liberal wing of the Democratic Party.

"We've been submitting similar bills since '49, and now the President decides he wants to support civil rights?" Humphrey asked.

"The President and his administration have been strong supporters of civil rights since assuming office," Nixon replied.

"Oh really? Then why doesn't he go to the South and endorse the movement?"

"President Eisenhower is afraid that would inflame the southern wing of *your* party even more."

"You're making excuses for him for being aloof on this issue."

"If you feel so strongly about it you can make sure the liberal Democrats support the bill. We need them and the Eastern Establishment Republicans."

"You'll also need Knowland and the Old Guard Republicans. Have you guys been working on them yet? They'll never listen to us."

"You know I can't talk about debates within the party."

Nixon's mind returned to the present as the Senate distributed bills to the committees. The Senate's clerk read the House bill's title in an unusually low voice.

"I object!" Russell announced. Nixon smirked. Russell was so predictable. "The clerk is too soft. This is an administration ploy to bypass the Judiciary Committee!"

"Overruled!" Nixon declared.

"I appeal to the chamber!" Russell retorted.

"Very well," Nixon muttered. "All in favor?"

Forty-five senators shouted, "aye!"

"All opposed?"

Thirty-nine senators shouted, "nay!"

"The 'ayes' have it," Nixon concluded. Russell slumped backward in defeat. Nixon smiled. His plan worked. He successfully took the bill out of the stalemated Judiciary Committee and got the entire body of the Senate to put the bill on the Senate's calendar. Nixon was one of the administration's leading advocates for civil rights; he was happy to contribute to the bill's success. He was also pleased that it was mostly Republicans who supported him and Democrats who supported Russell. He was dismayed, however, to note that one Democrat who voted against his resolution was his friend, Senator John Kennedy of Massachusetts.

☆☆☆☆☆

JULY 3, 1957

IKE ATTEMPTED TO lower his adrenaline and reduce how much he was sweating as he stood behind the press conference podium. The previous days were exhausting. Ike had spoken to the nation's governors on June 24, saying that the states were failing in their duty to protect voting rights and the federal government had to intervene. This sparked outrage among Southern Democrats and conservative Republicans who accused Ike of undermining states' rights. Then, yesterday, Russell condemned Ike on the Senate floor, rejecting Ike's claim that the bill was a "moderate, decent" measure. Russell said Part 3 of the bill would let Brownell "destroy the system of separation of the races in the Southern States at the point of a bayonet." This, he claimed, would restore the terrible occupation of Reconstruction. Finally, Russell doubted that "the full implications of the bill have ever been explained to President Eisenhower." This challenged Ike's intelligence and pushed the sensitive point of Ike's interest in civil rights issues.

Ike sought to regulate and calm his breathing as he was besieged by one question after another.

"Is the bill a cunning device, as Senator Russell called it, to enforce integration of the races in the South?" a reporter asked.

God damn Russell, Ike thought, frustrated. *Why can't that cheerless, hawk-faced patrician accept that it's the twentieth century and be less of a headache?*

"I believe the legislation that my administration is supporting to be a very moderate move," Ike answered. *This issue really is between a rock and a hard place. Anything that reforms the status quo horrifies one side. Anything that doesn't tear the entire system down is too weak for the other. Why can't people moderate so we can work through this like adults?*

Ike called on an African American journalist. *It's nice giving them national exposure.*

"Mr. President, would you support refocusing the legislation to address the right to vote, instead of school desegregation, which Senator Russell and other critics claim is its true goal?"

Ike's eyebrow rose. *What does that even mean? School desegregation isn't even in the bill.* He tried to dodge the question, as he so often did as part of his indirection strategy.

"I was reading that part of the bill this morning, and there were certain phrases I didn't completely understand. So, before I make any more remarks on that, I would want to talk to the Attorney General and see exactly what they do mean."

The room was stunned. Did the President say he didn't understand his own bill? Ike's stomach clenched as he saw the reporters' reaction.

Why the hell did I say that? That was unforgivably stupid.

"Mr. President, do you mean to say you have not read the bill or that you simply don't remember its details?" the African American reporter asked.

"That's... I..." Ike was not sure how to respond. *Damn it! That usually works! If I don't want to answer something I can usually plead ignorance and tell the press to go find an advisor to ask. But this gave Russell the red meat he needs to kill my bill! I'm going to meet with that son of a bitch immediately!*

☆☆☆☆☆

JULY 10, 1957

ANN WHITMAN EYED Russell like a hawk as he entered the Oval Office to meet Ike.

"How have you been, Mr. President?" Russell asked as he shook Ike's hand.

"Pretty busy. I'd say my hair was thinning, but, you know," Ike said, gesturing to his scalp that reflected the sunlight penetrating through the window.

"I assume you're referring to your bill regarding the coloreds?"

"I am."

"Shall we cut the small talk and get right to it?"

"Let's." Ike gestured to a chair for Russell that was placed on the opposite side of the Oval Office desk from Ike's seat. Ike was determined to remind Russell who was President and who wasn't.

"Mr. President, last year Southern Negroes voted for you, a Republican, at twice the rate that they did in 1952. That's to say that forty percent of them voted for you. Now, I understand you want to rebuild a Republican coalition among—"

"Senator, you should know me well enough by now to know that this has nothing to do with party politics."

"Then why cause all this chaos?"

"Because it's justice. And I challenge your use of the term 'chaos.' The bill was meant to preserve rights without arousing passions."

"I'd say it failed to accomplish *either*!" Russell exclaimed, his Georgian accent accentuating the last word of that sentence. "Allowing the Attorney General to interfere in the Southern electoral process will lead to a system resembling Stalin and the Soviet secret police! Aren't we opposing communism abroad specifically to avoid that happening here?"

That one's a doozy. Even from a violent exponent of the segregation doctrine, Ike thought.

"It's absurd to compare this moderate civil rights bill to Stalin, and you know it."

"It allows for *criminal* suits without a jury option! That's Stalinist in my book!"

"No, it allows for *civil* suits that will lead *to* a jury trial." Ike had reviewed the bill that morning in preparation for this meeting. He would not be caught off guard again.

"Those are criminal suits in disguise!"

A vein bulged in Ike's temple. *The blatant lies!* He took a deep breath. "I don't see us agreeing on the facts here, Senator."

That was fine with Russell. He knew Ike was a Republican and could appeal to Ike's desire for stability.

"This bill threatens the Southern way of life, Mr. President," Russell preached, trying to sound emotional. "You and I both know that stability is indispensable to civilization. Without it, we're nothing. We'll be like the cavemen of yesteryear. And this bill is more encouragement for the colored revolutionary movement that's bent on spreading chaos and disruption."

There's that word again. "Chaos," Ike thought.

"A system as unjust as the present-day South is for our Negro citizens can never remain stable. Negroes will lose patience entirely with our democracy and withdraw from our political process and society." *There's gradualism, and then there's literally doing nothing!*

"Is that such a bad thing?"

"Of course it is!"

"Why?"

"It's unjust! That sort of polarization is the exact opposite of the stability you were talking about. And more than that, it's not who we're supposed to be as a nation!" Ike exclaimed.

"What does that even mean?" Russell scoffed. "'Who we're supposed to be as a nation?'"

"We hold these truths to be self-evident, that all men are created equal, that they are endowed—"

"Jefferson was referring to *white* men, like you and me. Not the Negroes or anyone else."

"No, it was meant to expand to everyone over time. Negroes, Jews, women, everyone. The Declaration belongs to all Americans."

"Mr. President, you just called the Founders hypocrites!"

"How's that?"

"How could Jefferson have meant everyone when he himself was a slave owner?"

"Because they knew better than to restructure all of society in one shot. The Revolution was the first draft, not the final product, and 'all men are created equal' was a goal to be gradually reached over time."

"I agree more with the Supreme Court's interpretation of the Founders that said they never meant the Negroes to be full citizens of this country. That seems more accurate to me."

"You don't mean *Dred Scott*!"

"That's the one. I don't condone slavery, obviously, but I think this nation was founded *by* white men *for* white men. Not for anyone else, including nig—"

"Don't you *dare* say that word in my house!" Ike screamed, jumping from his chair. His palms slammed into the Oval Office desk, which blocked him from landing on Russell. Whitman shuddered from the other room, taken aback by her boss' explosion. "You will never say that wicked word in this office," Ike said softer.

Russell glared at the President, taken aback at what was clearly an instinctual reaction.

"Let's talk about another Supreme Court decision. Article 2 of the Constitution says your office, the executive, is invested with executing the law. You should uphold *Plessy v. Ferguson*, which correctly held that the races could be separated as long as they were still treated equally. *Plessy* is sacred! It must be respected."

"Why is *Plessy* sacred?" Ike asked, having recomposed himself.

"It came from the Supreme Court!"

"So did *Brown v. Board.* Why isn't that decision sacred, too?"

"Back in the good old days we had wise men on the Court. Nowadays we just have politicians," Russell answered, referring to Earl Warren.

Ike's eyes narrowed slightly. *I'd bet my best Angus cattle...*

"Can you name any of the justices on the Court when *Plessy* was decided?"

This time Russell narrowed his eyes and bit his tongue. Ike called his bluff.

☆☆☆☆☆

JULY 20, 1957

IKE, ADAMS, AND Morrow greeted Johnson in the Oval Office. Johnson, who lived, breathed, and ate politics, went straight into discussing the bill.

"Mr. President, you know that I started my career by teaching poor Mexican kids in Texas, right?"

"I believe you've told me that story before."

"Oh good. And then you know that I dedicated my life to ridding this great nation of poverty and discrimination. I want to build on FDR's programs to do that."

"You have a rosier memory of the New Deal than I do, but I likewise want to fulfill Lincoln's vision of America, where every citizen has a right to rise up through hard work. Following in Lincoln's footsteps is a large part of why I'm so adamant about this civil rights bill." Ike paused, slightly embarrassed at what he said. "Not that I mean to compare this moderate bill to the Great Emancipator."

"Of *course* not," Johnson said. "I'd keep that sort of talk between us, Mr. President. We don't want Uncle Dick thinking you're a reenactment of old Honest Abe! You think he's a nasty piece of work now!"

"I said nothing of the sort," Ike said, determined to be polite.

"But you're thinking it!"

Morrow glanced at Adams. Was this banter going anywhere?

"As I was saying, Mr. President, my life's mission is to end poverty and discrimination. Unfortunately, the South's mighty sensitive about this sort of thing, and they don't take kindly to your bill. Especially with you being a Republican and all. Reminds them of Thaddeus Stevens and that bunch," Johnson said, referring to the Radical Republicans of the Civil War and Reconstruction.

"Lyndon," Ike began, "You're the best vote counter in Washington. Don't you have the votes to pass this *moderate* bill?"

"That's the thing, Mr. President. I'm not here to tell you I have the votes to pass it. I'm here to say I have the votes to kill it."

Morrow and Adams looked at each other in surprise. Ike's hands became fists.

That sounded like a threat.

"Why would you kill this bill? You just said—"

"I didn't say I'm *going* to kill it. Just that that's one outcome of this."

"What are you getting at?"

"The administration needs to compromise with the South. Make this bill easier to digest. Soften it."

"*Soften* it!" Morrow interjected. "The bill is weak enough as it is! It already *is* a compromise!"

"It's not soft enough for me to pass it!"

Adams spoke before Morrow could speak again.

"What exactly would need to happen to achieve this compromise?"

"Part 3 has to go."

"The part that lets the Attorney General take preventive relief on civil rights cases?" Adams asked.

"Exactly," Johnson answered. "There's no way the Senate will pass anything with a section that gives the federal government that much power."

"That and Part 4 are the bill's teeth!" Morrow exclaimed.

"I'm telling you what we have to work with."

"What *we* have to work with?" Ike asked. *First he threatened to kill the bill. Now he's placing us on the same team. What game is he playing?*

"Yes, *we*. We two Texas boys are going to pass this here voting rights bill. I'm just telling you it's going to require a couple of compromises to get passed at all. The question is whether you'd rather have a weaker bill or no bill?"

"Obviously it's better to have no bill and stand for principle than to make a wicked bargain with Russell and the South!" Morrow claimed.

Ike squinted. *I'd hate to lose Part 3, but the other three parts will still help the Negroes. Especially Part 4 and the civil suits meant to protect voting rights. Is Part 3 worth losing all of that?*

"I would be open to removing Part 3 if we can pass the rest of the bill," Ike said, overruling Morrow. Morrow tensed, feeling betrayed by the President.

Adams jotted a note and gave it to Ike. *Shouldn't you talk to Brownell first?*

Ike quickly shook his head *no* to Adams and turned back to Johnson, who smiled.

"I admire your pragmatism, Mr. President. That's how you invaded Normandy and secured the Korean Armistice!" Johnson flattered.

"Pass the rest of the bill intact," Ike commanded, a military man to his core.

"Well, now, let's not be hasty," Johnson said, raising his hands to look like a stop sign.

"What else?" Ike asked.

"The other thing I need to pass this bill is an amendment to Part 4 that will replace the Justice Department enforcing voting rights with trial by juries. That will dilute the fear that this bill will allow for criminal trials without a jury option."

"Those are civil suits, not criminal trials!" Ike exclaimed.

"You expect the average Southerner to know the difference?" Johnson asked.

"I expect the average Negro to know that a jury trial amendment means juries of all Southern white folks who will side against their interests every time!" Morrow responded.

"That will change with time," Johnson answered.

"How, when you're nullifying their voting rights protection?"

Johnson turned back to Ike, ignoring Morrow. He sensed the President was hesitant to again compromise his bill. Johnson took several steps closer to Ike, his six-foot, three-inch body glaring over the President's five-feet-ten-inches.

"You want to sign a civil rights bill, don't you Mr. President? You'd like that as part of your legacy?"

Ike's jaw tightened. He was determined to not let Johnson's violation of his personal space intimidate him. He looked Johnson in the eye.

"A bill without Part 3 and with a jury trial amendment on Part 4 isn't worth the paper it's written on."

"Mr. President," Johnson began, putting his arm around Ike's shoulders, drawing him in close, peering down at Ike, and forcing the President to look up to stare him in the eye. "I know politics is unfamiliar to you. You're a professional Army officer, where you give orders and subordinates follow. Politics is a different animal. In politics, you've got to know when to compromise. You've got to know when to eat it. Those who are overly righteous don't make the history books. No one knows their names."

"I'm not agreeing to a jury trial amendment, Lyndon," Ike said, defying Johnson's intimidation tactics.

Johnson poked Ike in the chest with his index finger.

"This amendment will get your bill passed. Let's get it done!"

"No."

"If you don't mind me saying, Mr. Majority Leader," Adams began, "but I can't help but notice that a compromised bill fits your interest perfectly. It doesn't rock the electorate's boat too much by drawing the Northern Negroes back to the Republican Party, and it doesn't lose you many voters among Southern whites."

Johnson released Ike from his grip. He shrugged at Adams' comment. The former New Hampshire governor was a clever political operator who saw Johnson's game.

"No one said politics was pleasant."

I never realized this guy was such a phony! Ike thought. *He's only interested in his own power. What about George Washington's example?*

"Lyndon, public servants have a duty to the country. To compromise a voting rights bill for personal political purposes is disgraceful," Ike said.

"I was sincere when I said a softer bill is the only way to get this through the Senate. The one you have now will fail like the one last year did," Johnson replied.

Ike hesitated.

"I could see keeping my agreement to drop Part 3 to pass the rest of the bill. But I still won't agree to the jury trial amendment. That would nullify Part 4."

"You don't have a choice, Mr. President."

"My answer is 'no.'"

"You destroyed the Nazi Gestapo in Germany! I'm saving you from creating one in the South!"

"That's an absurd analogy. And I'm saying 'no.'"

Johnson looked disappointed.

"I'm sorry to hear that, Mr. President. I'd thought you were a stronger ally of civil rights than this, but you'd rather have no bill than a softer one. I'll salvage it as best I can, even if it's without your help."

"I will use everything in my power to stop a jury trial amendment."

"Best of luck to you, Mr. President." Johnson left shortly thereafter.

Ike, Adams, and Morrow were spent after the meeting. Morrow turned to Ike.

"You did the right thing, Mr. President."

Ike ignored the compliment and turned to Adams to address a more pressing concern.

"Make sure someone is standing in between him and me the next time we meet."

☆☆☆☆☆

AUGUST 2, 1957

JOHNSON AND KNOWLAND led the Senate debate about the jury trial amendment. Nixon waited in anticipation. He knew it could go either away. The vote would determine the success or failure of President Eisenhower's major initiative for the beginning of his second term. Ike spent the political capital from his reelection on this bill. More importantly, the voting rights for millions of African Americans were at stake.

The final vote was 51 to 42 in favor of the amendment. Nixon and Knowland privately spoke after their defeat.

"This might be the most disgraceful day I've ever seen in the Senate," Nixon said. "How could they vote for something that neutered voting rights?"

Knowland wiped tears coming down his face.

"The bill is so weak now. Between this and the removal of Part 3 it's almost worthless. I don't get how it happened! How did so many Republicans defect and side with Johnson and against Ike?"

"Johnson pulled off a master chess move. He whipped enough of his party in line and convinced the Republican Old Guard that states' rights were at stake. I'm more confused about how liberals like Humphrey and Kennedy, who constantly criticize Ike for being too passive on civil rights, could vote for this thing."

"Maybe they were afraid of a filibuster?"

"That's bound to happen anyway. The segregationists will want to kill a bill even as weak as this one."

☆☆☆☆☆

IKE MET WITH his cabinet later that day. His face was pale; he sat silently, absorbing the sting of defeat. The cabinet secretaries sat in awkward silence, waiting for the President to begin. Ike finally looked up to face his advisors.

"We've taken political defeats in the past four years, but this one is the worst." No one said anything. "Why the hell did so many key Republicans jump ship! They're not going to be the Party of Lincoln for long if this is how they treat civil rights!"

Labor Secretary Mitchell began, "Maybe they—"

"I don't want to hear any excuses for them! I don't have much forgiveness in my soul for this betrayal of our party and of decency!" Ike folded his arms and looked like an upset child. "Rarely in our legislative history have so many extraneous issues been introduced into the debate in order to confuse both legislators and the public! And the liberals, like Humphrey, they threw away their values! Humphrey blames me for this amendment because I wasn't decisive enough. He *voted* for the damn thing!"

The room became quiet until Commerce Secretary Weeks said, "At least Johnson is such a great leader. He managed to turn the bill into something that can be passed."

Ike's eyes widened.

"How stupid can you get?" Ike asked, ignoring his characteristic politeness. "Johnson threw away the enfranchisement of millions of citizens for his own political advantage. That's what happened today."

Ike slumped back in his chair. *I beat Hitler in the war. How the hell did Johnson outfox me? Social change has to come gradually, but he's delayed it too long. There's a limit to what the Negroes will endure. They're going to get frustrated if this takes a few more years. Patience is one thing but stalling for no reason is unreasonable to ask of anyone, especially a group that's suffered so much. The races will polarize as much as if it went too fast. Negroes will get angrier at whites, who will be offended and get angry back. Such a mess.*

☆☆☆☆☆

"WHEN SOMEONE TRIES to hit me with a brickbat, I start looking around for something to hit him with," Ike explained to Ann Whitman, pacing around the Oval Office. "I'm not going to stand for Johnson's misdeed."

"Are you going to veto the bill?" she asked.

"That would play right into the Democrats' hands," Ike replied. "They'd be able to use me vetoing a civil rights bill as a rallying cry in next year's midterm election."

"Then what's your plan, Mr. President?"

"I have to punish the pseudo-liberals like Humphrey and Kennedy for allying with Russell and his folk."

"How?"

"The House and Senate have passed two different versions of the bill. The House passed the good version; the Senate passed the sham version. It will have to go into reconciliation so both chambers of Congress can pass the same version. I'm going to tell the Republicans to resubmit Part 3, and that I'll veto the bill if Part 3 isn't there. That way it will be clear who supports civil rights and who's blowing smoke."

"Isn't that a gamble though?"

"So was Normandy," Ike said with a smile. "I feel as though I've really bounced back from that jury trial amendment."

"You look like it."

"Maybe my West Point boxing coach was really on to something when he said I have to smile after getting knocked down."

☆☆☆☆☆

IKE'S THREAT TO veto the compromised bill riled Johnson and the Democrats. Johnson was desperate to pass the bill, which he needed to campaign in the Northern states in 1960. But the South would not accept Part 3's readmission. Most of Washington thought the bill was doomed.

Brownell and the Justice Department brokered the compromise, which allowed for federal judges to try defendants accused of violating voting rights without a jury if the fine was under $300 or less than forty-five days of jail time. Johnson agreed to the compromise. Ike conferred with Knowland and agreed. Ike and Johnson had breakfast on August 26 to ratify their compromise.

Strom Thurmond, a leading defender of segregation, conducted a twenty-four hour filibuster to kill the bill. His effort was in vain. Ike's civil rights coalition of thirty-seven Republicans and twenty-three Democrats passed the bill through the Senate. Fifteen Southern Democrats voted against it.

Johnson smiled with relief after the vote. He slowly rose to his feet and left the Senate's chambers to discuss the vote with the press. He sold them a story that credited himself as the architect of the compromise and the bill's passage.

Nixon watched the Senators congratulate each other for a job well done. It appeared hollow to him. The first civil rights bill Congress passed since Reconstruction was more symbolic than substantive.

Adam Clayton Powell Jr., the most powerful African American in Congress, approached Nixon.

"This is the second Emancipation Proclamation!" he exclaimed, referring to Abraham Lincoln's signature achievement. Nixon did not agree.

Every thought leader in the country sent Ike their opinion on whether to veto the compromised bill. Morrow told Ike to veto the weak bill in protest of Johnson's actions. Jackie Robinson, one of the biggest sports stars in the country and a civil rights advocate, told Ike to wait for a stronger bill. But Martin Luther King Jr., leader of the Civil Rights Movement, advised Ike that a weak bill was better than no bill at all. Ike agreed with King and signed the bill on September 9.

☆☆☆☆☆

JUNE 23, 1958

DR. MARTIN LUTHER King Jr. stood with his closest advisors in the corridor outside of the Oval Office. He was stoic. His crisp black suit and blue tie presented a thin frame, while he restlessly rotated a fedora between his hands. His advisors were more frustrated than nervous.

"How much do you really expect to come of this meeting? The President was born in 1890. That's six years *before Plessy v. Ferguson* ruled 'separate but equal' was constitutional!" A. Philip Randolph said to King, emphasizing the word *before*.

"I know, but President Eisenhower has produced some decent results for a man of his generation," King said softly, trying to avoid Ann Whitman overhearing the conversation from across the room. "He gave us Warren, he intervened at Little Rock, and he signed the civil rights bill last year—"

"That bill was almost *useless*!" Roy Wilkins exclaimed in a stage whisper. "I heard Eisenhower doesn't even like cities, because he 'can't relate' to their social problems, whatever that means."

"I'm not disagreeing with your concerns," King replied. "But I think his record, as imperfect as it may be, shows we can convince him to go to the Deep South and endorse our movement. With his stature as a war hero and popular President, he can convince a lot of fence sitters to embrace our cause."

"He *is* a fence sitter, Reverend! He's a white moderate!" argued Lester Granger. "If he fought World War II the way he does for the movement, we'd all be speaking German right now!"

"You're not giving him enough credit," King responded. "Thurgood Marshall told me that he always tries to get Eisenhower-appointed judges when submitting a case. They *all* support civil rights. I think that says something."

"Maybe," Randolph said. "Will your friend Dick be joining us?"

"Not that I know of," King replied. King met Vice President Nixon in Ghana in March 1957 and again in Washington last June. King had asked Nixon to endorse the Civil Rights Movement in a speech in the South. Nixon declined but did host a meeting on more inclusive government contracts in the South shortly thereafter. Nixon advised Ike to meet with King, but Ike insisted on doing it only after the voting rights bill had passed, to avoid the South using the meeting to attack the bill. That meeting was imminent.

The Oval Office's door opened.

"It's nice to finally meet you gentlemen," Ike said, shaking hands with each civil rights leader. He gestured to some furniture in the Oval Office. "Please, take a seat. I've been eager for this meeting for a long time."

The President was joined by Morrow, Rocco Siciliano, who served in the Labor Department, and by Attorney General William Rodgers, who had replaced Brownell following his departure. The eight men took their place on the furniture in the Oval Office. Ike and King sat opposite one another.

Randolph handed Ike a written statement.

"What's this?" Ike asked.

"The NAACP commends you for your action in the Little Rock Crisis last September, after you signed the voting rights bill," Randolph explained. "The NAACP has the firm conviction that you are a man of courage and integrity who's shown leadership in this field."

"I'm honored," Ike replied.

"Mr. President, we want to start by asking the White House for aggressive action to combat segregation," Wilkins said. "We'd like a White House conference on the enforcement of school desegregation, stronger civil rights legislation, and for the Justice Department to investigate the bombings that have occurred in the South."

Ike was taken aback by such an extensive list.

I'm not even sure where to begin with all that!

King glared at Wilkins. Wilkins should know better than to make demands before he and Ike could exchange pleasantries.

"What my colleague is saying, Mr. President, is that such actions would mobilize the emotions of the spirit which, in turn, would aid in the fight for the abolishment of segregation," King explained.

Granger did not want King to be so diplomatic. He told Ike, "Expectations are rising in the Negro community. There's fear that progress has halted after the voting rights bill and the Little Rock Crisis. This concern is why some members of our community responded angrily to your call for 'patience' back in May."

Ike's eyebrows furrowed. "I'm dismayed to hear that after five and a half years of effort and action that you gentlemen are saying there's heightening bitterness on the part of the Negro."

"That anger is not directed at you, Mr. President," Granger said, "but at the communities where there is still resistance to integration."

"I've tried to guarantee that any federal actions in this field are done with diligence and care," Ike replied.

King bit his tongue. The meeting was superficial and beating around the bush. He was determined not to blow his meeting with Ike and shifted tactics.

"Mr. President, what did you think of the Montgomery Bus Boycott, back in '55?"

Ike smiled.

"I greatly admired that campaign. I thought it was constitutional and progressive. As I recall, it was the first time I heard your name come up, Reverend."

King chuckled.

"It was the first time most people heard my name. But that effort succeeded because it built sympathy and rallied the public opinion of average Americans. That's why we're hoping you'll come and speak in the South."

That would throw out my indirect approach to civil rights, Ike thought. *The South's already mad at me for Little Rock. This would just upset them further.*

"I'm afraid that would kill any credibility I have left in the South after what happened at Little Rock. I wouldn't be any more help to your movement than a dead pigeon's shadow."

"You don't give yourself enough credit, Mr. President," King said. Both men's advisors watched with curiosity as the two giants engaged one another. "You're a popular war hero. Even those who disagree with your politics must appreciate your service to our country."

"The South compared me to Hitler after I sent the 101st Airborne to Little Rock, so I'm not sure I'm as popular as you think I am."

"I ask you to remember Theodore Roosevelt's Bully Pulpit. He used it to end the Gilded Age and begin the Progressive Era."

"I don't think that would work on this issue. My condemning the South would just upset them," Ike shifted his posture forward. "The only acceptable way this movement can end is if the races have a lasting peace. They can't be antagonistic or polarized. That would be a tragedy for our democracy."

"I'm not disagreeing. I just think your vocal endorsement in the South would be more helpful than you seem to."

"I don't think I would be as useful to you in that capacity than if I continue to work behind the scenes," Ike said, revealing part of his strategy on civil rights. "Besides, I'm a soldier, not a revolutionary."

"George Washington was both." Ike's jaw clenched; he did not appreciate being disfavorably compared to his hero. "I feel this has been a pattern with your presidency. I know you value actions more than words, but words are still important. Like your failure to endorse *Brown*."

"I endorsed it!" Ike exclaimed.

"You said you would obey it, Mr. President. It was hardly a ringing endorsement."

"The President must execute the law, which includes opinions by the Supreme Court and federal courts. So, let's say I endorsed *Brown* more enthusiastically, which would have reflected how I *really* felt. That could lead to an expectation that I give my opinion on every Supreme Court decision. And what happens when I disagree with an opinion? I couldn't allow the public to have any doubt that I would faithfully execute the law. That would have been inappropriate and harmful to this republic."

"And what about your failure to send a letter or telegram of remorse to Emmitt Till's mother following his murder in 1955?"

Ike's face turned red.

"Hoover and the FBI told me that she might be a communist. That was all that I had to go on to make a decision. You may not remember, but McCarthy was targeting my administration at that time, and I couldn't risk him—"

"I understand that your heart lacked malice," King said. "But your failure to show remorse in that situation made Negroes feel that their President did not care about the tragedy."

"I have regretted my inaction in that circumstance every day since, Dr. King. But I don't think that misstep is representative of the efforts my administration has taken to help you people."

Morrow and Rodgers squirmed at Ike's use of the phrase "you people." The President did not realize he rhetorically divided himself from the African Americans leaders. Randolph and Granger exchanged a glance that read "typical." King ignored it.

Ike continued, "I know my strategy of action instead of talk doesn't win political points with the so-called sophisticated liberals—"

"There's a point of agreement between us, Mr. President. Trust me, the black man has his own complaints about white liberals."

"Such as?"

"They think they know what we want when they don't. Plus, they do a lot of talking and not a lot of listening."

Ike laughed.

"That's what I'm saying, though. I'm committed to action that will guarantee that all Americans get the rights promised to them under the Constitution. I didn't mean for patience on civil rights issues to imply inaction, just that it will take time and come in stages."

"Maybe our different interpretations of history will expose the gaps in our thinking. What's your view of history, Mr. President? Mine is that the moral arc of the universe is long but that it bends toward justice."

"I believe that much of American history is trying to find the Middle Way. Our Constitution was the compromise between extreme factions. And I think that compromise was correct and gave us the first stable republic since Caesar crossed the Rubicon."

"The Founders' compromises also allowed for slavery's continued existence."

"The Founders wanted three things. They wanted a Union of the thirteen states. They wanted it to be a republic. And they, at least the ones we still care about, were hostile to slavery. But they could get two out of three. A republic of only the Northern states could have existed without slavery. A monarchy under George Washington could have abolished slavery. But the Founders compromised on slavery to reach the other two goals. I do think that the Middle Way is what eventually destroyed slavery, though."

"The Civil War was the Middle Way?"

"That's not what I meant. Lincoln took four years to end slavery, despite pressure from the abolitionists to go faster. He knew that to go any faster would cost him the Border States and then the entire war. Kind of like my concerns about provoking a Southern backlash if I push too quickly on integration. Instead, he took two years to issue the Emancipation Proclamation and another two for the Thirteenth Amendment.

"The third example I would use is Theodore Roosevelt, who you mentioned earlier. He ignited the Progressive Era by breaking up monopolies and trusts while resisting the calls from extremists like William Jennings Bryan and Eugene Debs to end capitalism entirely. As a result, TR built a model of regulated capitalism that allows for capitalism's blessings without all of its vices."

"We're getting a little off track, Mr. President. I think my colleagues and I are concerned that the Middle Way may not be enough for addressing the fact that whites are the dominant race in America and what that means for Negroes and other minority groups."

"Saying whites are the 'dominant race' sounds more like Nazi Germany than the United States."

"Every Negro knows it is true."

"I still don't think that's fair or appropriate. Your strategy of nonviolence, as admirable as it is, and it *is*, would not have worked under Hitler's reign. It took the largest coalition in military history to stop him."

"My hero, Mahatma Gandhi, said pacifism from Britain and the Allies would have sparked so much outrage at Germany from the rest of the world that it would have forced Hitler's overthrow."

"I seriously question that premise. Only Operation Overlord could stop Hitler. And as much as the situation in this country needs changing, it doesn't require a solution nearly so drastic."

King sighed. He placed his hands together as he slowly explained, "Mr. President, I believe that we agree on the goal of racial justice. We're just disagreeing on the approach." He sought to build a connection with Ike. "I believe that this situation is dire and requires rapid change. Anything less is partaking in injustice. But you are temperamentally conservative and resistant to such a revolution. I question if you could be committed to anything that would involve a structural change to American society. You insist that any evil defacing the nation be extracted with tweezers because the surgeon's knife is an instrument too radical to touch this best of all societies."

"I would describe my approach more as one emphasizing change that does not disrupt the rule of law or the stability that a society needs to survive. Anarchy would unleash humanity's darkness."

"No one's calling for anarchy, Mr. President. But stability enforcing injustice is wrong. I don't think we need to fear revolution or rapid change. Institutional racism and similar structures are holding people back from the potential of brotherhood. That's how we'll have peace."

"You make it sound like humans are naturally good."

"I choose to think that they are."

"I disagree. Humans are selfish creatures who need to restrain themselves to have peace. That's why stability is so important. It creates rule systems that force humans to restrain their inner wickedness."

"That's a very pessimistic view of humanity."

"It's one grown out of experience in two World Wars and the Cold War."

The meeting ended shortly thereafter, with no bridge closing the gap between Ike and King.

☆☆☆☆☆

AUGUST 6, 1965

THE GETTYSBURG FARM was peaceful as evening rolled around. Cattle were in their stable. Mamie and Barbara Eisenhower watched a soap opera marathon in the living room.

Former President Eisenhower read a newspaper in a little chair in the adjacent room. A bust of Abraham Lincoln sat on the mantle and watched Ike as he read the *New York Times*. The headline read, "President Signs Bill on Negro Vote Rights" and contained an image of President Lyndon Johnson signing the Voting Rights Act of 1965. Various advisors and civil rights leaders, including Dr. King, stood behind him. The act was modeled on the 1957 bill.

Ike put down the newspaper after finishing the story.

He smiled and thought, Justice has finally been done.

Ike's Long Game

Don't see, don't feel, don't admit, and don't answer; just ignore your attacker and keep smiling.
—William Ewald, on Eisenhower's response to criticism

SEPTEMBER 14, 1957

THE FIRST THING you need to know about this story is that I had lots of trouble with my insides. They were in constant pain, especially when I was stressed. There wasn't a moment that I'm going to describe to you when that wasn't the case.

My built up frustrations could be seen in the painting I worked on while I waited for my advisors to arrive at the Newport White House. I'd opted to paint a wintery landscape with a few leafless trees and a lonely horseback rider. A dark, almost black creek that cut the snowy ground in half was the piece's defining feature. I used watercolors and based it on a photograph, which was true of most of my paintings. I would never claim to be a great artist, nor do I care to be. Painting was simply a way to relax, a way to put the surface of your mind on the canvas while the rest of your mind is making decisions. As a youngster, I would have said I'd grown up to be a sissy if you'd told me I painted as a hobby. It took Winston Churchill, my old friend, to convince me otherwise.

1957 was the low point of my relationship with Congress. The Democrats, a strange amalgamation of Northern liberals and Southern reactionaries, had defeated or undermined several important pieces of legislation that my administration proposed. Two stand out.

407

The first was a school construction bill. Education was as important to America as defense, yet we had a shortage of 159,000 classrooms. The states were building 69,000 a year, but that wasn't enough to get ahead of the shortage. I proposed the federal government spend $1.3 billion over four years. The idea was to focus on the poorer states, so as to secure equal opportunities for every American child. Federal involvement was necessary to solve the issue, but I was determined that it only be temporary. Permanent federal involvement in schools' operating costs would increase federal power over the educational curriculum, which would be a calamity of the first order and set America on the path to dictatorship as Washington bureaucrats controlled what entire generations of children learned and believed.

Both extremes attacked my proposal, which was the case with most of my administration's policies. The liberals claimed it was barebones, because they never saw a problem that they didn't think could be solved with permanent federal involvement. The conservatives claimed it was too liberal, even though I maintained that it was a more conservative position than the one held by the late Senator Taft, their leader for a generation. The Senate passed the administration's bill, but it died in the House when an amendment was attached that would speed up racial integration in schools. The amendment's author knew their racist colleagues would kill the bill with it attached.

That leads me to the voting rights bill, the second piece of legislation that was prominently crippled by Congress. You're certainly aware of the background information. America's Founding Fathers compromised on slavery, betting that it would disintegrate on its own. That bet failed, leading to the Civil War. Abraham Lincoln's political genius preserved the Union and ended slavery, but he was tragically assassinated before his work was complete. Discrimination against Negroes persisted for decades in spite of America's founding commitment to freedom for all. My administration sought to pick up where Lincoln's generation left off and set Jim Crow on the path to extinction. America allowed a barefoot boy from Kansas to lead a global military coalition in a world war and become President. It was my duty to make that journey possible for all American children, regardless of race, religion, or gender. It is unacceptable to have second class citizens in America, the world's foremost democracy.

The voting rights bill sought to create a civil rights commission, a civil rights division within the Justice Department, authorize the Attorney General to seek preventive relief from courts in civil rights cases, and allow the DOJ to engage in civil suits to protect voting rights. I don't normally engage in personalities, but as this is a private story, I am willing to say that Lyndon Johnson, the Senate Majority Leader, weakened the administration's bill in order to preserve the Democrats' bizarre voting coalition that I referred to earlier. The Attorney General's power to seek preventive relief from courts was removed and the DOJ's power to engage in civil suits was handicapped with rigid standards and minimal punishments. Thus showing politicians' innate selfishness.

The voting rights bill was the culmination of my strategy on civil rights that had engaged each branch of government. Truman had made a lot of noise on civil rights but got nowhere; my administration opted for an indirect approach. We integrated everything that was under federal jurisdiction, including the District of Columbia. We did this by threatening to withhold funding from any agency that refused to cooperate. The courts were next. We treated support for civil rights as a litmus test for judicial appointments. The idea was that this would allow the NAACP and like-minded groups to win more of their cases and advance the cause.

This strategy led to *Brown v Board of Education*, the most important Supreme Court case of the century. The Fourteenth Amendment, enacted shortly after the Civil War, guaranteed equal protection under the law. But courts in the Jim Crow era interpreted this so narrowly that it became nonexistent. *Brown*, in essence, was about whether segregated schools could be equal. The Court ruled that they could not, which was correct in my view. My administration filed an amicus curiae brief arguing such. My administration's appointments to the Court directly led to this outcome, which pleased me greatly.

There is confusion over my thoughts toward *Brown*, since I vowed to enforce it but kept my thinking otherwise private. The liberals, in their infinite wisdom, criticized me for taking this approach. I suppose they would rather I gave my opinions on every Supreme Court case, even if that raised concern about my willingness to enforce decisions I denounced. I definitely agreed with the *Brown* decision, though I did wish the Court would have started integration with graduate and undergraduate schools, as people are less emotional with young adults than with children.

Almost 60 percent of the country supported *Brown*, though that did only include 15 percent of the South. The South was misguided on racial issues and would take time to catch up with the rest of the country and the civilized world. Changing their way of life wasn't going to happen overnight. On the other hand, moving too slowly fed justified anger in the

Negro community who sought the rights guaranteed to them by the Constitution. Failing to stick to this Middle Way would trigger long-term racial polarization, which I knew in my bones would destroy this republic. That's much of what angered me about Johnson's weakening of the voting rights bill.

I hoped life would calm down once Congress' session ended, unmourned by me. Mamie and I thought it was a good time to go on vacation, and we left Washington for Newport, Rhode Island. Mamie was recovering from a hysterectomy. I looked forward to golf, bridge, and grilling steaks with John Moaney, my valet and friend. That relaxation was stillborn as the biggest domestic crisis of my presidency emerged.

Little Rock reminded me of the Rodgers and Hammerstein musical *South Pacific* in which the French lead character referred to the American heroine's town as "Small Rock." The situation grew out of *Brown*. Every school district in the country was required to announce how it planned to comply with the decision. Little Rock's school board announced in 1955 that they planned to begin integration in 1957 and finish by the early 60s. A group of white mothers tried to stop the process, but a federal court ordered it to proceed.

Orval Faubus, the Arkansas governor, deployed the National Guard to prevent the nine Negro youngsters that were set on entering Little Rock's Central High School from doing so. This triggered a mob of five hundred extremists who tormented the nine. Thus, my worst fear of advancing civil rights became realized as the Arkansas government, sanctioned by the state legislature, defied federal court orders and threatened to nullify the Constitution. Faubus sent me a telegram, asking for my cooperation in the crisis he started. I promptly replied that he could expect me to defend the Constitution by every legal means at my command.

As I understand it, Faubus was a socialist as a teenager who became a New Deal Democrat when he entered public life. Now he was taking advantage of the passionate resistance to civil rights to promote his own career. A demagogue and opportunist. He was nothing more than an example of human selfishness, the great enemy of my life and that can only be overcome by devotion to duty. My first experience with selfishness was my temper, which I've spent my life fighting to control. Hitler's desire for world domination is the most extreme form of selfishness I can think of, although Khrushchev was another would-be world ruler. On our side there were the great many individuals in and out of public service who preferred to wage nuclear war instead of wage peace, consequences be damned. Then there was McCarthy, extremists who saw their perspective as the only acceptable answer, and the racists who were happy to oppress the Negro. Humanity must restrain its selfishness if it is to build peace.

My advisors arrived at my painting room in our Newport White House. I put down my paintbrush and turned to them. Leading the pack was Chief of Staff Sherman Adams. A former New Hampshire Governor, Adams possessed a no-nonsense attitude that I appreciated. This did not endear him to politicians, who found him rude and accused him of being a Rasputin-like figure. They must not have seen Adams at social gatherings, where his singing was often the life of the party.

Next was Attorney General Herbert Brownell, my principal advisor on legal issues and civil rights. This dated to even before I became President, as he led efforts by the Eastern Establishment Republicans to draft me to run in 1952. Lastly was their escort, Sergeant John Moaney, my Negro valet to whom I referred earlier. John was my closest companion, other than Mamie. He followed me everywhere; through World War II to the presidency. He even came with me to NATO, even though it meant separation from his recent wife.

I turned to Adams first.

"Where's Jim Hagerty and General Morgan?"

"On their way."

Next, I turned to Brownell.

"Any updates?"

"Little Rock's school board asked a federal judge if they should undo their order to the Negro students to avoid Central High while the situation continued. The judge said that the integration must continue."

That was good. We can never appease extremists.

"Who's the judge?" Adams asked.

"Ronald Davies. He's on the District Court for the Eastern District of Arkansas," Brownell answered.

"Is he one of ours?"

"Yes," I interjected. "Can Davies rule on Faubus' actions?"

"Yes," Brownell replied, "even if Faubus made no effort to carry out the federal court order, which he hasn't."

I furrowed my brow and crossed my arms.

"To do nothing would set a precedent that governors and states can choose which federal court orders to follow. I don't see how we can let that stand."

"I agree, Mr. President. That's why my team and I at DOJ developed a contingency plan for this as soon as *Brown* came down."

"Which is?"

"We've already launched an investigation of whether Faubus sought to trigger violence by deploying the Guard."

"Who's involved in the investigation?" Adams asked.

"The FBI and the marshals' offices that Davies has at his disposal."

"Has the investigation found anything important?" I asked.

"The main discovery was to confirm that there were *no* agitators in Little Rock, which Faubus claimed he was protecting against. This mess is entirely *his* doing. That means he risks being held in contempt of federal court and that we can withhold federal funds from the Arkansas National Guard."

"What about using federal troops?"

"We hold that option to enforce the District Court's order."

"What if Faubus rejects our claim about the agitators and says he has a duty to 'prevent violence' by using the Guard?" Adams asked.

"We could counter by saying the federal government has a duty to protect children, who *he's* endangering."

"And if he denies that?"

"Then the federal government will have to stand firm and use federal troops."

"Which is exactly what I hope to avoid, if at all possible," I interjected again. "Faubus is almost here, and we need to discuss the plan for this meeting." I had their attention. "We need to anticipate that Faubus is going to ask for a delay in withdrawing the Guard. I'll ask you, Herbert, about that idea, and you have to say in confidence that that would be illegal. He might get mad at *you*, but *I'll* still look like an honest broker, which we'll need if we're going to resolve this situation diplomatically."

"This is a *terrible* idea, Mr. President!" Brownell exclaimed. "Faubus has soiled himself and is undeserving of meeting the President of the United States!"

I sighed as Brownell's face turned red. I had heard this argument before and had overruled it the first time. Adams spoke.

"Faubus knows he's made a mistake and is looking for a way out."

"Or he's trying to make President Eisenhower look *weak*, which he is *succeeding* at. The President already comes off as weak on civil rights issues because he refuses to use the Bully Pulpit. This will be a domestic equivalent of the Munich Agreement!"

"I want to exhaust *all* of our diplomatic options before resorting to force," I countered. "Especially if it means sending young boys against a mob. In the South. As a Republican."

"We have to give Faubus an out to make a retreat without losing face," Adams concurred.

"I've made my opposition clear," Brownell said as he constrained his temper.

Brooks Hays, a Democratic Congressman from Little Rock's district, brokered the meeting between Faubus and myself. I had given Hays the specific telegram that Faubus sent me to request the meeting. Faubus agreed to use it. He arrived at the Newport White House by helicopter. Adams and Hagerty, my Press Secretary, greeted him in front of reporters. They led him to me.

Faubus and I were alone. I did my best to not glare at him, this man who threatened our Constitution and the rights of millions for his own political gain. He appeared to constrain his nerves. He must have known he was over his head. Faubus spoke first after we sat down.

"I served under General Patton in the Second World War. Third Army. He was a great man."

"He certainly was an effective subordinate. On the Western Front."

Faubus squirmed as I shot down his attempt to establish a connection. I cut to the chase.

"I hope you know, Governor, that you're going to have to undo the situation that exists in Little Rock. States can't defy the Supreme Court."

He snorted.

"What, are you trying to do this quickly so you can get back to your golf?"

"No," I muttered, with tension in my voice, "I'm trying to give you a way out."

"Me! There are ugly plans afoot in Arkansas against me. Now what I require from you, Mr. President, is a ten-day break. A time for breathing that will let temperatures a chance to cool off, to give emotions a chance to subside. I also need the assistance of federal marshals to restore order."

"I don't intend to grant a governor who is *defying* a federal court order control of federal marshals. What you *need* to do is leave the National Guard in place but to change their orders to escort the Negro students *into* the school instead of keeping them *out*. If you do that, the DOJ will recommend that Judge Davies *not* find you in contempt of federal court."

"I can't stand for the federal government and the *North* to step all over the *Southern* way of life. And I fail to see how it benefits *you*, Mr. President, to antagonize the South."

"I hold to *one* purpose in this situation, Governor. There *must* be respect for the Constitution—that means the Supreme Court's interpretation of the Constitution—or there will be chaos."

"The Constitution belongs to *all* of us, not nine unelected—"

"We wouldn't have a coherent legal system if every individual could interpret the Constitution their own way. Now, the federal government has jurisdiction over this issue and it's my duty to enforce the Supreme Court's ruling. That means a state will lose if it defies the federal government in this situation and, frankly, no one will benefit from a trial of strength between a President and a governor. I don't want to see any governor humiliated."

"I've come too far to do what you ask of me, Mr. President. Backing down now would cost me reelection."

"To be blunt, Governor, *you* created this situation. It's on *you* to resolve it and to put the good of your state and the country ahead of your own career."

"Easy to say when it's not *your* career," Faubus muttered as he leaned back in his chair and then leaned forward again. "Am I right in understanding that you have a portrait of Robert E. Lee in the Oval Office?"

"Among others, yes."

"I see myself as acting in Lee's tradition. Loyalty to the state over the federal government. Surely you can see—"

"The legality and acceptability of nullification may have been questionable before the Civil War, but Appomattox settled it for all time."

Faubus' face sank at my interrupting him. It was clear we were getting nowhere, as I predicted. Time for Plan B.

"Let's go for a walk," I suggested. Faubus nodded and followed me. We entered an outer office. Waiting for us were Brownell, Adams, General Morgan, and Brooks Hays. Ann Whitman, my personal secretary, sat outside the room.

Faubus' eyes darted between us, aware he was surrounded. Six chairs were placed in a circle. I led the group to the chairs and told Faubus to sit next to me.

"I feel like a choirboy," Faubus joked. I briefly summarized the private meeting I'd had with Faubus to the others and Faubus' request for a delay. I then turned to Brownell.

"Herb, can't you go down there to Little Rock and ask Judge Davies to postpone the implementation of this order for a few days, ten days, or three weeks? Whatever time it might be decided is best to try to solve the problem?"

Brownell shook his head, as planned.

"No, that's impossible. It isn't legally possible." He eyed Faubus. "The governor may not agree with the Supreme Court's decision, but he must obey it."

Faubus was silent and frowning, studying my reactions, aware that this was scripted. He finally spoke, primarily to me.

"I am preserving peace and good order with the National Guard."

"The order was outrageous, Governor," I shot back.

"I had no choice! *Your* Attorney General sent the FBI and federal marshals to Little Rock to arrest me!"

"That was based on a request from Judge Davies!" Brownell exclaimed.

Faubus turned to me in exasperation.

"Do you see the type of people you have in your administration?"

"I support Mr. Brownell and am determined to uphold the Constitution against mob rule," I said, making my stance plain. The room settled into an awkward silence until I retrieved a letter from my pocket. "This is from a gentleman, a businessman, I believe, who offered me free advice. He recommended that I remove every Southern officer from command within the Army because they are going to stage a revolution over this Little Rock situation. So, I ask you, Governor, how far do you plan to go in opposing the federal government?"

Faubus squirmed back in his seat again. His eyes darted to and fro.

"I hope you know, Mr. President, that I am a loyal citizen and that I recognize federal supremacy."

A sudden smile overtook me. He folded!

"Remember, Governor, I don't believe you should necessarily withdraw the Guard when you return home. Just change their orders to support integration rather than oppose it. That will resolve this situation without you losing face."

"I appreciate that," Faubus responded.

I turned to Hagerty.

"Please explain how constructive this meeting was to the press, Jim."

I heard Mrs. Whitman scoff from the other room and couldn't help but notice how bothered Brownell looked. They lacked my optimism that the breakthrough was genuine. It would turn out they had reason to do so.

☆ ☆ ☆ ☆ ☆

SEPTEMBER 23, 1957

I SAT IN my office in the Newport White House, staring into space and lost in thought.

"Mr. President?"

I blinked a couple of times as I returned to reality.

"Oh, hello, Herbert," I said to Brownell. He was holding a paper.

"What were you thinking about," he asked softly, "if you don't mind?"

"I was thinking about Icky. My little boy. Died when he was three of scarlet fever. Mamie and I barely survived it. Drove us apart for years. These young people—whether they be students or soldiers—they're our most precious resource as a nation. We have to do right by them. What's that you have there?"

"It's a telegram from Mayor Mann, Little Rock's mayor."

"Can I see it?"

Brownell handed it to me. It read:

> The immediate need for federal troops is urgent. The mob is much larger in numbers at 8 a.m. than at any time yesterday. People are converging on the scene from all directions and engaging in fisticuffs and other acts of violence. Situation is out of control and police cannot disperse the mob.

I grimaced; depressive pain swelled in my chest. This was overwhelming.

"You were right about Faubus," I muttered, "The lying SOB betrayed me."

"The Democrats are on the offensive again," Brownell said, bringing more bad news.

"It's their damn party!" I exclaimed.

"Nonetheless, they're claiming you failed to uphold the Constitution by appeasing Faubus and that you told him to withdraw the Guard to unleash the mob."

"Did Johnson say that?"

"I believe it was Senator Humphrey and former President Truman."

I scoffed and dismissively waved my hand.

"That party's leadership is a bunch of hypocrites. They claim to care about civil rights, but they undermined the voting rights bill."

I felt a vein throb over my temple as I thought about the constant criticism I received about this issue.

"What does Mann mean when he says the mob is larger today?" I asked.

"The white mob's been growing since Faubus removed the Guard upon returning to Arkansas. It must be over a thousand people by now. He unleashed their hatred and isn't lifting a finger to contain it or help the local police. Mann's retreated the Little Rock Nine to safety. Reporters and Negro neighborhoods are being attacked."

"When's the last time Faubus made an appearance or an announcement?"

"He left the state for a conference of Southern governors."

I put a finger to my lip.

"If we make a move against the mob, is there a chance that Faubus will shut down the public school system? Can he do that legally?"

"That's a risk we have to take."

"Is it? That's seemed the most likely outcome since you and I began this integration process years ago. That segregationist governors will shut down public school systems across the South rather than accept integration. Then both Negro and poor white children will suffer as the well-to-do go to private schools."

"Mr. President, failing to act will set the Civil Rights Movement back fifty years. Segregationists will know that the federal government won't enforce court orders. Our whole strategy—the one you and I devised together—of putting civil rights supporters into the judiciary will be undone."

I nodded, conceding the point.

"It goes even beyond that. It would allow states to nullify federal law. It would reverse Appomattox."

"Exactly."

The decision was made. As general and President, I had sought to build a world secure for future generations to live in peace and be productive so they could maximize the value of their lives. I wasn't going to allow a small-town politician to undo that.

I called Army Chief of Staff Maxwell Taylor to come to Newport. He arrived within an hour, joining Brownell and me. Taylor and I had a complex relationship. He served under my command in World War II as the head of the 101st Airborne Division. But he was critical of the New Look, my signature national security policy, which sought to contain the Soviet Union through a cheap nuclear deterrent.

"I was updated on the Little Rock situation on the way here," Taylor began. "Do you intend to use force?"

"The issue isn't whether to act but by what means," I responded. "The local federal marshal lacks the capacity to restore order in this situation."

"What about the FBI?" Taylor asked.

"I already recommended that," Brownell chimed.

"I don't think they're strong enough either," I said, affirming my rejection of the idea. "The FBI's presence would just trigger an escalation by the mob."

"Is there any federal force that wouldn't cause that?" Taylor asked.

"A federal force of overwhelming power would restore order." I'd learned the value of overwhelming the enemy when I served under Fox Conner in Panama and applied the principle in World War II and in designing the nuclear deterrent.

"Like the Guard?"

"I want something that will deploy faster and not pit brother against brother."

"What then?"

"I want to use the 101st Airborne." I had a special connection with this group. I spoke to them the night before they were dropped into Normandy and deployed them to a critical road junction during the Battle of the Bulge.

Taylor was stunned.

"You want to send paratroopers into an American city?"

"The situation needs to be stabilized."

"A move that drastic hasn't been made since—"

"Since Reconstruction, I know. But we have no choice. If the day comes when we can obey the orders of our courts only when we personally approve of them, the end of the American system, as we know it, will not be far off." I turned to Brownell. "Draft an executive order that will nationalize the Guard and deploy the Airborne into Little Rock. After that, draft a proclamation that will order our citizens to cease resistance."

Brownell chuckled.

"I was hoping to fly to New York to catch the boxing match tonight. I suppose that plan's off."

My eyes locked on his. I disliked it when others tried to bring humor into serious discussions, especially now. Brownell shifted in his shoes under the weight of my glare.

"There's good legal precedent for this," he muttered "going back to George Washington and the Whisky Rebellion."

"This *mob's* a rebellion," I declared. "And it's helping our enemies. *Pravda* is saying that the Soviet action in Hungary last year doesn't compare to what the Negroes in the South are enduring. We have to show the world that we're a nation of laws. But we don't know what we're opening the door to here. The South might try to privatize the entire school system. We have to be ready for that. We also need a contingency if rebellions break out across the South." I looked to Taylor. "Put units across the Southern states on special alert to deal with any possible outbreaks related to school segregation."

"Yes, Mr. President."

☆☆☆☆☆

SEPTEMBER 24, 1957

I RETURNED TO the White House in Washington to address the nation. Mamie stayed behind in Newport, still recuperating. The conference of Southern governors released a statement supporting Faubus. They intended to undermine my speech, but I didn't care, and neither did the country. In times of crisis, the people turn to the White House for leadership. I hoped to deliver it.

I'd toned down Brownell's draft on my way to Washington. Words in public pronouncements should not draw attention to themselves, and I particularly did not like to use words that I knew Hitler used in his speeches, like "aggressive." I sought to focus more on the constitutional issue than the civil rights one, since that's what most people would respond to.

I called Bill Graham, my spiritual advisor, before giving my speech. He said that sending in federal troops was my only viable option. I also called Mamie to get her thoughts. She supported my decision.

I was exhausted as I sat behind the Oval Office desk. I squirmed in my seat; my insides still hurting me. I felt constricted and uncomfortable in my vest. I told Hagerty not to bother with the teleprompter. I had some notes before me, but I ended up not looking at them. Four portraits sat behind me as I went on television: Washington, Franklin, Lincoln, and Lee.

"Good evening, my fellow citizens:

"For a few minutes this evening I should like to speak to you about the serious situation that has arisen in Little Rock. To make this talk, I have come to the President's office in the White House. I could have spoken from Rhode Island, where I have been staying recently. But I felt that, in speaking from the house of Lincoln, of Jackson, and of Wilson, my words would better convey both the sadness I feel in the action I was compelled today to make and the firmness with which I intend to pursue this course until the orders of the Federal Court at Little Rock can be executed without unlawful interference.

"In that city, under the leadership of demagogic extremists, disorderly mobs have deliberately prevented the carrying out of proper orders from a federal court. Local authorities have not eliminated that violent opposition and, under the law, I yesterday issued a proclamation calling upon the mob to disperse. This morning the mob again gathered in front of the Central High School of Little Rock, obviously for the purpose of again preventing the carrying out of the court's order relating to the admission of Negro children to that school.

"Whenever normal agencies prove inadequate to the task and it becomes necessary for the Executive Branch of the Federal Government to use its powers and authority to uphold Federal Courts, the President's responsibility is inescapable. In accordance with that responsibility, I have today issued an Executive Order directing the use of troops under Federal authority to aid in the execution of Federal law at Little Rock, Arkansas. This became necessary when my Proclamation of yesterday was not observed, and the obstruction of justice still continues.

"It is important that the reasons for my action be understood by all our citizens. As you know, the Supreme Court of the United States has decided that separate public educational facilities for the races are inherently unequal; and therefore, compulsory school segregation laws are unconstitutional.

"It was my hope that this localized situation would be brought under control by city and state authorities. If the use of local police powers had been sufficient, our traditional method of leaving the problem in those hands would have been pursued. But when large gatherings of obstructionists made it impossible for the decrees of the Court to be carried out, both the law and the national interest demanded that the President take action.

"I know that the overwhelming majority of the people in the South—including those of Arkansas and of Little Rock—are of good will, united in their efforts to preserve and respect the law even when they disagree with it. They do not sympathize with mob rule. They, like the rest of our nation, have proved in two great wars their readiness to sacrifice for America. And the foundation of the American way of life is our national respect for law.

"At a time when we face grave situations abroad because of the hatred that Communism bears toward a system of government based on human rights, it would be difficult to exaggerate the harm that is being done to the prestige and influence, and indeed to the safety, of our nation and the world.

"Our enemies are gloating over this incident and using it everywhere to misrepresent our whole nation. We are portrayed as a violator of those standards of conduct which the peoples of the world united to proclaim in the Charter of the United Nations. There, they affirmed 'faith in fundamental human rights' and 'in the dignity and worth of the human person' and they did so 'without distinction as to race, sex, language, or religion.'

"And so, with deep confidence, I call upon the citizens of the State of Arkansas to assist in bringing to an immediate end all interference with the law and its processes. If resistance to the Federal Court order ceases at once, the further presence of Federal troops will be unnecessary, and the City of Little Rock will return to its normal habits of peace and order; and a blot upon the fair name and high honor of our nation in the world will be removed. Thus, will be restored the image of America and of all its parts as one nation, indivisible, with liberty and justice for all.

"Good night and thank you very much."

☆☆☆☆☆

I CALLED MAMIE after the speech to check up on her again. Next, I was informed that 500 paratroopers had entered Little Rock. The mob dissolved and order was restored. The jumpers successfully escorted the

Little Rock Nine to their classes and stayed with them through the day. Less pleasant was the opinion of every public person in America flooding into my office.

Civil rights leaders such as Martin Luther King and Jackie Robinson praised my decision and speech. As did many newspapermen, with Walter Lippmann as an exception. Most upsetting was a World War II veteran who served under my command in Europe sending me his medals, claiming to be ashamed he ever wore them. Most predictable was Faubus, who declared Arkansas to be occupied territory. Most outrageous was Georgia Senator Russell, who accused me of using the paratroopers to illegally mix the races and claimed the jumpers were no different than the Nazi SS.

I hit the roof when Mrs. Whitman brought me that telegram. I wrote out my reply on White House stationary for Mrs. Whitman to send back:

"Few times in my life have I felt as saddened as when the obligations of my office required me to order the use of force within a state to carry out the decisions of a federal court. My conviction is that had the police powers of the State of Arkansas been utilized not to frustrate the orders of the Court but to support them, the ensuing violence and open disrespect for the law and the federal judiciary would never have occurred. The Arkansas National Guard could have handled the situation with ease had it been instructed to do so. When a state, by seeking to frustrate orders of a federal court, encourages mobs of extremists to flout the orders of a federal court, and when a state refuses to utilize its police powers to protect against mobs persons who are peaceably exercising their right under the Constitution as defined in such Court orders, the oath of office of the President requires that he take action to give the protection. Failure to act in such a case would be tantamount to acquiescence in anarchy and the dissolution of the union.

"I must say that I completely fail to comprehend your comparison of our troops to Hitler's stormtroopers. In one case military power was used to further the ambitions and purposes of a ruthless dictator; in the other to preserve the institutions of free government."

Hagerty informed me that nearly 70 percent of the country approved my decision, a number that neared 80 percent outside the South. However, over 60 percent of the South disapproved. The Little Rock Crisis triggered an epiphany within my mind. Southerners were malicious, and not naive, regarding racial issues, and professionals such as doctors and lawyers partook in the mob, not just hooligans. A politician from Georgia wrote me to say I would suffer violence if I dared enter his state. A group in Kentucky put me on a mock trial for treason. I'll leave it to you to guess the verdict.

All this pales in comparison with the worst news of all. Brownell visited me in the Oval Office during my public opinion bath. He held a paper.

"What's that, Herbert? Another message of denunciation?"

He handed it to me.

"It's my letter of resignation."

My throat sealed shut. It was difficult for me to speak.

"Are—are you unhappy with how we handled the crisis?"

"Mr. President, you know I never intended to stay past the first term. I did so reluctantly because of the voting rights bill and the Little Rock Crisis, but all that's over now."

I felt tears swell up in my eyes, I but fought to hold them back.

"I don't know what I'll do without you. You've been my right hand and my guide on the civil rights question since the beginning."

"Don't worry, Mr. President. We'll keep in touch."

I noticed Mrs. Whitman waiting by the door.

"Come in," I instructed as I wiped away a tear. She handed me a telegram. "Who is this one from?"

"Louis Armstrong."

"The musician?"

"Yes, sir."

I read the message:

"Daddy, if and when you decide to take those little Negro children personally into Central High School along with your marvelous troops, please take me along."

My eyebrow rose. Mrs. Whitman and Brownell exchanged a glance.

"Is it negative?" Mrs. Whitman asked.

"No," I replied, "but he called me 'Daddy,' and I'm not sure how I feel about that."

☆☆☆☆☆

OCTOBER 3, 1957

I MET WITH the Southern governors and told them that I could withdraw the jumpers from Little Rock if Faubus cooperated. Tennessee Governor

Clement called Faubus and explained this to him. Faubus agreed but then flip flopped again.

I held a press conference, which I saw as a direct means of communication with the American people. I called on the first reporter.

"Robert Clark, INS. Do you foresee, Mr. President, another scenario in which you would deploy federal troops into a situation in the South, as you did at Little Rock?"

"Oh, Robert, I can't possibly answer a hypothetical like that."

"That isn't a 'no,' sir."

"I don't think it's wise for me to answer either way."

"I'll move on then. Sir, you probably are aware that some of your critics feel you were too slow in asserting a vigorous leadership in this integration crisis. Do you feel, sir, that the results would be any different if you had acted sooner instead of, as your critics say, letting things drift?"

I smiled.

"I am astonished how many people know exactly what the President of the United States should do."

The press corps laughed. I continued.

"I don't think it's reasonable to say that my administration has acted indecisively on this issue. We studied the problem from the time of the *Brown* decision and considered the risks and benefits of pursuing integration at various speeds. Now if you excuse me, Robert, I think I'd like to call on somebody else. Yes, you there."

"Sara Cooper, sir. Sir, you said yourself that you can't legislate emotions; and, as you just said, it isn't good to use troops; and you said that we need education, and you said a while back we needed patience. We saw patience did not work. Now, what will you do? Many people are asking, what will you do?"

The right side of my lips rose as I pondered that question which challenged my approach to the civil rights issue. My arms folded briefly.

"I don't know how much more *can* be done. I've written church leaders and met with teachers and with the Southern governors' conference. Now, the leadership of the White House can be exercised only, as I see it, through giving the convictions of the President and exhorting citizens to remember America as well as their own private prejudices.

"Now, this is not, I admit, a very persuasive thing. As I have told this group before, I've been myself challenged on even more academic questions than this in Russia; and I wasn't too successful in convincing the other fellow, although I thought I was very eloquent."

The press corps laughed again. The conference ended shortly thereafter. Several reporters approached me once the cameras were off to express their approval of my handling of the Little Rock Crisis.

That was new!

I have to admit that this was not my best performance before the press. I was exhausted. I desperately needed a break after my battles with Congress that I did not receive because of Faubus' schemes. My insides continued to ache and burn almost every minute of every day. Now I *truly* needed a break from stress.

I didn't get it.

☆☆☆☆☆

OCTOBER 4, 1957

THE R7 ROCKET was launched from Tyuratam Range in Kazakhstan. It went 560 miles above the Earth's surface and was the first man-made object to escape the Earth's terrestrial orbit. I'm not the person to ask about the technical details, but the rocket disassembled, and a beach ball-sized sphere exited. The sphere wielded four radio antennas.

Beep, Beep, Beep.

☆☆☆☆☆

MAMIE AND I sat on the balcony named for my predecessor at the White House as we played scrabble. Mamie rested her chin on her hand as her elbow sat on the table before her. She took a long time to decide, impassive.

"Are you ok, dear?" I asked. She took a moment to respond.

"I can't believe I'm sixty."

I scoffed without thinking.

"I'm on my sixth year of my sixties. They're not too bad. I wouldn't worry about it."

She grunted. Her face came alive as she finally played her move. She spelled out "Bltps." My face scrunched up as I looked at her creation.

"There's no way that's a word."

"Yes, it is! It's a type of Russian cheese!"

"It doesn't even have vowels!"

"You're being a bad sport!"

"I'm not going to stand for this!" I exclaimed. I grabbed the dictionary I had placed on the railing behind me. This wasn't my first experience of Mamie making up words. I opened it to the B section when Colonel Andrew Goodpaster, my Staff Secretary, stepped onto the balcony. He looked worried.

"What is it?" I asked, desperate that his message would not disturb my break that had only begun that day.

"We have a situation, Mr. President. We need to go to the Oval Office."

I sulked for a moment. Then I turned back to Mamie and lifted my dictionary, so it was facing her.

"This isn't over."

☆☆☆☆☆

"THE SOVIET SATELLITE orbited Earth in two hours. Subsequent orbits took ninety-five minutes. It sent signals back to its masters with two transmitters," Deputy Secretary of Defense Donald Quarles explained. We stood in the Oval Office with Goodpaster, Adams, Secretary of State Foster Dulles, and UN Ambassador Lodge. "TASS has already broadcast this news to the world." Quarles was referring to the Soviet news agency.

"I see," I muttered. "Does it have a name?"

"They're calling it 'Sputnik.'"

"What does that translate to?"

"'Traveling companion.'"

"Did the Soviet Union just win the Cold War?" Lodge asked. Lodge was part of a Republican political dynasty and had served as Senator, a tenure that was interrupted by his resigning to fight in World War II.

Adams scoffed.

"Oh, please! This is nothing more than a celestial basketball!"

"We can't afford to be arrogant, Sherman!" Lodge exclaimed. "This is going to strengthen Soviet prestige around the world and weaken ours. And we can count on a deliberate effort from the Democrats in the new Congressional session to destroy public confidence in the President."

"All that will be done in a week!" Adams replied.

"This is more serious than a mere prestige issue," Foster interjected. "The Soviets can claim they were successfully testing the technology for an intercontinental ballistic missile and will be able to fire nuclear weapons into any part of the world."

That made my advisors a shade paler! I had to restore calm.

"There's no point in trying to minimize what the Soviets have accomplished," I asserted. "This wasn't a surprise, either. The Soviets informed the International Geophysical Year of this project." I was referring to my administration's initiative to foster dialogue on scientific matters between West and East. "Our newspapers have been anticipating this for months. As far as Soviet ICBMs are concerned, the CIA's U2 Program has shown that they're still several years away from being able to launch a missile into the United States."

I approved of the U2 program after Khrushchev rejected my Open Skies proposal that would have allowed our governments to monitor one another in 1955. The U2s flew over the Soviet Union eighty thousand feet in the air, which the Soviets could see but not hit with antiaircraft fire. The pictures they brought back could show parking spot lines. I plotted each U2 route myself with CIA deputy director Richard Bissell. They gave us vital information about Soviet national security and were the equivalent of 1940s code breaking.

"Congress doesn't know about the U2 Program!" Lodge declared with a rising inflection. "Our critics will claim this is a defeat, no matter the facts. I can already tell you that Senators Symington and Jackson are going to say that your obsession with the national debt allowed the Soviets to get ahead of America in space and missiles."

"Maybe I'm stupid on this thing, but I don't think America must be first place in everything," I countered. "Prestige is a shallow concept, and I would opt for substance over fluff. We need to concentrate on security, stability, and prosperity, which the nuclear deterrent allows. And we need to think about the long-term; forty and fifty years down the line. What type of situation we're going to leave for future generations, like my grandchildren. We'll wreck all of that if we let this scare us and blow up the debt when it isn't necessary."

"I'm just saying that we can expect to take it from all sides on this— that the Soviets beat us because you're more interested in golf. And Johnson will surely bring Warner von Braun to testify to Congress on how we're not spending enough on space."

"I'm not inclined to care what that Nazi thinks."

"But Johnson will do it to hurt you and help himself."

"It's not as if we don't have a space program," Quarles chimed, "though it had a late start because Truman only spent seven million on it before leaving office."

"Can you remind us when our satellite program started?" Adams asked.

"1954. It's called Project Vanguard, a civilian effort under the National Advisory Committee for Aeronautics."

"What about ICBMs?" Adams asked.

"Different military branches are competing—"

"Can someone explain the connection between satellites and the ICBM?" Lodge interrupted to Quarles' frustration. "I think I missed that part."

"Satellites and long-range missiles use the same booster," I said as simply as possible.

"Then why not give the satellite science to the Air Force and Navy to speed up both projects?"

"Because the satellite technology was meant to be given to the world for the benefit of human learning and advancement. That means it needs to stay under civilian control and not the military."

"So, we'll just let the Soviets keep getting ahead of us? This will affect the midterm elections next year," Lodge said.

"I would argue that the Russians have in fact done us a good turn, unintentionally," Quarles suggested.

"How's that?"

"They've established the concept of freedom of international space by flying Sputnik over so many countries without asking for permission."

"That's true," I muttered as I put a finger to my chin. "They won't be able to object to us flying satellites over them because they've already done it to us. I'm hoping that we can use satellites for intelligence gathering within a few years." I referred to the Corona Program. "I know the Soviets' anti-aircraft fire can't reach the U2s, but it still makes me nervous to send planes over Russia without Khrushchev's permission."

"Frankly, Mr. President," Foster began, "if Secretary Quarles is right and this confirms that airspace doesn't count as sovereignty, then we can say that U2 falls under that."

"I suspect that Khrushchev will make a distinction between our world and the heavens," I countered. The conversation had run its course, or at least that's what I decided. "I really don't think this is as big of a deal as it may seem on the surface. We know from the U2s that the Soviets aren't as technologically advanced as they may claim."

"Maybe it's time to reveal the U2 to the public," Foster suggested. "That way we could dispel any concerns about the Soviets leading us."

I shook my head.

"That would embarrass the Russians and put us in an awkward moral position."

"It would dispel any fears the country might have about Soviet missiles," Lodge argued.

"My decision is 'no.' Let's not overreact and target our investments into long-term substance like infrastructure, schools, and an appropriate amount of defense as opposed to short term prestige. Now if you gentlemen excuse me, I have to get to a bridge game."

☆☆☆☆☆

OCTOBER 9, 1957

"THERE WILL BE a statement by the President that we will now distribute to you ladies and gentlemen here," Hagerty told the press corps. "From this moment on, however, we are under Press Conference rules, and nobody can leave the room or the balcony. My girls will now distribute the statement."

"He is still coming at 10:30, is he not?" Ray Sherer of NBC asked.

"Yes," Hagerty replied.

The statement explained the history of our satellite program, based on the conversation I discussed earlier. The statement also congratulated the Soviets for putting a satellite into orbit. I arrived behind the podium at 10:30. To say I wasn't excited for this would be an understatement. Lodge's prediction of a national panic was accurate, and I awaited a pounding.

"Please, sit down. Good morning, ladies and gentlemen. Do you have any questions you'd like to ask me?"

Charles von Fremd of CBS asked the first question.

"Mr. President, Khrushchev claims we are now entering a period when conventional planes, bombers, and fighters, will be confined to museums because they are outmoded by the missiles which Russia claims she has now perfected; and Khrushchev's remarks would seem to indicate he wants us to believe that our Strategic Air Command is now outmoded. Do you think that SAC is outmoded?"

"No," I replied. "I believe it would be dangerous to predict what science is going to do in the next twenty years, but it is going to be a very considerable time in this realm, just as in any other, before the old is completely replaced by the new, and even then, it will be a question of comparative costs and accuracy in the methods of delivery.

"It is going to be a long-term. It is not revolutionary, a revolutionary process that will take place in the reequipping of defense forces, it will be evolutionary."

This answer hid a growing concern of mine that Khrushchev was right in the sense that bombers were becoming outdated and having all our nuclear weapons in bombers at Air Force bases made them vulnerable to attack by theoretical Soviet missiles. But I wasn't about to tell that to the press!

I never liked speaking on television; it made my stomach do somersaults, but the months of intense stress and increased pressure of Sputnik led me to sweat in all the wrong places. I called on the next reporter.

"Hazel Markel of NBC. Mr. President, in light of the great faith which the American people have in your military knowledge and leadership, are you saying at this time with the Russian satellite whirling about the world, you are not overly concerned about our nation's security?"

Oh, God, another panicked question. This agitated me. I wanted to stamp out this scared attitude as best I could.

"So far as the satellite itself is concerned, that does not raise my apprehensions, not one iota."

Every reporter in the room feverishly wrote down that quote. I couldn't have guessed how much that was going to bite me in the butt! It fed right into my critics' argument that I was indifferent to the Soviets beating us in satellites and missiles, even though I knew from the U2 that they weren't.

"I see nothing at this moment, at this stage of development that is significant in that development as far as security is concerned. We could have produced an orbiting satellite before now, but to the detriment of scientific goals and military progress. Now does anyone have a question on another topic?"

A hand went up. It was Bill Lawrence from the *New York Times*.

"My question is still adjacent to this Sputnik business. Is that alright, Mr. President?"

"That's fine, Lawrence," I answered regrettably.

"Thank you, Mr. President. Would you say this question of our investment in science vis-à-vis the Soviets has affected your thinking of federal funding for education since the debate this summer over your administration's legislation?"

"*Hm*." I stepped back for a moment and pondered the question. This one *was* more interesting than I expected. I chose my words slowly.

"I still believe that there are very grave dangers that would accompany any initiation of general federal support for these institutions. In saying this I do not mean, of course, to be opposed to support in special areas to meet special and pressing needs of the government."

"Would you describe your main objections, if you don't mind?"

"I would say that it's two-fold. My first concern is that the government would have to take money from the country's taxes to give it to localities, implying a centralization of wisdom in Washington that doesn't exist.

"The other, of course, is that institutions like schools leaning on the federal government can lead to federal domination of them. And I just think that leaves open a lot of dangerous possibilities of future bureaucrats or Presidents or whatever taking advantage of that dominance to control the education and beliefs of entire generations of young people. That, to me at least, would appear to be a step toward tyranny."

"Thank you, Mr. President."

The press conference moved on. It was frustrating at the time, but the next day I learned how badly my critics judged my performance. A liberal political cartoonist drew me hiding under bed covers, saying, "Do not disturb—not one iota."

☆☆☆☆☆

OCTOBER 13, 1957

STRESS ATE AT my bones as the public criticism continued. Senator Mansfield, with more than a little hyperbole, claimed that Sputnik threatened America's existence. Edward Teller, the father of the hydrogen bomb, claimed that it was the worst attack on our country since Pearl Harbor. I lost weight, falling below the 175 pounds I tried so hard to maintain.

I instructed Adams to arrange a meeting with the country's top scientists. My scientists came to the White House for our conference. They were all Democrats, as far as I knew, but I didn't care. Science doesn't have a political party and I found that scientists were the only people who came to Washington who weren't out for themselves. What bothered me more was that they looked young enough to be my sons.

James Killian, the President of MIT, shook my hand as the meeting started.

"You look well, Mr. President."

I chuckled.

"Thank you, but you're talking to an old dodo."

"Am I right in understanding that it's your birthday tomorrow?"

"That's correct."

"I won't ask for the number."

"Oh, I don't care. I'm turning sixty-seven."

"I just want it on the record that I didn't ask."

"Noted." I turned to the other scientists. "Welcome to the White House. I personally think that the press is overblowing the Sputnik issue, but there are a couple of concerns I wanted to discuss with you. The first is that the American people appear hysterical over this issue, and I'd like your thoughts on what we can do to reassure them of our country's scientific prowess in a way that is constructive and worth the money. The second is that I want to explore all feasible ways to speed up the development of America's satellite and missile programs. Let's start with you. Can you tell me your name again?"

"I'm Dr. Isidor Rabi."

"And where are you from?"

"Columbia."

"Wonderful. What are your thoughts on the issues that I've described?"

"Today we can see a number of advantages on our side. But the Russians have picked up a tremendous momentum. Unless we take vigorous action, they could pass us swiftly, just as in a period of 20 to 30 years we caught up with Western Europe and then left it far behind."

"You really think Sputnik signals that big a challenge on the scientific front?"

"Yes, Mr. President. That's my interpretation of what's happened in the past week and a half."

"And what about you?" I asked another scientist at the conference. "Can you give me your name and credentials? I'd like to know who I'm talking to."

"Dr. E. H. Land. I'm the president of the Polaroid Corporation. It's a pleasure to meet you, Mr. President."

"Likewise."

"I would go further in my estimation of the problem than Dr. Rabi. The main thing that I'm worried about is how little Americans appear to value science compared to the Soviets."

"Really?"

"Yes, sir. Americans are no longer great builders for the future but rather are preoccupied with mass producing things we've already achieved. That's not the path to future progress. The Soviets, on the other hand, are pioneers. They regard science as an essential tool and as a way of life. In Russia, science is being pursued, almost universally, both for enjoyment and for the strength of the country. America would read a tremendous return if your administration could inspire our youth to pursue a whole variety of scientific adventures. We have to find a way to give science the popular appeal in this country that it has in the Soviet Union."

"Well, wait just a second," I said, "my administration did approve of the Enrico Fermi Award through the Atomic Energy Commission. It awards a gold medal and a $50,000 prize for physicists."

"But the Fermi Award is for adults, yes? Or am I misunderstanding it?"

"Hm. Fair enough."

"Yeah, I mean, I thought it had gone to Dr. von Neumann, Dr. Lawrence, men like that."

"You're right. It was my mistake. My apologies. But I would question the assumption that the Soviets are trying to inspire their people to enter scientific pursuits. My impression of their higher educational system is that they cull the best minds and ruthlessly spurn the rest. I think you're right to say that we need to do a better job inspiring America's youths. But that is a long-term issue with unlimited follow-through. Something along those lines will help reduce the public outcry over Sputnik."

"Can I offer an idea?"

"Of course, Dr. Rabi."

"In the modern age, the President is going to face a greater number of issues that contain a scientific component. It might prove useful for you to establish a full-time scientific advisor to the White House staff. That would help stimulate interest in science. And I think Dr. Killian would be the perfect choice."

Dr. Killian blushed at the suggestion. I smiled and nodded.

"I'll mention that to Adams later today."

My meeting with economic advisors the next day was less pleasant. Treasury Secretary Anderson and Federal Reserve Chairman Martin both warned of an emerging recession as a result of the Sputnik panic. They predicted that unemployment would rise by over a million and that our federal revenue would be $4 billion short of earlier estimates.

What a great birthday gift.

☆☆☆☆☆

NOVEMBER 4, 1957

THINGS GOT EVEN worse in the succeeding weeks. I had nothing to tell the critics or the country that wouldn't have jeopardized national security, like revealing the U2 program. We were weeks away from a satellite launch, while the Soviets launched a second one that was six times bigger and twice as fast as Sputnik. It carried a dog named Laika. Khrushchev called the satellite "Mutnik," which I felt was corny. The American people were less scared than angry about this second launch since Khrushchev sent Laika to her certain death as she entered orbit.

My administration appointed a panel of national security experts to analyze the Cold War regarding the nuclear arms race, space race, and the like to recommend America's response to Sputnik. The idea was to bring new minds into the government who could think outside the box. The panel produced a report titled "Deterrence and Survival in the Nuclear Age." My National Security Council and I met with the leaders of the report in the Cabinet Room of the White House. We exchanged pleasantries and took our seats.

The panel's leader was Walter Gaither, a lawyer, banker, and the president of the Ford Foundation. I was vaguely familiar with him. I was more concerned with the man sitting to his right, who I would have bet the Gettysburg Farm was the true author of the report. Paul Nitze. Nitze was the author of NSC 68, which Truman had implemented during the Korean War. NSC 68 identified Soviet expansion as an existential threat and recommended that the US spend 60 billion dollars on defense annually, quadrupling what it was spending before the report. Nitze's argument was that a Soviet nuclear strike on the US was inevitable by the mid-1950s and that we needed a colossal conventional military to carry on the fight. I thought that argument was crazy as hell because it put us on the trajectory to World War III and was guaranteed to bankrupt America by the end of the decade. Put simply, it gave us the options of forfeiting the Cold War or going nuclear. I threw out NSC 68 upon assuming the presidency and replaced it with the New Look, which is the cheaper nuclear deterrent that

I described earlier. Nitze was a leading critic of my strategy of threatening massive nuclear retaliation in response to communist aggression and advocated for Flexible Response instead, which proposed using the military to combat the communists in smaller situations than my threshold allowed for and which was gaining popularity among my critics.

I invited them to begin their presentation. Gaither took the lead.

"Our report identifies six points of concern.

"Point one is that the Soviet Gross National Product, although currently a third of ours, is expected to grow faster than ours, particularly when judging against the current recession.

"Point two is that despite their lower GNP, the Soviets are still able to spend as much on defense as we are.

"Point three is that the Soviets have enough fissionable material for at least fifteen hundred nuclear weapons in forty-five hundred long- and short-range jet bombers, and 250 to 300 long range submarines, as well as extensive air defense systems.

"Point four is that the Soviets are currently producing ballistic missiles with a seven-hundred-mile range and have been for over a year.

"Point five is that the Soviets could, by 1959, launch an attack on the US homeland with 100 ICBMs that carry megaton nuclear warheads.

"Point six is that, if such an attack happens, our civilian population would be unprotected, and the bombers carrying our nuclear arsenal in the Strategic Air Command would be vulnerable.

"This evidence clearly indicates an increasing threat from the Soviet Union that will become critical by 1959 or 1960. This means the next two years are vital to American national security and failing to act at once, in our opinion, creates an unacceptable risk."

The National Security Council swallowed every word of these basic conclusions. I remained skeptical because this wasn't my first tango with Nitze. I had to get them to reveal their end goal.

"What do you recommend?"

"The first step would be to build a system of fall-out shelters across the country."

"What's the price tag on that project?"

"We think $25 billion would be a good start."

My face must have become a shade paler when I heard that number. Gaither continued.

"We'll also want to improve our air defenses, expand our conventional military forces, step up our anti-submarine activities, increase the Strategic Air Command's offensive power—"

"How much are you thinking?" I interrupted.

"We recommend expanding our intermediate missiles from 60 to 240 and our long-range missiles from 80 to 600."

My God!

Gaither turned to Nitze.

"You're particularly passionate about the last point. Would you like to do the honors, Paul?"

My stomach clenched.

Nitze said, "We think it is vital to America's survival to alter our strategic doctrine on nuclear weapons. Right now, the authority to order a nuclear strike is monopolized by the President. We propose that the nuclear arsenal be disbursed so local commanders who, when conducting operations around the world, can authorize a nuclear strike on a limited scale against enemy forces. This would make nuclear weapons a usable part of our arsenal and relieve pressure on our conventional forces without them being the apocalyptic all-or-nothing option they are currently."

What? What? *That was the point!* The nuclear deterrent was meant to prevent war and to make the use of nuclear weapons so massive that no one would ever *dare* use them. It would both hold back the communists *and* hold back people like Nitze and my advisors and the critics and everyone else who treated using nuclear weapons as the default option in national security. Allowing them to be used by field commanders on a limited scale opened the door to their continued use and, eventually, Armageddon. That's why the only sane solution was to threaten an all-out nuclear response and strive for disarmament. But I was ready for the same argument that my administration had over and over again. My advisors pushed me to use nuclear weapons in every crisis—in Korea, in Vietnam, in defense of Formosa, and when the Soviets threatened intervention over Suez and *did* intervene in Hungary. And here it was again. *Again!* Me, all alone, simultaneously holding back communism while also holding back the consensus of the American government.

"I'm afraid to say that you boys missed several points," I began and crossed my arms. "The Free World already has forces around the globe to threaten the Soviets at multiple points, so this enormous buildup you've described really isn't necessary. But I appreciate what you've done and will be happy to review your report, though it can't be a blueprint for our national security."

"To what specifically do you object?" Nitze asked. He clearly was trying not to glare at me in anger.

"Well, the first thing is that I have no intention of giving up my control of the nuclear arsenal or diverging from the New Look."

"Mr. President, the New Look isn't a credible threat."

"It seemed credible when it checked Mao's aggression toward Formosa and Khrushchev's during Suez."

"I would question the extent to which it *was* the factor that resolved those situations. Either way, Sputnik and increased Soviet technology means that Massive Retaliation has lost whatever credibility it might have had. The Soviets can hit the US now. No one's going to believe that we'll wage World War III—that we'll sacrifice Chicago to defend Bonn."

"I don't agree, and we might as well move on to—"

"Wait a moment, Mr. President," said Chairman of the Joint Chiefs Nathan Twining. He leaned forward in his chair. "This is an interesting idea."

"You can't be serious," I replied.

"Why not?" Twining's family had a continuous presence in the US military since the French and Indian War. He served in the South Pacific in World War II.

"Nathan, using nuclear weapons on local or regional objectives is *crazy*. World opinion would *despise* us."

"But it would save American lives." Twining put his left index finger to his lip.

I threw my hands out to the side in exasperation.

"Not in the long run. America can't use its military without regard for the political repercussions of such a course of action. Imagine if every Air Force officer you ever served with had access to nuclear weapons to defend themself. Their radar would inform them of a flock of enemy bombers, and they'd be on the spot of making the ultimate decision of risking attack or unleashing nuclear arms! What would a field commander do in such a contingency? Does he not use every weapon at hand to defend himself and his forces? I would bet ten out of ten times that he would defend his troops and obliterate thousands or millions of civilians in the process."

"The panel is right to say that Massive Retaliation isn't credible," Twining argued. "Like, for example, you wouldn't start World War III if the Vietminh attacked South Vietnam tomorrow, I assume. The logical move would be to bomb Chinese bases and supply routes."

"But if you're using nuclear bombs on those targets you're causing World War III anyway," I argued, raising my right hand to symbolize the escalation.

"That means our only other option is to appease the communists every time they make a move. We'd be letting them chip away at the Free World one piece at a time because we're unwilling to use nuclear weapons on a limited scale or carry through on Massive Retaliation."

Foster Dulles cleared his throat.

"As the co-architect of Massive Retaliation, I would like a word. I visit President Eisenhower in the Oval Office every evening at six to discuss the state of the world. And in those discussions, we've discussed why it is that the Soviet government has repeatedly rejected our peace offers. Atoms for Peace, Open Skies, so on, and so on. It couldn't just be the global ambitions of the communist dictators. Nor their Slavic temperaments. The fact that *we're* religious and *they're* atheists? Perhaps. That sounds closer. That feeds into the fact that *we* believe in morality while *they* believe that any measure is acceptable to advance communism. But one thing that the President and I have agreed on, from the beginning, is that they're not suicidal, which means that they wouldn't risk nuclear retaliation. The truth is that we *don't* need ICBMs the way they do. We can target their hydroelectric developments with a nuclear strike *today* and tank the Soviet economy for a generation. That alone means Khrushchev won't start a war, and it's why President Eisenhower and I felt comfortable drawing a line and threatening war over Korea, Formosa, and Suez. All that to say that I don't foresee any serious changes in the strategic balance following Sputnik and therefore would advise the President against implementing this report."

I was stunned. Foster Dulles joining me was a nice change of pace in these debates. But how extreme do you have to be to lose Foster Dulles?

"Even if you disagree with our argument about the limited use of nuclear weapons, the administration would still be wise to authorize the other pieces of the report," Gaither asserted.

"Do you break down the numbers on costs?" I asked.

"Of course, Mr. President."

"May I see?"

Nitze handed Gaither a paper, who in turn handed it to me. I took a deep breath after I scanned it. Another debate on the horizon.

"Gentlemen, are you aware that these recommendations would have the government spend nearly $200 billion on defense?"

"Yes, Mr. President," Gaither replied.

"And that that's over five times what we're spending right now?"

"We believe that this shows the scale of inadequacy in our current defense preparedness." Gaither's forearms rested on the table while pages of his report were scattered around him.

"You would have us spend $25 billion just on fallout shelters in case of a nuclear attack. But do you have a contingency for how we pump air into the shelters if a nuclear strike destroys our nation's power grids?" I asked.

"We would have to figure that out."

"$25 billion alone is a huge sum of money." I looked Gaither in the eye. Then I looked at Nitze, Twining, and the others. "It would require the military to take over the economy to implement it. The military would take over our society. Maybe forever. This plan would have us adopt the system of Adolf Hitler."

"I'm afraid I don't—"

"I was a staff officer for Douglas MacArthur when he was Army Chief of Staff back when Herbert Hoover was President. You boys were probably still in school then. But President Hoover asked General MacArthur for a contingency plan for how the government and the private sector could cooperate in case of an eventual world war. It won't surprise you to learn that MacArthur pawned off this research project on me. Took a long time. But I drafted a blueprint for how such cooperation could occur. Ten years later, when the Japanese attacked Pearl Harbor, President Roosevelt pulled my blueprint out of whatever dusty file it had been sitting in to implement the Arsenal of Democracy. The Arsenal of Democracy defeated fascism and saved civilization. But it never really went away. Because, you see, the Cold War immediately replaced World War II and we had to maintain a large-scale military to defend our allies and contain communism.

"I agreed with all of this. It was the only option short of letting the communists rule the world. So, we couldn't disarm. But I've always been keenly aware of the other extreme, as well. That is to say, there is more than one way to lose the Cold War. We could arm ourselves to the teeth, beyond what is needed. To allow America to become a Garrison State. And it seems to me that this report acts as a perfect blueprint for the

Garrison State. I don't see the point of opposing tyranny abroad if we're going to implement it at home in the process.

"Then there's the fact that spending $200 billion on defense would be the *fastest* way to lose the Cold War because even if we built a Garrison State it would *bankrupt* the country. Power built on debt is power that will crumble. Excessive spending causes deficits, which in turn causes inflation, which will reduce the equipment and manpower that each dollar can buy. So, this astronomical amount of defense spending plays *right* into Khrushchev's hands by throwing liberal democracy down the toilet in exchange for a Garrison State that destroys the purpose of what we're protecting and shatters our economy beyond repair.

"I said in a speech after Stalin died that the jet plane that flies over your head costs $750,000, which is more than a man who earns $10,000 a year would make in a lifetime. No society can sustain that. Now, of course, the communists are refusing to make peace, so we'll have to sustain something of the sort for the time being, but to me it's clear that those costs need to be contained to only what is *necessary*. Otherwise, again, we would bankrupt ourselves and forfeit the Cold War. Where did that leave us? Well, not with NSC 68. That was for damn sure. That blueprint wasn't much better than this one. No, the only option that allowed us to both contain communism and preserve a healthy economy, for the long haul, so we can outlast the Kremlin, was to build a nuclear deterrent. It's cheap and it's frightening to both sides of the Cold War, which makes World War III less likely. I don't see how a deviation from the New Look can result in anything but disaster."

The room was silent. Foster finally chuckled at my monologue.

"It seems to me, sir," Defense Secretary McElory began, "that you're keeping us locked on a suicide course. I've agreed with everything the panel has said so far, and I don't understand why we hired them if you're going to reject every finding and save every nickel—"

"If you go to any military installation in the world where the American flag is flying and tell the commander that Ike says he'll give them an extra star for his shoulder if he cuts his budget, there'll be such a rush to cut costs that you'll have to get out of the way," I declared, my hands in fists.

"I would add to that that the report is greatly overstating the risk of a Soviet strike," Foster said. "The risk is low enough that we shouldn't accept such a great financial cost."

"You would put dollars over lives?" Nitze asked.

"If I'm being frank, this report doesn't even understand the problem of the Cold War," Foster shot back, quickly pushing his glasses up the bridge of his nose. "You've only looked at it from a military perspective. But the international struggle is not just military. The Soviet Union made its greatest gains—its greatest seizures of territory and people—from 1945 to 1950, when it had the ravages of war to repair and when only the United States had the atomic bomb. You haven't once mentioned our greatest asset, which is our global alliance system. And this proposal would throw that system away because we'd be spending so much on things like a national shelter program that the Europeans would never be able to afford, and we'd be clearly writing them off."

Gaither and Nitze were red in the face. So were several of my advisors. I tried to issue an olive branch to nullify any hurt feelings.

"My team and I will study your recommendations. One by one. But we really mustn't panic nor become complacent. We should decide what needs to be done and do it—avoiding extremes. I personally think that putting more of SAC on alert was your best idea. We need to disperse our SAC bases to make them less vulnerable to a Soviet strike."

"Thank you, Mr. President," Nitze said, accepting my olive branch. "Another idea detailed in the longer report is to build blast shelters that would protect SAC runways by tunneling them into mountains."

My eyes would have seen my brain if I didn't catch myself.

"That would also be too expensive to be feasible."

War broke out again. Gaither jabbed his finger onto his table.

"Even spending only $22.5 billion on the shelter program could save fifty million lives when the Soviets attack."

"If a wave of a hand could create those shelters we'd of course be better off with them than without them," Foster countered. "But it's hard to sustain simultaneously an offensive and defensive mood in a population. For our security, we have been relying above all on our capacity for retaliation. From this policy we should not deviate now. To do so would imply we are turning to a fortress America concept."

I turned to my right hand.

"You really are a militant Presbyterian, aren't you?"

That raised laughter around the room. Nitze continued glaring at me as the meeting ended. I was sorry he was so frustrated by our disagreement, but I couldn't accept his argument that World War III was inevitable, and we just had to get ready for it. The entire focus of my presidency was to avoid nuclear war and to build a lasting peace. The world would need to rebuild, even if it was only the United States and the Soviet Union that were destroyed, which they almost certainly wouldn't be. Who would fill the vacuum and become the dominant power under that hypothetical? Probably the Germans.

Now, wouldn't that be an ironic end to my career?

☆☆☆☆☆

NOVEMBER 25, 1957

I MET MOHAMMED V, the king of Morocco, at Washington National Airport and escorted him to the Blair House. He was to have dinner with Mamie and me at the White House that evening. I had a short nap and a light lunch before returning to the Oval Office to do some work and sign some papers.

Do you remember when I said things had gotten worse? Well by this point they were even worse than that. Our first satellite test exploded, to Khrushchev's delight. Worse than that, Nitze leaked the Gaither Report's existence to the press after I rejected most of the report's recommendations. I hit the roof when I heard that. Senator Johnson demanded I release the report. I refused and Johnson began a Senate investigation into my administration. Nitze then released the report to the *Washington Post*.

All my critics jumped on me at once. My Army friends, men I'd served with since West Point and who'd been mad at me for cutting the Army's budget to invest in the Air Force, claimed I was a traitor for disagreeing with Gaither and Nitze. In reality each branch wanted more and more funding because each wanted to win a war by itself, as if they learned nothing from World War II. There was never a limit that I could spend on them that would let them say the country was safe. Oh, and believe me when I say they were giddy to authorize limited nuclear strikes. And Congress believed their every word because the Pentagon had 130 staff members working as Congressional liaisons.

The Congressional Democrats called me a reactionary fossil for prioritizing the national debt. Why am I not surprised about the radical spenders? They said I was more interested in money than in people, even though there's nothing more inhumane to *people* than deliberately taking away the value of their money, which is what deficits and inflation cause.

Most insidious of all was the claim that I had allowed the Soviets to get a lead in the nuclear arms race and therefore threaten our existence. I believe this "Missile Gap" notion came from Joseph Aslop, a reporter who was my *worst* critic. He declared me as bad a President as James Buchanan. And, oh boy, did Senator Johnson jump all over the Missile Gap! He wailed like a banshee on the Senate floor about "how long" would America have to wait before I took the Missile Gap seriously. I'm not embarrassed to tell you that I mimicked his routine in the Oval Office, to the amusement of my advisors. God, how much my relationship with Johnson had fallen. In my first term we collaborated on defeating the Bricker Amendment. I'll spare you most of the details, but the amendment intended to strip the presidency of its power to negotiate with other countries. I told Jim Hagerty at the time that if it's true that when you die the things that bothered you the most are engraved on your skull, I'm sure I'll have the mud and dirt of France during the invasion and the name of Senator Bricker. Now, I would say it's Johnson—between undermining my voting rights bill, opposing the intervention in Little Rock, and claiming the Soviets would be dropping rockets on us from space as easily as children drop rocks on cars from freeway overpasses.

I'd never been criticized on this scale before. It really got to me. Claiming I was soft on defense. Me! My whole life was dedicated to defending this country. And they were having an effect. My approval rating fell below 50 percent for the first time.

Enough whining. I had to sign the forms on the Oval Office desk before I got ready for dinner with the king. I picked up a pen. That was weird. Felt a bit dizzy. I had to ignore that and reached for the first form on the pile. My fingers couldn't grip it properly. What the hell? I tried again and pulled it to me, though I crumpled it in the process. Whoops. I tried to scan the form, but I couldn't read the words. What is this? I dropped my pen without noticing. Okay, Ike, pull it together. I picked up my pen, only to drop it again. Picked it up. Dropped it. And again. And again.

I leapt to my feet to clear my head, but my hip cracked into the desk, causing me to lose my footing. My hand darted out and grabbed my chair to catch myself from falling to the ground. I sat back down and clicked a button on my desk that buzzed Mrs. Whitman. She came within a moment. I looked to her in desperation.

"Some . . . ting's wong—" I coughed, trying to clear my throat. "I— can—"

"Mr. President?" she asked as she reached for my hand to comfort me.

"Almost—" That was good. *A complete word.* "Almost landed on the table."

Table? I meant "desk." What the hell was this? Why did I say the wrong word? That wasn't like me! God, I felt so helpless!

"You stay right here, Mr. President," Mrs. Whitman said. "I'll be back in one second! You just stay here!"

I felt desperate, scared, and alone for the moments until she came back. She brought Colonel Goodpaster with her. Goodpaster monitored my strange behavior for a few seconds.

"He's had a head seizure."

"What should we do?" Mrs. Whitman asked.

"We have to get him to his room." Goodpaster touched my arm. "Mr. President, I think we should get you to bed."

I nodded. Goodpaster guided me to the East Wing. He helped me undress and tucked me in.

What happened next was quite strange. I wasn't asleep but I wasn't exactly awake either. My brain entered a fog. I started seeing endless trees and I felt sweaty and humid. I knew this place, though it took a moment to crystallize.

Panama. Where I'd served for three years in the early 1920s, after Icky died. Why was I in Panama? Was this supposed to be Heaven or Hell?

"Major Eisenhower?"

That voice. I knew it in an instance. It was soft spoken. Formal. Polite. I turned and saw *him*. The most important mentor of my life.

"General Conner."

"It's been a long time, Major."

My eyes welled up. I knew he didn't mind.

"I need you, General. More than I have in a long time. You were everything to me. You saved me from a court-martial. From the misery of Icky's death. You built me into the officer I am."

"I saw the potential within you from the moment we met. And you fulfilled my vision for you."

"That there would be another world war—"

"And that you and George Marshall would lead us to victory. You even used the lessons we discussed regarding multinational coalitions and Clausewitz. I was honored to live to see it."

Tears ran down my cheeks.

"That means more to me than you can know, General. Especially after these past few months. I'm so tired. I wish I could retire to Gettysburg with Mamie. Build up a library of Plato and Shakespeare, like the one you had. Though mine would have some westerns, too."

"You can't do that, Major. Not yet."

"But why!"

"Because you haven't finished your duty."

"My duty!" My face fell. "I am so *tired* of my duty. It's shaped every moment, every decision, of my life since I was *ten*. I'm sick of thinking about it. When is it done?"

"It never is. But you particularly can't give up now."

"What do you mean?"

"You have to stop the Gaither Report from being implemented."

"But it seems that *everyone* else says it's the right thing. Maybe I'm wrong."

"No, Major, you're not. Remember when we discussed the Civil War?"

"Do I? We spent a year on it in Panama."

"And who did we settle on as the true visionary of that war?"

"Ulysses Grant."

"That's right. And why was that?"

"Because he knew that the only way to defeat the Confederacy was to destroy their center of gravity. Lee's Army."

"That's right." Conner smiled at me the way he used to. A rarity, but always appreciated. "And you used the same concept to defeat the Nazis. You and I both know that America's center of gravity is its economy. Khrushchev wants us to overreact and destroy it for him. Your critics might not understand that, but you do. You have to stop it."

I nodded. Then my face sank again.

"I'm so tired of the criticism."

"Don't listen to it. You can't control what others say. Only your own actions. Greatness is knowing that virtue is enough."

"But how?"

"Take back the initiative. Define the debate on your own terms. And never forget to take your job seriously but never yourself."

I smiled.

"Thank you, General."

I awoke from napping a few hours later. I saw on a clock that my dinner with the king was approaching. I felt a bit better, so I put on a bathrobe and entered Mamie's adjourning room. She stood with John, our son, and with Dr. Snyder, who'd cared for me for years. They were mortified to see me standing.

"Get back to bed, Ike!" Mamie exclaimed. I ignored her.

"I suppose you are dis—" I couldn't think of the word "discussing." "I suppose you are talking about the dinner tonight." Maybe I wasn't better. God, that was annoying!

"We're not having this conversation!" Mamie declared.

"There is nothing the matter with me. I am perfectly alright. I need to get ready for dinner."

"Dad, that's a really bad idea," John said. "Vice President Nixon has already agreed to go in your place."

"If I cannot attend to my duties I am simply going to give up this job! Now that is all there is to it."

"Mr. President," Dr. Snyder began, "you had a spasm in one of the small capillaries in your brain. You need rest."

"What I need—"

"I won't go if you go!" Mamie declared. I grit my teeth but then saw her pale face. She was scared. For me. I finally nodded and agreed to go back to bed.

Dr. Snyder woke me up to check on me a few hours later. Mamie stood beside him. My eyes locked onto a painting that Mamie and I had in our bedroom.

"I love that . . . pain . . . ting," I struggled to say. Dr. Snyder ignored me. "That . . . cas . . . tle. We went there. Re . . . member, dear? Scott . . . land."

"Yes, Ike. I remember. Do you remember what it's called?"

The words wouldn't come to me. I shook my head.

"It's Culzean Castle."

"That's . . . right."

"How is he, Dr. Snyder?"

"The spasm is why he's struggling with his words, but he should recover within a couple of days."

"Will he be able to go to church with me on Thanksgiving?"

"Yes. I'll schedule an appointment for him at Walter Reed for a checkup."

"Thank you."

I turned to them, my eyes wide.

"I hope you . . . know. I plan to . . . go to the NA . . . TO conference next . . . month."

"Oh, no!" Mamie cried. "Dick Nixon will go in your place." My face thrashed to and fro. "Yes he will!"

"I'll go!" I insisted. "Or I'll . . . resign!"

I got my way, as it turns out. That happens every blue moon or so. I performed well at the NATO summit, proving to myself that I was back in the game.

☆☆☆☆☆

JANUARY 25, 1958

"ARE YOU READY for me, Mr. President?" Adams asked as he entered the Oval Office.

"Yes, Sherman, come in. Let's go over our agenda for this year." I sat behind the Oval Office desk while Adams sat on the other side.

"Where would you like to start?" Adams asked. He crossed his legs and placed a file folder on his lap.

"Can you give me an update on the Little Rock situation?"

"Of course. There's good news and bad news."

"Start with the good if you don't mind. I could use some good news." My clasped hands sat on the Oval Office desk.

"The good news is that the Airborne has been officially withdrawn. The Guard's still in place, but that's just to keep an eye on the situation."

"And the bad?"

"Faubus has announced that he intends to close the schools in Little Rock next school year and to privatize them in order to thwart any additional attempts at integration."

I groaned as I laid back in my chair. I rested my chin on my right fist.

"This was exactly what I sought to avoid in this whole integration issue."

"The DOJ will take him to court. He won't get away with this."

"I *know*. But it'll still keep the schools closed for the next school year. And it's so disruptive for these youngsters."

"Of course, Mr. President. Do you wish to move on to the next issue?"

I nodded and lowered my fist as my hand fell into my lap.

"My stroke in November scared me. It was my third health crisis in three years. I want a contingency in place in case I'm disabled before I leave office."

"That's a pretty cold-blooded way of talking about your own health."

"This is *important*, Sherman. I'm comfortable leaving the country in Dick's hands if push comes to shove. He performed well after my heart attack in '55. But we need a plan to guide us in case the situation isn't obvious."

"Such as?"

"The end of the disability would be determined by the President upon his declaration, in writing, that he is ready to resume his office."

"What if others disagree?"

"I think it should be the Vice President who disagrees. In that case, a committee would be formed by the three senior cabinet officials, the Speaker of the House, the President pro tempore of the Senate, and leaders of the minority parties in each chamber."

"What happens then?" Adams asked as he jotted down notes.

"I would be examined by four medical officials that the Cabinet chooses and who the American Medical Association determines as competent. I would leave office if they, and the committee, all determine it to be appropriate."

"This will require a Constitutional Amendment to be official."

"I don't really want to spend whatever political capital I have left on that. Just remember it if the situation arises."

"On what do you want to spend your political capital?" Adams looked up from his yellow note paper.

"One of this administration's biggest mistakes was to not properly anticipate the public's reaction to Sputnik. I assumed that because it wasn't a national security threat in actual terms that the people and the press would understand that. Well, they didn't, and I took the biggest beating of my life. Khrushchev is trying to scare us into bankruptcy and the supporters of the Gaither Report are trying to help him. We need a response that's more thoughtful and constructive than spending all our money on defense."

"We've already appointed Dr. Killian as your scientific advisor. What else do you have in mind?"

"Do you remember our education bill that failed in Congress last summer?" I leaned forward.

"Of course."

"I think we can frame the Sputnik issue as one of a lack of science education for our young people. So we would ask Congress to pass a new education bill that focuses on math and the sciences."

"Clever." Adams smiled, a rarity. "What would it include?"

"We should do a five-fold increase in the programs of the National Science Foundation. That will allow for greater scientific research and education and for training more science teachers. We should also enable the Department of Health, Education, and Welfare to set up ten thousand scholarships per year based on needs for capable high school students that are interested in math and science. We should also have federal grants that can match state grants that will help colleges expand their graduate programs."

"And this will all be permanent?"

"Yes," I said reluctantly.

"So, you've changed your mind on federal involvement in education?"

"I'm not sure you liberals swayed me as much as wanting to get more Democrats to vote for it. If I had my way, we would still make this a temporary arrangement."

"Well, you're still going to have to convince Rayburn." Adams was referring to the Speaker of the House.

"I know."

"He doesn't like your emphasis on needs testing and instead wants to give every student $500."

"But that doesn't make any sense. Some students don't *need* help getting an education. We need to help the ones that *do*."

"Maybe we can have some fun debating with him. He'll also want funding for students to learn foreign languages. Another pet project of his."

I chuckled.

"I feel like my lack of inclination on that issue might come from my own bad experiences. Surely, I've told you about my French tutor from when I served in Paris under Pershing."

"I don't believe you have."

"Oh, this was a funny one." I crossed my arms and laid back in my seat. "After a couple lessons he refused to teach me or take my money because I was so bad at it, he said it was unfair to *me!*"

Adams laughed.

"That's ironic given the amount you've lived abroad."

"Tell me about it! Certainly would make dealing with de Gaulle easier."

"Would anything really help that situation?"

"Probably not."

"Is the education bill the only legislative issue you want to frame with Sputnik?"

"No," I replied as I leaned forward again. "I also want a new civilian space agency. Not that I dislike NACA, but I want it retooled and better able to direct our space program."

"A successful test of Explorer 1 on the 31st will certainly build momentum for that."

"Exactly."

"And you *do* want it to be civilian and separate from the military?"

"Yes. Military research will require secrecy. I want space exploration to heighten global peace and imagination. We can make agreements with the Soviets on the peaceful use of space that can serve as a model for other untapped areas of secret, like Antarctica and the deep seas."

"Sounds wonderful."

"I think so. Dr. Killian and I think this new space program should focus on satellites that can improve life on Earth for everyone. Speed up communication, help with intelligence gathering. Things like that."

"What about putting a man on the moon?" Adams asked, extending his hand in a suggestive posture.

"Oh, Sherman, please! What a waste of money that would be!" I paused for a moment. "Now putting someone on Mars is a different story."

"How so?"

I shrugged.

"There might be life there."

"This is wild to think about, Mr. President. These bills will trigger a scientific revolution."

"Oh, it's remarkable how much science has changed since my youth, yet alone since Waterloo. We need to embrace the future. But we also shouldn't throw away what's worked in the past. Our values, and such. The world is shrinking, but countries will still matter and we need to respect that. I'm hearing predictions that, in the future, many segments of the economy might be automated. That's going to displace a lot of people and we need to think ahead to make sure those people are still respected and have self-worth so we can have the best of the past and the future."

"So," Adams said as he put his arm on his knee, "you seek a peaceful world of science and traditional values? That's what we'll spend your last three years building?"

"We're not out of the woods yet. Khrushchev's still a threat." I felt a surge of anxiety at my foe's mention.

"I know. But I'm optimistic about a disarmament agreement."

"I'd say I'm optimistic but cautious. And should we fail, I want to leave behind a security apparatus that guarantees us from attack."

"How so?"

"The one thing Gaither and Nitze were right about was that the Strategic Air Command is vulnerable because it's all bombers and Soviet missiles would easily target them. We need to put our nuclear arsenal in different tracks that will guarantee the Soviets can't hit them all and thus enable us to launch a second strike."

"I lack your military background, Mr. President. Can you elaborate?"

"Yes. Twining and I think that if we left some nuclear bombs in bombers, but put others in ground-based missiles and still others in submarines, that there's no way the Soviets could hit them all in one shot. We'd *always* be able to retaliate. That strengthens deterrence to the point where the communists wouldn't *dare* hit us, which eliminates the need for the rest of the Gaither Report."

"That's brilliant."

"Thanks," I chuckled. "It'll be the most powerful weapon system in human history. But it'll keep the peace."

Adams nodded. I shifted in my chair and looked at a portrait of George Washington, my hero, that sat on the wall behind me.

"God help this country when it has a President who doesn't know as much about the military as I do."

☆☆☆☆☆

DECEMBER 19, 1958

THE ATLAS ROCKET entered Earth's orbit. It carried SCORE with it. SCORE stood for the Signal Communication by Orbiting Relay Equipment. SCORE weighed over 150 pounds and had two tape recorders that were ready to transmit a radio signal to be picked up around the world.

NASA gave me the honor of being the first voice broadcast from space. My recording was the following:

"This is the President of the United States speaking. Through the marvels of scientific advance, my voice is coming to you from a satellite circling in outer space. My message is a simple one. Through this unique means, I convey to you and all mankind America's wish for peace on Earth and goodwill to men everywhere."

Last Act on the World Stage

The United States never lost a soldier or a foot of ground during my administration. We kept the peace. People ask how it happened—by God, it didn't just happen!
—Dwight Eisenhower

YOU'RE IN A pretty bad fix at the present time."

P resident Kennedy squinted as he absorbed what Air Force Chief of Staff Curtis Lemay had said. Did one of the Joint Chiefs mock the President?

"What did you just say?" Kennedy asked.

"You're in a pretty bad fix," Lemay repeated.

"Well, you're in there with me. Personally," Kennedy mumbled. The young President fought to control his nerves in front of the Chiefs as he unclasped his hands and put one skinny leg over the other.

Lemay's mouth evolved into a sinister grin. It was fun to bully the President, especially when the President was a mere patrol boat skipper with no other military experience.

President Kennedy, Attorney General Robert Kennedy, and Defense Secretary Robert McNamara were meeting with the Joint Chiefs of Staff. A U2 spy plane had photographed a Soviet missile buildup in Cuba on October 14. Kennedy's Executive Committee of advisors had advised him to blockade Cuba a few hours before this meeting with the Chiefs. The Chiefs did not agree with their civilian master.

452

"What about the risks of not hitting all the missiles?" Kennedy asked. "There's no guarantee an air strike would hit them all. And wouldn't an American attack on Cuba lead to the Soviets seizing West Berlin in response? And in the face of the Red Army we would have to unleash a nuclear response." Kennedy hoped the Chiefs were following his logic and understood why the Executive Committee thought bombing the missile sites was too dangerous. "I'm not saying this would start with nuclear weapons being used but it could lead to it. A nuclear war would start in the middle of Europe."

Lemay was unfamiliar with the chain reaction that Kennedy described. Lemay, who usually had a cigar sandwiched between his teeth, leaned forward.

"Air power can destroy any enemy. The United States has a huge advantage in intercontinental missiles over the Soviet Union. Why shouldn't we flex our muscles?"

McNamara anticipated Kennedy's reaction to Lemay's bluster. Lemay was McNamara's mentor and superior in World War II. Together, they directed the fire-bombing campaign of Japanese cities, killing hundreds of thousands. McNamara wondered if he and Lemay would have been executed for war crimes if Japan had won the war.

"This isn't an arm-wrestling contest between us and the Kremlin. We're talking about global stakes," Kennedy replied. Kennedy, like McNamara, was skeptical of the Joint Chiefs, having lost his respect for military officers and their bad advice in World War II.

"Simply doing a blockade of Cuba, or a quarantine, as you called it, is no more than a second Munich Agreement," Lemay said, referring to Neville Chamberlain's appeasement of Hitler in 1938 that encouraged Hitler's continued aggression.

"It may be even worse than that," Joint Chiefs Chairman Lyman Lemnitzer added. "Failing to take action over the Soviet missile sites in Cuba will be repeating the pattern of weakness that your administration has demonstrated in foreign affairs." Lemnitzer was a West Point graduate who served under General Eisenhower in the invasions of North Africa and Sicily in World War II.

"What pattern of weakness?" Kennedy asked, frustrated with the Joint Chiefs' disrespect.

Lemnitzer listed the events on his fingers.

"There was the Bay of Pigs, which failed to topple Castro and humiliated our country around the world. If we'd been allowed to deploy air power that would have gone differently."

Kennedy contained his frustration. He had gone over the Bay of Pigs hundreds of times in his head since its failure. His main conclusion reaffirmed his mistrust of his military advisors.

"Khrushchev cleaned your clock when you met him in Vienna. Then you did nothing when he built the Berlin Wall. Our concern is that this pattern of weakness is encouraging communist aggression and making our allies question American power."

"I'll acknowledge I screwed up in Vienna," Kennedy began, "but the Berlin Wall *did* stabilize the situation of the Soviets wanting to stop so many East Berliners fleeing to freedom. It lowered the risk of a clash between NATO forces and the Red Army."

"The Kremlin sees that sort of passivity as weakness, Mr. President. It's what led them to put their missiles in Cuba. It's why you need to take decisive military action to dislodge them and Castro from our flank and liberate Cuba."

"I really think that could escalate, potentially to a nuclear war."

Lemay chuckled.

"I wouldn't be afraid of that. The United States could fight a nuclear war if necessary and win it."

☆☆☆☆☆

"If World War III does happen, it's not going to be because of Nikita Khrushchev or Fidel Castro. It's going to be because of Curtis Lemay!" Kennedy exclaimed as he, Robert Kennedy, and McNamara returned to the Oval Office. The President was agitated, which usually happened when he visited the Pentagon.

"The Chiefs have one big advantage over me. If we do what they want us to do, none of us will be alive later to tell them they're wrong if it doesn't work." Kennedy took his seat behind the Resolute Desk. "I should have never trusted those sons of bitches with the Bay of Pigs thing. I knew the military brass were full of shit since the war."

Robert Kennedy and McNamara exchanged a glance, unsure what to say that would help the President.

"How could Khrushchev do this to me!" Kennedy exclaimed, resting his forearms on the Resolute Desk. "Things were going so much better between us! We were practically pen pals after how much we were writing each other this summer!" He slumped back in his chair. "How could he do this to me?"

"Geopolitics, I guess?" Robert said, unhelpfully. "Communist dreams of expansion?"

"But why did he put them there though?" Kennedy asked, referring to Cuba. "It's as if we began to put a *major* number of MRBMs in Turkey." He was referring to medium-range ballistic missiles. "Now that'd be *goddamned dangerous*, I would think."

McNamara's eyebrows pinched in confusion over his glasses.

"Well, we did it, Mr. President."

Kennedy looked up at McNamara.

"After the Bay of Pigs, you *did* put missiles in Turkey, to be tough on communism. Our missiles are now in range of the whole western Soviet Union, including Moscow and Leningrad."

Kennedy's face turned pale, embarrassed.

"Oh, that's right!"

"The Bay of Pigs probably didn't help either," Robert Kennedy added. "Attacking Castro like that made him and Khrushchev defensive and paranoid."

Kennedy turned to his younger brother and Attorney General.

"Did Mongoose cause this?" he asked, referring to the ongoing CIA operations to kill Castro.

"It's possible," Robert Kennedy replied with a shrug.

Kennedy turned back to McNamara.

"We won't trade Berlin away over this, if that's what Khrushchev's thinking. Most of the Executive Committee thinks I should quarantine Cuba. Some of the softer ones, like Stevenson and Rusk, don't think I should even do that. They only want to use diplomacy. But they lack the balls to stand up to Khrushchev on this."

"I think you should reconsider their perspective," McNamara countered. "First of all, I'm not sure why everyone is so scared of Soviet missiles in Cuba. It barely changes the nuclear balance in the slightest. The Soviets already have SLBMs off our coast," McNamara said, referring to submarine-launched ballistic missiles, "which would require less time to prepare to launch. Even the ICBMs from the Soviet Union itself have a shorter prep time. So, the missiles in Cuba actually give us more time to work with. Plus, with the amount of surveillance we have over Cuba, we'd be able to detect a missile launch from there much easier than we would one launched from the Soviet Union or from a submarine."

"Not removing them would be *political* suicide," Kennedy replied, immediately dismissing McNamara's argument. "The Republicans will kill us in the midterms next month. And Goldwater, or whomever else they nominate, will use this against me in '64. The Chiefs are right that this looks bad following the Bay of Pigs, Vienna, and Berlin."

"I'm not sure it's wise to escalate this situation into dangerous territory when it's *politically* problematic but not a *military* issue," McNamara responded. Kennedy shook his head in disagreement. "My second point is that, at the very least, we should reach out to Khrushchev through some back channels and determine what they think they're doing. He doesn't even know yet that we know about the missiles."

"Robert, he *lied* to me," Kennedy replied. "I can't trust him to negotiate in good faith. He'll probably drag out the negotiations long enough for the missiles to be operational."

Kennedy broke eye contact with his advisors. He wrestled with the situation, working through various factors. How would the public react to him doing nothing? What if he was too aggressive and things spiraled out of control? Would the Soviets seize West Berlin in retaliation for attacking Cuba, even if they knew that would lead to NATO retaliation? What terms would Khrushchev want if he opened negotiations without a quarantine? Would the European allies think he was weak for resorting to diplomacy, or did they still think he was unhinged for his obsession with Castro? Why did so many advisors have different opinions? At least his advisors were talking to each other more now than they did during the Bay of Pigs.

Kennedy froze on that last point. One key reason the Bay of Pigs failed was that Kennedy heard his advisors' advice individually. This made it hard to tell who was right. This time his advisors were communicating and weeding out weak ideas. Having his advisors debate was one of the most important lessons he had learned in his two years as President.

Kennedy reflected on how he learned that lesson. He met his predecessor, former President Eisenhower, at Camp David following the Bay of Pigs' failure. Kennedy walked Ike through the decision process that led up to the Bay of Pigs. Ike's main conclusion was that Kennedy needed to have his advisors debate more directly next time. The weaker arguments would give way to the stronger ones. It had been the best advice Kennedy had heard about crisis management, and it came from the architect of D-Day and the victory in Europe. He certainly had more credibility on military issues than the Joint Chiefs.

"I have an idea," Kennedy said with a desperate smile. "What if we asked for Eisenhower's advice on this? He knows what it's like to be a Cold War President. He faced a few crises during his tenure. He knows about when to use force and when to try diplomacy."

Robert Kennedy shook his head.

"I don't think that would be a good idea. We've attacked him a lot lately in the midterm campaigns, and he's started throwing some barbs back. Besides, his failure to act is how Castro took over Cuba to begin with."

"We can't afford to botch this one, Bobby," Kennedy replied. "My only concern is that, since he *has* been more critical of me lately, he may react badly if I say I need his help on a foreign crisis. He'll lecture me on how I shouldn't have cancelled U2 flights over Cuba for six weeks to focus on Berlin, or something like that. Especially after he warned me the Soviets would try something bold in Cuba after the Bay of Pigs failed."

"Could we get someone in the cabinet to make the first contact?" Robert asked.

"What about John McCone at CIA?" McNamara asked. "He was Ike's Atomic Energy Commission Chairman. He'd probably volunteer if we asked him."

Kennedy nodded, feeling better.

"I'll call him right now."

☆☆☆☆☆

OCTOBER 17, 1962

"I DON'T WANT to discuss the current administration's dreary record on foreign policy. It's too sad to talk about," former President Eisenhower declared to a Republican crowd this brisk Boston morning, attacking Kennedy on his home turf. "Under the direct and courageous foreign policy of the 1950s, we lost not an inch of ground to tyranny. We witnessed no abdication of responsibility. No walls were built. No threatening foreign bases established." Ike was referring to the reports of a Soviet military buildup in Cuba.

Ike and Kennedy had been on polite terms throughout 1961. They met in Palm Springs, California, in mid-1962 and got along well. Relations deteriorated between the President and former President as the midterm elections approached. Kennedy criticized Ike's record as a "do nothing" President and said FDR did more in one hundred days than Ike accomplished in eight years. Ike finally had had enough of Kennedy's criticisms and went on the campaign trail to promote the Republican Party. October 1962 emerged as one of the busiest months of his political career. He spoke in Baltimore, Denver, Boise, Omaha, and Minneapolis. He even campaigned for Richard Nixon, his former Vice President and protégé, who was campaigning to be governor of California.

"In the 1950s we defeated the communists in crisis after crisis. Now they're defeating us. The current administration is more interested in intimidating the steel mill owners, centralizing government power in Washington, and turning the government into Santa Claus with runaway spending."

The war of words between Ike and Kennedy in the 1962 election led to Ike removing his restrictions on attacking Kennedy's foreign policy. He even tossed aside his standard politeness. But Kennedy was not Ike's only target.

"How many of you remember this book?" Ike asked, lifting a copy over his head. "You might not, as it came out a few years ago. It's called *The Uncertain Trumpet*. It's a critique of our Massive Retaliation policy of the 1950s and is the basis for our current foreign policy."

Maxwell Taylor, head of the 101st Airborne in World War II and Chairman of the Joint Chiefs for part of Ike's presidency, wrote *The Uncertain Trumpet* to criticize Ike's reduction of conventional military spending in exchange for investments in America's nuclear deterrent. Taylor argued that the cuts to defense spending made it difficult for the US to deploy its forces abroad. That was Ike's intent as part of his strategy to keep America out of war. Taylor argued for a larger conventional force that would give the US a Flexible Response for combating communist aggression. The Kennedy administration adopted Flexible Response in exchange for Ike's Massive Retaliation, much to Ike's dismay.

"The Flexible Response doctrine articulated in this book, which has been adopted by the current administration, is bound to drag us into more Korea-type wars in Asia or elsewhere. It's our duty to contain communism, but that doesn't mean we need to police the world."

Ike's speech ended shortly thereafter with polite applause from the crowd, excited to see a war hero and former President.

☆☆☆☆☆

CARS HONKED AND red and gold leaves blew in every direction as the Chrysler Imperial that Mamie bought for Ike's sixty-fifth birthday zipped down the road. He swerved around traffic, trying to get home to his Gettysburg farm before dark. He expected a phone call. John, Ike's son, gripped his chair in the passenger seat while his wife, Barbara, and his mother, Mamie, held on for dear life in the back seat. Ike barely drove a car between Pearl Harbor and leaving the presidency twenty years later. His driving skills had deteriorated to say the least.

They robbed me of my legacy. Khrushchev, Castro, and Kennedy, the men running the world right now. None of them get along, but they seemed to work in conjunction to ruin the end of my presidency and make the public forget my ideas. That's why it's so important for Nixon and other Republicans to win and carry the torch, Ike thought as he abruptly changed lanes. *What did I even accomplish? I won the war, along with the other Allies, but the Cold War threatens to destroy the victory we won. I ran for President to avoid World War III and end the Cold War. I did manage to keep America at peace and I was so damn close to a deal that would have defused East-West tension. That would have been a career achievement on par with the Normandy Landings. But then Khrushchev botched it with that U2 fiasco and Kennedy stole the election from Nixon and threw out my entire legacy. Like how Wilson's effort to build the League of Nations failed and the people replaced him with Harding, his opposite. All my efforts to constrain defense spending and the debt—gone! What did I waste eight years in the White House for?*

Mamie and Barbara gasped for the third time in thirty seconds as Ike cut off another driver, who honked at the former President. Ike did not notice.

"That damn Crook-chev," Ike began, using his nickname for Khrushchev, "is the worst opponent I've had since Hitler. He might even be worse than McCarthy." John nodded in agreement, his eyes glued to the road. "He clawed and backstabbed his way into Stalin's inner circle, and then became Stalin's clown to keep his head. He wants to rule the world. You know that, right? Khrushchev's ultimate goal is world domination. Just like Hitler. Except Khrushchev doesn't want to rule a world of corpses, whereas Hitler was ready to burn the world down to be king of its charred remains. Khrushchev's happy to bluster and saber rattle with nuclear weapons to get his way. He's hoping we'll spend so much on defense in response that we'll bankrupt ourselves. And Kennedy's intent on helping him."

Khrushchev's such a thug, Ike thought. *Recklessly threatening nuclear war. I threatened Massive Retaliation as President, but that was a carefully crafted effort to contain communism. He's just playing with fire to get more power. I remember when he told me during the Berlin Crisis that he had the power to turn my grandkids into ash. Who the hell says that at a diplomatic summit? I had to remind him that missiles fly two ways!*

John groaned. His father was never so full of self-pity than he'd been since Kennedy's election. John knew his father was disappointed by the U2 incident and felt a lack of legacy, but Ike had always cared about his duty to the country. It had never been about himself. John was afraid that was changing since Ike entered retirement almost two years ago.

"What are you whining about?" Ike asked.

He and John had always had an awkward, if loving, relationship, resulting from the loss of Ike's first son, Icky. Ike never managed to show John the affection he wanted after losing his first-born.

"George Washington kept the peace, but the French Revolutionary Wars continued after he left office," John said. "Maybe your record is like his."

"At least he was succeeded by his Vice President. That election wasn't stolen."

"Is there actual proof that Kennedy stole the election?"

"That's common knowledge! He also ran on the 'missile gap,' claiming that I let the Soviets get ahead of us in the arms race. That was damn wrong! And the CIA told him it was wrong! But he kept saying it, because I couldn't disprove him without revealing the U2 program to the country!" Ike spat.

Most cars on the road slowed down to give Ike plenty of room to maneuver.

"Why is everyone driving so poorly?" he asked quietly. "And stealing that election was just the beginning of it. Damn shenanigans in Illinois and Texas."

"I've heard the list, Boss," John replied. John was a shy man, uncomfortable in large groups. He struggled more to find his place in the world than his father did.

"Then you get to hear it again. Kennedy was a mediocre senator from a rich family who bought him the presidency. He voted against my civil rights legislation and has done nothing on that issue for two years, yet the press hails him as a civil rights champion! He's wasted an ungodly amount of money on a pointless moon race and on fallout shelters and defense. Not to mention that he compromised my covert plan to topple Castro and then blamed me when the Bay of Pigs failed! Nixon would have toppled Castro by now."

John relaxed as he saw the Gettysburg farm emerge in the distance. The sun was starting to set, and no one wanted to experience Ike driving at night. John attended West Point, fought in Korea, and was an assistant in his dad's White House. He would need all that experience to pull his dad out of his rut.

"Welcome back to the Old Frontier," Ike muttered as he drove onto his farm and parked the car.

Mamie stumbled out of the back seat.

"I was afraid I would never see my grandchildren again," she said to Barbara.

The Eisenhowers entered their small white home that was surrounded by endless fields of shiny green grass.

"Welcome home, *Gennul*!" John Moaney exclaimed. "I think Doris almost has dinner ready!" John and Doris Moaney were an African American couple that had started serving Ike and Mamie during World War II, and had stayed with them ever since.

"Thank you, John. It's nice being home and off the campaign trail for a few days," Ike said as he put his coat on a coat rack. "Where's David?"

"Your grandson finished his chores a few hours ago and is doing his homework," John answered.

"He better not be listening to that Elvis again," Ike complained. "I can't stand that stuff. What happened to good music like Fred Waring and the Pennsylvanians?"

"Oh, Gennul, that's before my time! I was always more of a Sinatra man myself!"

"Oh, John, no! He didn't serve during the war! And he has ties to the mob!"

"That may be true, Gennul, but he has the sweetest voice I've ever heard come out of a white boy!"

Ike chuckled. "Where is David, though? I want to make sure he's using the right paint on the fences."

"Oh, Ike, let David be. He's reading for class," Mamie said. John and Barbara exchanged a glance. They didn't want to bother David, but they weren't sure Ike was in the mood to be challenged.

"Farm upkeep is important, Mamie! And don't you have one of your shows to watch?" *David needs to work if he's to become a responsible adult and do his duty to society. He should achieve some career success before he gets married. Should also associate himself with individuals who are better than him in certain respects. Cynics call that apple polishing, but it's the only way to get anywhere in the world. He's a good kid though. A clean kid. No drugs. God, I can't imagine how ashamed I'd be if he were caught with cannabis. That's such a red line for me. I was a huge Robert Mitchum fan until he was caught with cannabis. Haven't gone to his movies since.*

"Oh, no! I'm missing *As the World Turns*! Come on, Barbara!" Mamie exclaimed as they rushed to the living room.

Ike chuckled. *At least I can watch a western this evening.* He put a knife away that was sitting on a counter. John Eisenhower watched his father with curiosity. John knew the story of how Ike played with a knife as a child and left it on a counter where Earl, his younger brother, reached for it and lost his eye. Ike was innately cautious with sharp objects and was determined to keep them away from his grandchildren.

John Moaney opened David's door. "Can't Help Falling in Love" died out as Moaney told David his grandfather wanted to see him.

"Why does he offer me money for good grades if he's going to distract me?" David asked.

Fair point, Ike thought. The phone rang from Ike and Mamie's bedroom before David emerged. Ike went to get the phone. The bedroom had green walls and pink sheets that Mamie adored and Ike tolerated. *Already?* Ike wondered, having been alerted that CIA Director John McCone planned to call him.

"General?" McCone asked.

"This is he," Ike replied.

"Is now a good time?"

"Yes, now's fine. I made sure to drive home at a quick pace so I'd be here for your call."

"Thank you for your consideration, General," McCone said. He cut to the chase, "General, I called to talk about the situation in Cuba."

Why now? Ike thought. *The situation's been in the news for weeks.*

"Our U2 planes have determined that the Soviet missiles in Cuba aren't defensive, as we originally thought. They're offensive in nature."

"I see," Ike replied, still skeptical.

"My thinking is that Khrushchev knows that we have substantial nuclear superiority. He also knows that we don't really live under fear of his nuclear weapons to the extent that he has to live under fear of ours. Also, we have nuclear weapons nearby, in Turkey."

"That was probably an unwise move on the administration's part," Ike responded. "It was unnecessarily provocative to put missiles in Turkey. Now they're returning the favor. My question is 'why has the administration waited so long to respond to the buildup?'"

"I think the fact that the missiles are offensive in nature changed their calculation."

The fact that we're a few weeks from the midterms is more like it, Ike thought. *Kennedy's using this as a publicity stunt.*

"Do you have any advice for the administration, General? The thought is, given your war record and time as President that you're a good person to talk to."

What does that even mean? Kennedy's asking for me to endorse this publicity stunt? What else could this be? It's not like it's that complicated a situation.

"First of all, I would advise you and the administration not to overreact. This is just some new saber rattling on Khrushchev's part. I know it's scary because it's off our flank, but the Soviets aren't stupid. They're not going to wage World War III over Cuba."

"So you think it's safe to use military force if necessary?"

"Maybe, but I wouldn't start there. Try diplomacy first. Remember that Churchill always says that Jaw-Jaw is better than War-War. Besides, attacking Cuba will upset Latin America. Removing the Soviet missiles isn't worth the cost of angering the entire Hemisphere."

"Would you consider the missiles a threat to our vital interests?" McCone asked, knowing that was Ike's standard for using force.

"Probably. It's definitely not preferable to have these things on our flank. But I'm still not sure it's worth upsetting Latin America. It would look bad and undermine our diplomatic efforts."

McCone hesitated, unsure why Ike was so nonchalant about the situation.

"General, is there any way you could drive down to CIA headquarters tomorrow? I would love to give you a presentation and discuss this situation further."

Why is he overreacting so much? Just quietly contact Khrushchev and open negotiations. I can't let Kennedy trick me into helping the

Democrats. There's no way I'll commit myself to publicly endorsing his actions here.

"Is that really necessary?" Ike asked.

"I hate disrupting your retirement, General, but I would really appreciate this."

Ike rocked his head to and fro as he weighed the decision.

I can easily see Kennedy using foreign policy for political gain. But would McCone and the CIA help with that effort? I wish I could ask—

"Little Ike?"

Ike froze. He hadn't been called that for years. He slowly turned and saw a small woman standing behind him. Spectacles covered her eyes, a collar of white flowers sitting atop her black outfit. Her weight rested on a brown wooden cane, which Ike did not recognize.

"Mother," Ike whispered.

"Hello, Dwight," she replied. "I hear tension in your voice." Ike nodded. Ida smiled. "You always did need more guidance than my other boys."

"You—" Ike stuttered. "You've been gone for sixteen years."

"My son needs me," Ida replied. "Nothing's going to stop me from helping him. Nothing's stopped me before."

"I don't know what to do, Mother. I don't trust Kennedy."

"What's the worst that can happen?"

"He manipulates me into helping him in the midterms."

"But if the country needs you?"

"He robbed me of my legacy!"

"'Legacy?' Is that what they call 'duty' now? My my, much has changed in sixteen years. More than in my eighty-four years."

"I spent my whole life trying to do my duty!"

"I know. But you're the same stubborn boy you always were. The same boy who gambled his life by refusing to let the doctor amputate his leg when it was infected. Because it would have stopped him from being an athlete. Look how that turned out."

Ike chuckled. *I forgot about that.*

Ida continued.

"If memory serves me, you put Ed in charge of keeping the doctor from you as you went in and out of consciousness."

Ike's smile dissolved after a few moments of bliss.

"Mom, I was a President."

"So?" Ida spat back. "Does that make you better than anyone else? Should I be more proud of you than of my other boys, who I always loved equally?"

"I'm not saying that," Ike retorted, annoyed at the accusation of arrogance. "I don't act like I'm better than others. I changed the sign that said 'Childhood Home of Dwight Eisenhower' to 'Home of the Eisenhower Brothers' in '45 when the war ended."

"I know you did," Ida said. "I was pleased to see that. But you seem like you're losing the self-control I instilled in you."

"Mom!" Ike exclaimed, like the child she raised. "Kennedy hurt me!"

"So?" she asked. "Your reaction to him is *your* choice. He can't make you angry. Anger only hurts the one harboring it. You don't think you hurt me when you went to West Point to become a soldier? Despite my view of war's wickedness?"

Ike paused as his mother's words sank in.

"I never tried to overrule your decision," Ida continued. "I never stopped supporting you."

Tears emerged in Ike's eyes. He fought to hold them back. *She really did support me, even though I went down a path she considered immoral. Milton said it was the only time he saw her cry. I ignored the pain she went through at the time. I was only twenty. Maybe I can see it easier now that I'm a father and grandfather.*

"That doesn't mean I didn't have any warning that you would make that choice," Ida said.

"What do you mean?" Ike asked as he wiped away a tear.

"Lightning struck the ground the moment you were born. I knew you were destined to become a warrior."

"You never told me that."

"I didn't want to encourage you to wage war when you were supposed to wage peace."

"Mom, I am a man of peace! I ended the ultimate threat to world peace in 1945!"

"Through war, Ike, through war. Let's not pretend you did it entirely through prayer."

"I became President to build a lasting peace! I came close, too!"

Tears swelled up in Ike's eyes again as he remembered the U2 incident.

"I tried so hard to do my duty. To end the need for battlefields and nuclear arms. And I failed."

"No you didn't, Ike. Duty isn't always contingent on outcomes. No one could have succeeded given the circumstances. And you kept the peace when no one else could have." Ike smiled. "You also have the chance to do your duty again, maybe for the last time."

"How do you mean?"

"Help Kennedy."

"But—"

"No, 'buts,' Dwight! Control your emotions! Do I have to remind you of Halloween 1900?"

Ike froze. Then he sharply shook his head to and fro.

"You wanted to go trick-or-treating with your brothers, and your father and I thought you were too young. You lost your temper and punched our tree until your small knuckles bled. Your father, though I love him, whipped you. I tried a different tactic. I let you cry until there were no more tears within your young eyes. And then I spoke to you. Do you remember what I said?"

Ike nodded.

"He that conquereth his own soul is greater than he who taketh the city."

Ida nodded.

"*Self-control*, Dwight!" She emphasized the words. A tear slid down Ike's cheek. "Not selfishness. It doesn't matter who gets the credit. Do what's right."

That was the most important conversation of my life. It built my whole value system, Ike thought of the Halloween long past.

"I'm sorry I've gotten off track, Mother."

"Your heart is *pure*, Ike. That's how you stood up to that awful German man. And, frankly, Kennedy's not that bad either. Give him a chance."

Ike nodded, having trouble speaking, his voice breaking up.

"I love you, Mother."

"I love you too, Dwight. I always will. Now go save the world. Like you always do."

Ike's daydream ended.

"General?"

Whoops, Ike thought. *Didn't mean to leave McCone for that long.*

"Ok, John, I'll come."

"Thank you, General."

"What time do you want me?"

"Noon?"

"That works."

"That's very good. Thank you, General. You have a nice night. I'll see you tomorrow."

"See you tomorrow. Goodnight." Ike hung up the phone. He sighed, no longer in his mom's idealism. *Is Kennedy setting a trap? Or is this a genuine situation?* Ike emerged from his room. John Eisenhower was waiting.

"What was that about?"

"The administration is requesting my advice on a situation, but I can't tell if this is a crisis or a ploy for the midterms." John's eyebrow rose in skepticism. "What?"

"Dad, you've lectured me about duty since I was born standing at attention. If there's a chance that this is a legitimate crisis for our country, doesn't your duty require you to act?"

Just like his grandmother, Ike thought. "That's what I decided. I'm weighing if I should call Milton before heading over tomorrow." Ike was referring to his brother, Milton Eisenhower, who was an unofficial advisor on Latin America when Ike was President.

I thought I had done my duty when Germany surrendered. Then I thought my duty was done when I'd kept the peace for eight years. I guess Mother was right, I have to do my duty one last time.

☆☆☆☆☆

OCTOBER 18, 1962

ALLEN DULLES, IKE'S CIA Director, chose Langley, a picturesque location on the Virginia side of the Potomac River, as the location to build CIA headquarters in 1953. Dulles believed the location would give the headquarters security and privacy, as well as attract competitive candidates with its lush, green surroundings. Ike laid the cornerstone for CIA headquarters in November 1959. Three years later he returned to offer his services once more.

Ike greeted McCone and the intelligence officers upon his arrival.

"It's nice to see you again, Mr. President," one officer said.

"It's 'General,' now!" Ike replied.

"If you wouldn't mind taking your seat over here, General," McCone suggested, politely. "We'll start our presentation."

M. B. ZUCKER

Ike complied. *So nice being with bright young people again,* Ike thought.

The presenters explained that the Soviet military buildup in Cuba had been underway for weeks, but the administration had taken Khrushchev's word that they were defensive missiles. The administration permitted the CIA to take its first U2 flight over Cuba in six weeks on October 14. The presenters gave Ike the resulting photographs and the photographs from subsequent days.

"As you can see, General, the U2 photographs show that the sites are expanding and are being equipped with MRBMs and IRBMs that are offensive in nature," McCone said. "We think the IRBMs have a range of two thousand miles. That means they could strike anywhere in the continental United States, with the possible exception of the Pacific Northwest."

"But the Soviets were already able to hit us?" Ike asked.

"Yes. Soviet ICBMs and SLBMs could already hit the US."

"Then the President is concerned primarily for prestige purposes?"

"The administration thinks it will hurt US credibility with our allies and with the Third World if the Soviets can establish offensive nuclear missiles off our coast and there's nothing we can do about it."

"I see," Ike replied. *This is why I was so determined to stop the spread of communism in this hemisphere. We helped the Guatemalan Army remove the communists from power in that country and were careful to tell the Latin Americans that we will support any reformist movement short of communism. I don't know why I was so indecisive in dealing with Castro. Maybe I was a spent force after the U2 incident.*

"The administration is considering three courses of action," McCone continued. "Option 1 is to destroy the missile sites through bombing. Option 2 is a bombing campaign in conjunction with an invasion of Cuba to remove Castro. Option 3 is to blockade Cuba with measures that would ensure that the thousands of Russians on the island would be able to evacuate."

"What about simply contacting the Kremlin, maybe through backchannels? Strictly using diplomacy?"

"That's not an option the White House gave us."

Because that wouldn't make enough noise for the midterms, Ike thought. *But why are they even considering an air strike without an invasion? What if they didn't hit all the missiles?*

"I see no profit in Option 1," Ike said. "There's more merit in Option 2 or 3. I would support the President in either of those options." Duty overrode partisanship about supporting the Commander-in-Chief during a crisis.

"You don't have a preference?"

"I don't possess enough background information to judge between them. I don't know of any communications the President has had with Khrushchev, Castro, or our allies on this topic."

"You must have some opinion, General."

Ike chuckled.

"You know me too well. Even though we would be justified to use force to get rid of this thing, I would be wary of invading Cuba primarily because of how that will be viewed in the Latin American countries. For that same reason, I think a surprise attack would be militarily correct, but a political mistake because it would be viewed poorly and open the door for other countries to launch surprise attacks when it suits them."

"I think the Latin Americans would understand our wanting to eliminate this type of threat before it was operational."

"I wouldn't be so sure of that. From my experience, most of the people across Latin America are inherently suspicious of the US, and they'll say we're using the missiles as an excuse to topple Castro. That sort of mentality is part of why so many Latin Americans applauded Castro's rise to power, even though he's a little Hitler. If you attack Cuba without their approval, you throw away the possibility of a coalition effort."

"So, you would prefer Option 3 to Option 2?"

"I would," Ike replied. He started feeling restless and turned his hand into a fist to increase his adrenaline.

I should be painting on my porch right now. Watching the horses gallop through the grass. I'm so tired of war, ever since '45. Wanted to live in peace. I tried so hard to make that happen, and yet here I am.

"I'll confer your advice to President Kennedy," McCone said.

"If you don't mind, gentlemen, I'd like to ask you about some specifics."

McCone turned to his officers. No one was bothered by the request. They trusted Ike.

"What would you like to know, General?"

"When the topic of using force comes up, either here, in the administration, or in the Pentagon, are most of the conversations about conventional weapons or nuclear?"

McCone and the intelligence officers were stunned. They did not speak for several moments.

"General, of course we're only talking about conventional options. No one is thinking of using nuclear weapons as the first resort. Things with the Russians could escalate to that, but we'd never start there," McCone answered.

"I see," Ike replied.

Amazing. They act like it's obvious not to use nuclear weapons as a first resort now, but it was a different story when I was President! These same boys recommended just that, whether it was Taiwan, Suez, or Berlin, Ike thought, referring to the three largest foreign crises of his presidency. *I wonder where this change, this taboo, came from. Either way, Kennedy sure is lucky if he doesn't have all of his advisors telling him to use nuclear weapons every time something happens in the world. I wish I'd had that luxury!*

"I guess I'd tell Kennedy that I prefer the blockade idea. Also, that I don't think he should overreact to this situation. It looks scary, but I'm not convinced this is that serious a threat to our national security. No matter what, I don't see the Soviets going nuclear over this."

"Thank you for taking the time to drive down here, General, and for speaking with us. I'll inform the President of your thoughts as soon as possible."

"I hope I helped," Ike replied.

☆☆☆☆☆

"I WANT YOU to know, Mike, we're calling it a quarantine. That's right, not a blockade," Kennedy said on the phone, behind the Resolute Desk of the Oval Office. "A blockade would violate international law, not that that's my big priority. And the quarantine is probably the first step toward an invasion of Cuba. No, I don't care if it's illegal."

Evelyn Maurine Norton Lincoln, Kennedy's personal secretary, entered the Oval Office.

"He's on the phone with the Senate Majority Leader," Robert Kennedy said, asking for Lincoln's patience.

"International law matters so much as it's convenient on this issue," Kennedy said.

"What do you need?" Robert asked Lincoln.

"The CIA Director is here to talk to the President."

Kennedy's eyes widened. He moved the phone away from his mouth. "McCone is here?"

"Yes, sir."

"Bring him in!" Kennedy ordered. He put the phone close to his mouth. "Mike, I'll have to call you back. Something's come up." He hung up the phone.

McCone was rushed into the Oval Office and greeted the Kennedy brothers.

Kennedy cut to the chase.

"You talked to General Eisenhower?"

"Yes, sir. He came down to CIA headquarters. We gave him a presentation to bring him up to speed and he gave us his thoughts."

"What did he say?" Kennedy asked, impatiently.

"He seemed to undervalue the threat posed by the missile sites."

Kennedy looked to Robert.

"Is he playing us to help the Republicans?"

McCone spoke before Robert could answer.

"The General is surrounded by Republicans who have an axe to grind against you, Mr. President. But I think General Eisenhower really wants to do the right thing."

"Is he mad at me for what I've said in the midterms?"

"I'd say 'yes, he is,' but that I worked with him or at least reasoned with him a bit. He was entirely genuine in his analysis, though it seemed like a flash judgment as opposed to a considered opinion given the time constraints."

"And he doesn't think the missiles are a big deal?"

"He seemed more concerned with the opinion of Latin American countries than with the national security threat posed by the missiles."

"He's probably mad that we got the credit for the Alliance for Progress instead of his brother," Robert said, referring to Milton Eisenhower's efforts to encourage economic cooperation between the US and Latin America.

"He preferred the blockade of Cuba to the other options I said we were considering. He was particularly against a bombing campaign without an invasion."

"Interesting," Kennedy whispered, contrasting Ike's position with the Joint Chiefs. "What did he think about invading Cuba?"

"He thought it was justified given the missile sites but advised against it so as to not upset Latin America."

Kennedy nodded and turned to his brother.

"This certainly makes me feel better about ignoring the Joint Chiefs."
He turned back to McCone. "Will he publicly support a quarantine?"

"Again, he was initially reluctant, but I think he would do it if I asked
him."

"Could you do that?"

☆☆☆☆☆

OCTOBER 21, 1962

IKE SAT UNCOMFORTABLY in his chair as the make-up artist brushed his
forehead.

"Please don't move, General. I don't want your scalp to reflect the
lights once you're on air," said the artist, who was thirty years Ike's junior.

Ike groaned. He'd hated when his aides made him wear makeup on
television while President so he would be less pasty. His feelings had not
improved since leaving the White House.

*What kind of man becomes a makeup artist anyway? I supported civil
rights for Negroes and asked Congress to pass the Equal Rights
Amendment for women, but this seems excessive. It's so unmanly.*

"Were you in the Army?" Ike asked, establishing his standard for
manhood.

"Yes, sir," the artist answered. "I was in the 101st Airborne."

Ike's jaw clenched, no longer questioning the artist.

Ike's interview started shortly thereafter.

"I respect Mr. Miller greatly, and I think he's done a great job as
chairman of the Republican National Committee," Ike explained, "but I
did not agree with him when he suggested that this situation in Cuba is the
biggest issue in the midterm elections."

"But General, you yourself have made reference to the Cuba situation
in your campaign speeches, including in the speech you made in Boston
last week," the reporter said, challenging Ike. "So has Mr. Nixon, who is
challenging Pat Brown as governor of California, and other Republicans
you've campaigned for."

"Listen," Ike chuckled, "partisanship stops at the water's edge.
Foreign affairs and national security are too important a topic to use for
partisan attacks."

"So, you take back the comments you made in Boston?"

"I'm not saying that," Ike replied, balancing his duty to the Oval Office with not being a hypocrite. "What I'm trying to say is that, while Republicans can argue over history and long-term trends, those who attack President Kennedy's handling of international crises weaken and divide the nation. Any pronouncement he may make respecting an impending crisis is almost sacrosanct as far as I am concerned."

"So, you're making a distinction between a foreign crisis and day-to-day foreign policy developments?"

"That's right," Ike answered.

☆☆☆☆☆

OCTOBER 22, 1962

"I'M THRILLED HE'S giving me cover with regard to the Cuba situation," Kennedy said. "Hopefully some other Republicans will follow his lead and cut me some slack."

"Hopefully," Robert Kennedy agreed.

Kennedy waited by the phone, anticipating Lincoln telling him that his predecessor was on the line.

"I'll have to call Hoover and Truman in the next couple days. So, they don't feel left out."

"Hoover?" McCone asked, unsure why the FBI Director, his rival, was being added to a list of Presidents.

"I mean Herbert Hoover," Kennedy answered.

"Oh, okay."

"The General is on the line!" Lincoln exclaimed.

"Thank you, Evelyn!" Kennedy replied as he put the phone up to his ear. He heard a buzzing sound and then a click. "Hello, General?"

"Hello!" Ike bellowed from the other side of the line in Gettysburg.

"How have you been doing, General?"

"As well as retirement could treat me, Mr. President," Ike answered. "Time with the wife and the grandkids and all that."

Kennedy chuckled, anxious.

"How about you, Mr. President?"

"Well, I really have my hands full here, as you might expect."

"Oh, of course, I know the feeling." *This is just a taste of what I was dealing with for eight years,* Ike thought. "What's your schedule like with this thing?"

Kennedy was relieved to have the opening to jump into the crisis.

"I've got the leadership coming back at five o'clock this afternoon. Then we'll begin this blockade. Then we'll begin surveillance." The list flowed out of Kennedy, eager to vent to his predecessor. "First, Khrushchev will make the statement that any attack on Cuba will be regarded, the same that he made at the time of the Suez business," Kennedy said, linking his crisis to the biggest crisis of Ike's presidency, "that it will be regarded as an attack on the Soviet Union and will be responded to with all of the weapons at their command.

"Number 2 is we have to assume that while this surveillance continues with the U2s that these Soviet and Cuban SAM anti-aircraft sights might shoot one down. At that point we would be discussing what actions we would take in attacking the SAM sights, so I would assume that this blockade would only be the first of an increasing number of steps in a military campaign.

"We're not going to be in any position to carry out an invasion for some days because we have to move those troops around from San Diego," Kennedy continued, "but we're going to do all of those things and we'll just stay in touch with you this week, which as I say, we anticipate it will be getting more intense."

That was a lot of information, Ike thought.

"Now as I understand it," Ike began, pausing to restructure his sentence. "John McCone talked to me about three possibilities."

"Right," Kennedy agreed.

"The first of them," Ike began, referring to the idea of an air strike without an invasion, "I told him the only real thing was that was sweetly wrong. Apparently everyone else—"

"That's right," Kennedy interrupted, still anxious but wanting to agree with Ike so Ike would think they were on the same page. "The reason is we didn't think we'd get all the missiles. We'd have all of the disadvantages without finishing the job." Kennedy meant bombing Cuba without invading the island would lead to global condemnation but not destroy Castro's regime.

Ike continued, ignoring the interruption.

"With the second one, the invasion idea, the difficulty is that I don't know about all of the communications you've had with Latin American governments, and NATO, and so on. But between the invasion and the blockade, no matter what you decide, I'll support it." *There's no point in trying to convince him to contact Khrushchev through a backchannel. I need to just do my duty and support my Commander-in-Chief.*

"Right, right," Kennedy agreed.

"Now, the one thing I don't understand is that I suspect the program of invading and occupying Cuba would require a number of increasingly serious steps."

"Well, what we anticipate is first Khrushchev's statement, or you know, the usual one. But then of course the surveillance," Kennedy said, shifting back to his earlier point. "Now, of course, we have to assume that they might shoot down one of these U2s. In that case, it would make our surveillance impossible. In that case, of course, we will then have to judge what action to take. But I don't expect they'll discontinue work on these missile sites or withdraw them. I think we'd have that danger in any case."

"I think, Mr. President," Ike began, "that the problem that is bothering you the most after this speech you're making tonight will be the outcry from around the world, and from Latin America, and so on. And from the United Nations and so on. The only thing I said to John McCone was that if you do an attack without talking to South America this will become a unilateral effort. And there won't be any way to change that, so you'll be stuck with it being unilateral."

Kennedy was unsure why Ike was so obsessed with Latin American opinion.

"Well, we can try to get the two-thirds under the Rio Treaty," Kennedy replied, referring to a collective defense treaty that bound most of the Western Hemisphere. "And if we don't get the two-thirds we can do it under our own self-defense."

"What time's your speech tonight?" Ike asked, shifting topics.

"7 o'clock," Kennedy answered. "Then we'll go to the UN to get support for the withdrawal of these missiles. Hopefully the speech will assist Adlai, our UN Ambassador."

"Yeah, well, thank you for speaking to me about this," Ike said, expecting Kennedy to hang up soon. "I personally think you're making the only move you can here with this blockade."

"It's tough," Kennedy continued. "We may get into the invasion business before many days are out."

"From a military standpoint, that is the clean-cut thing to do. But having to be concerned about world opinion—"

"And Berlin," Kennedy said, interrupting Ike again. "That may be what they try to trade off for the missiles."

Ike hesitated.

"Personally, I just don't quite go along, you know, with that thinking,

Mr. President. My idea is this: The damn Soviets will do whatever they want, what they figure is good for them. And I don't believe they relate one situation to another. And they already know that West Germany's in NATO, and if they go in there, that's all there is to it, and there'll be nuclear war. They'll want to make sure they don't get a terrific blow themselves. Now, I could be wrong, but I don't think the two situations are related."

Kennedy sensed Ike was genuine and decided he could be candid. He decided to address his biggest concern at the heart of the issue.

"General, what about if the Soviet Union and Khrushchev announces, and I think he will, that if we attack Cuba, it's going to be nuclear war? What's your judgment as to the chances they'll fire these things off if we invade Cuba?"

Ike hesitated.

"Oh, I don't believe they will."

"You don't think they will?" Kennedy repeated. "In other words, you would risk that if the situation seemed desirable?"

Ike stuttered. He did not want to endorse any military action he thought was unnecessary.

"Well, what else can you do?" Ike asked. "They've placed these missiles off of our flank and we won't feel safe unless they're gone. Something may make these people shoot 'em off. I just don't believe this will." *That's why I don't get why his administration is overreacting so much. Khrushchev's saber rattling. He's probably exerting pressure to make a trade. This doesn't need to be a major crisis.*

They shared a tense, awkward laugh.

"Stay alert," Ike advised, knowing the conversation was ending.

"Hang on tight!" Kennedy awkwardly exclaimed as he hung up the phone. He slumped in his chair and let himself relax. That phone call with the man who beat Hitler and kept the peace for eight years gave Kennedy the strength he needed to override the Joint Chiefs and announce his decision.

☆☆☆☆☆

PRESIDENT KENNEDY ANNOUNCED his decision to quarantine Cuba in a televised address. He decided that to contact Khrushchev through diplomatic channels was not strong enough; the Soviet dictator could not be trusted. On the other hand, air strikes or an invasion risked escalating out of control. His decision was based on the advice of the bulk of his advisors. He also knew Ike planned to publicly support him, reducing partisan pressure.

No speech struck so much fear into hearts around the world.

"Good evening my fellow citizens.

"This Government, as promised, has maintained the closest surveillance of the Soviet military buildup on the island of Cuba. Within the past week, unmistakable evidence has established the fact that a series of offensive missile sites is now in preparation on that imprisoned island. The purpose of these bases can be none other than to provide a nuclear strike capability against the Western Hemisphere.

"Upon receiving the first preliminary hard information of this nature last Tuesday morning at 9 a.m., I directed that our surveillance be stepped up. And having now confirmed and completed our evaluation of the evidence and our decision on a course of action, this government feels obliged to report this new crisis to you in fullest detail.

"Only last Thursday, as evidence of this rapid offensive buildup was already in my hand, Soviet Foreign Minister Gromyko told me in my office that he was instructed to make it clear once again, as he said his government had already done, that Soviet assistance to Cuba, and I quote, 'pursued solely the purpose of contributing to the defense capabilities of Cuba,' that, and I quote him, 'training by Soviet specialists of Cuban nationals in handling defensive armaments was by no means offensive, and if it were otherwise,' Mr. Gromyko went on, 'the Soviet Government would never become involved in rendering such assistance.' That statement also was false.

"Neither the United States of America nor the world community of nations can tolerate deliberate deception and offensive threats on the part of any nation, large or small. We no longer live in a world where only the actual firing of weapons represents a sufficient challenge to a nation's security to constitute maximum peril. Nuclear weapons are so destructive and ballistic missiles are so swift, that any substantially increased possibility of their use or any sudden change in their deployment may well be regarded as a definite threat to peace.

"For many years, both the Soviet Union and the United States, recognizing this fact, have deployed strategic nuclear weapons with great care, never upsetting the precarious status quo which insured that these weapons would not be used in the absence of some vital challenge. Our own strategic missiles have never been transferred to the territory of any other nation under a cloak of secrecy and deception; and our history—unlike that of the Soviets since the end of World War II—demonstrates that we have no desire to dominate or conquer any other nation or impose our system upon its people. Nevertheless, American citizens have become adjusted to living daily on the bull's-eye of Soviet missiles located inside the USSR or in submarines.

"The 1930's taught us a clear lesson: aggressive conduct, if allowed to go unchecked, ultimately leads to war. This nation is opposed to war. We are also true to our word. Our unswerving objective, therefore, must be to prevent the use of these missiles against this or any other country, and to secure their withdrawal or elimination from the Western Hemisphere.

"I want to say a few words to the captive people of Cuba, to whom this speech is being directly carried by special radio facilities. I speak to you as a friend, as one who knows of your deep attachment to your fatherland, as one who shares your aspirations for liberty and justice for all. Now your leaders are no longer Cuban leaders inspired by Cuban ideals. They are puppets and agents of an international conspiracy which has turned Cuba against your friends and neighbors in the Americas—and turned it into the first Latin American country to become a target for nuclear war—the first Latin American country to have these weapons on its soil.

"The path we have chosen for the present is full of hazards, as all paths are—but it is the one most consistent with our character and courage as a nation and our commitments around the world. The cost of freedom is always high—but Americans have always paid it. And one path we shall never choose, and that is the path of surrender or submission.

"Our goal is not the victory of might, but the vindication of right—not peace at the expense of freedom, but both peace *and* freedom, here in this hemisphere, and, we hope, around the world. God willing, that goal will be achieved.

"Thank you and good night."

"HOW COULD HE do this without alerting me?"

Khrushchev took a swig of vodka in his Kremlin office, and then slammed his glass on his desk in a fit of rage. Andrei Gromyko, his foreign minister, sat motionless, other than sliding his finger along the top of his glass, shaken by the sudden escalation of tensions.

"What kind of a moron would take this action and threaten our Navy *and* our ally without even *trying* to negotiate! In front of the *whole* world!" Khrushchev spat. "When that rich brat put his Jupiter missiles in Turkey, I denounced it, but I didn't even threaten force, yet alone blockade the country!"

"Who would have thought Kennedy would find the balls to do this after standing by when the Berlin Wall was built?" Gromyko added, hoping to calm his boss. It didn't work.

"I did nothing more than give him a taste of his own medicine, for what he did in Turkey! Do you realize how humiliating it would be to withdraw the missiles now? How can I *swap* the Cuban missiles for his Turkish ones now? The whole world would laugh at me! And what is the Communist Party going to say? I'll be lucky if they don't take me out back and *shoot* me!" Khrushchev screamed for emphasis.

His body shrunk as he laid his fingers along the sides of his glass. His piggish eyes glared at his drink.

"We were supposed to quietly swap missiles behind the scenes. Not start a global crisis that could turn into a nuclear war." He sighed and looked up at Gromyko. "Eisenhower never would have done something like this. He was much more mature than Kennedy."

☆☆☆☆☆

OCTOBER 26, 1962

IKE AND JOHN walked in silence around the Gettysburg battlefield, father and son each reflecting on another time America was on the brink of destruction. John noticed that ice started developing on the soil, once covered in Confederate blood, and heard soft *crunch* noises as they walked along the trail. Gray clouds cast their shadows.

Ike envisioned great armies of blue and gray locked in combat, some of it in medieval, hand-to-hand fighting, as he had hundreds of times before. He eyed ridgelines where Confederate forces retreated on the second and third days of the battle.

If Grant's victories are an example of what to do as a general, this battle was a model of what not to do, Ike thought. *Lee miscalculated as to why he failed to break Meade's flanks on Day 2 and launched a frontal assault on Meade's reinforced center on Day 3. I can't for the life of me figure out why Lee, usually too aggressive per his limited resources, told Longstreet, "Do it if you can," regarding Pickett's Charge. So passive and indecisive. I'd have fired Monty if he gave that type of order to the 21st Army Group. Can you imagine that? World War II without that psychopath? That may have alleviated at least some of the misery of commanding the Western Front. But it amazes me how America is in danger again after a whole generation sacrificed themselves on this battlefield. That they had to go to Europe to save freedom from the Germans. Twice. And then the crises of the 1950s and this thing in Cuba. Why can't there be peace? Why is man so stupid? I tried so damn hard to secure peace! God damn Khrushchev to Hell!*

Ike slowed down, his body locking up from frustration. His face flashed with red as a blood vessel throbbed over his temple. John stopped, noticing his father's mental anguish.

"Dad…"

"What?" Ike exploded. "What the *hell* do you want?"

"I think you're tired from getting in late last night."

"You think I've never had late nights before?"

"No, but you need your rest these days. You're seventy-two."

"I'm fine! God, between you, your mother, Rose," Ike began, referring to Mamie's aid who put Ike and Mamie to bed each night.

"Forget it," John sighed.

"What? I shouldn't have supported the President? I thought you were the one who told me I have to do my duty this one last time." Ike had attended a Republican rally in Pittsburgh the night before, where he told the crowd, "We are, one and all, deeply concerned with recent events occurring off our southeastern coast. Until this urgent problem is solved to the satisfaction of our nation, every loyal American will without hesitation carry out and conform to any instruction pertaining to it proclaimed by the Commander-in-Chief." It was part of his campaign to give Kennedy partisan cover during the crisis.

"I think you're doing the right thing by supporting Kennedy. I just don't like that you're planning to campaign again for the Republicans in the midterms."

"I won't discuss foreign policy," Ike replied.

"I don't think it's appropriate."

"That's not appropriate? What about doing nothing about the Soviet buildup in Cuba for months and then starting a crisis over it two weeks before an election? I would think that's even more inappropriate!"

"Dad…"

"Don't 'Dad' me! None of his behavior makes sense. I've never seen a President overreact this much to a situation. The Soviet missiles don't change the security situation. And to make a public standoff over this is incredibly reckless. It might be the most irresponsible decision ever made by a President if he escalated this for the midterms."

"You're assuming the worst about him." John was no fan of Kennedy. He was a Republican, like his father, and agreed with most of his father's criticisms of the President. But he hated seeing his dad fuming like this. This wasn't the smiling optimist he knew all his life.

"Maybe you're right," Ike said quietly. *I wish Kennedy didn't frustrate me so much.*

They continued walking. John broke the silence after a few moments.

"How do you think you would have handled this?"

"What?"

"The Cuba situation."

"It wouldn't have happened if I were President."

"What do you mean?"

"First of all, I think there's a difference between starting up with a five-star general and a naval lieutenant. Second of all, I decided against putting missiles in Turkey since it was inside the Soviets' red lines and was too provocative."

"But what if it did happen? If the Russians put missiles in Cuba while you were President, what would you have done?"

"I think I'd have used diplomacy. Quietly reach out to Khrushchev and figure out what game he was playing."

"Would you have done a quarantine?"

"Probably not. If I did, I certainly wouldn't have proclaimed it to the world and make it virtually impossible for Khrushchev to make a deal or back down."

"I guess my question pertains more to the way you ran your National Security Council."

"What about it?"

"It's known how rigid it was, how it was like a military command post. Was it flexible enough to deal with a situation like this?"

"Son, my NSC discussed every possible foreign crisis we could think of and made contingencies for dealing with them. Of course we were ready if something like this happened."

"But—"

"And frankly, we had our *fair share* of nuclear crises. We had to threaten a nuclear strike to get the Korean Armistice. Then there was when the Vietnamese communists defeated the French in Dien Bien Phu. You remember that? The French were asking me to launch a tactical nuclear strike. *While* the McCarthy hearings were going on, mind you! Then there was when Mao bombed Taiwan, and I had to take us to the brink of nuclear war to deter him. Then Suez and Hungary exploded *at the same time* during my re-election. You think I could deal with those situations simultaneously but not this? Then there was Sputnik, and then Mao attacked Taiwan *again*. Then Khrushchev gave us that ultimatum on Berlin. And I had to threaten a nuclear response. *Again.* So spare me this notion that this is the only time we've had a close call with the communists.

"On top of all that, do you have any *idea* what advice I was getting? From my own advisors, from the Pentagon, from Capitol Hill, from academia, and from the public? They all, unanimously, were pushing for me to use nuclear weapons. *Every time!* There wasn't a situation that passed where I wasn't pressured to hit the communist world with our whole arsenal. Did you know the Joint Chiefs wanted me to launch a nuclear strike on China when they were being stubborn about returning our POWs from Korea? Not just McCarthy, or some nut from the John Birch Society. The *Joint Chiefs. Over and over again.* And not just them. *Everyone.* The Chiefs pressured Kennedy to use conventional weapons on Cuba. He had to oppose them, which was tough, but he didn't have the entire establishment *and* the public telling him to *start* with nuclear weapons *every* time something happened in the world. And that doesn't even deal with the fact they all wanted to spend every cent this country had on defense."

"You never explained it to me like that before."

"Of course I couldn't. I was the President! I couldn't complain or vent to someone about what I was going through! It was just me, having to oppose this tsunami of bad advice all the time. No one to turn to. I had to resist all of them *while* finding a solution that denied communism the chance to expand. And I know this goes against my belief in a soldier's duty, but it seems like *no one* appreciates it or what that was like!"

Tears emerged in Ike's eyes. It felt good to let out what he'd been pushing down for nearly two years. John watched his father, unsure how to help. He decided to push back on his dad's interpretation of events.

"I know you kept us at peace, Dad. But maybe people ask 'what good was it when we're still dealing with this nuclear issue? Just look at what's going on in Cuba.' Maybe they feel like what you did didn't last."

Ike brushed away a tear as he considered his son's statement. He nodded.

"You know, I've been thinking about my legacy a lot lately. It felt like any chance I had to leave a legacy, a *real* legacy, was destroyed by the U2 fiasco and Kennedy's election. I had wanted to achieve nuclear disarmament and then hand over the country to Dick Nixon, who would continue most of my policies. That would have been such a great climax to my career. And then it was ruined. The CIA talked me into that *stupid* U2 flight before the Paris summit. The pilot survived getting shot down, didn't kill himself as per his protocol, and then told the Soviets *everything* he knew. Khrushchev, instead of looking past the whole thing to build peace, used the opportunity to *embarrass* our country and threw away the hopes for disarmament. Then Kennedy won. And he threw out my policies for balanced budgets. Nope. Taxes cut, spending increased, bigger military. Threw out everything I'd worked on with delight. And now he's escalated this crisis. I know it may seem scary, because it's right off our coast, but I honestly do believe that the ones I faced were far more complicated. I mean, honestly, this Cuba thing is so much more straightforward than Suez. I had to sanction our allies while threatening nuclear war with the Soviets. War was already breaking out. This Cuba thing should not have been that big of a deal."

"I'm sorry, Dad. I hate that you feel like your legacy was robbed from you."

"Well, wait a second. That's the interesting part of all this," Ike said, raising a finger to signal his son to slow down. "I noticed something during my meeting with the CIA officers that I'd never noticed before."

"What was it?"

Ike smiled.

"They were only talking about attacking the missile sites with conventional weapons. Not nuclear. And it sounds like the Joint Chiefs were advising the same thing. No one treated nuclear weapons as a tool of first resort."

"And that was different when you were President?"

"Exactly!"

"Why do you think that is? Did they think you were more likely to use a nuclear bomb than Kennedy?"

"I think it has more to do with the point in time. You see, Truman used the atomic bomb on Japan, which ended World War II. That put this idea into our consciousness that the bomb was so powerful that it would solve any problem. That's why everyone thought that dropping a bomb on Moscow or Peking would end the Cold War. Like *that*." Ike snapped his fingers. "That's why they were predisposed to use it as a first resort in foreign crises. That's why they were constantly telling me to use it."

"What changed?"

"What I'm thinking is that I avoided using it long enough that people changed their minds about its use. Like they finally got that even the limited use of nuclear weapons, like at Dien Bien Phu or at a Chinese military base or something like that, would have *legitimized* their use in foreign affairs. It would have been acceptable for *anyone* to use them whenever they felt it necessary. And that's not the world we live in today. Instead, there are norms between nations that they *shouldn't* be used. A taboo. Especially as a first resort. That would be unthinkable today."

"And you think your keeping the peace is why that shift happened?"

Ike nodded.

"I'm starting to think that *that's* my legacy. My administration kept the peace long enough that the use of nuclear weapons didn't become normalized. I may not have achieved disarmament, but that at least must have seriously reduced the likelihood of them ever being used. It's like Washington's precedent of surrendering power except on a global scale." Ike smiled. "That must count for something! Even if historians and the public don't see it."

☆☆☆☆☆

OCTOBER 27, 1962

KENNEDY LAID ON his back, his head resting on a pillow, his eyes unblinkingly staring at the ceiling. Mimi Alford, a nineteen-year-old intern, rested her head on his chest, on the brink of sleep. Kennedy had no such luxury. The number of events from the past few days overwhelmed him, playing through his mind one after another.

The American and Soviet navies were in a standoff on the coast of Cuba. Khrushchev went to the opera on October 23 and told an American opera singer he wanted to negotiate a peaceful resolution to the crisis. Pope John XXIII called for peace. Khrushchev wrote to Kennedy saying the missiles were merely defensive. Kennedy wrote back and refuted that claim. Adlai Stevenson, Kennedy's UN Ambassador, presented indisputable evidence of the Soviet missile buildup in the General Assembly. Khrushchev wrote Kennedy again, claiming Kennedy was not appealing to reason. A second letter said Khrushchev sought to deescalate the crisis before it led to nuclear war. A third letter demanded Kennedy withdraw American missiles from Turkey.

West German Chancellor Adenauer advised Kennedy not to back down. French President de Gaulle said risking World War III over something insignificant like missiles in Cuba made him question Kennedy's judgment. Dean Acheson, Secretary of State during Truman's second term, advocated for an invasion of Cuba. A U2 plane was shot down over Cuba. Assistant Secretary of Defense Paul Nitze said the communists had fired the first shot and the US needed to retaliate.

The situation was spinning out of control. Kennedy envisioned an all-out American nuclear attack across Eastern Europe, the Soviet Union, and China. The Soviets would respond with a nuclear attack of their own across North America and Western Europe. Hundreds of millions would be dead. Kennedy could barely fathom such destruction. He thought of his children, Caroline and John Jr.

"I'd rather my children be red than dead," he said, not caring if he woke Mimi.

☆☆☆☆☆

ATTORNEY GENERAL ROBERT Kennedy greeted Soviet ambassador Anatoly Dobrynin in his Justice Department office. Dobrynin was taken aback by Robert's exhausted appearance. He looked like he hadn't slept in days. Robert was desperate to begin the meeting. Kennedy's Executive Committee instructed Robert to respond only to Khrushchev's more diplomatic letter, which offered to trade the Soviet missiles in Cuba for the American missiles in Turkey.

"The Cubans shot down one of our U2 planes earlier today," Robert said.

"Where was it?"

"Over Cuba."

"Maybe that's why."

"Don't get cute with me. They can't shoot at our planes and not expect us to start shooting back. The situation is deteriorating. Fast."

"I am aware."

"Then you need to communicate your understanding to Mr. Khrushchev. Those missile bases need to go and they need to go right away. He has to commit to us tomorrow that the bases will be removed. The President and I can't hold back the Joint Chiefs for much longer. The generals are itching for a fight."

"Is that an ultimatum?"

"It's a statement of fact. Mr. Khrushchev needs to understand that if *he* does not remove those bases then *we* will. The Soviet Union may take retaliatory action, but Mr. Khrushchev needs to know that both Americans *and* Russians are going to die before the war ends."

"What about Turkey?"

"There could be no quid-pro quo."

"What does that mean? Are you and the President not interested in a trade?"

"What it means is that the American missiles will be pulled out of Turkey in four or five months. President Kennedy can't mention anything in public with regard to Turkey."

"Why not?"

"It would embarrass him domestically. The Republicans would use this against us. That's why this conversation about Turkey is extremely confidential. Besides my brother and I, only two to three people in Washington know about it."

"I understand. I shall convey this information to Khrushchev immediately."

☆☆☆☆☆

OCTOBER 28, 1962

"HELLO?" KENNEDY ASKED, excited.

"One moment," Lincoln, his secretary, replied.

"Oh, is the General on the other line?"

"We're ready," Lincoln responded.

"Hello!" Kennedy exclaimed, not missing a moment.

"It's General Eisenhower, Mr. President," Ike replied.

"General, how are you?"

"Pretty good, thank you. How are you?"

"Oh fine, General. I just want to bring you up to speed on this matter because I know of your concern about it," Kennedy said. "On Friday night we got a message from Khrushchev which said he would withdraw these missiles and technicians and so on provided we pledge not to invade Cuba. We got a public one the next morning that said that he would do that if we withdraw our missiles from Turkey. We then, as you know, issued a statement that we couldn't get into that deal."

Kennedy was determined to mislead Ike. He didn't want his predecessor, a Republican, to know about the missile swap.

"We then got this message this morning," Kennedy continued, referring to Khrushchev's agreement to end the crisis and withdraw from Cuba. "So now we've got to see how this unfolds and there's a good deal of complexities to it. If they withdraw these missiles and technicians and cease their subversive activity, well we'll just have to set up satisfactory procedures to make sure that these actions will be carried out. So, I would think if we could do that, we would find our interests advanced, even though it may be only one more chapter in a rather long story as far as Cuba is concerned."

"Of course," Ike replied. "Though, Mr. President, did he have any other terms for this agreement?" *Khrushchev is withdrawing from Cuba and accepting global embarrassment in exchange for what? A promise not to attack Cuba? Kennedy must have exchanged our Turkish missiles or something like that. This is too one sided, otherwise.*

"No, except we're not going to invade Cuba."

"Yes."

"That's the only condition we've got. But we don't plan to invade Cuba under these conditions anyway. So if we can get them out, we're better off."

"That's correct. I'm quite pleased. I just wonder if he was trying to, knowing we would keep our word, whether he would try to engage us in any kind of statement or commitment that one day could be very embarrassing. Suppose they started to bombard Guantanamo," Ike explained, referring to the permanent US base in Cuba.

"Right," Kennedy muttered.

"What I'm getting at is, I quite agree that this is a very conciliatory move that Khrushchev's made."

"Right. Oh, I agree. That's why I don't think the Cuban story is over yet. I think we will maintain sufficient freedom to protect our interests if they engage in subversion or attempt to engage in aggressive acts. Then all bets are off."

"That's all I'm saying," Ike agreed.

"In addition," Kennedy continued, "my guess is that by the end of next month we're going to be toe-to-toe over Berlin anyhow. So, I think this is important for the time being because it requires quite a step down for Khrushchev. On the other hand, I think we all know that they always prove that their words are unreliable, so we just have to stay busy on it."

"As I've said, I really do not think that these people equate Cuba with Berlin or any other things. Any spot in the world, and they don't care where it is, the question is, 'are you in such a place you either can't, or won't, resist?'"

"That's right."

"But now I think you need to insist on our conducting inspections in Cuba to guarantee that they're complying with this agreement," Ike commanded, as if speaking to a subordinate officer. "What you say you will do, whether it is an inspection by us, and in whatever concession we are prepared to make, do this very specifically: make sure it is written down. And then by all means do everything you say you are going to do. Because if you don't, pretty soon you will find that you possibly can't do it."

"The problem," Kennedy explained, "is that Khrushchev had initially agreed to the inspections but reversed course once Castro refused to comply with that."

"You're risking Republican criticism if you concede too much to the Soviets and Cubans," Ike warned. "I don't think you should give any 'blank check' that we won't interfere in Cuba at some time in the future."

"I see."

"For instance, you had an opportunity last December when Castro proclaimed himself to be a 'Marxist-Leninist.' Then you might have taken action against him, and your actions would have been approved by the United States."

"We didn't even think of that."

"Well, we're past that point anyway," Ike conceded, trying not to be rude.

"That's right. Well, I'll keep you informed, General."

"Alright, thank you."

"Thank you, General." Kennedy hung up the phone.

Ike put down the phone and wandered to his front porch, where John was watching Susan and Mary Jean, two of his daughters, play in the grass.

I guess he did alright. If he didn't, I'd never get to see this again, Ike thought as he sat down with his son.

"It's warmer out today," John muttered.

Ike nodded.

"I heard from a friend of mine in the Pentagon that Lemay thinks this deal is the biggest defeat in our history."

"You don't agree with that though?"

"Of course not. That blind aggression is why I put Lemay in charge of the Strategic Air Command. Keep the Russians on their toes. But I don't agree with the press hailing Kennedy either. This was a blip."

"What do you mean?"

"If I'm right, my presidency led to a shift in thinking about nuclear weapons, setting in place the conditions to prevent another world war. That suggests this Cuba crisis was more of a secondary issue that spiraled because Kennedy made it so public. So, this will get the attention when it probably shouldn't. I hope historians see it correctly one day."

"Me too, Dad," John replied, happy his father felt better but still troubled that he remained so concerned about his legacy. His inner peace wouldn't last. They sat in silence for a few minutes.

Ike frowned. *He that conquereth his own soul is greater than he who taketh the city.*

"Actually, I take that back."

"Take what back?"

"That I hope historians see it correctly one day. It doesn't really matter."

John smiled.

"What matters is that this crisis, and the crises of my presidency, and the World Wars, become artifacts of an older time," Ike continued.

"Do you think they will?"

Ike nodded.

"Western civilization will outlast Soviet communism. That regime will collapse, probably before the millennium. And history will view the twentieth century as a period of butchery, but one that paved the way for a golden age for humanity. It will be an age when the conference table will finally replace the battlefield as the method for solving problems between countries and peoples. That's the world my grandchildren will get to live in. And their grandchildren, and the ones after them. A world that's finally at peace."

Further Reading

The Eisenhower Chronicles is a work of historical fiction, but it relied on the brilliant work of professional historians for research. I recommend all of them to interested readers.

The Eisenhower Diaries and *Eisenhower: In War and Peace* by Jean Edward Smith were useful for every story of this novel. Smith's work is the most notable cradle-to-grave biography of Ike. His *FDR* was an important source for "Choosing a Supreme Commander."

Mrs. Ike, Susan Eisenhower's biography of Mamie, her grandmother, informed my portrayal of Mamie throughout *The Eisenhower Chronicles*. This book also provided context for Ike's thought bubble about his drive through the Alps in "Choosing a Supreme Commander."

The following works were important to all six stories in Part I:

Crusade in Europe, Ike's World War II memoir.
Letters to Mamie, the official collection of letters Ike wrote to Mamie during the war.
The Supreme Commander: The War Years of Dwight D. Eisenhower by Stephen E. Ambrose. This is the best non-fiction book on Ike in World War II.

Additionally, the following works were important for individual stories in Part I:

Most Reasonable of Unreasonable Men: Eisenhower as Strategic General by Todd A. Kiefer provided much of the basis for "A Plan to Save Civilization." The scene of Ike explaining his proposal to General Marshall and other commanders was inspired by *Ike: The War Years*, a TV film.

The idea for "The Tragedy of Leroy Henry" was derived from a brief description of the case in *Ike's Final Battle* by Kasey S. Pipes. *The Guns of Last Light* by Rick Atkinson was another source used for this story.

"The Soldier versus the Tyrant" was helped by *Ike: An American Hero* by Michael Korda and *A Time for Trumpets* by Charles B. MacDonald. Hitler's portrayal was largely influenced by *Hitler: A Biography* by Ian Kershaw and by Bruno Ganz's performance in *Downfall.*

Eisenhower: Soldier and President by Stephen E. Ambrose and *Eisenhower: The White House Years* by Jim Newton were important to every story in Part II.

Additionally, the following works were important for individual stories in Part II:

His Excellency: George Washington by Joseph J. Ellis and *Washington's Farewell* by John Avlon informed George Washington's portrayal in "The Office Once Held by Washington: Part I."

Ike's Final Battle by Kasey S. Pipes was useful for "The Office Once Held by Washington Parts I and II."

Waging Peace: How Eisenhower Shaped an Enduring Cold War Strategy by Robert R. Bowie and Richard H. Immerman provided the context for analyzing NSC 68 in "The Office Once Held by Washington Parts I and II," "Better Scared than Dead," and "Ike's Long Game."

Ike's Bluff: President Eisenhower's Secret Battle to Save the World by Evan Thomas shaped my understanding of Eisenhower's foreign policy and the nuclear deterrent, which was key to "Better Scared than Dead," "A Dove in Hawk's Clothing," "The Outbreak of World War III," "Ike's Long Game" and "Last Act on the World Stage." This is the best non-fiction book on Ike's foreign policy.

Ike and McCarthy: Dwight Eisenhower's Secret Campaign against Joseph McCarthy by David Nichols was key to "The Road to McCarthywasm." This is the best non-fiction book on the Eisenhower-McCarthy rivalry.

Mandate for Change, Ike's memoir for his first term as President, was particularly useful for "The Road to McCarthywasm."

The Soul of an American President by Alan Sears, Craig Osten, and Ryan Cole provided context for Ike's faith in "A Dove in Hawk's Clothing."

Waging Peace, Ike's memoir of his second term was an important source for "The Outbreak of World War III," "Son of Father Abraham," "Ike's Long Game," and "Last Act on the World Stage."

Eisenhower 1956: The President's Year of Crisis by David Nichols is an excellent volume on Ike's handling of the Suez crisis and was useful for "The Outbreak of World War III."

Iron Curtain: The Crushing of Eastern Europe by Anne Applebaum provided context for Henrika Kato's story in "The Outbreak of World War III."

A Matter of Justice by David Nichols and *Ike's Final Battle* by Kasey S. Pipes are both great books on Ike's civil rights record. Both were useful for "Son of Father Abraham" and "Last Act on the World Stage." *A Matter of Justice* and Ike's memoir, *Waging Peace*, both informed my portrayal of Senator Johnson during the Civil Rights Act of 1957 debate.

Eisenhower's Sputnik Moment: The Race for Space and World Prestige by Yanek Mieczkowski informed the Sputnik section of "Ike's Long Game." This is the best nonfiction book on Ike's handling of the crisis. *Eisenhower: The White House Years* by Jim Newton informed the Gather Report debate.

Going Home to Glory, a memoir by David Eisenhower, Ike's grandson, about Ike's retirement, was useful for "Last Act on the World Stage."

The Presidents Club by Nancy Gibbs and Michael Duffy informed the portrayal of the relationship between Ike and JFK in "Last Act on the World Stage."

"The Real Cuban Missile Crisis," an article in *The Atlantic* by Benjamin Schwartz, shaped my portrayal of JFK's handling of the Cuban Missile Crisis in "Last Act on the World Stage."

About the Author

M. B. Zucker has been interested in storytelling for as long as he can remember. He discovered his love of history at fifteen and studied Dwight Eisenhower for over ten years. Mr. Zucker earned his B.A. at Occidental College and his J.D. at Case Western Reserve University School of Law. He lives in Virginia with his wife.

Follow Mr. Zucker on Twitter at @MBZuckerBooks and @MichaelZucker1 and on Instagram at @m.b.zucker.author

Contact him at mbzucker1890@gmail.com

HISTORIUM PRESS

www.historiumpress.com

A Subsidiary of
The Historical Fiction Company

www.thehistoricalfictioncompany.com